Big
Girls
Do It
Bigger

The *Ultimate* Collection

ISBN: 0989104451
ISBN 13: 9780989104456

Big Girls Do It Bigger

The *Ultimate* Collection

JASINDA WILDER

Big Girls
Do It
Better

*M*y mom says I was always fat. She once tried to tell me she had to buy my baby clothes in the husky section at Sears, but I don't for a second believe that nonsense. Mom exaggerates. She took me with her to my first Weight Watchers meeting when I was five. All I remember is all the talking about food making me hungry.

I've always had a passion for life and I think that translated into a bit of overindulgence. What can I say? I've never met a cupcake I didn't like.

Two things always get me into the most trouble: food, and my mouth. That's how it all started with Chase. I had just finished my shift DJing at a bar appropriately called "The Dive" when I drove by Ram's Horn and decided I needed a snack. Let's just say the tips at The Dive were usually liquid and I tended to get tipped well. I stumbled in the door and bumped right into trouble of the tall, dark and handsome variety. He apologized as I looked away, flushing in embarrassment and lust. This guy was HOT. I couldn't make myself meet his eyes. Not pretty but plus-sized me. I mumbled an apology and scurried to my usual corner booth and hid behind the menu.

Why am I such a klutz and why do I always embarrass myself in front of men? I thought to myself, pretending to peruse a menu I knew by heart.

"Can I sit with you?" His voice was like a mellow, throbbing bassline.

Of course you can sit next to me, Mr. Sexypants, I thought. I was blushing scarlet from my forehead all the way down to my ample cleavage.

"Sure," I mumbled, trying to act like I didn't really care either way.

I looked up at him again, wishing he wasn't twice as sexy as I remembered when I looked ten seconds before, but he was. I wanted to say something cool and nonchalant, but all I could was focus on keeping the menu to single images, rather than double.

Mr Sexypants ordered water, because he was just that cool. I thought about ordering salad, so I could be cool too, but when I actually opened up my mouth to speak I said pie.

Lemon pie? Really? Awesome job, Anna, I scolded myself. *No way will a guy this hot ask me out, now that I've gone and ordered freaking pie.*

My mind was racing now. Why in the world was this guy sitting here with me? Why hadn't I just gone home, and why did I do so many shots of Jäger after work?

I played with my hair, twisting a lock of my bottle-blond hair between my fingers. It smelled like smoke.

"Do you come here often?" Mr. Sexypants asked.

"No, not really. I DJ down the street at The Dive."

Why did I just tell him where I work? This guy could be a killer.

"You're a DJ?"

"Yeah, I sing and play music at a few local bars."

"Oh really?" he said, flashing his absurdly straight and white teeth at me. "I sing too."

Of course Mr Sexypants would be a singer.

"Really?" I said. "Like at church?"

"No, in a band. We're called 6 Feet Tall. We just got back from playing at CBGB's in New York."

I smiled and ate my pie and twirled my hair again. *Is this actually happening to me right now?* I put my hand down onto my leg and pinched myself. *Yep, really happening.*

I glanced down, more to get away from Mr Sexypants and his fiery brown eyes than anything else, and that was when I remembered what I was wearing: knee-high black hooker boots, fishnet stockings, and a size-eighteen sequined leopard-print mini dress.

Dear God, I bet he thinks I'm a stripper. I went ten shades of scorching red all over again.

"How's the pie?" He asked, still with that too-damn-cute little smirk. He knew exactly what he was doing to me, and he was enjoying watching me squirm.

"Uh...great, thanks." I scarfed down the last couple bites. "I really need to get going."

"The pie is on me," he said. "I was lonely in here studying and I'm glad you came in. I needed a break and some company. My name is Chase, by the way."

"Nice to meet you Chase. I'm Anna." I shook his hand, trying desperately to ignore the sparks of heat that ran up my arm at the touch of his strong, calloused fingers. "Good luck with your band."

With that I got my big butt out of that booth and into my car as quick as I could. I turned the key in my car and looked at the clock: three-thirty eight am. I needed to get home before my roommate Jamie started calling the police to look for my dead body. She hated my job and was always worried guys were going to attack me leaving the bar. I've tried to explain to her that serial killers don't kill fat girls but she doesn't care. I turned to check for a car before I started to pull out and my car door opened.

"I didn't want you to go without getting your phone number." His bassline voice washed over me as his massive presence filled the passenger seat.

Holy shit! What do I do? If I give him my number I'm easy. If I don't I may never see Mr. Sexypants again.

"My mother taught me not to give my phone number to strange men."

"So I'm strange, now, huh?"

"Ok, well not strange, but I don't know you." It took all my control to keep my voice even.

"What if I want to get to know you?" He smiled at me again and I swear I forgot what my name was.

And then he kissed me. Not a tiny, friendly, introductory kiss either; it was a deep, almost-tongues-touching kiss. A soul-scorching kiss. My foot slid off the brake and the car started rolling, and he had to jump out of the way to avoid being run over.

"Sorry about that," I mumbled, trying not to touch my lips where his had just been. *Can my face get any hotter?*

"I'll see you again, Anna, and soon." He shut the car door before I could finish mumbling "Goodnight."

He smiled at me as he turned to run back inside the restaurant.

I didn't remember the drive home, so wrapped was I in thoughts of Mr. Sexypants and the incredible kiss.

The next morning it all seemed like a weird dream.

Being a DJ sounds like a way cooler thing than it is. Most people think it's all sexy bars and talented singers crooning into a microphone just before their break into the big time, or hysterical groups of hot guys singing their theme song in a rousing, raucous chorus. Nothing could be further from the truth. You have to buy your own equipment, for starters, and that stuff ain't cheap. Then you have to load it into your car and unload and set it up in the bar's usually-too-small stage-space. Then you have to have all the music tracks and the song selection binders and the request forms, and you have to know how to use a mixer to get the sound right, and you have to be comfortable in front of crowds and you have to be able to sing yourself. That's all before the people come up, asking you if you this song or that one, and can I get you a drink, and I bet DJing isn't too hard. And then they get drunk and they think they're all Tony Bennet or Nikki Minaj. Let me tell you, out of an entire crowded bar, maybe two or three hundred people depending on the size of the bar, maybe one or two people will have even halfway decent singing voices. If I DJ three nights a week, I might come across three or four people who can actually sing and who know how.

Chase knew how. I mean, he was *good*. He had the natural talent plus the technical skill to use it properly, as well as the stage presence to have the best effect. He swaggered into The Dive the following week, wearing tight leather pants and a sleeveless black T-shirt. It was a look not many men could have pulled off, but he wore it like he'd invented it. I mean, *damn*, those pants hugged his ass like a second skin, and his arms were brawny, bulging, and writhing with gorgeous tattoos. He was lean in the hips, wide in the shoulders, and...

I was completely screwed.

And that was *before* he picked up the mic. He let a few others go first, some not-quite drunk regulars that had decent voices, people I could rely on to get the night started. Chase picked "All I Want" by Toad the Wet Sprocket. He took the mic in one hand, curled the cord around the other hand, standing with his weight on one foot, head down, tapping a toe to the opening notes. Most people, when waiting for their Karaoke selection to start, glance at their table of friends for encouragement, or stare with nervous eyes at the prompter for the lyrics to start turning blue.

Chase milked the moment like a true performer. He drew everyone's eyes, and he knew it; rather than just waiting for the cue to start performing, he was building tension, making sure every eye was on him. The music shifted from the intro to the first verse, and Chase lifted the mic to his mouth, drew a deep breath...and blew me away. The man could sing. He knew how to transition from the low notes to the higher ones without cracking, knew how to belt it without screaming. He worked the crowd, getting those who knew the song to join in on the chorus, got the rest clapping and trying to sing along. He turned a dingy dive bar into a concert hall before his first number was over.

Of course, at the time, all I could see was his glorious body and dark skin. All I could feel was the rush of pure desire coursing through my body to pool in a damp pool beneath my thighs. I was remembering the heat and pressure of his lips on mine one week ago, and desperately wanting more.

His eyes burned into me as he owned the stage. Every time he glanced my way—which was often—I found myself pinned in place, my legs turned to jelly by the blaze of raw lust burning in his eyes.

Why is he looking at ME like that? I kept asking myself. There were dozens of other women in the bar, prettier, richer, skinnier women literally half my size. Just about every other woman in the bar was oozing desire for Chase, practically lining up around the little raised stage area, all of them wearing sexy little outfits that sized in the single digits instead of double.

Yet Chase had eyes only for me, with my size-eighteen mini skirt and three-inch heels that made me stand nearly six feet tall. I knew I looked good for me, but compared to all these other skinny bitches with their size-zero little asses and itty bitty titties, I knew I didn't have a chance in hell with a guy like Chase. But yet here he came, burly arms swinging, eyes fixed on my like he was a lion stalking a gazelle across the savannah. I was no gazelle. I was more of an elephant. At least, that's what my ex used to tell me.

I'd told myself after breaking up with Bruce that I'd never again date a guy that called me names. Hell, he didn't have to compliment all the time, he just couldn't outright call me a whale like Bruce used to. I know I wasn't skinny and I owned it, but it still hurt every damn time.

"You've got a great selection," Chase said, voice rolling over me, flustering me so badly I dropped the CD I was holding. He was suddenly somehow mere inches from me, gazing down at me with what could not possibly be, could never be, surely wasn't *desire.*

"Selection?" What was he talking about? My selection? Was he talking about my boobs?

Am I popping out of my top? I looked down at my chest, suddenly unable to put two thoughts together.

Chase laughed, a low, amused chuckle. "Your song selection. You have a lot of songs to choose from."

I glanced back up to meet Chase's eyes, and as our gazes met, Chase let his slide down to my cleavage and hung there, an obvious, intentional ogle.

"Oh," I muttered. "Yeah...well, you can't be a DJ without music."

"True. But your selection is especially...vast." He *was* talking about my tits, now.

"You sounded great," I said, because it was true, and a complete thought.

"Thanks." He reached past me, his arm going over my shoulder and brushing my face, his lips now mere inches from mine with the whole bar watching.

I thought he was going to kiss me, but he just bored his gaze into me and grabbed a song request slip from the waist-high counter running along the wall behind me. He picked a mini-pencil and scribbled something on the slip, and then handed it to me.

"Sing with me," he said. It wasn't quite a direct command, but almost.

I was tempted to say no just to show him he couldn't order me around, but damn it, I *wanted* to sing with him. I knew, in the same way I knew when I was nailing song just right, that Chase and I would sound incredible together. My deep alto voice would provide a perfect counterpoint to his powerful tenor.

We would make beautiful music together, I thought. I had to suppress a naughty giggle then, because the thought had nothing at all to do with singing.

"I would love to," I said, before I'd even taken the slip from his fingers.

Our fingers touched when I grabbed it from him, and I felt again an electric current zapping through my entire body from that one split-second contact.

What I wouldn't give to feel his hands on me. I couldn't stop the thought from zooming through my addled head. If I felt such electricity from just our fingers touching, then...oh my god, what on earth would it feel like to have his hands on my tits? Pinching my nipples and slipping his fingers into my—

I actually, literally gasped as I forced the thought from my mind. Chase was still gazing at me, and now the gleam of lust was bearing down on me full force, unmistakable and undeniable and totally, completely focused on me.

"Stop looking at me like that," I said.

"Like what?" His voice was pitched low so only I could hear, even though with the fill music pounding from the speakers he could have spoken in a yell and no one would have heard. He spoke low on purpose, so I'd have to get closer to him.

It worked, and I wasn't protesting.

"Like you want me." It was hard to get the words out. I didn't believe them, and I was afraid he'd laugh at me.

His eyes sparked and flashed, and the corners of his luscious mouth tipped up in a smirk. "Oh, but I do."

"You can't," I said, in a voice barely audible even in a silent room

Of course, he read lips too.

"Why not?"

"Because I'm—" I started, and then had to cut myself off and grab for the mic, because the fill song had ended and the next number was up and needed introducing.

I read the name and song title, my brain working on autopilot. Chase was still standing there, his brow furrowed in a slight frown. When I sat back down, he moved to rejoin me, but had to step aside for a line of people making song requests. I was forced to push him from my mind after that, busy with sorting CDs and prompter tracks and announcing songs, and by the time I looked out at the crowd again, he was gone.

I took my break at midnight, slipping out behind the bar with a bottle of beer. This was my quiet time, my five or ten minutes away from the crush of the crowd to gather my thoughts and let my nerves settle.

"You never put our song in the line-up." Chase's voice came from behind me, from the shadows of the building.

I squealed, whirling around with my fist flying. The Dive was in an area where it didn't pay to let your guard down. I'm not a small girl, and I know how to punch. I've flattened men, before, with my fists and with pool sticks and with beer bottles. I've knocked teeth loose and caused concussions. I'm not a brawler, but I can take care of myself.

Chase caught my fist easily, almost casually. He held my closed fist in his for a moment, then curled his fingers around my wrist and pulled me to him.

Oh Lord, I thought, resisting with all my strength and finding it futile. *Here it comes. I knew I shouldn't trust him, I knew he'd turn out to be—*

His other hand drifted up as he slowly and inexorably dragged me against his chest. I flinched away from him, trying to get away from his hand, which I was sure contained a knife, but then I realized it was empty and reaching for my face. The backs of his fingers brushed my cheek, almost tenderly, and then he wrapped his hand around the nape of my neck and pulled my lips against his.

His kiss made my knees buckle. He was still holding my wrist up near our faces, as if worried I might haul off and hit him for kissing me. I thought about it. I really did. This guy was trouble. He just wanted me cause he thought I'd be easy, and desperate. A lot of guys assumed that, and a lot of guys had gotten a rude awakening for it.

But Chase, the way he was kissing me...it didn't feel like a guys who assumed he'd be in my pants. He was kissing me like he *hoped* he'd be in my pants, like he was planning on working to get there.

Now *that* I could work with.

His fingers loosened on my wrists, and I tugged my hand free. I didn't hit him, though. I let my arm drape across his shoulders, then, of their own accord, my fingers were tangling in the soft, dark hair on his neck and pushing subtly to deepen the kiss.

He groaned, a low, animal sound in the very bottom of his throat, a primal growl that had my belly trembling. I wanted to hear that sound again, wanted to feel the power of his voice and know that I'd caused it. So, naturally, I grabbed his ass.

Oh, my sweet Lord. The man's ass was a perfect globe of muscle, and I swear by all that's holy it was made to fit in my hands. Once I had a hold on that fine piece of leather-cupped flesh, I couldn't let go. I was actually, factually electrified as if I'd grabbed a high-voltage wire.

His chuckle was the same amused leonine rumble of pleasure, but laced with amusement. He slipped his hand from my neck and let it trace a sensuous, teasing line down my back to rest just above the swell of my hip, no more sexual a touch than if we were dancing in a club. I wanted him to move it down the rest of the way, to mirror my hand's placement.

Our kiss broke for a moment, and he pulled his face back far enough to meet my eyes. The lust was there in spades, but now it was mixed with too many other emotions for me parse them all out. His eyes were boiling, rife with the same desire he'd looked at me with since I bumped into him at Ram's Horn, but mixed in with it was a different kind of desire, as if he'd like to just sit and talk, or just kiss me all night. I didn't think it was possible to express so much with just a look, but Chase managed it.

He also managed to get both his arms around me and grab my ass with both hands. He had long arms.

Then he kissed me again, and this time it wasn't a kiss meant to surprise, like the first two, quick and hard and shocking, all lips and startling power and zero finesse. This time, he kissed me slow, languorous and deliberate and skillful. He let our lips touch, and then he slipped his tongue out to touch my teeth and explore the contours of my mouth, the corner where my upper and lower lips met, the hollow beneath my tongue, and then farther in to slide along the surface of my tongue.

I may have moaned, then, a soft murmur of my vocal chords. Chase tugged my hips flush against his, and I felt a hard length between us. It was just a bulge against the leather of his pants, but it was enough to get me wetter than rainforest between my legs, and I knew then that I would stop at nothing to get even a glimpse of this man with out his pants on.

My hands circled around away from his ass finally, and tried to slip between us to unbutton his pants, and yes, I was aware that we were in public, mere feet away from several hundred people and oh hell no I'm not an exhibitionist. What can I say? Even through his pants I could tell the man was endowed like a god, and all I wanted was a little taste.

"Just a taste." The words actually came out of my mouth.

"You can have more than a taste, sweetness," Chase said.

I don't think he realized I was talking about his cock.

"I didn't mean your lips," I said.

What the hell is wrong with me? My brain seemed to be disconnected from the rest of me. This guy was playing me, and I knew it. I wasn't just letting him play me, I was actively throwing myself at him.

Chase pulled away long enough to meet my eyes. "I know," was all he said, smirking.

That smirk, that stupid, knowing smirk. He didn't know, but my flush of embarrassment gave me away. He moved his hips away from mine, keeping that smirk on his lips. I wanted to wipe it off his face with my fist, or my lips. I wasn't sure which. He was touching me and kissing me like he owned me, and it infuriated me and intoxicated me at the same time.

Intoxication may have had the upper hand.

My hand found his stomach, and rested there as I warred with myself over whether or not I could bring myself to touch him any lower down. I wanted to, of course I did, but I wasn't that kind of girl. I just wasn't. I was the girl that let guys convince her into bed. I didn't pursue them, because that never went well. I'd tried it, and it sucked.

Rejection always hurts, but when you like the same hot guy as a skinny bitch, well...the rejection is usually a bit rougher for girls like me.

But Chase was pursuing me, wasn't he? That was the argument the horny side of me offered up. It was starting to sound like the logical side of me too, which was odd. Usually the horny side and the logical side were telling me exact opposite things. So, when they started agreeing with each other, I listened.

I snuck my fingers underneath his shirt to touch his stomach, and the slab of muscle my hands found was ribbed and cut into deliciously soft yet hard divots and squares. It was a tempting playground, and normally I'd jump at the opportunity to rub my hands on the kind of abs Chase had, but in that moment I was in search of another, more dangerous place to explore.

The leather was rough and pebbled under my fingers as I dragged my hand south from his stomach to the waistband of his pants. I forced myself to let the moment last, to draw it out. The bulge was growing larger as my hands neared it, and I felt a tremble in his hands on my hips, just the merest leaf-shake of his fingers, but it was enough. He wanted it, too. I mean, of course he did. He's a guy. All guys want their cocks touched.

But this was different, right? He wanted *me* to touch him. And it was right there, waiting for me. Sure, I didn't even know his last name, but he was this ridiculously gorgeous guy decked out in leather pants—my Mr. Sexypants for real, tonight—with a ripped body and what promised to be a positively, deliciously enormous package, and he was all but claiming me as his.

I was perfectly willing to be his, to be played by him, if it meant just one night with a guy this gorgeous. This was a once in a lifetime opportunity, and I was determined to take it.

Yes, I was psyching myself into it, so what? It was a new experience for me, and I needed some self-motivation.

It worked. I found the button and slipped it through to let the tight pants spread apart, and then drew the zipper down, forcing myself to go slow, because you can't rush beauty. Then there was just a thin layer of stretchy cotton between my hands and his cock, just black DKNY boxer-briefs that didn't stand a chance against my daring fingers. His pants were tight, though. Too tight. The zipper opened them enough to let the bulge spring free, and I pulled the band of the boxers away from his belly to get a glimpse of the glory contained therein.

Fuck me sideways! The man is hung like a porn star! It was too good to be true, surely. He would let me get a glimpse, maybe let me suck him off—which I would gladly have done right there and then—but that would be it. No way he'd take me back to his apartment and fuck me proper.

Determined not to let such a golden opportunity go to waste, I touched him with my forefinger, just one reverent brush of the pad of my finger along the pre-come-glistening tip. He was sensitive. He gasped, sucked in his belly and throbbed his hips into my hand. Oh, oh, oh my god, did he fill my hand.

Touching his cock was like eating a chip; I couldn't stop after just one. I had to have more, had to get both hands around him, and yes, he was a two-hand man. Maybe, two and half hands, even, because for a big girl I have small hands. I wrapped my fingers around his girth and shoved his boxers farther down with the heel of my hand so I could fit my other palm around him.

He sucked in his breath and arched his back. "God, Anna. You're driving me crazy."

"I like hearing you say my name." I didn't mean to say that, but it slipped out, and Chase didn't seem to mind.

"Anna," he gasped.

I was smearing his pre-come on his cock with a hand-over-hand motion, and he was writhing into my grip. He was nearly there, about to explode on my hands, and I wasn't about to stop. He put his hands on my ribcage, just beneath my breasts.

"Yes," I whispered, "touch my tits."

What am I doing? The voice of reason, my more prudish nature, which shies away from such behavior as this, was speaking up now. *Are you really about to blow this guy behind The Dive?*

Yes I was. I told my inner prude to shut the hell up and read a book or something. My inner prude didn't like it when I touched myself, even alone, and didn't like it when I thought lusty thoughts about hot guys. My inner prude could get fucked...which was the entire point of all this, after all.

I felt the veins of his shaft pulsing under my touch, so I worked one of my hands into his pants and cupped his heavy, tight testicles as I continued to work his length with the other hand. He was bucking up and down now with his entire body, bending his knees and thrusting up with his entire torso, driving his cock through my slippery grip. His eyes were hooded and his breathing was coming in desperate gasps.

I wanted him to come, and hard. I wanted him to want me to make him come again, and again, and I was determined to make sure he damn well never forgot this experience, even if it was all we'd ever have together. I didn't care about getting off myself, momentarily; I knew I could go home and break out Mr. Pinky McVibrator and use this memory to come at least once, if not twice. I was multi-orgasmic, you see, if only with myself. No guy had ever made me come more than once, but I hoped someday, someone would.

I was trying desperately not to hope it would be Mr. Sexypants himself, my god-cock Chase, who was now mere seconds from spooging into my hand.

"Anna, wait," Chase gasped, trying to back away. "This wasn't...I wanted to—with you—"

I didn't let him get away. He curled in over his stomach, and I knew it was time. I dropped to my knees, wrapped my lips around his head and sucked for all I was worth. He couldn't speak, couldn't move, couldn't do anything but thrust his cock into my mouth and shoot his load into me. He shot, and he shot, and he shot, and I took it all, tasting the smoky, salty thickness against my tongue and my throat and for once not minding at all, for once actually understanding those girls who claim to love giving head.

I'll do it, every once in a while, just to make the guy feel good and to remind him who had the power, but I'd never enjoyed it before. I didn't dislike it, it just wasn't a "hooray, I'm sucking cock" kind of thing for me.

But Chase...oh, he came beautifully. He stretched his mouth wide and arched his back, fluttering his lovely, pulsing cock into me, holding back, restraining himself from cramming himself straight through the back of my throat like I knew he could have. Even as he came, he was trying to think of me.

That was when I knew I was *really* in trouble. You know how many guys out of the....let's say less than half a dozen...that I'd slept with and gone down on had ever, even during sex itself, *ever* thought of me? None. Zero. As soon as they got off, that was it for Anna. And let me tell you, I'd never been able to finish myself off under those circumstances. It's hard to feel sexy when the guy you had sex with turns over and starts snoring, leaving you hot and bothered and sometimes on the very cusp of coming, and if they'd just kept at it for a *few* more minutes, seconds even, I could've gotten there with them, but they just didn't care.

It was a little thing Chase did, not jamming his cock down my throat while he came, but it meant a lot to me, and I knew I had to cut and run before I got attached. The fantasy was bound to come crashing down around me any minute, and I wanted to get free while I still had a good memory to hold on to.

When I'd milked him of every last drop, I tucked him back into his DKNY boxers and zipped up his pants and buttoned him up.

"You have a beautiful cock," I told him, rising to my feet, "and you taste awesome."

I kissed him once, a fast, hard crush of the lips.

"Thanks for a good time, Chase," I said.

And with that, I turned and made my exit.

"Wait," Chase growled, grabbing my arm. "You can't just leave. That wasn't what I—"

I kept moving, despite his grip on my arm. "I have to finish my set."

He grabbed my other arm, then, and pulled me forcefully back around to face him.

"I wasn't done with you yet."

I jerked free, starting to angry that he'd ruined my exit, and was in the process of ruining my memory of him. "Let go, Chase. You got what you wanted, didn't you? I've got to go back to work."

Chase's eyes narrowed and his brows furrowed. "Got what I wanted? You did that, not me."

I gritted my teeth in irritation. "Yeah, I know. You didn't ask for it, not in so many words, but guys like you know how to get what you want without asking for it. Especially from girls like me."

"Guys like me." Chase frowned and squeezed my arm hard enough to make me wince.

"Yeah. Guys like you. Talented, gorgeous, guys who can get anyone they want."

"How do you know what I want? And what do you mean by girls like you?"

I absolutely refused to answer that question. Why was he pushing this? *Why can't you just let me have my memory?*

I jerked free and walked away as fast as I could, just as my partner Jeff came looking for me. I haven't mentioned my partner yet, have I? Jeff...a stable, steady guy, a good business partner, just barely better-than-average looking, and an incredible singer. We DJed together, splitting the profits and making quite a bundle, usually. We'd never been more than friends and partners, even though I knew he had a major crush on me.

"Where have you been, Anna? Everyone's waiting," Jeff said. He knew me well enough to see I was upset. "Is everything okay? What happened?"

I was glad he hadn't come around the corner twenty seconds earlier; he wouldn't have done or said anything, but it would have hurt him to see me doing that to Chase, and I didn't want to lose a good partner.

"I'm fine, Jeff. Don't worry about it." I turned him by the shoulders and pushed him back to the front door of The Dive before Chase came around looking for me.

Which would be in....three...two...one...

"Anna, wait." I felt his hand on my arm, and spun around with my fist flying.

Of course, he caught it like he had the first time. Thank god, Jeff was already inside, so he didn't see anything.

"Chase, seriously. We both know the score here."

"Score? What score? Don't be like this. What you did felt great, better than great, but that wasn't what I was going for. I don't know why you're getting so upset, all of a sudden. I like you, I want to—"

"Anna, let's go!" Jeff stuck his head out the door, saw me stumble as Chase told me he liked me.

"Hey, listen, buddy, I don't know what your game is, but Anna's not interested." Jeff thrust his chest out and strutted towards Chase, thinking he was defending me. Jeff was sweet, and meant well, and was obviously fearless, since Chase was several inches taller and several pounds of muscle heavier.

I pushed Jeff back inside. "It's fine, Jeff. He's not bothering me. He was just leaving."

Chase's face darkened. "No I wasn't." He strode past me, ignoring Jeff completely. "You owe me a song, at least."

Jeff glance at me, and I shrugged, stifling a sigh.

We sang "Broken" by Seether and Amy Lee. I couldn't hold on to my conflicted feelings, not with Chase's dulcet growl braiding perfectly with my voice. The bar was silent as we sang, even the bartenders going still to watch. The tension rippling in palpable waves between Chase and I took the performance into overdrive, sparks crackling as our gazes met, his angry and confused and determined, mine hard and agonized. The lyrics fit our conflict perfectly.

Sometimes, when you perform, time itself seems to stop and watch, if you hit your notes just right. The music seems to glide between the pores of your skin to bubble through your veins in place of blood, and you can't help but clutch the mic with both trembling hands and let the song flow out of you like blood from a wound. In those moments, when the music has replaced everything and even your awareness of your own body has faded, you can't even breathe, can't do anything but let the song own you, let the performance rocket through you. There's no people, no problems in your life, no buzz of alcohol in your blood or pain in your heart...and if you're sharing that moment with another person...it's more intimate than sex. It's a bonding experience like no other, except maybe going into combat, from what I've heard. You and the other person lock eyes, bend at the waist to belt the notes into the mic and invisible, sun-hot flames burn between you, linking you. You could be the only two souls alive in the world.

When the song ended, I was exhausted, feeling as wrung out as if Chase and I had just gone three rounds in bed. The tension was thick enough to cut with a knife, and neither of us knew how to approach it. The chemistry required to share a song like Chase and I just had, that was rare. You could harmonize perfectly with someone, and even give great performances together—like Jeff and I did every week—but to be able to join your souls together for the length of a song, and inter-pret the music and lyrics to have deeply personal meaning...you just didn't come across that every day.

The next several numbers felt flat, even to me. The rest of the bar seemed to feel it, reluctant to take the stage and sing, not when the memory of Chase's and my song still rang loud in the small space.

Eventually, a chant began. "Sing, Sing, Sing...."

The whole bar caught on, until the chant was echoing off the ceil-ing and the patrons were pushing Chase and I onto the stage.

Jeff, ever the professional, knew exactly what to do. He stuck in a CD and sat back in the shadows.

When the first notes pounded from the speakers, Chase and I rolled our eyes and sighed in tandem. Jeff had put on "I'd Do Anything For Love (But I Won't Do That)" by Meatloaf.

Of course he knew the song. I knew, right then, before we'd sung a single note, that we'd bring the house down even more than the first time. He'd provide the perfect harmony, and of course the song would fit our tension yet again.

We killed it. No one could breathe, and I think I saw a few teary eyes as Chase and I sang, the roiling emotions between us ratcheting up even further with every note. I hated Jeff for putting on this song. I was trying SO hard not get attached, not to let my emotions lead me to a broken heart, which I knew was all that waited for me on the other side of anything with Chase. And of course the man was bleeding himself dry selling the performance, pushing himself the edge.

The crowd went wild when the last note faded. We held hands and bowed, as if we were on stage at Harpos or somewhere. s

Jeff put on fill music and I vanished out the side door. Chase followed, of course.

"Chase, I can't do this—"

"Come home with me."

We spoke at the same time, and I was so shocked by his words that I could only stand, stunned. Then he kissed me. You know how in *The Princess Bride* it says in the history of the world there's only been five truly great kisses? Well, this one blew them all away. Yes, I know that's the next line from the movie, but I've never thought that kiss between Westley and Buttercup was all that great, for one thing, and for another, this kiss between Chase and I...the stars froze in the sky, and the moon went dark, and all the world stopped and stared, awed at the sheer, breathtaking passion blazing between us.

At least, that's how it felt to me.

When we broke apart, Chase pulled a business card from his back pocket, which already had his address scribbled on it in neat, blocky capital letters. No phone number, or email address, just his physical house address.

"I'm going home," Chase said. "If you want to know what I was going to do to you, come over after your set. If you don't, you'll never see or hear from me again. It's up to you."

I took the card in trembling fingers. "Chase...I..."

He kissed me again to cut me off. "It's up to you, Anna. If you're too afraid, I'll understand. Just remember, you never know what's possible until you risk finding out."

And then he was gone, roaring away on a sleek black Ducati motorcycle.

I stood on the sidewalk in front of Chase's house. It was a modest one-story ranch-style home, a square of grass in front, a detached garage, cracked driveway and a tasteful lamppost in front. The front porch light was on, despite the fact that it was past 3am.

I forced my feet to leave the sidewalk and take the steps up to the front door. My finger hesitated on the doorbell, and then, with closed eyes and a hammering heart, I pushed it.

Chase was at the door within seconds, still in his leather pants but without his shirt.

Holy hell. I'd felt the muscles of his stomach, had seen his biceps, but nothing could prepare me for the sight that greeted me through the storm door. Pure male perfection, cut muscles, defined with artistic clarity, dusky skin taut and hairless, inked across the pectorals and biceps with stunning full-color red dragon wrapping entirely around his torso, writhing with every breath, every shifting of his muscles.

I froze, unable to tear my eyes away. Chase opened the door, took me by the hand, and pulled me in. He'd meant for me to move past him, but I ended pressed against his hot skin and bulky muscles, hands slipping and sliding across his broad shoulders and ridged back, up his sides and to his chest.

"Why am I here?" I breathed.

Chase grinned down at me. "Can't you guess?" He pulled me into the house, closing the front door with his foot.

I shook my head. "Nope. I'm a terrible guesser." I pressed my lips to his shoulder blade, and then his neck. "Are we here for pretzels? I *am* a little drunk."

"You don't seem drunk," Chase said. His hands were resting on my hips, letting me kiss his skin.

"Not drunk, then. Tipsy. Enough to wonder if this is real."

"It's real. I hope." He dragged his fingers through my hair, wrapping his fist into it near the nape of my neck. He tilted my head backward so I was looking up at him, lips parted in anticipation of his kiss.

"Why would you hope it's real?" I said. My mouth was running away from my brain again, and I couldn't stop truth from spilling out. "I'm the one who must be dreaming."

He kissed me, and it wasn't quite the kiss he'd given me in the parking lot a few hours ago, but it was close.

"Your lips don't feel like a dream." He ran his strong hands across my mini-skirted backside. "Your ass doesn't feel like a dream. It feels real enough to me."

"Are you sure? There's an awful lot of fabric in the way," I said.

"True. We should fix that." Chase's fingers explored the skirt until he found the zipper, tugged it down, slipped his hands between the skirt and my skin to push it down.

His hands on my bare skin felt like tongues of fire along my flesh. I couldn't help a moan from escaping my lips. Chase buried his nose against my neck at the sound, digging his fingers into the flesh of my ass. I was wearing a thong, a bit of blue fabric across my vag with a few strings around my hips and down my asscrack. He traced the line of the strings, dipping down between the globes of my butt to cup each cheek, then up to my stomach.

"Lift your arms up," he said.

I complied without thinking. He was commanding me, and I normally hated being ordered around, but the gentle promise in his voice had me raising my hands over my head. He drew my shirt over my head, leaving me standing in the middle of his living room clad in only a matching bra and panties. Chase stepped back away from me.

"God, you're beautiful," he said, just loud enough for me to hear.

"Wow," I said. "You're good. You almost sound as if you believe it."

Chase tilted his head, looking honestly confused. "Of course I believe it. Would I lie to you?"

"I don't know. I've know you for a week."

"True," Chase said, grinning as he inched back toward me. "Then you'll just have to believe me. I would never lie to you. I promise."

"Okay, sure. Now kiss me again."

"I want to look at you first." Chase stopped just out of arm's reach. "You're a goddess."

I rolled my eyes. "Yeah, right." I planted my hand on my hip and put my weight on one leg, posing for him even as my mouth betrayed me. "I'm an elephant. Nice try, though."

Chase went from gazing appreciatively to gripping my arms in anger within the space of an eyeblink. "Why the fuck would you say that? You're beautiful. You're perfect. I wouldn't change a thing about you."

"You're hurting my arms," I said. "And it's true. You're sweet to try to flatter me, but I know what I look like."

Chase loosened his grip, but didn't let go. His eyes bored into mine. "Never, ever say that about yourself again, Anna. You. Are. Beautiful." He stepped into me, and now his skin was brushing against mine, the leather of his pants rough against my hips, his bulge hard and thick against my stomach. "I know you won't believe me if I say, so I'll just have to show you."

Smart man. He could tell me I was beautiful till the cows come home, or till I went home, rather, but as much as I'd enjoy hearing him say, I knew I wouldn't believe it, not deep down. I'd heard the opposite for too long from too many different people, the very ones who should have been saying what Chase was saying now.

He took me by the hands and led me down a short, narrow hallway to the master bedroom, a simple, tasteful space, light and airy and masculine, neat and smelling of candles.

He'd lit candles. The man had lit candles. A dozen of them, all around his room, on his dresser and on the trunk at the foot of his bed. I melted. The walls around my heart cracked, although the pragmatic core of me stayed on the defensive, knowing better than to let me think the four-letter word that rhymes with "glove" and is impossible between a guy like Chase and girl like me. He'd fall for a woman as perfect as him, someone who was worthy of his beauty. Not me.

"Why are you doing this for me?" The words were choked from my lips.

Chase kept pulling me in, towards the bed, wide and neatly-made, covered with a simple comforter and a few pillows. "Because I like you. Because I want you. Because you deserve it."

"No I don't. Not with you."

"Why not?" He stopped pulling and stood holding my hands.

I couldn't meet his gaze, kept my head down and stared at his bare feet. "Because I'm..." I drew a deep breath and forced the words past quivering lips. "Because I'm...big."

Three little letters, but they contained so much fear, so much revulsion and self-loathing and history and pain. Nothing had ever, ever in my life been so hard as to speak those three little letters.

Chase's fingers clenched mine, and his eyes went from fiery with lust to wavering with sudden understanding and something awfully like compassion. The compassion was the hardest to see, stabbing through my pragmatic self-defensive walls around my heart.

"Big?" His voice was incredulous. "You think I couldn't want this with you, just because you're not a size zero. Unbelievable."

He kissed my shoulder, the right one, on the round curve where my arm began.

"You're perfect the way you are, Anna. You're a work of art." He kissed my chest, just above my left breast. "Don't ever, ever change. Don't ever let anyone tell you you're anything less than a glorious, beautiful goddess."

"Shut up, Chase." I was resorting to toughness in a desperate attempt to keep the burning in my eyes away. "You're full of shit."

"Look at me, Anna." His voice was gentle, but firm. He touched my chin and forced me to obey. His eyes were burning with the fiery lust once more. "Listen to me."

"No. Just shut up and fuck me already." I looked away, watched a candle flicker.

"I don't want to fuck you, Anna. I want more to do so much more than that."

"Don't mess with me, Chase. This is supposed to be easy. I know what this is. It's sex. One night of hot monkey sex, and then you go back to your life. You marry a sexy little skinny bitch and you have kids and get it on in all sorts of positions I could never do."

"You don't know what this is, if that's what you think. And if you think I want that for my life, then you don't know shit about me."

The tone in his voice pulled my eyes up to his once more. "I don't even know your last name," I said.

"Delany." He reached around my back and unhooked my bra with one dexterous hand.

He brushed the shoulder straps off and the bra fell into his waiting hand. He set it aside and gazed at my breasts.

"Chase Delany," I whispered, as he leaned in towards me.

"That's me. And what's your last name, sweetness?" He put his lips on my chest, an inch beneath my throat, and I instinctively arched my back into his hot, wet mouth.

"Devine."

He stopped at looked up at me. "Seriously? Your name is Anna Devine?" His mouth returned to my flesh, and this time his lips found the rising mound of my breast. "You really are a goddess, then, Anna Devine."

"I'm...I'm not. I'm—"

He straightened and his gaze nearly knocked me over in its intensity. "Say it." He took one my tits in his hand, hefting the significant weight of my thirty-eight triple D breast, then the other, running the pad of his thumb across my taut nipples. "Say it, Anna Devine. Say, 'I'm a goddess.'"

I met his gaze, steady and hard, and pressed my lips together.

His eyes twinkled. "You'll say it. You'll say it before I'm through with you."

He knelt down in front of me, staring up at me through the mountains of my breasts, his hands around my waist to rest on the swell of my ass. His fingers curled through the strings of my thong and he drew it down over my hips, dragging it slowly, never taking his eyes off me.

Oh Lord, I thought, as he brought the panties down past my knees. *He is not...no...he can't be serious...oh sweet Jesus, he is.*

His tongue ran up my inner thigh to the hollow where my hip met my leg. My muscles twitched and my breath caught. He kissed me belly, low, just above the mound of my pussy. He was still gazing up at me, even as his tongue dipped down to run up the other side of my thigh, brushing just past my labia once more.

"What are you doing?" I put my hands in his hair, meaning to tug him up.

"Worshipping a goddess."

He smiled at me, then pushed at my thigh with gentle, insistent fingers. My stance widened on its own, my legs spreading apart to give him access. Every fiber of my being was screaming *YES YES YES PLEASE!* but my fears and insecurities were whispering that this would all be snatched away at the last second.

If it was, then I'd enjoy it while it lasted, I told my fears, and they were silenced.

Well, his tongue silenced me, if I'm being honest. His nimble, probing, licking tongue, swiping up between my lower lips, a wet heat against my most sensitive area. I couldn't even gasp, then. He pressed his mouth to my opening and his tongue flicked in, darting against my clit, a single tender brush, but it was enough to make my legs buckle. I forced myself upright, not wanting to fall down on top of Chase and crush him. That would be bad. It would end the first—and probably last—time any man had ever put his mouth anywhere near me like this.

His arms went back up and circled my waist, supporting me. I put my hands on his thick shoulders and threw my head back as his tongue went back in, and this time stayed in. He licked in slow, lazy, wide circles around the cluster of nerves, sending shockwaves through my body. I moaned. I couldn't help it, not with his tongue drawing from my trembling loins an ecstasy I'd never knew existed.

The slow circles narrowed and sped up, and the shockwaves narrowed in waveform, rolling over me until I was dipping my knees at each pulse of his tongue against my flesh, pressing my mound in his rough stubble, his powerful arms supporting me.

I cried out, a rasping whimper, and went limp. He caught me, lifted me, actually factually lifted me clear off the ground and onto the bed before I could catch my breath. And then, before the world stopped spinning, he was back into me, holding my legs apart, resting my knees on his shoulders and spearing his tongue into me, relentless, merciless.

The shockwaves were so close together now they were indecipherable from each other, a single cresting, crashing tidal wave. The tsunami broke and I came with a shriek, my inner muscles clenching as pure, sinful pleasure washed through me in a flood.

He didn't relent with my cry, though. He kept licking and spearing, putting two fingers inside me and curling up to find my G-spot.

Light exploded behind my eyes as explosions rocked my body, one after another, a thrilling detonation for every swipe of tongue against my damp nub, a billowing concussion for every caress of his fingers against the rough patch of skin deep inside my walls.

I curled in, knees tight, fingers tangled in his hair and pulling him against me as I came and came and came, and still he didn't give in. I had to make him stop so I could catch my breath, so I could let my muscles release.

"I've...I've never had so many orgasms...before," I said.

"You haven't even started to come for me," Chase said, nipping the darkened skin of my areola with his teeth.

"No, I mean I've never had so many orgasms before, ever. Combined, in all my life." I couldn't stop my fingers from tangling in his hair again as he took my nipple in his mouth. "At least, not that weren't self-induced."

"Then we'll have to make sure you lose count," he said, around a mouthful of breast.

I ran my hands down his back, marveling at the cords of muscle bunching as he moved. I'd found my breath, and now my own lust was starting to boil. I wanted to feel him, needed to see him nude before me. I'd seen him earlier, but that was with his pants still on. I needed them off, needed to see him in all his glory. The button and zipper were undone in a single jerking motion. I pushed him off me, off the bed.

He let me push him, stood up and waited as I tugged the pants down. They were tight and didn't want to cooperate, but I got them off without help, and then he was standing in front of me in just a tiny bit of black fabric stretched tight across his waist. He was huge in his boxers, and I licked my lips at the memory of him in my mouth.

Just another taste.

"You can taste me all you want," Chase said, and I realized I'd spoken aloud.

I moved toward him, lying horizontally on my stomach across the bed. My hands went around his waist and dug underneath the elastic to touch his hips, pushed the boxers down and I was gripped his muscular ass with both hands. The waistband caught on his engorged tip, and I had to pull the fabric away from his cock to get them down around his thighs. His shaft was standing at attention, bobbing against his stomach as he breathed. He was naked, then, and I could only stare.

"God, you are so gorgeous," I said.

And oh my god, was he ever. Eight-pack abs, broad pectoral muscles and thick arms, a perfect V leading down to his cock, which was, in a word, perfect. His legs were like tree trunks, his ass a wonderland of muscle and flesh, his hair a sweep of black inky strands, his face a symmetrical sculpture of angles and planes, hard and masculine. And his eyes, deep, dark brown, almost black, glittering orbs of expression.

I took in his beauty, drinking him in as I couldn't ever get enough. But, inevitably, my gaze was drawn back to his cock, which was just begging to be touched, held, kissed. I reached for him, took his handle in both fists and let myself just explore his length with my fingers and palms.

He closed his eyes as I touched him, moving his hips in imperceptible rolls. I watched as the little hole at the tip began to leak clear fluid under ministrations. I couldn't stop my tongue from licking out, didn't try to.

He took my face in his hands. "I take it back. No more tasting. I can't take it, not without exploding all over you."

"What if I want you to?" I drew him toward me by his cock. "What if I want you to come all over me? Is that what you want? To come on my face? On my tits?"

I moved my hands on him in an increasing rhythm as his hips began to buck. His eyes flew open and he took my wrists in his hands.

"No." He forced my hands away from his throbbing cock and drew me against his chest, pressing his lips to me. "I don't want that. Not yet, anyway. I want to be inside you."

He pushed me down, and I let him guide me to the head of the bed. His weight was on top of me suddenly, his heat radiating into my skin, our bodies pressed together in delicious points of contact. His knees forced my thighs apart and he was poised to spear into me, but he hesitated once more.

"Chase, please," I heard myself say. I wanted him inside me. I didn't care if I had to beg to get it.

"First things first." He leaned over to the bedside table and opened a drawer, pulled out a string of condoms and ripped one free.

I touched his arm. "I'm on the pill and I'm clean."

He froze. "I'm clean too, but even the pill isn't—"

"I'm not worried."

He still hesitated, and I took his hips in my hands, pulled him toward me. He resisted.

"I trust you," I said. "Just take me."

I didn't tell him what my doctor had told me: I was highly infertile and would likely never conceive. Bruce and I had discovered this together. Bruce, my ex-husband. The other thing I wasn't telling Chase yet. I didn't tell him this, but I thought it. I wondered how he would react, then comforted myself with the knowledge that I'd likely never have to find out.

Chase's lips found mine, covering my mouth with his and claiming a kiss that shook me down to my toes. His hand caressed my breast, his palm brushing my nipple, sending lightning thrills through me, and I rocked my hips into his. He finally gave me what I wanted: his lovely, perfect, glistening, turgid, incredible god-cock, deep inside me, stroking slow and gentle and careful.

"Oh...my...god..." I breathed, as he drew out, fluttered at my entrance, and then plunged back in. "Chase...don't stop, please."

"Never, never" he said, his words rhythmed to the crush of his cock into me. "God, you feel so good, so goddamned perfect."

One of his hands was pinching my nipple and rolling it between two fingers, and the other was on my hip, encouraging me into him. I was forcing myself to go slow, to enjoy every last particle of sensation, every nanosecond of this time with this incredible man above me. What I wanted, however, was to buck desperately into him, to pull him into me until I couldn't take him any more.

His thrusts were deliberately measured, as if he too was fighting for control. I didn't want control, suddenly. I didn't want him to be able to keep the rhythmic pace he was setting. I wanted to make him wild, to make him break loose with insanity.

I wrapped my legs around him and abandoned all pretense. My face buried into his shoulder, teeth biting his skin, I let myself have him how I wanted him, with animal ferocity. His eyes found mine, wary.

"Don't hold back," I told him. "I'm not delicate. You won't break me."

He responded with tender lips at the taut peak of my nipple, fingers diving down to find my clitoris and drive me even wilder. The explosions began in my belly, spread to my lungs and my toes, and then to my inner muscles, and last to my brain. The intensity of this orgasm, with him flush against me, muscles surrounding me in walls of strength and heat and man, with Chase gasping in my ear, whispering my name...it put all other sensations in my life to shame.

I saw the heavens, felt pure ecstasy, unadulterated glory. I whimpered as the climax began, and then, when he kept pushing into me, the whimpers turned to moans, and the moans to sobs, and then, at the full, furious apex of wonder and joy bursting through my body and soul, I screamed.

He wasn't done yet.

He rolled with me and the world tipped and tumbled and suddenly I was on top of him, his hands on my hips pulling me into a roll.

I tried to move off of him, but he held me in place.

"Chase, no, let me down. I'll hurt you. I'm too heavy for this."

He just grinned and thrust into me, silencing my gasps as his shaft began to push back up the peak towards climax once more, and I couldn't help but move my hips to match him.

"I'm not delicate," he said, throwing my words back at me. "You won't break me."

"Yes I will," I said.

But I didn't move to get off him. I couldn't stop myself. I'd never been like this with a man. No one had ever been brave enough to try this with me, or strong enough. But Chase, oh, the man held me in place and rocked into me, and his grunting and gasping drove me wild. He was losing control, now, his cock throbbing into me in wild pulses, his head tilted back and his eyes closed, his hands reaching for my tits again and fondling them and lifting them; he arched his back, and with the strength of his core lifted me off the bed with each thrust. I took him, all of him, swallowing his immense size with each downward crush of my hips onto him.

He opened his eyes and watched me, his lips curling in a wicked smile of satisfaction and respect.

"Yes, yes," he groaned, driving into me with each syllable. "Just like this. God, god, oh god, Anna, yes. Oh, I'm so close now."

I was at climax again, and I leaned forward, put my hands on his chest and let my weight fall on his shoulders. Something in me snapped, then, as he supported me with just his body, holding me off the bed with his hips and his hands and his shoulders, coursing into me, wild and abandoned to the passion flaming between us.

Snapped, melted, fell...the words all mean the same. I lost myself to him, then. Heartbreak or no, I knew I was gone, no longer belonged to myself but to this man who strong enough to take me like this. I knew the double entendre in the thought, even as it passed through me; he was strong enough to take me, physically and emotionally.

Fear at the thought of belonging to him emotionally waved through me, but I pushed it away, drowned myself in the crashing ocean of pleasure.

He gripped my hips in bruising fingers to drag me down onto him harder and harder with each thrust of his cock.

Time slowed and stopped then, as I felt his muscles tense and clench around me, felt his cock tighten and release. He roared, a bellow of male pleasure, and I felt the hot jet of his seed wash through me, a pulse of liquid and a thrust, a growl, and then he pulsed again, filling me with yet more seed, and now I was exploding on top of him, coming apart in his hands. I fell forward and our lips met as we came together, my inner muscles clamping around his still-thrusting, still-coming shaft.

I wept, then. I completely and totally lost it, overcome by sheer orgasmic pleasure and by fear and wonder and abandonment and that one word I didn't dare even think. Four letters, sounds like 'dove.' Means vulnerability and pain and trust.

It was there, even if I didn't dare think it.

It was there in his eyes as he came inside me, and that was what caused me to weep and collapse against him, limp and shaking and still seeing stars, still coming. He was shuddering into me, all pretense of rhythm lost as he gasped ragged inbreaths, and long quaking out-breaths. His arms wrapped around my back and neck and clutched me to him.

"Say it," he breathed into my ear.

"I am a goddess." I sobbed the words, one syllable at a time.

"Yes, yes...you are. You're my goddess." Chase kissed my throat and my shoulder and my chin and my forehead, holding me in his powerful arms. "My goddess. My Anna Devine."

I wept against him, a helpless rain of tears mixed of so many emotions positive and negative I couldn't have begun to explain it all, had he asked.

Which of course he did.

"Why are you crying, Anna?"

"I didn't know...I didn't know it could feel like that," I said. Which was true, but only a bit of the truth.

"And...?" His eyes pierced me, willing the truth from me. I rolled off of him and into his embrace. "Tell me, Anna. Tell it all to me."

I shook my head, calming now, but still shuddering with sobs and aftershocks.

"I can't," I said. "It's too much."

"Try. Just a little, for now. Just a little at a time."

"Why do you want to know?" I gazed at him, trying to keep my eyes neutral. I know he saw though. I'm shit at keeping my emotions out of my eyes. I know he saw the fear and the budding L-word in my eyes.

"Because I want to know you." He spoke the words slowly and deliberately. "I want—no, I *need*—to know who you are. Please."

"I'm just me. Anna Devine."

"Tell me in two words who you are. Start there."

The words came unbidden. "Big. A singer."

He shook his head. "You're not big. You're perfect."

"Stop saying that. I am not. I know what I am. I can't change it, and I'm fine with that. But don't you try to deny it."

"I'm not denying it. I'm saying you're perfect the way you are. I made love to you as you are."

Goddamn it. He said the word. I shook my head and a fat tear plopped onto his chest. "You had sex with me as I am. There's a difference."

"Why are you so afraid? Why can't you believe what I'm saying? Not every guy in the world likes women to be stick figures. Not every guy in the world want his woman to be all skin and bones. I happen to like curves, just like I like your attitude, and your style. I like the way you screamed when you came for me."

"Stop, Chase. Just stop. Don't tease me with this shit." I pushed up to an elbow, trying to summon the strength to leave his warm, comforting embrace before I got hurt any further. "I can take the truth. Just don't jerk me around."

He pulled me back down and pressed his mouth to my ear. The next words he spoke broke me.

"I made *love* to you, Anna Devine. I made *love* to a goddess."

I wrenched out of his arms. "STOP!" I was across the room, crying again. "Don't you fuck with me like this. I can't take it. You're lying to me."

He moved slowly, inching across the bed toward me as if approaching a skittish animal. "I mean it, Anna. I mean every word." He stretched out a hand, and I shrank away, but he touched me anyway, and the same electric spark shot through me as the first time our hands had touched. "I know we just met, but I know what I'm feeling, and I'm not afraid of it."

"I am."

"I know you are," he said, both hands on my shoulders now. "But you don't have to be. I can tell you've been through some serious shit, and you've got scars, just like I do. But you can trust me. You trusted me with your body, now take another chance, and trust me with the rest of you."

I was stiff, but he was insistent and gentle and determined. He pulled me toward him until his broad chest was pillowing my face, and the soft *thump-thump* of his heart beat was all I could hear.

"Take a chance," he repeated. "I won't hurt you."

It was stupid, and I knew it, but I let him guide me back to the bed and into his arms.

I slept better than I had in all my life, feeling safe for once.

Safe, and loved.

I woke the following afternoon to an empty bed and a house smelling like coffee and bacon and sex.

I found Chase sitting with a cup of coffee in one hand, his cell phone in the other, and a grim look on his face.

"What is it?" I asked. "What's wrong?"

He looked up at me, wearing a T-shirt from his drawer.

"It's complicated," he said, getting up to make me a cup of coffee. "I just heard from my agent. My band is getting signed to a major record label."

I sat down next to him and sipped the coffee. "Then what's with the sad face?"

He set his phone down and covered my hand with his. "I have to be in New York by tomorrow afternoon. I'm not sure when, if ever, I'll ever be back."

Then I understood. He had to leave me. I nodded slowly.

"I get it." I scalded my mouth on the coffee, glad for the pain to distract me from my burning eyes. I'd almost started to hope.

"This was the phone call I've been waiting for my whole life," he said, staring at the phone as if it had betrayed him. "And up until a week ago, it would have been the best news of my life. Then I met you."

I squeezed his hand. "It still is the best news of your life. Don't let me...don't let some girl you had sex with stop you from being happy about this. I'll be fine. I knew all along this would be one-time thing."

He glared at me, eyes hard but wavering with emotion. "I didn't. And—god, Anna, I wish you could see yourself like I see you. You're not just some girl I had sex with. I told you last night what it was to me."

I couldn't face the emotion in his voice, how fraught with tension he was. I stood up and gathered my clothes, dressed in the bathroom, and found my purse.

"Thanks for a great time, Chase. Congratulations, and good luck in New York." I didn't turn to look at him as I spoke.

I opened the door, pushed open the storm door and took a step out, and then his voice froze me solid.

"Come with me," he said.

The Long
Drive
Home

*T*he drive home from Chase's house was the longest trip of my life. My roommate Jamie would have called it "the walk of shame."

The walk of shame is when you've got your panties in your purse, you're a little sore between your thighs but not quite sexually sated, and you have a walk from his door to your car in the pre-dawn chill that seems several miles long. You can almost see your breath in the gray hazy light, even if it's July. Your car has dew on the windows and the seat is cold against your legs, and the steering wheel is hard and frozen against your palms. The engine rolls over sluggishly, and you don't want to turn on the heater because you know by the time it warms up you'll be almost home.

You don't turn on the radio, because you want to be alone with your thoughts. You might wish you'd been able to stay over a bit longer and get some real sleep, because you've got work later in the day and you know you won't be able to sleep now but you'll be a zombie later. You might be ashamed of yourself because he seemed so awesome and sexy in the bar, and even when you got back to his place. The sex might have been okay, or even pretty good, and you got off but it just didn't quite satisfy you on some indefinable but visceral level. And now you're on the way home at four or five in the morning and you have awful morning-after-the-bar breath and a queasy drank-too-much stomach.

You know you'll never see him again, because you didn't offer your phone number and he didn't ask, which meant he just wanted a hook-up for the night. You might be pretending you wanted the same thing. You tell yourself as you drive just over the speed limit through the brightening yellow dawn that it's fine. It was fun, you had a good time and that's all it was meant to be. But, deep down, you were hoping it would turn into something more. You hoped that maybe he'd wake up while you were getting dressed and offer you coffee. You'd hold the mug in both hands and discover that he's just as sexy as you remember, if not more so, and god, he's actually funny and charming, and coffee would turn into breakfast at National Coney Island and an exchange of phone numbers and email addresses and suddenly he'd be your boyfriend.

Instead, you're alone in your car, he's asleep still and you noticed as you stuffed your tits into your bra that he's got a snaggle tooth and his eyes are too far apart and his mouth is lopsided, and you sort of remember his cock not being all *that* big, and really, the orgasm was more of a low rumble than anything resembling fireworks. Of course, the morning after a hook-up, no one is attractive. You think, as you run that yellow light, that he'll wake up and flick on Sports Center and drink coffee and wonder if you were as hot he remembered. Of course, you wouldn't be there so he'd have the luxury of relying solely on his memory rather than facts, whereas you got a good look at Mr. One Night Stand while he was sleeping and you *know* he wasn't as hot as when you were half-drunk.

This is what I was thinking as I drove home. Chase would still be sitting at his table, trying to reconcile his lifelong dream coming true with the fact that it meant he and I couldn't ever really be anything more than one night of hot sex.

Hot sex. That term bugs me. I mean, who thinks of sex in terms of anything other than hotness? If it's lukewarm sex, it's probably only happening once. If it's cold sex, then it's probably not even getting finished.

So Chase and I didn't have hot sex. No, we had earth-shaking sex. *Universe*-altering sex. Life-changing sex.

There's the truth of it. That one night of heaven with Chase Delany had changed me. He'd *wanted* me. He'd wanted me despite the fact that I was "plus-size." Not despite, but *because of.* I nearly cried right there in the car remembering his eyes and his voice as he looked at me, as he touched me. As he made me come harder than I'd ever thought a girl could come, and made me admit, out loud, that I was a sex goddess.

Cupcake goddess, maybe. Jaeger goddess, maybe. Sex goddess? Me? Psshh. Yeah, right.

Anna Devine is *not* a sex goddess. But I'd felt like one with Chase. I'd realized I could make him feel good. I could give him pleasure. He wanted what I had. He wanted me. *Me.* It came back to that one fact as I sat at a red light, wishing I had more coffee. He wanted to be with me, to have sex with me, to touch my body, to kiss my skin.

My experience with sex thus far in my life had not prepared me to feel that way. My first time wasn't fun. We'd been virgins and it had been awkward and uncomfortable and messy. It's kind of funny now, looking back, but it hadn't been then. He'd gone on to date the prom queen, and had never looked at me again after that night in Hazel Park in the back of his '91 Lincoln Continental. It was almost like he'd used me to get rid of his virginity, wasted it on the fat girl so he could get the real experience with a girl who was actually hot. That's what I'd felt afterward, and when I ran into him at a reunion five years later, I'd realized I was probably right. He'd turned into a local politician, and you know how *those* guys are.

After that, sex was something bestowed me, seemingly more out of pity than anything else. Lay there with him above you, not looking at you. A little kissing to start off, then he'd grab your tits and squeeze too hard, pinch your nipples too hard. Shove his hand down your pants and grope a few inches too low with clumsy fingers. Let him tear your clothes off, fumble with your bra strap, try not to shield your breasts with your arms as he climbs on and rams into you without so much of a courtesy lick, or at least lube. God knows you don't feel *prepared*, as it were, so it's dry as a desert, but he doesn't care. He's already coming and he just uses his own spooge to lube you up for a few more stuttering strokes, smearing you from back to front with all kinds of mess. Roll off, turn over, snore. You're left unsatisfied, frustrated, wanting an orgasm yourself, but your own fingers just aren't doing the trick and he's done for the night, so there you are, frustrated with no relief in sight.

Or you have guys who expect you to go down on them because you're the big and desperate girl, so *of course* you'd willingly and *gratefully* give him head, just for the gracious gift of getting to touch a man's actual flesh-and-blood cock rather than something rubber and battery powered. Once upon a time, I had been that girl.

But when a guy tried to jab his cock through the back of my throat, and then hit me when I protested, I vowed to never ever act out of desperation again. A man would want me, or I wouldn't do a damn thing.

Which only made what had happened with Chase all the more confusing. Chase was a god among men. He was the kind of guy who gets out of limousines to the staccato lightning of flashbulbs, the kind of guy who sets fashion trends and appears in *People* on a weekly basis. And he'd come after me. It felt surreal. The entire thing, the kiss in the Ram's Horn parking lot, the song at The Dive, the endless paradise of last night…it couldn't have been real.

I pinched myself hard enough to leave a mark, but the memories persisted in being real. My pussy insisted on being pleasantly sore. It was real. He was real. He'd wanted me.

No matter how many times I said it to myself, I couldn't believe. He had to have an ulterior motive, right? Why else would he have brought me back to his house? He could have had anyone. He had only to beckon and flocks of supermodels would come honking and squawking to his side, eager to please him. But instead, he'd wanted me. Anna Devine. DJ, plus-size, chronically lonely and under-sexed.

I'd given up on sex being something incredible, since it never lived up to the fuss everyone made out of it.

And then Chase happened. I wasn't a pretty-enough plus-size girl, or kind-of-hot for a big girl, and sex wasn't just "meh" anymore. I was beautiful and desirable, and sex was incredible.

I wanted to swing the car into a U-turn and race back to Chase's house, throw him down on the bed, or even the kitchen table, and ride him to climax again and again. I wanted to feel him above me. I wanted to taste him, touch him, feel the sweat bead on his skin and hear him groan as he came.

But I couldn't. He was leaving for New York, and he wasn't coming back. He'd invited me to go with him, but it had been a last minute thing, impulsive, ridiculous. I couldn't actually just up and go to New York City on a whim, with a guy I'd just met.

Sex with a guy I'd just met was one thing. A life-changing move across the country to a city where I knew no one is another thing entirely.

But god, he'd made me feel so good. Not just physically, but about myself. For one night, I knew what it felt like to be a woman wanted by a man. How could I let that go?

I made it home, snuck past Jamie's half-closed door and crawled in bed. I wouldn't sleep, I didn't think, but it felt so good to be in my own bed. It was freezing at first, the sheets cold from long hours of disuse, but after a few minutes they warmed up and I felt myself drowsing.

I fell asleep thinking of Chase. I fell asleep holding on to the feeling of being desired.

Big Girls
Do It
Wetter

*G*od, I was so close. I wanted it *so* bad. I was on the edge, just moments from making myself come, but...I couldn't. I'd tried, and tried, and tried. I lay on my bed, Mr. Pinky McVibrator in both hands, using all my tricks and all my best memories, but...nothing. I could get close, writhing on the bed, gasping and moaning and full of aching pressure between my thighs, but no matter what I did, I couldn't get myself past the edge into orgasm.

I had the vibrator turned to high, the humming audible in my silent bedroom, I had it plunging inside me, two fingers circling my aching, sensitive nub, and I had a firm image of Chase in my mind. In my fantasy, he was tied to a bed, hands and feet bound by his silky neckties, erection throbbing and dripping dew against his belly, just waiting for me to climb aboard and ride him like a prize bull.

I could almost feel him inside me, but...it didn't take me there. His hands weren't around my waist, urging me onward. His voice wasn't in my ear, whispering my name. He wasn't giving me gentle commands and wrapping his brawny arms around me.

He wasn't here, and I couldn't come without him.

It had been four days since I'd last orgasmed, and it was an eternity. Four days since I walked out of Chase's house, still aching between my thighs from the vigor of his lovemaking.

He watched me go, sadness in his eyes. He'd argued for a moment or two, but he realized I wasn't going to change my mind, and let me go.

I wanted to go with him. New York? Alone with Chase and his wonderful god-cock? Thanks, yes. But...he was going for his career. It was his big break. He didn't need me there, hanging on him, waiting for him to come back.

Besides, I'd known him for a week. One week. Two meetings. He'd kissed me the first day we met, and we'd slept together the second time.

Slept together. Such a trivial, meaningless phrase in the face of what really happened. Chase showed me what sex was like, what it could be, even for a big girl like me.

Big girl. I'd rolled that phrase around in my mind since he left. What did it mean, really? What did it signify? My clothes size? The number on the scale when I dared step on it? The shape of my body or the heft of my breasts and the swell of my backside?

No, what I realized was my use of the phrase "big girl" in reference to myself was nothing more than a self-categorization. I identified myself as that, so that's what I became.

Yeah, I know. Diets and exercise and eating right and it's not about what you eat but how much and why...blah blah blah. I'd tried it all. I could get to a certain point, and then my body just stopped shrinking. It just held where it was and refused to change anymore, until further efforts turned into bashing my head against the wall. So I kept myself at the point where I wouldn't lose any more weight and learned to accept it as the best I'd get.

But then I met Chase, and he thought I was beautiful. He didn't say it—well, he did, over and over again—but it was his actions that showed me he thought I was beautiful. It was in the way he touched me, in the way he kissed and me held me and made love to me. It was the fact that he considered it making love rather than having sex or fucking.

All this, from one night. Lordy lord. I was so mixed up, so completely screwed up in the head, now, and it was all Chase's fault. I was addicted to his body, to being in bed with him, from one night.

I had a friend in high school who tried crack once at a party. She tried it once, got high on it once, one single time, and that was it. She was hooked. OD'd a few years later.

Well, Chase was my drug. Once, and I was hooked.

The problem was, he was gone, and I couldn't get him back. Not without chasing him across the country. Chasing Chase.

I tossed the dildo across the room, not bothering to clean it first. There was no point.

DJing that night was hellish. I'd begged off my last shift the weekend Chase left. I went home, got drunk with my roommate and stayed that way all day, marinating in my despair. Jaime never asked what was bothering me, because she's awesome that way. She knew I'd tell her when I wanted to, when I was ready.

I wasn't ready.

So now, with my first shift halfway through, I was a mess. I was cranky, bitchy, and off my game.

Jeff was setting up the speakers and mixer board while I sorted CD's and song books.

He was holding the speaker above his head with one hand and trying to spin the knob to tighten it in place, but it wouldn't catch for some reason, and he was getting frustrated. Those speakers are heavy, remember. Most people can't lift them above their head with one hand. Jeff's a beast like that. I watched him, grunting and sweating as he fiddled with the knob, his habitual long sleeve T-shirt falling down around his forearms.

I suddenly realized how attractive Jeff really was. Maybe it was my raging libido or desperate need to get off, but right then, with his face contorted in irritation, his muscles bulging against the fabric of his shirt...he'd never been sexier to me.

Sure, I'd noticed in an off-hand way that he was attractive, but I'd never considered him before, and I suddenly wasn't sure why not.

"Anna, give me a hand, will you? This thing is stuck." Jeff's voice snapped me out of my rumination.

He put both hands to the speaker and held it while I got the knob to work. He was inches from me, the musk of male sweat in my nostrils, the heat of his body radiating into me. So close, yet so far.

I had a sudden, crazy desire to press my body into him, to see what his arms felt like around me. I was leaning, shifting my weight...and then he was gone. His eyes were on me, though, and I knew he'd felt it.

I shook my head. *What the hell am I thinking?* I couldn't afford distractions, not with Jeff. He was my partner, my business friend. Nothing else. It couldn't work.

Plus, he just wasn't Chase.

Yeah, but he's not far behind. My libido was piping up now, telling me what it wanted. And it wanted a taste of Jeff, a look at him without his long sleeve shirt, to feel his hands on me.

Jeff stood around six feet tall, maybe an inch less, but bulky. Where Chase was a toned, proportionate specimen of male perfection, Jeff was more naturally powerful, heavy upper body and thick, muscular legs, all padded with a layer of softness that belied the power of his body. I'd seen him in action, breaking up fights in the bar, lifting hundred-pound speakers easily. He had short, thick brown hair, expressive dark brown eyes, almost black, and a broad, attractive face. He wasn't a handsome man, not classically beautiful like Chase was, but rather rugged, attractive in a rough-hewn way. Jeff wasn't much for words, but he managed to express a huge amount with a simple look, a quirk of the eyebrow, a small smile, a narrowing of the eyes.

We got the equipment set up, got the first songs worked through and adjusted the quirks in the mix. Jeff and I did our first number together, "Summer Nights" from *Grease*. We always killed that one. Everyone loves that song. It's catchy, fun. The older crowd knows it from when the movie first aired, and the younger ones either know it or just like the poppy tune. Jeff's high, clear tenor suits the male part, and I can push my voice high enough to fit the female thread.

But the spark, the heat and tension driving that drove my performances with Chase...that wasn't there. It was just missing, and I couldn't sell the performance like I usually did with Jeff.

He noticed.

When we took our break in closed, darkened bar kitchen, he followed with a pair of Jaeger shots.

"You were flat at the end," he remarked, handing me my shot.

I downed it and gave him the rocks glass back. Jeff was blunt, and he always had been. I knew it, and it didn't usually bother me.

"Well, awesome," I snapped, feeling a sudden rush of irritation. "Thanks for that."

Jeff gave me a puzzled look. He tells me when I'm flat; I tell him.

"I didn't mean it like that, and you know it. Just letting you know." He muttered it, irritated.

"Well next time keep your opinions to your goddamn self. I know when I'm flat."

"What the hell's your problem?"

"None of your fucking business, Jeff."

His eyes narrowed and his mouth turned down. The confused hurt on his face was palpable. I felt bad, knowing he'd done nothing to deserve my irritation.

"Jesus, Anna. Take a pill. Goddamn." He stuffed his phone back in his pocket and went back out into the bustle and noise of the bar.

Great, I thought. *Now I've pissed him off.*

The last thing I wanted to do was apologize, but I didn't want Jeff mad at me. He wouldn't say anything, just give me hard, sad glances and keep it to himself. It was worse than being yelled at.

I followed him out and cornered him behind the mixer. "Jeff, I'm sorry." My hand was on his arm; I hadn't meant to touch him, but now I couldn't move my hand away. "I'm being bitchy, and it's not your fault."

He shrugged, not looking at me directly, but over my shoulder. "No big. We all have bad days."

"Yeah, well, this may end up being more than a bad day, just fair warning." I didn't want to end up talking about it. "So, if I'm a bitch to you, don't take it personally."

Jeff eyed me, then, a long, searching look. He had his suspicions what was bothering me I think. He was too spare with his words and emotions to ask though.

"We can talk about it after. I'll buy."

I shrugged, uncomfortable. I *did* want to talk about it, actually, but I wasn't sure Jeff was the right person.

"Maybe. We'll see. It's just one of those things, you know?"

Jeff lifted an eyebrow at my vague statement. "Well, the offer stands."

We made it through the night, and I managed to keep my irritability to a minimum. I only snapped at Jeff few times.

When the customers were mostly gone and it was time to pack the equipment, Jeff waved me away.

"Go home, Anna. I got it."

Home. Jaime would be out still, over at her boyfriend's house, most likely. Silent, empty, lonely home.

I shook my head. "I'm fine. I'll help."

He rolled his eyes but let me carry the mixer to his SUV. When we finished loading, we bellied up to the bar and Darren, the owner and manager, slid us a pair of beers. We'd been DJing at Green's Tavern for years, and Darren let us stay after hours to drink until he had to leave.

We drank the first beer in companionable silence. Jeff spoke up halfway through the second.

"So. Problems with the boyfriend already, huh?" He spoke without looking at me, a Jeff-quirk.

"He wasn't my boyfriend." I *so* didn't want to get into the messy details. "Just a guy. But yeah. The problem is, he's gone."

Jeff took his time to formulate a response. "And you didn't want him to leave."

He was trying hard to hide the jealousy in his eyes, but he couldn't quite manage it. At least, not from me.

"It's complicated. It wasn't anything. Just one night. But then he had to leave, and he won't be back. Sucks."

Jeff spoke in short sentences, sometimes leaving out words. I had a tendency to start sounding like Jeff after a while.

"Sorry to hear it. He was good for you?"

Jeff was being careful. He knew I knew about his feelings for me, and he also knew I wasn't interested. What he didn't know was my mind and body seemed to be changing their minds.

"Yeah. He was great for me. Treated me like I was beautiful."

"That's 'cause you are." The words seemed to slip past his lips as if he'd tried to hold them back. "Shit." This last was mumbled into the mouth of his beer bottle.

I twisted on my stool to look at him. Our knees were almost touching, but not quite. I could feel the space between our knees as if static electricity was sparking between us.

"I am?" I tried not to make it sound flirty, but didn't succeed.

Jeff drained his beer and popped the top of the third. Darren had left a few on the bar for us while he counted the register. His actions were short and jerky, the bottle clinking against his teeth as he lifted it to his lips.

"Don't, Anna. Not if you don't mean it." He was examining the bar top as if it held an answer. "You know how I feel. So don't."

"How do you feel?" I wasn't looking at him either. It was just easier.

Jeff didn't answer for a long time. "Quit playing games with me," he said, eventually.

I shifted my legs so our knees touched. Jeff jerked, as if the contact had physically shocked him.

"Damn it, Anna. Don't fuck with me." Jeff stood up and slammed his beer bottle down. "I need a shot, goddamn it."

"I'm not, playing games, Jeff. I promise."

"Then what is this? What are you doing? I've spent six years as your friend and partner, nothing more. I haven't—what I feel hasn't changed in all that time. But now, suddenly...you—" Jeff reached over the bar and pulled a bottle of whiskey out, found a shot glass and poured a finger into it; he slammed the shot, and then another. "Times like this I miss smoking."

He'd quit cigarettes two years before, and I'd never heard him voice a craving. He'd also never drank anything but beer or Jaeger.

I matched his shot count. Darren was at the end of the bar watching us. He'd nodded at Jeff when he first grabbed the bottle. I was feeling dizzy, now, but I didn't stop. I finished my beer and grabbed another. The dizziness was welcome, the lightheaded forgetting a pleasant distraction from my emotional turmoil.

Jeff was facing away from me, staring out the window into the darkness of an empty street, traffic light cycling from red to green.

"You're just using me as a crutch to get over what's his name," Jeff said, apropos of nothing. "Not fair to me."

I stood up unsteadily and made my way next to Jeff. I didn't touch him, although I wanted to.

"Maybe I'm just realizing what's been in front of me the whole time," I said.

"Horseshit," Jeff spat. "Besides, I don't want his leftovers."

Oh, ouch. I'm leftovers, now?

"What the fuck, Jeff? I'm not sloppy seconds, I'm your friend. And I'm just wondering what else it might be, or could be. I don't know."

I turned away to stomp to my car, only I wobbled on my heels. Jeff caught me and I shrugged him off. I was pissed off now, even though I knew Jeff was just pushing to protect himself.

"Fuck off, Jeff. I'm going home."

Jeff grunted in irritation and caught my arm again. "Not like this you're not. You can barely walk. You aren't driving anywhere." He was both irritated and feeling his alcohol, so his accent was getting thicker.

"I'm fine."

"You're not." Jeff pulled out his wallet, tossed a bill on the bar and waved a goodbye to Darren. "I'll take you home. And Anna, I'm sorry. I didn't mean it. I was just pissed off."

I let him help me into the passenger seat of his Yukon. It smelled vaguely of pine-scented air freshener, and something that was indefinably Jeff-smell, clean and male. He leaned over me, buckled me in, dug in my purse for my keys and locked my car. His presence in front of me had me inhaling his scent, wondering what the skin by his jaw tasted like.

Things were spinning, the dashboard wavering in front of my eyes, and the floor beneath my feet seemed to jump and wiggle.

"Guess I'm worse off than I thought," I said, hearing the slur. "Don't know what's come over me. I've done more shots than this and been fine."

Jeff snorted a laugh as he slid into the driver's seat and started the van. "You haven't eaten today. Your stomach's been growling since nine o'clock. Plus, you don't usually drink whiskey."

"What about you?" I focused on breathing and keeping my head straight on my shoulders.

"Had a big dinner. And I used to drink whiskey by the gallon. "

I couldn't summon any more arguments. Maybe it'd be fine, maybe it wouldn't.

"Don't take me home," I mumbled. "Don't want to be alone."

Jeff glanced sidelong at me. "You can crash at my place."

I realized I'd never been to Jeff's place, and I didn't know if he lived in a house or an apartment. He drove slowly and carefully, seeming none the worse for wear. I was having trouble keeping track of time, and it might have been five minutes or an hour before we pulled up in front of a tiny house on a corner lot, deep in a subdivision. It was a shack more than anything, maybe one bedroom, if that.

Jeff helped me out and gestured to the house. "It's not much, but... well, it's home."

I slumped against him, letting me support my weight. I was feeling better than when I'd gotten into the car, but still dizzy. Jeff's arm was around my shoulders, and I let my head tilt to the side and rest on his arm. It was comforting, somehow familiar. He held me easily, and

I didn't resist the urge to burrow into him. He smirked down at me, a lift of one side of mouth, just a tipping of his lip, but it was enough to tell me liked having his arm around me. It was a good start.

Inside, the house was tastefully decorated in light colors that made the tiny living room and galley kitchen seem bigger than they were. Jeff helped me lay down on the faded gray couch. It was deep, soft, and comfortable. I was tired all at once, my eyes heavy.

I was wearing a long skirt and boots, and the skirt was tangling between my legs and catching on my boot heels. I tugged at the boots, got one off but the other defied my efforts. The zipper of my skirt was in the back, and I knew it was hopeless.

"Jeff, I need my other boot off."

He was gentle as he pulled the boot off my foot and set it neatly with the other by the door. He moved to cover me with a blanket, but I stopped him.

"I need the skirt off too. It gets tangled."

Jeff's face contorted into something like panic. "I don't—your skirt? Can't you do that?"

I might have managed it if I stood up, but that wasn't happening. Plus, this was fun.

I twisted my hips to the side. "Please? I'll be more comfortable."

Jeff's jaw tightened, and one hand curled into a clenched fist before he uprooted himself and knelt beside me. His hand reached out, hovered over the zipper just above the swell of my backside. His eyes locked on mine; he wasn't afraid, or nervous, but I couldn't decipher the emotion in his eyes. Desire? Hesitation? Longing?

He took the zipper in two precise fingers, not so much as brushing the fabric, and drew it down, eyes riveted on my face.

He's proving something to me, I realized. *He won't touch me since I'm drunk.*

When the zipper was at the bottom, I lifted my hips and he tugged the stretchy black fabric down, gripping near my legs where there was enough loose cotton to allow him to not touch me. The skirt slipped over my hips and he drew it off my feet, folded it and set on the floor by my boots. He stood up, facing away from me.

Oh no you don't, I thought. He wasn't going to get away with not so much as looking at me.

"Jeff?"

"Hmmm?" He stopped and grunted the question without turning around.

"I'm thirsty." And I was, all of a sudden. Positively parched.

His shoulders slumped and he shook his head. He filled a glass with water and brought it to me, keeping his eyes downcast until he reached the couch. His eyes met mine, flickered away, and then back.

When I'd gotten dressed, all I could find clean was a slinky purple thong, so that's what I was wearing. It barely covered me, even in front. I certainly hadn't had Jeff in mind when I'd put it on, but now I was grateful.

His eyes flickered down to my low-cut T-shirt, which had hiked up to bunch just beneath my breasts, and down to my hips and legs.

"Goddamn, Anna. You're not making this easy on me."

"I'm not making what easy?" I asked.

"Being a gentleman."

"What if I don't want you to be a gentleman?"

Jeff closed his eyes and let out a long breath. "You're drunk."

"A little bit."

I kept my eyes on his and let him look. He fought it still, trying to focus on my eyes, but at last he gave in and let his gaze rove down my body, lingering on the miniscule patch of purple silk between the narrow V of my thighs. He turned away, at last.

"Such a gentleman," I said, taking the glass from him and sitting up to drink it.

"I'm trying," he said, "but you're not making it easy. "

"Sorry," I said, but my tone of voice implied otherwise.

Jeff smirked. "No you're not. You're just being difficult. Teasing me."

I faked a hurt look. "Me? A tease? Never." I smiled sweetly, all innocence. "I always follow through."

Jeff's eyes narrowed, and his hands twitched at his sides, as if trying to keep them from touching me.

"If you're playing a game with me, Anna, I swear, I'll never talk to you again. I mean it."

"I'm not playing a game. I promise." I finished the glass of water and set it on the coffee table before laying back down on the couch.

I only posed for Jeff a little bit.

He closed his eyes briefly before crouching next to me and drawing the blanket over my hips. His knuckles brushed along my skin from knee to hipbone, an electric spark crackling between us at the contact. I wanted him to run his hand up my leg, but he didn't. He thought about it, though.

"Good night, Anna." He rose and went into his room, closing the door behind him.

When I woke up, head pounding and stomach roiling, Jeff had a full breakfast spread out, eggs sunny-side up, bacon, toast, orange juice, coffee.

"Thought you might be hungry." Jeff was sitting at his table, a round thing barely big enough for two people to sit at.

I slipped into the chair across from him, still basically naked from the waist down. The table was clear glass, and his gaze fell from my face to my legs. I pretended not to notice and dug in to the food, which was simple and delicious.

"Thanks for breakfast," I said.

"Welcome," Jeff grunted.

He got up and dug around in a cabinet, found a bottle of Aspirin and gave me two.

"And thanks for taking care of me last night," I added, swallowing the Aspirin gratefully.

Jeff shrugged, uncomfortable. "That's what friends are for, I guess."

He drummed a rhythm on the glass with two fingers. I set my hand on his, just rested mine on top, at first. When he glanced up at me in surprise, I slipped mine beneath his. His palm was warm and calloused on my hand, and he looked from our hands to my eyes, and back.

His eyes burned into mine, questioning.

"Is that all we are?" I asked. "Just friends?"

Jeff looked our hands again. "Well, it's all we have been." His eyes flickered up to mine. "Till now." It was almost a question, but not quite.

"Until now," I agreed.

I wasn't sure what this was, or where it was going, but I wanted to see. Jeff had been my friend for a long time, keeping his feelings for me on the down low, never letting them interfere. He'd never tried anything, never asked me out, never told me liked me, or tried to seduce me. We'd gotten drunk together on a number of occasions, but he'd always been a perfect gentleman, just like last night. Only, last night I'd finally seen a glimpse of his desire for me.

So then, how did I know what he felt for me? *I don't*, I realized. *Not for sure.* But I did know, though. It was in the little things. A look he would give me while setting up, meeting my eyes for a few beats too long, a wistful gleam in his eyes. The way he'd never let me do anything too hard, keeping all the heavy lifting for himself. Fending off drunks and keeping losers from hitting on me.

I looked at him, at the slope of his shoulders and the tension in his eyes. He was waiting for this end, for me to tell him we'd just be friends. He'd never tried anything with me, but he wanted to.

"Jeff? Can I ask you something?"

"You just did, didn't you?" He smirked, that rare little expression of humor.

"You know what I meant." He lifted a shoulder, and I plunged ahead. "Why haven't you ever tried anything? As more than friends I mean?"

A long silence, and then a shrug of one shoulder. It wasn't even an answer, but somehow there was a wealth of expression in it. The shrug seemed to mean hidden fear, worry of rejection, a whole slew of things he could and would never say aloud, or even admit to himself in so many words.

"You never know until you try, right?"

Jeff opened his mouth to speak, but closed it again. After a deep breath, he tried again. "I didn't mean what I said last night, but I do have to know. Why now?"

"Sometimes...you just wake up one day and see what's always been there."

"I guess." He threaded his fingers through mine, a gesture that held something of finally giving in to hope.

He seemed about to say something else, but he shook his head, drew his hand out of mine and stood up.

"I'm gonna take a shower. I won't be long," and then he was gone.

I heard the bathroom door closing and the shower start, and I was left sitting alone, wondering why he'd pulled away. He'd seemed on the verge of something, but had swerved aside.

I knew he wanted me, I'd seen that last night. So...maybe it was up to me? Maybe he wouldn't believe I actually wanted him unless I showed him, in no uncertain terms.

Why shouldn't I go after him? His hand brushing my leg had been electric, thrilling. What would sex be like? Even more electrifying, likely.

There's only one way to find out.

My body was moving before my brain was aware of the decision being made. At some point, my shirt ended up on the floor, leaving me clad only in a front-clasp bra and thong.

The bathroom door was unlocked. My heart was pitter-pattering in my chest as I entered the steam-clouded bathroom. His shower door was clear glass, fogged by steam but still translucent enough to show me his body, thick and heavily muscled. His manhood was limp and pointing down; from what I could see, it would be enormously thick. I wanted a better, closer look. I wanted to touch, to taste. Desire was pooling in my belly, and it wasn't only for release, for relief from the sexual frustration raging through me, but for Jeff, for the man I'd worked with for so long, knew so well, but didn't know at all, in some ways.

He heard the door creak open. "Damn it, Anna. I'm in the shower."

"I like the way you say that. So irritated, but still affectionate. 'Damn it, Anna.' "

"What are you doing in here? I'll be done soon."

He wasn't turning away, but wasn't moving to open the door either. I crossed the tiny bathroom in one step, slid the stall door open. He was beautiful, in his own way. His body wasn't sculpted, but it was still hugely muscled, his arms as thick as my thighs, his stomach not flat, but slightly rounded and hard as a boulder. His legs were massive, thighs like ancient oak trees.

His cock twitched at the sight of me. His thick, short brown hair was pasted to his head as water sluiced onto his shoulders and poured down his body. I stood and let him look, taking in the view of his body, my tongue running over my lower lip in appreciation for his physique.

"I'm sober. You don't need to be a gentleman this time."

"Why?" He was still fighting the urge to stare.

"Does it matter?"

"Yes. It does to me."

My legs were being spattered by the shower. I waited for him to move, thinking about his question. Why now?

"I guess I just realized what I wanted. I don't know." His eyes were raking my body now, lingering on my breasts; I stepped closer, nearly in the shower now. "That's the best answer I can give you right now. I don't know."

"What do you want, then?" He hadn't moved toward me, but he looked like he was on the verge of it.

"You," the word came out of me in a whisper.

"Me." He shuffled forward a half-step, his hand lifting for me. "You're sure? This is a line we can't uncross."

I just nodded and took a deep breath, swelling my breasts in my bra. Jeff was semi-rigid now, pointing straight forward. I let myself look, let him see me looking. He rested one hand on my waist at first, a hesitant questing touch. I moved closer, and his body blocked the spray of water. He was hardening with every passing moment. I kept my hands at my sides.

Both of his hands were on the concave curve of my waist now and sliding up, rivulets of hot water dripping down my sides. Up farther, then, closer to my breasts. He met my eyes, still hesitating.

"I'm not going to change my mind." I unclasped my bra and set it aside. "Touch me."

He was fully erect now, and I couldn't help comparing him to Chase, just for a moment. He wasn't as long as Chase, but he was thicker, and perfectly straight, whereas Chase had been slightly curved.

I wanted to take him in my hands, but I kept still, waiting for Jeff's hands to finish their upward journey and heft my breasts in his large hands.

"Don't play me, Anna." His voice was low and husky, his hands stopped on my ribcage.

"Oh for god's sake." I closed the gap between us and pressed my lips to his.

He was startled, frozen for a moment, then he softened into the kiss and dipped his tongue past my teeth. His kiss was gentle, achingly tender for such a hard, gruff man. His calloused palms caught the undersides of my tits and cupped them. His murmur of pleasure buzzed against my sternum. I put my hands on his shoulders and ran them down his back to curl around his hard round ass. At my touch to his backside, Jeff pressed into me, crushing his erect shaft between us.

I stepped back, pushed Jeff into the shower and stripped off my thong before joining him in the shower. Now I touched his cock for the first time, wrapping one hand around him, slicing a thumb across his bulbous, leaking tip.

Oh my sweet lord, I thought, clutching his cock with greedy hunger, *he's huge. SO thick.* He would fill me, and then some.

He rumbled again, one corner of his mouth tipping up in a smile, his eyes half-closed. My hair was still in a pony tail, and I tugged it free, letting the stream of scalding water wet my hair against my scalp and neck. Jeff ran his hands across my face, brushing sopping strands of hair away from my face, and down the back of my head. His hand rested on the nape of my neck and pulled me into a kiss. My hand was still fisted around his thickness, and I kept enough distance between our hips to allow myself room for stroking. He was at once soft and hard, a skin of silk around a core of steel.

My breathing was turning to sighing gasps as I felt him throb in my fist, felt his hips pump him into me. His fingers found my nipples, hard and sensitive, sending zaps of arousal thrilling through my body. One hand kept toying with my nipple, and the other circled my waist to clutch my ass, caressing, digging into the muscle and flesh, caressing again, spanning the crease to grasp the other cheek.

All this with the delicious heat of the water dousing us, wrapping us in warmth.

"I can't believe you're here in my shower with me," Jeff said.

"Me either," I said, "but there's nowhere else I'd rather be."

"You're sexy." Jeff's fingers descended the plain of my belly to skim over the hillock of my pussy as he spoke, stroking the entrance with a single finger. "So goddamn sexy. Come for me, Anna."

I leaned back against the wall and out of the stream of water, spreading my thighs apart to allow him access.

"Make me," I told him.

He didn't answer, just pressed his lips to the mound of one breast, lapped his tongue down the wet surface to flick against the taut bead of my nipple. I pressed my palm against his iron-hard neck, pushing his mouth deeper around my breast. His other finger continued the teasing exploration of my pussy, tracing the lines of the labia, tickling the crease between my leg and hip, dipping in between my thighs to streak across my perineum.

He penetrated me at last, one gentle, questing finger into my aching channel. I clenched my buttocks and arched my hips forward, and he skinned the inner walls with the finger before pulling out to furrow against the nub of my clit. I gasped as he touched me there, eyes closed and whispering "yes" with an inbreath. Two fingers then, slipping back in and exploring my pussy, retreating out, grazing my clit, and then three fingers.

My hips were fluttering, my hands gripping his cock as handle, holding on to him as I pushed into his fingers. Pressure was rising, now, magma welling in my belly, surging up to ready for a volcanic eruption. His fingers stoked the heat, one finger in, curling to slash across my G-spot, eliciting a moan that echoed in the shower. Two fingers again, pulling out of my pussy to dovetail around my clit, pinching it, slipping back and forth.

His other hand was busy with my breasts, pinching and rolling my nipples, teeth now nipping the rippled skin of my areola, tongue laving the sides and across my chest and ribcage.

Finally he set a rhythm, three fingers diving in and back out, pressing onto my clit with every stroke. One small quiver in my belly at first, a buckle of the knees into his upstroke. My hands, slipping up and down on his manhood now, slow pumps around his swollen, straining head.

Another stutter, lower down, a swelling tremor pushed into a rolling waveform. Jeff sped the rhythm of his fingers' plunge, billowing the heaving my hips into a desperate gyration. Then he slowed, just before the upwelling explosion overtook me.

"Faster, please, faster," I breathed.

He complied, surging faster, biting my nipples and using both hands on me now, two fingers circling my nub, three fingers diving in. My hips were moving on their own now, pulsing upward. My hands worked his shaft in time with my hips' motion, and then...

every muscle buckled and tensed as my long-pent orgasm finally coursed through me, a rocketing surge of heat and ecstasy in my belly, pussy muscles clamping around his frenzied fingers, his mouth on my neck and lips and tits, my knees lifting me up and dropping me down.

"Inside," I gasped. "I need you...inside me."

"Don't have protection," he breathed against my breast.

"Birth control." I couldn't form full sentences.

Jeff's arms curled up around my ass, and then one hand lifted my leg by the knee. I guided him into me, leaning into his body, the shower spray, growing lukewarm now, blasting against my neck and the top of his head. He pulsed into me, a slow, careful thrust.

"Goddamn, Anna. You're so tight."

I opened my mouth to tell him it was just because he was so huge, but he thrust again and I could only gasp, breathless, as my pussy stretched to fit him. My labia formed an 'O' of taut-stretched flesh, burning and throbbing so wonderfully, my orgasm still pounding through me, constricting my inner muscles around his thick, slick member.

His thrusts timed with the contracting pulsations of my orgasm.

"Oh god, Jeff, yes..." I scraped the words past rasping vocal chords.

Every fiber of my being quivered; my eyelids fluttered, my thighs trembled, my fingers clawed down his broad back, my toes curled in, my breath caught on an inbreath and held; a plunge, and I came again, riding the crest of the last explosion, another plunge, and I came again, clutching to Jeff with all my waning strength.

He never sped his thrusts, held himself to slow, measured pushes, going deeper with each one.

"Anna." He grated my name past clenched teeth as he came, thrusting hard and deep to the rhythm of my name. Two syllables, a full thrust inward on the initial emphasis, our hips bumping together on the 'N', retreating on the outbreath 'A'.

I felt his seed hit my inner walls, felt him throb within me as he continued to come, and come and come, lips crushed to my shoulder.

He held my leg firm around his hip all the while, pulled on my knee for leverage, his free hand roaming my torso, breast to belly and back up, fingering my hypersenstive nipples.

The water was going cold now, and he finally let my leg down and pulled out of me. I shut the water off and pulled him against me, curling into his heat, our damp skin sticking together, our breathing matched gasps.

He moved away first, pulled a thick white towel from a rack and spread it open, drew me out of the shower. What he did next made my breath hitch. He scrubbed every inch of my body with the towel, beginning with my shoulders and moving down my back, across my belly, around each breast, my arms and sides, then my buttocks and thighs, down my legs and back up. The last thing he did was gently spread my thighs apart and clean my tender folds, wiping carefully downward and in to clean me of his still-leaking essence, his touch featherlight and almost reverent.

I couldn't help but do the same. Another dry towel hung on the rack, and I rubbed it across his muscles, cupping his sack and massaging his flaccid member with it. It was a moment both tender and erotic, and I didn't know what to do with it.

I followed him to his bedroom, a tiny space filled with queen-sized bed and a low dresser, and nothing else. No pictures, no posters or paintings or anything. The window was open, letting the brilliant noonday sunlight stream in, bathing everything yellow-white. The bed was neatly made already, the corners crisp, the blanket tucked in under the pillow in a line as straight as razor. On the dresser was a wide, shallow metal dish, filled with loose change, a single bullet shell, and a battered set of dog tags.

I sat down on the edge of the bed, naked, still trembling from the aftershocks. Jeff stood in front of me, looking down at me with an inscrutable expression on his face. He was just out of arm's reach, hands at his sides, his posture relaxed, but his gaze was intense, focused on me, sweeping and searching.

"What?" I asked.

He shook his head and closed the distance between us, standing between my knees. His cock was right at eye-level, point down and seeming to be waiting for me to touch it. I looked up at him, gave him a smile as I put my hands on his hips, traced the line of the muscles on his thighs.

I dragged my fingernail down the outside of his thigh and back up the inside edge to his groin. I watched his eyes as I traced my finger from the very bottom of his sack upwards, feeling the skin tighten under the pad of my finger, and then lifted his cock with my finger, tracing its length as well. His gaze was fiery, dark eyes glittering. His hands rested on my shoulders, not pushing or pulling, just touching me.

I ran my fingernail down his cock again, this time from the root against his belly down to the tip, then scratched the tip with my nail. The flesh of his cock was tightening, but he wasn't growing hard yet. He hadn't sprung into an instant erection, and I found myself enjoying the process of touching Jeff during his refractory period, learning the way his body looked and felt.

I scootched back on the bed and moved to one side, patting the blanket beside me. He hesitates, then climbs on the bed beside me. As he turns his back to me, ever so briefly, I see the reason for the long sleeve shirts. He's been burned badly on his back, shoulders, and arms, running down to his elbows and across one forearm.

He saw me notice. "Car accident, years ago."

I roll to lay my head on his chest, and his arm snakes around my body to cup the curve of my hip, resting there with familiar, tender affection.

"What happened?" I ask.

He blows air through puffed out cheeks. "Long story. My buddy and I were driving the Seeney Stretch, up in the UP. Hit a deer, flipped a couple times. I was in the passenger seat. Got tossed out of the car, which prolly saved my life. Well, my buddy Brett wasn't so lucky. Got trapped under the car when it stopped rolling upside down. I was pan-icked. I'd known Brett all my life. Had to get him out, so I tried to flip the car on my own. I did, too. Adrenaline rush, that kinda thing. Flipped it over so I could drag Brett out. Problem is I was pushing on the bottom of the car, where things were hot. Burned me."

That was the most I'd ever heard Jeff say all at once in my life.

"Did your friend..."

Jeff just shook his head and I let it go, turned my attention to slid-ing my palms along his body, fingertips exploring the heavy, unde-fined bulk of his muscles. I realized he's much bigger than I'd ever thought. His shirts made him seem smaller, somehow, but in reality, I think he would be much, much stronger than Chase.

"I'm sorry to hear that," I replied, belatedly.

"Long time ago." He shrugged, and turns his gaze to my body, nestled naked against his.

Our warm flesh merged in one long point of contact. I felt com-fortable there, held in his arms. Safe. The oddest thing was, even post-sex, still naked and feeling his hot skin and hard muscle, I felt just as at ease with Jeff as if we were setting up for a shift at The Dive.

His palm moved from the swell of my hip to the hollow of my waist, then down to graze my ass, curling around one cheek and hefting it, following the crease down to the fold where ass meets thigh and back up. He rolled so I landed on my back, supporting his head on his elbow. His free hand continued its slow exploration of my body, leaving nowhere untouched. He circled my kneecap, up the inside of my thigh, dips into my navel and the sides of my belly, my ribs; he spends forever on my breasts, lingering on every square inch of skin.

At last, at long last, he moved his attention downward, tickling my belly, my thighs, and finally slipping one long index finger to the keyhole gap of my pussy. I moved my legs apart, greedy for his touch, hungry to be stimulated, turned on, toyed and played with and sated. He didn't touch me to bring me to climax, at first. It was the same way he touched the rest of my body, as if...as if memorizing my body, creating a mental map of my curves to remember.

"You're beautiful, Anna." The way he said it, his was voice softer than I ever remember him speaking, a world away from the gruff voice he uses most of the time.

It was three words, but coming from Jeff it was worth ten thousand words. He was spare with words, to the point where sometimes getting him to use complete sentences could be a chore, like dragging answers from a teenager.

"Thank you."

He gave me his Jeff smile, the upward quirk of one corner of his mouth, just a twitch of the muscles, but a smile nonetheless.

I leaned up and kissed him, a slow meeting of lips, a gradual exploration of mouth-space with tongues. His arm wrapped around my back and pulled me closer, rolled me to my side facing him. One arm was trapped between us, and I used that one to touch his manhood, stiffening now under my caress. My other hand slipped up his back and rested between his shoulder blades, stayed there.

Encouraging his cock to full girth was a slow process, deliberately so. I could have used my mouth to speed it up, but I enjoyed just touching him, holding him, feeling its weight in my hand, brushing the tip in slow, small circles, cupping his balls in my palm, sliding up his length and back down in lazy dips and rises, twisting around him in spirals.

I wasn't even aware of movement, of a change of position. I blinked, breathed, and found Jeff above me, kneeling between my thighs, his hands on either side of my face, his flinty near-black eyes soft on mine, searching my face.

I didn't need to guide him in with my hands. He found my entrance without taking his eyes from me, as if his body knew exactly where to merge with mine. He slipped inside me with exquisite slowness, utter gentility, as if I were delicate. In the shower, he'd claimed me slowly, but his desire had been there beneath the surface, boiling within him like magma surging to the core of a volcano; he'd forced himself to go slow, as if savoring the experience.

Now, he went slow out of pure desire to simply take his time, in no rush, no hurry. He dipped down and kissed me, his tongue flicking out to meet mine in the rhythm of his hips' lunge against mine. My arms floated up as if borne on unfelt winds to wind around his neck as he kissed me; he slipped one thick forearm beneath my head as a pillow, and with his other hand cupped and caressed my breasts, whisking his palms across my nipples, tweaking them, circling and lifting and squeezing, as if he could never get enough of touching them.

All the while, his slow, inexorable thrusting into me, breathing unchanging, eyes locked on mine when we weren't kissing. And, just because it was Jeff, he was silent.

Then, when the fluttering of climax began in my belly and I moaned in his ear, wrapped my legs around his waist, he allowed himself one barely audible "mmmmm" in my ear, and then another when I dug my nails into his back.

He slowed, then. Just when my climax began, and his neared, he slowed, dragged it out. He wrapped his other arm under my head with the first, and now his thrusts were merely at the surface, barely entering, shallow dips, quick plunges and back out. I whined high in my throat, protesting the change. He only kissed me, and then plunged deep, once, drawing a gasp from me. Back to flutters, then, kissing me at each thrust, touch of the lips and thrust, again and again, his tongue darting between my lips each time.

The deepest stroke yet, then, burying himself inside me, "mmm-mmm" in my ear, breath on my cheek. Again, and deeper. Oh lord, another, deeper, and so slow. A rhythm, then, back to the exquisitely slow strokes, deeper than ever, hips grinding at each apex.

The only sound was our breathing, an occasional whimper, a soft "mmmmmm" from Jeff; sunlight streaks across our bodies, bright and hot.

The climax rose, brought from a small flutter to a sudden hot impending pressure, a kind of crushing need in my belly, deep inside me. This was like nothing I'd ever experienced. He took his time, pulsing into me, building up to the peak in steady blocks of pleasure, backing away from the edge each time, but not enough to allow us to slip back down and lose the burning need for release.

I couldn't have said how long he'd been above me, tireless and supporting his weight so no part of him rests on me. Minutes? Days? I didn't know, and didn't care. The unhurried pace was delicious, each stroke filling me completely, each thrust delivering wondrous pleasure throughout me.

I knew, when climax came, it would be blinding in its intensity, would carry on for an eternity. I had no doubt he would bring me there, in his own time, and I was perfectly content to let him take me there in his own time.

Slow strokes, deep and gentle, were replaced by longer, harder thrusts, after a time. I wrapped my legs around his ass again, pulled him against me at each thrust.

He wrapped an arm around my leg, and then other, and he was supporting his weight on my legs, kneeling above me, driving so deep, deeper than I'd ever been taken, so perfectly, incredibly deep, I thought perhaps he may lose himself inside me, and it struck me that perhaps this was exactly his desire, to bury himself within me and never leave.

In that moment, I wouldn't have argued.

The climax erupted, then, with my legs near his chest, held by his arms. It wasn't a sudden detonation, it was an inevitable overwhelming floodtide, washing through me not in waves but in a gradual upsurging. Our pace increased, but imperceptibly, until he was driving into me with relentless speed, but still gentle, never pounding.

"God, yes," I whispered, my first words since we began. "More."

He released my legs and curled over me, and I wrapped my arms and legs around him, clung to him, held tight to him as he found his release, and now I came with him. It wasn't hard, or explosive, or shattering. It was an intense falling into perfection, a coming home.

When he laid down next to me once more, I pillowed my head on his chest, felt his arms wrap around me, and fell into the deepest, most restful slumber of my life.

It was late evening when I woke up, facing away from Jeff, with his arm around my belly. His erection was a hard lump between my ass cheeks, and I knew by his breathing he was awake.

I'd never before woken up aroused, but in that moment I felt a rush of dampness hit my pussy and drip through me, my nipples standing on end. I pushed my ass into him, took his hand and brought it to my breast. He writhed his cock into me, caressing my breast.

I rolled to my stomach and rose up on my forearms and knees. "Take me like this," I said.

Jeff rose up to his knees behind me, palmed my ass with both hands and spread me apart, and now I felt the first touch of his tongue to my sex, an erotically slow lick up the length of my pussy, followed by another, each striking deeper, starting at my nub and moving upward to my perineum. Each swipe of his tongue had my hips bucking, had me rocking forward and back into him.

Gentle and slow and relentless and methodical, this was his way, bringing me to a gasping, whimpering climax in a puddle on the bed. Then he entered me, dipping a finger into me and following it with his cock and driving deep. I was collapsed on my face, still shuddering from the first orgasm when he drove into me, and I immediately, automatically rose back up to push back into him.

What I wanted, then, was for him to lose himself in me, to make him forget the gentility. I wanted his pleasure in me to be...rapturous, a turn around for the way he'd so carefully brought me to climax.

I rocked backwards into every thrust, moaning with each motion.

"Yes, Jeff, yes," I said, "Take me, take me hard."

"Don't wanna hurt you," he grunted.

He was moving faster now, gliding into me with his hands on my back, pulling me into him.

"You won't, I promise."

I slammed my ass into him, forcing him deeper, and again, and now he was beginning to lose control, growling low his throat, a long rumble as he pushed into me.

"Yes, yes," I gasped, "Just like this. God yes, it feels so good."

He was gripping my hips now, jerking me onto his cock, all technique abandoned, moving furiously. The explosions began, going from zero to full bore with seconds, from devouring his cock and loving it to frenzied orgasm with the space of a single thrust.

He came into me, clawing his fingers down my spine, thrusting slow and so wonderfully hard, my tits bouncing. His seed filled me, a hot jet spurting throughout me, drilled harder and deeper as he continued to climax.

I was shrieking with every thrust of his cock into me, sometimes whimpering his name, sometimes a wordless wail of ecstasy. His crushing thrusts slowed, finally, and he withdrew, pulling me down back into his arms.

"Goddamn, Anna. You make me feel so good," Jeff said, breathless.

I rolled into him, kissed him hard and full of passion. "*So* good. *So* good."

Silence, filled with our hands exploring each other's bodies, an almost idle survey of skin.

"I'm hungry," Jeff said. "How about some dinner?"

Maggiano's was busy, humming with subdued energy. It was a Saturday night, and from what I knew, you had to have reservations to get a table here on the weekends, but somehow Jeff had managed it.

I stood next to him as we waited for the host. He was dressed simply, in blue jeans and a crisp, spotless white button down and leather dress shoes, but he made it look formal, almost dressy. I realized again how attractive he really was.

When the host led us to our booth, Jeff's hand found my skin between my shoulder blades, where the back of my dress left my back bare, and even that small amount of contact left me trembling. A gentle, casual touch, but it was enough to make me want to feel his hand brushing down my back, sweeping across my naked backside again...

My sexual frustration was gone, but in its place was a raging, insatiable hunger. Now that I'd felt Jeff, had him, been in his bed and experienced his slow, thorough plundering, I couldn't get enough.

His dark eyes roved the restaurant, his big, warm hand holding mine gently. His presence next to me, his hand in mine...it felt natural, easy, and comfortable. But at the same time there was a sense of nerves in my belly, nerves and something else, a burning, fluttering of desire. His eyes found mine, and my heart pattered, thumping in anticipation.

We sat side by side in the booth, the light low and soft yellow, conversation from other tables washing over us in a dull blur of sound, Frank Sinatra and Ella Fitzgerald filling the spaces. We drank expensive wine, lingered over soup and salad, knees brushing, me asking questions and him answering in his typically spare way. I learned he'd been in the army for four years, done two tours in Iraq and been stationed in the Philippines. He skipped over the army bit, saying only that he'd been a grunt, seen combat, and that was it. I could tell he didn't want to talk about it. I knew if I asked, he'd tell me, but he'd rather I didn't ask.

As we ate, I let my hand wander underneath the table to rest on his thigh. I was feeling...daring. At first, I simply left my fingers on his leg, but, over the space of several minutes, let it drift incrementally higher until Jeff lifted an amused but surprised eyebrow. He gasped audibly when I moved my hand high enough to feel his package, a thick lump even through the denim of his jeans. A few subtle zipping strokes of my hand on his groin had him hardening under my touch.

"What are you doing, Anna?" Jeff whispered to me.

"Doing? Nothing. What am I doing?"

He growled, a low grunt of irritation, arousal, and amusement. "Teasing me."

I circled my palm on him, felt him get hard enough to need adjusting. I tucked my fingers in the waist band of his jeans and pulled them away, allowing his erection to spring vertical.

"Teasing?" I ran my tongue over my bottom lip, stroking his denim-covered length underneath the table. "I never tease. I make promises."

"Promises. I'll bet." He squirmed in his seat, fully erect now. "We're in the middle of a restaurant. How're you going to keep this promise?"

I smirked at him, mimicking his tipping of one side of his mouth. "I didn't say *when* I would keep my promise, just that I *would*. And I will."

"Well I call that teasing." Jeff's eyes twinkled, and the corners of his eyes crinkled, worth more than an outright laugh from any other, more verbose, kind of man. "And two can play that game."

We were done with dinner, sopping up the last of the pink vodka sauce from our plates with focaccia bread; our server came by with a tray of desserts.

"Did you save room for dessert?" Our server was a young man with a faux-hawk and a carefully-trimmed goatee.

At that very moment, when the server approached and directed his question at me, Jeff slipped his fingers under my dress, between my thighs, and into my pussy, all in one sudden motion. My eyes flew wide and I gasped. Jeff's face remained impassive as he fingered my clit in slow strokes.

"Ma'am? Are you alright?" The server's brow furrowed in worry; my gasp had been sharp, a surprised intake of breath.

"Yeah...I just...oh...stubbed my toe on the—the table leg." Fortunately for my excuse, there was a central bar holding the table up.

"Are you alright?"

I stifled another gasp as Jeff sped his finger's attention to my wet, sensitive nub. "Yeah, yeah I'm fine."

"So, dessert?" He pointed at the various items on the dessert tray: New York-style cheesecake, lemon cookies, apple crostada, crème brûlée, tiramisu and spumoni...

I stopped listening when he got to spumoni, although to be honest, I only heard half of what he said. My brain was scrambled by Jeff's strong, relentless finger circling my clit, by the need to stifle my usually-vocal reaction to my rising climax. I was *so* close, my thighs were trembling and I was using every shred of my self-control to not undulate my hips into his hand.

"Ma'am? Would you like to make a dessert selection?" The server was getting antsy and confused by my vacant, distracted behavior.

"Order what you want, Anna," Jeff said. "I'll eat whatever."

And now he's making pussy-eating jokes. Bastard.

"I'll have...ahem—" I was reaching climax now, and speech was nearly impossible. "Crem brulee, please." I wasn't sure I liked crème brûlée, couldn't remember ever having it; my mouth spouted an answer having completely bypassed my brain.

"Very good, ma'am," The server said, and then was gone, thank goodness.

I slumped down in the booth, breathing through my nose in long, controlled huffs, fists clenched tight, nails digging into my palms, fire pooling in my belly and crashing through my body...

...and then Jeff stopped, withdrew his hand and left it on my thigh.

"Goddamn it, Jeff!" I spoke through gritted teeth, wanting to scream in frustration. "Not fair!"

"Turnabout's fair play." The humor was in Jeff's voice, in the subtle softening of the corners of his mouth, the almost imperceptible lift of one eyebrow.

"Well *that's* not cliché."

"I wasn't *teasing*, Anna. I was making a *promise*."

"Oh, you bastard."

"Don't tease me, I won't tease you." His finger brushed between my thighs again, and they split open on their own, with alacrity. "But, if you ask nicely, I may finish what I started."

I grabbed his hand and tugged it higher, toward my wet, aching opening. "Please, Jeff?" I used my tiniest, most innocent voice. "I'm sorry. I won't ever tease you again."

Jeff smiled, both sides of his mouth lifting this time; a real, bonafide grin. I felt victorious, having wrested a full-fledged smile from a man as taciturn as Jeff Cartwright.

"I'm not sure you'll keep that promise, but I'll go easy on you this time." His finger brushed the fabric of my thong aside and delved into me. "But you have to be quiet. I wouldn't want to be embarrassed."

I gasped and fluttered my eyes. Of course, the server came up with my crème brûlée at that very moment. He only eyed me this time, frowning in puzzlement.

"Will there be anything else?" The server asked. He had our dessert in one hand, and the tray in another, presumably to show another table.

"I think I'd like to take a look at the desserts, actually, now that I've seen Anna's," Jeff says.

Jeff was circling my clit now, wringing a climax from me in record time. I forced myself to hold still, to keep my ass planted in the seat and my mouth shut. Miniscule whimpers kept escaping me, though, and the server was giving me increasingly perplexed glances as he pointed out and described each dessert.

"And what's in the tiramisu?" Jeff asked.

My teeth were grinding so hard my jaw ached, my fingernails were digging into my palms hard enough to draw blood, and I was exploding from the inside out, tongues of fire blossoming from my sex up through my belly and into my thighs and chest and down to my toes, curling them in my strappy platform sandals. If I were in a bedroom, I would be shrieking, moaning, clutching to Jeff for dear life as I rode the wave of ecstasy. Instead, I sat, still and silent, pitiful whimpers drifting from my lips at intervals as Jeff listened to the server patiently described ladyfinger pasties soaked in espresso, layered with blah blah blah OH GOD help me he wasn't stopping, surely he felt my muscles clenching around the fingers he'd slipped in and up to my G-spot, surely he knew I was coming, dying, but no, he kept stroking, kept pushing me higher.

A wave rocked through me, and I couldn't stop the gasp from escaping. To cover, and to mollify the server's concerned expression, I faked a cough. Which then turned into a real cough, and now Jeff *and* the server were looking at me in concern. I took a sip from one of the glasses of ice water, the ice now melted and the glass covered in dripping sweat. I put the glass to my lips, and a took generous mouthful of lukewarm water. What did Jeff do? He slipped his finger out of my pussy and explored backward, past the stretch of skin and pressed onto my second, tighter opening.

I spewed water all over the server. I mean I sprayed it all over the front of his apron, his shirt and tie, his order book...everywhere. *How humiliating.*

Jeff actually, factually chuckled. A real laugh. At my expense, sure, but a laugh. It was almost worth the embarrassment. He stifled the chuckle with a sip of wine.

When I could breathe again, I muttered an apology. "Sorry, it went down the wrong pipe."

The server looked disgusted, swiping ineffectually at himself with a napkin that had been dangling from his back pocket. He turned and walked away without so much as glancing at me or Jeff, still trying to dry himself off. When he was gone, I rounded on Jeff, my eyes blazing.

"What the hell was that?" I demanded.

Jeff just smirked at me. "I didn't want to leave you hanging."

Not like I had him, was the implication.

"But did you have to do it with the server there?" I squirmed in my seat, still feeling the aftershocks, and the surprise of his finger in my asshole. "And you *really* didn't have to put your finger *there*."

Jeff retained his innocently blank expression. "Where?"

"You know where." I leaned close, feeling more shy than I'd ever been; I'm not a shy girl. "You stuck your finger in my ass. That's why I spat water all over that poor server."

"I did? Gee, Anna, I'm sorry." Jeff's tone belied his words. He was all but laughing out loud. He knew exactly what he'd done. "Didn't you like it? You seemed like you did. I would never do anything you didn't like." That last sentence was delivered with an intense sincerity, all joking put aside.

"No, I did like it, honestly. It just surprised me. I've never been touched there." I kissed his jaw and whispered in his ear. "I wouldn't mind if you did it again, in private."

Jeff nodded, as if filing the information away for later. "Your crème brûlée is getting cold."

I giggled. "I just said the first thing that came to mind. I don't even know if I'll like it. I was a little...distracted."

It turned out I did like crème brûlée, and so did Jeff. Jeff paid the bill—ignoring my attempts to help pay it—and we left.

We got to Jeff's house, and I discovered he lived not far from me. Sexual tension filled the car, the smell of my arousal musky and intense. I wanted to touch Jeff, to feel him fill my hand, but he wouldn't let me. He held my hand in a firm grip on his thigh, a safe distance away from his crotch.

"I'd rather wait until we can do things right," was all he'd say.

I managed to wait until we were inside and Jeff was kicking off his shoes before I attacked him. I sidled up behind him and pulled at the buckle of his belt and then worked my way down the button-fly of his jeans. He slipped his shoes aside and straightened, putting his hands behind him on my hips. His head tipped back as I pushed his pants and boxers down to let his still-rising erection free. I wrapped eager fingers around him, the other hand cupping his sack and stroking the skin behind it.

Still cradling his balls in one hand, I caressed his length as lightly as I could, focusing my ministrations on his tip until the first pearls of moisture began to leak from him. I smeared my palm along his tip, and felt his knees buckle as I did so.

I circled around in front of him, pushed him backward to the couch until his knees hit and he sat down. I knelt in front of him and pulled his jeans and boxers off, and then settled between his knees.

"Anna, you don't have to, just because I—"

"I want to," I cut in. "I want to taste you. I want to feel you come like this."

He didn't argue. I took him in both hands, pushing my hands down on him in a hand-over-hand cycle. When his breath started to come in gasps and his hips to move, I leaned forward and fit him into my mouth. I had to stretch my jaw as wide as it would go to take him. He smelled and tasted clean and of male musk. His skin was salty and slick and smooth. I started a slow bob of my head, careful not to graze him with my teeth. He leaned his head back against the couch and tangled his fingers in my hair, not pulling or tugging, merely holding. One hand pumping him at the base, I slipped my hand underneath him and put my middle to his the stretch of skin behind his balls and pushed, gently, as he began to move his hips. He was struggling to keep still, I could tell. I lowered my head to take him deeper until he brushed the back of my throat, feeling him throb harder against my lips. His body tensed as I drew him out and wrapped my lips around his head, working him with my hand and sucking hard. My cheeks hollowed and he gasped a shuddering breath, arched his back, and tightened his grip on my hair.

"I'm...I'm coming, oh god..." His warning accompanied the jet of viscous, salty come against the back of my throat.

As soon as I felt him tense and climax, I put a second finger to his taint and massaged in circles, lips on his head, hand pumping in a blur. He shot a second time, and then a third, his back arched in a rigid curve.

When he finally went limp, I let him go and sat on the couch next to him, resting my hand on his belly.

"God, you come a lot," I said.

"Sorry," he said.

I laughed. "It's not a bad thing," I said. "I don't mind."

"Thank you," Jeff said. "That was...incredible. It's been a long time since I've—never mind."

"What?" I put my head on his shoulder and looked up at him. "A long time since what?"

"Since I've had that done to me."

"Do you like it?"

"Well, yeah, obviously. Like I said, it was amazing. But now it's your turn."

He stood and pulled me to my feet, drawing me into his bedroom. He kissed me as he unzipped my dress and let it fall to the ground around my feet, and we got lost there for a few minutes, clinging to each other and kissing.

"I could kiss you forever," Jeff said. He unhooked my bra, kissing my shoulder as he slipped the straps off.

He nudged me onto the bed, stripping my panties off as he did so, and then he was kneeling above me, staring down at me with an expression on his face that told me more clearly than any words how beautiful he thought I was. I wanted him, right then. I wanted to feel him fill me with his cock and hold me down with his weight as we came together. He wasn't ready yet, though, and he lowered his lips to my breasts first.

Each kiss of his lips to my skin was a slow, reverent, moist caress, moving with agonizing slowness over my body. With each kiss, my body turned hotter, my skin prickling in anticipation of his next kiss.

My nipples puckered and stiffened as he pinched one and licked the other. I was dripping from between my thighs, wanting, needing to feel his mouth move there next, but he didn't, even when he kissed his way down my belly to my pubis and hipbones. I spread my legs apart, willing him to put tongue inside me, but he licked my inner thigh instead, just outside my labia, then across my belly and down the other thigh.

I tugged a pillow from the head of the bed and stuck it under my back, elevating my hips to make it easier for him. He kissed my calf and behind my knees instead, then the soles of my feet. He ran his hands up my legs ahead of his kisses, touching his lips to my quad muscles, and then my hipbones again, and finally, at last, to my pussy. It was a kiss, at first, just his lips stroking my entrance, then a single shallow lap of his tongue.

Oh, lord, I thought, *he's really drawing this out.* His slow and methodical pace, his mouth and hands' detailed attention to every inch of my body brought my desire into furious life, making me desperate for him to lick me, to be hard and ready to push into me, fill me with his cock.

He refused to rush, though, and when he at long last dipped his tongue against my clit, I moaned out loud and pulled his head shamelessly against me. He rewarded me with a swift circle of my clit and a finger striking into me, curling in to stroke my walls and find my G-spot. After one swift circle, he resumed his unhurried bottom-to-top licks, focusing the apex of each swipe on my aching nub.

I'd come already, and hard, and I was anticipating another body-shivering explosion.

I wasn't disappointed.

He never increased his pace, even when he had to know by my breathing and moaning and desperate undulation of my hips that I was close. He paused once to spit into his hand, smearing the saliva against my asshole. His other finger was deep inside my pussy and stroking slowly, his tongue gliding in lazy circles around my clit.

He touched a finger to my tightest hole, paused and looked at me for approval.

"Do it," I breathed. "Gently."

He didn't answer, just pushed his finger against me, not trying to shove in but to coax the opening to stretch. His tongue and other finger had slowed to almost stillness, but not quite. And then he was inside, just his pinky finger. I gasped and drew my knees up, trying to relax the muscles. He left his finger there, letting me acclimatize to his presence, and then moved deeper with his characteristic gentle, unhurried pace.

His tongue began to move again, flicking my clit, and his finger in my pussy to stroke the rough patch of my G-spot, and now the fire and pressure began to burgeon. My breathing was a long-drawn, high-pitched moan, rising into a panting whimper as the climax rose to frenzied peak, his pinky working its way ever deeper until I felt his knuckles against me. I clawed my fingers into the bed and didn't even try to dampen my scream of climax, feeling ecstatic detonations rip through me, and now my pussy clenched around his fingers and my asshole clamped around his pinky and he was moving both hands in tandem, his pinky more slowly and shallowly, and I was blind and deaf and mute, every muscle, every fiber, every synapse of my being on fire and in twisting paroxysms of delight, and he did not relent.

When finally he removed his fingers from me, I went limp, nearly with ripples of pleasure.

Jeff brushed his lips against my ear and whispered, "I'll be right back."

I couldn't have moved if I wanted to, and right then, all I wanted was to lay and bask in the glow of a glorious orgasm.

He came back, put his hand in mine and helped me sit up. "Come on," he said to me, pulling me to my feet.

"Where are we going?"

"You'll see." He nipped my throat with a kiss and led me to his living room and out onto his back porch.

I hesitated on the threshold of the door-wall. "Outside? But...I'm naked."

"So am I," Jeff said. "There's a privacy fence, for one thing, and I only have neighbors on one side, for another, and for a third, I've got a wall around the hot tub."

Hot tub? Hell yes. I perked up at that. I loved hot tubs, but rarely got to use one.

I let him pull me outside, and sure enough, he had a ten-foot tall fence between his backyard and the neighbors. In addition to the privacy fence, he had built a three-sided wall around the hot tub.

The night was pitch black, and the tub glowed with submerged yellow light. A small, round, three-legged table stood to one side, a massive, four-wick white candle flickering merrily, and a bottle of wine. It was a small touch, just a table, a candle and a bottle, but it was enough to show he'd made an effort. It wasn't just sex, for Jeff.

Oh, shit. The thought was a flash through my head, but enough to make me wonder what I'd gotten myself into. And then Jeff's arms were around my bare waist and pulling me into a breath-defying kiss and all thoughts and worries were gone.

We broke apart long enough to step into the hot tub. It was scalding, and I wasn't ready to sink down into it yet. I held to Jeff, one arm around his neck, the other toying with his cock, testing his readiness for round two. Oh, he was ready.

He grew rigid under my hand, standing upright, unfolding, uncoiling. I put on foot up on the side of the tub and lifted up onto my toes, a gush of wetness spreading through me in eager hunger to feel him spear into me, fill me past-full. Jeff rumbled deep in his chest as he probed my pussy with his tip. I sank down from my tip-toes, plunging him up into me. He spread me apart, pushing into me and rising up on his toes until he was hilt-deep.

He sat down, easing us into the water. I put my legs on either side of his hips and he braced himself with his feet on the far edge of the tub, his hands supporting his weight and mine on the seats.

Holy shit, he's strong, I thought. He held us without straining, both of our bodies' weight held by the power of his arms and core. I sought the tub bottom with my toes, but he held me aloft, smirking he as began to thrust.

"Jeff, you're crazy," I gasped.

I was waist deep in the water, and he let us sink down, floating nearly weightless, and then he powered upward, spearing deep and then pulling out, only to thrust again. I curled over him, mouth quivering, breathless, as he moved. I was near climax almost instantly, burning all over again, boiling with pressure.

He finally sank to a sitting position on the bottom, and I wrapped my legs around his waist, the water at his chin and at my throat. He tilted his head up and I pressed my lips to his, tasting the tang of my essence on his tongue. He rolled his hips into mine, barely moving inside me, just enough to keep the pressure building.

The wine was open, and I reached for the bottle, tilted it to my lips and drank. It was a sweet red, inexpensive but delicious.

"I forgot glasses, didn't I?" Jeff said, taking the bottle from me.

"It's fine," I answered. "I'm not above drinking from the bottle."

We took turns drinking from the bottle, our hips rolling in synch all the while, until my climax was nearing peak, until I couldn't hold the bottle, so unsteady were my hands. The water was hot, the air with a bite of near-fall cool, and the night silent but for our breathing and the gentle bubble of the water.

Jeff set the half-empty bottle down and took my waist in his hands, lifting me and pulling me down in an increasing rhythm now. I bowed my back and bit his shoulder as the fire began to spread, turning from a slow blaze into a wild inferno, heat spreading through me until my hair stuck in damp tendrils to my forehead and cheeks, until I was sure the boiling of the water around us was due to the heat radiating out of me.

Jeff began to groan, lifting and pulling me, thrusting upwards, never letting our hips part, driving himself deep, and then his groans turned into my name, "Anna, Anna, *Anna*," pulsing deeper into me with each syllable. He pressed his lips to my throat and began to thrust harder, splashing water now, his arms curled up around my shoulders and dragging me down, down, down, harder, harder, harder, and I came, came so hard stars burst behind my eyes and my fingers gouged into his back and my head tipped back to gasp whimpering gusts of air into my heaving lungs.

He came, then, exploding into me, thrusting upward so hard I had to fall forward and clutch myself to his hot, dripping chest and cling to him as he lifted me clear of the water, the wet heat of his seed crashing against my inner walls in an endless flood.

"Oh my lord...oh my Anna," Jeff whispered, sinking down and stroking my hair from my face.

"God, that was intense," I breathed, nestled against his chest, his cock still buried inside me.

"I don't want to leave you," he said. "I mean, I want to stay inside you."

I wiggled my hips down onto him. "So don't. Let's stay like this until you're hard again, and then we can do it all over again."

He reached for the wine and we drank, me still sitting on his lap, the water bubbling around us, flushing us with heat.

I've never been a make-out session kind of girl. I like kissing all right, but as a means to an end. When I kiss a man, it get my juices flowing and all I want to do is keep going.

Then Jeff kissed me, post-coital, in the hot tub, and all that changed. It was a slow, delicate kiss, moving and shifting in its own rhythm, drawing me into it, pulling me down into the substance of the moment. For the first time in my life, I lost myself in a kiss, drowned in the taste of the man, the feel of his body around me, his strength supporting me, his manhood slick inside my sex.

It was just a kiss at first, and it continued thus for a timeless eternity, minutes and hours passing out of awareness, until I wasn't sure which way was up, where I was or even who I was, outside of the roaring passion of our lips' and bodies' matched fervor.

And then, gradually, he grew within me, hardening and lengthening, almost imperceptibly at first, but more noticeably with every passing second. His hands lifted to find my breasts, and with that sensual touch my awareness of sensation beyond the kiss broadened to include his cock inside me and his hips beginning to move and my pussy beginning to glide on him then...

The world obliterated. There was nothing but orgasmic brilliance, instant ecstasy from the very first full thrust, lasting for a time without time as he crushed into me, and I came again and again, until I was limp on top of him and still coming, shudders rocking through me with each roll of his hips, so much unending climactic fury that I couldn't contain it, could only writhe helpless on top of him until he began to grunt, moving in a thrashing rhythm into me, his breathing in my ear almost panicked; when he came, I fell over the edge of sanity into something else, and he clutched me as if he too had passed beyond the ability to contain the spreading infinity coursing between and in and through us.

Jeff had a way of making even a night spent in his living room seem exciting and fun.

One night, our DJ shift ended early, since the bar hadn't seen a single customer—other than Earl, the old graybeard in a John Deere cap who drank there every night—in more than two hours. We packed up, got takeout Chinese, a six-pack of cupcakes, a couple bottles of wine, and went back to Jeff's house.

We ate on the couch, watched *Bones*, and got drunk. This may not sound like fun, but it was. Well, maybe not *fun*, like bowling or go-karts or kinky sex, but satisfying. Pleasant.

After we threw away the leftovers and Styrofoam and those stupid square white boxes, Jeff pushed me down onto the couch, refilled my wine, and then shot me a mischievous smirk. I sipped my wine and waited. Jeff scooped up the remote and changed the channel to *Bravo*. Apparently he knew my dirty little secret: namely, an addiction to *Real Housewives*. I'd never tried to make him watch it with me, though, figuring no self-respecting guy would like it. New Jersey was on, my personal favorite.

He still had the silly grin on his face, though, letting me know he wasn't done. I wasn't sure how much better it could get, though. I mean, *Real Housewives of New Jersey* and wine?

It got better. He unwrapped a bumpy cake cupcake, handed it to me, and then knelt down in front of me.

"What are you doing?" I finally asked.

"You'll see. Just sit back and watch your show. Pay no attention to me."

He had something up his sleeve, I just knew it. He waited until I was immersed in my show, then rested his hands on my knees. I glanced at him, but he only shrugged and grinned.

"You're being weird, Jeff."

"No I'm not, I'm just drunk." Jeff laughed. "Now sit back."

I sat back, confused but curious.

Jeff's hands slid up my thighs to cup the curved sides of my ass, then arced across to unbutton my pants with a swift, feather-light touch.

"What are you doing?" I demanded.

"Nothing," Jeff said, unzipping my pants and tugging them down.

I lifted my ass up and with a single tug the jeans and panties were off.

"This doesn't seem like nothing," I said.

Jeff just smiled and touched his stubbled mouth to my knee, then the soft, sensitive skin of my inner thigh.

"Want me to stop?" Jeff asked, his lips nearly to my crotch now, moving to the other leg and tickling my flesh with hot, wet kisses.

I opened my mouth to answer, but my breath was stolen by his lips grazing my mound, his tongue laving over my labia. My hands were occupied, holding wine and a cupcake, and I realized this was his plan all along. He knew my favorite things, and was giving them to me all at once.

I closed my eyes and shut out Theresa's shrill voice, sipped my wine as Jeff's tongue speared into me. The wine burned hot and dry as it slipped down my throat, and Jeff's tongue licked waves of heat and moist desire through my nether lips. I took another sip and followed it with a taste of icing as Jeff slipped two fingers between my swollen labia and inside me, curling up to stroke the hypersensitive patch of skin high inside my walls.

This was sensation overload. The icing was sweet, the chocolate rich and crumbling, the wine potent and robust, and Jeff's fingers and tongue licked and swiped and swirled. Waves of rising climax sliced through me, fire and spasm and pressure all at once.

In the background, Caroline and Jacqueline and Theresa argued in overlapping voices, and I only heard every third word, the familiar themes of their recurring issues washing over me.

Jeff's unoccupied hand traced up my belly and under my shirt, tugged the cups of my bra down to free my nipples, and now his fingers rolled the taut responsive nubs, pushing the volcanic pressure of pending orgasm higher and higher. I gasped and bucked my hips as he increased his pace, his tongue circling my clit in narrowing concentric rings, his fingers on my G-spot and my nipples matching the rhythm, and I was on the edge, about to explode, god so close, and then...he slowed to nearly a stop. I wanted to scream, opened my mouth to say something in protest, but then he abruptly resumed his frenzied rhythm and I was barreling towards the edge once more.

At exactly the moment I was about to reach climax, Jeff slowed once more. When I took a breath to speak, Jeff pushed the wine toward my mouth, and I took another dutiful sip, feeling my head spinning from the wine, my palette exploding with the contradicting tastes of dry red wine and rich chocolate and sweet white icing.

Once more Jeff's tongue swiped in quick circles, his fingers stroking in time with his tongue, my nipples pinched and rolled and flicked, and now I was near the edge again.

"Let me come, Jeff," I gasped. "I'm so close, please...oh god, yes..."

He matched the rocking of my hips, driving his long, quick tongue into me and as I whispered his name he swept his tongue directly across my clit, striking the stiffened bundle of aroused nerves with the tip of his tongue. At the same moment, he pinched my nipple hard, stroked my G-spot with one finger, and I came in a blinding rush. Every nerve ending on fire, my body exploding, my breathing caught and stopped. My spine arched into a bow-shape, wine sloshed over my thumb, and Jeff continued spearing his tongue into my clit, pushing my orgasm higher, the pent up pressure billowing through me in a flood of ecstasy.

When the fires cooled and Jeff rolled back on to his butt, I could only lay limp and gasp for breath as aftershocks rocked through me. I felt Jeff's tongue lap at my hand where the wine had spilled.

"You seem to have crushed the cupcake," Jeff said with an amused chuckle.

I opened my eyes and glanced at my hand. When I came, my fist had clenched involuntarily, and now chocolate crumbs were spilling over my hand. Jeff just laughed and took the remainder from me, threw it away, and sucked up the crumbs with a hand vacuum before sitting down next to me with a glass of wine.

"That was incredible," I said.

"You liked it?"

I laughed. "I'm not sure how it could have gotten any better," I said.

"Then my work here is done," Jeff said, a satisfied grin on his face.

I noted a tell-tale bulge against the zipper of his jeans. I knew Jeff well enough to know he wouldn't ask for a return favor. He wasn't looking at me as he carefully and methodically devoured a bumpy cake. I was struck by an idea.

I slipped off the couch and knelt between his knees. Jeff just quirked an eyebrow and took a slow, deliberate bite, and then washed it down as I unbuttoned his pants. I unzipped him and pulled the jeans and boxers off, then took a cupcake from the plastic container. Jeff seemed less sure of what I was doing, suddenly. I broke the hardened chocolate shell of the bumpy cake to get at the icing beneath.

Wrapping one hand around the base of Jeff's cock, I dipped the fingers of the other hand into the icing. I smeared it over the tip of his shaft, dipped into the icing again and spread it down the length of him.

"Icing has always been my favorite part of a cupcake," I said.

Jeff grinned, then hissed as I licked up his cock from the root to the tip. His head flopped back against the couch as I swiped my tongue along his icing-covered flesh again, licking him as if his cock was an ice cream cone. I cupped his balls in one hand and gently massaged them as I wrapped my lip around his tip and took him into my mouth, backed away, and then bobbed down again. He gasped as I moved my fist up and down his length, sucking on his engorged, icing-smeared head. My saliva and the icing became a slick lubricant, and my fist slipped on his length without friction, and now I sucked hard enough to hollow my cheeks. He arched his back, stuttered a garbled warning just before he jerked his hips and came. I continued to move my fingers and mouth on him as he came, drawing the seed from him until he was softening in my hand.

Jeff looked at me with heavy-lidded eyes, a hazy smile on his face. I went to the kitchen, wet a paper towel and cleaned him carefully. I didn't imagine it would be fun to be sticky, after all.

We sat, half-naked, and finished our wine, and Jeff actually watched the show with me, although he muttered, "they're all fucking nuts," every five minutes the entire time.

I knew one thing for sure: I'd never look at cupcakes the same way, after that night.

A little over two weeks passed, and Jeff and I spent almost every spare moment that we could together, working, sleeping, eating, and making love...having sex...fucking. I wasn't sure what to call it, what word to use in reference to our coital activities.

Nothing we did was wild or kinky, just vanilla, multi-positional sex, but he rocked my world every single time. He was unfailingly slow in all things, never rushing to take me, never moving into me until I had found climax at least once, never allowing me to come down from climax until I was limp as a dishrag and completely sated.

He was wonderful. He was attentive. He was polite and considerate, and incredible in bed, and...

I panicked.

The panic began with an envelope, with a New York, New York return address, and the one name that could throw me for a loop: Chase Delany. Eleven letters, and I was sweating, my heart hammering, confusion pumping through me, and I hadn't even opened it yet.

Jeff had swung me by my apartment to get clothes and check my mail and appease Jaime for having vanished for two weeks. I sorted through the mail: *bill, bill, junk, bill...holy shit what is this?*

Jeff noticed me freeze with the envelope in my hands.

"What is it?" He asked, concern tingeing his voice."

"A letter." My voice was small and tight.

"From?"

A pause too long. "Chase."

An even longer pause. "Chase." A lift of the chest and a slow out-breath was his only reaction. "Might as well open it, then." Jeff's eyes were shuttered, cold, and guarded.

I opened the letter. A plane ticket to New York fell out of the envelope, and I unfolded the letter with trembling fingers:

I need to see you.

Chase

I tossed the letter on my lap and sighed, a long, shuddering, almost-but-not-quite crying whimper of desperate confusion. My thoughts were a jumble of noise and curses and hysteria.

What do I do? What do I do?

The thought repeated itself, over and over. Jeff kept silent and drove. I thought of Chase, of the one night I'd had with him. He made me feel alive as never before. He'd awakened my hunger not just for sex but for life. I would never have even considered being with Jeff if it wasn't for my time with Chase.

And god, Chase had done things to me that I didn't know were possible. He'd done, hot, kind of kinky things that I really had liked, and wanted again. And again.

Jeff...god, the man didn't need any of that to rock my existence.

But Jeff wanted more. Expected more. Needed and deserved more. It wasn't just sex for Jeff. And I wasn't sure I wanted that, at least not yet.

New York? With Chase? It could be incredible. Who am I kidding? I KNOW *it will be incredible.*

Jeff finally pulled his Yukon over to the side of the road. We were on a dirt road in the middle of nowhere, fields on both sides, a glowering gray sky heavy around us and threatening rain, trees in the distance. AM talk radio whispered in the background, only audible in the silence as Jeff waited for me to speak. He wouldn't ask. If I didn't say anything, he'd just wait until it was clear I wasn't talking and that would be that.

"He...he wants me to visit him in New York." The words were like small, hard stones tumbling out of my mouth.

A long, fraught silence. "And you want to go."

"I don't know, Jeff. I don't know." I picked up the plane ticket and stared at it like it could answer my dilemma. "Yes, I do. But I also don't."

Silence, Jeff staring out the window as raindrops plopped in slow, staccato rhythm on the windshield, abruptly blossoming into a downpour.

"Say something," I said.

"So go. Don't let me hold you back. If New York is where you want to be, then go. Be happy. We had fun while it lasted."

"Jeff, I—"

"It's fine, Anna." Jeff pulled the gearshifter into Drive, slowly and carefully, as if he wanted to slam it, but didn't. "You *do* want to go. I can see it in your face, but you're worried about hurting me. Don't. I'll be fine."

He took me home, driving in silence. When we pulled into the parking lot of my apartment complex, he put it into park and finally met my eyes.

"Be happy, Anna. If that means going to New York to be with Chase, then go."

"Jeff—"

He cut me off with a kiss, slow—as all things with Jeff are—and delicate. A farewell.

"Goodbye, Anna."

It was a dismissal.

I got out of the car and went to my door. Jeff pulled out backwards and drove away without looking at me.

My flight was for ten the next morning.

I was on it.

Big Girls
Do It
Wilder

*O*ne glimpse of Chase Delany in leather pants, a tight T-shirt, and shit-kicker boots was all it took to get my libido raging, and to drive away any lingering doubts about coming to New York.

Well, the doubts were still there, they were just pushed down under a torrent of lust.

He stood waiting for me, thick arms crossed over his broad chest, dark hair messy and sort-of-but-not-quite spiked, brown eyes blazing. He looked like he could, and would, drag me to the nearest bathroom and fuck me in a toilet stall. How do you resist that kind of naked lust?

You don't.

He pulled me into a hug, palms circling on my back, drifting lower and lower, and then he grabbed my ass in full view of everyone in the airport. I opened my mouth to protest, and then he kissed me, hard enough to take my breath away and make me forget what I was saying.

I'd almost forgotten how he could do that.

"Come on, hot stuff," he said, "I've got a cab waiting."

He pulled me into a fast walk, and I forgot to ream him out for groping me in public. *Besides,* I asked myself, *how much do I really mind?* Not so much, came the answer. He was claiming me. I didn't mind being claimed. And oh boy, the promise of the things he would do with his hands, when we were in private, had my blood racing.

"How was the flight?" He asked.

"Fine. Nothing eventful. How's things with the band coming?"

"Great! We're in the studio right now, recording our first LP. Once that's in post, we're going on tour, just local stuff at first, New York, Buffalo, Atlantic City, DC. We'll be opening for some big name bands though, so it'll be great exposure." He squeezed my hand, his excitement palpable, radiating off him in waves. "Have you ever been to a recording studio? I'll bring you with me. You'll love it. It's so fun."

He chattered all the way through baggage claim and out to the taxi line. The taxi ride into the city was full of more Chase-chatter with barely a pause for breath. He didn't ask me much of anything about how I'd been since I'd seen him last.

His hand crept up my leg as we sat in the back of the taxi, and slow crawl up to the hem of my skirt. I let his chatter wash over me and focused on wondering how far his hand would venture, and how far I'd let it. The cabbie's eyes flicked back to us every once in a while, and I wondered how much he could see through the rearview mirror. I tried to think about being in a car, driving, looking in the mirror into the backseat.

You can't see much, can you?

I smirked, and decided to let Chase explore as far as he wanted, just as a dare. I let my legs loosen a little, and Chase's fingers made their first exploratory move under the hem. It wasn't much of a skirt, really. Short enough to need my legs crossed when sitting in view of others.

Chase was going on about isolating the instruments and layering them in post-production, and how his bassist had trouble playing his part without the rest of the band. I nodded, made agreeable noises at the appropriate places, and slid my bottom down a bit farther.

His fingers were tickling my inner thighs, working upwards. Another shift of my legs, and his forefinger was brushing my pussy through the thin silk of my panties. I bit my tongue and forced myself to keep still. He glanced at me and grinned, a cat's-caught-the-canary smile. Then his middle finger worked its way underneath the band next to my leg to slip into my folds, which grew wetter the farther he got.

He never slowed his patter as he found my clit with one finger, and now he circled it, slow and soft. I swallowed hard and tried not to gasp when the climax began almost immediately. God, was I ready. It was as much anticipation as anything. The memory of what Chase could do, and would do.

A soft sigh escaped me, and the cabbie glanced back, a smile crinkling the corners of his eyes. *He knows*, I thought. But I didn't care. I was close, raging and ready. He never increased his pace, just kept a slow and steady stroking rhythm, even when the cabbie struck up a conversation about...I don't even know what. Something inane. My thoughts were a jumbled mess, scattered and lost in the blaze of a rising climax that wouldn't pass the edge.

I put my hand over his and pushed, wanting him to go faster, harder, but he only let a corner of his mouth tip up in a mocking smirk.

The bastard is playing with me, I realized.

By the time the cabbie let us out at Chase's address, a modest walk-up shared with the rest of the band, I was a quivering, knock-kneed wreck. Chase grabbed my single suitcase from the trunk, paid the driver, and led me in. He gave me a tour, a long, detailed tour. He introduced me to his friends/bandmates/roommates, and made sure they engaged me in witty banter. Witty fucking banter, when I was a few good touches away from coming, and hard.

I was on the edge still, every step brushing my thighs together and making my nub ache harder. It didn't help that Chase took every opportunity during the tour and the conversation to touch me in some surreptitious way, just enough to keep my desire alive and burning.

I was snarling with unfulfilled sexual need and irritation by the time Chase showed me to his room and closed the door behind him, twisting the lock with a flourish. He held my bag in one hand, the other in his pocket, a shit-eating grin on his face. I was flushed, my hair sticking to my temples, my legs shaking like leaves.

"Miss me?" Chase asked. Cocky bastard.

I attacked him. I mean, I just about flying tackled him. He dropped the suitcase with a loud thud and caught me against his chest, our tongues clashing and colliding, hands ripping zippers open and peeling clothes off.

Chase pushed me away, chest heaving, and pulled my shirt over my head, going slowly now, and then pushed my skirt down past my hips.

He was hard, his erection bulging against his pants, and I reached for him, but he moved out of reach.

"My turn first," he said, unhooking my bra. "I've missed you. I need to see you."

I wasn't sure if that was a self-centered thing, or a compliment. It didn't matter. He had me naked in front of him, and he was running his hands over my body as if it were the most precious thing he'd ever seen, and simply couldn't get enough.

I was wet and trembling, aching. I wanted him to push me down onto the bed and slip inside me, take me hard, or slow, or anything.

"Take me, Chase," I breathed. "Take me, please."

"Are you begging me?" Chase asked, rolling a nipple gently between a thumb and forefinger.

I arched my back, thrusting my breast into his hand, writhed my hips into his thigh.

"Yes." I wasn't above begging. "Please, Chase. I want you."

Chase stepped back, taking his hands off me. "Say it, baby. Beg me."

He wanted me to play the game. Well, I could play too. He was hard, and I knew he wanted me. His eyes betrayed him. The twitching curl of his fingers betrayed him.

I moved toward him, putting an extravagant sway to my hips. I slipped my hands underneath his chest to his nipples and pinched, hard. He grimaced and tried to escape, but I followed him. I bit his earlobe, breathing into his ear, and dug a single finger under the waistband of his leather pants, brushing the tip of his cock. His stomach jerked inward, and his hands flew to my waist, cupped my ass, pulled me against him. I circled around behind him, kissing his neck, his jaw, and his ear again.

"Beg you?" I whispered. "How about you beg me?"

Chase squared his shoulders and set his jaw. "I don't think so."

I laughed, and reached around his waist to unbutton his pants. His hands groped behind to reach for me, but all he could reach at this angle were my hips. I let him touch me. My hips ground into his ass, and I tugged his pants down, just enough to free the tip of his cock.

"I'm so wet, Chase," I whispered, rubbing the pad of my thumb on the drop of pre-come oozing from him. "I'm wet for you. I'm aching. I want you inside me. I want you to fuck me, Chase."

He tried to turn around, but I danced to follow his motion, and he went still. "It's not nice to tease a girl. Don't you know that?" I said. Chase groaned.

I dipped my hand into his boxer-briefs to take his full length in one hand. He rolled his hips, but I let go, scraping the tip with a fingernail in slow, gentle circles.

"How about you beg *me*," I whispered. "You know I want you. I could drop to my knees and suck you off, right now. All you have to do is beg."

Chase sucked in his breath between his teeth, but otherwise kept silent and still. I pushed his pants down a bit farther, past his hips. My teeth at his earlobe again, I took his balls in one hand and his cock in the other, stroking and massaging. Chase refused to move, even when I began pumping him. A change in tactics was required, then. I pulled his shirt off with one hand, still sliding my fist up and down his length. He couldn't stop his breathing from changing, though, and I knew he was nearing the end of his control.

Next came the pants, which were more of a struggle with one hand, but I did it, along with some judicious use of my feet. He was naked too, then, and my hands were doing their slow work on his cock, his breathing growing ragged, his hips beginning to tremble despite his attempts at control. At last, a moan escaped his lips, and that was my cue.

I let go of his shaft and massaged his sack, pressing a finger in a gentle circle to his taint. He groaned, growled, and thrust his hips, close, so close, but unable to come without me. He grabbed for my hands, but I resisted his attempts to guide me back to him.

"Anna," he said, his voice ragged. "Goddamn it."

I moved in front of him, pressed my body against his, slid my pussy against him, ground into him, slipped my hands over his body, kissed him everywhere.

Time for the real teasing.

I dropped to my knees, kissing his torso on the way down, took him in my hands again, caressed his cock in a hand-over-hand motion. He threw his head back, anticipating.

Anticipate away, baby, I thought. *Not gonna happen how you think it is.*

I even went so far as to wrap my lips around his head and suck until my cheeks hollowed. He was close, I could feel him tensing, about to come, and I spat him out again, glancing up at him, a wicked smile on my face.

"Oh, I'm sorry, were you about to come?" I said, trying to sound innocent.

Chase growled at me and tangled his fingers in my hair, but didn't apply any pressure.

"Not gonna work," he growled.

I lifted an eyebrow in a 'we'll see' gesture. I took him in my mouth again, stroking him with my hands now as I bobbed on him, put a finger to his taint again and massaged, faster now, hands sliding up and down, lips sealed around his head, and his knees began to move....

This time his growl of frustration was loud and irritated.

I crawled onto the bed, laid down on my back and spread my knees wide. Chase's eyes followed me, hungry and predatory. I slid my hands on my skin, rubbing up from my belly to take my breasts in my hands, thumbing the nipples, hefting the heavy mounds, then down between my legs. Slow, then. A single finger tracing the crease between my labia, dipping in to swipe the slick juices.

"Look how wet I am," I said, showing my glistening finger. "You want me?"

Chase crawled up on the bed, eyes burning. I slapped my knees closed and covered my breasts with my arms, as if suddenly demure.

"Tell me you want me," I said.

Chase rocked back on his knees, brow furrowed in irritation. "You know I do."

"Say it."

"I want you."

I shook my head. "Tell me what you want to do to me."

"I want to tie you up and fuck you until you can't walk."

I widened my eyes as if shocked. Chase grinned and scooted off the bed, rummaged in a dresser drawer and pulled out four neckties. He held them up, two in each hand.

I spread my hands and feet wide, waiting for him. This time, he tied my hands and feet both, and I felt a rush of true nerves, then. With my feet free, I wasn't as vulnerable. I was completely at his mercy.

I was spread-eagle before him, and now he climbed up on the bed between my legs, ran his hands up from my knees to my thighs, dragged a thumb down my pussy, not entering, but teasing.

He could tease me as long as he wanted, touch me until I was near to orgasm and then stop. For hours, if he wanted. I refused to let fear show on my face. I squeezed my eyes shut and pretended indifference as he teased my entrance with a finger.

A single push inside, one finger. I gasped, bucked my hips. I kept my eyes closed, enjoying the sensation without sight. Two fingers, then, curling up to caress my G-spot, and now I whimpered. Two fingers and a tongue, stroking my walls and licking my clit, and I jerked my hands against the bonds holding me in place.

Climax rising, rising, fire burning, and Chase kept going, bringing me to the edge.

"Don't stop, please, please don't stop," I said.

He didn't stop. He flicked and stroked and licked me over the precipice, and I moaned, refusing to scream. He didn't stop, though. I was hypersensitive, every touch like fire on my skin, and I wanted him to stop, to give me a minute, but he didn't. This was a new torture. He withdrew his fingers and used his tongue alone, moving in circles and squares, side to side and up and down, and now...holy shit, another orgasm blossomed through me and I bit off a shriek of ecstasy, pleasure so potent it was like pain.

His weight descended on me, and now I felt a new pressure probing my entrance, his cock, now, finally. But he didn't enter me. Oh, how I wanted to beg him, but refused. He pushed the very tip inside, gripped himself in his hand and moved his cock in circles inside me, brushing my clit, and now it was there, his moist tip against my throbbing nub. He thrust, ever so slightly, sex in miniature. I sucked in a ragged breath at the flush of lightning bursting through me.

And then he pulled away, probably about to come himself. His lips found my breast, and his fingers the other, and now I entered a new realm of heaven as he licked and laved and tongued and pinched me.

There was no warning. He thrust inside me in one push, driving to the hilt, hard. My eyes flew open and I breathed a whimper, straining against the ties. His mouth remained on my nipple, and he didn't thrust again, just stayed there, buried to the root, our hips grinding together. I tried to move into him, but he held my hips down with one hand.

He was inside me, and another climax was building. I wanted him to move, *needed* him to thrust.

"Please..." I couldn't help myself.

He didn't move. He grazed his teeth on my stiffened nipple, then moved to the other. His hand held me down, kept me from rolling my hips.

"Damn it, Chase, please!"

I was past games. I'd come twice without him inside me, and it just wasn't the same. I wanted him deep, wanted to feel his length sliding inside me.

"Please what?"

"Enough teasing. Just fuck me."

"Hard, or soft?" He accompanied his question with a slow pull out and a hard thrust in.

"God, yes, just like that. Both. Either. I don't care!"

He moved again like he had before, a torturously slow withdrawal, until only the very tip was left inside me, and he hesitated there, stopping the flutter of my hips with his powerful hand, and then he crashed back into me. I gasped when he plunged in. He did it again, and again, slow out, fast in.

Then he switched, pulling out quickly and driving in as slow as he could. More teasing. I wanted rhythm, I wanted him to move and move and move, hard and fast or slow and soft, I didn't care, but I couldn't find release like this. It felt delicious, but it wouldn't bring me over the edge.

He switched tactics again, now adjusting the depth of his strokes, shallow, shallow, setting a rhythm but only a few inches in and out. Maddening. Deeper now, yes, I whispered encouragement, gasped his name as he neared what I wanted, deep thrusts hard inside me.

I felt him abandon the games. He settled his weight on me, forearms planted underneath my neck, his lips crushing mine in hungry kisses. Finally, thank god, he drew out and plunged in, deep, as far as he could go, and again, a slow rhythm at last.

"God, Anna. I missed you. I missed this, so much."

I missed it too, but I couldn't speak to say it. The anticipation of this, all the many minutes of teasing had me desperate for him, had the explosion wild and rampant through me, but I couldn't move anything by my hips in the shallowest of rolls. I wanted to wrap myself around him, hold him as he drove into me, faster now, but I couldn't.

I tugged at the ties, jerked my feet, bucked wildly as he moved above me.

"Oh god, oh god," I moaned, needing to be freed, "let me go, let me go!"

He was gone, lost in the frenzy, and I could only gasp his name. He came, hard, so hard, and the fiery liquid of his seed filling me sent me over the edge, the mad thrust of his cock inside me sent me over the edge, his body going stiff in the throes of orgasm sent me over the edge.

This climax made stars crash in blinding bursts behind my eyes, and I couldn't stop the shrieks this time. Fire in my veins, in my muscles, in every cell, but still he thrust, pushing me past orgasm into desperation, back into pleasure so powerful it hurt.

At long last his motion slowed and he untied me with trembling fingers.

Something twinged in my heart, a brief but sharp pang of some emotion I didn't recognize. I didn't like it, didn't want to categorize it, and I pushed it away. I curled in to rest my head on Chase's chest.

"God, I needed that," Chase said, after a long silence.

"It was definitely intense," I said.

Chase gave me an odd look, which I interpreted to mean he'd expected me to say "me too." Which was dangerously close to having to realize it hadn't actually been all that long...

Shit. This is awkward.

The look passed, and I let myself drowse, feeling Chase's arm around me, his thick pectoral muscle a perfect pillow.

I woke up to Chase shaking me gently.

"Come on, sleepyhead. We've got reservations."

"Hmmm-what?" I forced myself to a sitting position, the sheet pooling around my waist. "Reservations?"

"For dinner. This place my buddy knows about, real tiny, but really great food." He grinned and tugged the sheet off me. "So get moving. Dress up nice."

I'm not even sure if the restaurant even had a name, honestly. The menus were small squares of thick white paper printed in black calligraphy. There was no name, no prices, no descriptions, just the item name. Very...minimalist.

The food was delicious, though. Incredible, actually. Strange pairings like steak and roasted apple, or garlic hummus and pork chops with candied asparagus. Bizarre. I found myself having a really great time, which shouldn't have surprised me, but did. I'd never been on a date with Chase. Never spoken to him outside of Ram's Horn and our one night together.

I felt panic bloom in my chest as I thought about that. I didn't know Chase *at all*. I didn't know where he'd grown up, if he'd been ever married or engaged before, if his parents were alive or if he had siblings or if he liked vegetables.

What am I doing here? I shouldn't have come. This was stupid. I should have stayed in Detroit with—

I cut my train of thought off ruthlessly. I wouldn't, couldn't think about *him* while I was with Chase. That was too close to a whole mess of emotions I didn't want to think about.

"Anna?" Chase's voice cut through my tangle of thoughts.

"Hmm?"

"I asked if you'd ever been backstage before."

"You did?" I shook my head and tried to clear the thoughts away. "Sorry. I'm just...sorry. No, I haven't."

Chase frowned, then waved a hand in dismissal. "Anyway. I got a text while you were sleeping. Our agent booked us to play a club in Harlem tomorrow, opening for a local band. It's a great opportunity for the band, and I figured you could watch from backstage. It'll be fun."

"Sure, sounds great."

We finished eating in silence, and finally Chase set his fork down with a clatter. "You seem distracted."

"Sorry, Chase. Just...I was dealing with some drama back home when I got your letter."

"Anything you want to talk about?"

"No, not really," I said.

"Okay, well, I'm here if you do."

Throughout dessert—paper-thin crepes filled with handmade apricot preserves, dusted with powdered sugar—I learned Chase had an older brother in accounting, in Connecticut, and a younger sister studying law at Duke, parents both passed on, no grandparents, no uncles, no cousins. He'd been engaged once, three years ago, but it had ended due to her being a cheating skank.

I in turn told him about my sordid past, or some of it. I mentioned my mostly-normal mom, including her predilection for popping Oxy like Tic Tacs, and I mentioned my brother, who'd joined the Marines out of high school and never came back. I also didn't mention my dad, who'd been quick with the Jack Daniels and quicker with his fists. I didn't mention the guy with the knife in the alley, my first time DJing, when I was eighteen, before I met Jeff.

I suspected there were things he hadn't mentioned, and I didn't push.

I don't have to tell Jeff any of this, because he already knows. The thought was errant and unwelcome.

We left the restaurant and strolled down the street, Chase looking sexier than he had any right to in a different pair of leather pants, these faded, beaten gray, with a white button down and a plain black tie loosely knotted around an open collar.

"How many pairs of leather pants do you have, exactly?" I asked.

Chase laughed. "Too many. They're my thing, you might say."

"Do you ever *not* wear leather pants?"

"Not if I can help it. They're suitable for all occasions. You can even wear them to weddings, if you pair them right."

I had to admit he did look sinfully sexy in leather pants, which reminded me of my nickname for him when I'd first met him: *Mr. Sexypants.*

Another errant thought flew through my head, a reminder how long ago it seemed that I'd met Chase and had that night in his bed. The weeks with Jeff had seemed endless, longer than they really had been. A lifetime, almost.

Why do I keep thinking about Jeff? I'm with Chase.

I shook my head and threaded my arm around Chase's. "So, Mr. Sexypants. What's next?"

"Mr. Sexypants?" Chase quirked a corner of his lip up in an amused smile.

"That's the nickname I gave you the night we met."

"I can dig it." Chase tangled our fingers together. "Well, we can go have some drinks, or we can go back to my place and fuck like bunnies."

"Sounds good," I said.

"Which?"

"Both. Well, first the one, then the other."

Chase nodded, and we hailed a cab, ending up at a crowded bar stuffed with cheering sports fans and half-naked women. I felt over-dressed in my miniskirt and halter top. I mean, seriously, most of the women I saw were wearing almost nothing, booty shorts halfway up their asses and a bra, if that. Chase's eyes wandered, as men's eyes will, but he soon turned his attention back to me. We drank vodka and cranberry juice and tried to talk over the noise. We were crushed into a back corner, standing up. I was up against the wall, Chase pressed into me, and we soon abandoned all pretense of conversation.

He focused on my neck for awhile, his lips cold from his drink, his breath hot, and every kiss he planted in his slow descent to my breasts made my nipples stand higher and harder with desire. I couldn't help noticing we weren't the only couple thus occupied, as most of the dark corners were taken by couples in similar positions. A few seemed to be actually going at it, the girls on their date's laps.

His mouth finally found the edge of my shirt and could go no farther down, not without pulling my breast free, and hell no to that. Not in public. I didn't care how dark the corner was.

The problem was, I wanted it. He'd found my erect nipple even through the shirt and bra, scratching at it with a fingernail till it stood harder, and yes, his other hand slid up my skirt and stroked my damp panties. He was hard, his bulge against my belly, and I could almost but not quite make myself reach into his pants. No one was paying attention to anyone else, and any noises we might have made would have been swallowed by the too-loud music, the blare of the TVs, and the cheering, laughing, screaming, chattering buzz of the bar patrons.

My blood was racing, my heart hammering. He'd worked one finger around my panties, and I was lifting up on my toes as he worked it in slow circles.

Do it, Anna. No one's watching.

I dug my hand into his pants and touched him, felt sticky wetness smear my palm as I stroked him. He groaned against my chest, a sound felt in my bones rather heard. I pulled his face up to mine and kissed him, heat blossoming in my belly as his tongue explored my lips.

A door opened not far away and a couple snuck out, hand in hand, sated grins on their faces. I tugged Chase to the door I'd seen the other couple leave, discovered it to be a bathroom, of sorts. It clearly catered to this purpose, with a chaise lounge in one corner.

Chase grinned at me, then pushed me toward the lounge. I moved to lay back on it, but Chase had other ideas. He gripped my hips and turned me facing away from him. I knew what he wanted, and I went along with it. Shimmying my panties off and stuffing them in my purse, I knelt on the lounge chair on my hands and knees. Chase grinned and licked his lips, then pushed my skirt up over my hips.

He caressed my ass with a gentle hand, then smacked me, hard enough to make me shriek in surprise. More smooth circles on my ass cheek, then a smack. This time, he speared two fingers into my wet pussy at the same moment he smacked me, and I had to grip the arm of the lounge with one hand.

The bathroom door didn't have a lock. I realized this as Chase straddled the lounge chair standing up, positioning himself behind me. Anyone could walk in and see me getting railed from behind. It shouldn't have made me wetter, but it did.

A zipping sound, and then his fingers were replaced by his cock, and I bowed my back upward as he thrust into me. His hands gripped my hips and jerked me into him. He wasn't gentle, and I liked it. Oh god, did I like it. He pounded into me, one hand on my hip, the other fingering my clit as he plunged. I didn't bother trying to muffle my moans as he drove into me, harder with each thrust, flesh slapping.

"God, you're so tight," Chase groaned. "I love fucking you like this."

"In...a public...bathroom?" I had to gasp the words past the grunt that escaped me at each thrust.

"It's hot, but no. I meant from behind."

I heard the door unlatch, and then a surprised male voice: "Whoa. Nice."

"Fuck off," Chase growled, and the door closed again.

I should have been mortified, but wasn't. I should have been, but I realized I'd had more than a few vodka cranberries, and the shame was a low burn in the back of my head that I knew I'd feel later. But now, oh god, now I didn't care, not with climax so close, not with Chase's cock slamming into me, and his finger working my clit as he thrust, adding an edge to the fire exploding through me, and the knowledge that someone else had seen me like this only fueled the fire, added a frenzy to it, and now I was falling over the edge.

"Give it to me," I groaned, "yes, give it to me."

"Say my name," Chase said. "Say my name."

"Chase, Chase." I breathed it.

Then he pushed a finger onto my asshole, not pushing in un-lubricated, thankfully, just circling, and I screamed into the arm of the lounge, my head thumping against the fabric as he pistoned his hips into me.

He came, then, slowing his thrusts but driving deeper than ever and his fingers dug into my skin and he froze with his hips to my ass, deep and spurting seed through me.

"God, Anna. You make me come so hard." He spoke slumped over me, breathing in stuttering gasps.

We cleaned up and left the bathroom, getting looks from more than one person, telling me we'd been heard as well as seen.

"Let's get out of here," I said to Chase.

Even my heady buzz couldn't cool the flaming of my cheeks.

"You don't want another drink?"

I stalked towards the door, trying to get away from the amused eyes I felt on me. "No. Not here at least."

"Honey, it's fine—"

Honey? I wondered where that endearment had come from.

"I want to go," I cut in.

"Okay then."

We left and walked back to Chase's place in silence. I wasn't sure what I was feeling, and I didn't know how to express it.

"Anna, look, I—"

"I'm not mad. I've just never done anything like that before. They *knew*. They heard us."

"It wouldn't be the first time people have gotten carried away in that bathroom, I'd wager."

I gave him a cross look. "Well it's the first time for me, and I don't know how to feel about it."

Chase pulled me to a stop at the bottom of his steps and held my arms. "Did you enjoy it?"

"Yeah. It was great. But—"

"Do you know any of them?"

"No, but—"

Chase stepped closer, and I could feel the heat radiating off him, his dark eyes burning into mine, intense and piercing. "Look. I've never been there before, and neither have you. We didn't know anyone there, and we never will. Who cares if they heard us? Who cares if someone saw us? They were probably just jealous it wasn't them getting hot and heavy in the bathroom."

"You've never been there before?" I was softening, and I realized I had been mad at him.

"No," Chase said. "I've heard about from a few different people, but I've never been there. I didn't even know about the bathroom. That was you."

"I saw a couple come out, and they'd obviously just boned in there, so I figured..."

"It was hot. I've never had sex quite so publicly before. It was kind of..."

"Exhilarating," I filled in.

We grinned at each other, and then we started laughing.

"Whoa. Nice." Chase said, mimicking the gravelly voice of the guy who'd walked in on us.

"He was talking about me," I said.

"Not arguing there," Chase said, smirking. "Come on, let's go in. I have some Red Stripe."

A few more beers and I found myself in Chase's bed, pinned down by his weight and his hands on my wrists as he slowly and thoroughly plundered me. As I did every time, I came hard, and more than once, before Chase finally fell asleep.

I laid awake for another hour or so, trying to sort through the jumble of emotions the day had engendered. 'Trying' is the operative word, though. It was too tangled to figure out at three in the morning, half-drunk, and sexually exhausted.

We spent the next day on a tour of New York. Chase took me on the subway, in cabs and on foot, showed me the big tourists spots and then a few of the more underbelly sort of places. We had dinner at another tiny, out-of-the-way restaurant, and then it was time to get to the club where Six Feet Tall would perform. I helped set up, watched them warm up, and then the club started to fill up and Chase showed me a spot backstage.

Backstage turned out to be a busy place, bustling with techies, assistants, band members, and a host of other people whose functions I couldn't have even guessed at. Chase was in his element, wearing the sexiest pair of leather pants yet, ripped and tattered and weathered, knee-high boots with buckles and spikes and straps, and nothing else. His marvelous body was bare from the waist up, chiseled and cut, and even larger than ever, if that was possible. He'd rubbed oil into his muscles, and he had leather cuffs on his forearms that spanned from wrist to elbow, looking like something a medieval warrior would wear.

I couldn't take my eyes off him. He strode back and forth the back-stage area, clutching his mic in one hand, eyes bright and focused. His dark hair was wild, spiked, messy, as if he'd just fucked hard. Which he had. We'd found a bathroom and Chase had backed me against a wall, lifted my leg around his hips and driven into me wildly until we both collapsed into each other. The sex had energized him, it seemed, made him buzz with pysched passion for his impending performance.

When the lights dimmed to black, he rounded on me, kissed me hard and fast.

"Kill 'em, baby," I said.

He grinned at me, then trotted out on stage with his band in tow.

Baby? Where the hell did that *come from?*

I shrugged it away as the lights came up with the drummer pounding a fast rhythm on the bass kick-drum. The bassist came in next, slapping his strings in a complicated riff, and then the guitarist wound in with a slippery, snaking tune. Chase stood bathed in a spotlight, hands at his sides, head down, motionless. I could pretty much hear all the women in the audience creaming themselves from this vision of him, huge and cut and dominating, even silent and still.

This was a rock band, no holds barred, just this side of metal, but with real melody and musicianship. The music continued, picking up pace and energy until it reached a crescendo, and then, on a single syn-chronized note, the band fell silent and Chase filled the space with his voice, a low vocalization that rose and rose and rose. The band kicked in, then, perfectly timed with the shift in his singing.

God, they were good. So good. The crowd went nuts, screaming, waving, suddenly pumped for a kick-ass opening number. His lyrics, oh man. Deep, full of feeling and poetry. Intelligible and meaningful,

118

unlike the tripe spouted by so many other bands these days. He meant every word.

And then, of course, after a few heavy-hitting numbers, the lights dimmed and the energy dropped. Chase sat with his legs dangling off the low stage, mic held in both hands, close to his face, eyes downcast as if seeing long ago memories, and crooned a ridiculously touching ballad of heartbreak and loss and love. Of course, he sold it as dramatically as he did the angsty, angry numbers.

They finished their set and I visited the bathroom while they loaded their gear. I found myself in a corner stall, sitting on the toilet and listening to a pair of girls primping at the mirror, discussing Chase.

"Ohmigod, is he *hot* or what?"

A second voice made a shrill squeal, and I could practically see her waving her face with her hands. "I mean seriously. He's huge. I bet he's hung like a fucking horse."

The first girl popped her lips, reapplying lipstick, probably, and then said, "Hung like a horse is right. You could totally see his package through his pants, and he wasn't even hard. I bet he's awesome in bed."

"I've heard he's into some weird shit. I know this chick who hooked up with him after a show once. She said he's hung like a fucking god, and that he's *amazing* in bed...if you like being tied up and spanked, among other things." A pause, then, "He can spank me as hard as he wants, I'd let him do *any*thing. He can even put it in my ass."

"Marcia! That's nasty. And if he really is that huge, wouldn't it hurt?"

"Not if he's slow about putting it in. He's gotta work up to it, use his fingers first, and a lot of lube. It's really fucking hot, if he does it right."

"You've done anal?"

"Hell yes. I let Doug fuck me in the ass all the time. It's hot. The fun part is, no condoms, and you can do it even during your period, if you're in the mood."

119

"God, that's *so* nasty. And I'm *never* in the mood when I'm on my period. I would never let Brian put it in my ass. He's asked a couple times, but I always say no. *This* ass is exit only."

"Well mine isn't. That singer is so hot, he makes me wet just looking at him." A pause, hands being washed and dried. "I wonder if I can get backstage to meet him."

"I know one of the bouncers here. I'll get you backstage. I might even join you for a threesome with him. I'll bet he'd be down with that, if he's as kinky as Jenny said he was."

I was alone again, and I nearly vomited.

I found him by the stage, cornered by who I imagined were the girls from the bathroom. He hadn't seen me yet, so I stayed in the shadows, blatantly eavesdropping.

"So, do you have plans for later, Chase?"

"If you don't, we could grab a few drinks, maybe go by my place... hang out for a bit. You know, just see what pops up."

Chase looked awfully tempted. He actually hesitated. I saw him search the bar for me, and I sank back farther into the shadows by the hallway to the bathrooms.

"As much as I'd like to, ladies, I *do* have plans for tonight. Maybe another night though. My next show is in a few days, and all the details are up on my band's website."

God. He knew exactly what they were proposing. I still felt ill. *Why am I jealous?*

I tried to shove it away. So what if he'd hooked up with someone before I got here. I had, hadn't I?

It wasn't just hooking up with Jeff, though. That meant something.

Shit. What did that mean? It meant something? Then why am I jealous of Chase? Why does the thought of him having a threesome with some groupie sluts bother me?

Because I could picture it, easily. And I could see him honestly considering it, before realizing I was still here in New York with him and turning them down. But then he'd basically set up a rain-check, hadn't he?

Maybe he didn't realize what they were getting at.

Yeah, right.

Where was I going to be in a few days? Here in New York still? The return flight was open-ended. We hadn't established a length of time for my visit. I'd told Jeff...well I hadn't told him much of anything. He'd DJ without me.

Is Jeff hooking up with someone, now that I'm here in New York? That lovely thought made me sick again, and I wanted to throw up yet again. Jealous of two men. Not good.

"Anna? Are you okay?" Chase's voice filtered through my fog of thoughts, and his hands gripped my arms.

"Sorry, yeah. I'm fine." I couldn't quite meet his eyes. If I did, I'd say something about the groupies from the bathroom, and that would complicate things. I didn't need more complication, or drama.

"You looked...I don't know...angry, or sick, or something. You sure you're okay?"

I forced a smile on my face. "Yeah, just...yeah. I'm fine." I made myself kiss him, knowing the groupies were watching from the bar; after a moment, I didn't need to make myself, because I was lost in the kiss. "Great show! You killed it! That ballad was wonderful."

"You liked it? I just wrote it the other day. That was the first time I've performed it live. I was so nervous I nearly harfed."

"It was incredible. You totally sold it."

"It was for you."

"It was about losing the love of your life." I gave him a confused look.

Chase grinned. "Well, I really wanted you to come with me."

"So you wrote a ballad about it?"

"Yep. I was heartbroken."

I crossed my arms under my breasts and gave him a skeptical eyebrow-raise. "Uh-huh. You're lucky you're cute, 'cause you're totally lying."

"Am not," Chase said, running his hands down my sides to my hips.

"Not cute, or not lying?"

"Not lying. I'm totally cute," he said.

"You sounded like a school girl just then. You should never say 'totally'." I smirked at him, my irritation largely forgotten, what with all the witty banter and his wandering hands.

"I'm a rockstar. I can say whatever I want," Chase said.

He nipped my earlobe, then my neck, and his hands were on my ass, and then he was pushing me up against a wall and kissing me. I felt eyes on us, watching us, hating the attention I was getting and they weren't. Or weren't...yet.

I'm so mixed up. I don't know what I want.

Chase sensed me tense. "You're not okay. What is it?"

I shook my head. "Not here, not now. Let's go somewhere."

"There's an after-party uptown. We can talk in the cab on the way."

When we were in the cab and on the way to the after-party, Chase turned to me, his hand resting on my knee. "So talk. What's bugging you?"

How much to tell him? Argh.

"Well, it's just...I was in the bathroom, and I heard these girls talking to you, the same ones who were trying to get you to go their place with them. They were talking about hot you are, which you *totally* are," I smirked at him as I used his word, "and the one girl was talking about how much she wanted you. Again, understandable. You're basically sex on legs. And the other girl was saying how she knows a girl who hooked up with you after a show, and that you're into some different kind of stuff. And I...I just don't know why it bothered me so much. But that's not true; I do know. It just reminded me that I don't know why I'm here, or what we are, and that I don't have any reason to be jealous. And no, I don't want to try and figure all that shit out right now, I just want to go to the party with you and have fun and celebrate your awesome show."

"Um, wow, okay." Chase said, sitting back with a sigh. "That's a lot of things. I don't even know where to start."

I shrugged and squeezed closer to him. "So don't start. You asked and I told you. I'm really, really not trying to be all girly and talk about my feelings. Mainly because I'm still trying to figure out what I'm feeling. Let's just have a good time."

"But now you have me thinking. Yeah, I hooked up a few times before you got here, but—"

"Chase, for real. Let's not worry about it now."

"But—"

"Chase. Listen to me. Stop thinking like a guy for a second. You don't have to jump in and fix anything. I'm here, you're here...just let it go for now. I'm not ready to talk serious yet."

Chase searched my eyes, then shrugged. "Okay, I guess I get that. Later, though, okay?"

"Sure. Later." *Later, when I've figured out what the hell I'm even feeling, much less what I want to do about it.*

The after-party was massive. Hundreds of people, band members, fans, techies and roadies and groupies and I didn't even know who else. The huge loft apartment smelled like booze and body heat and cologne and perfume. There was a makeshift bar along one wall and corner, staffed by a catering company, two men and two women, clean-cut, nondescript and efficient. Alcohol was flowing freely, the noise level nearly deafening. I saw no one I recognize except Chase's band mates: Dave, Austin, and Gage, each whom I'd met a total of once, when I first arrived.

Chase got a vocal welcome, and I felt him turn on the charisma. On the way up, he was just Chase, laid back, quiet, holding my hand. He was still in his battered leather pants, but he'd put on a white linen shirt, the sleeves cut off and the edges artistically frayed, unbuttoned to his navel. Then, as soon as the door opens and we walked into the loft, he transformed into a different person entirely. It was like his entire being just...turned on, and he exuded this powerful, irresistible charm and charisma. He was dynamic, just standing, walking, talking, when in this mode. Every eye was on him, watching him, hoping he'll talk to them. He was funny, entertaining, attentive to the person he's speaking to...

Which meant everyone was looking at *me*. Judging me. Assessing me. I wanted to let go of Chase's hand, just get away and catch the first flight back to Detroit, away from the attention and the rockstar drama. It was ridiculous. I mean, he wasn't even famous yet, and he was being swarmed by people who want his attention, and that meant I was being grilled, questioned, chatted up and flirted with. The women all wanted Chase to notice them, to talk to them, to flirt with them. To take them home. Except, he was with me. He flew me here from Detroit, and brought me to the show and now this party, when he could probably have had any two or three women here, at once.

I didn't know whether to be jealous and upset that he probably *has* taken multiple women home, and flattered that he likes me enough to want me there, instead of these women. I chose flattered, because it was easier. The jealousy got pushed down and ignored, to be dealt with later.

The party lasted well into the night, or more accurately, the wee hours of the morning. When things started to blur, I asked Chase to take me home. He seemed like he wasn't ready to leave the party yet, but he did. He made his rounds of goodbyes, which took nearly another hour, by which point I was yawning and starting to come down from my buzz.

By the time we got back to Chase's place, I was too tired to do anything but fall asleep. Chase, bless his sweet heart, curled up behind me and let me sleep. My last thought, before succumbing to sleep, was that I'd have to reward him later.

We slept the day through, had late breakfast/early lunch at a diner a few blocks from Chase's walkup. We talked, a lot. He had a degree in musical theater, oddly enough. He'd almost joined the Army out of high school but hadn't at the last second. I told him about my first boyfriend, the one who'd cheated on me with my best friend's brother. That really messed with my self-esteem, needless to say. He'd told me he'd never really been attracted to me, and had thought it was just because I was fat—his words, not mine. It turned out he wasn't attracted to me because I was fat, *and* because he was gay. I got over it, mostly. I chalked that one up to bad luck and learned to feel better about myself, to accept my body as uniquely mine, and uniquely beautiful.

Chase spent a long time after that story reminding me how perfect he thought I was. He took me home, brought me to his room and stripped me slowly, peeling my dress off, kissing my flesh as he bared it.

I stood stock still and let him kiss me, let the touch of his lips on my flesh ignite the always-banked fires of desire within me. He unzipped the back of the dress, brushed the sleeves off my shoulders and let it fall around my feet. Then, standing in front of me, he began at my shoulders, kissing his way down my body. He was slow, for once, lingering at my breasts, then down to my belly and my thighs.

By the time he had kissed his way back up to my lips, I was trembling with desire, my nipples hard with need. I wanted him to touch me, wanted to feel him hard against me, feel his hands on me, feel him fill me. His kisses had inflamed my passions, and I had to bite my tongue to keep from begging him.

He hadn't even taken his shirt off, and I found myself aching to touch him. I tugged at the hem of shirt, but he pushed my hands away.

"Not yet," he said. "Soon."

He went to his dresser and removed a long, wide strip of black cotton. "Trust me?" When I nodded, he wrapped the blindfold around my eyes and tied it in back. "Can you see?"

I couldn't. I fought back an initial rush of panic. It was loosely tied, and my hands were free so I could pull it off if I wanted to. I forced myself to relax and focus on the other senses.

I had the aftertaste of dinner in my mouth: corned beef Rueben and fries with a Coke. I heard a rasping metallic *click* and then tiny *whump* of flame coming to life from a lighter, then the snap and pop of a wick catching: a candle being lit; these sounds were repeated several more times. I smelled the candles, smelled Chase—male sweat, faint cologne, leather. I was aware of Chase moving around the room, hearing his footsteps on the old, creaking hardwood floors, following his smell and the intangible feeling of his presence. Now he moved close to me, not touching me.

Goosebumps pebbled my flesh, on my arm, and then my side, a strange, not-quite physical sensation. It moved from my side and down my hip and my leg, and then back up the other leg.

"What is that?" I asked. "What are you doing to me?"

"Guess."

"I can't figure it out. It's like—god, it's weird!" Then it hit me. "You're not touching me, but almost, right? Moving your hand right next to my skin but not actually making contact."

"Bingo."

He rewarded me with a leisurely removal of my bra. No other part of him touched me except his hands on my back as he unclasped the hooks. *Not* being touched had never been so erotic. I tried to anticipate where he'd put his hands next, but he always managed to surprise me. He slid the straps of my bra off my shoulder, and I expected to feel his hands on my breasts, perhaps skimming underneath to heft their weight, or rolling a nipple; he kissed my back where the strap had been, a slow tonguing kiss across my back. I felt his hair tickle the back of my left arm as he moved across my body. I lifted my arm as he kept circling around, planting kisses as went, and then he was kissing the side of my breast, one hand on the small of my back, the other wrapped around one leg, kissing, kissing; he was kneeling next to me, I realized. He still hadn't touched my nipple, or removed my panties. I was tingling everywhere, every inch of my flesh burning with anticipation of his touch, his kiss. My folds were wet, waiting, wanting.

I put my hands in his soft hair, smelling of shampoo and pomade. His hand on my leg finally, finally slipped up to dip beneath the leg hem of my panties, pushing up to the crease of my hip, achingly near my wet, hot core, where I wanted his touch so badly. I was trembling, waiting for him to move just an inch to the right.

He pulled his hand free and I moaned in dismay. He tugged he waistband of my panties down enough to kiss a fiery line across my hipbone to my belly just above my sex, slow, hot kisses that had my knees buckling.

Just a little lower, please!

"Soon, baby," he said.

I'd spoken aloud without realizing it. "Please, Chase. Touch me. Kiss me."

He just chuckled as he kissed my opposite hip, then down my leg, pulling my panties down as he went, a single centimeter at a time, it seemed, agonizingly slow. Then, after an eternity of torturous delight, my panties were off and tossed aside and he was kissing up my calf, holding the leg in both hands, sliding his palms up my thighs to cup my ass, kneading the muscle. I spread my legs apart as he neared my groin, lips now mid-thigh and still rising, and yes, oh please...

I nearly fell backward when he lapped at my pussy with a long swipe of his tongue across the labia. I moaned, tangled my fingers in his hair and let my head fall backward. He held my ass in both hands as he kissed and licked, flicked and tongued, moved his head from side to side and up and down. I felt my legs dipping in the rhythm of his mouth's motion, helpless to stop myself, and now the fires were raging out of control, burning and exploding, my muscles tensing in preparation for the imminent explosion....

He moved away, and I whimpered. "I was so close, why'd you stop?" I sounded whiny in that moment, but I didn't care, I wanted his mouth on me again, or his hands.

I reached and felt the empty air around me, but he'd moved out of reach. I smelled for him, listened for him, simply felt for his presence, but he was nowhere my senses could find.

I heard his voice, over to my right, against what would be the closet wall. "Take two steps back."

I hesitated. "Where am I going?" I thought about the layout of the room, and answered my own question. "The bed, right?"

"Two steps, and then stop."

I took one step backward, then another, and felt the edge the bed bump the back of my knees. I stopped, and waited. My heart thudded in my chest, and I smelled his hair before I felt his presence. My four other senses had never been so sharp as now without my sight. I felt his fingers brush my belly, barely contact at all, a whispering touch, like feathers, or a breath; I gasped and shivered.

The featherlight touch turned to a gentle but unmistakable push. I leaned back to sit on the bed. Chase kissed my kneecap, and my thigh, and then I was falling backward, laying down with my legs hanging off the bed. A hand clasped around my wrist and extended it above my head. Then, beginning at my palm, Chase kissed his way down my arm. I sucked in my breath when he reached my breast, slipping his lips around its circumference, narrowing to my aching, stiffened nipple. He only lingered there for a moment, grazing it with his teeth but once. I wanted to crush his head to my breast, or guide his hand to my pussy, or simply beg him to touch me, touch me. I didn't though. The game, the drawn-out, rapturous, torture was exquisite.

He repeated the process for my other arm, lifting it above my head and kissing his way down to my breast. This time, however, instead of merely moving away from my breast, he kept lapping and licking downward, tracing the lines of my ribs, the hollow of my diaphragm, the expanse of my belly. All the while his hands were brushing and whisking and whispering across my skin, just the pads of his fingertips touching now, and then his palm circling the taut peak of my nipple.

His tongue found my drenched, throbbing folds again, dipped in to pull from my trembling lips a moan of relief. Yes, now he would let me release, now...

He tongued my clit until I was writhing on the bed, sight gone, the only sound my voice, the only scent the musk of my arousal, lost in tactile ecstasy, so close, so close, wavering on the verge, teetering on the brink...one last touch of his tongue...

I grabbed wildly for him when he pulled away again, and he only laughed. My entire body was on fire, quivering with need, primed and set for explosion. My senses were so attuned now that I could hear the rustle of his pants legs as he moved, hear the soft susurrus of his breathing. Every inch of my flesh was on fire, waiting for the next place he would kiss or touch me.

I heard the leather of his pants zipping as he moved to stand next to me. "Sit up and turn to face my voice."

I did as he'd instructed, wondering what was next; he took my hands in his and placed them on his chest. I could feel his heart pounding under my palm. He moved my fingers so I felt a button on his shirt. I realized what he wanted and complied eagerly, unbuttoning his shirt and pushing it off. I wanted to rip his pants off, but, according to the way he was playing this game, I made myself wait. Instead, I explored his torso with my hands, all my attention now focused in my fingers. I traced each muscle, each line and angle and curve from shoulder to wrist to abdomen, lingering, and now I couldn't stop myself from replacing fingers with lips. I kissed him slowly, deliberately. Each time I neared the V-cut above the waistband of his pants, I lingered, let my fingers toy with the button.

When he was shaking and tense, I slipped the button free and unzipped his pants. I moved with delicate attention, following the muscles downward, pushing the pants away inch by inch. I stripped them off, then, unable to wait any longer. He was in his boxers now, and I let my hands learn the shape of his body through the underwear, the curved stone of his buttocks, the hard angles of his hips, the rigid shaft of his straining cock. He'd leaked a dot of moisture at his tip. I moved his boxer-briefs down on one hip, licked the hollow where leg met hipbone, then across until my lips were brushing next to his cock. He sucked his stomach in, a reflexive motion of anticipation. Instead of touching him, yet, I revealed his other hip, mirrored the kiss across his groin.

Now, at last, I tugged the elastic over his cock, slipping him into my mouth as I exposed him. He gasped past clenched teeth as I took him in to my throat, groaned when I wrapped my fingers around him, and rumbled deep in his chest when I bobbed my head and moved my hands along his shaft. I sucked until my cheeks hollowed, sliding my hands on him faster and faster, his hips bucking him into my mouth.

His breathing was ragged, and he was buckling at the knees.

"Oh, god, I'm gonna come," he said.

I let go immediately and moved back on the bed, laying down on my back and waiting, legs spread in invitation. I heard him growling, imagined him flexing every muscle in an effort to hold back.

"You didn't come, did you?" I asked. "You better not have. I want you to come inside me."

He groaned again, and I felt weight on the bed. "No, but nearly."

"Good. I want you inside me, right now. Please, Chase."

I reached for him, where I thought he was. I felt hair, took a handful and pulled gently until I could reach his jaw, and then his shoulder and then his hip, and then he was above me. I grasped his cock in my fist and guided him to my entrance.

"No more games. Just take me," I rocked my hips as I spoke, and he sank in to me.

He shuddered, tensed, and I felt his lips brush mine, shaking as he held himself back from the edge.

"God, you feel so good," he whispered, "I'm there already, again, I can't..." He sounded ragged, desperate.

The feel of him inside me, filling me past full, knowing he was so close, it brought me in a single rush, before he'd thrust even once, to the edge of climax. I tangled my fingers in his hair and pulled his head down to mine, crushed my lips to his. I thrust my tongue into his mouth and as I did so, rolled my hips against him, driving him to the hilt.

He held himself stone-still, every muscle tensed. He was still holding back.

"Give it to me," I breathed, rocking into him, one hand still gripping his hair, the other clawing down his back. "Don't hold back anymore. Give it to me. Hard. Now."

He roared, a feral sound, leonine, primal, and bucked his hips, sliding his cock into me, once, deep, and hard. Again. Again. I gasped, bit his shoulder. He arched his back outward, pulling almost out and tensing, holding. Still withholding. I dug my nails into his hips and jerked him toward me, pulling with all my strength against his resistance. Still he played the game, holding back.

I rolled sideways and he went with me, pulling me over him. I draped myself on top of him, waiting, let him fade back from the edge. The game continued. Above him like this, I held the power of pace. He was sunk to the hilt, our hipbones grinding. I sat straight, stretching him backward, placed my hands on his belly, my weight spread between his body and my knees. I waited, absorbing the sensations rocketing through me: his cock, hard and huge and throbbing with pent pressure, his body beneath me, muscles tense and rock-solid, his hands resting on my hips, my heart beating wild in my chest like a fleeing rabbit, my nerve endings all afire now, silence except our breathing, the scent of sex thick in the air.

I lifted up, just a few inches, held my weight there for a moment, and then sank down. I gasped, he groaned. More. I lifted higher, sank back down harder, hips thumping, blood thrumming. He growled again. I felt his buttocks clench against my thighs.

"Give it to me," I said, leaning close to his face. "I want it."

"No," he said, crashing his lips to mine and spearing his tongue into my mouth. "Make me."

I rocked up and back down. "With...pleasure...."

No rhythm, only sporadic rolls of my hips, a pause, lift up and sink down. His hands found my breasts, pinched my nipples, sending jags of lightning bursting through me. Then he cheated. He dug a single finger between our merged bodies and found my clit somehow. I rocked back instinctively, lifted up, gave him access.

A few slow circles drove me mad; he moved his finger faster, and then I came, almost without warning, a nuclear detonation blasting through every cell of my body.

I couldn't stop the rhythm then. I fell onto him, clutched him against me and let my hips run wild.

Hips don't lie, as the song goes, and mine danced on his with truthful desperation. I couldn't play the game any longer. I whimpered against his neck as I pulsed my pussy onto him.

He arched his back upward, arms wrapped around me, clinging to me as he came. I was still riding my first climax, and when he came I soared over the edge again, the heat of his release washing through me, each piston-drive of his cock sending me further and further into a frenzy of orgasm. We were bucking in syncopated abandon now, riding each other beyond climax, beyond mere physical release into something else, into an escape from singular self into a duality of ecstasy.

We were caught up in a storm, and all we could do was cling to each other through it, let it pound through us. When it passed, we were both limp and panting, sweating, spent.

I rolled off him and nestled into his arms, feeling his heart beat against my cheek.

We showered, changed, and Chase hailed a cab, but wouldn't tell me where we were going. The cab pulled up to Macy's.

"What are we doing here?" I asked.

"Shopping," was his cryptic reply.

"Well no shit, it's the world's largest department store. Shopping for what?"

He just grinned. It seemed a bit like a leer, honestly, lecherous and eager for what he had planned. I rolled my eyes at him and let him drag me by the hand up the escalators and to the lingerie department.

"Lingerie? Really?" I stopped at the entrance to the lingerie department.

"Yes, really."

"Are you saying my underwear aren't sexy enough for you?" I teased.

"I'm saying you can never have too much sexy lingerie."

We browsed together, Chase showing me what he liked—always grabbing an item several sizes too small. Eventually, we settled on a red and black lace bustier with matching panties, and a hot pink and purple ruffled set.

I tried a few of the less adventurous bras, and then stepped back out, fully dressed, with an idea. It was near closing time and the store was empty, with one store assistant prowling around. I waited until she was sorting through a stack of panties on the other side of the department, then pulled Chase with me into the changing room.

I stripped for him, peeling off my clothes to a silent rhythm, then pinned him against the stall wall with my body. I was down to just my panties, rubbing my bare breasts against the soft cotton of his shirt. I felt his cock burgeon in his pants, met his gaze as I unzipped him.

"Hello? Is anyone still in here?" The store clerk called out.

"Yes," I said. Chase had frozen, not even breathing. "I'm just trying on a few last things. I'll be done in a minute."

"We're closing in five minutes. If you're going to make a purchase, it needs to be soon."

"Okay, I'll be right out." I stifled a laugh, tugging Chase's underwear down to free his erection.

I glided my hand on his length, put my mouth to his ear and whispered, "I want you right now." I felt Chase's cock throb and tense as I spoke. "Put it in my pussy."

I stroked him, one hand massaging his sack, until he was rolling his hips into my hand. When he was nearly ready, I stripped my panties off of one leg and faced the wall, bending at the waist with my hands braced.

Chase didn't need another invitation. He slipped a finger into me, finding me already wet. He plunged into me, and we both had to bite our lips to stifle our moans.

"Hello? I really need to cash out, dear," came the clerk's voice. Her shoes peeked under the door, tiny little white sneakers, the footwear of a woman who spends her life on her feet.

I was just within reach of the top of the door. Chase had frozen, and I plunged my hips back into him to get him moving. The exhilaration of this moment, being completely naked, with Chase's cock driving into me from behind, and only a thin stall door between us and complete humiliation...I nearly came right then. I caught up the hangars of the items I wanted and hung them over the door.

"Ring these up and I'll be right out to pay," I said. My voice wasn't quite steady, but she didn't say anything, if she'd noticed.

Chase was moving slowly, trying to avoid making any noises as our bodies joined. I was riding the edge of climax now, and so was Chase.

"Will that be cash or charge?"

God, the woman was relentless. *Leave me alone for five seconds!*

Chase handed me a wad of cash and I handed it over the top of the door.

"I don't know how much it'll be, but that should cover it," I said, a little breathless.

The clerk took the cash and finally left us alone.

"Now, Chase!" I whispered. "Come for me, right now!"

I drove my ass onto him, feeling him plunge hard to the hilt deep inside my pussy. Again, even harder, and the stall shook. A third time, and I rocked backward to absorb the impact, feeling him drive deeper than he'd ever been, both of us silent, breath caught. I felt him tense, drive one last time into me, and then he was coming, flooding me with his seed. I felt him come and I joined him an instant later, resting my head against the wall as he fluttered into me, my inner muscles clenching around him in spasms.

He pulled out of me, tucked himself back into his pants and slumped back against the wall. "Damn, Anna...just...damn."

I smirked at him, feeling sated and daring. I dug in my purse for a little packet of tissues, and cleaned myself before dressing again. I told Chase to stay in the dressing room until I called him.

I walked up to the cashier's stand, my thighs quivering with aftershocks. I could barely walk, but I had to cover up and act as if nothing had happened. The woman, mercifully, had everything bagged up and the change ready, and she vanished into a back room with barely a "thank you."

I snuck Chase out of the changing room and we left Macy's laughing like teenagers.

After Macy's we went to Times Square and mingled with the bustling crowd, holding hands and talking aimlessly. We sat on the giant steps with the signs around us, kissing as if we were alone, making out until even the New Yorkers shouted at us to get a room.

We spent the entire following day in the recording studio. I sat in the producer's booth watching in rapt interest as they laid down track after track, sometimes going back for a dozen takes of the same section of song, the same riff, the same vocalization until they got it right.

I knew my way around a mixing/EQ board, and I quickly learned to understand what the producers and sound engineers were doing at the giant board on the other side of the acoustic room.

The whole process made me wonder if I could ever find my way on the other side of the glass, where Chase and his band was. I'd always loved singing, and had settled on DJing as a way of utilizing my musical talent, modest as it seemed to me. As any girl with a decent voice, I'd harbored dreams of "being a singer" but as I got older and learned a bit about the business, I came to realize how distant and unlikely a prospect that was. Now, sitting in a real recording studio, in New York City no less, those dreams all came rushing back to me.

I was lost in my thoughts and was startled when Chase came up behind me and kissed me on the neck.

"Thinking deep thoughts, huh?" he asked.

"What? Oh, yeah. Guess so. I didn't hear you come in."

"I called your name twice, babe. You were zoned out. What were you thinking about?"

I looked up him over my shoulder. "Oh, just how cool it is to be here, in a studio. Thanks for bringing me."

"Thought you might like it." He glanced at the producer, a younger-looking man with full-sleeve tattoos on both arms and wide-gauge earrings. "We have a few minutes left on our time, right Jake?"

Jake nodded, glancing at his watch. "Yeah, a couple. Wanna lay down a bonus track with your girl?"

Chase just gestured to the door to the booth. "Shall we?"

We sat down in the booth and Chase settled the expensive headphones on my ears.

"What do you want to sing?" Chase asked.

I thought carefully. I didn't know if they were going to actually include this recording on the CD or not, but if they did, I wanted it to be knock-out.

"I don't suppose you know 'Don't You Wanna Stay' do you?" I asked Chase.

"Jason Aldean and Kelly Clarkston? Surprisingly enough, I do," Chase answered, with a sheepish grin. "I learned it when I did a karaoke contest with a friend. We actually won with that song."

The producer tapped at the computer keyboard for a moment, and then the introductory strains filled my ears through the headphones. Chase started it off, the slow, sad melody turned aching and haunting by his clear, powerful voice. *He really is amazing*, I reflected. I heard my part coming up, and Chase nodded to me. I took a deep breath and added my voice to his, and once again I felt that intangible, bone-deep knowledge boil in my blood. We were *on*, we were hitting it just right, our natural chemistry and talent flowing together. I could see the producer nodding, a surprised expression on his face. We were killing it.

I felt my skin prickle and adrenaline surge through me, felt the notes flow from me without thought, without effort. Chase's hand was in mine, and then my eyes closed and all I knew was the music and those wonderful lyrics, which had suddenly taken on new meaning.

Every kiss we'd shared filled the spaces of my mind, every moment spent naked together, every look, it all took on new importance. I really had no clue what this was with Chase, or how long it would last.

The song ended all too soon, and Chase and I ripped the headphones off to embrace each other.

"That rocked!" Jake said. "Chase, your girl's got some real pipes on her. I may have to steal her, one of these days. For music, I mean."

"You just want to steal her, period," Chase said, with a wry grin.

Jake shrugged. "Yeah, well, you'd better get out of here before I do. Good work, guys."

We left the studio to have a later dinner, and I had the song running through my head the entire time, as well the thoughts the lyrics had engendered. Chase must have sensed my pensive mood.

"What's up, buttercup? You seem lost in thought again." He pushed back from his plate and searched my eyes from over the top of his glass of beer.

I shrugged. "Oh, that song has just always had a lot of meaning for me. It always makes me think, I guess."

"So what are you thinking now?"

I still wasn't sure if I wanted to have that conversation with Chase yet, if at all. It was too easy to just float along one day at a time and let the relationship, such as it was, just be a nameless, uncategorized thing. To put a box around it, to give it a name and boundaries would be to change it.

After a long, thoughtful silence, I shook my head. "Nothing. Nothing important."

Chase frowned. "You know we have to talk eventually, Anna."

"No we don't. One day at a time. Carpe diem and all that."

He laughed, a mirthless, resigned sound. "Isn't this backwards? Aren't I supposed to be the one avoiding the discussion?"

I shrugged again, a coward's non-answer. "How about another beer and then we go back to your place?"

Back in his bedroom, we lay down, fully clothed, on his bed, just holding each other. The avoided conversation loomed between us. It really was backwards, him being the one who wanted to put a name to what we were, to establish our thing together as a *relationship*. I didn't want to do that. Why I didn't want to was a more complicated thing, and that's what I ruminated on as I lay in Chase's arms, content to be held for the moment.

Why didn't I want to commit to this being an actual relationship, monogamous and working toward some kind of future together? Chase was incredible. He was charming and thoughtful, gorgeous, talented... an amazing lover. He was going places, career-wise. He wanted me. That was a big one. He wanted *me*. I'd still not quite gotten over that. I think I was expecting it to change at some point, for him to wake up and realize he did in fact want a girl who was not me, who was in some way either more or less than me, depending on how you looked at it. But he hadn't so far, and judging by his response to my avoiding the relationship discussion, he wanted more with me. Something long-term.

Why wasn't I jumping at that?

Jeff.

I'd left something unfinished with him, back in Detroit. I hadn't said when, or if, I was coming back. I'd just left, perhaps precipitately. I'd hurt him. That was clear in his eyes, in the tense slump of his shoulders when he drove me home.

He'd never said what he wanted, with me. But he hadn't needed to. It was clear, somehow. Jeff had a way of implying his desires without saying them, of communicating his thoughts nonverbally. I couldn't have pinpointed what it was he'd done, or how he'd looked at me that told me he wanted a relationship, but I knew he did. Maybe it was the fact that he'd held a crush on me for all the years we worked together, never voicing it, never moving on it after a few initial, hesitant flirty moments I'd pretended not to notice. Maybe it was his slow, sweet, reverent love-making.

I shut down thoughts of that. I couldn't let my mind go there, not when I was in Chase's bed.

The realization hit me like a ton of bricks: I had to choose. Stay here, indefinitely, and eventually decide that I was staying with Chase. Or, I had to go back to Detroit and face Jeff. That's what had been niggling at me since I'd arrived here. I didn't know how to choose. I didn't know what I wanted. *Who* I wanted, long-term, if either of them.

"Quit thinking so hard and just be here with me," Chase said.

"Are you a mind-reader?"

He turned into me and kissed my cheek, then my chin. "Sometimes. You wear your thoughts on your face, though, so that makes it easier. You're thinking too hard. We don't have to figure anything out. Just be here with me, in this moment, right now."

I nodded, his stubble scratching my temple. "You're right. I'm sorry, I'm just—"

"Let it go for now."

I lifted up on an elbow. "So distract me."

Our lips met, a hesitant touch at first, almost as tender as if it were our first kiss. Slow, and delicate. Explorative. It wasn't a kiss meant to go anywhere, at first. It was just meant to be a kiss, the expression of affection. His kiss told me what he felt about me. His lips showed me in a visceral way that he thought I was valuable, and beautiful.

The feeling of being desired, the knowledge that a man as hot as Chase thought I was beautiful...that was something I couldn't ever get enough of. I still couldn't turn off my brain, even kissing Chase like this. He had unlocked something inside me, that night in his bedroom in Detroit. He'd unleashed something powerful and insatiable. He'd made me understand my own worth as a sexual woman. There was a phrase I'd heard a million times before but never really truly grasped until this moment in Chase's New York apartment:

He'd shown me my inner goddess.

I did feel, in that moment, with his arms slipping around me, his body sliding against mine, his fingers exploring my body and starting the slow unwrapping of my clothes, that I was a goddess. I had power. My body, my desires, my needs...I could affect a man, hold sway over him, manipulate him or lift him up or draw his pleasure out, multiply it, deepen it. I could, for the minutes or hours I was with a man in bed, be all of his universe, the only thing that mattered in his existence, in those moments. It's not about experience or lack thereof, or what you've learned or with whom. That power comes from within a woman, and it must be understood on a blood- and bone- and soul-deep level.

Time had vanished and reappeared, and I was naked with him, limbs tangling in a writhing twist of flesh and sweat and heat. I had no memory of removing clothes, of anything but his lips and his hands and his body against mine, and it didn't matter. Nothing mattered. Only him, only me, only us together.

There were no games, no kinks, no blindfolds or positions or bindings, just bodies mingling and merging. Lips collided and tongues mated, hands and legs and arms wrapped and touched and twined. I felt him move into me, fill me, glide with serpentine grace to merge our bodies in a manner more intimate than ever before. Walls and defenses and worries melted away, futures and pasts and choices had no meaning.

Climax happened gradually, together. We mounted the heights of pleasure together in a timeless dance of flesh, moving and breathing until we were left motionless and breathless together.

There was something massively important in that experience together. I couldn't look at it too carefully, not yet. I just let it permeate my being, sweep my thoughts away. His breathing and mine matched, slowed, deepened, merged until there was nothing but breath, nothing but contact of cooling flesh and drowsing mind.

We slept then, and dreamed no dreams but each other.

I stood in the shadow of a curtain backstage, watching Chase and his band Six Foot Tall perform. We were in a tiny club outside Hoboken, New Jersey, and the crowd was wild, raucous, and rambunctious. They demanded hard numbers, fast beats, and constant spectacle. Chase seemed to instinctively know he couldn't try to bring the tempo down, but kept the band playing their hardest original numbers as well as some stock cover songs.

They'd gone over an hour and a half without breaking, and I could tell they were exhausted from the intense pace of the show. Chase was dripping sweat, wiping his face with a rag between numbers and guzzling bottles of water. He spent a lot of the show at the edge of the stage, hanging off the speakers and getting as close to the crowd as possible.

By the time two hours had passed, they were out of original material and had played all the stock hard rock covers they knew. The stage lights had been doused and the band had thanked the crowd for coming out, but the little club was being rocked by chants of "Encore, encore, encore!" As minutes passed and the band failed to reappear, the crowd became increasingly restless.

Finally, Chase turned to me. "I don't know what to do. We're out of material except ballads and soft shit they won't want to hear."

"Well at this point, if that's all you have left, that's what you have to do, right? They sound like they're about to riot. You guys have to play something."

Chase stared at me, then snapped his fingers and pointed at me. "I've got it. Come on."

He pulled me by the hand onto the stage, the lights still down. The band took their places, waiting for Chase to announce what they would play.

He turned to me. "You still know how to sing 'Broken'?"

I nodded, numb. "Yeah, of course, but—"

He pointed at the guitarist. "Start it up, bro."

The guitarist nodded, his long braided beard wagging. His fingers slid down the fretboard and he picked out the opening notes. The bassist rolled his shoulders, and then joined in, thumping the rhythm. The drummer waited another beat, then *ratatatted* in on the snare.

A techie garbed in black scurried out onstage, handed me a cordless mic, and then the lights came on, bathing Chase and I in a single spotlight. I looked out at the crowd, the faces swathed in shadows, heads bobbing to the familiar song. Scattered cheers and applause met us as the band ramped up into high gear, and then music was washing through me and my rush of nerves receded.

I had a sudden flash of the first time I'd done this song with Chase, in an appropriately-named bar called The Dive. Then, we'd sung to a karaoke track in front of maybe a hundred people. Now, the club was stuffed to the rafters, easily three hundred people packed in tight, holding clear plastic cups of pale amber beer over their heads, sloshing it over the rims as they jumped and cheered.

Chase started the first verse, and then my voice lifted and wove around his, finding the harmony as if we'd practiced a dozen times. The natural onstage chemistry Chase and I shared kicked in, sparks buzzing between us, and then everything faded away but the driving guitars and the chugging base and the pounding drums and Chase's blazing brown eyes locked on mine.

We bridged from the chorus to the second verse, and the crowd was wilder than ever. Chase took my hand as we finished the song, and I felt a brief, sharp pang of sharp emotion burn through me, mixed up feelings of awe for Chase's natural ability to play the crowd, adrenaline at the experience of performing on an actual stage with his band, and something awfully like deep affection for Chase.

The song ended, the lights went down, and the crowd continued to cheer. Chase pulled me off the stage, as elated with post-performance adrenaline as I was. The band was behind us, chattering and clapping each other on the back.

Chase ignored the band and the still cheering crowd, pulling me toward the red and white exit sign. He pushed open the door and led me out into the warm summer night. The alley behind the bar was dark and silent, lit only by the ambient city lights and the half moon.

The alley was filled by the cargo van the band used to transport their equipment, and Chase led me to a patch of darker shadows between the wall of the club and the white metal of the van. He pushed me back up against the wall and crushed his lips to mine, heat billowing off of him, sweat from his upper lip mingling with my own, his mouth cold from the water he'd slammed on the way out to the alley. His body pressed against me, pinning me to the wall, and his hands moved from cupping my face as he kissed me, smoothing down my body to the heavy curve of my breasts, and farther, to the hem of my skirt just above my knees.

His cock was a hard rod between us, and the furious fire of his kiss lit the boiling fuel of my desire, turned into a white-hot blaze by the rush of adrenaline. I reached between us and opened his leather pants, pushed them down, curled greedy fingers around the silky steel of his shaft. He dragged my thong down and I stepped out of the panties as they dropped to the ground between us.

His fingers delved into my pussy, already wet and aching for him, not needing any priming. I lifted my leg and wrapped it around his waist, and he held it in place with one hand. I gripped his cock in my hand and guided him to my quivering entrance, bit his lower lip as he penetrated into me. He lifted up on his toes to drive himself inside me to the hilt, holding me aloft with one hand around my leg and the other around my ass, pulling me tight against him.

Our lips met, crushed together but not kissing, breath merging as Chase drove up into me, rocking his body upward, spearing me until my breath caught. I buried my face in his neck, nipped his skin, muffled a gasp against the salt of his flesh, holding on to his shoulders and whimpering.

Within a dozen thrusts I was reaching climax, the leg supporting me buckling under the pressure of the ecstasy driving through me.

"Oh god, Chase, I'm coming," I gasped, clinging to him, breathing the words in his ear.

Hearing me say that spurred Chase to move even harder, lifting up on his toes, pushing me back into the wall with every thrust of his cock inside me. I came on an up-thrust, biting his shoulder to muffle a shriek, biting hard enough to draw a grunt of pain from Chase, which turned into a drawn-out groan as he came. He plowed into me, harder and harder, his mouth huffing loud moaning breaths into my hair as he shot his seed into me, a flood of heat washing against my walls.

My inner muscles locked around his cock as I came, my body trembling and quivering and shaking, every nerve on fire, my arms and legs shaking from a mixture of pleasure and exhaustion.

Chase finished, slowed his thrusting and pulled out of me, letting my leg down. We both back against the cold metal of the van just as Chase's band-mates came out into the alley looking for us. I tugged my skirt down mere seconds before they shoved the door open, but our out-of-breath panting and just-fucked hair gave away what we'd been doing. They just grinned and shook their heads as they lit cigarettes, which drove Chase and I—both non-smokers—back inside to look for drinks.

I visited the bathroom to clean up and then met Chase at the bar, where he had a Jameson and ginger ale waiting for me. I sat next to him, realizing I'd left my panties on the ground in the alley. We drank with the rest of the band until the bar closed, fans surrounding us, everyone wanting to party with the band. The other guys continued on to an after-party, but this time Chase took me back to his place.

We rode each other again, this time more slowly, our moans of united climax rising in harmony.

It was nearly dawn before we finally fell asleep.

For the first time since arriving in New York, I found myself alone for several hours. Chase's band had to rehearse their set for that night's show, and since I was going to see it later anyway, Chase suggested I "do some shopping or whatever."

I decided to do the tourist thing. I'd been to New York a few times before, but I'd never really just explored, I'd always been with friends or family with a set itinerary. This time, I went to the Statue of Liberty, explored the area around Times Square on foot, ate at a hole-in-the-wall pizzeria, took the subway in a circle around the boroughs, just wasting time and seeing the every-day-life parts of the city.

I made it back to Chase's apartment with enough time to take a nap, shower, and change. Well, that was the idea, at least. I got the nap in, exhausted from a long day on foot, but the shower didn't exactly happen as planned.

Chase came back from rehearsal, amped up and adrenalized. The hot, leisurely shower I'd anticipated turned into Chase pinning me under the stream of water, one of my legs around his hip as he drove up into me. There was no romance or technique to it, this time. Chase often spent an inordinate amount of time giving me pleasure before he let himself go; this time, the focus was on him, and I liked it that way, in that moment. I tangled my arms around his neck and held tight as he drilled into me, grunting, plunging. He was primal, raw power. He came with a shudder and a growl of teeth in my shoulder.

We finished cleaning up and toweled off, and by that time, Chase was ready again. He didn't make any overt moves to take me again, but I could tell he wanted it.

I waited until he had gotten his boxers on before I made my move. He was pulling his shirt over his head and momentarily blind. I knelt in front of him, jerked his boxers around his knees, and wrapped my lips around his head, letting my teeth lightly graze him, enough to shock. He gasped and flinched.

"God...what are you doing?" Chase tugged the shirt and looked down at me as I stroked his base. "We just went...and I have to be at the club in a few minutes..."

I licked him from root to tip before answering. "If you don't have time, then I guess..." I backed away slowly, giving him time to consider.

"Well, we might have a *few* minutes," he said.

"I thought so. I mean, I wouldn't want you to perform...frustrated." I used both hands then, pumping him slowly, just the very tip in my mouth, sucking gently.

Chase tried to answer, but could only gasp as I slid him deeper into my throat, moving my hands down his length as I did so. His fingers tangled in my damp hair and he fluttered his hips, restraining himself from thrusting. I went slow for a moment, stroking, sucking, and massaging, until he was limp-kneed and gasping. He was slick and hard in my hands, veins throbbing and sack taut, ready to burst. I moved a fist on him, quickly now, a finger massaging the muscles of his taint, lips locked around his engorged head. He threw his head back, groaning, tightened his fingers in my hair, and then he couldn't help his thrusting hips. I took him deep, not quite gagging as he brushed the back of my throat. Harder, faster, until he was dipping at the knees and rocking his hips to the rhythm of my bobbing.

"God, goddamn...I'm coming..."

I hadn't needed the warning. I could feel him tense, feel his balls contract and release in my palm. He came hard, shooting a jet of hot, thick, salty come down my throat, and then again, and a third time. I kept moving, kept sucking, until he was curled down over his belly and rumbling, jerking. He lifted me up to my feet and held me in a hug, breathing hard.

"Wow, what was that for?" Chase asked.

I shrugged. "I wanted to. I like making you feel good, especially before your show. If you guys kill it like you did the other day, I might even do it again."

Chase chuckled. "Well then, we'll have to kill it, won't we?"

They opened for one of New York's biggest up-and-coming local bands, and they killed it. They started their set with one of their hardest numbers, a thrash piece that had the crowd moshing within minutes. That set the pace for the rest of the show, each song harder than the last, and the crowd ate it up. Chase was in rare form, climbing up on a stack of speakers for an entire number, getting the crowd participating in chant-back choruses, jumping off the stage and working through the crowd, even singing from on top of the bar at one point.

By the time their set was over, the crowd was in a frenzy, and actually demanding an encore. After approving it with the stage manager, Chase and the band went back out and did a cover of the Ramones' "Blitzkrieg Bop".

I had watched from the bar, wanting to experience the show from a different angle. When they finished their set, I made my to the backstage entrance. Chase had introduced me to the stage staff before the show. I saw the other guys from the band near the door to the alley, and I made my way to them.

"Hey, Anna!" Gage, the bassist, greeted me with an effusive hug.

"Great show, guys!" I said.

I congratulated all of them, then looked around for Chase, but didn't see him.

"Where's Chase?" I asked.

Gage shifted from one foot to the other, not meeting my eyes, glancing at the back door to the alley and then away. "He's...in the bathroom."

My stomach dropped. I suddenly knew what I'd find if I opened the alley door, but I didn't want to believe it.

I'd spent the show amazed at Chase's talent, wondering again what my hold-up was with him. I'd come backstage with the intent of telling him I was planning to stay in New York for awhile longer, maybe even having the relationship discussion tomorrow.

"The bathroom?" I narrowed my eyes at Gage, fist clenched. "Don't bullshit me, Gage. Where is he?"

Gage shifted again, biting at his lip ring. "Just give him a minute, Anna."

I shoved Gage out of the way, and wrenched the door open. The metal knob was cold in my fist, squeaking as I turned it. The door was heavy, solid and rusted. I put my shoulder to it and pushed. It burst free, sending me stumbling into the alley.

I heard Chase's voice. "Wait, girls, not here, not now, just wait...I don't want Anna to find me—"

My heart clenched and my eyes burned. Chase was backed up against the alley wall, the same two girls from the bathroom at the last show pawing at him. One of them was kneeling in front of him, stopped in the act of opening his pants. The other had his hand in hers against her breast, which was bared, her camisole pulled down.

"Too late," I said, barely above a whisper.

"Anna, wait, please! It's not like you think!" Chase pushed the girls away and stumbled toward me.

I shook my head, spun on my heel and stomped out of the alley toward the main street. My eyes burned and blurred, and my chest seemed to be clutched in a vise. I heard Chase behind me, calling my name, begging me to wait, trying to explain.

I saw a cab trundle past, lit up. I ran toward it, whistling with two fingers. The cab stopped and let me in. I managed get "airport" out before shattering into sobs. I heard a palm slap the window, saw Chase through tear-blurred eyes, running after the cab, panic on his face.

"Want me to stop for him, lady?" The cabbie asked.

"No. Keep going."

"None of my business, but he looks awful shook up. Sure you don't wanna give him a chance?" I saw the cabbie's pale brown eyes meet mine in the rearview mirror.

"Just fucking drive, goddamn it."

The cabbie shrugged and kept silent the rest of the way to the airport. I didn't have my suitcase, but there was nothing vital in it anyway. He could keep it. I had my purse, my phone, my charger, and my ticket. My phone buzzed and rang nonstop, text after text, voicemail after voicemail. Eventually I turned it off and tried not to have a panic attack.

By some miracle, I made the next flight home.

I cried all the way back to Detroit, soft, silent tears dripping down my chin.

Big Girls
Do It
On Top

I'm not the crying type. I've been through too much in my life to go bawling every time something shitty happens. I cried when my dad died a few years ago, and I cried when my dog died when I was thirteen. Not much else in between, mainly because everything else in my life just kept coming, one thing after another, and if I started crying, I'd never have stopped.

I sobbed all the way from New York to Detroit. I did it quietly, face to the window. My seat mate, an older woman with salt and pepper hair and a ridiculously adorable button nose, asked me what was wrong, but I just shrugged and kept my face to the window, watching the clouds pass by. She sighed and muttered something rude, then went back to her issue of *People.*

I wasn't sure exactly what I was going to do in Detroit. I knew I had to face Jeff, but I couldn't bear the thought of doing so right away. I knew I'd hurt him badly. I knew he'd be pissed when I finally got the balls to talk to him. Knowing Jeff, he wouldn't have a lot to say, but his thick, tense silence would speak volumes.

When my plane landed, I had no one to pick me up. My mom lived in Flint, and we didn't get along. Jeff was part of my problems. The only choice left was Jamie. She showed up an hour and a half after I landed. I spent most of that time in a little bar, nursing a margarita and attempting to get a hold of my crazed emotions.

A part of me wanted to fly straight back to New York and punch Chase in the face. Another part wanted to give him a chance to explain. The third part of me wanted to run to Jeff and beg him to take me back. The fourth and, at that moment, the strongest part wanted to just forget both of them and bury my head in the sand.

Being pulled in four different directions emotionally is confusing and exhausting.

Jamie is really my only friend aside from Jeff. We've been room-mates for nearly three years now, through two moves, several tragedies between the two of us, and innumerable break-ups, mostly on her end. She's a serial dater. She's the girl who has a new boyfriend every few weeks or months, but nothing is ever serious and she rarely ever gets truly emotional about breaking up with them. They're just hook-ups for her. I've never understood how she can go from guy to guy and not get attached. She claims they're fun for a while, but then she gets bored.

I'm not that type. I get attached. My thing with Chase should've been just a fling: fun for a while, then over. I shouldn't have been dev-astated when I found him in the alley with those girls. But I was. I felt betrayed and confused. And now, with a couple thousand miles between us, I realized I'd been stupid to think it ever could have been anything for Chase but what it was: a fun distraction. He talked a good game, made it seem like he really cared, like it meant something to him.

He was a rock star, and I was his flavor of the week.

I'd turned my phone on to call Jamie, after having turned it off in the airport so I wouldn't hear Chase's deluge of texts and calls trying to explain away his bullshit.

I scrolled through the missed call log: he'd called me eighteen times and left ten voicemails. I dialed my voicemail and started hit-ting the "seven" button: delete, delete, delete. I couldn't help hearing snatches of the messages:

"Anna, I know what you think you saw, but please, give me a chance to explain. It wasn't—"

Delete.

"Goddammit, Anna. You have to listen. Please answer the phone—"

Delete.

"Seriously, Anna. It's not what you thought. I swear—"

Delete.

"Anna, for fuck's sake—"

Delete.

"Anna, this is the last message I'll leave. You're not answering, and your phone's going straight to voicemail, so I'm guessing you're not even listening to these. You're making a mistake. This is all a misunderstanding. I didn't do anything with those girls. They threw themselves at me. I would never...I care about you...I lo—"

Delete.

Oh, yeah. He went there.

I was shaking with rage, standing at the curb waiting for Jamie's battered blue Buick LeSabre. He wanted me to believe it was all them? Horseshit. I wanted to throw the phone across the road and watch it smash, but I didn't, because I couldn't afford a new one. I deleted his twenty-three texts unread.

I had one message that I hadn't read yet. I'd seen the unread mail icon but ignored it while I was in New York. It wasn't a text; it was an email. From Jeff.

ANNA:

I DON'T BLAME YOU FOR GOING TO NEW YORK. SERIOUSLY. I GET IT. I'M NOT SAYING I LIKE IT, OR THAT I'M NOT HURT, BUT I GET IT. JUST BE SMART, OKAY? DON'T LET YOURSELF GET HURT. I DON'T KNOW THIS CHASE FELLA, AND I'M NOT GOING TO BUTT INTO YOUR BUSINESS, WHEN YOU CLEARLY DON'T WANT ME IN IT. JUST BE CAREFUL. I DON'T KNOW WHAT I'M TRYING TO SAY.

HERE'S MY POINT. I'M YOUR FRIEND, ASIDE FROM ANYTHING ELSE. IF THINGS DON'T WORK OUT FOR YOU, OR IF THEY DO, I'LL STILL BE YOUR FRIEND. I CAN'T GUARANTEE ANYTHING ELSE, BUT AT THE VERY LEAST, I'LL BE YOUR FRIEND. AND YOUR BUSINESS PARTNER.

I GUESS THAT'S ALL.

JEFF

It was dated the day I left for New York. It made my eyes burn. I'd gotten my crying jag under control, but reading Jeff's email made tears prick my red and burning eyes all over again.

Stupid Jeff. He should be pissed off. He should be too angry to want to see me ever again. He had to know why I went to New York, what I was doing with Chase. He'd admitted in his roundabout Jeff sort of way to being hurt; for him to admit that in writing meant he was very deeply wounded.

But he was still willing to be my friend and business partner? How the hell was that possible? If he'd done that to me, I'd never have spoken to him again. He was a better person than I, apparently.

The racketing roar of a car without a muffler disrupted my thoughts. Jamie's LeSabre pulled up next to me. The trunk popped, and Jamie hopped out. She was a few inches shorter than me, making her not quite five-seven, and she was built a bit more willowy and svelte than me, which always made me jealous. She wore most of her weight in her hips and breasts, which were more than ample. She often talked, only halfway joking, about getting a breast reduction, if only to save her some back pain. She was a natural redhead, pure Irish orange-copper locks falling past her shoulders in absurdly perfect waves, and pale cornflower-blue eyes, freckles, the whole nine yards.

When I said she was willowy and svelte, that was relatively speaking. She's still what most people would call "plus-size." Which is why she's my best friend. We understand each other. We tell each other, when life hands us pain due to the fact that we're not diet-obsessed stick figures, that God just gave us an extra portion of awesomeness. And then we watch *Breakfast at Tiffany's* and share a pint of Ben and Jerry's, washed down with a bottle of wine.

In this moment, with Chase in New York and Jeff shoved aside until I had the courage to face him, Jamie was the only person I could stomach. She was my only real family, and the one person who'd understand what I needed in that moment: cupcakes and alcohol.

She had a six-pack of Tim Horton's muffins (three left) and a grande skinny mocha waiting for me. Yeah, she's that kind of friend.

"I honestly didn't expect you to come back," Jamie said as I slid into the passenger seat.

The engine roared, and I held onto my mocha with one hand and the oh-shit bar with the other. Jamie is an...exuberant driver.

"I'm not sure I did, either," I answered, unwrapping the low-fat blueberry muffin.

"So what the hell happened?"

I ate the muffin and thought about how much to tell Jamie.

"Everything happened," I answered, after a few bites. "He took me backstage for a couple shows, which was awesome. We hung out a lot, which was also awesome. And then I caught him with some groupies in an alley. Which was not awesome."

Jamie frowned at my Spark's Notes version of events. "Come on, Anna. Spill. Don't be selfish with the gossip."

I rolled my eyes. "It's not gossip, Jay. It's my life. And it hurt."

Jamie backhanded my shoulder. "I know. We can get to the hurt later. For now, tell me the good stuff. Is he good in bed?"

I realized I hadn't really talked to Jamie about Chase at all since I'd met him.

"He's...god, where do I start?" I closed my eyes and grabbed the oh-shit bar as Jamie merged onto the freeway. When we were cruising at a relatively tame eighty-five, I started talking again. "Chase is a rock star in every sense of the word. Nothing I've ever done, with anyone, can even remotely compare to Chase in bed."

"Is he big?"

I choked on my muffin. "I didn't exactly measure, Jay, but yes, he is. And that's all I'll say. A girl's gotta have some secrets."

"Not from your best friend, you don't. But seriously, if he's that good, why come home?"

"I told you, I found him porking some chicks in an alley."

Jamie frowned. "Are you sure? If he's as hot as you claim, which I wouldn't know because you wouldn't introduce me, then girls would be throwing themselves at him, right? So maybe it wasn't how it looked. Did you give him a chance to explain?"

I ignored the niggling worm of doubt in my gut. "I didn't need to. I know what I saw."

Jamie looked at me, and it wasn't a look I liked. "So you just left? You just got on a plane and left, without listening to anything he had to say? Nothing?"

"Whose side are you on?" I suddenly wasn't interested in the other two muffins.

"I'm on yours, which is why I'm pissed off. You should have at least given him a chance." She narrowed her eyes at me, as if coming to a realization. "You ran because you like him. Right? It wasn't just the girls. That was an excuse. You have *feelings* for him."

"Feelings" was a swear word in Jamie's dictionary. Feelings led to pain, which she'd had enough of in her life. Just like me.

"I flew to New York on a whim to see him, Jamie. Yes, I have feelings for him."

Jamie gave me an exasperated look. "No, dumbass. You *like* him, like him. Meaning, you're worried you're falling in love with him, so you bolted."

The guardrail out my window was suddenly interesting. "No. That's not it."

Jamie shrieked, "It is! You love him. But you're chicken."

I rounded on her, pissed off now. "And you wouldn't be? If you found yourself falling in love with a guy way out of your league, you'd be shitting yourself, too, and you know it."

"True. But I'd be honest about it."

"And I'm not?"

Jamie didn't answer right away, tongue poking out the side of her mouth as she focused on weaving around a train of slow-going semis. When I could breathe again, and she had decelerated down to ninety, she gave me a serious look.

"No, you're not. You ran without telling him what you were feeling. Let's just say, just for argument's sake, that you're wrong about what you saw. And let's say he invited you to New York because maybe, just maybe, he has feelings for you, too. And then some girls jumped him in the alley, and you walked out and saw something incriminating, and left without so much as a how-de-do. How would he feel, do you think?"

My stomach clenched. "Who the hell are you, and what did you do with my best friend? Because it sure as hell sounds like you're advocating a real relationship with actual feelings here."

Jamie kept her eyes on the road, both hands clenched on the steering wheel. I'd never seen Jamie use both hands to drive. She always had one hand on the gear shifter, even though her car was automatic.

"Listen, Anna. I know I'm like the all-time queen of humping and dumping guys. I act all 'fuck feelings' and whatever, and that's true enough. I mean, it's not an act. But, deep down, when I'm doing the walk of shame to my car at three a.m., I do wonder what it would be like to really have a guy care about me. Like, want me, and want me to stay over." She gave me long, sad look. "I find myself wondering what it would be like to have a guy want me for me, not just because I'm easy, you know?"

"You're not easy, Jay—"

"I am, too. I am and I like it that way. Usually. But sometimes, I wish a guy would see past the tits and ass. The problem is, I don't let them, because it keeps the ones who might feel something at bay."

"You've really thought about this, haven't you?"

She nodded, rubbing across her cheek with a forefinger. Almost like she was crying, which was absurd. Jamie didn't cry.

"Yeah, of course. More than I'd ever admit to." She looked at me, let me see the diamonds glittering in her eyes. "I'm just saying, Anna, if Chase was for real, then...I don't know. Maybe you should have given him a chance."

It was hard to breathe for a few minutes. This was the deepest Jamie had ever let me see into who she really was. I mean, best friends, yeah, but deepest, darkest, most vulnerable secrets? Not usually.

"It was more than that, Jay." I picked at the fraying seam threads of her leather seats between my thighs. "I was confused."

"Confused? By what?"

"I think...I thought—"

"Spit it out, sister."

I took a deep breath and said what I'd been worried about for days. "I have feelings for Jeff, too."

"Shit on a shingle."

"Exactly." I pulled my hair out of the ponytail and ran my fingers through it. "I think they both have feelings for me, too. Or...did. After leaving Jeff like I did, I'm not sure where that stands. I really made a mess of things."

Jamie took my hand and squeezed it. "When you said no one could compare to Chase in bed..."

I shook my head. "They're completely different. I don't know how to think about them at the same time, you know? It's like trying to compare apples and cheese."

"Apples and cheese go great together..." Jamie winked at me.

"Oh, hell no."

"It's never even crossed your mind?"

"Both of them at the same time?" I looked at her with horror. "You should know me better than that. I would never, could never, with *anyone*. Much less two men I care for. I don't know how you could do that and then look at either guy the same way again."

"You'd be surprised," Jamie said.

"You mean, you—?"

"ANYWAY," Jamie said, a little too loudly, "if they're so different, then it should make it easier to decide, right? Just pick the one you like sleeping with more."

"I wish it was that simple," I said. "I don't know how to explain it. Chase is wild. We do crazy things. Like...whoa. But Jeff? Jeff is just slow and sweet and...."

Jamie raised an eyebrow. "Keep going. Tell me about wild and crazy."

"Like, in the bathroom of a bar. And in a changing room. Tied up. Blindfolded."

"No fucking way. Blindfolded?" Jamie grinned at me, incredulous. "I've done it in public places before, no problem. Fun and risky, but whatever. Old news, and gets uncomfortable, just like in cars. But, seriously? Blindfolded? Tied up? Tell me about it! What's it like?"

"Intense. Tied up requires serious trust. Even if you have a safeword, you have to trust him to listen if you use it. But god, is it hot. You have no idea what he's going to do next. You can't do anything back to him, you just have to lie there and let him do whatever he wants. He can make you wait for hours, if he has the patience. Blindfolded is different. Without sight, everything else is more vivid. Smell, hearing, touch..."

Jamie moaned and slid down low in her seat. "Okay, enough. You're making me horny and jealous. I don't have anyone I trust enough to do that with. Sounds incredible."

"It is."

"Soooo....what's the problem?"

"I didn't say there was a problem. I had no idea it could be like that. Just no clue."

"So, then, what about Jeff?"

I didn't answer for a long time. "With Jeff it's not as...exciting. Like, not as wild and unpredictable. But he's amazing, in his own way. It doesn't need to be crazy to be just completely satisfying, on a soul-deep level. He takes me places, emotionally and physically, where I didn't know two people could go together. It's just a totally different experience. I'm not sure I can describe it."

Jamie was silent for awhile. "So you have two amazing guys. Both have feelings for you, and you have feelings for both of them, but they're totally different."

"Basically. And I've messed it up with both of them. I mean, I'm not sold on Chase being innocent. But if he is...?"

"All you can do is make the best choice you can and try to fix things with whichever one you pick."

"It's a shitty choice. Whatever I do, someone gets hurt. And with Jeff, I'm not sure there's any picking left. I ran to New York to fuck Chase less than forty-eight hours after sleeping with Jeff. How does that not make me some kind of slut?"

"Beating yourself up won't help. And it wasn't like that."

"No? How was it then? I get a letter with a plane ticket. All the letter said was, 'I need to see you.' And I just went. Left Jeff just when things were getting interesting."

"By which you mean an emotional connection was starting?" Jamie said.

"Yeah, basically. I mean, with Jeff, I think there always was. I've known him for so long, and we know each other on a completely different level, you know? Jeff was my business partner, and besides you, my best and only other friend. Sleeping with him didn't change our friendship, really. It just...deepened it. At least, until I left. I don't know if there's anything left to go back to. He did send me an email saying he'd still be my friend, but I don't know how far that goes. I really hurt him."

Jamie bit her lip. "He said that? In an email?"

I nodded. "Yeah. He sent it just after I left Detroit. I didn't see it until just now, though. I never really used my phone in New York."

"If he said that, that he's still your friend, then I'm willing to bet he's still in love with you. He'd give you a chance. I know Jeff well enough to know he'd probably forgive you."

"I'm not sure. And should he?"

"Of course he should. People do shitty things. You forgive them and move on."

"Is that why we never let anyone in? Because we forgive and move on?"

Jamie laughed. "Well, people that aren't us. We're messed up."

We rode in companionable silence for a while. We were nearly back to our apartment when Jamie spoke up again.

"So what are you going to do?"

I shrugged. "I don't know. I really don't."

"Well, don't wait too long. The longer you put it off, the harder it'll get."

"Yeah, you're right." I agreed with her out loud, but inside, I was wondering if maybe I should just pretend nothing had happened. Get a job somewhere else, stop DJ-ing so I didn't have to see Jeff, and move on with my life, without either man.

It was the coward's way out, but it would be easier than dealing with Jeff's hurt eyes and hard silence.

I hid in my room for two days, then took some independent DJ-ing jobs. I drank too much with Jamie. I ignored the waning amount of texts from Chase.

Basically, I tried to pretend nothing had happened, or would happen. I don't know if Jeff even knew I was back in Detroit.

With every passing day I wanted more and more to see Jeff, if only to apologize. Being here, in my apartment, passing places where I'd DJ-ed with him, places where we'd had dinner before work…it all made me realize what I'd given up with him.

A week passed. Jamie held her tongue until I was halfway through the second week.

"Anna, you're being a coward and an idiot," she told me over our second bottle of two-buck Chuck. "If you don't woman up and do something besides avoid the situation, we're gonna be fighting. For real."

"I can't, Jay. I don't know what to do."

"Not doing anything isn't an option. You're better than this. If you don't want to be with either of them, fine. I think that's stupid, but it's your choice. If you have two men in love with you, you *have* to pick one of them, I'd think. It's hard enough to get *one* guy to feel something for you besides 'I want to fuck you.'" Jamie frowned at me in irritation. "Girl, I'm telling you as your friend, if you don't *do something*, you're gonna wake up one day and realize you made the biggest mistake of your life."

Her eyes welled up and she looked away, downed her glass of chardonnay. I suspected she was speaking from experience, but this seemed to be deeper than we'd gone. We'd always been "have a good time and don't talk about the past" kind of friends.

"What was his name?" I asked.

Jamie didn't answer for a long time. When she did, her voice was barely above a whisper. "Brian. We met a few months after I graduated from high school. My brother had just gone to jail. He'd gotten caught after a heroin-induced series of B and E's. Mom was high all the time, Dad was off with one of his hooker girlfriends. I had no one. No one came to my graduation, no one cared that I was valedictorian, despite not having parents who gave a shit. I'd known Brian all through high school, but in an opposite sides of the same circle of friends kind of way. Then, one day, I was out on the tracks, smoking down, feeling sorry for myself, wondering what the hell my life meant. Brian showed up, just swaggering down the tracks. Long metal-band hair, all-black clothes, skin-tight jeans and combat boots and spiked bracelets, the whole bit. He saw me smoking, sat down next to me, and we shared the J together. Didn't talk until it was gone.

"He...he got me. Had a similar home situation, and we just kind of talked about it enough to realize we were like the same person, you know? I didn't feel as alone, suddenly. He turned into my best friend. My only friend. We were inseparable after that. I think I saw him every single day for, like, a year. It was just friendship at first. Then one day we got really high and split a forty. He had his own place with a buddy who was twenty-one, bought beer all the time. We lay in Brian's bed, smoking and drinking.

"I don't even remember how it happened. One second we were just blazing and talking and whatever, and then we were kissing and our clothes were off, and...it just happened. You know, I always call bullshit when people say, 'oh it was accident, it just happened.' And most of the time, it is bullshit. It was a choice, and you just chose not to stop it, because really, you wanted it, and the consequences didn't seem so bad in that moment. But that night, with Brian, it really did just happen. I don't remember there ever being any sexual tension, or flirting, or whatever. It just...happened. I remember it all. Every sweet, incredible moment is burned into my brain forever.

"It freaked me the fuck out. I've got damage, Anna. You know that. I've got guy issues, and it all goes back to my dad not loving me or whatever. I've had that shit psychoanalyzed dozens of times. Knowing why I've got issues doesn't make 'em go away. Well, Brian had mommy issues like I've got daddy issues, and together, it just made things impossible. He wanted to work it out, give it a try. We got each other, on a fundamental, emotional level. We didn't have to explain our walls and hot-button issues. And the sex was great. After that first time, we couldn't stop, you know? We just kept fucking every chance we got. But it was never any deeper than that, as in we never talked about what our relationship was, or about our feelings. Well, when he finally confronted me on the issue, told me we had to either talk it out or stop seeing each other...I bolted.

"He chased after me for weeks. Called me, hunted me down wherever I went, told me loved me, wrote me songs. I pushed him away. Finally he took the hint and left me alone. Forever. And now, every day, I realize what a mistake I made. I should have let him love me, should've tried, shouldn't have been such a goddamned coward. It's too late, though. I tried. I looked for him, and I actually found him, but he'd gotten engaged to this great girl, and he was happy and just looked at me all sad, like, 'Too late, baby. Your loss.'"

Jamie had never talked about herself that much at once in all the time I've known her. She stood up and left, went into the bathroom and stayed there for a long time. Crying, probably. Getting it out in private.

When she came back, her eyes were red but she was back to normal. "Anyway, all that with Brian is the reason I am like I am. My therapist used to tell me the reason I go through guys like I do is because I'm looking for Brian, or someone like him."

"Is that why?" I asked.

She nodded. "Pretty much. I mean, do I look at every guy I go out with and ask myself if he's like Brian, or compare them to see if he matches up to Brian? No, not consciously. But I think down deep, subconsciously or whatever, I dismiss the guy before I've given him a chance just because he's not Brian and never will be. The problem is, Brian is gone. No one will ever be him. Someday I'm going to have to let go of him and my idea of a guy based on him. I think maybe I keep hoping some man will come along and just sweep me away, but so far, it hasn't happened, and I'm starting to wonder if it ever will."

"Let me ask you something, Jay. If a guy did come along who was somehow just different from all the others, would you let him sweep you away? Because so far, in my experience, it's not that easy. Getting swept away is scary, in reality. It's not all love stories and fairy tales." I looked at her over the rim of my wine glass. "You don't know what's happening, and everything you feel is freaking intense as hell, and nothing makes any sense and it's just...scary. It's not like, oh, hey, hot guy who likes me, let's go live happily ever-fucking-after. When you're as damaged as we are, a guy tries to sweep you away and you're like oh, hell no, I'm running. Screw this. I'm gonna go back to what's familiar."

Jamie nodded. "Yeah, that sounds about right." She smiled at me. "So if you've got that much figured out, then why haven't you done anything about Jeff or Chase?"

"Because I'm scared shitless, that's why." I laughed. "Avoiding them both is easier than being rejected. I hurt them, and now I don't have the guts to ask for forgiveness."

Jamie frowned, pointed at me with the index finger wrapped around her wine glass. "Well, woman the hell up, *chica*. You've fought off guys in bars, broken cue sticks and beer bottles over the heads of drunk assholes, and been through more insane shit than most guys I know and come through fine. Well, mostly fine. The point is, don't let this own you, girl. I'm serious. If you let this go, we'll be for real fighting. Don't be an idiot. Find Jeff and apologize and beg him, on your hands and knees, to take you back. Or fly to New York and get Chase to take you back. Something. Anything. Get them both here and have a threesome. Don't just sit around with your head up your ass. That's the only wrong choice in this situation."

She didn't give me a chance to respond. She downed her wine and wove her way unsteadily into her bedroom.

"I'm right, Anna, and you know it. Get off your ass. Right now."

"I'm drunk right now," I pointed out.

"Well, tomorrow, then. Drunk is never the right time to make major life decisions. *Talk* about major life decisions, yes. *Do* something about them? Not s'much. G'night, Anna."

"Night." I watched her flop onto her bed and start snoring immediately.

I've always envied her ability to go right to sleep. It always takes me a while, even drunk. I finished my wine, set her glass and mine by the sink, turned off the lights and shut Jamie's door. Alone, the silence was deafening. I heard Jamie's words in my head, rolling over and over: *Do something, anything. Get off your ass, girl.*

I lay down in bed and stared at the ceiling, thinking.

Enough running, Anna. No more cowardice.

I told myself I was going to call Jeff in the morning. Better yet, go to his house. Face him in person.

Oh, hell.

Jeff's Yukon was in his driveway, his front door was open, and I could see him through the storm door, sitting at the kitchen table in front of his laptop. My stomach was in my throat, my heart pounding in my chest like a high school drum line.

I was in my car, willing myself to get out. It wasn't working. My feet were planted to the floorboard, my ass rooted to the ripped cloth seat. My eyes were already burning, my throat thick, my hands trembling.

I had no idea what I was going to say.

Jeff's back was to me and he had earbuds in, so he didn't see me pull up in his driveway or hear my car rattle down the street. He was oblivious. Would he slam the door in my face? Would he lead me inside and tell me he forgave me?

I forced myself out of the car. Took a step. Another. A third, and then I was at the door, the glass pane rattling under my trembling knuckles. Jeff looked over his shoulder, the pen in his mouth dropping to the floor.

He pulled the earbuds out of his ears and tossed them aside, closed the laptop, and moved across the small living room. He stopped in front of the door, his features schooled into neutrality. No anger showed, no sadness or condemnation. Blank.

After an eternity, he opened the door, but he didn't let me in. He stepped out onto the concrete slab that was his front porch. My eyes were blurry and stinging for some reason. I wasn't crying, though. Really.

Okay, so maybe I was, a little.

A long, fraught silence hung between us.

"Jeff, I—I'm sorry. I just wanted to stop by and say that I'm back in Detroit, and—I don't know." I couldn't look at him. "That's it, I guess."

He hadn't said anything yet, hadn't even changed his blank expression. I turned to leave, heart heavy and cracking.

I felt his hand wrap around my elbow. "Anna, wait." I tried not to let hope blossom too fully in my chest. "Why don't you come in and have some coffee?"

It was two in the afternoon, but for Jeff, coffee was an all-day thing. Leftover habit from the Army, I guess. I nodded and followed Jeff inside. I'd only been gone a few days, but it felt like longer. It felt like a lifetime. I realized, as I watched his broad back retreat into the kitchen, how very much I'd missed him. Had going to New York been the worst mistake of my life? It was hard not to think so, in light of my feelings of Chase's betrayal, whether he was guilty or not.

I sat down at the little round table, remembering breakfast here with Jeff, after what had been one of the best nights of my life. It hadn't been wild or acrobatic or daring, just satisfying on an emotional level. It was companionship.

I'd left it all behind for a few days of fun that hadn't panned out into more. And what if it had? What if I'd just stayed in New York with Chase? He'd be a huge rock star someday soon, traveling the world, playing shows in exotic locations. It was just a matter of time. Would I have gone with him? Stood backstage and watched every show every day for months on end? Sat in hotel rooms, waiting for him to get back? Attended insane after-parties like the one in New York? Would any of that have fulfilled me? Would he have been faithful all that time?

There were too many questions pounding in my head, and Jeff was sitting across from me, a huge mug with the U.S. Army logo stamped on it held in both of his hard, calloused hands.

"New York didn't work out for you, huh?" Jeff asked.

I shook my head. "I don't want to talk about New York."

Jeff's eyes narrowed. "He hurt you."

A short, tense silence, in which I tried to keep my feelings bottled up inside where they belonged. I couldn't just dump it all on Jeff.

"I said I don't want to talk about New York. I came to apologize for hurting you, and that's it. I—I didn't mean to hurt you. That doesn't help, I guess, but I had to say it." I sipped my coffee to buy time to think, burning my tongue. "I got your email when I got back in to Detroit. I don't know how you can say you're still my friend after the way I—after I—"

Jeff interrupted. "Anna, you'll always be my friend. You can't hurt me bad enough to kill that. I care about you. No matter what."

"You're a better person than I am," I said. "I'm not sure I could do the same, if the situations were reversed."

"I don't buy that," Jeff said. "You're a good person."

"No, I'm not. I wouldn't have left if I was."

"Well..." Jeff seemed conflicted. "You did leave. It did hurt. But does that make you a bad person? That's not for me to judge."

"This is a confusing conversation. I just came to apologize. I'm not...I'm not trying to get—to ask you to..." I couldn't get the words out.

I stood up and walked to the sliding glass door, watching a robin hop across Jeff's backyard. Jeff was making me even more mixed up inside. He seemed both deeply hurt and impossibly understanding. I didn't know how to deal with either one, much less both at once.

"To what?" Jeff said. "You're not asking me to what? Spit it out."

I shook my head. "No. It's stupid to think of it, and not gonna happen. I don't deserve it, and I don't even know if I want it."

"Say it."

"No." I felt Jeff coming up behind me, standing an inch away, his body heat radiating into me, not touching me, his breath ruffling my hair. "Don't, Jeff. I apologized, and now I'm leaving."

"You didn't apologize," Jeff said. "Just told me you were sorry. That's not an apology."

I turned around, angry now. "You want me to say the words? Fine. Jeff, I apologize for hurting you. Please forgive me." The words started out angry, irritated, but ended up as a cracked-voice sob.

Jeff's hands clutched my shoulders, held me at arm's length. "I forgive you, Anna." His dark eyes pierced into mine, a welter of emotion in his gaze.

"You shouldn't."

He laughed. "Of course I should. Friends forgive each other."

"Okay. So now what?"

"You tell me."

"It's not that easy," I said. "You can't just say 'I forgive you' and have everything go back to the way it was."

"Of course not," Jeff said. "But it's a start."

Jeff sat down at the table again and sipped his coffee. I joined him, and we drank in silence.

"What happened?" Jeff asked.

"You don't want to know."

"Sure I do. You're my friend. Something happened to rile you up and send you back to Detroit."

"Jeff, you really don't want to know. We're more than friends, and you know it. At least, we were. I don't know what we are now, but you don't want to know about New York."

"Don't tell me what I want," Jeff growled, anger finally showing in his voice. "We were more than friends. We still are. Now tell me what the fuck happened in New York."

"What do you want to know?" I felt myself on the verge of exploding, and I couldn't stop it. "Do you want to hear that Chase and I fucked like bunnies? That it was crazy and wild and I never wanted to stop? Or do you want to hear that even when I was with him I couldn't stop thinking about *you*? That I felt guilty with him because it felt like cheating on you? Is that what you want?"

"Anna, I—"

"Or would you like me to get more detailed? Do you want a play-by-play description of positions? Is that it? What do you want, Jeff? You can't honestly still want me after this, can you? What was it you said before we ever hooked up? Oh, yeah, I remember. You said you didn't want Chase's sloppy seconds. Well, I've got news for you, Jeff. That's what you'll be getting. Chase's really sloppy fucking seconds."

Jeff's eyes wavered, angry, hurt, confused, and still pinning me to the wall with impossible understanding. "Anna, now hold on, I already told you, I didn't mean that—"

I didn't let him finish yet again. "You want to know what happened? Why I came back? I found Chase in an alley after his show with a couple of girls all over him. I bolted. I didn't give him a chance to explain. I just left. I was on a flight home within two hours. It just made me so mad. It may not have been what I thought it was, because girls have a tendency of throwing themselves at Chase." I looked away. "Just like I did."

"Fuck," Jeff sighed. "The way I saw it, he threw himself at you. Granted, I didn't see it all, but that's the impression I got. He didn't seem like your type, to be honest."

"My type?"

"Yeah, I mean, he's all pretty boy rock star or whatever, and I've never seen you go after guys like that."

"Because I never thought I was enough for a guy like him."

"Damn it, Anna. You're beautiful. I know you have a hard time believing that, or seeing it in yourself, but it's true." Jeff touched my jaw, turning my gaze back to his. "*I* see it, Anna. You were always enough for me."

"Even after—"

"Yes. I'm not saying I'm not hurt and pissed off at you. I am. What I'm saying is, I'd be willing to try, if you were. If you want to give Chase another chance, then I guess that's your choice. I wouldn't, personally. I mean, even if it wasn't like you thought, and he wasn't really doing anything, he'd end up doing it one day. No guy can have women throw themselves at him like that and not give in sometime."

I didn't know what to say. Was he serious?

"Jeff, I—I don't know."

"You don't have to know right now," Jeff said. "Hell, I'm not even sure. I know I care about you. I know I'm sorry you got hurt. I know I've really missed you."

"Do you feel like I betrayed you?"

Jeff sighed. "Yeah, kinda." He refilled his coffee and spoke without looking at me while doctoring it. "I felt like we had a damn good thing going, and it could've been more, could've been even better. But then that pretty boy sends you one stupid letter and you run off to him without a second thought."

He sat down and looked at me. "Listen, I do understand. It was one of those things where you would've spent your whole life wondering 'what if.' You had to find out. Now you know, and you can move on."

"You're amazing, Jeff. I don't know what to say." I couldn't believe he was even giving me the time of day.

"I care about you. I'm not saying I'll trust you all the way again right off the bat. We'd have to take things slow for a while, because I am still a bit sore, you know? But you're back, and I...I just can't seem to picture my life without you in it, somehow."

I couldn't help crying at that. It was quiet tears, slow and burning down my face.

"Don't cry, Anna. You're gonna be fine. We'll be fine. One day at a time, okay?"

"I've been back for almost two weeks, you know that? I've spent every moment wondering what you'd say, how you'd react, thinking you'd be so mad."

"What, you think I'd yell at you? Scream and call you names?" Jeff seemed almost insulted by the thought.

"Well, I don't know! All I knew was I'd hurt you, and I didn't deserve—"

"Forget the talk about deserving. We are who we are. People who really love us will do so even when we hurt them."

"So you love—"

"Let's go get something to eat," Jeff interrupted. "I'm hungry."

It was awkward at first. We drove in Jeff's truck, a tense silence between us. Neither of us knew what we were, where we really stood. We hadn't settled anything, really. We'd just sort of...stopped talking about it. What else was there to say, really, though? Either things would work out, or they wouldn't. No amount of talking would get us past what had happened.

The funny thing was, I realized as we sat down together at Max and Erma's, we'd both just kind of assumed we'd try to...not pick up where we'd left off, but move on, be together in some way.

Jeff didn't bring up New York or Chase again. He talked about some interesting DJ gigs he'd done, did a few funny impressions of a drunk guy trying to sing "Brown-Eyed Girl," which was a song he hated, even when done by Van Morrison, and even more so when butchered by some wasted bar patron.

We'd always been comfortable together, an easy come-and-go to our conversations, silence that could stretch out for long periods of time without either of us needing to fill it with aimless chatter. At first, things were stilted, hesitant, and difficult. Awkward at best. But by the time we were done with our burgers and were sharing a brownie sundae, we were finding our old rhythms, our previous comfort.

Once again I was struck by how long it had seemed we'd been apart. So much had changed. I had changed, somehow. I didn't see Jeff as a given commodity. That's really the truth of it. Jeff had been a consistent part of my life for so long that I had taken him for granted, assumed he'd be there no matter what. And then I left for New York on a whim, and somewhere along the way I realized he might not always be there, that maybe I'd pushed him away.

The thought of Jeff not being in my life, of not having his quiet, steady presence to rely on, scared me. He belonged in my life. I couldn't fathom working a gig without him to help set up. Couldn't fathom waking up and not being able to call him, or have lunch with him.

He was giving me another chance, and I vowed to not mess it up.

A little over two and a half weeks passed in which Jeff and I spent a lot of time together, as just friends—albeit friends with sexual chemistry sparking at every moment, in everything we did. Every conversation was rife with innuendo. Every touch threatened to ignite an inferno between us.

The breaking point came during a shift DJ-ing at a Mexican place in Lake Orion two weeks later. We set up, ran through the first set without a problem. Some good singers did their numbers, and of course, as the night went on, some drunks did the usual murder to "Sweet Home Alabama" and "Margaritaville."

We took our break, ran a few more numbers, and then, as the fill music was playing between numbers, a guy maybe thirty-five or so sidled up to Jeff and me. He was tall, with brown hair and a goatee, a western-style shirt with pearl snap buttons and pointed breast pockets, a huge belt buckle, and cowboy boots, complete with a Stetson. His wife was sitting at a round high-top table, similarly decked out, but with jean skirt.

The gentleman leaned an elbow on the mixing board and addressed Jeff. "Can I make a special request?"

"Sure," Jeff said, setting a pencil and request slip down in front of the man and pointing at the songbook. "We've got plenty of country songs to choose from."

"Hell, no. I don't want to sing, and you don't want me to. I can guaran-damn-tee you that. If I get started, I'll clear the place in three bars flat."

"Well, then, what can I do for you?" Jeff asked.

"I want you and the lady here," he said, pointing at me, "to sing a song together. It's my wife and I's tenth anniversary today, and we'd sure appreciate hearing our favorite song."

My wife's and my, I mentally corrected, but didn't say out loud.

"Well, if we know it, we'll sing it," Jeff said.

"We'd like to hear 'Let's Make Love' by Tim McGraw and Faith Hill."

Jeff cast a glance at me. We knew that song. We'd listened to it just the other day, trundling down a narrow dirt track road in the middle of Milford, cruising and listening to music. The harmony fit our voices perfectly, and then, in the car, it had been hard enough to ignore the lyrics and keep driving.

Performing it together would be...intense.

"We know it," Jeff answered. "We'll sing it. And congratulations. Ten years together. That's really awesome."

"It takes a lot of hard work, a lot of compromise, and a lot of forgiveness," the man said, clapping Jeff on the shoulder. "If you love her, show her. That's the real trick. It takes a real man to let his feelings show to his wife."

Jeff just nodded and sent the man on his way back to his table. He hopped onto the high chair and flung his arm around his wife's shoulders, nuzzling her neck and whispering something in her ear that made her giggle and swat him on the arm.

Tapping a few commands into his laptop, Jeff brought up the song track and lyrics. We'd spent a lot of time over the last few weeks converting all our old CDs to digital tracks, so now we just had one laptop as opposed to several huge binders of discs. Jeff handed me one of the cordless mics, and we stepped out onto the stage together as the opening strains of the song came up.

In my mind, I see the music video: black and white images, a lovely blonde woman and a rugged, handsome man in a cowboy hat and duster dancing in front of the Eiffel Tower. The chemistry between the pair, as they dance together and begin singing, is clearly not acted, or performed, but real and genuine. It makes the lyrics of the song that much more powerful.

Jeff's clear tenor starts in, a bit low for his register but on key and... god, he's never sounded better. His eyes fix on mine, and his hand reaches for me. Sparks fly as his palm brushes across mine, our fingers tangle, and he turns to face me, no need for the prompter or the crowd—gone silent now, caught up in the moment, as I am. My part comes, and I hear my voice rising up, pitch-perfect and clarion clear, and I know I'm on, I can feel the rightness in my bones, I can feel the music boiling in my blood and the buzz of adrenaline from performing, even for the hundred or so bar patrons. None of that matters, though, because it's the song, the lyrics, the moment. Jeff is clutching my hand, pulling me close, our bodies almost touching, our eyes locked as if connected. I couldn't look away from him if I wanted to. This is beyond chemistry, beyond spark.

Something is happening, in this moment, as I sing, as he sings, as we harmonize, as the music coils around us like serpents of visible flame, burns through us like dulcet fire.

They say the eyes are the window to the soul; as we sing, those windows are flung open and our souls collide. It's the kind of moment you never forget. The song doesn't end, in my memory. It just keeps going, and we keep singing. Our hands are joined, we're singing from one mic, the crowd is stunned, eyes are glistening.

The couple who requested the song, the cowboy and his wife, they're dancing together in front of their table. No one else is dancing, or even moving at all. Even the bartenders and the servers are paused, trays of drinks set down, pints of beer half-filled. A few cooks are even peeking out from the doors of the kitchen. The couple dances, cheeks pressed together, heads inclined a little, bodies pressed close into a hold that's more embrace than anything else. They dance slowly, swaying in gradual circles. You can feel the love pouring between them, and you can't help but wonder what it must feel like to love someone that hard. How well must they know each other by now? Ten years of every single day? Ten years of conversation shared, secrets spilled, fears faced, and love made? They must be nearly one person by now, a single whole made from two inseparable halves.

Ten years is a long time to love someone. Your biological family is different, you know? They have to love you. Or, they're supposed to, but they don't always, which makes it even worse, I think. But to choose someone, one man, one woman, out of the thousands and millions of people in the world, all the different individuals you *could* love, *could* be with, you've chosen that *one* person, and you've stuck with them for an entire decade. You hear about people being married for twenty, forty, sixty years. I can't fathom that, not in any sense. Ten years I can imagine. I've known Jeff for six years. I can see us spending another ten together, if I don't fuck it up.

Our song, in reality, does end. The music fades away, and Jeff and I continue to hold hands. Our eyes are locked, mics held down by our sides. The crowd is still silent, as if waiting.

I'm waiting, too, I realize. I'm holding my breath, looking up at Jeff with his dark eyes glittering into mine.

He kisses me, a slow inevitability, lips touching in hesitant tenderness. His hand drifts up to my face, cups my cheek, thumb brushing my ear, and then the hand holding the mic is wrapping around my back and holding me closer, tighter, and the kiss is going deeper, and the crowd, silent, watching us kiss, seems to know better than to even breathe.

Time stopped for that kiss, I swear. Time was stopped for the whole song, and that kiss was part of it. When we broke apart, the crowd burst into frenzied cheering, clapping, whistling. The cowboy and his wife approached us, shook Jeff's hand, and gave me a hug.

"That was the best anniversary present we've ever gotten," the cowboy said. "I swear, y'all sounded just like Tim and Faith, if not better."

"Thanks," Jeff said. "Congratulations again."

"No reason for congratulations," the wife said. "It's just love."

The couple left then, but before they were out the door, the woman came back and leaned close to me. "That boy loves you, honey. Don't let him get away."

The same thought had crossed my mind.

We finished the shift, energy and tension sparking between us. Every time our fingers touched, every time our eyes met, I saw him in the shower, naked body heavy with muscle and dripping with rivulets of steaming water. I felt him above me in his wide, soft bed, dark eyes burning into mine as he moved, his rippling muscles pulsing his thick manhood into me.

It had been over a month since I left New York, and almost six weeks since that night in the hot tub. That was the one moment I saw in my mind, in my dreams, more than any other. Jeff, his solid bulk beneath me in the boiling water, our bodies moving in synchronized splendor, heat throbbing between us, fragments of our souls merging in the cool of the night and the spark of the stars and the thrum of our united passions.

I wanted him, so badly. We'd waited, through some kind of unspoken agreement, putting time between us and...all that. I didn't think I could wait any longer. Not now, not with the incredible performance we'd just shared, that song, those lyrics.

Jeff seemed to feel it, too. He got the equipment put away in record time, and we took our pay and left, not stopping for a drink or two like we usually did. The other gigs we'd done together in the past couple weeks, we'd had a couple of drinks, or gone to get some late night food. We hadn't gone back to either of our places.

Now, we stood by our cars, keys in hand, mere inches separating us.

"Thought maybe you'd come over for a bit," Jeff said, after a pregnant silence.

My lip curled in amusement. "Just for a bit?"

Jeff's eyes glinted his amusement. "Yeah. Just for a bit. I need my beauty rest, you know."

"Yeah, you sure do. Wouldn't want to keep you up too late, or tire you out."

"No, we wouldn't want that." Jeff pinched my chin gently between his thumb and forefinger, leaned in and kissed me.

It was delicate, gentle, a caress of the lips. The kiss communicated so much that he hadn't said in words. His slow and thorough devouring of my mouth and my tongue told me he'd forgiven me, he'd moved on and left the past behind us. His hand curling around my waist and pulling me against him told me he wanted me, told me he desired my body.

"Let's go," I said, "or we won't be going anywhere."

Jeff nodded and pecked me on the lips before getting into his Yukon. I think we made it back to his place in record time. I don't even remember the drive, honestly. I was so caught up in my thoughts of Jeff and what I wanted to do with him that I seemed to look up and find myself in his driveway.

He opened my car door, took my hand to help me out and to my feet. He didn't let go of my hand, even to unlock the front door. He reached to his left pocket with his right hand rather than let go, which was awkwardly funny enough that I laughed at him.

Inside, Jeff closed the door with his heel, then slowly turned to face me, taking my other hand in his.

"I said it once before, and I'll say it again: Don't play me, Anna. Not again. I can't take it again. Once I can forgive and forget. Not twice."

"I won't, Jeff, I promise. I'm here, and I'm not going anywhere."

"You promise?"

"I said so, didn't I?"

Jeff squeezed my hands, his eyes serious. "Say it again. Say, 'I promise I'll never leave you again, Jeff.'"

I took a deep breath. "I promise I'll never leave you again, Jeff."

My heart was hammering in my chest as I spoke the words. I felt like I'd crossed a line I could never uncross. I'd promised to never leave him. A quiet but fierce voice in my soul told me I'd just made a promise I could never, ever break. Jeff was the epitome of the strong, silent type. He didn't say much, but when he did, he meant it, and you listened. He didn't express his emotions much, but when he did, they were deep, rooted in his very identity. If I broke this promise to him, he wouldn't get over it. If I was to ever walk away from him, it'd be forever.

He was watching me carefully. Watching for hesitation, watching for regret, for some part of me being held back.

"I'm serious, Jeff. I won't."

"Better not." He was smiling now, inching closer, dark eyes vivid in the gloom of his unlit house.

I closed the gap between us, pressed my body up against his. He'd hugged me since I'd been back, but he hadn't held me. Now, he wrapped his arms around me, snugging me into the hollows of his body, my curves fitting into his angles as if we'd been cut from the same puzzle.

I pressed my cheek to his chest, heard and felt his heart thump-thumping, smelling the scent of Jeff—sweat, cologne, something else indefinable, something that was just Jeff, male and comforting—and feeling like I'd come home.

"You belong here," Jeff murmured.

He didn't mean his house, and I knew it.

"I'm home," I said.

My heart was expanding, ballooning, bursting. It hurt, in an odd, frightening way. It was a good thing, a feeling of belonging, of being protected, but it was scary. I knew I couldn't go back to the way I was before this moment. This was indelible, imprinted on me.

Neither of us had spoken the words, the three words that make things like this seem so permanent, but we didn't need to. It was there, writhing in the spaces between the other words, the pauses for breath when he dipped down to kiss me again, it was in the gap between his fingers as they at long last slipped under the hem of my shirt to brush my aching, waiting skin.

I mirrored his action, sliding my palms up his back, tracing the cords and ridges and planes of muscle. This felt like our first time, in a way. We were going slow, exploring, questing. His lips danced down to my chin, along my jaw to just beneath my ear, and I tipped my head back, eyes closed, as he continued to plant hot, moist kisses down my throat to the hollow at the base, just above my breastbone.

My palms carved around to press against the slabs of heavy muscle along his sides and stomach, up to his chest, to the hard little nubs of his nipples, and then his arms were above his head and his shirt was off, tossed aside. I was growing impatient, wanting more, wanting all of him now. An ache was starting deep in my core, throbbing between my thighs, spreading heat and the wetness of desire through my sex. Jeff's hands were everywhere now, pushing my shirt over my head and unclasping my bra as his mouth trailed between my breasts, tongue flicking each nipple in turn as the bra fell away.

"Take me to bed, Jeff," I whispered.

Both of us topless, Jeff led me to his room, left the light off so our only source of illumination was the silver wash from the gibbous moon and spattered, sparkling stars. We stood for a moment in the pale square of light from the window, looking at each other, not touching or speaking, only regarding, waiting for the other to move first.

Jeff only smiled at me, and stood waiting. I unbuttoned my pants, shimmied out of them, posed for Jeff in my panties, my weight on one leg, the other bent so only my toe touched the ground, crossed in front of my other leg. I crossed my arms across my chest, then slid my palms under my breasts, lifting them, pinching my nipples, watching Jeff's reaction.

His zipper bulged out as I toyed with my breasts, then grew even larger when I pushed my panties off and kicked them aside. Jeff still hadn't moved, so I continued touching myself. I ran my hands down my ribs, past my belly and to the mound of my aching pussy. Jeff's tongue ran along his lips, and now his fingers unbuttoned his jeans, and then paused. I dipped my middle finger between my labia, and Jeff unzipped his pants. I circled my clit slowly until a gasp escaped; Jeff kicked his jeans aside and hooked his thumbs under the elastic of his boxer-briefs. I put one hand to my breast and rolled a nipple between my fingers, swirling two fingers around my clit with the other hand. Now Jeff drew his boxers off, revealing his thick, rigid cock, straining erect and leaking pre-come, begging to be touched.

I was done with games, suddenly.

I pushed Jeff backward to the bed, followed him as he crawled back to lie on his back. He curled his hands around my hips, traced my curves, hefted the weight of my breasts, looking up at me with a frightening tenderness in his eyes along with the desire. His hands continued their upward journey, his rough palm sliding along my cheek, cupping there as he lifted up to kiss me, then slowly and carefully sliding my hair out of the elastic band of my ponytail. My blonde waves fell down around our faces, and now his other hand slipped down my belly and between my thighs as I knelt above him.

I moaned into his mouth as we kissed, his fingers working magic, spreading fire up from my pussy to the rest of my body, a climax rising before he'd even entered me. I reached between us with one hand to grasp his cock, our foreheads touching as I ran my fingers up and down his length. I rubbed his tip in circles with my thumb, slid down to the root and massaged his balls before caressing his length once more.

Jeff continued to circle my clit with a gentle finger, pushing me up and over into orgasm. I whimpered, collapsed on top of him.

"Take me now, Jeff, please."

I guided him into me, a vocal moan filling the room as he penetrated deep into me, filling me.

"Sweet Jesus, you feel so good," Jeff said, thrusting slowly. "You feel like heaven."

My lips were crushed against his breastbone as I lifted my hips and slid back down his hard length, my arms against his sides, my hands on his shoulders, only our hips moving. His hands rested on my ass, curled around the taut-flexed globes.

"I'm gonna come again," I moaned.

"Yes, come for me, Anna." Jeff pulled on my ass, lifting me up and letting me fall, his body thrusting against mine.

I sat up straight, balancing on top of him with my hands on my thighs, riding him hard, rolling my passion-slick slit onto his cock with a frenzy of sighs and shrieks. I came, holding myself upright with my palms planted on Jeff's chest.

Jeff's arms wrapped around me, pulled me down to him, and then we moved in a dizzy roll and he was above me, in me, all around me. I locked my legs around his waist and my arms around his neck, clung tight to him, pressed my quivering lips to his and rocked into him, felt his turgid cock pushing deep into me, huge and hard and wonderful.

Another orgasm washed through me, this one coming in waves, a crest of ecstasy thrilling through me with each thrust of his cock. He was close now, his rhythm growing frantic, his thrusts harder and deeper. I drove my hips against him to match his rhythm, to match the frenetic fury of his rising climax.

"Come with me, Jeff," I said. "Come hard."

Jeff's eyes flew open and met mine, his gaze blazing with intensity. He plunged hard into me, paused with our hips flush, then pulled out again. As he drove himself into me once more, he came, flooding me, his gasp of pleasure a low-voiced growl.

He arched his back and thrust again, wet heat shooting into me once more, and now his forehead bumped mine and his ragged breathing echoed loud in the silver-lit room.

"I love you, Anna." He whispered it into the silence between breaths, into the stillness between thrusts, into the space between heartbeats.

His eyes were on mine as he said it, our bodies merged, our essences mingling, united in the flush of climax.

Tears started in my eyes, burned as they trickled down my cheeks to drip past my jaw beneath my ear.

"I lo—" I choked back a sob. "I love you. God, I love you." Saying it felt like a release.

I did love him. I couldn't imagine ever leaving him, ever being without him. I felt like I'd spent all my life waiting for him, and just never knew it, couldn't see it, or understand that he was what I needed. He'd been there, too close to see.

We were still moving together, roiling in the silence of soughing breaths, my tamped-down sobs of weltering emotions punctuating the rhythm of our lovemaking.

This wasn't sex, wasn't fucking, wasn't even just shared pleasure. This was, finally, a true expression of joined emotions, and I knew I couldn't ever match this experience, not with anyone else, not for as long as I lived.

Jeff didn't wipe away my tears, didn't shush me, or tell me it was okay, or ask why I was crying. He just kissed me tenderly, whispered my name.

We lay side by side, facing each other, our eyes speaking a thousand words that didn't pass our lips.

We fell asleep, woke up in the early dawn spooning, his erection hard against my ass. I guided him in and we rocked like that, back to front, his hand on my hip, his breath on my shoulder, slow and unhurried and uncomplicatedly sensual. We came at the exact same moment, and when we did, our fingers tangled across my breast, over my pounding heart.

We slept again, woke up past noon, and showered together, making love yet again, standing up in his shower, just like the first time.

A few more days passed, just like that. We didn't leave each other's side for more than a few minutes. We made love constantly, and the words "I love you" came more easily.

One of the few times we were apart Jeff wouldn't tell me where he was going. He left around two in the afternoon and didn't come back until almost five, and wouldn't answer one question, just insisted that I wait and find out. His eyes shone with amusement, telling me I would probably enjoy the surprise, so I left off questioning him and went along with it.

He came home, his home—which I was starting to consider home as well—and told me to get changed, to put on a dress or skirt of some sort. He stood in the doorway of the bedroom, watching me change. I slipped off the stretchy yoga pants and cotton panties I'd been wearing, as well as the T-shirt and sports bra. I took my time picking my outfit, naked, waiting for Jeff to sidle up behind me and start something, but he didn't, just watched with a smile on his face.

I picked a knee-length skirt and a button-down shirt, and a matching set of red lace lingerie. I started to put on the panties, but Jeff spoke up from the doorway.

"Leave 'em off. Go commando. We're gonna be somewhere private, so no one'll know but me," he said.

I stared at him for a moment, considering. I never went anywhere without panties on. It was just...not something I did. I didn't know any girls who did go out without panties on. It seemed skanky, somehow. I'm sure there were girls out there who would go to the bar with a little skirt on and no panties, but that wasn't me. Jeff had promised we'd be in private, though, so I went along with it, slipping the skirt up over my hips and zipping it. It felt strange, like being naked.

When I was fully dressed and had done a little makeup, against Jeff's protestations that I didn't need it, we left, Jeff driving. We drove for almost an hour, going far out into the country. We eventually came to a wide, rolling grassy field, a huge spreading oak tree in the middle, casting long shadows in the golden light of early evening. Jeff pulled the truck to a stop on the side of the narrow, empty dirt road and parked. From his trunk he retrieved wicker picnic basket and a folded quilt.

"We're going on a picnic?" I asked.

"Yep. Never been on an actual, factual picnic like this before, so I thought it might be a fun change from dinner at a restaurant. 'Sides, it's a beautiful evening."

I stuck my hand through his arm as we walked together across the field toward the tree. "I've never been on a picnic like this, either," I said. "Whose property is this?"

"An Army buddy of mine. He owns several hundred acres, I think. Most of it is farmland, but this here is just an empty field he doesn't use for much of anything."

"Does he know we're here?"

"Nah, but he won't care. He never comes out this way. His crops are all closer to his house, 'bout a mile that way," Jeff said, pointing off to the east.

We reached the tree, spread the blanket under the canopy of its branches. Jeff had put together an impressive spread of food, sandwiches, potato salad, pasta salad, fruit salad, key lime pie, sparkling mineral water, and a bottle of expensive champagne. We ate leisurely, drinking the water. I wondered about the champagne, but didn't say anything.

When we were both full, Jeff packed the basket once more. Jeff lay on his back and pulled me into his embrace, holding me close, his hand stroking my back. He was wearing a white button-down, and I popped each button open until his torso was bare. I spent awhile tracing the contours of his chest before I moved on to his belt, unbuckling it, unclasping his pants, unzipping them. He was semi-erect, growing larger as I watched.

There was an oddly shaped bulge in the pocket of his pants. I dismissed it, though, eager to feel his flesh firming in my hands. I pushed his pants and boxers off, set them aside.

I climbed astride him, thankful now that he'd had me leave my panties off. I was already bare to him, completely clothed even as he speared into me, gasping and his eyes crossing, fluttering, closing.

My skirt billowed around our hips, covering his belly and the joining of our bodies. I wanted to feel the air and the sun on my skin, though. I led Jeff's hands to my buttons, and he undid them, brushed the fabric from my shoulders and stripped off my bra, rocking into me all the while. His hands brushed over my ribcage and caressed my breasts, squeezed them, and rolled my nipples in his fingers. He lifted up to take a taut peak into his mouth, nipped lightly, sending jolts of electricity through me. He was pounding up into me, our bodies gyrating in sync, fire blossoming between us, in the merged heat and sweat of our flesh. I rocked above him, rode him to climax, palms flat on his chest.

When I came, I screamed at the top of my lungs, shrieked his name. I'd always been fairly vocal during sex, and found it hard not to be. This was the first time I'd let myself go wild, totally uninhibited, and god...screaming that loud made me come even harder, turned Jeff into a primal beast beneath me, his fingers locked around my hips and driving me down onto him, harder and harder, his cock plunging up and lifting me clear off the ground, his roar of climax every bit as loud as mine. Hearing him bellow as he came inside me drove me to a new orgasm, and now our voices were raised together in the golden evening light.

I rode him, coming, until he softened within me, and then I collapsed on top of him, still shuddering with aftershocks.

"God, that was amazing," Jeff gasped, clinging to me.

"Incredible," I agreed. "I don't think I've ever come so hard or so long in my life."

"Me, neither," Jeff said.

Silence between us then, for many long minutes, only the susurrus of the wind and the clatter of branches and the distant twitter of sparrows.

"Anna?" Jeff was rummaging in his pants pocket for the odd bulge I'd noticed.

"Hmmm?"

He lifted up on elbow, his shirt open and draping across one of my bare breasts. His hand was closed around the whatever-it-was. My heart was hammering in my chest, thudding with a sudden rush of nerves brought on by the serious expression on Jeff's face.

"I love you, Anna," Jeff started.

"I love you, too—"

"Hold on, now, sweetheart. Let me finish."

Sweetheart, he'd called me. It made my heart melt and tangle more thoroughly around his.

"I love you, Anna," he started again, as if reciting something he'd memorized. "I know this is maybe a little crazy and a little sudden, but I just know it's right, it's meant to be. I love you too much to ever let you get away again."

I had a sudden flood of panic as I realized what he was leading up to. My eyes stung and burned. My breath caught, and I felt as if time had stopped. The breeze, which had blowing all the time, had gone still, and the even birds were silent.

Jeff opened his hand, showing me, yes, a black box. He opened it with one hand, revealing a slim platinum band topped by a princess-cut diamond, glittering in the sun.

"Will you marry me?"

Shit. Shit shit shit.

I didn't know what to say, what to do, what I was even thinking or feeling. Tears fell unheeded, tears of joy and confusion. I loved him, so much. I wanted to be with him. But...this? Now?

"Anna?"

"Jeff, I—I love you, so much. I do. My heart is saying yes, but—"

"But?" Jeff was puzzled, confused, hurting.

"I'm not saying no, Jeff, I'm not."

"But you're not saying yes."

"I'm saying, can I have some time to think? I mean, this is so sudden, so unexpected. I only want to be with you, and I...I want to say yes, but...I just need a day or two to really think about it."

189

Jeff nodded slowly. "I guess I get that. But you're...you're not saying no?"

I shook my head and put my hands on his clean-shaven face, kissed him hard and deep. "No, Jeff. I'm not saying no. I just need to process it before I say yes. I don't know if that makes any sense or not, but I just—"

"No, it does. I did sorta spring this on you kind of suddenly. I love you, sweetheart. If you need some time to think, then that's fine by me. Take whatever time you need."

Not long after that, we packed up, the champagne unopened, and left. Jeff seemed quiet, or rather, more subdued than usual. I felt bad, knowing he'd hoped it'd be a joyous occasion, an exuberant yes. I just couldn't give him that, not yet. I hadn't even considered him proposing, not for a long time yet.

We went home, and for the first time in days, we went to sleep without making love.

We had a DJ shift the next day, at, of all places, The Dive. The place where I'd first met Chase. As we unloaded and set up, my gaze went to the alley where I'd first touched and tasted Chase. A pang went through me.

I didn't precisely miss him, per se. He'd been vital to me feeling my own worth. Before him, I'd never thought of myself as beautiful, really. I'd accepted myself, and even liked who I was, but didn't think of myself as an object of male desire. Chase had changed that. He'd shown me men could think I was beautiful. He'd wanted me, he'd shown me in glorious detail what sex could and should be.

Without him, I wouldn't have ever had the courage to approach Jeff.

My thoughts were a whirlwind as we set up and started the first set.

Jeff had proposed. *Proposed*. He wanted to marry me.

But what if I'd been wrong about Chase? What if he'd had real feelings for me, too? If I was being honest with myself, I'd felt things stirring for him, which was part of the reason I'd bolted at the first opportunity. Sex with Chase was great, and he'd given a priceless gift in helping me see my own power as a sexual woman.

What if I'd been wrong? The thought wouldn't go away.

Jeff wants to marry me. Why was I hesitating? I loved him. I knew it, felt it as true deep inside me, in my bones and my blood, in my heart and my mind, in the core of myself as a woman, I knew I loved him. What was more, I trusted Jeff, completely.

We had a dead spot, no one signing up for songs, so I sang, to prompt some requests. I did "Alone" by Heart. It was a song I'd loved pretty much my entire life, and it was something I could perform in my sleep and nail it every time. I knew each note the way I knew my own face in the mirror. It was comforting and familiar when all the rest of me was tumultuous, chaotic, confused.

I stepped outside after my song ended, caught my breath and tried to calm my jangling nerves. When I went back in, Jeff was cueing up a song, a strange, tight expression on his face.

A male figure was standing just off to the side of the stage area. I didn't recognize him at first, since he'd shaved his head and was wearing plain tight blue jeans instead of leather pants, and a tight white T-shirt instead of something flashy and rock star. He turned, mic in hand.

Chase. What the hell is he doing here?

My heart shot into my throat, my fists clenched, my stomach dropped away. If I was confused before, there simply wasn't a word for my emotions when Chase's eyes locked onto me.

He looked good with a shaved head. It set off his eyes, the sharp contours of his gorgeous face. He'd gauged his ears and had new ink crawling up his forearm.

He didn't smile when he saw me, didn't walk toward me, just stared at me, hard, intense, poised.

The music started, the opening bars of a song I knew all too well: "With or Without You" by U2. Oh, hell. God, he sounded good. He sang the entire song standing sideways on the stage, pinning me in the doorway with his fiery gaze.

I can't live...with or without you...

It was clearly a message, each word spoken directly to me. He was pouring his heart out to me, telling me what was inside him. By the time the song ended, I knew one thing for absolutely certain: I wasn't over Chase Delany.

Oh, god.

Tears were sluicing down my face, chest heaving. The song ended, the music faded, Chase spotlighted on the tiny stage. No one spoke, no one moved, no one even breathed. Everyone was waiting. For what?

Out of the corner of my eye, I saw Jeff standing behind the mixer, a glass of Coke in his hand.

Chase reached into his pocket, pulled out something small and round and glinting in the dim barlight. He held it up, slowly lowered himself to one knee.

No, no no no. Please no. Oh, god, no. Please don't—

Chase spoke into the microphone, his eyes drilling into mine: "Anna, I know this is crazy. We haven't known each other all that long, and I know we had a big misunderstanding. But the thing is, I'm in love with you. I fell in love with you from the very first moment I laid eyes on you. I can't live without you. I want you to come on tour with me. I want us to see the world together.

"Anna, will you marry me?"

The glass in Jeff's hand shattered.

A single sob tore from my throat. I shook my head, turned, and slammed against the crash bar and out into the night.

Big Girls
Do It
Married

Chapter 1

*C*hase proposed to me.

Holy shit.

What was I supposed to do? Jeff had proposed to me the day before. Two proposals of marriage in two days. Seriously? Who does this happen to?

Me, apparently.

I shoved open the door and ran out into the night, sobs ripping from my throat. I heard voices behind me, Jeff's and Chase's. They both called my name, told me to wait.

Then I heard Jeff's voice again, deeper, harder, growling. "Back off, pretty boy. You had your chance."

"Who the hell asked you?" Chase, angry.

I stopped, sensing trouble. Jeff had sounded threatening. Chase had sounded equally threatening. Two proposals, and now the two men were about to fight over me. I'm sure some girls might find that sexy or something, but not me. There's nothing hot about the two men in love with you making each other bloody over you. Two men in love with you is messy, period. Flattering, yes. But it's complicated and difficult, and I don't recommend it.

I turned in time to see Chase push past Jeff, who was trying to keep Chase from coming after me. Jeff shoved Chase, spinning him in the process. A fist flashed, and Chase went down with a grunt, bleeding.

"Stop!" I ran over to them, pushed Jeff away, knelt down beside Chase.

Jeff backed away, fists clenched, eyes narrow and angry. "Anna?"

That single word, my name dropping from Jeff's lips, held a thousand questions, a thousand recriminations. I looked up at him. He wasn't just angry at Chase.

"Jeff, I didn't know he would do this. I haven't seen or spoken to him since I left New York." I stood up and met Jeff's eyes. "I promise, I didn't know he'd do this."

"Okay, then." The anger faded from his eyes, but the hardness didn't. "Leave, pretty boy."

Chase stood up, angry. "Fuck you. I'll leave when I want, cowboy. I have a right to talk to her. She doesn't belong to you."

Jeff pushed forward, but I stopped him with a gentle hand to his chest. "Jeff, no. Please. Let me talk to him. Go in, run the shift. I'll be there in a few minutes."

He hesitated, looking from me to Chase and back again. I realized I was the one he didn't entirely trust.

"Jeff, please. I'll be fine, I swear. I mean, don't worry, okay? It's not like that."

He grunted, his lip curling in a frown, but he turned on his heel and went back into The Dive.

Chase waited till Jeff was gone and then turned to me, wiping the blood sluicing from his nose on the back of his arm. "Anna, listen, I—"

"Chase, what the hell were you thinking?" I turned away from him, because looking at him made my head and my heart and my body all go in different directions. "You can't just show up where I work and propose to me in front of hundreds of people."

"It's not hundreds," Chase pointed out. "There's maybe seventy people in there."

"What fucking difference does it make how many people there are, Chase? You embarrassed me!" I turned back to him, my face flushed hot with anger. "Putting me on the spot like that isn't the way to win me back, if that's what you're going for."

"Embarrassed you? I asked you to marry me!"

"Yeah, but I wasn't ready!" I was yelling loudly, but I didn't care at the moment. "You can't just show up after a month of silence and propose, Chase. It doesn't work like that."

Now it was Chase's turn to yell. "I tried for weeks to get a hold of you, Anna! You ran without giving me a chance to explain. I sent a million texts, called and left a million voicemails. You never so much as acknowledged me."

The hurt in his eyes made my heart clench.

"Chase, I can't have this conversation now. I have to work."

He sighed and rubbed his forehead with his knuckles. "Fine. When, then?"

"Tomorrow, lunch. Call me and we'll meet." The hurt on his face turned to hope, forcing me to backtrack. "Look, I'm not agreeing to anything. I'm just saying I'll meet with you and give you a chance to explain. That's *it*. Okay?"

He nodded and stepped into me for a hug, his arms sliding around my waist. I was disoriented for a long moment, feeling the anger and embarrassment and confusion warring with my physical desire for and comfort with him. I managed to push him back and step away.

"Chase, stop." My voice was small; I couldn't meet his eyes. "Stop trying to confuse me."

"I wasn't—"

"I have to go." I turned and walked away without a backward glance.

The bar was buzzing. No one met my eyes or spoke to me. Jeff was setting up the song queue when I got back to the karaoke stage; the glance he shot my way was equal parts worry, anger, and resignation.

I waited until the song was under way, a big blond man doing fair justice to "Crash" by Dave Matthews Band.

"Jeff," I said, leaning close to him, my hand on the back of his shoulder. "I know what that must have seemed like to you. But please, please believe me, I had nothing to do with it. I haven't seen him, texted him, emailed him, called him, nothing, since I left New York."

He shrugged, not quite looking at me. "Okay."

"Goddamn it, Jeff." I picked up a Keno pencil and snapped it between my fingers, toying with the halves. "I need you to believe me. I didn't know he would do that. I didn't want him to."

Jeff blew a long breath out, puffing his cheeks and rolling his shoulders. "All right, Anna. All right." He put his hand on my knee and squeezed lightly. "I'll make the choice to trust you."

I had to tell him I was meeting Chase for lunch tomorrow, but now wasn't the time. It'd have to wait until after we were done working.

The shift dragged on forever. Each song seemed to take an hour, and each performance was worse than the last. Finally we finished, loaded up, and went home, once again not staying for a drink. I could use one, but I'd rather wait until we were home so I could get Jeff relaxed before pissing him off all over again.

We got back to his place, carted the equipment back into his garage, and plopped down on his couch with beer and a bag of pretzels. Jeff sat down and propped his legs up on the coffee table, waiting. I curled up next to him, feet crossed underneath me.

We drank in silence for a few minutes, and then Jeff nudged my thigh with his beer bottle. "You got something to say. Spit it out."

I bit my lip, then let my head flop back onto the couch as I answered. "I told Chase I'd meet him for lunch tomorrow, give him a chance to say his piece." I held up my hand to stall his objections. "I was very clear with him. I told him it wasn't for anything but to give him a chance to explain. Nothing is changing."

"The hell it isn't," Jeff said. "I asked you to *marry* me yesterday, Anna. You said you needed time to think about it. Then pretty boy shows up and asks you, too. What am I supposed to think?"

"His name is Chase," I said. "Not 'pretty boy.' I know you don't like him, and I don't expect you to. But don't be a dick about it, okay?"

"So should I just take the ring back, then?" Jeff asked.

My heart throbbed at the tone in his voice, despair tangled with anger.

"No, Jeff. Please, you're not being fair. I know how this must seem to you—"

"I don't think you do, Anna." Jeff set his beer bottle down and turned on the couch to face me. "I've been in love with you for six years. You know that? This isn't just a sudden thing for me. I've loved you since the very first song we sang together. Remember what it was?"

"'I'll Be' by Edwin McCain."

"Yeah. You acted like you didn't notice I was in love with you, so I didn't push it. I liked being your friend. I liked working with you. I wanted you in my life any way I could get you, even if that meant never saying anything about how I felt." Jeff looked down and scratched at the couch with a fingernail. "I love you, Anna. But I'm not waiting around anymore. You gotta choose."

"You're making this something it's not, Jeff. There's nothing to choose. I love you. I had no idea he was even here. You think that's the kind of proposal I'd like? In public? A complete surprise?"

Jeff shook his head. "He's an idiot. He doesn't know shit about you if he thinks that would work. But that's not the point. I don't think you're over him. I think you still wonder about him, about New York. I saw your face. You hated the shock of it, but the fact that he'd shown up and was doing something to get your attention, that hit you hard."

I couldn't answer for a long time. I stared at the carpet until the pattern wavered.

"Maybe you're right," I said, finally. "What the hell am I supposed to do? I would have been fine if he'd just stayed in New York. I would have wondered every once in a while, but I would've been fine. Now? I don't know."

I was talking to myself more than Jeff, but he answered anyway.

"Well, go and talk to him, then. I'm not gonna say I don't care, 'cause I do. Do what you have to do."

"I'm just meeting him to hear what he has to say. That's it."

"And what if he says he loves you, and he wants you to go to New York with him? What if he kisses you, and begs you, tells you that you were wrong about what you saw? What if he has proof he didn't do anything? What then?"

I couldn't answer. Those questions were banging in my head, too. I shrugged. "I don't know," I whispered. "But...don't leave me, okay? Give me a chance. Please?"

Jeff drained his beer. "Do what you have to do." He stood up and looked down at me sadly. "We'll take things one step at a time."

He poured the suds at the bottom down the drain and set his bottle on the counter, then reached into his shorts pocket. He took out a black ring box and set it on the table, turned without looking at me or the ring, and went into his room.

I sat on the couch, staring at the ring box, drinking my beer and wishing the answer would strike me like lightning. It didn't. I moved to the table and sat down in front of the little black box, but I didn't touch it yet. I set my beer down, wiped my damp fingers on my shirt, and opened the box.

The ring was as breathtaking as it had been the first time I saw it. I lifted the ring out of the box and held it between my finger and thumb. The light refracted on the myriad facets, glinted from the platinum. My eyes burned, my sight wavered, and then a single tear dripped to the glass surface of the table.

What the hell am I supposed to do?

No answer came.

I stared at the ring for a long time, trying to sort out what I felt for Jeff and what I felt for Chase. Sitting there alone, all I could think was that they were both important to me. They both said they loved me. They both wanted me.

Me. *Me.* Anna Devine.

How was I supposed to make this choice?

I couldn't.

I put the ring back, closed the box, and shut off the lights before going into Jeff's—our—bedroom. I lay down next to him, afraid to touch him.

Sleep was a long time coming.

Jeff was gone when I woke up. He'd left a note:

ANNA,

I NEED SOME TIME. WENT TO THE GYM TO WORK OUT, THEN TO THE
SHOOTING RANGE WITH SOME ARMY BUDDIES.
JUST KNOW, WHATEVER HAPPENS, I LOVE YOU. I WANT YOU TO BE HAPPY.

JEFF.

I stared at the note, written in Jeff's all-caps scrawl, tersely worded. Those last six words haunted me: "I want you to be happy." I knew Jeff. I knew what he was saying. He loved me enough to let me make my own choice. He'd made his feelings clear, and that was that. He'd let me go, if that's what I wanted.

It would have been easier in some ways if he'd recriminated with me, fought for me, stayed angry. But that just wasn't Jeff. He would fight for me, though. He'd punched Chase, after all. Although I suspected the punch was more about his own jealousy than protecting me. I hadn't needed protection, after all.

The morning passed slowly. I ended up back at my apartment, which was sans Jamie again. I showered, changed, and tried to figure out what the hell I was going to do. Like the night before, no answers came.

Eventually I texted Chase rather than waiting for him: *Meet me at National Coney Island in Royal Oak in twenty minutes.*

A few minutes passed, then he responded. *K. OMW. See you there.*

I gathered my courage and left.

He was waiting for me. My belly quivered at the sight of him, like it always did. How could it not? He was so beautiful. He'd changed, though. His thick black hair, usually carefully spiked in an intentionally messy way, had been shorn to the scalp. He'd gauged his earlobes, and now had quarter-inch-diameter black plugs. He was wearing a sleeveless T-shirt, and I could see new tattoos spiraling around his left bicep and shoulder. Shaving his head, which I normally found unattractive, brought the sharp planes and angles of his face into high relief and made his eyes stand out, vivid brown so dark it was almost black.

He was tapping a message in a cell phone when I arrived, and so didn't see me until I sat down on the opposite side of the booth.

He started at my appearance. "Shit, you scared me," he said, laughing. "Thanks for coming."

"I don't want you to think my meeting you means I've agreed to anything. It's a courtesy."

He nodded, sipping his Coke. "I get it."

The waitress came and we ordered. When she was gone, Chase took a deep breath and started talking.

"First, you were right about the proposal. I'm sorry, that was kind of a dumb idea, in retrospect. I just—I had to get your attention somehow."

"Well, you have it, for now."

"I guess the most important thing I need you to understand is that I wasn't doing anything with those girls. I know how it looked, but it wasn't like that. They surprised me in the alley, okay? I was out there getting some air after the show, and they cornered me, jumped all over me. You came out as I was telling them I wasn't going to do that with them, and they needed to get off me because I didn't want you to find me in a compromising position and get the wrong idea."

"Which is exactly what you're saying happened."

"Right," Chase said.

Our food came, and we ate in silence for several minutes.

"Here's my question," Chase said. "I don't think the business with those girls was the real reason you ran off on me."

"So what do you think it was?"

"I think you were afraid of falling in love with me. I think you felt things happening and you panicked. The whole wrong timing business just gave you an excuse to run."

"You may be right," I agreed, not looking at him. "But it doesn't matter now."

"How could it not matter? Feelings like that don't just vanish in a month or two, Anna. You still feel something for me. I know you do. I saw it in your face when you first saw me at the bar."

I shrugged. "Maybe there are still feelings there, but I'm with Jeff now. I can't just run off on him again."

"Again?"

"Whatever—"

"No, not whatever, Anna, what'd you—"

"Let it go, Chase," I said, making my voice hard. "Listen, we had a great time in New York. You really showed me things about myself that I needed to see. Thank you for that. You opened my eyes and helped me realize I'm more than just my pants size. I can never repay you for that. But it's not enough to base a relationship on." I swirled the ice in my glass with my straw, staring down at the cubes as they bobbed and clinked in the brown bubbles of the Coke. "And besides that, you're a rising star, Chase. You've got a sick amount of talent. Your band is going to be huge, I promise you. You don't need a girlfriend holding you back."

"How would you be holding me back?" Chase asked.

"I need a man who's going to be faithful. I need someone who'll be there with me. *Here* with me. I don't want to live in New York."

"I'd be faithful—"

"I'm sure you'd mean to be. But when you're famous and girls like that are throwing themselves at you every night, and not just one or two, but dozens every show, eventually, you wouldn't be. You'd give in, and it would make things tough. You don't need a girlfriend. You need the freedom to live the rockstar life. I mean, don't do drugs or anything, 'cause that's stupid. But you know what I mean."

He nodded, dipping a fry in cheese and then ranch. "I get what you're saying, and you're right to an extent. But I love you. I'm in love with you. I can't just ignore that."

"Chase...I know where you're going with this." I reached across the table and took his hand in mine. "You can't give up this opportunity. You could be the next huge thing, you know? Like Daughtry or whoever. I was gonna say Nickelback, but everybody hates Nickelback, right? Whatever. The point is, you can't walk away from this. Not for me.""Then come with me. We're going on tour in a few weeks. A U.S. tour at first, then if everything goes well, a European one."

"You want me to tag along with you on a world tour? And do what? Sit backstage every show? Wait for you on the tour bus?"

"Sure, why not? It could be fun. You'd meet bands, go with me to signings and events and stuff."

"No, Chase. I don't think so. I know you mean well, but that's not a life for me. I'm not meant to be an arm-candy, wait-backstage kind of girlfriend. I want more than that. I *deserve* more than that."

"What are you going to do here, then?" Chase asked. "DJ karaoke for the rest of your life? Have Jeff's kids and be a soccer mom?"

Anger boiled through me. "Fuck you, Chase." I stood up and threw money on the table, turned around, and stomped off.

I'd made it out of the restaurant and to my car when I felt him grab my arm and turn me around. I jerked my arm free. "What if that's what I want? What if I like DJing karaoke? What if I want to marry Jeff and have his kids and be a soccer mom? You have something against soccer moms?"

"No, Anna, that wasn't my point. If that's what you want, then fine, go for it. My point was, you're more talented than that. You've got a great voice. You've got stage presence, and you know how to put on a performance. If you came to New York with me, I could probably score you a meeting with a record exec. You might get a deal, be a singer for real."

My heart stopped. "You could do that?"

"Easy. My producer said you had a stunning voice. He said he'd consider signing you himself."

I had a moment of dreaming: me, alone on a stage, performing; spotlights on me, my name on the marquee.

But then reality butted in.

"Chase, that's not me," I said. "Yeah, sure, the idea of being a singer, recording and touring and all that, it sounds great on paper. But if I did that, when would we ever see each other? The music I'd make isn't like yours. We wouldn't tour together. We wouldn't record together. So we'd have different careers, and wouldn't really be together. So if I'm not with you, why would I leave? It just doesn't compute, in my mind. I guess what it comes down to, really, is that I don't have a desire to be famous. I just...I don't know what I *do* want for my future exactly, but a life of paparazzi and magazine articles and whatever, that's not me."

Chase put his back to the car and pinched the bridge of his nose. "You're really dead set against letting this work, aren't you?" He sighed. "Fine. I guess I'll see you around."

"God, Chase. It's not that I'm against it, it's just that I don't see it working out with us."

"You're not even willing to try?"

"I don't know."

Chase's eyes bored into me. I felt the brunt of his emotions hitting me, his hope and his love and his fear. He really did love me. "You're afraid, Anna. You're afraid I don't really love you, or that I can't be faithful while I'm on tour. But you do love me. Or at least, you *could*, if you'd let yourself."

"You're right, Chase. Is that what you want to hear? Yeah, I left because I was falling in love, and it scared me. But it wasn't you, or the idea of being in love with you that had me panicking. Some of the things that happened in New York bothered me, and I'm not talking about seeing you with the girls. It was...I don't know how to put it. It wasn't me. It was fun, and I enjoyed it, but I don't think it was things

207

I'd do normally. You have a way of bringing out the wildness in me, and I'm not sure I'm comfortable with that."

"You're talking about the bathroom thing."

"That's part of it, yes."

"It doesn't have to be like that—"

"Chase, stop. If that's the thing you like, then you should be free to do it. I'm just not sure that's the scene I'm into. I tried it, and...I don't know. The sex was great, but being walked in on, being seen? Sex is private to me, I guess. Sex is always great with you. But I need a relationship that's not just sex."

Chase looked hurt. "You think our relationship is just about sex?"

"I think that's a big part of it. I'm intensely attracted to you. Every time I see you I get all quivery inside. You turn me on just by being you. You're out of my league in a major way. I love having sex with you. It's seriously incredible. But there's got to be more. We barely know each other. I'm not sure what we have in common, long term." I had to physically restrain myself from touching him to comfort him, he looked so forlorn. "And I *really* want long term."

"But I can do long term. I can."

"I'm not doubting that. I'm doubting whether you can do long term with *me*."

Chase turned away from me. "I can't win this argument, can I?"

"It's not an argument," I said, softly.

"Then what is it? Me, begging?" He shook his head, then turned back to me, put his hands on my waist above the swell of my hips. "Anna, I love you. I don't know what else I can say or do to convince you. I'll say it once more. Please, be with me."

My throat felt thick. "Chase, I—I don't know. I don't think I can. If I leave Jeff, he'll be heartbroken. I can't do that again."

"What about me? If you turn me down, *I'll* be heartbroken. Or don't you care about that?"

I tried desperately to pull away from his touch, but I couldn't. "Of course I care, Chase. No matter what I do, someone gets hurt. Please, don't make this harder than it has to be."

Chase's eyes narrowed. "It doesn't have to be hard. Just come with me. Jeff is a big boy. He can deal. Just come with me. I can make you happy. You know I can."

Something in my belly and below it trembled and turned to liquid. The heat in his eyes told me exactly what Chase had in mind when he said he could make me happy. I knew he was right. He could make me happy. My entire body shook with raw, potent desire. For a moment all I could think was how badly I wanted to drag him back to my apartment and rip his clothes off, let him make me happy.

I wrenched myself out of his grip. "No. Not like this."

Chase watched with a tight, pained expression. I got in my car, started it, and backed out. He stopped me with a palm slapping against my window.

I stopped and rolled my window down. "What do you want now, Chase?" Exasperation was rife in my voice.

He reached into his pants pocket and pulled out a black box.

Goddamn it. I was starting to hate those little boxes.

"Chase, for god's sake—"

"Just listen, damn it." He reached through the window and put the box, closed, on my lap. "Take it. Think about it. I love you. I'll give up being a rockstar to be with you. I'll stay here. I'll go wherever you want. I'll even sell my bike and drive a minivan if that's what you want. I just want you."

And then he was gone, leaving me trembling and hearing his words.

I managed to make it home before collapsing into sobs. Even in the midst of my confused, heartaching tears, it felt weird to be in my own bed in my apartment. I'd spent so much time over the last few weeks at Jeff's house that my place was starting to feel less and less like home. Jeff was home. I managed to get my bawling under control and lay on my bed, staring at my room. This small space had once been my haven. I'd come here after work, half-drunk and lonely and horny, and I'd read a book or a magazine, or watch TV on the tiny set Jamie had given me on my birthday.

I was comfortable here. I knew where everything was, where everything belonged. The pile of clothes in the corner by the dresser wasn't just a pile of clothes. It was a specifically sorted pile of clothes; shirts were on top, pants, shorts, and skirts on bottom. The magazines stacked on top of the dresser were piled in order of how much I liked each issue. The bra hanging on the doorknob was clean, the one hanging in the bathroom was dirty. It looked like a mess to a casual observer, but it was my mess, and it was an organized mess.

Now, after the military cleanliness of Jeff's place, it just looked messy. Jeff would shoot me irritated glances if I left my clothes on the floor. He wouldn't get mad or yell at me—he'd just pick it up and make me feel guilty with a few calculated glances. Now, lying in my bed, looking at the piles of crap, I realized I didn't feel comfortable here anymore. It had felt like my nest before spending so much time at Jeff's.

I wanted to be back at Jeff's. What did that mean? Did it mean I loved him more than Chase? I hadn't really liked being at Chase's place. It was a room in a house he shared with his band. It was clean enough, nice enough, but it just hadn't felt like home.

Jeff's house was home. Jeff was home.

But Chase...he was exciting. He made me dizzy with desire, pure lust, unadulterated greed for his body. He was a rockstar. He'd be famous. I could be famous just for being his girlfriend.

Jamie wouldn't hesitate. The chance to be with a real live rockstar, an up-and-coming player on the music scene, that wasn't an opportunity to pass up. Especially not when the sex was so mind-blowing.

I found myself out of bed and cleaning up as I thought. My bed got made, the clothes stacked on it folded, put away. Dirty laundry was set outside my door to wash, magazines and books were put away on the bookshelf opposite my bed. I even vacuumed.

None of this, however, got me any closer to knowing what to do.

I felt better about my room, and was able to actually relax without feeling claustrophobic. I also knew if Jeff came over, he'd be comfortable. He'd tried coming over once, but after that one visit, he'd never suggested coming back. It may have had something to do with the loud and vocal sex noises coming from Jamie's room, but my mess was the largest part of it, even if he'd never said anything.

Chase wouldn't have minded. He'd have cleared a path to the bed, added our clothes to the mess, and turned his attention to my body.

Was that something to base a decision on? Suddenly, every little factor and facet of the two men was brought into focus. Jeff was clean, neat, organized, methodical. He was steady, stable. Not predictable, because he'd shown a capacity for constantly surprising me. But I could always depend on him.

Even now, stewing in my room, I knew I could expect to hear from him soon. He'd get tired of waiting and wonder where I was. He'd want to know what I was doing, even if it was just to make sure I was safe.

Was Chase dependable? My gut told me he'd be there if I needed him. He really would give up his rising career in music if I told him that was the price to be with me. He'd turn his back on it all and stay here with me. He'd play local gigs, maybe start DJing with me. He'd give me what I wanted. But...he'd always wonder what could have been if he'd followed his dreams, stuck with the career rather than the girl. Would he resent me?

God, my head was spinning. They were two totally different men, both amazing in their own ways. They were both claiming to be in love with me, and I was faced with the choice between them. This was the stuff of Regency romance books: The plucky and intrepid and oh-so-charming heroine was presented with the impossible task of choosing between the wealthy nobleman offering her a comfortable future and the poor but handsome and completely devoted peasant who loved her unconditionally. Yeah, that was me. Except this was my life. No one was writing this story. I had to make the choice and live with the consequences.

I knew one thing: I'd hurt one of them, whomever I chose, and I'd always wonder in part of my mind what life would have been like if I'd chosen the other.

The buzzer jolted me out of my thoughts. I buzzed the person through without checking to see who it was. I opened the door to see Jeff lifting his fist to knock.

"You *are* here," he said by way of greeting. He didn't move to come in.

"Of course. Where else would I be?"

He frowned. "Gone. New York with pretty—with Chase. You weren't at home—I mean, at my house, so I wasn't sure where you'd be."

I took his arm and pulled him in, shutting the door behind him. "I talked with Chase and then came here. I needed to think." I flopped down on the couch and stared at the signed Bon Jovi poster of Jamie's hung over the TV. "I'm confused, Jeff."

He sat down next to me and stretched his arm out behind my head. I nestled into the hollow of his arm automatically. I don't think either of us realized I was doing it until he had his arm wrapped around me.

"Confused about what?" Jeff asked.

"Everything," I said. "Talking to him just made things worse."

"Could have told you that before you went," Jeff remarked.

"Yeah, and if you had, I would have gone anyway."

"True," Jeff chuckled. "You're stubborn like that."

"I just don't know what to do. You're both so different. But you both claim to love me." I glanced up at Jeff to see him flinch. "Sorry, I guess it's not fair to you to talk about this with you."

"Who else are you gonna talk to about it? I'm still your friend, Anna. That ain't ever gonna change."

"But you're part of the problem." I sighed. "I didn't mean that. You're not a problem. The situation is a problem, and it's my own fault."

"I know what you meant. But if you need to talk, then talk."

"I just don't know what to do."

"You already said that," Jeff pointed out. "Break it down for me like I'm not one of the choices in front of you."

"You both claim to love me. That by itself is hard to swallow. Just a couple months ago I was lonely and depressed. I had you and Jamie, and that was about it. I didn't think I'd ever find anyone to love me, and I hadn't had sex in months and didn't feel beautiful." I pulled my hair out of its ponytail and ran my fingers through it. "Now, everything is different.

"Honestly, a lot of the reason I've begun to realize I'm beautiful is due to Chase. I know you don't want to hear that, but it's true. He started it all. He pursued me, and he made me see myself through his eyes, to a degree. He wanted me. I hadn't felt wanted in...well, ever."

"I wanted you," Jeff said, his voice quiet.

"Yeah, but you didn't do anything about it, Jeff. I didn't know you loved me. I thought it was a crush. You let me pretend it wasn't there for six years."

"I didn't think you wanted me back."

"Would you have ever made a move on your own?" I asked.

"I don't know. Maybe. Maybe not. I wish now I had made a move sooner."

"Me, too." I ran my fingers across Jeff's cheek. "You make me feel beautiful. My point about Chase is that he got me thinking about myself in a different way. I wouldn't have ever had the courage to try anything with you if it hadn't been for him."

"Well, I guess I owe him some thanks, then."

"Me, too," I said. "In a big way."

Jeff got up and went to the bathroom; when he came back he smirked at me. "Your room looks different. Cleaner."

I shrugged. "Your house is always so clean. I've spent so much time there that now my room seems nasty. I couldn't relax until I'd cleaned it up."

Jeff grinned. "Well, glad I'm instilling some good habits in you at least. It was kinda gross the last time I was here."

I slapped his arm. "Gee, thanks, asshole."

He laughed. "Hey, you know what I meant." He scrubbed the smile from his face with his palm. "So you went to talk to Chase, and it made things worse. Why, though? I thought you were just going to hear him out."

"Yeah, well...I guess the problem is I didn't ever really believe he'd done anything awful. It was an excuse. I was feeling things for him that scared me. Plus, I had you on my mind, and I knew I felt things for you, too, and that scared me even more. Like I said when I came back, I felt like I was cheating on you with him, and seeing him with those groupies just made it easier to run. I think I was hoping he'd let me go and this problem I'm having now would be avoided."

"No such luck."

"No," I agreed. "No such luck. And now I've got both of you saying you love me, and I have feelings for both of you, but they're completely different feelings."

"And you don't know what to do," Jeff said.

"Nope."

He blew a long breath out between his teeth. "Well, I can't make the choice for you, obviously. And you know what I want. I want you, I want you to pick me. I think I'm best for you. I think I understand you. I think I can give you what you want and need. I think Chase is exciting and fun, and I'm sure he's talented and going places and all that. But I don't think he's right for you. He may be faithful to you if you pick him and go with him. I can't say he's a bad person. I don't know him well enough to make that call. Maybe he's great. Maybe you'd have the best happily ever after with him. Maybe. But I don't think so." He slid off the couch and knelt in front of me, positioned himself between my knees so our faces were level, within kissing distance. "I love you, Anna. I'll love you forever. I'm being completely honest here when I say I want you to be with me instead of him. But more than anything else, I want you to be happy. No matter what. If you think he's the best choice for you, for your life, then go with him and be happy. I let you go to New York without fighting because I knew you'd always wonder if you didn't, and because I could tell nothing I said would change your mind. I didn't want you to go. But you did, and here we are."

I shook my head. "God, Jeff. That really doesn't help." A sob bubbled out past my lips.

"I didn't say I could help. I said I'd listen. I said you could talk to me about what was bugging you. I can't be anything but honest about what I want, and I can't be objective, either."

"Well, what fucking good are you, then?" I asked. "Kidding. That's the problem, though. You're my best friend, aside from Jamie, and usually you'd help me sort through this."

"Where is Jamie, anyway? Why can't she talk to you about it?"

I shrugged. "I don't know where she is. And I don't think she'd be objective, either. Her taste in men is...different from mine. She has her own issues. I just don't think she'd be able to help me. No one can." Another sob whimpered from me, this one more hysterical.

I was trying to keep it together, but I couldn't, quite. My shoulders shook and my eyes burned. I didn't want to cry.

Jeff didn't have an answer for that. He moved up onto the couch next to me and drew me onto his lap. "Just breathe, Anna. It's going to be okay. It's a shitty thing to have to choose, and I can't say I know how you feel, 'cause I don't. But remember, we're both adults, okay? Yeah, the fact is, one of us will be hurt when you choose the other. But it won't be the end of the world. I'd be heartbroken, and it'd be real long fucking time before I cared for anyone else like I do you, but I'd be okay, in time. I don't know Chase, but I don't imagine he'd flip out off the deep end, either. Hurt heals, Anna. Choosing sucks. Pain sucks. Hurting someone you care about sucks, but that's life. Life hurts. Sometimes we're faced with a shitty fucking choice that leaves everyone involved hurt somehow. All you can do is make the right choice for you and move on."

He put his forefinger under my chin and lifted my face to his. I blinked hard, sniffed back tears, and bit my lip to keep from bursting apart. Jeff's dark eyes were soft and tender and compassionate. His body was a hard, strong shelter around me. It didn't fix my problem, but with his arms around me, I felt loved, I felt able to keep breathing despite the crushing pressure on my chest.

He kissed me, a slow, feather-soft touch of his lips to mine. "Quit holding it in. You don't have to be strong all the time. You're upset. It's okay to feel it."

His palm rubbed my back, and his fingers brushed tendrils of hair away from my eyes and traced the line of my jaw. I held it in a moment longer, my body trembling with the effort. It began as a single tear down my cheek, then a second. I sniffed, tried to breathe deep enough to hold on to my composure. A sob wrenched my gut, and then another, and then I was wracked by shuddering sobs, a veil of tears obscuring my vision. I was lost then, carried away and helpless. Jeff was my anchor, the only solid thing in my world.

He held me, wiped the tears away, used the hem of his shirt to clean my face.

"I can't do it," I said, when I had enough breath to speak. "I just want to run away from both of you. I can't hurt you. I can't hurt him. There's no right choice." I hiccupped. "I need a cupcake."

Jeff kissed my forehead, then each cheek, and then, last, my lips. "Don't worry about right or wrong. Just worry about what's best for you."

"But I don't *know* what's best for me!"

He kissed my lips again to quiet me, and this time he kept kissing. The sweet, familiar taste of his lips swept me away, his body beneath mine cradled me close and comforted me, and his hands ghosting over my curves pushed thoughts to the background.

Distraction was welcome. A fragmentary thought flitted through my head: *This is only going to confuse me further, later.* But I didn't care. Kissing Jeff was all that was right in my life. My tears subsided and my sobs quieted and my confusion drifted to the background, all subsumed beneath the storm of need for Jeff.

I moaned as his tongue swept into my mouth, and then twisted on his lap so I was facing him, my knees digging down into the crack between couch back and cushion. This was all I needed.

Desire erupted within me, gouging all thoughts from my mind. All I knew was Jeff's mouth, his cock hardening beneath me, his hands on my waist and slipping upward to cup my breasts. I arched my chest into his hands, dragged my fingers through his close-cropped hair and down his sides. My fingers caught the bottom of his shirt, and I lifted it up over his head.

He broke the kiss and pulled back, searching my eyes. "I don't want to make anything harder for you," he said.

I stood up, his shirt balled in my fist, and led him by the hand into my room, closing the door behind us.

He stood uncertainly with his back to the door. "Anna, I don't wanna confuse you—"

I peeled my shirt over my head, unhooked my bra, and then took a step closer to Jeff. He backed up, his hands reaching for me even as he tried to protest. He bumped against the door, and I crushed myself against him.

"Shut up and make love to me, Jeff. I know it's not gonna fix anything, but I need it. I need you. Please."

I popped the button on my jeans and shimmied out of them, then turned my hands to Jeff, tracing the heavy muscles of his chest and the broad, hard bulge of his belly. He ran his hands down my arms, his eyes raking over my body, hungry, burning with lust and shimmering with love. I pressed a kiss to his shoulder, then his pectoral muscle. He thumped his head against the wooden door, rumbling in his chest as I opened his pants and shoved them down.

His thick, hot, hard cock filled my hands, the veins pulsing against my palms, his sack tightening as I cupped it. I ran my hands up and down his length, murmuring in pleasure as I kissed his chest, then his stomach, sliding to my knees in front of him and caressing the cool curve of his ass.

He caught at my shoulders as I knelt, bent to lift me up. I glanced up at him, took his hands in mine, and tangled our fingers. Breaking my gaze away from his, I lowered my mouth to his cock, wrapped my lips around the tip, and carved circles around his crown with my tongue.

"Anna," he groaned.

I wasn't sure if it was a protest or a sound of pleasure. Both, probably. I took him deeper, let him bump against the back of my throat and then backed off. His hands tightened on mine, refusing to let go. I licked his length from base to tip, then swirled my tongue around him, tasting him, teasing him. He moaned again, and I took him deep into my mouth once more, opening the back of my throat until I couldn't take any more.

"God, what are you doing to me?" Jeff asked.

I spat him out and smiled at him. He used the momentary distraction to pull me to my feet. His lips met mine and his hands gripped my hips, pulling our bodies together, crushing his cock between us.

"Anna—" he began, but I silenced him with my mouth, as he had me.

I pushed away from him, lay down on my bed, feet drawn up, knees apart, waiting. Jeff took a step toward me, then another. I cupped a breast in one hand and skimmed my fingers down my belly to my cleft.

Jeff's hands clenched into fists and released, and then I saw the last of his indecision fade away. His lips curled into a sensual smile, and he crawled onto the bed. He prowled toward me, his head going between my knees, his eyes locked onto mine across the expanse of my body, and then lowered between my thighs. I felt a tremble of anticipation waver in the muscles of my legs and belly, gushing through my pussy as a wave of heat and wet desire.

My knees fell apart as his tongue ran up the inside of one thigh, my back arching and my fingers tangling in his hair. I had no thoughts, no mind, no problems, no past or future when he touched me this way, when he kissed my most sensitive and intimate flesh. His fingers touched my folds, found them wet and slid in. His tongue lapped against my lips, then dipped in between them as his fingers curled up as they drew out. I moaned, gasped, whispered his name, pressed his head closer to me. His tongue searched up along the cleft of my labia, found the aching nub of my clit and circled around it, drawing my hips up and my back into a convex bow shape. He knew exactly how to draw the whimpers from me, how to touch me and give me the most pleasure. This was all I needed, all the answers I could ever find, here with him, alone and naked and vulnerable.

Slow swipes around my clit, careful slips of his finger against my G-spot, were replaced by swifter licks and more insistent sliding in and out. I moved my hips into him, whispering his name as climax boiled through me. At the moment of orgasm, my body wracked with shuddering waves, Jeff slid up and drove into me, piercing me in one smooth motion, gliding deep. I shrieked and curled into him, clutching his heavy, hard body against mine, wrapping my legs around his waist and crushing our hips together.

Jeff moaned into my mouth, his thrusts long and slow. His hand cupped my breast, hefted it and squeezed it, and then his fingers rolled my nipple until I shuddered, an aftershock turning into a full-blown orgasm, each thrust of his hips now driving me to further heights of desperate orgasming desire.

I couldn't get him deep enough, couldn't feel his body far enough inside me, pressed hard enough against me. I bit his shoulder as I continued to come, thrusting madly against his measured strokes.

"Harder, Jeff. Harder, please!" I said, each word a whimpered plea.

He answered me with his body rather than words, crashing his cock deeper into me, arching his back and lifting my breast to take a nipple into his mouth. He nipped gently, just hard enough to make me jerk in surprise and come with a curse.

Jeff's motions became ragged and arrhythmic, no longer slow, measured thrusts into me but hard and fast and deep. He cupped the back of my head and lifted me up into a kiss, biting my lower lip as he came, a quick hard pulse of hips against hips and a flood of hot seed inside me. Feeling him come drove me to climax yet again, this one harder than all the rest, curving my body into a spasm of ecstasy.

"Oh, god, Jeff, yes, don't stop," I moaned, feeling the climax drawing out as he continued to thrust, riding the waves of pleasure.

I held him close, feeling him quiver within me, still hard and still pushing deep and pulling out. He kissed me again, kissed me hard and thrust deep.

I felt him softening and pushed him to his side, curling against his chest. He kissed the top of my head, lifted my chin to kiss my lips.

"I love you, Anna, no matter what," Jeff whispered. "I'll always love you. Only you."

Something sharp and hot and bone-deep shifted in my soul. "I love you, too, Jeff. You're my best friend. I don't know what I'd do without you."

In that moment, satisfied in my heart, mind, body, and soul—if only for a fraction of time—I thought I knew what I wanted. If I could have stayed there in that moment forever, I wouldn't have had to make a choice. I nestled close to him, as close as two bodies could be, and wished with all my being to stay there like that forever.

Jeff didn't ruin the moment with further words. He only held me, and left the silence full of our words of love. Decisions could wait. Right then, there was only him and me.

Daylight came, and with it knowledge of Jeff's body spooned behind me, his palm splayed across my belly and his other arm wedged between us. His morning erection was a hard rod against my ass, but his breathing was slow and deep, soft snores telling me he was still asleep. I'd woken with him like this before. It was one of my favorite things, honestly. Early morning light filtered through the window, the air beyond the blankets wrapped beneath our chins was cold, and the warmth of our naked bodies comforting and familiar.

I tangled my fingers in Jeff's hand and moved it to cup my breast, then slipped my fingers down to my pussy. I didn't often touch myself, not anymore. Jeff's hand tightened on my breast as I circled my clit, letting moans whisper past my lips as I spread damp heat through myself with slow-moving fingers. When I began to near climax, I lifted my leg, reached behind me to guide Jeff's stiff cock to my moist entrance. With a sigh of pleasure, I drove him into me, moving my hips in slow flutters on his hard shaft.

I felt his breathing change, felt his body begin to move in time with mine. His fingers on my breast flattened as he stretched, groaning, thrusting into me as he arched his back.

"Goddamn, what a way to wake up," Jeff said, his voice sleep-muzzy.

I tilted my neck back to kiss his jaw, gyrating my hips into his. He moaned, cupping my face in his broad, callused palm, then ran his hand down my throat, pausing to dip in the hollow between throat and chest. Farther down then, to the expanse of skin above my breasts, down between the gravity-pulled flesh, palm spreading to lift a breast, rolling the nipple with gentle, piercing pressure, then resuming the southward journey across the ivory plain of my belly, up the gentle mound of my pudendum. He thrust slowly as he touched me, making love to me with his hand, his lips pressed against the back of my neck.

He rolled with me, pulled me to lie on top of him, back to front, his body pillowing me, his manhood impaling me deep, deep, my knees drawn up between his. His breath huffed in my ear, my name whispered on his lips, and now both his hands roamed my flesh, held my breasts aloft and cupped them and pinched them and paid homage to them, and then his hands curved down my sides to the swelling rise of my hips and to the round muscle of my thighs and inward, to my pussy. He slid into me with a roll of his hips; I lifted my head and craned my neck to watch as he pulled out and pulsed back in, his slick length pistoning into me, his fingers delving into the shallow cup around my clit.

I fell back onto him with a shrieked sigh, feeling a spear of fire shoot through me. His fingers rolled my nipple, the left one, the more sensitive one, and his fingers traced around my throbbing clit in alternating fast-slow, rough-soft circles. I writhed on top of him, my body gone haywire and out my control, my hands gripping his head and clutching at his hands and clawing at his hips.

"Anna, Anna," Jeff said, a note of pleading in his desperation-rough voice, "I love you so fucking much, Anna. You are so beautiful, so amazing."

The utter vulnerability in his voice shredded my heart. I couldn't stop moving, not with climax rocking through me. I couldn't deny the raw love in his words, in his touch. I wanted to deny it. It scared me. I didn't know what to do with it.

Even as I continued to come apart on top of him, I felt fear ripping at me. I didn't know if I could love him as he loved me. He had no doubts, no hesitation, no reason to hold back. He was in love with me, and he'd owned it.

"Jeff..." His name was all I could push past trembling lips.

He pushed into me, his long middle finger curling down and in to find my G-spot at the very moment I peaked in climax, driving me to scream his name, unable to control even the volume of my voice. I'm sure every neighbor within three apartments heard me, and I didn't care. Not then, at least.

He came as I screamed, clutching both of my breasts and holding tight with primal strength, bellowing and thrashing into me, lifting me high with his thrusting hips. I wrapped my arm behind his head and rode him as he bucked into me, the other hand gripping his thigh with clawed fingers.

He stilled, and I lay back on top of him, panting. After a moment, I rolled off him, carefully pulling him out of my cleft.

"Holy shit," Jeff said. "I haven't even had my coffee yet."

I laughed. "I woke up and you had a hard-on. Seemed a shame to let such a beautiful erection go to waste."

He laughed with me, but I noticed the humor didn't quite reach his eyes. There was sadness lurking in his deep brown eyes, something hard and hollow. He kissed me, a quiet touch of lips, and then left the bed. He cracked my bedroom door and peered out, looking for Jamie, seemed satisfied that she wasn't around, and then disappeared into the bathroom. I heard the shower start, and I was alone in my room with my thoughts.

Now that I didn't have Jeff to distract me, an overwhelming wave of pain rolled through me. Jeff loved me so completely. How could I walk away from that? He expected me to, that much was clear from the sadness in his eyes. He'd tried to hide it, and I don't think anyone else would have seen it but me. It was buried deep. It was in the shine of his eyes, the way his glances lingered on me, in the wrinkles at the corners, in the downward tilt of his mouth seen only for a moment before he forced a smile on his lips.

I glanced at the floor, at the pile of clothes. Jeff's jeans sat on top, and I could make out a square bulge in one of his pockets. I knew what it would be even as I lifted the heavy denim, jingling with change and keys. I dug in the pocket, found the small soft black velvet box. When I opened it, the diamond glittered in the early morning sunlight.

The ring was so beautiful. It was simple, not extravagant or gaudy. Just a band of platinum with a single stone, elegantly cut. Like any girl, I'd always loved diamonds, always dreamed of wearing them. I knew what made an expensive ring; this had cost Jeff a *lot* of money. He wasn't a rich man, not by any stretch of the imagination. He drove a truck he'd bought five years ago, and he took immaculate care of it, kept it clean, tuned the engine himself once a month. His house was paid for, I was pretty sure. He had some money saved from his time in the Army, but his only income was DJing. He didn't have the kind of money lying around that he could just suddenly decide to buy a ring as pricey as this one.

He'd never asked me my ring size. I couldn't help wondering if it would fit. It wasn't a conscious decision, but I found myself lifting the ring from the slit in the box, angling it to catch the light, then slipping it onto the ring finger of my left hand.

It fit perfectly.

My throat closed up at the sight of Jeff's ring on my finger, knowing he'd bought it with me in mind. He'd spent a huge chunk of his savings on this piece of metal and mineral.

He wanted to marry me. He wanted to spend every single day for the rest of his life with me. Both of us came from broken homes, parents who had divorced and left distrust and pain in the wake of their ruined marriages. One of the things Jeff and I had talked about, in the long soft hours of afterglow, was how if either of us ever married, it would be once, forever.

When you grow up shuffling between Mom's house and Dad's house as I did—watching them fight in the kitchen every evening in the years before the split, watching them snipe at each other every holiday, every time they ended up face to face with me in the middle—you end up hating the thought of divorce, hating the thought of making so poor a choice of husband that you hate him after a few short years of vicious arguments and tumultuous makeup sex.

I stared at Jeff's ring on my finger, thinking for the first time in many, many years about my parents. They'd split when I was nine, and they'd had me less than a year after they were married. I'd long suspected I was the reason they'd married. The math added up, to my adult brain. If I turned nine the year they celebrated their ninth anniversary, that pretty clearly pointed to a shotgun wedding. I knew both sets of grandparents well enough to be fairly certain if Mom had turned up pregnant at twenty, they'd have pushed my parents into a rush wedding.

Brian and Laura Devine hadn't been a happy couple. They were attracted to each other, that much was clear to me even at a young age. They were always touching each other. I'd heard them having sex all too often as a child, and had walked in on them more than once. They'd just yelled at me to get out, and then told me to mind my own business when I asked what they'd been doing. I learned quickly, without "the talk," what they were doing. As often as they had sex, they fought even more. I fell asleep more nights than not with the sound of their yelling voices. I never knew what they fought about, and I still don't. I can guess, now, though: everything. They were not a good match. They were both stubborn and headstrong and quick-tempered, passionate and physical. Neither was ever willing to compromise, or listen to the other side.

They were attracted to each other, and I understand now as an adult that they had an intense sexual relationship, but it was never enough to make the relationship work long-term.

I layered my understanding of my parents' relationship over top of my relationship with Jeff. Did we have a relationship outside of sex? I didn't even have to ask that question. We had been close friends and partners for years before we ever had sex together. I could assess Jeff's mood just by looking at him. I could almost hear his thoughts sometimes. I felt myself wondering what our relationship would be like in ten years, or twenty. If I felt now, after a few weeks of being with him, that I knew him inside and out, what would it be like in twenty years?

The thought set my hands to trembling.

I didn't want to be like my parents had been. I knew Jeff felt the same way. His dad had walked out on Jeff and his mom and brother when Jeff was eleven. No warning, no reasons, no note. Just packed a suitcase and walked out, in the middle of family dinner. Jeff hadn't ever seen him again, or heard from him. His mother hadn't remarried, Jeff said.

All this bubbled in my head as I gazed at my left hand with the spot of silver brilliance on the ring finger.

"Does it fit?" Jeff's voice startled me.

I tried to wiggle the ring off quickly, as if ashamed to be wearing it. Jeff knelt in front of me and laid his hand over mine. His eyes drilled into mine.

"Does the ring fit?" he asked again.

I nodded. "It fits perfectly," I said, my voice breaking into a whisper at the end. "It's beautiful, Jeff."

Jeff nodded. "It's beautiful, like you." He took my left hand in his right, adjusted the ring with his thumb, staring at it rather than at me. "If you're wearing it, does that mean...?" He trailed off, as if giving voice to his hope would banish it from coming true.

"I don't know. Yes. I don't know."

Jeff laughed. "Sounds like you're still confused."

I shrugged. We were both staring at the ring on my finger rather than meeting gazes.

"I was just looking at it," I said. "I was hoping looking at the ring would, like...I don't know, provide an answer or something. I ended up thinking about Mom and Dad."

He frowned, knowing how seldom I thought about my parents. "Your folks? Why'd you think of them?"

I drew a long breath and let it out. "I don't know, really. I just did. They were so unhappy together. They had great sex, but that was the extent of their relationship."

"It's kind of weird that you know that about your parents," Jeff said, making a face of disgust.

"That's how they were. I saw them together more than once. I heard them all the time." I hesitated, then let my thoughts pour out to Jeff. "I don't want to be like them. I don't want to have a marriage based on that. I don't want to be married if it's not going to last. I'd always thought I'd never get married, then Bruce happened. Fucking Bruce. I was only with him because I thought he was all I could get. I can't believe I wasted so many years of my life on him. After I broke up with him, I swore I'd never get married."

"He was an asshole," Jeff said. "I never liked him. I never thought he was good enough for you."

I let out a mirthless laugh. "God, Jeff, you don't know the half of it. He was beyond asshole and into some other territory. There aren't words for how fucking awful he was to me. He never hit me, but he was verbally abusive. He'd call me names. Tell me I was fat. I needed to lose weight so he'd be more attracted to me. Told me I was only good for one thing, and I wasn't even that good at it."

Jeff rocked back on his heels, the towel wrapped around his waist coming loose. "Are you serious? He said that to you?"

"All the time."

"I never knew." Jeff seemed shocked, hurt, insulted.

"No one did," I whispered. "I never let on to anyone. I thought it was all I was worth. All I deserved. I thought for a long time my parents had split because of me. I know differently now, of course. I thought guys like Bruce were the normal way for guys to treat girls. He was my first, you know? My first real boyfriend, and I thought I loved him."

Jeff moved to sit on the bed next to me. "Anna, I—"

"It doesn't matter now, Jeff. I'm fine. I learned after I left him that I didn't need to take that shit. I deserved better. Well, I learned that the hard way, in some ways. But I learned it. My point is, after him I never wanted to get married. He'd assumed we'd get married and I'd stay home and have his kids and fuck him whenever he wanted and cook his dinners. That's what he told me. It's why I left him, ultimately. He told me he was gonna buy me a ring and we'd get married the next summer and proceeded to explain what he expected of me." I laughed. "It's funny, though. I tolerated his verbal abuse for, like, three years, day in and day out. I took it, and thought it was fine. I thought it was worth it for the times he was good to me, when he'd buy me nice things and take me to nice dinners and stuff. But when he told me he expected me to cook for him and wash his fucking underwear, I lost it. I told myself I'd never tie myself to a guy, after that."

Jeff shook his head in disbelief. "Anna, listen, that's not what I—"

"I know, Jeff," I said. "I know that's not what you expect. I love you. I know you better than that."

"So what does that mean for us?" Jeff hesitated, then said, "What does that mean for what I—for...god, I can't even say it."

"I don't know. I love you. I can't imagine anyone else knowing me the way you do. But get married? It's such a scary thought, Jeff. I don't know why. I trust you. I know you. I like our relationship. I don't want it to change."

Jeff let the silence hang for a long time.

"Anna, listen. I know what you're afraid of. Like you said, you don't want our relationship to change. But you gotta understand something. Marriage isn't some magical thing. Putting the rings on and saying 'I do' doesn't make the marriage. It doesn't mean you'll love each other any better. All that comes from what you've already got. Marriage only means as much as you make of it. To your parents, it was something expected of them. It was a burden, a rope tying them together. They were meant to be...I don't know, ships in the night, or something. Passing by each other, a few nights of good times, then going on their way. But it doesn't always work like that. Sometimes a night of pleasure turns into a child, and a family that wasn't meant to be. I think that's how it was with my mom and dad. He didn't love her. He stayed with her as long as he could, but she wasn't enough. Jim and I weren't enough."

He took my chin in his fingers and forced my gaze to his. "But you and I, we've got more. You know we do. I told you I loved you enough to let you go. I do, and I mean that, but don't think I'll let you go easily, and don't think I'd ever get over it. You are what I want in life, Anna." He leaned in to kiss me, soft, slow, and sweet. "The time I've spent with you is better than anything I've ever known. I don't want it to ever end."

A tear carved a tickling line down my cheek, caught at the corner of my mouth by Jeff's lips. I slid my fingers around the back of his neck as he kissed my jaw, the corner of my lips, my cheekbones, my throat. My heart hammered in my chest, as if anticipating something my mind wasn't aware of yet.

Words came out of my mouth, and I heard them as if from someone else. "I'll marry you, Jeff."

When I heard myself say it, tears flowed, and I felt the meaning hit me. I did want to marry him. Only him.

Jeff's lips froze on my skin between my breasts. "What?" He straightened, fear of having misheard warring with joy in his eyes. "What did you just say?"

I took his face in my hands. "I said I will marry you. Yes. Yes. I love you, and I want to marry you." I kissed his lips, long and deep. "I don't want it to ever end, either."

"It doesn't have to," Jeff said, breaking the kiss just long enough to speak.

His fingers tangled with mine, and I felt the ring on my finger as a warm weight. It felt right, there on my finger. I've never been much for jewelry besides some simple earrings and a necklace. Rings always felt odd on my fingers when I tried them on. This one, Jeff's engagement ring, felt as if I'd always worn it.

I was still naked, sitting on the bed, chilled by the morning air, Jeff's free hand skimming up my ribs. The damp towel around his waist was tucked in near one hip, coming loose as he sat next to me. I kissed him, reached for the edge of his towel and worked it loose, pulled it free so he was bare to me. I trailed my fingers up his thigh to his sack, massaged it in my fingers.

Jeff growled, twisted on the bed, and in the space of a single heartbeat had me flat on my back, his cock probing my entrance and sliding in.

"You just showered," I said, caressing the ridged muscles of his broad, powerful back.

"I'll shower again," he said, tangling the fingers of both our hands together above our heads. "Say it again, Anna. I heard you, but I'm not sure it's sunk in yet."

I smiled, wrapping my legs around his ass and pulling him deeper into me. "I want to marry you, Jeff." I rolled my hips, feeling him slide deep and slip out. "Has it sunk in yet?"

He laughed, moving into me in a serpentine glide. "I don't know. I might need to hear it once more."

"I love you, Jeff..." My breath was ragged, my motions desperate as Jeff brought me to climax almost instantly. "I'll marry you."

He buried his face in my neck as he came with me. "Oh, god, Anna...you don't know what it means to me...oh, god...hearing you say that."

"I don't know why I hesitated," I said, as we moved together. "We belong together."

"We always have," Jeff whispered. "It just took you longer to see it."

"I see it now."

I did see it. Sweat mingling, breath merging, pleasure synchronizing the beating of our hearts, I knew then I would only ever love him, be with him. I couldn't fathom, in that moment, how I'd ever missed it.

In moments of sharing love so powerful it winds the fabric of your soul around his, you can't help but feel the perfection of true intimacy. It goes beyond the sharing of physical sensation, it goes deeper than the vulnerability of nakedness, or the expression of emotional connection. It becomes an instant of timeless unity, in which you and he cease to be discrete identities and become something new, something more.

You become each other for those brief eternities spent clinging together in sweat-slick surrender.

When compared to such raw completion, marriage ceases to be quite so frightening, and begins to seem the most natural next step: binding yourself, your whole self, voluntarily, to the man who knows you most deeply.

Chapter 2

I twisted Jeff's ring around my finger nervously. A cup of coffee sat untouched in front of me, tendrils of steam rising from the tawny liquid. My heart thrummed, my stomach flopped, and my mind raced.

What the hell am I going to say?

My purse sat open on the booth bench next to me. The black box containing Chase's ring stared at me, daring me to think I could do this without completely losing it.

"You sure you don't want nothin' to eat, hon?" the waitress asked.

I shook my head and willed her to leave me alone. I needed these minutes before Chase showed up to get my nerves under control. The last thing I could do right then was eat. Which should say a lot about how nervous I was. Food was normally my greatest comfort. A piece of pie, or an order of fries with ranch, or a bowl of chicken lemon rice soup would usually soothe me under most any circumstances.

These weren't usual circumstances.

I'd never broken anyone's heart before.

I saw his black Ducati pull into a parking spot, and I nearly vomited just watching him stride into the Denny's where we'd agreed to meet. It was public, which was bittersweet. I knew I needed a buffer against him. I didn't want to do this in public, but I didn't think I could handle being near him in private. I knew myself better than that.

He slid into the bench across from me, unzipping his leather jacket. He ran his palm over the sandpaper stubble on his scalp, heaved a deep breath, and planted his elbows on the table.

"This isn't a good news meeting, is it?" he asked.

I shook my head, not trusting my voice yet. I sipped my coffee, burning my tongue.

"Well, then, out with it," he said. "Don't beat around the bush."

My breath trembled as I drew it in to speak. "Ican'tmarryyou."

Chase laughed. "Slow it down. I'm not gonna faint, okay? When you wanted to meet me here, at a fucking Denny's, I knew what the answer was going to be."

"I'm sorry, Chase. I just—I can't be around you in private. It's too hard." I sipped my coffee again, more to buy time to think than anything else. "I care about you. I had a really great time with you, and I can't thank you enough for what you've done for me, but—"

"But I'm not enough. Not good enough."

"Goddamn it, Chase. No. You are amazing. You're an incredible lover, a great guy, and—"

"If you say, 'you'll make some woman really happy someday, but it's just not me,' I swear to god I'll lose my fucking mind," Chase said.

He flagged down a waitress and ordered a cup of coffee.

"I don't know what else to say. It's the truth. You're amazing, and you deserve someone amazing. I'm not that someone. It's cliché and stupid and I hate the way that sounds, like it's a line from a bad romance movie. But it's true."

The waitress brought Chase's coffee, giving him a long, hungry once-over before walking away; Chase seemed oblivious to her attention.

Chase stared into his coffee. "It's not just about me, is it." It was phrased like a question, but his tone made it a statement.

"What do you mean?"

"I mean, is it that you don't love me, or that you love *him* more?"

I hesitated for a long moment before answering. "A little of both, I guess. I love Jeff, with all my heart. He...he asked me to marry him the day before you—before you showed up. I would have said yes anyway. You coming here like you did, it really threw me off. I do care about you, Chase. Maybe, yeah, there might be a part of me that wonders if I could have fallen in love with you. If we could have been great together. But...all the rest of me says I belong with Jeff."

He dumped several creamers into his coffee and followed it with several packets of sugar, stirring it until it sloshed over the side and ran down to pool on the table. He drank his coffee too fast, staring over the top into the middle distance.

"I should have come after you sooner," he muttered, almost to himself rather than me.

"I don't think it would have mattered, Chase. Maybe if you had followed me to Detroit that same day, and forced me to listen to you then, *maybe*. But do we really want to play 'what if'? I don't. It is what it is."

Chase growled. "I hate that phrase. It's so empty and...fucking meaningless. 'It is what it is.' Just another way of saying, 'I don't feel like coming up with a real explanation.'"

"Haven't I given you an explanation?" I asked, irritation replacing nerves. "I told you honestly what I'm feeling, and why I'm saying no."

"I still think you could have loved me, if you had given it a chance. But you didn't, and now it's too late." Chase's voice was low and thick with emotion.

"I don't know what to tell you. What if part of the reason I ran like I did was because I knew it wouldn't have worked? I don't want to end up like my parents. They had a great physical relationship, but nothing else. I think that's us."

Chase's gaze snapped to mine, and he slammed his mug down. "You think that's all we have? That's all I'm good for?"

"God, Chase, quit being so damn melodramatic. No, that's not what I think. You're good for more than sex. I think you're sweet and talented and so much else. But I do wonder. Is that all we have? I don't know. Maybe not. But the question is there, and that's reason enough for me."

"And you know you have more with Jeff."

"This isn't about Jeff. I'm not talking to you about Jeff."

"Do you talk to him about me? About us?"

He's not taking this well. I didn't know how he would take it, but I wasn't expecting this.

"Chase, that's not the point." I focused on breathing and sipping coffee until I was calm enough to be rational. "What else do you want me to say? Do you need to hear it bluntly? I do not want to be with you. I want to be with Jeff."

Chase took a deep, shuddering breath. He wouldn't meet my eyes. "I guess that's it then. Hearing you say it that way..."

I placed the ring box on the table in front of him, next to his coffee. Chase gingerly opened the lid, took another shudder-wracked breath. He was barely keeping it together, I realized. My own eyes burned, feeling the hurt radiating off him.

He lifted the ring out of the box, stared at it for a second, then put it back. He slapped the lid closed and put the box in an inside pocket of his leather jacket. He finished his coffee, silence aching between us.

"Bye, Anna. Good luck with life."

He slid out of the booth and practically ran out of the Denny's. As he turned away, I could have sworn I saw him touch his eye, like a tear was streaking his face, but then he was gone, leaving me to wonder. His bike roared to life, and he peeled out of the parking lot at a breakneck pace.

I managed to keep it together long enough to pay the bill for both coffees and get into my car before I broke down. I cried long and hard for Chase. He had given me something priceless in my newfound confidence, my belief in my own beauty and sexual power. I didn't think he could ever understand that, and I wished I'd tried to impart some of that to him, but it was too late.

I forced myself to stop crying. I'd cried more in the last few days than I had in most of the rest of my life. It was done, he was gone, and I could move on. I could go back to being happy with Jeff.

I drove home, found a note from Jeff on my counter:

ANNA,

HAD TO GO HELP AN OLD ARMY BUDDY MOVE. I'LL BE BACK LATER THIS EVENING AND WE'LL GO OUT. I'VE GOT RESERVATIONS AT MAGGIANO'S.

IF YOU NEED TO TALK, CALL ME. HOPE THINGS WENT WELL. YOU KNOW WHAT I MEAN. I LOVE YOU.

JEFF. XOXO

Yes, he actually wrote "X"s and "O"s on the bottom of the note. It was cute enough to make my heart melt even further. I folded the note and put it in my purse, along with all the other notes Jeff had written me. I wasn't sure why I was saving them, other than it felt wrong to throw them away.

My roommate Jamie came home not long after I did. We'd rarely seen each other lately, as we were both gone a lot. She always had a boyfriend, someone to spend the time with, but it was never serious. I'd spent most of my time at Jeff's lately, so this was the first time I'd seen her since our conversation after I got back from New York.

"Anna, I feel like I haven't seen you in forever," Jamie said, giving me a hug.

I hugged her back, holding tight. "It's been a while," I agreed.

"You've been with Jeff, then?" she asked, pulling away and looking at me.

Being my best friend, she sees everything in my eyes. But she still asks.

"Tell me."

"There's nothing to tell," I said. Talking about it would only upset me all over again.

"Bullshit," Jamie said.

She dumped her purse on the table, stuck the charger in her phone, and plopped down at the kitchen table, sipping from her venti skinny white chocolate mocha. She always got the same thing from Starbucks. I teased her about it pretty relentlessly, since she's never, ever had anything else for as long as she's been going to Starbucks.

"It's not bullshit. I don't want to talk about it."

"So there is something." Jamie rolled her eyes and sighed. "You know you're going to tell me. It just depends on how much wine I have to ply you with first."

"Ugh. You are such a pain in the ass," I said.

"Yep. That's why I'm your best friend. We pry information from each other when necessary. This is one of those times. I can see it in your eyes. You've been crying."

"All right. Fine. Let me make some tea first." I filled the carafe from the refrigerator, set it on the warmer, and depressed the button. When the water had heated, I poured it over two bags of Irish Breakfast tea, added sugar, and sat down next to Jamie.

"All hell broke loose, Jay," I said, by way of introduction.

"Uh-oh."

"Yeah. Jeff forgave me. We got back together, and things were great. *Are* great. Now, at least. But...he proposed." I showed her my hand, with his ring on my finger.

Jamie spewed coffee into her hand. "What?" She wiped at her face and hands with a napkin. "He *what*?" She took my hand in hers, practically yanking me over the table to examine the ring.

I withdrew my hand after a minute, staring at the ring myself. "He proposed. Asked me to marry him."

Jamie shrieked, clapping. "Tell me! Spill! Now!"

I laughed. "Jesus, Jay! Calm down! I'm spilling, already. He took me on a picnic—"

"Like, an actual, factual picnic? Like, outside? With a blanket and a basket of food—?"

"Yes, Jay," I cut in. "An actual, factual picnic. Beneath a huge oak tree, on a handmade quilt, with a basket of food and champagne and everything. It was...so romantic. We had this *incredible* sex, and afterward, he pulled one of those little black boxes from his pants pocket and proposed."

"And you said yes, right?" I didn't answer immediately, and Jamie freaked. "Oh. My. God. You didn't. You *hesitated*."

"I was scared! You know how I am about marriage, and my parents. I...yeah. I hesitated. I told him I needed to think about it."

"You needed to think about it." Jamie repeated my words like they were an accusation. "You're an idiot. If he loves you, and you love him, what is there to think about?"

"I'm not done, Jay," I sipped my steaming tea, and then started again. "He took it pretty well, I guess. Told me he understood how it might be a surprise and to take as much time as I needed. I wanted to say yes, I really did, but I just...I couldn't. Some part of me wouldn't let me. I don't know. Well, we had a gig the next day. At the fucking Dive, of all places."

"Isn't that where you used to sing with Chase?"

I nodded. "Yeah. Exactly. Well, we get through the shift okay, and then I took a break near the end. When I came back in, Jeff had this weird look on his face. I wasn't sure what to make of it, but then I saw *him*."

"No! Chase showed up?" Jamie covered her mouth with a hand, leaning forward.

"Just wait. It gets better."

"How could it get better?" Jamie demanded. "Jeff proposes, you say 'I'll think about it,' and then Chase shows up?"

"He looked different, so I didn't recognize him at first. He'd shaved his head—"

"Oooh! Does it look good on him? Not all guys can pull off that look."

"Yes, of course it looks good on him. The man can make a paper bag look sexy. With his head shaved, his eyes are just that much more vivid. He'd also gauged his ears and gotten a new tatt, and I'm not always a huge fan of ear gauging, but again, it's Chase, so it works."

"What happened?" Jamie slapped the table. "Get on with it!"

"You're the one who keeps interrupting!" I said, exasperated. "So *any*way, I saw him, but I didn't have time to do anything. He has a microphone, and he's got the lights on him, and he turns, sees me coming in from the side door, and he fixes me with this intense, typical Chase stare. Now, keep in mind I haven't seen or spoken to him since New York. He called and left all these voicemails, sent me a million texts. You remember. Well, I didn't answer any of them. It had been over a month since I'd been back here, and it had seemed like he'd given up. So then he shows up out of the blue, where I'm working. With Jeff, who just proposed. Of course, Chase had no way of knowing that, but still."

"What did he do? What'd he say?""God, impatient much? I'm getting there. So he's got everyone's attention. He just...he commands the room, you know? He doesn't even have to try. He's got that larger-than-life magnetism. So everyone was looking. I mean *everyone*."

"And then he proposed."

"*What?* Are you fucking serious?" Jamie seemed nearly apoplectic. "He shows up out of the blue, after not having spoken to you in, like, two months, and then he asks you to marry him? In public?"

"Exactly. I nearly had a heart attack. I mean for real, I think my heart actually did skip a few beats."

"What did you do?"

"I freaked! I ran like a bat out of hell. I swear, in the seconds before I ran out the door, you could hear a pin drop. I've heard the expression before, you know? But have you ever actually been in a room full of people that is completely and totally silent, with every single eye on you, waiting for your response? It's absolutely terrifying. It's worse than fucking up a performance. With that, you have the music to prompt you, you can keep going and everyone knows, but the song keeps going. This was so much worse. I wanted to die."

Jamie, for all her bravado and manic energy, truly did love me and understand me. "Oh, honey. I can't even begin to imagine what that must have been like. How did Jeff take it?"

I winced. "He had a glass of Coke in his hand when Chase proposed, and he actually squeezed the glass so hard it shattered. Naturally enough, his first thought must have been that I'd been talking to Chase behind his back or something. But I think when he saw my reaction he knew I hadn't been. Chase and Jeff both ran after me, and...Jeff tried to push Chase away, saying something like, 'you've had your turn'—"

"Oh, god, that couldn't have gone well."

"No, not even a little bit. Chase pushed him back, and Jeff decked him. I mean, he leveled him. Completely flattened him. And let me tell you, having two guys fight over you is not in any way cool. It's awful. I mean, having your guy protect you from some asshole is one thing. I can see how that'd be hot. But when you care about both of them? It's heartbreaking."

"God, Anna. How awful."

"Yeah. So I made Jeff go inside and told Chase I couldn't deal with him right then. I don't think Chase understood at first how I might not have completely appreciated a proposal quite like that."

"Idiot."

"No, he meant well. He just wanted to get my attention, I guess. I'd run off and ignored him, and he was upset. I don't say it was the best way of doing it, but I can understand where he's coming from." I sighed before making the next admission. "You were right about Chase, and my feelings for him, and all that, though. He'd—"

"Well, of course I was," Jamie said, waving her hand as if it was the most obvious thing in the world. "I knew it, I just knew it would take you time to realize it yourself."

She peered at me, and then the ring. "Wait, so is that Jeff's ring or Chase's? I thought it was Jeff, but if you're admitting you have feelings for Chase, then I'm not so sure, all of a sudden."

"I do have feelings for Chase. But what I realized was they were more like my mom and dad's feelings for each other. I wasn't sure we had an emotional relationship. He's great, honestly. It's not that I don't think he's capable of having that kind of relationship, 'cause I think he totally is. I just don't think it's there for him and I. Him and me, he and I—whatever."

"I think it'd be 'him and me.'"

"Oh, like you have any idea," I teased. "But seriously, though. Chase is amazing, in a lot of ways. But I don't think we have a relationship that would last forever. The sex would stop being exciting, or... well, no, it wouldn't. But a relationship has to have more than sex to it, or it doesn't work. I learned that from my parents."

Jamie was conspicuously silent, staring through the tiny hole in the lid of her cup at the dregs of her mocha.

"You'll find him, Jay," I said, quietly, laying my hand over hers. "Just stop looking for a while. Just be content being you. Go without sex for a few months. When you find the right guy, it'll be that much more amazing."

"A few *months*? I can't go a few *days*, Anna. I'd die. I'd be a cranky bitch." She curled her lip in disgust. "God, what does that say about me? Am I a nympho? I am, aren't I? I'm an actual nymphomaniac A sex addict."

"You are not. You're just trying to fill the hole in your heart with sex, like I do with food. It won't work, though. That's what I'm learning."

"Why are we talking about me?" Jamie said. "Shut up about me. I'll be fine. So what did you do?"

"I met Chase for lunch the next day and told him I'd give him a chance to explain, but that it wouldn't change anything. So he went and tried to get me to marry him anyway. He was charming and convincing and totally Chase. And it was confusing as hell. He gave me a ring, and he told me to think about it. I went home and cried my eyes out, and then Jeff showed up."

"What did he do?"

"He...he reminded me why I'm so completely in love with him. He didn't push me on his proposal at all. He didn't even bring it up. He knew I was upset, and he comforted me. He let me talk about what was bugging me, and he actually listened, even though it was about him and Chase. He...he's so much more than I can ever deserve. He always thinks about me first. He told me he loved me enough to let me go, if

I decided I wanted to be with Chase instead. He just wanted me to be happy."

"He said that?" Jamie seemed choked up at the idea, though she kept it under control.

"Yeah. He just held me, let me talk, let me cry. When a guy knows whether to just hold you and let you cry or talk to you and try to make it better, you know he really knows your heart."

"And Jeff knows you like that?"

"Yes, he does."

"So is that when you knew?"

I shook my head. "No. I knew when I couldn't imagine a day without him in it. I knew when making love to him wasn't just a physical thing anymore. It was an all of me thing."

Jamie slipped the cardboard sleeve off the paper cup and started ripping it into pieces, not looking at me. "Sounds great."

"Jamie—"

"No, seriously. I'm happy for you. Jealous as hell, I don't mind admitting." She finally met my eyes. "If you fuck this up with Jeff, I swear I will kill you."

"I know. Believe me, I know."

"So you said yes to Jeff?"

"Yeah. Last night. I saw Chase today. I got back from talking to him just before you did."

"So you told Chase no, then?" Jamie asked. I nodded. "How did he take it?"

"Not well. Not well at all. I mean, how do you take something like that? Is there a good way?" I ripped the tag from the tea bag between my fingers and added it to the pile Jamie was making with the cup sleeve. "He argued. He protested. He was mad."

"Can you blame him? You're amazing. And you didn't really give him a chance, did you?"

I shrugged. "It doesn't matter. I'm convinced it wouldn't have worked. I love Jeff. I belong with Jeff."

"So did Chase go back to New York?"

"I don't know. I'm assuming so."

Silence for a bit, then, "So when is the wedding?"

I laughed. "I don't know. We haven't exactly discussed any of that yet. I just told him yes last night, and I haven't seen him yet today. He's helping a buddy move. We're going out later."

Jamie nodded and stood up, scooped our trash into her empty cup, and threw it away. "Well, like I said, I'm glad for you. I'll help you plan your wedding when you're ready. Just...be smart, okay? I love you too much to watch you mess this up."

"What's that mean?" I asked, irritated. "Why do you keep thinking I'd mess this up?"

She shrugged. "Because we're alike. And I'd totally mess it up."

"Give yourself more credit, Jay. And me."

She laughed as she closed her bedroom door. "Credit where credit is due, Anna. You nearly did mess it up, you know." She opened the door again, poked her head out, and said, "If Chase shows up again, just say no. And then send him my way."

I just sighed at that. She was incorrigible.

I took a shower and spent a long time doing my hair and makeup for my date with Jeff later that night. I was still wrapped in a towel, not having decided on what to wear, when the door buzzed. I was expecting Jeff, so I didn't even think twice about hitting the buzzer and opening my apartment door. My towel was loosely wrapped around my chest, a toothbrush in my mouth as I held the door open. Expecting Jeff, I started to loosen the towel, thinking I would give him a surprise before we left. The thought had my juices flowing, anticipation of Jeff's hands on me, his lips on me.

Chase clumped in his shit-kicker boots into the entryway. Shock hit me like a bolt of lightning. I started to close the door in his face, simply out of self-preservation. His eyes were dark with desire, his hands shoved into the pockets of his tight leather pants, stubble smeared across his face and scalp. His face was twisted with a haze of emotion, and I felt the familiar rush of uncontrollable desire for him pierce through me, riding the heat of my already aroused hormones.

He took a step toward me, and then another. I backed up one step, but then he caught me in his strong arms and crushed me against him.

Conflict warred in me. I struggled with my desire, with guilt, struggled against his implacable strength.

And then he kissed me, and I was lost.

Chapter 3

My head swirled, whirled, skirled. Lunacy and madness boiled in my brain, heat moved within me in convection circles of desire, clouding my heart and body.

I pushed against him, or I thought I did. I intended to, meant to. But somehow I was moving into the living room, the back of my thighs bumping against the edge of the couch. I moaned, meaning to say "no," but all that emerged from between our locked lips was the moan. It sounded, even to me, all too much like encouragement. My body was betraying my heart and mind. I knew this was wrong. I didn't even *want* this. Not really. I didn't love Chase.

But his lips burned against mine, his tongue explored my mouth, my gums and teeth and tongue. His hands were branding my arms, sliding down to the damp towel, touching the swell of my hips and then up the silk of my thighs.

No, no, not this, not like this. My thoughts were fragments of denial.

I lifted my hands to his chest and pushed, pushed, *pushed*. He didn't budge. He only kissed me harder. His fingers brushed the dip of my hip where leg met pubic bone. So close, and I knew all too well how much fire he could spread in my body with a single finger.

No! The word wouldn't come out.

His hand slipped up my front, spreading the edges of the towel apart to reveal my skin, my belly, my breasts, and then the wet terry-cloth was falling down around me and I was bare to the air, my breasts crushed against the cotton of his black T-shirt, my pussy brushing against the supple leather of his pants, his erection hard against my belly.

Fingers brushed the bottom of one breast, traced a circle around my nipple, traitorously erect. I forced my body to remain still, to not arch into his touch.

I heard footsteps on the stairs. The front door was wide open. Anyone walking by could see me, naked, clutched to Chase, lips locked in a kiss.

If Jeff sees me like this, he'll never forgive me.

The thought provided enough impetus to rip away from Chase. I pushed with all my strength against him, stumbled backward, tripping over my towel.

"No!" The word scraped past my throat, a ragged denial. "No, Chase! I'm not with you. I can't do this. I don't *want* to do this. Go. Just...go."

I crouched, one arm across my breasts, the other across my privates, to lift my towel and wrap it awkwardly around me. Chase had seen me naked, making a mockery of my modesty, but to me it was a gesture of refusal.

"Anna, please, I know you said we weren't right for each other, but I couldn't just leave, not without—"

"Barging into my home and jumping me?" I was angry, now, embarrassed. I couldn't see past Chase's broad shoulders, but I felt a presence beyond him. "The door is wide open, Chase. Do you even *care* what I want?"

"But we've been together before, in other places—"

"That's *over*, Chase. *We* are over." Anger was quickly ebbing away, stealing my strength. "You need to leave. Please. Just leave."

Chase didn't move. He just stood there staring at me, eyes wavering, alternating between the hard anger of rejection and the soft hurt of love denied. He took a step toward me, and I backed away.

I heard Jamie's door open behind me, but I didn't turn to look at her. I heard a foot shuffle on the carpet behind Chase. I squeezed my eyes closed in a vain, wishing for none of this to have happened. I could feel Jeff's anger, even without seeing him. It was a palpable force.

I stepped to the side, and there was Jeff, dressed in pressed khakis and a crisp white button-down, sleeves rolled up to just beneath the elbow. His brown hair was getting longer, enough to run my fingers through, and his dark brown eyes were blazing.

"Jeff, it's not what you—"

"Shut up, Anna," he said, his voice calm and deadly quiet. He turned his eyes to Chase. "I'll give you one chance to walk the fuck away before I break you in half, pretty boy."

Chase seemed to swell up, get bigger. His fists clenched. I knew what was coming, and I had to stop it.

"No!" I stepped forward, pushing Chase between the shoulder blades. "Just go, Chase! Get the fuck out! Go! I don't want you here!"

Chase turned to me. "Anna, I'm sorry, I just—"

The anger in Jeff's eyes—directed at me, it seemed—spurred me to scream, "*GO!*"

Chase's face closed down, turned hard and impenetrable. He spun on his heel and stalked past Jeff, who closed his eyes, fists trembling, jaw clenched, as if it was taking all his restraint to keep his hands to himself.

Chase paused with one foot on the stair, then turned back. "This was all me, Jeff," he said. "This wasn't her. Don't be mad at her." Then he was gone.

Jeff's eyes flicked to me, taking in the towel clutched to my breasts, hanging down my front so my bare hips peeked out from the sides of the towel.

I heard Jamie's soft footfalls behind me, then she was in front of me, as if to shield me. I backed up, bumped against the wall and slid down to my bottom, letting the towel pool over my lap.

"Jeff, he just showed up, okay?" Jamie said. "He took her by surprise. Don't—"

"Give us a minute, Jamie, will you?"

"Jeff—"

"It'll be fine. I'm fine. She's fine. We're fine. Just...go make sure he's gone, okay?"

Jamie searched Jeff's face, seemed to see something that satisfied her, and left, closing the door behind her.

Jeff turned to me, and suddenly his face was soft once more, the anger gone. He crouched in front of me, lifted the towel to cover me. He took my hands and lifted me to my feet. Adrenaline had been rushing through me, but it abandoned me right then, and my knees buckled. Jeff caught me, lifted me effortlessly, carried me into my room, closed the door behind us with his heel, and set me on the bed. The towel covering me slipped once more as I fell back against the pillow, and Jeff tugged the sheet up over me.

The bed dipped as he sat beside me, brushing my hair out of my face. "Everything is okay, Anna," he said. "I saw what happened."

"What'd you see?" I could barely muster a whisper.

"I came up the stairs and saw your door standing open. I panicked for a second. I worried someone had broken in, but then I saw pretty— I saw Chase kissing you. I saw red, and I nearly lost it. I wanted to rip him apart."

"He just showed up," I said. "I thought it was you coming up. I had just gotten out of the shower, so I was in my towel. I was...I was thinking we could...you know, before we went to dinner so I was...turned on. I was thinking about you. I wanted you. And then it was him, and he didn't even say anything. He just walked in the open door and kissed me. I didn't want him to kiss me, I swear. It took me by so much surprise that I couldn't think. And...I honestly do have this automatic reaction to him. I know you'll probably think it's bullshit, but it's like this instinctive reaction, and I can't control it. I just...can't think."

Jeff's mouth opened, but I spoke over him.

"I tried to stop it right away, but I couldn't—"

"Did he force you?" Jeff asked. The anger in his eyes flared up again.

"No, not like that. No. He didn't hurt me, and he would have stopped. He did stop, when I managed to get myself together and tell him to. I don't know why—I can't—"

"I get it, Anna." He took my hands in his, tugged me toward him. "I saw. You pushed him away. I heard what you said."

"You're not mad at me?" I was suddenly shaking, terrified, even though he was still here holding my hands, that he'd leave me. "I heard your footsteps on the stairs, and I—I knew if you saw him kissing me, you'd—you'd leave, you wouldn't love me."

Jeff pulled me to my feet and pressed our bodies together, holding the sheet in place. "I love you. I admit, when I first saw you guys like you were, I did think you'd chosen him after all. I was set to walk away."

"Jeff, I don't know what it is with him. I know I'm not in love with him. And I didn't want him to kiss me. But when he did, I still felt...I don't know how to put it—"

Jeff cut me off. "Anna, you had a thing with him. He's a good-looking guy. I can see how he'd be exciting to be around, I really do. Don't like to think about you with him, but I can see it."

"That's it exactly. He was exciting. He *is* exciting." I wrapped my arms around his waist. "But he's not you."

"And I'm not exciting," Jeff said with a lift of his eyebrow.

"Jeff, you're exactly who you're supposed to be, and that's who I'm in love with. Exciting wears off. For me, at least. You're what I want."

"So you like me even though I'm boring, huh?" Jeff smiled as he said it to make it seem like a joke, but I sensed he wasn't entirely kidding.

"You're not boring," I said. "You're exciting in your own way."

"How's that?"

"You're sexy. You're sweet and steady and considerate. You're amazing in bed."

"Steady?" Another inquisitive lift of the eyebrow.

"Yeah, steady. Dependable. Responsible." I planted a kiss on his jaw next to his chin.

His mouth slanted down to catch mine. "Those aren't exciting traits, sweetheart."

"No, but they're yours, and they're what I've fallen in love with. You're always there when I need you. I don't think a lot of guys would have stuck around long enough to find out the truth about what just happened. They would've taken one look and run." I ran my fingertips through his hair, tracing around his ear to the back of his head. "You didn't. You gave me the benefit of the doubt."

"Yeah, that part wasn't easy. I knew you liked him, and I had to wonder if maybe you liked him more, since he was all rock star and whatever. Leather pants and tattoos and shit."

"You could wear leather pants," I said, smiling at the mental image.

"I'd look stupid," Jeff said.

"I don't know about that," I said. "I think you might look pretty damn sexy."

"Hmmm. Don't know about that."

"Maybe I'll buy you a pair. You can wear them just for me."

"Guess we'll see." Jeff's palms ran over my shoulders and smoothed down my spine, stopping at the swell of my ass. "You should get dressed, or we won't make it to dinner."

His eyes were wide and dark with desire, now. I wanted to erase the memory of the last ten minutes from my mind, and his. I leaned away from him to let the towel drop to the floor between us. Jeff breathed deeply, his nostrils flaring, his eyes raking down my body.

"We have a few minutes, don't we?" I breathed.

"Maybe just a few," Jeff agreed, pushing me backward to my room.

I let him push me until the door was closed behind us, then, keeping my eyes locked on his, I turned to face the bed, climbed up on to it on all fours and presented my ass to him.

Jeff grinned, reaching for his belt buckle. I watched him over my shoulder as he stripped down. He was about to take his socks off when I spoke up.

"Leave the socks on," I suggested.

He paused. "Why? Isn't that weird? Sex in socks?"

I giggled. "Sex in socks. Sounds like a kinky Dr. Seuss book. It's funny. A guy wearing nothing but a giant hard on and dress socks is just...funny, in a hot sort of way."

Jeff laughed crawling onto the bed behind me. "Sex in socks it is, then." He knelt behind me, running his hands over my ass, up my back and down again. "You look so hot like this, all spread out for me.""Come on, Jeff, take the leap, put it in and take me deep," I said, in a sing-songy Dr. Seuss voice.

Jeff sputtered into laughter, bending over me. "Oh, god, Anna. You did *not* just rhyme at me, did you?"

"I think I did. Can you come up with anything better, kid?"

Jeff slid his palm up the inside of my thighs, a slow and gentle touch. His finger drifted up to my spread opening, dipped in and back out. "Of course I can rhyme. I'm a singer, I do it all the time."

He spoke in a soft lilting voice, slipping two fingers into me, curling into my G-spot and scraping across it. His other hand joined his first, brushing across my clit with his finger, drawing a gasp from me.

"That doesn't count—we're rhyming about sex. I wanna see those muscles flex."

"When it comes to rhyming, you kind of suck." He touched drew his finger around my clit in slow circles until my hips began to rock with his rhythm.

"Quit talking so...we can fuck," I gasped.

Jeff laughed, a deep rumble in his chest as he delved his two fingers deeper into my wet pussy, then pulled out and touched his pinky finger to my other, tighter hole. I sucked in a sharp breath at the unexpected contact, then relaxed and pushed back into his hand, encouraging him. He pressed lightly at first, pulsing with his pinky in slow waves until I felt the hard ring of muscles give way, allowing his smallest finger in. My entire body convulsed as he pushed in, ever so carefully. Each time he circled my clit, causing me to quiver and buck my hips, he pushed a little deeper with his pinky.

I collapsed forward onto my forearms, my face buried in the blanket as he penetrated me, unable to think or string words together. My thighs shook with the onset of orgasm, and as the climax rose, I felt Jeff remove his fingers from my pussy and replace them with the broad tip of his cock, touching at first, splitting my nether lips with his hot, hard head.

His pinky stayed in place, though, and when he thrust himself slowly in, he matched his inward pulse with his pinky. My hands fisted into the covers and I pulled myself forward as he pulled out, then, with a shuddering outbreath, slammed my body backward into him.

I couldn't stop the muffled shriek from escaping my lips as his finger drove into me to the last knuckle, his cock driving into my farthest wall. Jeff growled low in his throat, one hand gripping my hip and pulling me into him. He was holding himself to his typical Jeff pace, slow and deep strokes. I wanted him to lose control, if only for a moment. I rocked my hips again, a high-pitched gasp erupting from me, and I felt Jeff jerk into me, once, hard, and then force himself to slow down and go gently.

I turned my head to look at him over my shoulder. His eyes were closed, his head thrown back, his spine arched into a curve as he pushed into me. I rolled my hips, a small pulse at first, and his lips parted as he matched the thrust; I moved harder, and he thrust in synch with me.

I began to rock my ass onto his cock with desperate force, feeling the orgasm still bubbling inside me, not quite there yet, but so close. I let my need overtake me, still watching Jeff as he began to sway forward, bending at the waist to crash harder and harder. His palm slid up my back to rest between my shoulder blades, and I rose up on my hands again, shuddering back and forth with my entire body to meet his thrusts.

Now the climax rose again, and this time it boiled through me, cresting as he came inside me, growling through gritted teeth as he thrust hard, fast, and relentless. I let my voice rise unfettered to match his, plunging backward into his crushing thrusts, wave after wave of orgasm blinding me, ripping screams from me, pleasure so potent it seemed nearly painful threading between the pulses of my heartbeat, the pulses of Jeff's hard body against my soft one.

The waves lessened with the slowing of his thrusts, leaving me limp on the bed. Jeff extracted himself from me and lay down beside me.

"God, every time I think making love to you can't get more intense…" Jeff said, panting.

"I swear it gets better every time," I said, "which I didn't think was possible."

Jeff curled up behind me, kissing the back of my neck. "I can't believe you started rhyming."

"It was pretty cheesy, wasn't it?"

He laughed, his breath huffing hot on my skin. "It was awful. But cute."

"Awful?" I protested, twisting in his arms to face him. "Like your rhymes were any better?"

He just laughed and kissed me. "Of course they were. Let's go get cleaned up again."

We rinsed off, dressed, and left, barely making our reservation in time. Jeff seemed distracted through dinner. I let it go until the very end of our meal.

I sipped from my wine and then reached for Jeff's hand. "What's bugging you?" I asked.

"Nothing's bugging me," he said, idly twisting the ring on my finger.

"Okay, whatever," I said, my voice dripping with sarcasm.

He grunted a laugh. "Fine, then. I guess I'm just wondering, now that you've agreed to marry me, how long of an engagement you're thinking."

"I hadn't really thought about it at all, honestly. I've only had, like, a day to get used to the idea that I said yes." I rolled the cloth napkin into a tight spiral. "What are you thinking?"

He shrugged. "I don't know, either. I know I love you, and I'm personally ready whenever you are. If it were only up to me, I'd say only as long as it took to plan the wedding."

"The wedding," I said.

Agreeing to marry him had seemed simple and natural enough, but I hadn't given a thought to the actual wedding yet. I'd been pretty preoccupied with other concerns, after all.

"Yeah, the wedding. I thought all girls spent their time planning the whole thing out with their girlfriends?"

I laughed. "Well, yeah, but by the time you're an adult, things have changed, you know? Like I said the other night, I never saw myself getting married. I don't know. I haven't really thought about it much. I guess I'm not a typical girl like that."

Jeff smiled. "Baby, there's nothing typical about you, and that's exactly what I love about you. This just means we can figure it out together."

"I thought guys hated planning weddings. Just agree to whatever his fiancée wants, and all that."

"Well, I'm no more a typical guy than you are a typical girl. I want to be a part of it."

"I guess not. So we're a matched pair like that, huh?"

"Guess we are. So where do you start planning one of these things, anyway? I don't have any idea."

"Neither do I, really," I admitted, "but I'd say location? Or date?"

"Hmmm. Do we want it around here? Like in a church?"

I laughed. "Where else would you have a wedding but in a church?"

Jeff frowned at me. "Um, outside? On a beach?"

"Oh, good point. So what do you want?"

"I don't know. I like the idea of something fun. On a beach in Florida, maybe? Or even somewhere more exotic, like Jamaica?"

"You know how expensive that would be?"

He shrugged. "Yeah, suppose it would be kinda pricey, but worth it, to my thinking."

I tried to picture myself on a beach, somewhere tropical, in a wedding dress, facing Jeff. "It would be awesome, wouldn't it? And it's not like there'd be a lot of people to invite."

That sobered Jeff up quickly. "Guess not. For either of us, huh? I'd invite my mom and brother, probably Darren, my buddy from the Army."

Who would I invite to my wedding?

"There really isn't anyone for me besides Jamie," I said, the realization hurting more than I'd anticipated.

"Oh, come on," Jeff said. "I know you don't have the best relationship with your mom, but you'd at least invite her to your wedding, wouldn't you?"

I shrugged, uncomfortable with the direction of the conversation. "I don't know. I haven't seen her in a long time. Years."

Jeff's brow furrowed. "Really? Not even for holidays?"

I stared into the rippling red surface of my wine. "Jamie and I both are pretty much alone, so we've spent the last few holidays together. Her past is even more messed up than mine, if you'll believe it."

"Except for the other morning, I've never really heard you talk about your parents much. Or your past at all, come to think of it." He frowned into his wine glass. "Actually, I don't even know if you have any siblings. I've known you for six years. How is it I don't know that?"

"I don't talk about it. Nothing to say." I shrugged, trying for a casual dismissal.

Jeff didn't buy it. "Come on, Anna. Talk to me."

I set my glass down. "There's not much to say. I have an older brother in the Marines, career. Joined up the day he graduated high school, eight years ago now. Then there's my cousin who lives in Miami. She's got her own life. We used to be close, except for every other weekend. But she got married as soon as she could and moved to Miami."

"You don't talk to her, either?"

I shrugged again. "We email back and forth a few times a month. I went down to visit her and her family...I think it was last summer? When I went to Florida a while ago."

"Last summer. I remember you going to Florida," Jeff said. "So you'd invite her at least, right?"

"Yeah, I suppose I would. Miri is great. She and her husband Kyle have boys, twins."

"Twins? Does that run in your family? Or is it from her husband's side?"

"You're really full of twenty questions tonight, aren't you?" I asked.

"I want to know you. I realized after talking about your folks how little I know about your family."

"Family." I spat the word, said it like a swear word. "I don't like my parents. That sounds awful, I guess, but it's the truth. There's a reason I don't talk to them. Or about them. My dad...he was the problem. Hopeless drunk. Held a job no problem, but he'd drink a bottle of Jack like it was nothing. Smacked us around a bit. Mom, mainly, me and Jared, too, if we got in the way.

"Jared busted loose as soon as he could. He'd stood up for Mom and me as much as he could, took some pretty hard knocks for us when Dad was at the bottom of the bottle. But when he had a way to get out, he took it, and I didn't blame him for it. I'd've joined too, but the military wasn't for me, and I knew it. Mom moved out with us when I was thirteen. Fourteen, maybe? Jared had just turned sixteen, so yeah. I would've been fourteen. Filed for divorce. Of course, my dad still got visitation every other week, which was pretty fucked up, since he drank even more after we left. He didn't hit us when it was just us. He was always going after Mom. He'd get drunk and turn on some stupid kids' movie. *Bambi* or something. We didn't argue, just wait till he passed out and turn on something else. That was pretty much it. We'd see him twice a month, he'd buy us some crap, take us for ice cream. He finally figured out we hated the Disney movies, so he started playing movies Mom wouldn't let us watch. But we started getting older, and he just...he didn't know what to do with me."

"My brother has a daughter who's a teenager. Teenagers are difficult."

"Especially when you didn't want kids in the first place, like in our case."

"Oh, come on, Anna, I'm sure that's not—"

"I heard him say it, Jeff." I took a too-big swallow of wine and coughed. "I was listening out my window after Dad dropped Jared and me off, one Sunday night. He and Mom were arguing. Dad said he had to skip visitation for the next few weekends. Called it 'business.' Mom called it bullshit. She wanted him to spend more time with us, and he kept making excuses. Eventually my mom badgered him into getting so pissed off he just admitted it. 'I never wanted kids, Laura!' is exactly what he said. Mom flipped the fuck out on him. I refused to see him after that. I guess I always knew he didn't want me, but to hear it..."

"That's a shitty thing to say."

"Yeah. He knew it, too. He saw me in my window, tried to explain how that's not what he meant, but—"

"But the damage was done." Jeff's eyes were full of compassion.

"Yeah. That was when I was fifteen. I didn't really see him except for a handful of times since. He died a couple years ago. Cirrhosis of the liver."

"What about your mom?"

I pinched the bridge of my nose. I hated talking about my parents. "Jeff, this is history. I hate—"

"It's important to me."

I finished the wine and spun the cup by the stem between my fingers. "God. Okay. Well, my mom is more complicated. I love her, I do. She raised me by herself after she and Dad split up, and she did the best she could. Then she met her new husband, Ed. She changed when she met him. I don't know even know what it is, exactly, but she's just...different. She was always high-strung, passionate and outspoken and all that—"

"Gee, I wonder why that's familiar," Jeff said, grinning.

"Yeah, I wonder," I laughed. "But when she met Ed and starting dating him, she got more...just bitchy. I can't explain it much better. She's just not as nice anymore. It's something to do with Ed. He's an okay guy, it's not like he's not a perv or a complete dickhead or anything. He's just—I don't know—passive aggressive? Never openly disagrees with you or does anything outright rude or insulting or whatever, but he just makes these little digs, so subtle you have to think about whether or not he actually insulted you. By the time you figure it out that you're pissed off about it, it's long past the time you can say anything."

Jeff grimaced. "Ugh. I had a lieutenant in the Army like that. Except when someone like that is your superior officer, it's even worse, because if he does insult you, you can't do dick about it."

"Yeah, see, my mom thinks Ed can do no wrong. She thinks he's like...mini-Jesus or something. I don't know. Mom and Ed have been married for, like, almost fifteen years."

"How old is Miri?" Jeff asked, after a brief pause in the conversation.

"Um...twenty-three? Twenty-four? I'm twenty-six, and she's a little over two years younger than me. So yeah, she'd be twenty-four. She got married to Kyle when she was twenty, just barely. Their twins, Eric and Dawson, are three. Why do you want to know all this?"

"You never answered me about whether twins run in your family," Jeff said.

I sighed. "I don't know. It might, I guess. I think I remember some talk of one of my relatives being part of a set of twins, but I don't know for sure." I narrowed my eyes at Jeff. "Why does it matter?"

"Well, my brother has twin girls. So if it runs in both of our families, then if you and I ever had kids, there's a big likelihood we'd have twins."

"You're thinking about kids already?" Something like panic shot through me. "Jesus, Jeff. I haven't even fully processed that we're actually going to get married yet. Can we slow this down a tiny bit?"

Jeff didn't answer for a long moment. "It was just a thought, honey. I'm not saying I'm ready for kids, or trying to have a conversation about it. It was just a realization. If you have twins on your side, and I do mine, then its something we should be prepared for, if and when we're ready to start thinking about kids. That was my only point, I promise."

I let out a long breath. "I'm sorry, I guess I'm just feeling like things are moving a bit fast."

Jeff tangled his fingers in mine. "How so?"

"Just everything. Things with Chase over the last couple days really messed with my head, I think. You proposing was a surprise in itself. Now all that with Chase is settled, and suddenly we're engaged, which I'm happy about." I rubbed my thumb on his knuckle. "I don't want you to think I'm not happy or excited about this, Jeff. I am, I promise. It's just a lot, when a matter of weeks ago I wasn't even sure who I was really in love with. I'm overwhelmed, I guess."

"I guess that's understandable," Jeff said. "Things've been crazy for you lately."

"No kidding. I just...I want things to be normal for a hot minute. Just you and me. Let me get used to the idea of being engaged. It still doesn't feel real."

"I hear you. We'll give it time. No rush. We can plan when you're ready."

That sounded good to me.

Chapter 4

Jeff let it be for about three months. We went out together, we worked. We made love. He never brought up the wedding, never asked me if I was ready to plan, or even dropped any hints.

I fell even harder in love with him for that. I knew it was on his mind. I could see it in his eyes when he looked at me, when he took my hand in his and touched my ring with his thumb.

I think maybe the first hint I was ready for wedding plans came when I realized I'd thought of the engagement ring on my finger as "my ring" as opposed to "his ring." It seems like a silly distinction, I guess, but it was an important one to me. No one had ever given me anything worth a lot of money. My cars had all been bought by me with money earned by me. I'd been given earrings and necklaces before, but nothing expensive or extravagant. We were spending a lot of time at his house, and as much as I was beginning to think of it as "home," it was still *his* house, not mine. My car was old and starting to break down from one thing after another, so Jeff would often have me drive his Yukon if I needed to go somewhere, but it was still *his* truck, not mine. I had *my* cell phone, *my* clothes.

So, to me, the ring on my finger—worth more than my car several times over, I was pretty certain—was *his* ring. A thing he'd bought and had given to me, to mark me as his. But it wasn't mine.

I was at the store, buying milk, bread, beer, frozen chicken breasts, feminine pads, razor heads, and hand soap. The cashier paused in the process of swiping and scanning my items to glance at my left hand, resting on the little ledge with the card reader. My ring glinted in the fluorescent lights, and the cashier, a tiny, awkward-looking woman with sharp features and oily brown hair, reached out and touched my hand near the ring.

"Wow, that is *gorgeous*!" she said, her wide, genuine smile showing nicotine-stained teeth.

I smiled at her, then glanced at my hand. "My ring? It is pretty, isn't it? Thanks."

My ring? The realization of what I'd just said hit me like a bolt of lightning. *Is it my ring? Or his?*

The cashier was speaking to me, but I didn't hear her.

It is my *ring, isn't it?*

I realized she was waiting for me to answer a question. "I'm sorry, what'd you say?"

"I asked when the wedding was?" She resumed scanning the last of my items and totaled it. "Forty-six eighty-two, please."

I counted out the cash, wondering what the correct answer was. We didn't have a date. We'd been engaged three months, and we had no date, no venue, no caterer, nothing.

"Um, we haven't set a date yet. We kinda just got engaged not too long ago," I said, eventually.

"Oh, well, congratulations, then."

"Thanks." I took my receipt and left, my head spinning.

I sat in Jeff's truck, the bags of groceries on the floor behind the passenger seat. Our groceries. Things for me, things for him, things for us. I was going to go home—to Jeff's house—and make dinner for us. I had half the closet full of my clothes. Space in the cabinet for my toiletries. Coats in the front closet. My phone charger in the kitchen.

I'd never lived with anyone before. Jeff hadn't asked me to officially move in, or made any comment about the mysterious influx of my things into his house, but my stuff seemed to suddenly have their own specific place in the house, and I found myself putting them there.

Jeff wasn't my boyfriend or my lover, or my fuck-buddy. He was my fiancé. I'd agreed to marry him. *Marry* him.

Sitting in the truck, *his* truck, I realized I'd only said yes because that seemed like the right answer. It was a way of making the decision between Jeff and Chase. It wasn't because I'd actually expected to get married, to have a wedding.

Get married. Have a wedding. The phrases rolled off the tongue easily enough, slipped through the mind quietly enough. But to put images to them, make them reality, that was different. Married meant only Jeff, for as long as I lived.

I tried the thought on: Anna Cartwright. Wife of Jeff Cartwright.

Hi, this is my husband Jeff.

My husband, Jeff.

Suddenly I saw flowers, lighting a candle, Jeff's hand on mine. Jeff sliding a ring, a simple band, on my finger. Jeff in a tuxedo.

Me, in a dress. All I could see of the dress, in my imagined fantasy, was waves of white, and my skin, and Jeff kissing me. Movie images, not reality images. But I could see it.

Where did you start planning a wedding? I had no idea.

I pulled out my phone and called the one person who might know. "Hey, Jay. So...if I was, hypothetically speaking, wanting to start planning a wedding, where would I start?"

Jamie was silent for a long time. "Um. I...don't know. I've never thought about getting married before. I'm not that kind of girl any more than you are."

"Yeah, so now you know my problem."

"Does Jeff know you're thinking about this?"

"No, I just now realized it."

"Oh. So...what happened that you're suddenly thinking about it for real?"

"It was weird. I'm at Meijer, grocery shopping. Well, I was, I'm in the car now, but...the cashier asked about my ring, and I realized I was thinking about it as *my* ring."

She got the significance of it immediately. "Oh. Wow."

"Yeah. Wow. And then I realized I was shopping for *us*. And I'm going to take the groceries *home*. To my *fiancé*. And it all just kind of sunk in."

"Well, I think most girls start by looking at dresses. That's what they show on TV, at least. I don't know. That's where I'd say we start. Maybe it'll make it all seem more real, or whatever."

"What kind of dress do I get?" I wore skirts, and even a few full-length dresses every now and again. I mean, it's not like I'm a tomboy, wearing jeans and sweatshirts all the time. I'm a woman, and I like fashion as much as any other girl. I read *Cosmo* and *OK* and magazines like that. I like romantic comedies. But I don't know anything about wedding dresses.

Jamie laughed, but it was a confused, disbelieving laugh. "Well, how the hell should I know? It's not like I sit around watching *Say Yes to the Dress*."

"Do too. I've caught you watching it."

"That's a dirty lie. Take it back."

"The first step to recovery is admitting you have a problem."

I heard a blender in the background, and she sounded distant as if she was holding the phone between her shoulder and ear. "I'm not an addict. I can stop any time. It's just because I get so bored sometimes. All those long nights alone."

"You haven't spent more than three days alone at home in all the time I've known you."

"Shut up. So when are we going to look at wedding dresses, Miss 'I'm ready to get married finally'?"

"Tomorrow? Lunch and then we can go to…a wedding dress store. Somewhere."

Jamie was silent for a few beats. "I think you have to make an appointment. It's not like going to buy a new skirt."

"Oh. Well. I guess I'll have to Google wedding dress boutiques or whatever and make an appointment? Or maybe we can go and just look, at first. Kinda get our feet wet."

"Your feet, maybe. Mine are staying dry. And out of wedding dress shoes."

"That's what you say now. If I'm getting married, then so are you. Just watch."

"God, now you've gone and cursed me, you meddling bitch."

We laughed, more at each other than because anything was funny. "I'll call you when I know what the hell I'm going to do."

"'Kay, see you later."

"Jamie?"

"Yeah?"

"You're gonna be my maid of honor, right?"

Silence. "Um. Obviously. Unless you have a secret *other* best friend I don't know about." Jamie laughed to make it a joke, but I could tell she was emotional. "Except I'm not really a maid. I think you have to be a virgin to be a maid. Or at least, virtuous. So I'll be the skank of honor."

"You're not a skank."

"Yep. That's me. The skanky-ho of honor."

"Jamie, seriously."

"The horny slut of honor."

I sighed. Her self-deprecation wore on my patience sometimes, more frequently now than ever. I used to think it was just her way of joking, but I was beginning to think she was serious.

"Jay, knock it off. You're being stupid."

"Okay, fine. Whatever. Call me."

"Bye."

Jeff came out and took the bags from me, and we put things away in companionable silence. I leaned back against the kitchen counter, spinning my ring in circles, wondering how to start talking about it all.

"Spit it out," Jeff said, brushing a strand of hair away from my mouth with his finger.

"I'm ready," I said.

"You're ready?" Jeff watched me spin my ring around my finger. "Sure? I've been trying not to—"

"I know you have," I said, sliding my arms around his waist, "and I can't even begin to thank you for giving me time."

"So what made you ready?"

I explained what had happened at Meijer, and how I'd talked to Jamie in the parking lot.

Jeff frowned. "She's your best friend, and I get that. But I guess I wish you'd talked to me first."

"It's instinctive, on some level," I said. "Something big happens and I call Jamie, or tell her when she comes home. Except now this is more home than my apartment, but she's still my best friend and I tell her everything."

"I know. I'm just saying. I want to be the first person you call when something happens." He kissed my cheekbone. "I'm not saying you can't tell Jamie things. She's your friend and that's important. I'm not trying to take that away."

"I know. It'll take a while to adjust my thinking, I guess."

"So. Where do you wanna start?"

"Well, that's what Jamie and I were talking about. I think she and I are gonna go look at dresses."

"When?"

I set out the chicken to thaw and flipped through a cookbook, looking for something to make. "I don't know. Jamie says you need an appointment first, but I don't even know where those kinds of stores are. Bridal stores, dress boutiques, all that."

"Are you looking forward to it?"

I shrugged. "I don't know. It could be fun."

Jeff leaned against the counter next to me, flipping his phone in his hand. "So should I start looking for churches around here? Or do you want to do a destination wedding? We could do the Florida Keys. I have—"

"Lemme guess, an Army buddy," I said, still flipping pages but not really seeing anything.

Jeff laughed. "Yeah. I must be kinda predictable, huh? Well, anyway, yeah, my buddy Arnie has a house on the beach down there, lots of room. There's even a country club nearby Arnie's a member of, he could arrange for the reception to be held there."

I quit flipping pages and looked at Jeff. "Then everyone would have to travel down there to be at the wedding."

"Well, yeah, that's the point of a destination wedding. I'm pretty sure most everyone on my side wouldn't have a problem taking a few days, especially if we have it in the summer, when people take summer vacations anyway."

"Wouldn't it be crazy hot in Florida in the summer?"

"Late summer, then. Have it in the evening."

"I guess this means I have to actually decide about my mother, huh?"

Jeff glanced away, out the window, and then back at me, as if containing a subtle irritation. "Yeah, guess so. That's the real reason you didn't want to think about the wedding. Right?"

I nodded. "I can call my mom. Jared, too. Maybe he can get leave if we give him enough time. If we have it in Florida, Miri and Kyle and the boys can be there. Doubt they could take a vacation to anywhere far."

"I guess Florida sounds good. We can talk more later. Depends on Mom and Ed, though."

"All right."

"I don't know, Jamie. I'm not sure about this one. There's too much tulle and lace. It's not me."

Jamie tilted her head, biting the corner of her lower lip, eyebrows furrowed. "Yeah, you're right. It's too...frou-frou. Something simpler next."

I turned to the may-I-help-you person, a woman a few years older than I named Brandi, slim, with pale white skin and flaxen hair pulled into a high, severely tight ponytail.

She nodded. "I think I have something that might work. I'll bring it into the changing room."

Jamie and I went back to the changing room and Jamie helped me out of the dress.

"This is stressful," I said, adjusting the straps of my bra tighter. "Half of the dresses I try on I'm falling out of, the other half make my ass look huge. And the rest are ugly."

"That doesn't make any mathematical sense," Jamie said, hanging the old dress up.

"Shut up. It doesn't have to. I thought trying on wedding dresses was supposed to be fun."

"It is. You're just difficult. And the only dress that made your ass look big was the mermaid one."

I snorted a laugh. "That didn't make my ass look big, it made it look like my ass had its own damn zip code. Which I'm starting to think it does."

Jamie smacked my shoulder. "Shut up, hooker. Your ass does not have a zip code. It doesn't even have an address, 'cause our lease just ran out."

"Don't remind me. Are we renewing?"

Jamie shrugged, fidgeting with the dress on the hanger, studiously avoiding my gaze. "Why would we? You're getting married in a few months. You should just move in with Jeff now. Save yourself the trouble after the honeymoon. 'Sides, you already live there half the time anyway."

I let my hair out of the ponytail and retied it to get the strays off my neck. "Then what will you do?"

She still wouldn't look at me. "I don't know. I'll figure it out. Not your problem."

"You're my best friend. Of course it's my problem."

Brandi came in then, effectively ending the conversation. "I think you might like this. It's A-line, just a touch of lace around the hem and the bust. It's simpler than the others you've tried on, but I think it'll look lovely on you. I think the bust line will nicely accentuate your full figure."

I winced. *Full figure*. Means plus-size. Curvy. Voluptuous. More euphemisms for not size-zero.

Brandi noticed my reaction and touched my shoulder, stammering. "I—I mean—"

"What she means is, you've got great tits," Jamie cut in, "and this will make 'em look even better. Jeff won't be able to take his eyes off your boobs."

Brandi breathed a soft sigh of relief when I laughed, and then she turned to hang the dress on the hook and pull it out of the bag. I stepped into it, and Brandi helped me adjust it to my full-figure boobs and zip it up the back. I hadn't looked at myself in the mirrors as I got into the dress, and I wasn't sure I wanted to yet. This dress felt nice. It felt...comfortable. Not heavy or draggy like some, or too light and airy like others. I could feel a lot of skin bare to the air, and I knew, even without looking, that my breasts would indeed be on display in a big way. Jeff would like that, but I wasn't sure I wanted to look like a hooker or pinup girl.

I tugged the cups higher, stuffed my boobs deeper in, breathed deeply and let it out. I glanced at Jamie first, to get her reaction. She had her hand clamped over her mouth, and her eyes were shimmering.

Oh, shit. She's crying.

I closed my eyes, turned back to the mirrors, and then looked at myself. My eyes stung, suddenly burning. Jamie came up next to me and tugged my hair back out of the ponytail, fluffed it out, and then pulled a bobby pin from her own hair and pinned my bangs behind my head, leaving the rest loose around my shoulders. Her eyes were wet, tears flowing freely now.

"God, Anna. You look...incredible."

"You really do," Brandi said, setting a veil attached to a tiara on my head and arranging the gauzy white material around my shoulders. "You look gorgeous."

I sniffed hard, ran my finger underneath my eyes.

I didn't look at myself in the mirror too often. I did my makeup, of course, but I leaned close and didn't really look at the rest of me. Clothes shopping wasn't something I did frequently, since I always felt like I had for most of the wedding dress shopping experience of the last few weeks: insecure about my body, overwhelmed by all the different kinds of dresses, stressed about having to choose *one* dress out of thousands.

But this...was different. All the other times I'd tried on dresses I'd looked at myself and seen my belly, or my wide hips, or the bulge of my ass, or my arms, or my *full figure* bust line. I didn't see me as a bride, I saw a girl in a wedding dress. A girl playing dress-up.

This time, though, when I opened my eyes and looked at myself in the mirror, even before Jamie fixed my hair and Brandi put on the veil, I felt like a bride. I felt...beautiful.

For the first time in a long time, I really looked at myself. I saw a tall woman, a few inches shy of six feet, long dyed-blonde hair wavy and loose around my bare shoulders, full breasts displayed but not spilling out. I saw my eyes, hazel and wavering with unshed tears within a heart-shaped face, high cheekbones, and full lips. I didn't see a dress size or a bust line or an ass that went on forever.

I saw me: curvy and confident. I saw a woman with a body made for loving, hands made for holding, lips meant for kissing. I saw wide, expressive eyes and blush-pink cheeks. I saw me as Jeff might see me. I saw the body that gave him a hard-on just looking at it, naked and wet from the shower. I saw the woman he loved, the woman he desired.

I saw the woman he wanted to marry. No longer a girl playing dress-up, or a girl in a wedding dress, or an insecure plus-size girl.

I saw me, beautiful the way I am.

Jamie touched my eyes with a Kleenex and rested her chin on my shoulder. "This one?" I could only nod and try to hold back the tears. "I'm pretty sure you're supposed to cry when you find the dress," Jamie said.

I shook my head, refusing to let them fall. I was happy. I was overwhelmed. I wasn't going to cry.

"Anna. It's fine."

I shook my head again and swiped my finger underneath each eye. "I'm fine. Really. I just—"

"It's overwhelming," Brandi said, standing near the door. "You see yourself in The Dress, and you finally realize it's really real. Like, it's actually going to happen. The veil is what usually does it for most of my clients."

"That's it exactly," I said. "Until now getting married was just an idea. But now...I can actually see myself walking down the aisle."

"Better you than me, girl," Jamie said, fidgeting with the veil.

"That's what I always thought," I said. "But now that I'm ready for it...I'm getting kind of excited."

"I'm happy for you. Really. I can't wait to be in the wedding. You and Jeff are perfect together. But it's not happening for me. No way, no how. Never."

"You're impossible."

"Yep."

"So when you do end up getting married, I get to say 'I told you so,' right?"

Jamie laughed. "If it happens, which it won't, then sure."

"So is this the dress, then?" Brandi asked.

"Yeah, I think so," I said, my voice wavering. I looked at myself once more, head to toe, and this time my voice had conviction. "Yes. This is the dress."

It would clean out the savings I'd been setting aside for a new car, and probably max out my credit card to boot, but it was worth it. Jamie and I met Jeff for lunch after making an appointment to return for a fitting.

Jeff had already ordered for us and was waiting at a four-top table at Five Guys. "So, how'd dress shopping go today?"

He'd never come with us, obviously, but he always wanted to know what was happening.

"I found the dress," I said, sitting next to him.

Jamie took the spot opposite me. "It's gorgeous," she said. "Like, incredible. You just might faint when you see her for the first time."

"I'm sure I will," Jeff said.

"No, really. All the blood's gonna rush to your cock and you're gonna pass out. It's that sexy."

"Jamie, seriously? You're incorrigible." I threw a French fry at her head.

"What? It's true. I'm a girl and I got a hard-on."

"Ohmigod, Jamie. You're so freaking impossible."

"You know you love it."

"True. But seriously, though, Jeff. I really love it." I dabbed a fry in ketchup. "My credit card balance doesn't love me, but it's worth it."

"How much was it?" Jeff asked.

"You don't want to know."

"Anna. You can't go broke trying to do everything on your own."

"Neither can you."

"Anna."

I dabbed another fry. "Fivethousanddollars," I mumbled the words, all squished together and under my breath, and followed it with a bite of cheeseburger.

"Excuse me?" Jeff leaned forward, setting his burger down. "It sounded like you said five thousand dollars for a second there."

"Wow, I really like this song. I haven't heard it since the nineties," I said. "This is Gin Blossoms, right?"

"*An*na."

"Fine. Yes. It was five thousand three hundred and ninety two dollars, okay?"

"You spent fifty-five hundred dollars?" Jeff sank back in his chair. "Good lord. I thought you'd at least call me before you went and blew your entire savings. I could have helped you. We're doing this together. At least, that was the idea."

"Are you really pissed off about this? I wanted to. It was what I wanted. I'm finally getting into this, getting into the whole 'planning a wedding' thing, and now you're pissed off that I made a decision. You're not supposed to see the dress until the actual wedding anyway."

"I know that, but we could have split the difference or something. At least talk to me before you go and spend that much money. I thought that's what couples did?"

"Well, shit. I'm sorry I didn't consult you first. I guess I thought I was old enough to make my own decisions."

"That's not what I meant—"

"Wow, look at that soda dispenser," Jamie said, a little too loudly, getting up for a refill. "They have like, a dozen different kinds of Fanta."

"Jeff, let it go."

"Well, at least call your—"

"If you bring up my mother, I will straight up walk out. For real. I am *not* calling her to help pay for my wedding."

"Didn't you want your mom to be there when you picked your dress? It's kind of traditional, isn't it?"

"Jeff, you really need to stop pushing this family button, okay? Yeah, maybe it is traditional, but Jamie is more my family than my mom at this stage. Tradition can jump off a cliff. I just want a happy wedding. I don't want my family there. Just you and me and those who really matter. My blood family doesn't matter. Not anymore."

"I know I'm pushing it, but...it's important to me. Family is important to me."

"You're my family. Jamie is my family."

"What about Jared?" Jeff picked at the Cajun-seasoned fries.

"Well, he's been in the Marines since I was, like, sixteen, and he's only spent his leave Stateside, like, three times, ever, so I don't see him at all. He'll message me using the TextMe app every now again, but that's it."

"Where's he stationed?"

"The Philippines. He's been there for...three years? He was in Okinawa first, then Italy."

"What's his MOS?"

"He's an MP."

Jamie had come back to the table but had pretended to be absorbed in her phone. "He's hot. If he lived here, Anna and I would be sisters."

"I thought that was never happening, with anyone."

"For your sexy-ass brother, I might make an exception." She looked up at me and saw my irritated expression. "God, Anna. Kidding. I would never marry Jared. I'd fuck him till he couldn't walk for a week, though."

"JAMIE!"

"Shutting up."

We finished eating, and Jamie and I said our goodbyes. I promised to call her with the next step of our plans. Jeff drove us home, but before we went inside, Jeff spoke up: "So, this dress you picked out."

"You can't see it until I'm walking down the aisle."

"No, I know that, but—

"You want to know how I knew which dress was the right one?"

"Yeah."

"I saw myself like you see me. Just for a second, looking in the mirror. I saw the woman you love, the woman you want." I paused. "Would it be overly dramatic if I said it was kind of a defining moment in my life?"

"Really?"

"Yeah, really. To finally, finally feel my own worth in myself...I can't explain how huge that is for me. Not just through you, or through

Chase. But in myself. Actually *seeing* with my own eyes a woman worth being. Yes, it was a defining moment of my life."

"And I shit all over it, freaking out about the money."

I laughed. "Yeah, you kind of did. But I get it. You couldn't have understood if I didn't tell you. I don't care how much the dress costs. I'd sell my liver if it meant feeling that way again. And yeah, I know it's just one day. I don't care. If you want to pay for it, or split the cost, fine. Whatever. I really do want to do this with you. I'm just...I'm not used to being a couple. To doing things like that together. But I want to."

Jeff's deep brown eyes swept over my face, love radiating from him in palpable waves. "Thanks for telling me."

"I would've eventually. I just—"

"Needed a little prodding," Jeff said.

"Yeah."

"I'm pretty good at prodding," he said, a mischievous smirk on his face.

"Hmmm. I might have to test your prodding abilities. You know. To make sure they're up to expectation. We have very strict prodding standards, you know."

"What kind of test did you have in mind?" he asked, feigning curiosity.

"Come inside and I'll show you," I said.

His eyes lit up with a lustful hunger as we went inside.

"Take me," I gasped, my lips against the hair above his ear. "Take me right here, right now."

Lately, we'd gotten into a pattern. We'd work, go back to his place, have a glass of wine or a bottle of beer, and then go into his room, our room, and make love. It was a pattern I enjoyed. There were nights we simply went to sleep, holding each other. The sex, even when it was the same basic thing or two every night, was never stale, never boring. I could see us in ten years, still enjoying vanilla missionary sex just as much as now.

But this, the fiery hunger flickering in Jeff's eyes, the demanding way he pinned me back against the front door and chained my wrists by my face with his strong hands, this was sudden and powerful and lit me from within. He didn't kiss me at first. He held my hands in his, palm against palm, fingers lined up, his dwarfing mine. Then, slowly, he curled his fingers into mine, clenching tight. His lips explored my mouth, his tongue pushing between my lips to taste my tongue.

I kissed him with eyes wide open, watching his expression change moment by moment: lust, love, hunger, need, raw and potent strength. He circled both of my wrists with one hand, holding them up over my head. With his other he lifted my shirt up, stripped it off, releasing my hands long enough to pull it free and toss it aside. His mouth dipped to my shoulder, kissed the round bend from shoulder to arm, then upward to my neck, my jaw. Gentle, nimble fingers unclasped my bra, dropped it to my feet. While my hands were free to slip the straps off my arms, I tried to wrap my arms around his neck, but he caught my wrists again and pinned them above my head, kissing me with startling power.

I melted into the kiss, relaxed into his hold, pressed my bare breasts against the rough cotton of his button-down shirt. His free hand traced down my side, butted against the waist of my jeans and circled around to the front, toying with the button before releasing it. He lowered himself down, stretching his arm to keep my hands in place, his lips kissing a hot, moist line down my chest and between my breasts. He tugged my pants down, one side at a time until they pooled at my feet, and then he repeated the action with my panties.

My back was still against the front door, my heart thudding with anticipation. This was a new, demanding Jeff, in control and taking what he wanted from me. Excitement made my hands tremble and my lips shake against his, and when his teeth grazed my nipple, wet heat burst between my thighs. I struggled against his hold, wanting to touch him, needing to strip him down to skin and slide my legs around him.

He held me still, crushing me against the door with his body, kissing me with hard fury. His mouth demanded my acquiescence, and I gave it, opening to him, softening against him. When I was still and only our lips moved against each other, he leaned back and ripped his shirt open, buttons popping and ticking on the floor at our feet, then, with the fabric dangling from his arm, he deftly slipped out of his pants so he was naked in front of me.

I expected him to push me to our bedroom then, but he didn't. He pressed burning kisses around my breasts, focusing in on one and laving the nipple, circling it, nipping it. His free hand slid palm against my belly, fingers pointing down and moving between my thighs. He cupped me, and I whimpered, wanting to feel his fingers delve in, but he drew out for the moment, smiling against my lips.

"Tell me what you want, Anna," he whispered, his voice a rough, primal growl in the silent, evening-lit house.

"You," I answered, pushing my pussy against his hand, willing him to touch me.

He rewarded me with a single fingertip slipping between my nether lips.

"Tell me more. What else do you want?"

I bent my head down to rasp my answer in his ear, "Put your finger inside me. Make me come, Jeff."

He growled, a rolling animal sound of hunger. His finger dipped in, sought my juices and slathered them over my soft folds, finding the hard nub of my clit and softly swiping around it. I moaned and rolled with his moving finger, pushing my breasts against his bare chest.

"Yes, just like that," I said, "two fingers, now. Yes, god yes. Faster."

He obeyed my commands, moving faster until I almost couldn't stand it.

"Slower, slower. Slow down." I let myself fade away from the ragged edge of orgasm, until his fingers were barely moving against me. "Faster, not so hard. Soft. Yes, just like that. Oh, god, Jeff. I love the way you touch me."

Climax rose slowly, this time. I let it build gradually. My arms were starting to tingle over my head, but I ignored it.

"Put your mouth on my tits," I said. "Suck my nipples."

"Yes," was his only response.

His lips found one nipple, then the other, his fingers circling my clit. I opened my mouth to tell him to slow down, but then climax hit me without warning, gushing through me, ripping the strength from my knees. I collapsed, shuddering, and only Jeff's hand held me aloft.

Jeff's knee nudged my thighs apart, and I forced myself upright on trembling legs. I felt his hard tip brush against my thigh as he crouched and rose up. Gently, slowly, carefully, he guided himself into me. When our hips bumped and his cock filled me, I felt my legs go limp again, and I was held up by him, by his hands around my wrists and his cock within me.

I curled over him, my face against his shoulder, bit his salty skin. He gasped at the sharp nip, and then thrust into me, once, hard, and my whimper of pleased shock was muffled by his flesh. I was lifted up onto my toes, and then he was fading out and plunging back in, pressed back against the door by the power of his body coursing against mine. I let my weight fall against him, trusting his strength. The climax, still rocking through me, redoubled, inundating me with searing ecstasy. I let my voice rise in volume, giving in to the pleasure, shrieking and gasping as he began to drive into me with ever greater force.

His hand released mine and I wrapped my arms around his neck, clinging to him. He slid his hands beneath my ass and lifted me. I wrapped one leg around his waist, and he held it there, rocking up on his toes to crush ever deeper.

"Jeff..." I could only gasp his name as the waves of orgasm trebled in intensity, each crest indecipherable from the one before or behind. I squeezed my eyes shut and rode the climax, gasping with each surge of his body against me, the pitch of my voice rising until I was screaming unabashedly, back arched, face thrown to the ceiling, hips gyrating madly.

I felt him come, heard his bellow. His cock throbbed, pulsed, and released a flood of seed within me, hot and washing through me. His face buried in my breasts, he groaned as he came again, and again, moving his body into me in sinuous thrusts.

I hadn't thought I could come any harder without breaking apart at the seams, and yet I did, feeling him spasm and arch into me, feeling him lose himself in me.

"God, I love you," I whispered in the silence between our breaths.

"You're my eternity, Anna."

Tears dripped from me, a sudden rush of hot salt burning my cheeks. "Fuck. You've gone and made me cry after sex again."

"Good tears?"

"Good tears."

"Cry if you want. Doesn't bother me." He let me down, pulled out, and we lay on the couch, pulling a hand-knit afghan over us.

I was messy, and I didn't care. "I've cried so much lately. I don't know what it is."

"You're finally learning to feel your emotions?"

"Yeah, maybe." I nuzzled my face into his broad shoulder. "I just wish there weren't so many of them. I feel like a basket case sometimes."

"I love who you are, and I love every single thing about you, good or bad. I know you've been through some hard shit, and I wish I could take away the pain you've carried. I would take it on myself if I could. But I wouldn't change anything about you. Our pain and mistakes and faults are an integral part of us. They make our joy and successes and qualities all the more significant."

"That's...deep."

"Sit with a gun staring at nothing for days on end, you tend to have a lot of time to think."

"You know, all I really know about that is you were in the Army. I don't know for how long, or what you did, or if...if you saw combat."

"Yeah, don't talk about that much." He seemed to stiffen, his muscles tensing.

I waited, curled into him on the couch, my hand resting low on his belly.

"Not a whole lot to say, really. Saw combat. It was fucked up. Things you shouldn't see, shouldn't do." His words were clipped short, his voice barely audible.

I looked up at him, saw his closed eyes flickering, as if seeing the past.

"If it's too hard to talk about—"

"It's more that there's no point. It's not like I'm super hung up on it. I had PTSD counseling, I'm over it. Few bad dreams here and there." He looked down at me and drew a breath, let it out. "Here's the basics. I was a grunt. Infantryman. Did a tour in Iraq. God, it was fucking boring as hell for the most part. A whole lot of sitting on a roof watching dust blow around. Drive here and there in a Hummer, house-to-house patrols. My unit got ambushed, toward the middle of my tour. It was a pretty standard insurgent ambush. Lead vehicle hit a land mine, and when the others stopped, they opened fire. Lost some good buddies in that one. My nightmares are usually about that. Haven't had one in a while. So, if you wake up and I'm not in bed, that's why. I'll probably be outside in the backyard. Fresh air helps."

I heard an odd note in his voice. "What aren't you saying?"

"Perceptive one, aren't you?" He scrubbed his face with his hand. "My vehicle got hit by an RPG. They kinda missed, you know? Hit near it, not dead on, but enough to...well, no one made it out alive, 'cept me. Not sure why I made it, or how. I was trapped in the back seat, the whole thing burning, buddies dead, buddies dying outside. Taking heavy fire from all directions. That's the dream. It's more a memory, being trapped in a burning vehicle."

"Was this before or after the car wreck in the UP?" I asked.

He grunted. "Before. That's the reason I went nuts trying to save Brett. He was trapped. Like I'd been. Had to do something, *had to*. But I couldn't save him." A long silence, then, "So now you know. Never really talked about that before."

"How'd you get out? Of the vehicle, I mean?"

"Couple guys heard me yelling. Screaming, more like. Pulled me out, and we used the wreck as cover. Wicked enfilade fire. Couldn't see where they were shooting from. Hidden in a bombed-out building, a good fifty of 'em. We were almost double their numbers, but they had surprise. Took us a while to get organized. When we did, though... wiped 'em out. Every last fucking one."

He slid out from behind me, strode naked to the sliding glass door. I gave him a few minutes, just lay on the couch watching him. Eventually, I got up, wrapped the afghan around me, and stood behind him, palms on his chest. His heart was hammering in his chest.

"I'm sorry I brought up bad memories, Jeff."

He took a few long, deep breaths. "It's fine. I'll be fine. Just takes a bit for the memories to fade, you know? But they will."

"Want a drink?"

He shook his head. "No, not yet. One thing the counselor emphasized a lot was, when the memories are riding you, don't turn to alcohol. That's how it becomes a crutch. It seems natural enough. Bad dream? Have a drink. But the memories hold on, you know? They stick. And one drink turns to four. Turns to eight. Turns to passed out on the bathroom floor. Saw it happen to too many buddies to let it happen to me."

"I'm proud of you," I said.

"Proud? For what?" He turned his head so he could just barely see me in his peripheral vision.

"For dealing with it so well. I would never have known you'd been through anything so awful. I think a lot of men would have been bitter, or alcoholics. Or, I don't know. Just, I'm proud of you. You're so strong."

He shook his head. "Lots of guys have been through shit like that. Not all of them turn to drugs or alcohol. A lot of us are normal, well-adjusted men with normal, well-adjusted lives. We just...have some bad memories that haunt us sometimes. Women like you, who understand

and help us deal, you're how we get through the flashbacks and stay sane."

"I haven't done anything, though. Not yet, at least."

"You listened. You're here, holding me. Talking to me."

"Well, what else would I do?"

"You haven't asked the one question almost everyone wants to know, whether they ask it out loud or not: 'Did you kill anyone?'"

I let the pause hang. "I…guess I'm not sure why I'd ask. It's obviously hard for you to think about. I don't want you reliving it. I mean, I'm assuming since you said you saw combat, that you probably did."

"Exactly." He turned and put his back to the glass. "Enough about the bad old days. Come here and kiss me."

And so I did. I welcomed the distraction from my own memories, and the opportunity to help erase the pain in his eyes, to fill the haunted hollowness. I kissed him with all I had. I let the blanket fall to the floor and ran my hands on the ridges of his muscle, the ropy cords of strength in his arms and abs. I ran my fingers along the rough, burned skin along his back, so familiar to my touch now that I forgot it was there, what it was, what it represented. It was simply a part of Jeff, an element of his attractiveness to me.

I felt his body respond, stiffening and standing up between us; I took his manhood in my hands and caressed his length, softly, gently, with as much tenderness as I could summon. When he was throbbing between my palms, I released him and led him, walking backward, to the bedroom. I pushed him onto the bed and climbed astride him. My hair fell in blonde waves around our faces as I leaned down to kiss him, taking his turgid cock in my hand and guiding his hard length into my soft, wet cleft. My mouth quivered wide in an open-mouthed kiss as he penetrated me.

Our bodies glided in synchronized splendor, skin sliding slick and soft, our breath a slow susurrus in the dusk light. I moved on top of him, ran my palms on his chest up to cup his face, kissing him on the offbeat, lips touching in a syncopated rhythm. He'd given it to me hard and fast and sudden against the front door; now I was giving it to him slow and locked in melodic counterpoint of soul expression, eyes meeting, closing, meeting, hips bumping and pulling away, gasps turning to sighs.

This was not about climax. I felt his tension fade with every thrust, felt his memories sink into nothingness with every soft kiss. I couldn't heal him, but I could douse the heat of the nightmare, subsume the horror beneath the power of my love.

When it came, it was a tidal wave, sweeping us away. He clung to me as if I were a spar and he a shipwrecked sailor. He moved into me with a desperation unlike anything I'd ever seen in him before, as if he could bury the nightmare memories within me, be free of them forevermore simply through the act of driving deeper into me.

If that was true, I would accept it all.

His breath caught when he came, and a single sob escaped his lips. I kissed each of his cheeks, the single trickle of salt at each corner. I asked no questions, spoke no words, only held him closer and pushed him deeper within my folds, clutching his face against mine, forehead to forehead, breathing matched and his legs tangled with mine.

In time, we found a perfect stillness, contentedness in breathing, holding, being. Loving. I leaned over to kiss him and tasted salt on his lips, moisture on his face. I wiped his cheek with my palm, then the other.

"Sorry," he muttered, gruff, moving to sit up. "I don't know why I'm—"

"Shh. Don't." I pushed him down and kissed him again. "You're allowed."

He went still, and after a while he cleared his throat and brushed his palms across his face. "Thanks," he said. "I guess I just—"

"I know. I love you. Like I said, you're allowed. Doesn't make you less a man...less *my* man."

"And that's why I love you. Well, one of the infinite number of reasons, at least. Now, how 'bout that drink?"

Chapter 5

A few days later, I had just gotten out of an afternoon shower and was looking for a particular bottle of body lotion. I tore the bathroom and bedroom apart, but couldn't find it, which was when I realized I'd never brought that particular bottle of lotion over to Jeff's house. It was still at my apartment, which I hadn't stepped foot in for at least a month. Half of my clothes, most of my makeup, hair products, lotions, all that "girly shit," as Jeff called it, was at his house. But every once in a while I came across something I wanted that turned out to be at my apartment.

This is ridiculous, I thought.

I found Jeff out on his back porch, reading a book on his Paperwhite. He looked up when I came out.

He took one look at my face as I approached and set his Kindle down. "What's up, buttercup? You look like you're thinking deep thoughts."

I handed him one of the bottles. "Well, just sort of wondering something."

"Wait, can I guess what you're about to say?"

"Um, sure?"

He reached into his pocket and pulled out a single key. "This is more symbolic than anything, since you're basically living here already, but..." He handed me the key. "Wanna make it official? Move in for real, permanently?"

I took the key and blew out a sigh of relief. "The idea of asking had me in knots." I frowned. "I've been paying my half of the rent with Jamie still, because I know she can't afford it on her own. The lease ran out, and we've going on a month-to-month basis. That's the part I'm really not sure of. What is she going to do?"

"Have you talked to her about it?" Jeff asked, picking at the peeling label of his bottle.

"Sort of. Not really. It came up while I was trying on dresses, but not since. She's been my best friend and roommate forever. I'll miss her, but I also worry about her by herself." I took a long pull on my beer.

"She's a grown woman, Anna. She can take care of herself. She's not your responsibility. I know her well enough to know she'd kick your ass for thinking that way."

"I know. You're right. But I can't help it. It's not that I don't think she can take care of herself. She's even more hard-headedly independent than I am. She's a tough-ass. She'd never ask for help, or take it if it was offered. It's more emotionally. She's got damage, like me. Bad history. I just worry that she's unhappy and can't get out of the rut she's in."

"Well, look at it like this: What can you do about it, practically speaking, even if you were to keep living with her?"

"Not much, I guess. If she wasn't ready to talk about it, she wouldn't talk about it. She can be prickly like that."

Jeff nodded, pulling the label free and shredding it. "I've gotten glimpses of that. Just talk to her. Tell her you're moving in with me, and what your worries are. Be honest."

"Yeah, you're right. Thanks."

He smiled. "Of course, my love. "

I called Jamie the next day, and we met for coffee.

When we had plunked ourselves down in the big red chairs, I plunged right in. "I'm officially moving in with Jeff. We talked about it last night."

Jamie gave an extravagant sigh and eye-roll. "*Finally*. You've been pussyfooting it around that for weeks. About damn time."

"I thought you'd be, I don't know..."

"Hey, you're my best friend. Living with you has been awesome. But we both knew it was coming. You're barely there as it is, and I'm not there much more myself. I've picked up hours at work, and I've been seeing this new guy, so that's kept me busy—"

I snickered. "I'll bet it has."

"Like you have room to talk, hooker."

"Hey, mine put a ring on it," I said.

She lifted a skeptical eyebrow. "Haven't we already talked about this? I don't *want* a ring. I'm happy being the booty call. No-strings sex all the way, baby."I left the pause hanging. "Are you really?"

Jamie slid the cardboard sleeve of her white paper cup off and on, not meeting my eye. "How about them Tigers, huh?"

"Jay. Seriously."

"Damn it, Anna. I so do *not* want to talk about this. I've already told you how I feel. I'm not marriage material. I'm good in bed, I'm fun to drink with, and I can give a killer blow job. But I can't cook for shit, I don't do laundry, and I hate compromise."

"Jay, listen. I'm not married yet, so I can't say for sure, but unless something magical happens when you say 'I do,' getting married is just a way of publicly binding yourself to one guy. It's not an indentured servitude contract. No guy should expect you to cook and clean and all that shit, unless that's the way you want your relationship. Some people are happy with the more traditional roles. I'm a foodie, so I like cooking. But I hate cleaning, and Jeff's a neat freak. He does most of the cleaning around his house—our house. I just do enough to keep him from getting irritated with me. It's all about finding someone who gets you. Everything else is up to you and him, and what you want your relationship to be."

"So how is with Jeff and you?"

"I don't know. It just is. We never really sat down and laid out the parameters of our relationship. We just...found a rhythm. He gets up at, like, five every morning out of habit from being in the Army. He goes to the gym and showers and all that before I've even gotten out of bed.

I'm a monster in the mornings, and he's discovered that, so he gives me space. I didn't tell him, he just figured it out for himself. I realized it absolutely drives him batshit when I leave clothes on the bathroom floor, so I had to make myself stop doing it. He wouldn't say anything to me—he'd just clean up after me and had this way of making me feel guilty without ever really trying. I don't know how he does it."

"You make it work." She still wasn't looking at me. "That sounds great. I just can't see myself wanting to spend that much time around one person, all the time. Every day, every night. I don't know. The idea sounds nice, someone to count on, who knows me and stuff. But I've got skeletons in my closet, you know? Trusting someone with all that, it's scary."

"Hell, yeah it is," I said. "But it's worth it, if you decide to really trust him."

"How do you know you trust Jeff? I mean, if things don't work out, you'd be up shit creek, you know?"

"He knew about Chase. He let me go, and took me back. He made me work for his trust again after that, and I know, beyond a shadow of a doubt, if I ever messed up with another guy, Jeff would walk. It'd be done. And I know he's the one—as corny as that phrase is—because the idea of losing him makes my blood freeze. I get literally sick to my stomach at the thought of losing Jeff."

"Really?" Jamie was finally looking at me, and I could tell she was really listening, and thinking.

"Yeah, really. He's...part of me. I mean, he's been in my life as a friend and business partner for so long that it just seems like an extension of everything to be together." I gave Jamie a long, serious look. "And honestly, sex is only a part of it. Don't get me wrong, sex is, like, vital. But it's not everything. If he doesn't love you, it ends up being flat and empty."

"Meaningful sex? Gag." Jamie forced a laugh. "Kidding. I—fuck. I *do* want that, Anna. I do. I really, really do. I just don't know how to find it."

I considered my next words carefully. "I think...I think the trick is, love finds you. The harder you look, the more elusive it is. But when you finally give up and learn to be content just being you, *bam*, you're in love with last person you'd thought possible. And you can't fight it. Love is like quicksand—the harder you struggle against it, the deeper you fall in."

"Listen to you, all deep and wise like Confucius or some shit."

"I'm pretty sure Confucius never talked about falling in love."

"Okay, fine. Nicholas Sparks, then."

"Gag."

Jamie made an odd face. "Hey, he's actually a good writer. Don't knock him. *The Notebook* is ridiculously fucking adorable. Makes me all teary and pathetic."

I stared at her like she'd sprouted a second head. "You've read a Nicholas Sparks book?"

"What? I can read."

I laughed. "Well I know *that*, stupid. I just can't picture you curled up on the couch reading a book like that. Did you drink chamomile tea and dab your eyes meaningfully with a folded Kleenex, too?"

"You're being mean."

"I'm sorry, it's just a funny picture. You're not the Nicholas Sparks type, Jay. You're just not. You watch things with subtitles, and explosions and sex."

"What? I can't have a softer side?"

Her averted gaze told me she wasn't playing around anymore. "Of course you can, Jay. Look, I'm sorry. I didn't mean to suggest you *couldn't* be that kind of girl. I just haven't seen that side of you before. Honestly, I'm glad to hear you say that. I worry about you, sometimes."

"You worry about me? Why?"

"Just...you're so self-deprecating all the time. You've always got these boy-toys that never really go anywhere or mean anything, and I worry you think you're not...I don't know, worthy, or capable of anything more."

"What are you, a mind reader?" Her voice was too small, too quiet. "Seriously?"

"Not all the time. There are days where I like who I am and think there's a lot I could offer a guy. But then there's other times where I doubt myself. That's usually when I'm doing the walk of shame at six a.m." She fidgeted with a button on her sweater.

"Jamie, you can't think that way. You're amazing, and beautiful—"

"What are you, my girlfriend? Save the pep talk, hooker. I know what I am. I'll find Mr. Right eventually. That's not your problem. It's mine." She pointed at me, jabbing her forefinger at me. "Your only worry should be getting married to *your* Mr. Right."

"Okay, just promise me one thing?"

"No guarantees, but I'll try."

"Dump your current booty call. Go without sex for a while. No boys. No kissing, no BJs, no hand jobs, nothing."

"God, you make it sound like I'm—"

"I'm just covering all the bases," I said. "I'm for real. No boys. Take some time to learn how to be single, how to just be you. Stop trying to fill the hole and just be you."

"I'm not sure I can do that," she said.

"Yes, you can."

"I haven't been truly single in...longer than I'm willing to admit out loud."

"Exactly. Okay, are you ready for another Confucius saying?"

"Hit me up."

"Empty sex is like Pringles: You can eat million of them, but they never really fill you up. If you want to be truly satisfied, you have to eat real food."

"No more one-night stands, is what you're saying."

"No more two- or three- or four-night stands. No more two-week stands. No more two-month stands. No stands at all. Stop looking. Stop trying. Someday, probably sooner than you think, a guy will come along, and you won't be able to stop thinking about him. It will go beyond wanting his hot body—it'll be about him, the man. And when that happens, wait to have sex until you can't wait anymore. Until you feel like you're going to die if you don't have him right the hell now."

"Anna, I—"

I grabbed her hands and squeezed as hard as I could. "Shut up and promise me, Jamie."

"I don't make promises. They only get broken." She stared at the floor between her feet.

"Promise me."

She met my eyes. "This is really important to you?"

"Yes."

"Fine, then. But only because it's you. I promise."

"I'm serious about this."

"Yes, Anna. I said I promise. I'll go celibate. I promise."

"Okay, then."

"How did you come to this? I mean, it's not like you did it."

"If I hadn't found Jeff, I would have."

She frowned. "He was always right there."

"I know, but...I still found him. Found the real him, the one who'd been hiding from me until I was ready to really see him."

"When did you get so wise all of a sudden?"

I shrugged. "I don't know. I think it started with Chase. Realizing I was beautiful, and worth loving...it did something to me."

"You found your softer side."

I nodded. "Exactly. What I really want is for you to explore yours, and I don't think you will if you've got a boyfriend to distract you."

"I know what you mean. I will. I promise." She made a shoo-ing motion with her hands. "Now, enough about me. Go plan your wedding."

My dress was ready a little more than two weeks later. It had fit almost perfectly in the store, so it hadn't needed much. I picked it up and brought it home.

Home. It hadn't taken much to move me completely into Jeff's house. I didn't have much by way of furniture, and most of what I did have was old castoffs and second- or third-hand items that I left for Jamie to keep or discard when she moved. The rest of my things all fit into the back of Jeff's Yukon in one trip.

When I brought the dress in, Jeff watched me hang it up in the closet, eyeing the white bag as if he could see through the opaque material.

"So it's done, huh?"

"Yeah. It didn't need much alteration, so it didn't take long."

Jeff leaned against the doorframe. "So I've been thinking more about our wedding. Since neither of us have much of anyone to come, except Jamie for you and Darren for me, we should just...be a little crazy."

He reached into his back pocket and pulled out an envelope and handed it to me. I opened it and pulled out two airline tickets to Las Vegas. I stared at the tickets, then back up to Jeff.

"I've got us booked to get married at the Venetian early next week." He grinned. "Jamie and Darren are both on board already. They've got rooms, flights, the works."

"Are you serious?" I examined the brochure. "You want to get married in Vegas?"

"I know it's not the traditional white chapel wedding with the works, but—"

"No, it's perfect. I've been trying to think about planning a real wedding, and my brain just freezes. This is...perfect."

"For real?" He let out a relieved breath. "I booked all this, deposits at the hotel and the tickets and the honeymoon and everything, but I wasn't sure if you'd be on board. I was kinda winging it and hoping."

"Where are we going on our honeymoon?"

He shook his head, grinning. "Nope. Not telling. It's a surprise."

I sidled over to him. "Sure you won't tell me?"

"No way. I've got everything arranged. Trust me."

I kissed his neck. "But I *really* want to know. Is it the Bahamas?"

He tilted his head back as I kissed his throat, unbuttoning his shirt and kissing my way downward. "Not telling. It's not the Bahamas, though."

I knelt in front of him and gazed up. "Sure there's nothing I can do to convince you to tell me?"

He laughed and tangled his fingers in my hair. "Not gonna work. I want it to be a surprise."

I unbuttoned his pants and pulled the zipper down. He was thickening in his underwear, bulging out against the cotton. "How about a hint?"

"You can do whatever you want, but I'm not telling. No hints."

I tugged his pants and boxers down, freeing his erection. "Hmm. Well, I'll have to try and change your mind."

His head thunked back against the doorframe as I licked his length from base to tip. "Anna, you're not gonna get anything out of me."

"Nothing?" I asked, sliding my palms around his girth.

"Well, nothing information-wise. Keeping doing that and you'll get *something* out of me, though."

I took him in my mouth, just the tip at first, my fist around his base and pumping slowly. "Hmmmmmm." I spat him out. "I can be very convincing."

He closed his eyes. "I know. But it won't work this time."

Still sliding my fist at his root, I moved my lips down his shaft. He groaned as I began to bob my head, working him with my hands in the same rhythm. Another groan, and his hips began to rock. When I could tell he was close, I slowed my hands to an imperceptible glide and took my mouth off him.

"God...damn. Not nice. Oh, god. I'm so close."

I laughed, and licked the tip of him in small circles. "How close are you?"

"So close. I'm gonna come...any second."

I stopped moving my hand. "So tell me." I wrapped my lips around the tip of him and sucked gently, not enough to bring him over the edge.

"You're impossible. Fine. We're going to an island."

I started pumping again and lifted my mouth enough to speak. "An island? The Caribbean?"

He hunched over, and I felt his cock throbbing in my hands, his fingers fisting in my hair. "I'm coming, Anna..."

I slowed. "Tell me!"

He huffed a laugh. "No! Not the Caribbean. Somewhere obscure. That's all I'll say. Now please..."

I felt his balls clench, and I nearly didn't get him in my mouth in time. He came as I was lowering my lips around him, and felt his seed hit my throat. I slid my hands on him, working his climax until he sagged against the frame.

He pulled me to my feet and held me against his chest, tilting my face to kiss me. "That was very underhanded of you," he said, a smile in his voice.

"Yes, it was. I told you I can be convincing."

He laughed. "But how much do you really know? An island that's not in the Caribbean. Doesn't really narrow it down much, does it?"

I frowned. "No, guess not." I shrugged. "But I really just wanted to see how much you'd tell me before you came. You can have your secrets. It'll be fun."

"You'd better start packing. Our flight leaves tomorrow afternoon."

"Tomorrow? I thought you said you had us booked for next week? It's only Thursday."

"Yeah, but we're gonna be in Vegas, baby! We can go the casinos and do touristy Vegas stuff, and then get married. An Army buddy of mine got married in Vegas, and he said it was a lot of fun. He gave me some tips."

I laughed. "How many 'Army buddies' do you have? It seems like I hear that phrase every single day, but I've never met any of them."

He chuckled. "Well, I use the phrase pretty loosely. Darren is my closest friend, he was my bunkmate in basic, and we were in the same unit all the way through every tour we did. He was one of the guys who pulled me out of the Humvee. He's the one with the property where I proposed to you. But I do have a lot of other guys that I know who are more acquaintances than real true friends, like people I see a lot or trust. We stay in touch, usually via email, and every few months we all get together on Darren's property and get wasted."

"And Darren is coming to Vegas."

"Yep. He's already got his ticket and a room on the same floor as Jamie."

"Is he single?" I asked.

Jeff frowned thoughtfully. "I think so. Why? You gonna try to hook them up?"

"Well, no. I was wondering if it would happen anyway, more than anything."

Jeff shrugged. "I don't know. It may, it may not. Darren is a good guy, but he's been through a lot, like me. He's hard to get close to."

I laughed. "You just described Jamie."

"Well, maybe they'd be good for each other."

"Maybe. I don't know. I made Jamie promise to stop having sex for a while."

Jeff chuckled. "And she actually agreed?"

"Says she promises."

"Why'd you do that?"

I shrugged. "Something just told me she needs to change her approach to things. She'll never find what she's looking for the way she's going about it."

Jeff kissed my cheekbone. "I agree. But until someone is ready to see things on their own, nothing you do or say, or even make them promise, will make any difference."

"I had to try," I said.

"I get it. You're a good friend." He turned me around and pushed me into the bedroom, smacking my ass. "Now get packing. I want to get to the airport early."

Chapter 6

We spent the first few days being tourists. It was a kind of combined bachelor/bachelorette party, as in Jeff, Darren, Jamie, and I spent much of those first two days in varying states of inebriation. None of us were big on actual gambling, so we spent a lot of the time exploring various attractions, playing slot machines with handfuls of quarters. I stood next to Jeff and cheered for him while he played blackjack, winning a couple thousand dollars before folding.

I could see Jeff being a top-notch poker player, since the entire time he was playing, at one point with almost three thousand dollars on the line, he never cracked a smile or broke a sweat. His face never changed expression. The only sign of stress was a slight narrowing of the eyes and thinning of the lips.

Jamie and Darren seemed to hit it off as friends, but I never saw any evidence of attraction beyond that. Maybe she was merely trying to keep her promise to me. Darren was the kind of guy she usually went for, tall, muscular, rugged, with pale blue eyes and buzzed blond hair. He and Jeff were cut from the same cloth, it seemed. Both were quiet men with slow tempers and deliberate gentility. There was a darkness to Darren that Jeff lacked, however, a sense of his personal demons lurking ever just beneath the surface.

Then, on Monday, the day before our wedding, Jeff told me he had somewhere he was taking me. He refused to say anything whatsoever about where or what, though, no matter how I pleaded with him.

I'm not very good with surprises, it seems.

I dressed in a button-down shirt and a knee-length skirt with bright purple tights, and he took me to dinner just off the Strip, and then had a cab bring us to a small casino. It was a little place, faded, a ways away from the bustle and brilliance of the main Strip.

"What are we doing here?" I asked.

"You'll see in just a second," Jeff said, leading me through the casino floor to the theater area.

Music pounded, muffled. I saw signs for a music festival of some sort, a list of band names, none of which I recognized as I scanned the list. Jeff pulled me away from the sign and through a pair of doors. He already had tickets, and we were led into a concert area bustling with tattooed, pierced, spike-haired, ponytailed rock fans. The band on stage was loud, fast, and hard, rough vocals being growled into a mic by a thickset man with a braided beard down to his chest.

"Jeff, what is this?" I yelled into his ear.

He shook his head, pulling me with a firm grasp on my hand through the crowd until we were near the stage, off to the right and close to the edge of the crowd and only feet away from the VIP entrance.

The band on stage finished their song, played one more, a hard-driving instrumental number. When they exited, a metal song blared through the house speakers as the stage crew reset for the next band. In a surprisingly short time, the lights went down and the house speakers went quiet, and an MC brought a mic and stand out. A spotlight bathed the MC, who waited for the crowd to quiet.

"Our next band was a last-minute addition to the festival," the MC said. "I personally had a chance to see these guys play in New York a few months ago, and I was just blown away by their relentless energy and simply phenomenal talent. Please help me welcome, all the way from Detroit, Six Foot Tall!"

The MC swept an arm at the stage, on cue with the stage lights exploding to life. My heart stopped, my stomach clenched, and my blood went cold.

I turned in place to glare at Jeff. "What the fuck is this?"

"This is your last chance," he answered.

Further conversation was pointless. The drummer kicked a fast beat, and then they were off, a hard, driving number full of angst and anger. I couldn't make out much of the lyrics, but I had a feeling they were about me.

Chase was on fire. He wore nothing but leather pants and heavy black boots and thick, spiked leather cuffs on his forearms, spanning from wrist to elbow. He gripped an old-fashioned square handheld microphone in both hands and bounded from one side of the stage to the other, eyes blazing, thick muscles rippling on his bare, oiled torso.

I couldn't tear my eyes off him. I hadn't expected to ever see Chase again, yet here he was, in Las Vegas, the day before I was set to get married. Between numbers, I forced myself to turn and face Jeff.

"What is the meaning of this, Jeff Cartwright?"

Jeff's eyes were hard and serious. "I found out they were playing here the other day. I didn't plan this. But when I saw it was him, I had to know."

"Know what?"

Jeff pointed at the stage. "I'll never be him. I'll never be like him. I can't do that, I can't look like that. I can't be that. Can't, and won't." He reached into his back pocket and pulled out a VIP backstage pass on a lanyard. "I have to know if this is really what you want. If *I'm* really what you want." "I chose you—" I started, but Jeff held up his hand, pushed the backstage pass into my hands.

"Like I said, last chance to get out. To get that," he said, with a gesture at the stage, and then he turned and made his way through the crowd, away from me.

I watched Jeff disappear, and then turned back to the stage. At that moment Chase was standing in the spotlight as the guitarist plucked a mournful intro melody. His eyes roved the crowd and found me. Shock rippled through him, so potent he almost dropped the mic. His gaze moved down to the VIP pass in my hands, and then I saw hope blossom on his face, quickly shut away.

Why would Jeff do this?

I couldn't figure it out. I thought I'd made my choice. I didn't think I'd ever have to feel Chase's eyes on me, waiting, ever again. But yet, there I was. I felt a presence beside me, smelled Jamie's familiar perfume. She didn't say anything; she only watched as Chase lifted the mic to his mouth, his eyes never leaving me. The look on Chase's face was haunting, full of longing. If I didn't know better, I might think all this had been scripted or arranged. The song was clearly about me, and now, by my sudden presence, sung directly to me.

"This next song is...special. It's brand new, you guys are the first live audience to hear it played. I wrote it during a time of...heartbreak and loss. Just listen, you'll see what I mean." Chase paused, and it was obvious he was struggling with emotion. "I hadn't planned this, but the person...the woman I wrote this song about, is in the audience today. Makes this performance especially personal. Anna, this is for you."

The guitar picked up volume and tempo; Chase closed his eyes, breathed deeply, then his eyes flicked open and focused on me.

He lifted the mic to his mouth and began to sing:

"I found you
floating between the pores of time
I found you
a dream of pale flesh and bright eyes
a fever dream
The moment our eyes met
I saw the gleam of need
and I couldn't resist
I found you
and I pulled you close
I found you
and I fell for you
but you walked away
I found myself

lost in the long dark night
watching the stars burn
watching your image fade
I found myself
dreaming in the dark
loving a ghost
a vision of you
not dead but gone all the same
I found myself
broken by you
blooded by you
I found you
a dream of pale flesh and bright eyes
a fever dream
I found you
nothing but a dream
I found you
nothing but a dream."

The song began as a haunting lullaby, sprightly and sweetly melodic, but always beneath there was a low, thrumming bass line weaving around the guitar chords and lyrics. When the words changed from "I found you" to "I found myself," the tempo picked up and the rhythm guitar started to chug, the bass began to pick up volume and discordant power, and the drums started to sprint, deep pounding bass drums and galloping snares. By the end of the song all was raging, the words no longer sung but screamed, and his eyes, god, his eyes, locked so laser-bright on me, until the crowd near me turned to see who he was singing to, screaming at with such pain and anger rife in his expression. He pointed, kneeling, when he began the last chorus, he pointed at me. The spotlights found me, frozen in place, eyes wide and terrified, heart pounding as loud as the bass drum.

Guitars went silent, drums faded, Chase's powerful voice quieted. All was motionless, a statue-still tableau, Chase's eyes fixed on mine. Jamie was next to me, her fingers gripping my arm in painful vise grip.

"*Do something*," Jamie hissed.

What could I do?

"You bastard." I wasn't sure if I meant Chase or Jeff.

I ripped the lanyard off my neck and shoved it at Jamie. The silence held, so profound that each shuffle of a foot, each clearing of a throat, was loud as a gunshot.

My words, spoken loud to carry to the stage, were audible to everyone. "I made my choice, Chase. I didn't want—I didn't come here on purpose. I'm sorry."

I turned and ran. The crowd parted for me. The double doors leading out to the casino floor stood in front of me, and I pushed them open.

Chase's voice froze me, raw and deep, amplified by the mammoth sound system. "Are you happy?"

I turned slowly and let the doors thump closed behind me. "What?"

"I asked if you're happy with him."

"Yes." I nodded, so that if he couldn't hear me clearly, he'd know my answer.

A charged pause sparked between us, even separated by hundreds of feet and hundreds of people. His eyes, his body, his presence, I couldn't help my physical response to him. I still wanted him, still desired him. My muscles trembled in memory of what he could do to me, of being tied up to his mercy. I pushed the traitorous image away. I didn't want that anymore. Not with him. I focused on Jeff's face, his hands, his body, his love. I felt the doors open, a brief cold breeze and a sense of openness behind me, and then Jeff's hard body brushed against my back. I leaned into him.

"Then that's all that matters," Chase said. His gaze flicked up to Jeff, and his next words were for him. "Take care of her."

I felt Jeff nod, once, curt.

Another pause, during which Chase turned away and addressed the band. There were nods all around, and then the drummer snapped his drum sticks together on a fast four-count. On the fourth clack of the sticks, the entire band burst into synchronized sound, the bass, rhythm guitar, and drums all matching with a driving heavy metal beat. Chase stood facing away from the crowd, mic held loosely by his side, bent at the waist and headbanging to the rhythm. I felt Jeff pulling me away, and I turned into him.

The song was brutal, hard-charging and pulsating with angst. I heard the opening lines growled with primal rage: *"How can I escape your eyes? I can't, I can't...How can I escape your lies? I can't, I can't—"*

Then the doors slid closed and the sound was muffled. I fell against Jeff's chest, sobbing.

"Why? Why did you do that to me?" I stepped back and slammed my fists into his broad chest. "I didn't *fucking* need that!"

"I'm sorry. But when I found out he was playing in Vegas, I just—"

"Had to test me?"

Jeff blew a long breath between pursed lips. "Yes, honestly. I also figured if he was here, and you were here, knowing your luck you'd run into him at the worst possible moment. Like, you'd be about to say 'I do' and he'd walk into the Venetian at that exact moment."

I tried to fight the laughter bubbling up at the image. "Yeah, that's exactly what would have happened."

"I'm sorry, Anna. I didn't mean to blindside you, but honestly, I had to know. I'm not Chase. I'm not some exciting, sexy rockstar. I like a quiet life."

"Why are you so hung up on this?" I asked him. "If I wanted someone like him, I would have chosen *him*. I chose *you*. I want *you*. Part of the reason I love you so much is that you're confident in who you are without being cocky. Why is it whenever he's around, or he comes up, you get all insecure?"

Jeff's eyes hardened. "Because you chose him over me once before, remember? Hard not to be insecure about that when I know you're capable of it."

My heart panged at the pain written in the lines of his face. "I guess I deserved that."

"Guess so." He looked away, and when he turned back to me, his eyes were softer. "Listen, Anna. I'm sorry. So sorry. I know that was really unfair of me to do. It wasn't about testing you—I mean, I guess it was, but...I can't lose you again. I can't. I saw the flyer for this music festival and I saw his band name on it, and I just...I froze."

I opened my mouth to say something, I wasn't even sure what, but he held up his hand to silence me.

"When you left me to go to New York, I knew—" His voice broke with a welter of potent emotion. "I knew what you were going for. You thought you might love him. Maybe you didn't think it in so many words, but I knew. I saw it. You thought you might love him more than you loved me. I...letting you go was the single hardest thing I've ever done. I've buried buddies, Anna. I've buried best friends. But no lie, letting you go to him...that ripped me to shreds. You'll never know how hard that was—at least I hope you won't. I *cannot* go through that again. I watched you walk away, picking *him* over *me*. You went to New York and spent a week *fucking him*, when you'd just been with me. You know how hard that was for me? It was the longest week of my life. And then you came back, I knew you were back, I drove by your apartment and you were there, I saw you. I almost went up to the door, to talk to you, to—I don't know. Yell at you, or beg you to come to me. But I didn't. I waited. And you came back to me, wanting me because he'd hurt you. I wanted to kill him. No lie. But...you needed me. You need me."

Crowds flowed around us, oblivious, and music pounded on the other side of the door, Chase's band. Jeff paused, gathering himself.

"I need you, Anna. But if you want him, if there's any doubt in your mind that you might still care about him, then go. He's right through those doors, and he's still in love with you. He'll take you back. I had to know, Anna. I *had to.* I can't live through you picking him again. So if that's what you're gonna do, do it now." He held my face in his hands. "The last thing I ever wanted to do was cause you any more pain, and I'm *so* sorry. Forgive me for putting you through that. But I—I had to know."

I turned away from him to stare at the door, as if I could see Chase through it. I searched myself, scoured my heart and soul with brutal honesty; I owed Jeff that much.

I turned back to Jeff and let him see all of me in my eyes. "I choose you, Jeff. There's no doubt in my mind, no question. None. You are my heart and soul. He's my past. I'll never choose anyone but you for as long as I live. I wouldn't have agreed to marry you if that wasn't true." I let out a long breath. "Now, can we go? Or do you have any more *tests* for me?"

"Guess I deserved that," Jeff said.

"Guess so."

He took my face in his hands and kissed me. I resisted, turned away from his kiss for the one and only time in our romantic relationship. I was still angry at him for bludgeoning me with Chase.

"No." I ripped free from his arms. "I'm mad at you."

I walked out of the casino and hailed a cab, Jeff trailing behind me. I climbed into the cab and gave the driver our hotel name. Jeff sat in silence beside me, picking at his fingernails.

My lips tingled from the force of Jeff's kiss. It had been furious, demanding kiss, claiming me as his. My anger was fading, but I refused to give in to Jeff just yet. I could tell he felt bad, but I wasn't ready to let him off the hook yet. I hadn't deserved to be blindsided like that, not with Chase, not when I'd already endured the agony of having to choose. I didn't love Chase, but he hadn't deserved that shock, either, especially not during a public performance. The pain in his eyes had nearly broken my heart all over again.

I knew why Jeff had done it, though, and I didn't blame him, not now that my anger was receding. I *had* chosen Chase over Jeff once upon a time, and even though a deep, dark, secret place inside me held on to the memories of my time with Chase, I did regret having left Jeff. I regretted having hurt him, having broken his trust in me.

I couldn't change that, but I could prove to Jeff I only wanted him. I decided to prove it the only way I knew how.

We got back to our hotel room, and I waited behind Jeff while he slid the card into the lock reader. Seconds seemed to stretch out, the light turning green with a soft *click*, the door sliding open on oiled hinges, my heart thudding in my chest as if we were going into the room to make love for the first time, rather than the thousandth time. My hands shook, a cold sweat broke out on the small of my back, and a burning flush of desire flamed my cheeks, turned my panties damp.

A few short steps through, and then the door latched closed behind me. Jeff released my hand and kept walking, settling on the edge of the bed and leaning his elbows on his knees and his face in his hands.

I pressed my back to the door, watching him. He remained there, breathing, upset. I smiled, but he didn't see it. I plucked open a button of my shirt, and then another, and then the shirt was open and I dropped it on the floor at my feet. He didn't hear the rustle of fabric or the soft *plop* of cotton hitting the floor. I slid my feet out of my flats, unrolled my knee-high purple stockings, slowly unzipped the side of my skirt. He heard the zipper then. His eyes narrowed in confusion, and he straightened on the bed.

My bra joined the pile of clothing on the floor, followed by my panties, and then I was naked, too-cold hotel room air pebbling my skin and making my nipples harden. I swayed toward Jeff, and he crawled backward on to the bed. He sat up to take me in his hands, but I pushed him down with a hand on his chest. I peeled his shirt over his head, straddling his khaki-clad hips, leaning forward to draw the T-shirt off, my breasts swaying over his face. He nipped a breast with sharp, gentle teeth, but I refused to gasp. I slid down his body, unbuttoned his pants, and pulled them off.

His cock was rigid, lying flat against his belly, rising and falling with his short, panting breaths. I teased him with my fingers, touching his purple-veined length with my fingertips, tracing the groove beneath the head with my tongue. I wrapped both palms around his cock and took his tight sack in my mouth, gently sucking it between my lips, one side and then the other. He gasped, arched his back, groaned my name as I caressed his shaft and suckled his balls.

I waited until he was moments from coming into my hands, and then I released him and crawled up his body, rising up on my knees above him, palms braced flat on the wall, my slit poised above his mouth.

"Make me come, Jeff," I said, my voice hoarse, low and rough.

"Yes, my love."

He suited action to words and slid his palms up my thighs to the cleft of my pussy, slipping a single long middle finger into my wet folds, using his other hand to pull me down to his mouth. His tongue found my clit and swiped slow circles around it, each touch of his tongue a line of fire, burning pleasure into my heat-slick blossom.

I forced myself to stay still as his finger moved within me and his tongue speared against my clit. I arched my back and allowed myself a single soft whimper as waves of ecstasy rose through me. A hand cupped my breast, testing its weight, and then pinched my nipple at the same time as his tongue punched against my aching, sensitive nub.

He pulled his finger out, added his index finger, and slipped them back in, but this time his pinky finger was extended, and it bumped gently and insistently against the rosebud knot of muscle.

He paused, asking silent permission.

"Do it," I said.

His smallest finger kneaded the muscle, relaxing it, and then his fingers were gone briefly, replaced by wet warmth slicking the tighter entrance. He slipped his pinky into me at the same time that his tongue found my clit and his first and middle fingers found my pussy, and then I was writhing helplessly above him, explosions rocking through me, drilling sensation to the wildest heights of furious orgasm, wringing me into a gasping, begging puddle on top of him, his fingers gone, my ass on his chest, my body curled over and sliding downward, downward, pierced slowly and subtly by his thick, hot shaft. No chance of recovery for me, only pleasure so potent it became pain, too much to bear, but instead of begging him to stop, I heard my voice whispering ragged pleas in his ear:

"Jeff, my love, please don't stop, don't stop..." even though I couldn't take any more of him, couldn't come any harder without ripping in half, without bursting into helpless sobs.

He didn't relent, but drove into me with his characteristic slow, powerful strokes, pushing deeper and deeper.

I rolled off him without warning, as he was about to come. I heard his teeth grinding as he struggled to hold it back, and then he lifted up on an elbow and watched me settle on my knees and forearms, presenting myself to him, my face turned to the side, a seductive smile on my lips inviting him wordlessly.

Like a lion he prowled on his hands and knees behind me, his cock slipping between the globes of my ass. His nails raked painfully, sweetly down my back, gripped my hips, and then, with a single tilt of his pelvis, he was inside my pussy and driving, god, so deep. I bit the blanket to stifle a scream, climaxing a third time on the instant of penetration.

It didn't take him long to find his release. He thrust, thrust, thrust, and then a deep, rumbling growl announced his climax. He drove into me, hard, bowling me forward, his hands pulling me back, and then again, a primal plunge of his cock, fingers digging into my hipbones and clawing me back into him.

Even blanket-muffled, my scream of delight was loud in the still, cold air. His roar of release was louder.

We lay side by side, and I nuzzled my head onto his shoulder.

"I love *you*, Jeff. Only you. Forever." I tangled my fingers with his, my left hand in his right, dim light glinting dully off the facets of my engagement ring.

"Damn right, only me forever," he said, a smile in his voice.

"Cocky bastard," I laughed.

"It's why you love me."

"One of the many reasons."

He tilted my chin up with an index finger and kissed me, long and slow and drowning with passion. "I love you, Anna Devine," he said when our lips parted.

"After tomorrow I'll be Anna Cartwright," I pointed out.

"I like the sound of that."

"Me too." We drowsed in the dreaming dark, until a thought struck me. "You know, we never wrote our vows."

"Huh. You're right," Jeff mused. After a moment, he said, "Well, I've got an idea for mine. Just write yours from the heart. Doesn't have to be complicated. Tell me you'll love me forever and always, no matter what."

"I can do that."

"I know you can." He pulled me closer. "Now go to sleep. We've got a busy day tomorrow."

Chapter 7

I woke to my nose being tickled. I swatted at the offending sensation, encountering small, soft hands. I forced my eyes open to see Jamie sitting next to me on the bed, cross-legged, dressed in a tiny skirt and tight T-shirt. She had a tendril of her copper hair in her fingers and was brushing my nose with it.

"Wake up, sleepy-head," she said in a sing-song voice.

"Unh-uh. Go away." I slapped at her half-heartedly.

I knew her better than to think she'd leave me alone. She scrambled off the bed and pulled the covers off me. I curled in a ball, moaning in protest as the cold air hit my naked body.

"God, woman, you stink of sex. Get up and take a shower."

I rolled up to a sitting position and rubbed my eyes. "Where's Jeff?"

She waved her hand. "Oh, off with Darren. Picking up his tux and getting ready. Whatever guys do before weddings."

"What are we doing?" I caught the robe Jamie handed me and wrapped it around me.

"First, coffee. Second, a shower. Third, breakfast." She brought me a cup of Caribou coffee, because she knows I hate Starbucks' over-roasted coffee, even though I love their espresso drinks.

I sipped slowly as I stood up and went to the window to peer out the curtain. It was another glorious Las Vegas day.

I'm getting married today. It didn't seem real. Was it really going to happen? An actual wedding? Jeff had sprung this whole thing on me, and I had no idea what was going on. Panic hit me, and I focused on breathing through the hammering of my heart, sipping my coffee.

Jamie slid her arm around my waist and rested her head on my shoulder. "Hey, it's going to be great, you know. I can feel you panicking. Don't."

"Easy for you to say. I have no idea what's going on. Did he actually plan this thing, or is he just winging it?"

Jamie laughed. "He has this thing planned down to every little detail. You'll be shocked. I'm, like, mega-impressed. If I believed in romance, or weddings, I'd say this was the most romantic wedding ever." She sighed. "I believe in *this* wedding. I'm not going to ruin any of the surprises, but you should relax, because he's got it all covered. He loves you.""I know he does. I should know better than to think Jeff would leave this to the last minute, because he never leaves *anything* to the last minute. But...it's a Vegas wedding. I'm worried it's going to be something from a bad romantic comedy. Like, the minister will be this fat old Elvis impersonator, and we'll be driven away in a pink Cadillac with tin cans hanging off the back and it'll be the most embarrassing day of my life."

"You're ridiculous. Do you really think Jeff is that stupid or tasteless?"

I shook my head. "No, but that's what my fears are telling me will happen."

Jamie rolled her eyes. "Well, that's not what's happening, so quit freaking yourself out. I told you, he's *got* this."

I finished my coffee, and Jamie followed me into the bathroom, sitting on the closed toilet while I showered.

"You know, when I first heard your wedding was in Vegas, I kinda had similar expectations," Jamie said. "Some tiny little chapel way off the Strip, bad piano music, and yes, an Elvis impersonator for the minister. But Jeff showed me some of what he had planned, and I'm telling you, it's going to be amazing. You'll love it."

"What happens after breakfast? Which is what, bagels and cream cheese?"

"Breakfast is whatever you want. Order in, go out, whatever. We have some time. After that, we have part one of wedding day surprises. So get your ass moving."

"I thought you said we had time."

"Yeah, but not all day. 'Sides, I'm hungry."

Breakfast was omelets and toast at a nearby diner, and then Jamie hailed a cab and gave the driver a slip of paper with our destination written on it. We ended up at a spa a few minutes' drive away from the main downtown area.

"Come on, " Jamie said, climbing out. "This is part one. The full treatment at a day spa."

"Serious?"

Jamie grinned. "You and me, baby. Get ready for some serious pampering."

My throat closed up, and my eyes burned. I blinked away tears and followed Jamie inside. Jeff really had planned everything out, and the fact that he'd included Jamie in the day spa treatment made me choke up even worse.

I made it through the manicure before the question that had been tickling the back of my mind popped out. "So, Jay. What happened after I left the concert?"

Her long hesitation piqued my curiosity, and my worry.

"Um. Nothing?"

"Jay."

"Fine. I went backstage and hung out with the band. We partied. Darren showed up at some point, and things got crazy." She pretended not to notice my suspicious glare.

I picked up a cotton ball from the counter nearby and threw it at her. "Jamie. Talk. You're not telling me something."

"Ugh. Why does it matter?"

"Because you'd tell me if it didn't matter," I said.

"Hooker," she muttered. "Fine. Like I said, we partied. There were lots of people, girls were all over the guys from the band. Chase was all angsty and broody. Darren and I sort of hit it off, stuck together since we knew each other better than anyone else that was there. It was all groupies except for Darren and me."

"Darren is totally your type. Jeff says he's single."

"Yeah, but remember that promise you made me make?"

I lifted an eyebrow at her. "Break it already?"

"No." When my eyebrow lifted even higher, she protested loudly, "I didn't! I promise."

"Then what?"

"Nothing happened. I just...that song Chase sang to you? That whole thing was *hot*. I know he was hurt and you were hurt and it was all hurty. But...god, I can see why you were hung up on him. He's—"

"Fucking amazing. I know. Please don't remind me. I'm getting married today, remember? To Jeff. Chase is old news. History. He means nothing to me anymore."

I watched Jamie as she fidgeted in her seat.

"I know. I just feel bad for him, is all. He's stuck on you."

"This is a weird conversation," I said. "By way of changing the topic...so you and Darren?"

She shook her head slowly. "No, I don't think so. The vow of celibacy thing has its merits, I have to admit. Once upon a time, I would have fucked that boy silly. I still want to. But our conversation about empty sex keeps running through my head, and I just can't...I don't know. Darren is nice. He's hot, he's totally my type, you're right about that. But I can't see anything working with him long term. I don't know why. It just wouldn't work. I think he's...what is it? He's dark. I've done the dark and angry guy long enough. If I'm going to break this vow of celibacy, I want it to be with someone...different from what I usually go for. Someone better. Someone who could give me what you have with Jeff." She paused for a long moment. "I'm jealous, you know. Of you and Jeff. I've never told you that, but I'm finally able to admit it. I'm green with envy. You're so happy, and he's doing all this for you..."

"You'll find it, Jay. You will."

She was silent then, and I could sense there was something else she wasn't saying, but the prickles were out, and I didn't push it.

After the pedicures and facials and waxing, Jamie seemed to have pushed away whatever was eating at her. During the massage, Jamie blurted a question that floored me.

"Are you and Jeff going to have kids?"

"What?" I saw double for a second. "Kids? God, Jamie. I haven't even gotten married yet. I don't know. It's never come up."

"Well, can you see yourself with a kid?"

I thought about it. "Um. I guess? It's never crossed my mind. I honestly don't know."

"If you happened to get pregnant, like whoops. How would you feel?"

"God, Jamie, what's with the cracked-out questions? Are you pregnant or something?"

"Me? Hell, no!"

"Then what is this?" I groaned as the masseuse hit a knot and bore down on it.

"I don't know. You getting married and this whole vow of celibacy thing has really messed with my head."

I tried to picture myself as a mother and failed completely. "I don't know, Jamie. I don't know a damn thing about kids. I have no nieces or nephews, no friends with kids. If I got pregnant, I would be scared, I think. But...excited, too, probably, once I got over the whole shitting-myself-with-terror part. Do I really have to think about this? I'm panicking enough as it is without you jinxing me with a sudden pregnancy or something."

"Sorry, sorry. I don't know what's gotten into me. My brains been going a mile a minute for days now."

I laughed. "Maybe the constant sex was dulling your brain. Now that you're not in a constant state of sexual arousal, maybe you'll think more clearly."

Jamie snorted. "You couldn't be more wrong, girlfriend. I'm hornier than ever! Not having had sex in so long—"

"It's been less than a week."

She continued as if I hadn't interrupted. "—has turned me into a raging fucking horndog. I'm honestly worried I'll end up jump the first thing with a cock at some point." She shuddered. "I haven't even gotten myself off, Anna. It's awful. I can't stop thinking about sex. I feel like a guy. I should scratch my vag every time I think about sex and rename myself James. It's that bad. Like, all the time."

"Right now?"

"God, yes. Like, even talking to you, I'm thinking I could just roll over and whip this towel off and me and masseuse boy here can go at it on the massage table."

The masseuse, Todd, a toned young blond man with a carefully sculpted goatee, laughed. "Sorry, sweetheart. Wrong team. And we're not that kind of establishment anyway."

"Damn it," she laughed. "Just as well, I guess. It wouldn't be good to break my vow this quick."

Todd made an odd face. "You really took a vow of celibacy? Like no sex? At *all*?"

Jamie sighed theatrically. "Yes. No sex. At all. It's all her fault. She thinks it'll help me find the man of my dreams or some shit."

He bobbled his head back and forth. "Hmmm. Interesting idea. Is it working?"

"Not so far. But like she said, it's only been a week. If it works, I have a feeling it'll take longer than a week."

"Well, good luck," he said. "I can't imagine what that must be like. I'm already boy-crazy as it is. If I had to go a week without so much as a blow job I think I'd actually die."

Jamie giggled. "Yeah. Exactly how I feel."

"But you—" He cut himself off with a laugh, slapping her shoulder playfully. "Oh. You dirty little slut!"

"Thus the vow of celibacy," Jamie said. Then she craned her neck to look at the masseuse. "Are you allowed to call your clients names?"

He quirked an eyebrow. "You're buck-ass naked, honey. I can say whatever I want."

"Oh. Well." Jamie frowned. "I never thought about it that way."

"Most people don't," he said.

"Honestly, though," Jamie said, "it really does change the way you think, I'm discovering. Especially if you're boy-crazy like me. I've always had someone around. I got to rely on them for my self-esteem, in a way. Like, they make me feel sexy, and they want me, so it gives me a power over them. But that's different than feeling it from inside myself, you know? Not looking at every hot guy and wondering how fast I can get his pants off is actually kind of liberating."

"Really?" Todd asked.

"No kidding. If I can make this stick for a while, it might be a really good thing."

"Hmmm," Todd said. "I think my boyfriend is about to break up with me. Maybe I'll give it a shot. I think I'll set a goal, like two weeks at first, and see where it goes from there."

"I should get a medal if I make it two weeks," Jamie said.

I looked at her. She was acting nonchalant, but something in her voice had me thinking she had someone in mind who was threatening her vow. She met my eyes, and something passed between us, a kind of unspoken agreement. I wouldn't ask, and when she was ready, she'd tell me.

The next surprise of the day was an appointment at a high-end salon, where my hair and makeup were done with artistic care. Jamie was quiet for much of it, but with enough judicious use of outright mockery, I got her back into sassy form. After my hair and makeup were done, we went back to the hotel to finally get me into my dress.

"Jamie, you have to help me write my vows."

She looked at me as if I'd grown horns. "Two things. One: you haven't written them yet? And two: me? Are you crazy?"

I snorted. "No, I haven't. I've been sort of busy, if you hadn't noticed. But fine, I'll write them myself. Just give me some time alone before we put me in my dress."

"I think it's time for another cup of coffee. I'll be back later." She left the room with an airy wave.

I stared at the pad of hotel stationery, with absolutely no clue what to write. And then Jeff's advice floated into my mind: *Just write them from the heart. Tell him I love him forever and always.*

My pen scratched along the paper, the words flowing easily once I got started. The paper had a few wet blotches by the time I was done.

Jamie came back with a cup of coffee for me, and we drank together in peaceful silence. I let Jamie read my vows.

She handed the paper back with a sniff. "Damn it, girl. You've made me cry. We don't cry. And we just had our makeup done."

I handed her a Kleenex. "We do now."

"When did that happen?"

I shrugged. "I don't know. But I'm learning to be okay with it. Crying doesn't have to be a sign of weakness. It just means we're human. We're women, and we have emotions."

"Gah. Whatever." She rubbed at her eyes in irritation. "I still hate crying, even if you *are* right. Now, get your sexy ass up, and let's put on a wedding dress."

I focused on breathing. Breathe in, clutch the bouquet of roses in trembling fingers; breathe out, one slow step forward. Wide double doors were pulled open from within the chapel, revealing a dozen dark wood pews, each pew garlanded at the aisle-end with a bow of white silk and a single pink rose. The aisle itself was covered in pale pink rose petals.

My heart was beating so hard I thought the entire chapel could hear it pounding like a drum. When the doors opened, an older woman with silver hair began Mendelssohn's "Wedding March" on a grand piano. I was shaking so bad the roses trembled in my hands. My knees were weak, my throat thick and burning.

A male voice cleared his throat from beside me, a deliberate *ahem* to catch my attention. I turned and nearly fainted. Jared stood next to me in his full dress uniform. He looked so different, so much older. I hadn't seen him in so long.... He had new lines around his eyes, a leaner, rangier build. His eyes were like mine, hazel and expressive, and his hair was the color mine would be, chocolate brown. He gave me a bolstering smile and held his arm out for me, and I had to choke back a sob.

"Jared? When did you get here? And how?" I whispered, looking up at him.

He bumped me with his shoulder. "Jeff knew someone who got me some emergency leave," he whispered back. "Pulled some strings, called me, and here I am. Just got in an hour ago. Your boy up there is a keeper, sis."

"Yeah," I said. "That's why I'm in this dress."

He laughed. "Yeah. Now quit talking to me and look at your husband," Jared said. "I think he's trying to catch your eyes."

I'd been avoiding looking at Jeff because I was worried it would make me burst into hysterics. I was near to hyperventilating as it was, and with Jared's unexpected presence to walk me down the aisle, I was even closer to the edge of breakdown. I tore my gaze away from my brother and met Jeff's eyes. A single tear dripped down my cheek, and I wiped it away.

He was resplendent in a traditional tuxedo, his eyes wavering with emotion as he watched me. As if sensing my nerves, he smiled at me and mouthed *I love you*. My nerves receded, my tears evaporated, and I could move again. I'd been rooted to the spot at the doors, Jamie behind me holding my train. Now, with his eyes on me, loving me, I was able to take the first step forward.

The aisle wasn't all that long, but the measured walk from the doors to *him* seemed to take an eternity. With each step, I realized more fully how ready I was for this. I didn't think I would be, even when I agreed to marry him. I worried, all the way up until the moment I saw him at the altar, that I wouldn't be ready. But I was.

I'm ready. I want to do this.

With every step closer to the man I loved, I realized that this was exactly what I wanted, and you couldn't have dragged me away from the altar with a thousand wild horses.

At long last I reached him. A step up, a second, and then his hands were in mine, holding me, steadying me. His eyes burned into mine, the love in his gaze bringing tears of happiness to my eyes. I didn't wipe them away.

"Dearly beloved," the minister began, "we are gathered here today to celebrate the blessed union of this man and this woman…"

It really sank in then, as the minister began his brief sermon:

I'm getting married.

There was no "dearly beloved" besides Darren, Jamie, and Jared. But then I peeked out at the chapel and saw a man a few years older than Jeff who I took to be his brother sitting next to an older woman with graying hair and eyes dark brown like Jeff's.

I took a deep, wavering breath to steady myself, clutching Jeff's hands for dear life. I tuned in to the minister's words of advice regarding marriage, trite platitudes that suddenly took on new meaning as I contemplated the reality of being married to Jeff. Then came the vows. The minister turned to me first, and Jamie reached up to hand me my sheet of paper.

I needed several breaths to calm myself enough to speak. "Jeff, I wish I could explain to you how much you mean to me. I wish I had words to say how deeply entwined you are into the woman I've become. You've swept me off my feet and turned my life into a fairytale, because you are my happily ever after. I don't care what's happened in the past, and I'm not worried about what will happen in the future. All I need is you with me, every day. Most wedding vows have promises like 'in sickness and in health, for richer or for poorer.' I promise you those things. Of course I do. Money, health, those things are a part of life. What I promise you is forever. I promise you all of me. I promise you every last shred of myself, day in, day out, no matter what. Even when you're being a stupid jerk." I laughed, half-sobbing, and took a moment to compose myself.

"I'm never a stupid jerk," Jeff said.

I wiped my cheeks. "Yes, you are. Now shut up and let me say my vows. I'm not done." I scanned the paper and found my spot, near the end. "I promise to love you, even when I don't feel like it. I promise to take care of you. I promise to listen to you, because you're usually right. I promise, above everything, to be faithful to you, and *only you*, for as long as we both live. I love you, Jeff Cartwright."

The minister nodded and turned to Jeff. "And your vows?"

Jeff grinned. "Mine are a bit...different. Darren?"

Darren reached into his suit coat pocket and pulled out a wireless microphone, handed it to Jeff. Music began to play from the PA system, soft country strains. I recognized the song: "Wanted" by Hunter Hayes.

Jeff lifted the mic to his lips, and for the second time in two days, a man sang to me. This time was different. If I hadn't already known it, Jeff singing a sweet country song to me as his vows proved I'd made the right choice. I didn't feel on the spot, or pressured, or frightened. This was a soft serenade, a dedication set to music.

His arm went around my waist, my hand joined his on the mic and I sang the harmony, our bodies swaying to the rhythm, our eyes locked on each other. Everything faded except the music, except Jeff's deep, strong voice weaving around mine, the words of the song with their soul-deep, so-perfect meaning.

I didn't need the words of the song to hear Jeff's promises to me. They were written in his eyes. They were proven in the way he loved me, in the fact of this wedding. I would be wanted, every day. I would be loved, every moment.

The song ended, but Jeff stood holding me, one arm around my waist, one hand on the mic. "I know you heard what I was saying with that song," Jeff said, "but it's just not enough. Forever isn't enough. No words are enough. But yeah. I want to make you feel wanted every minute of your life. I want to wrap you up and protect you. I want you to know how completely I cherish you, I want you to know it when you wake up, and when you fall asleep. I want to make the things that hurt you not hurt so bad. I want my love to fill you when you're empty, and make you overflow when you're full. I want every moment of our life together to be your fairytale, your happily ever after. I'm no knight in shining armor, no prince charming, but I'll sure as hell try, every single day."

He paused, thinking. "Remember what I said to you, not too long ago?"

Somehow I did know exactly what he was going to say, and I said it with him. "The time I've spent with you is better than anything I've ever known."

He laughed, brushing my face with his rough palm. "Yeah, of course you remember. Well, that'll be true for always, every day until the day we die. I love you, Anna."

The minister waited until he was sure we were both done speaking. "Anna, repeat after me."

"I, Anna, take you, Jeff..."

I repeated the words, and my voice broke on "I do." I'd held it together up till then, but at those two words, I fell apart. Jeff's thumb swept my tears away, and his palm cupped my cheeks as he repeated the same words. His voice went low and rough at the "I do," his hand around the mic, still held between us, trembling.

"I now pronounce you man and wife. You may kiss the bride."

My arms went around him, my fingers curling in the hair at the base of his neck, our lips meeting, our bodies crushing together. I lost myself in that kiss, drowned in the revelry of belonging. He was mine, and I was his.

Cheering erupted from the entrance to the chapel, too many voices raised and hands clapping to be just the three people in attendance.

We broke the kiss and turned to look: a crowd had gathered at the doors to the chapel, drawn from the hotel by the sound of our singing, our amplified vows. We laughed together, and I wiped my eyes on the shoulder of Jeff's tuxedo coat.

My throat caught again as I scanned the chapel. I saw Darren, Jamie, and Jared, and there at the back, nearly hidden in the crowd of onlookers, was my mother. I looked to Jeff.

He shrugged, shaking his head. "I didn't know for sure if she'd be here. I called and invited her, but...I wasn't sure she'd come. I hope it's okay."

"I'm glad she's here." I stared up into his rich brown eyes. "Thank you for this. All of this. Thank you, so much."

He kissed me lightly. "I wanted to give you a wedding you'd remember. I know this wasn't a traditional thing, but—"

I shut him up with a kiss. "This was perfect. Absolutely perfect. It's exactly what I wanted. I can't believe you got Jared here to give me away!"

He turned with me, and we moved down the aisle toward the doors. "It was tricky, but I knew a guy who has an uncle in the Corps. You needed someone to give you away."

We made it to the end of the aisle. I felt Jamie fiddling with my train behind me, but I only had eyes for Mom. Suddenly I couldn't remember why I hadn't seen in her in so long; I knew I'd remember as soon as we tried to have a real conversation, but in that moment it didn't matter. She'd shown up for my wedding, and to the part of me that was still a little girl wanting her mother's approval, it was enough.

"Hi, Mom."

"Hi, sweetheart," she said, kissing me on both cheeks, European-style. "I'd say thank you for inviting me, but you seem surprised to see me."

"Well, it's a bit of a surprise wedding. I'm glad you're here, though."

Mom laughed. "What's a surprise wedding? You didn't plan this?"

I shrugged. "Not really. I mean, I knew I was getting married, but Jeff surprised me with pretty much everything else."

"Wow. Quite a surprise, then," she said, with a wry arch of her eyebrow.

Jeff seemed to sense my discomfort with the direction the conversation was taking. "I'm glad you could make it, Laura. I know it means a lot to Anna for you to be here. We'll see you at the reception. Jamie will make sure you know where you're going."

He pulled me into a walk, and I squeezed his arm gratefully.

When we were out of earshot, I leaned up to whisper into his ear. "See what I mean?"

He chuckled. "Yeah, subtle digs. I can see how that would wear on a person."

I rolled my eyes. "Oh, you have no idea. She was just warming up. And she's more forthright than Ed. Eventually she'll just come out and say what she's thinking. Ed won't. He'll just keep digging, keep poking." I craned my head to search the crowd. "I don't see Ed, speaking of whom."

"Guess he couldn't make it."

"Guess not," I said. "Fine with me. Now, where's the reception?"

"Oh, I reserved a private room downstairs. Cake, catering, that kinda stuff. Nothing fancy. Just an excuse to eat and get tipsy before we go on our honeymoon."

"Speaking of our honeymoon—"

"Nope. Still not telling." He glanced at me and grinned. "You're more than welcome to try and...convince me again, though."

I laughed. "Hmmm. Not a bad idea. Although I have something a bit more...involved in mind. And I'm not sure I can get on my knees in this dress anyway."

We were moving through the crowd of onlookers, who were enthusiastically calling out encouragement and congratulations. Apparently someone heard my comment about not being able to get on my knees, and I heard several bawdy suggestions to give it a try. Jeff and I laughed them off and made our way to the private room where the reception would be held.

It was one of the smaller conference rooms of the hotel, but something told me even a relatively small room like this wouldn't be cheap to rent out, even for an hour or two.

"Jeff, how'd you afford all this?" I asked.

He winked at me. "A man's gotta have his secrets, doesn't he?"

"Not from his wife, he doesn't."

He laughed. "I had a bit of money saved. I put it to good use. And that's all you'll get out of me."

"But all of this had to have cost—"

He spun me to face him. "It doesn't matter. It was worth it. You're worth it. It's just money."

"But, Jeff—"

He kissed me silent. "Honey. Let's not have this conversation now. Just relax and let me take care of you. Please?"

I relented with a sigh. "Fine. But only because you look so hot in your tux."

He ran his hands over my hips, pulled me flush against him. "You know, Jamie was right about the dress. I did almost faint when I saw you. All the blood rushed south."

I ground my hips against his, feeling the evidence of his arousal. "Wish we could sneak away somewhere and...take care of your...problem down there."

He chuckled. "I'm not sure that's physically possible in a wedding dress. All that tulle seems like it'd get in the way."

I laughed. "I don't think it's tulle, actually. But you're probably right. We'll just have to wait."

It was a long wait. The food was good, the drinks were plentiful, and the music loud. We were only half a dozen people, but we had fun. Jeff had even arranged for a small cake, two tiers, red velvet with thick buttercream frosting.

After a couple of hours, Jamie announced, in her brash style, that the party was over and we were leaving for the airport. I hugged Mom, said goodbye, and promised to call her when we got back. I spent the longest goodbye with Jared.

"I wish we had more time together," I said, hugging him.

He squeezed me tight, spoke into my hair. "I know. Me, too. But we'll see each other again soon. I've got a longer leave coming up over the holidays. I'll spend it with you and Jeff."

Jamie came next. "Have fun, Anna. Make sure you get up off your back at least once during the honeymoon, huh?"

I snorted. "Honey, real women do it on top. You should know that."

"Well, then, at least let him up every once in a while. Go swimming or something."

"Yeah, I'll give him breaks to eat. But not many."

She shook her head. "You're making me horny. Go. Get out of here."

I pinned her with a glare. "Remember your vow. Make it worth it."

"Don't remind me," she said. I lifted an eyebrow. "I will. I *will*. I promise. Quit worrying about me. You have a plane to catch, Anna. Get going."

Jeff had a limo waiting for us. We changed in our hotel room, leaving my dress and Jeff's tux for Jamie and Darren to take care of. We climbed into the limo and were soon speeding out of downtown Las Vegas for the airport.

Once we were underway, Jeff turned on some music, locked the privacy window, and then turned to me. "You were saying about later?"

The heat in his gaze sent quivers of desire fluttering through me. He'd put on a tight T-shirt, and his muscles strained against the thin cotton as he reached for me. We were sitting on opposite benches of the limo, our knees brushing. I felt an electric tingle shoot through me where his leg nudged mine, his touch as thrilling now as the first time I'd made love to him, in his shower at his house.

I had a flash of that encounter, his tanned skin and broad muscles sluicing with hot water, steam wreathing around him, his eyes wary and full of desire. He reached for me now as he had then, with gentle and implacable strength. He pulled me to sit on his lap, but I moved out of his reach, kneeling in front of him on the floor.

I'd changed into a calf-length skirt and T-shirt. I lifted my skirt slowly up past my thighs, swaying to the music. Inch by inch I showed Jeff—*my husband*, I thought, tasting the phrase—my bare thighs, my bare hips, my bare pussy. I stretched back in the seat, spreading my thighs as Jeff crawled across the limo to kneel between my legs. He ran his fingers up my calves to my thighs, parted my folds to press his mouth my cleft. He lifted my legs onto his shoulders, and I pulled him closer to me, tangling my fingers in his hair.

His tongue speared into me, and I let him lap at me a moment or two and then pulled him up to kiss him, fumbling with his belt, button, and zipper. He sprang free, and I pushed him to a sitting position and sat astride him. I lifted myself up and poised there, one hand braced on the roof, the other grasping Jeff's thick shaft.

I pushed his tip into my folds, nudged my clit with the broad head, and moved him in circles against my stiffened nub, eliciting small gasps from me. Jeff slid his palms up my belly and my sides, pulled the cups of my bra down to free my breasts. His fingers pinched my nipples, rolled them, and then his soft lips found my skin, and he kissed his way over the mounded flesh to graze his teeth over my nipples. My thighs trembled with the effort of holding myself up at an awkward angle, and with desire. I moved his cock in quickening circles around my clit until my knees were buckling with the rhythm, and when I could bear it no longer, I sank down on him, impaling him deep inside me. We gasped in tandem, a Muse song drowning our voices.

I felt the limo slow and move through a series of turns, telling me we were moving through the airport.

"I think we're almost there," I said, rising and sinking on his shaft slowly.

"Not yet," Jeff said. "I'm not there yet."

I giggled. "No, I meant at the airport."

"Oh." Jeff pulled my head down for a kiss. "Well, that's awkward. I'm not done with you yet."

I leaned onto him, my arms around his neck, looking down into his molten chocolate eyes. He thrust up into me, slow, deliberate strokes. He reached over with one hand and hit the intercom. "Give us a few minutes before you drop us off, please, driver."

"Yes, sir."

I thought I detected a faint trace of amusement in the driver's voice, but then Jeff's pistoning hips took on an increased urgency, and I lost all capacity for thought. I pressed my face into his neck and rolled my hips, keeping my weight on my shins to allow Jeff room to move. His hands slid down my hips to cup my ass and lift me up, then let me lower down onto him, driving him deep.

Climax washed through me, slow, powerful waves sweeping me away. I heard my voice whispering Jeff's name into the sweat-salted skin of his neck. His teeth nipped my earlobe, his hands on my ass moving me faster and faster now, and the rolling wave of orgasm crashed over me, so intense I could only cling limp to Jeff as he pushed, pushed, pushed into me, gritting his teeth to keep from roaring aloud as he came with a series of savagely powerful thrusts.

We shuddered together through the aftershocks, and then Jeff rolled in place to set me down and pulled out of me. He rummaged in a console, found a box of Kleenex, and used them to clean us both.

"You can drop us off, driver," Jeff said into the intercom.

"Very good, sir."

I pulled my skirt down and smoothed the wrinkles out, then stuffed my breasts back into my bra.

"You may want to, ah, fix your hair," Jeff said.

I rummaged through my purse and found a compact. "Oh, god. I have just-fucked hair." I pushed and pulled at the loose curls for a few seconds, then gave it up as a lost cause and pulled it back into a ponytail.

"Hey," Jeff said, "I happen to like the just-fucked look on you."

"Yeah, I bet you do," I said, grinning at him. "You give it to me often enough."

"I don't hear you complaining."

"Hell, no," I said. "You can give me just-fucked hair whenever you want."

"I'll hold you to that," Jeff said, pinching my ass as I moved toward the door.

The driver opened the door and we slid out, our bags waiting for us on the sidewalk. Jeff tipped the driver, and we moved through the crowd, Jeff in front, leading me by the hand. We checked our suitcases, and Jeff pulled me through the bustling airport to international departures, and from there to a gate buzzing with waiting travelers.

"Wait a second," I said, after scanning the departures screen. "You said we were going to an island. This says Paris."

Jeff smirked. "Surprise?"

I smacked his arm. "You lied to me!"

He laughed. "I didn't lie. It was...deliberate misinformation." He leaned close and whispered in my ear. "Besides, you had my cock in your mouth. I told you what you wanted to hear so you'd keep doing it."

"You're a sneaky bastard," I said.

"Yeah, well, you didn't think I'd actually tell you what I was planning, did you?"

I frowned. "Yeah, I kind of did."

He kissed me, laughing still. "Well, obviously it didn't work. You can try again later, though. Maybe I'll give up some of my other surprises, if you're...persuasive enough."

My arms slid around his waist. "Other surprises?"

"Yep. You never know what I might have planned."

"We're going to Paris. What else could you possibly have planned?"

He shrugged. "Like I said. You never know. You'll just have to wait and find out. Or you can try and...coerce it out of me."

I snorted. "You're really pleased with yourself about that, aren't you?"

"Yeah, a little. You really did almost get it out of me, though. A little more teasing, and you might have gotten the truth."

"So I just have to tease you long enough?"

"Shit."

I slid my hands into his back pockets. "I'll have to remember that." I kissed his mouth next to his lips. "So, why Paris?"

He bobbed his head side to side. "Well, it was just an idea that hit me. Remember when we sang that Faith Hill and Tim McGraw song together, for that couple's anniversary?"

I smiled at the memory. "Yeah, I love that song. The video is *so* awesome."

"That video is why I picked Paris. That song makes me think of us and of Paris, so it seemed like it might be a fun place to spend our honeymoon."

The boarding call echoed over the speakers, and we joined the crowd lining up.

"It's perfect," I said. "You and me in Paris, just like Faith and Tim."

"Exactly," Jeff said, smiling.

Chapter 8

*P*aris was everything I'd ever thought it would be. Winding streets, narrow alleys, quaint cafés, and expensive shops. It was beautiful and cultured and haughty. We spent the first few days too busy exploring the city to do much more at night besides fall asleep in our huge hotel bed. The third day we agreed to separate in a department store and buy something for the other, something reasonably priced and fun.

I bought lingerie, something sultry and lacy that I'd never wear except to turn Jeff on, the kind of thing I didn't expect to have actually stay on my body for long. It was a pair of black and red lace panties, cut high in front, and a bustier to match, strapless, pushing up my breasts to overflowing, cupping my every curve, displaying my body. The clerk wrapped my purchase in a plain brown paper bag, and I carried it with me to meet Jeff for dinner at Cafe Flo on the top floor of The Printemps department store. Words failed me as I walked in. The ceiling was stained glass, an impossible dome of a million, million colors, panes of hand-painted glass rising in an infinite jigsaw puzzle of pastels. The stained glass descended on all sides to maybe a dozen feet above my head as I stood staring up, neck craned to gawk at the elegant ceiling.

I wasn't the only one gawking. An older man bumped into me as he stared up, excusing himself in German. I saw Jeff leaning on a wall, watching me, a small opaque plastic bag in his hand, a store logo printed in French on the side. As I didn't speak or read French, I had no idea what kind of store he'd gone to.

I crossed the café and pressed myself against him, meeting his lips with mine. "What'd you buy me?" I asked.

Jeff grinned mischievously. "You'll have to wait and find out." He reached for my bag. "What about you?"

I held it out of reach, laughing. "I don't think so! You'll have to wait, too, buster. Unless you want to show me yours, in which I'll show you mine."

"I'm kidding," Jeff said, taking my free hand. "Let's eat, I'm hungry."

We ate at a mirrored table, which provided a view of the magnificent ceiling even as we dined. We talked about the various sights we'd seen, and would like to see. We finished eating and strolled slowly through the dark Parisian night back to our hotel. We stood in our room, the blinds open to let in the glittering topaz lights of the city and the lit spire of the Eiffel Tower in the distance. For a long moment neither of us spoke, just looked at each other, the room unlit, shadows long and our hearts beating in unison.

I tore myself away from his gaze and took myself into the bathroom to change into my new lingerie. Nerves pulsed like fire in my blood as I stripped naked, rinsed off in the shower, primped my hair and redid my makeup, spritzed perfume on myself, and then pulled the negligible bits of lace from the bag.

This was new for me. I'd been in my bra and panties in front of Jeff on any number of occasions. I was comfortable in my skin with him; he thought I was beautiful and spared no effort to make sure I knew he thought so. But to wrap myself in lace for him, to present myself to him as a gift...this was different. I slipped the panties on, fitted myself into the bustier, and plumped my breasts before looking at myself in the mirror.

When I did, I stopped breathing for a moment. I saw myself, yet again, as Jeff might see me. And then, with a shock, I realized I wasn't merely seeing myself through *his* eyes, I was seeing myself through my own eyes. It was a strange, almost dizzying, metaphysical understanding. I was finally learning to see myself as beautiful. Not simply because Jeff thought so, but through his endless repetitions, through his demonstration, through constant love and reassurance.

My hair floated loose in golden waves around my shoulders, framing my hazel eyes and high cheekbones. My bare shoulders were delicate, my breasts lifted high and full, spilling out for his hands to touch. My sides were held in to accentuate the swell of my hips and my lace-clad buttocks. My legs were long and bare, smooth and pale as porcelain.

I was a sensual, sexual woman, and in this lingerie I was a vision of tantalizing eroticism. My nerves faded into nothing, replaced by a river of heat in my belly. Jeff was waiting just beyond the door, and I knew how his eyes would widen when he saw me, how his hands would curl at his sides as if grasping my flesh, how his cock would tighten inside his pants.

I let out a deep breath and twisted the knob, pushed open the door, and stepped through to stand a foot away from Jeff. He had sat down on the edge of the bed, his shoes kicked off, and was rolling and unrolling the paper bag holding his gift to me. When he saw me, his eyes went wide and his jaw went slack.

A confident smile crept across my face at the stunned awe on his face.

"God*damn*, Anna. You look—just...damn." He stood up and took a hesitant step toward me. "Are you really meant for me? This isn't a dream?"

I laughed and stepped closer; mere inches separated us, but he hadn't touched me yet.

"Yes, my love. I'm all yours." I swept my hands down my curves. "This is your gift. Do you like it?"

"Do I like it? My god, Anna. I've never seen anything as beautiful in all my life as you right now."

"Then unwrap me."

"Not yet. First I want to just look at you." He gently pushed me toward the bed.

He opened the paper bag and withdrew two sets of fuzzy purple handcuffs and a matching purple velvet blindfold.

"You bought handcuffs and a blindfold?" I asked.

"Yeah, well, no. I mean, I bought them in Vegas and brought them here. This isn't what I bought you at the store," he said, toying with the blindfold. "I don't know how you feel about this kind of stuff, but I thought it might be fun. Exciting. You know? What do you think?"

"Jeff, I don't want you to think we need this stuff to be exciting."

"No," he said. "I don't. But I mean, do you want to?"

I smiled at him, a small seductive curl of my lips. "Slap those cuffs on me, bad boy."

Jeff licked his lips, then approached me with the first set of cuffs. I stretched my right wrist over to the bedpost, and Jeff gently curled the bracelet around my wrist and clicked it in place.

"Is it too tight?" he asked.

I shook my head. "No, it's fine." He hooked the other side of the cuff to the bedpost, then did my left wrist. "You can do anything you want to me, now. I'm at your mercy."

He stood staring at me for so long I started to squirm under his gaze. Eventually, he reached for the hem of his shirt and peeled it off, then slipped out of his pants so he stood naked in front of me. His cock stood straining straight up, thick and purple-veined, hard and begging to be touched. I lay, cuffed to the bed, wanting desperately to touch him, to take him into my mouth, to feel him slide between my lips and my palms and the folds of my pussy.

"Jeff...let me touch you," I said. "Come here so I can taste you. Let me put your big cock in my mouth." Jeff gaze went heavy and hooded. "Uh-uh. No. I wouldn't last three seconds if you did that. Just looking at you like that, cuffed and helpless, wet and ready for me...I'm so hard I'm about to come without even touching you."

"What are you gonna do?" I asked.

He grinned and stepped toward the bed, his cock bobbing as he moved. He took the blindfold and wrapped it around his eyes, tied it in back, and crawled onto the bed near my feet. He took my foot in one hand, slid his palm up my shin to my knee, traced the circumference of my thigh from one side to the other. His finger trailed up my other leg, tickling gently along the inside to the lace "V" of my panties. I writhed my hips into his fingers, feeling dampness moisten the black fabric as he barely brushed up the mound of my pussy to the band of my panties.

"Oh, Jeff...I love the way you touch me. Take them off, please."

He smiled beneath the blindfold. "Not yet, sweetness." He ran a finger underneath the waistband, teasing me. "I'm not ready for you naked yet. I'll get there, though."

He lowered his face to my leg, kissing up my thigh from knee to my hipbone.

"You take everything so slow," I said. "Have I ever told you how much I love that about you?"

He paused with his lips on my belly and turned his face to me. "You do?"

"Yes," I said, sucking in my belly in anticipation as he resumed kissing my flesh ever farther downward, now at the inside of my thighs. "It's so delicious. It—oh, god, yes, right there—makes everything... just better."

"You like it slow, huh?" A hint of something in his voice made me shiver. "Well, then, I'm gonna have to go *real* slow, aren't I?"

He pressed his mouth to my pussy through the lace and breathed on me, a long, slow, hot breath. I moaned and writhed on the bed, wanting his fingers in me, or his tongue on me, or something, but he refused to even slip a single finger under the elastic to touch my bare flesh.

Instead, he traced a fingernail over my pussy where his breath had blown, the lace and the flesh beneath still hot. I trembled and thrust with my hips, but he drew away and laved his tongue along the inside of my thigh parallel to the elastic band.

"God, Jeff, touch me, please!"

He only laughed, another blast of heat on my folds. "Already begging, my love? This is gonna be so much fun." He bit the soft skin of my thigh, hard enough to draw a yelp of protest. "You're handcuffed, Anna. Did you think I wasn't going to draw this out as long as I could? I have you helpless. I could draw this out for hours. I could feed you, and give you water, and never ever let you come. You're so expressive. I know exactly when you're getting close to coming."

Something like real fear shot through me; he was perfectly capable of torturing me with near-orgasm, I realized. "You wouldn't."

He tugged the waist of the panties down to the very edge of the crease of my nether lips and dipped his tongue in, a mere brush against the sensitive skin, but it was enough to make me cry out.

"Oh, no? You don't think I would?" His voice dared me to think otherwise.

"Please, Jeff..."

"Please what?" His tongue dipped back into the crease and slid toward my clit.

"Please, touch me. Let me feel you. I want you inside me."

"Oh...no. I don't think so. Not yet. You aren't screaming my name yet, baby. You're not even really begging me properly yet."

What have I done?

I'd known he would tease me, but he seemed to be dead set on truly teasing me into hysteria.

Jeff pulled the panties lower, exposing my clit, giving me hope. My body was on fire, every nerve ending alive with hope of stimulation. He hadn't touched me above my waistline.

My breath huffed in and out, and I made my first pull against the handcuffs. He laughed and speared his tongue against my clit, giving me my first taste of near-climax. He left the panties where they were and removed his mouth from my skin, exploring me now with his fingertips. He drifted from kneecap to inner thigh, traced up the line of my pussy, brushing briefly over my clit and across my hips, the merest grazing of the pads of his fingers, crawling slowly over my flesh. His fingers slid up under the edge of the bustier, touching my ribs and the padding of flesh over them, just beneath the wire of the bra.

Touch me! I pleaded silently, but the words wouldn't come out past my panting breath. He clawed his nails slowly and gently down my sides, gathering inward toward my wet, aching folds. My hips involuntarily left the bed as he drew closer, closer, nearing the goal, across the smooth-waxed mound and—

Down either thigh, drawing a desperate whimper from my lips. I wanted him to touch me, *needed* to feel his fingers dip inside me. I knew he wouldn't give me his cock, not yet, but surely he would slide a finger into me, give me a taste of release?

He curled his fingers into the panties at my hips and drew them down farther.

"Yes, yes...please," I whispered.

He kissed my belly, my side, my hipbone, the edge of my pelvis above the lace panties, and then...yes, he licked my clit, a single slow swipe of his hot, wet tongue, and then a second, even slower. While his tongue made its aching path against my clit, his fingers danced up my thighs and hooked inside my panties, brushing my cleft, and my entire body lifted off the bed, bridging with shoulders and feet. He lapped against me yet again, and now hope blossomed through me, tangled with the rising phoenix of orgasm.

Abruptly his tongue and fingers were gone, and he was kissing my shoulder, his weight hovering over me but not touching, a felt presence. I lifted my head to watch him, felt a thrill of excitement at the sight of his naked body over mine, covering me, his broad shoulder and back rippling with heavy slabs of muscle, the burn scars ridged ropes glinting in the moonlight and city light. His buttocks flashed pale and hard as he stretched over me, his palms planted on either side of my breasts, his arms tree-thick and his cock throbbing against my belly.

I felt an upwelling of love, a roaring inferno of passion for this man, even as he tortured me with sweet, ecstatic pleasure. His lips moved against my clavicle, touched my throat, gentle as a thought, slid stuttering slickly down my breastbone to kiss the heaped flesh of one breast, the right, and then the other. His cock bobbed against my belly, so close but so far; I strained downward against the handcuffs, seeking to get him inside me. He moved with me, though, kissing my breast inch by inch, only the exposed flesh. I waited for him to pull the cup down and begin the slow tease of my nipple.

After an agony of minutes spent kissing my breasts as if he'd never touched them before, never tasted them before, he finally tugged one cup down enough to let a nipple pop free. He kissed his way toward it, and I found myself holding my breath as he circled the hard-standing bead of nerves with his tongue.

He teased it with gentle nips of his teeth, light flicks of his tongue, moist pinches with his lips, and then, without warning, he bit the nipple hard enough to make me buck up off the bed with a squeal.

"Too hard?" Even teasing he couldn't help worrying about hurting me.

I shook my head, then realized he couldn't see me. "No," I gasped, "just...shocked me. Any harder would be too hard."

He didn't answer, went back to flicking my nipple with his tongue, licking in a rhythm that set my hips undulating. His fingers met my clit on my hips' up thrust, and I gasped at the sudden pressure, sudden burst of intense pleasure. As quick as the full thrust of his fingers against me appeared, it vanished again just as fast.

"No, Jeff, please, bring it back..."

For once he did as I asked, sliding his fingers along my belly to cup my pussy, a molasses-slow molding against my folds. His middle finger moved inexorably inward, slipping under the panties to dive inside me, the first full penetration.

I moaned, a long, throaty voicing of relief. He added his ring finger, and then moved them together deeper inside me until his pinky and index finger were splayed on either side of my labia. He swiped in, curled in, brushed the rough patch of my G-spot, and this time I shrieked aloud.

My hips were writhing as alive, bucking and gyrating, a silent plea to keep stroking me, keep going, don't stop. His fingers moved inside me, pushing the waves of climax higher and higher, until the waves were on the verge of breaking within me.

"Are you about to come, baby?" Jeff's voice spoke from between my legs, his breath huffing on my thigh. "Are you so close?"

I knew, even in my desperation, if I told him I was mere moments from coming, he'd stop.

"No?" My voice was a breathy squeak, and my hips gave the lie.

His fingers went still inside me, but didn't withdraw. "Oh, I think you are. I can hear it in your voice. Your pussy is so tight around my fingers, and the way you move against me? Yeah, you're close. I bet if I licked your clit, just once, you'd come *so fucking* hard, wouldn't you, baby?"

I couldn't help the answer ripping from my lips. "Yes! Please, give it to me, Jeff."

His tongue swiped next to my labia, one side and then other, stroked in beneath my clit, licked just above it. I undulated against him, dying to feel the wet heat of his tongue against my clit, desperate for climax.

The waves of orgasm floated away, lessened and shrank, and then, right then, he flicked the button of my clit with his tongue, just once, bringing me back the edge. But then his mouth swept upward along my belly to kiss my cheekbone, my forehead, my chin, my lips, exploring my face as his hands skimmed over my skin, over the lace of the bustier beneath my breasts.

He pushed his hands beneath my back, and I lifted up to let him touch me, anywhere and everywhere. He followed the line of clasps along my spine, exploring the catches. I rolled to my side, my arms twisted unnaturally. He unhooked the uppermost clasp, then the next, and his lips pressed burning kisses to my skin where it was exposed by the widening gap between the edges of the bustier. With each released eyelet, my breasts gained weight.

With each kiss to my skin, the velvet blindfold brushed my skin, soft and cold against the heat of my skin. I'd forgotten for a moment he was doing all this by touch alone. He knew my body so intimately, was so familiar with my every curve that he could explore me blindfolded, kiss my face and unerringly find my breast from mere memory. I imagined I was him for a moment, smelling the scent of my soap and the light dusting of perfume, silky skin beneath his lips, flesh firm in his hands.

The way he worshipped me told me I was beautiful. The loving and delicate way he kissed my flesh told me how desperately he desired me. The slight tremble of hands on my back as he released the final clasp to free my breasts told me how much he wanted to forget the game and ravage me hard and fast with primal fury. The fact that he continued to move with aching, tender slowness told me he cherished each salty touch of skin to his lips, each gasp elicited from my lips.

He hadn't said the words "I love you" since he handcuffed me to the bed and began his blind mapping of my body. He didn't need to; the feather-soft grazing of his fingers across my skin spoke the words for him, the gentle crush of his lips to my breast made the words clear to me, the effortless strength with which he lifted my body to strip off my panties showed me how much he loved me.

I stopped fighting, stopped wishing for climax, and closed my eyes, lay back in the bed and let him love me, as slow as he wanted. This wasn't about any kind of chemical orgasm any longer. This was pure adoration made physical. I was finally naked beneath him, my bare breasts cupped in his hands and lifted to his lips to kiss and taste and touch, my nipples sucked into his mouth and drawn taut, bringing fire rushing to my loins and bursting through me, a shuddering precursor of the earthquake to come.

He slid up my skin, the soft, leaking head of his cock stuttering along the inside of my thigh, bumping against my entrance. I held my breath, straining helplessly against the bonds restraining me from touching him. I wanted to hold him, needing to feel his firm flesh under my hands, but I couldn't. All I could do was lie tensed and coiled for the moment of his body's slide into mine. I drew my knees up, and my shoulders lifted off the bed as I sought to curl closer around him.

His lips caressed my breast, first the right, then the left, brushing underneath each one, carving around the sides, coming to a stop on my nipple. All the while his hands were cupping my hips and dipping between my thighs to tease me with a quick finger slipping in between my slick lips before retreating and tricking my clit with a circling tip. I gasped and whimpered, sounds brought forth from me without volition, my entire body now writhing against him, begging him to move inside me.

"Jeff, please, I'm begging you, please let me feel you inside me. I need it. I want it so bad. I need your cock inside me. Please!"

He sucked my lip into his mouth, silencing me, stroking my pussy with his fingers, drawing me toward the cliff of orgasm. His thick, hard cock was probing my entrance just beneath his hands, and now he braced himself above me, his broad, essence-slick head touching my clit, sending me into paroxysms of need.

"Beg me again, baby," Jeff whispered.

I wrapped my legs around him, struggled to pull him closer, but he resisted me, held himself in place. "Please, Jeff! Give it to me. I want to feel you inside me."

"Tell me more. Tell me exactly what you want," he said. "I love hearing you talk dirty to me."

"Yeah? You want me to tell you how bad I want your cock?" I gave myself over to his game. "I want it, baby. I want your cock. I need you to slip it into my pussy. I don't care if you go slow or fast, I just need to feel your big, hard cock fill me."

Jeff moaned, a low growl against my skin. He pulsed his hips, pushing his cock against my clit, and I gasped in pleasure as an electric thrill zapped through me. He did it again, and I crushed my pussy against him, moving with furious desperation.

"You want it inside you?" he asked. "Right now?"

"Yes! Please, yes!"

He kissed me, thrusting his tongue into my mouth at the same time as he drove his cock into me. "Like that?"

I let myself scream out loud. "Yes! Oh, god, Jeff, thank you...god!"

He buried himself to the hilt and held there, filling me but not moving. His teeth grazed my nipple, and I knew if he had thrust as he bit me I would have come, but he didn't. He held himself motionless, deep inside me. This was a new kind of torture. I was filled by him, but if he didn't move I wouldn't find the release I needed. He spent sweet, slow moments kissing my breasts, toying with my nipples, licking them in a quick rhythm to mock the motion I wanted his hips to make.

His body covered mine, his weight pressed down on me in the intimate crush of hard male angles on soft female curves. I moved, wiggled, writhed, not just for the glide in and slip out but to feel his skin against mine, to feel his knees inside my thighs, his chest against my breasts, his belly flat against mine. I moved against him only to feel the merge of flesh with flesh, the flutter of hearts beating in sync, the sinfully sweet slip of skin slick with sweat, sliding silk in the searing susurrus of sex. The words naming this union ceased to matter. This was sex, this was love, this was primal fucking and intimate lovemaking, this was the baring of self to self, mind to mind, heart to heart.

I heard no sound but his breathing, each inbreath my name whispered on his quivering lips. He moved then, as he spoke my name.

"Anna," and his manhood slid out of my sex, paused at the slick opening, his lips met mine in a soft, sugar-sweet kiss, and he moved into me, slower than the glacial slide of ice down mountains.

I didn't dare breathe, didn't dare so much as flutter an eyelid, held still so the only motion was the beating of my heart and the pumping of blood in my veins. Statue-still, stone-still. His shaft pushing into my desire-damp blossom was the slowest pulsing of a drifting wind, a gliding of silk on skin, a gradual infilling of my body with his. I gasped as he pushed into me, wept his name as he slid back out, whimpered in delight with the feel of his thickness slicking into my heat.

338

I jerked against the chains, tears dripping down my cheeks, seeking to curl closer, cling tighter, keep him in me, pull him faster. He kept the slowest motion possible, sliding into me like mercury merging, splitting apart and rejoining. He moved with the speed of continents spreading apart, a dozen heartbeats passing between the time of his tip drifting in and his hips bumping mine. I continued to weep, unabashed, feeling climax rise in me, a flood of release pooling like an ocean of potential energy poised on the brink of flash flooding into kinetic rush.

He didn't stop, now. He moved, slid, slipped. He kissed my tears and whispered my name, held my curves close, poured his love into me without words. My feet hooked around his waist, held him inside me. I clamped down with my inner muscles, desperate to keep him deep. He groaned when my vaginal walls clutched his cock, holding him tight. Move and breathe, pulse and pull. The push and pull of lungs filling and releasing, the pump of our hearts spreading lifeblood, these mirrored the sliding of his body into mine, the perfect merge of body into body.

Time slowed, stopped. His face buried into my neck, my breasts crushed up into his chest and my hips crashed against his and we came, we came, bursting together like a storm breaking on the shore, like waves splashing on the sand.

I shattered beneath him, broke apart under his body. I felt him fill me, each thrust of his cock into my throbbing channel like heartbeat, felt the jet of wet heat hit my walls, and then he thrust again and the wash of seed spread through me again, and my inner muscles clenched his shaft, lights bursting behind my tight-closed eyes, fire blossoming in my every fiber. I couldn't breathe for the detonation of my body, couldn't help but scream and weep and call his name, gasp his name, plead his name. Still he moved, slow and deliberate. His pace never changed, even as he came, even when I climaxed underneath him.

His hands cupped my face and we kissed, trembling lips on lips, love passing between like shared breath. I felt him push the blindfold down at last to dangle from his neck, and our eyes met, sparks flying, tears sliding down faces. He wept, too, and I kissed his cheeks, tasted salt.

He snatched the key from the bedside table and unlocked my wrists, the cuffs dangling free. I snaked my arms around his neck and crushed my mouth to his, freedom lending me renewed passion.

Time faded as we lay side by side, breathing, kissing, holding each other. I felt his manhood stir and gathered him in my hands, caressed him into hardness, sat astride him. He reached up and closed a cuff around his wrist, and I did the same to the other side, and then we were bound together, fingers tangled, hands sliding along bodies. My fingers traced my hips as he touched me. Together we grasped his shaft and guided him into me, and then he lay back and I supported my weight on his hands, fingers twined, my hips undulating on him. He stared up at me, the purple blindfold a swath of darkness against his tanned skin.

Motion became liquid, no longer in and out or up and down but wave crashing into wave. I gave into desperation, collapsed on top of him and rode him like a runaway stallion, fast and furious, my hair draped around my face and sticking to my sweat-damp cheeks and forehead, plunging my love-mad hips on his as hard as possible, crashing with bruising force.

Orgasm was a nuclear explosion mushrooming within us in tandem. I felt him splash his seed into me as I burst above him, around him. Again and again we came together. I felt him come, but his cock throbbed hard inside me and I continued to move on him, riding him, and then I felt him impossibly hard and huge and coming again.

Mouth pressed to mouth, quivering wide in silent screams, we came together, merging and morphing until I had no conception of myself without him.

His dark brown eyes glittered in the silver light of the fading moon, piercing mine, and finally he spoke the words aloud: "I love you, Anna."

"I love you more," I said.

He laughed, and rolled me onto my back and kissed me with the fire of a thousand suns.

We slept, and woke, and made love with starving hunger, and slept again. At some point the blindfold went around my eyes and I made love to Jeff in perfect dark, feeling only his body on mine, smelling the scent of sex and sweat and Jeff.

At some point day came and went, and only the hunger in our bellies told us of the passage of time.

When we slept again, it was the sleep of utter exhaustion and completely satiety.

We woke and showered and dressed, found a cafe and had a late lunch.

"The clerk at the front desk told me about this bridge that's somewhere around here," Jeff said around a bite of brie cheese. "Apparently you buy a padlock and write your names on it, both you and your lover, and then you lock it on the bridge and it will seal your love for as long as the lock remains on the bridge."

He pulled a small heart-shaped padlock out of his pocket, along with a Sharpie. "I got this as your gift. I thought it would be fun to do. I guess there's these bridges with love locks on them all over the world, in cities in Belgium and Japan and a bunch of other places."

He wrote his name on one side of the lock and handed it to me, and I wrote mine. For the first time, I signed my name *Anna Cartwright*. I smiled as I showed it to him.

"Anna Cartwright," Jeff said, leaning over the table to kiss me. "My wife."

"I like the way that sounds," I said.

"Me, too."

We took the lock to the *Pont de l'Archevêché*, opened the lock, hooked in an open spot, and clicked it into place.

"You know there are two such bridges as this?" a voice said in a thick French accent. An older man, with silver hair and a carefully trimmed beard, shuffled over to us. "You look as if you are in love, yes? Not only lovers, but in love?"

"We just got married a few days ago," I answered.

"Ah, well then you are in the wrong place, I think. This, the *Pont de l'Archevêché*, it is for lovers, you know? You have the key, still?" I showed him the key in my hand, and he took it from me, unlocked our lock, and handed it to me. "You must take this to the *Pont des Arts* and place there your lock. When you have locked it, you must throw the key into the Seine. There you are claiming the tradition of the committed lover, *oui*? It is a different kind of love, not only for the sex, but for the staying together, the always love. *Oui*?"

Jeff and I exchanged amused glances. "Thanks," Jeff said. "Wouldn't want to invoke the wrong tradition."

The old man narrowed his eyes. "You make fun, but this is serious. What can it hurt to believe? You should have more faith, *non*?"

"I wasn't—" Jeff started, but I stepped on his foot, and he smiled at the man. "Thanks, for real. Um, how do we get there?"

The old man gave us directions, and we found the bridge after a few wrong turns. The railings of this bridge had far fewer locks. Jeff and I put our padlock in place and withdrew the key. Before we tossed it into the Seine, Jeff pulled me against his chest and kissed me, hard and full of passion.

"I don't know if this how this works," he said. "But I think we should make a wish before we throw this key in."

I laughed. "I'm pretty sure that's how this works, but I'm game."

He wrapped his huge hand around my smaller one, holding the key together. "I wish for forty years of marriage with you," he said.

"Only forty?" I teased.

"Fine. How old are we? Almost thirty for both of us? How about eighty years, then? We'll be over a hundred. If we're still alive in eighty years, I want to still be married to you. Still in love. Still kissing you, just like this—" and he caressed my lips with his, slow and delicate, then hungrily, "every single day, until we fall asleep together and wake up in heaven."

"To kiss you every single day already is heaven," I whispered, "And that's my wish. A million kisses, and then a million more."

We threw the key into the Seine. It made a tiny splash, but I knew, deep in my soul, that the image of the key hitting the rushing river would be ingrained in my mind for as long as I lived. The feel of Jeff's hand in mine, a gentle breeze ruffling our hair, evening in Paris lowering gloom around us, these would be memories locked in my mind forever.

THE END

Big Girls
Do It On
Christmas

I took a deep breath and lifted the mic to my lips. "I would like to welcome everyone to The Whitney for Governor Blumquist's holiday party. My name is Anna Cartwright, and this is my husband, Jeff," I gestured to my right, where Jeff stood with his hands behind his back, looking sexy as ever in a trim, tailored steel-gray suit. "We're the DJs for this evening, we'll be doing a couple special performances and we'll also be taking song requests. I hope everyone has fun, and I'd like to wish you all a Merry Christmas and happy holidays. Thank you."

There was polite applause from the crowd, about four or five hundred people, I estimated. After I lowered the mic, Jeff pushed the volume back up, and "A Holly Jolly Christmas" started up.

Jeff and I had been asked by the Governor to DJ his holiday party. It was a huge honor for us, and a testament to how far we'd come as a DJ team. We'd taken to performing more frequently during our DJ gigs, and word of our high-energy performances had spread, it seemed. Our gigs went from being solely bar karaoke to DJing private events and parties thrown by wealthy individuals. This holiday party by the mayor was by far the largest and most upscale crowd we'd worked before, and Jeff and I were understandably excited and more than a little nervous. The party had just started, and our first duet wasn't scheduled for another twenty-five minutes, but I was already feeling the pre-performance jitters.

I was also antsy for another reason, a secret I was keeping from Jeff. I planned to tell him later that night, at the hotel. I just hoped he'd take it well. I wasn't entirely sure, though. I mean, he was Jeff, and little fazed him, but this was big news. It wasn't time yet, so I pushed it away to focus on the job at hand.

"Great intro, baby," Jeff said in my ear, squeezing my hand. "I've got the next few songs queued up, so we're good to go for a few minutes."

I smiled at him and squeezed his hand back, too full of a million butterflies to formulate a proper response. Of course, Jeff being Jeff, he caught on.

"What's up? You okay?" He asked, his rich brown eyes filling with concern.

"Yeah—" my voice caught, and I cleared it. "Yeah, just nervous, I guess. This is a big crowd."

"You'll be fine, sweetness. You know this song backwards and forwards."

"No, you're right, I know. I'm fine." I smiled again, but it must have been unconvincing.

"You sure it's not something else? You don't usually get this nervous for our duets."

"I'm good. Thanks, babe. I'm fine." I needed something to distract him. "How about something to drink?"

"Wine? Coke?"

I hesitated. "No, just some water with lemon, thanks."

Jeff lifted an eyebrow at me; I hated drinking plain water, and I always had. I drank soda, tea, coffee, beer or wine, never water.

"Sure, if that's what you want." He shrugged and got me a glass of ice water with a wedge of lemon.

The minutes passed quickly, people lining up requests for favorite holiday songs, and before I knew it, Jeff was queuing the track for, "Baby It's Cold Outside", our first duet.

My nerves lasted until I hit the first note, and then, as always, they receded until after I was done performing. The crowd was loudly appreciative of our song, which helped. Jeff was eyeing me suspiciously, which didn't. The Governor himself congratulated us on our performance, and requested we play "Carol of the Bells".

We played the requests, mingled with the crowd, enjoyed the delicious food, and then performed again, this time a harmony version of

"Jingle Bell Rock". The night wound down, and we performed one last time, "Have Yourself A Merry Little Christmas".

Jeff put on a few slower songs and then crossed to stand in the middle of the dance floor, holding out his to me. I smoothed my hands down my sides, and the look in my husband's eyes told me how I looked. I was wearing a floor-length evening dress, a dark red satin with gold piping around the deeply scooped bust line, sleeve cuffs, and bottom hem. It clung to my curves in the right places, belled out in the others. My hair was down and loosely curled, swept back from my face and held in place by a complicated arrangement of bobby pins. I was wearing a simple pair of black flats, a white gold necklace with a tear-drop sapphire pendant with matching earrings Jeff had gotten me for our first anniversary. I knew I looked beautiful, and more importantly, I *felt* beautiful.

I crossed the room and took Jeff's hand, let him sweep me into a waltz hold and circle the floor in smooth, slow circles. His hand rested easily on the swell of my hip, the other clasping my hand near our shoulders. Our bodies brushed and touched as we moved, and Jeff's eyes gazed into mine, blazing with affection.

As happened often, I felt a burst of pure love rush through me, joy at being his wife, his best friend. There were times, lying awake at night while Jeff slept, I wondered how I had gotten so lucky. He love me, he took care of me. He protected me and cherished me. I thought back, as I danced with him, to afternoon he'd asked me to marry him. If I could go back in time and talk to the me that had hesitated, wondered if I was ready, wondered if I could or should take the huge step and marry him...I would shake her by the shoulders and yell at her, make her say yes, emphatically, a thousand times yes.

My life could be very neatly split it two parts: before Jeff, and after Jeff.

Before I accepted his love, and learned how deeply I returned it, my life was dull, lonely, and drab. Empty. I often wondered how I had functioned without Jeff.

Now, as his wife, everything was bright and vibrant. I felt alive, complete. Even the colors of life, the blue of the sky, the gray of overcast clouds, the green of grass and leaves and the brown of Jeff's eyes, these seemed brighter. The feel of his hand in mine as we walked, the caress of his lips on mine, on my body at night, I felt these more acutely, as if his love and attention had woken up some long-slumbering part of my very being.

We finished our dance, by which time the party was over, the Governor having paid us and thanked us. Most of the guests had gone by the time Jeff and I had our equipment put away, and then Jeff settled in at an empty table with a glass of wine. I was, again, drinking ice water.

"You don't want a drink?" Jeff lifted his glass.

"Nah," I said. "I guess I'm feeling a bit queasy. I don't know."

He finished his glass in a couple big gulps and took my hand. "Well then, let's get back to the hotel."

We were flying out to Florida in the morning, an early flight so we could spend Christmas Eve with my cousin Miri, my Mom and Ed, and my Uncle Stuart and his wife. Jeff's mom and brother were flying down as well, and we were spending Christmas Day with them. Jeff and I were doing our gift exchange that night, in the hotel room.

The short drive from The Whitney to our hotel was quiet and awkward. Jeff seemed to have picked up on the fact that I had something on my mind, but knew me well enough to know I'd tell him when I was ready.

We'd checked in earlier in the day and left our luggage in the room, so when we got in, we sat down and traded gifts. Jeff had gotten me a Coach purse I'd been eying for weeks. It was big and black and leather; he knows me well enough to buy a purse I'd actually like. You know your man loves you when he can pick out a purse you'd like. I made the appropriate excited noises, and then handed him my gift to him. It was a small package, just a little square box wrapped in silvery paper, but all my nerves were on fire as he opened it.

Jeff had quizzical expression on his face as he peeled open the paper to reveal a Bulova watch box. I'd seen a couple old watches in a box on Jeff's dresser, but he never wore them. He opened the box and pulled out the silver Precisionist watch, grinning.

"Wow, honey, this is awesome. I love these watches, I just never bought one for myself." He slid it on and clasped it.

"Um, there's an engraving on the back," I said.

Jeff took the watch off and peered at the back. Shock rippled over his features, mingled with emotion. "'To Jeff,'" he read, "'with love on our first Christmas. A wonderful husband and an amazing father.'"

I bit my lip, watching him process the meaning of the engraving.

He glanced at me, his eyes wide. "Husband and father?" He rubbed his thumb over the writing on the back of the watch. "I'm your husband, but I'm not a father...am I?"

I nodded, and tried to speak. "Yeah—" My voice caught and I tried again. "I'm pregnant."

Jeff's features went through several stages of emotion. Shock, confusion, happiness, fear. "You're pregnant?"

I laughed. "Yes. I took at least a dozen tests. I'm definitely pregnant. I missed my period this month, so I took a test and it came up positive. I didn't want to freak out just yet, so I waited a couple days, and took another. And then another. All positive."

Jeff rubbed the back of the watch again. "Did you see a doctor?"

I shook my head. "No, not yet. I wanted to tell you first."

We'd just celebrated our one year anniversary a few months ago, and then in November we'd decided I would go off birth control. Not really *trying* to get pregnant, but not preventing it either. Apparently for us, "not trying" meant "get pregnant."

Jeff didn't say anything for a long time. I let him process, knowing he needed to think about things before he'd give me his reaction. I tried not to freak out and assume his lack of immediate joy meant he was upset by it. It wasn't easy to put off that assumption.

Finally, I couldn't hold it in. "So, what are you thinking?" I couldn't look at him. "Are you...upset?"

Jeff looked up sharply, then scrambled off the bed to kneel in front of me. "Upset? Baby, no. No." He took my hands in one of his and tipped my chin up to meet my eyes. "Just...surprised, I guess. I mean, I know I shouldn't be, since we stopped the birth control, but I guess I thought..."

"It would take longer?" I filled in.

"Yeah." He laughed sheepishly. "I mean, I get that it only takes once, but...I just wasn't expecting it this soon. But I'm happy. I'm thrilled, just...surprised."

"That's how I felt too," I said. "Why do you think I took so many tests?"

"So how far are you? Do you know?"

I shrugged. "Not exactly. I mean, the first time we made love after stopping the birth control was...seven weeks ago? So, at least that. Maybe less. I'll make an appointment when we get back from Florida."

"When will we be able to find out the gender? Do you feel okay? Should you put your feet up?"

I laughed and pushed Jeff backward so he fell onto his back on the floor. "Jeff. I'm barely a month along. I haven't even started feeling sick in the mornings yet. I'm not sick or weak. And I have absolutely no clue when we'll know the gender. Not till we're a lot farther along, though, I think." I slid off the chair and crawled to straddle Jeff, staring down into his eyes. "We're having a baby. Jeff. We're going to be parents!"

He took my face in his hands and kissed me. "We're having a baby, Anna." He laughed, only a little hysterical. "I'm gonna be a father. You're gonna be a mommy."

I moved my hips on his. "I know what your next question is going to be," I said, unbuttoning his dress shirt to slide my hands on his broad, muscular chest, "and yes, we can have as much crazy hot monkey sex as we want, right up until I give birth. That was the first thing I checked."

"Are you sure? I saw this Oprah once where they showed the penis hitting the baby in the head."

I laughed so hard I snorted. "Jeff, honey. Seriously. At this stage, I don't think the baby even has a real head yet. It's like a little bean, I'm pretty sure."

He slid his hands up my back under my shirt. "I just don't want to hurt you, or the baby."

I had his shirt off by this point, and slid down to unbutton his pants. "You won't. I promise. Now shut up and take my clothes off."

Jeff grinned and complied, popping the buttons on my blouse, unclasping my bra and sliding it off so my breasts swayed free over him. He hefted their weight.

"Does this mean your breasts are going to get bigger?" He asked.

I wrinkled my nose. "I'm pretty sure this means *all of me* is going to get bigger, but yes, those will too."

He smiled happily and pushed my skirt down past my hips, then brought his hands up to cup my ass. "Awesome. Bigger boobies."

"Aren't they big enough as it is?" I asked, stripping his pants off and settling astride him again. "They're double D's! They're almost as big as your head as it is, honey."

He brushed my nipples with his thumbs. "I love your curves. I can't wait to feel your belly grow, feel little feet kicking." He moved to sit up and guided me to the bed. "You may only be a month or two along, and the baby may not have body parts yet, but I'm not going to have sex with you on the floor while you're pregnant. Not happening."

I shook my head at him as I took his shaft in my hand and stroked him, gently tugging him toward me. I lay on my back and spread my legs wide, inviting him to me.

"You're gonna be freaked about every little thing for the next nine months, aren't you?"

He slid up between my thighs, his broad shoulders pushing them wider as he kissed the inside of my thigh. "Yep. Sure am. I'm probably going to drive you batshit crazy with my worrying by the time this baby is here."

He traced his tongue along my cleft, inciting a rush of heat and damp desire. I let him taste me, once, twice, his tongue circling my clit, and then I pulled him up to me and kissed him, my essence on his lips.

"I need you inside me," I said. "Right now."

He tilted his hips and pushed inside me. I gasped as he filled me, thick steel and hot silk. I clawed my fingers into his shoulders and swiveled my hips to get him deeper.

"You'll tell me if I—" Jeff started.

"Shut up and make love to me, Jeff," I said, writhing into him. "I'm not going to break."

He ignored my plea, sliding into me and back out with a tender delicacy that took my breath away. I was desperate for him, suddenly, but he was determined to be gentle. He was always slow with me, taking his time reaching climax. This, though, this was entirely new. He held all of his weight off me, bracing himself on his forearms next to my head, his knees at my thighs, his hips drifting against me, a breath of skin against skin like a soft summer breeze.

There was no huffing of breath in my ear, no grinding hips or pulling me fiercely against him, only his cock slipping in and caressing out so sinuously I barely felt the change from in to out. He moved inside me so smoothly it felt like one constant eruption, perpetual motion. Only his hips moved, all the rest of him was perfectly still, as if any slightest jarring would damage me.

I clutched his shoulders and let him stroke into me, let his overwhelming tenderness flow through me. The first pulse of climax was a gentle rolling press of heat low in my belly. Moments passed in molasses slow motion, each brush of his shaft into my tight, wet, channel feeding the fires in my stomach, spreading the heat down into my thighs as tremors, into my chest as quick gasps.

I held still for as long as I could, containing my impatience, kept my feet planted, my palms flat on his shoulder blades, my mouth pressed against his neck. He glided and glided, silky smooth, serpentine, settling silt slow.

At last I could take it no more and shoved at his shoulder to roll him onto his back, settled on my knees astride his belly, back straight, heavy breasts now cupped by hands. I reached between us to grasp his cock, smiling lustfully at the hard heat of him, slicked with my juices and his own, throbbing and thick. I lifted up with my thigh muscles, one hand holding my hair out my face, guided his tip into my folds and sank down. He filled me, then, and I began to move, using only the strength of my thighs, rising and sinking, withdrawing and impaling, locking eyes with him, making a point.

When burgeoning orgasm stole the power from my legs and forced me to collapse onto his chest, I dug my hands beneath his head and pulled him into a fierce, demanding kiss, grinding my pussy onto him, hard and faster as climax pulled desperation out of me and stretched it into something new, like sexual starvation fulfilled and renewed in a moment-by-moment cycle.

I swallowed his moans of pleasure with my mouth, swallowed with my quivering folds his plunging shaft, and when he came, I swallowed his seed with my inner walls. He groaned into my mouth, and I matched his vocal release, matched his physical orgasm with my own, shattering apart above him, sobbing spasming breaths into his chest when I couldn't hold myself up anymore, clinging to his neck and fluttering my hips against his with frantic speed.

When we had both gone still and I was nestled into his shoulder, I let my insecurities out. "You'll still think I'm sexy when I'm pregnant, right?"

Jeff just laughed. "Anna, you know I will. You are sexy in every moment, all the time. You're sexy when you wake up, no makeup, hair messed up, morning breath. You're sexy when you sleep, and you're sexy when you laugh. You're sexy when you sing, and when you dance. You were beyond sexy tonight in that incredible dress. And when you've got that glow of motherhood, round belly sticking out to here—" he molded his hand over my belly in an imaginary pregnancy bump, "you'll be even sexier."

I kissed his neck and then his jaw, stroking his chest with my fingertips. "You're sweet."

"I'm right."

I laughed. "Okay, baby." We drowsed in the afterglow for a while. "So...names? Just for fun?"

He chuckled, a sleepy rumble. "Barney."

I wrinkled my nose. "You're kidding, right?"

"Yeah, Anna, I'm kidding. You think I'd stick our kid with a name like Barney?" He turned on his side and rested his hand on my hip. "Well, we're not doing a junior, that's my only rule. No Jeff junior."

"No?"

"Huh-uh. I think it's tacky, personally. I've got no problem with people who do that, I just don't want to."

"Okay, well, if it's a boy, how about...Orlando?"

"Orlando? Like Orlando Bloom?"

"Yes. No. Shut up."

He laughed. "Actually I don't mind it. Xander?"

"*Hell* no. I'm naming my son after that gumpy putz from *Buffy*."

"God, fine," he said, grinning. "I was teasing."

"Seriously, now." I pinched his skin next to his nipple. "No more jokes."

"We have nine months, baby."

I sighed. "Well I want to think of names now."

He glanced at the ceiling, thinking. "Caleb." He held up his hand. "Before you say anything, it's not random. Caleb was a buddy of mine from Basic. He died in that ambush I told you about. He was...one of my best buddies."

I knew that one meant a lot to him. "Caleb Cartwright." I said, trying it out loud. "I like it, actually. What about a girl?"

He thought for a moment. "Niall?"

"That's an interesting one," I said. "Niall. Niall Cartwright. How'd you come up with that one?"

"I had a great-aunt named Niall, and I've just always liked it." He yawned and pulled me against him. "I like those names. Caleb and Niall."

I felt his breathing slow and even out. "Are you really happy we're having a baby?"

He didn't answer right away, and when he did his words were slow and heavy. "I couldn't be any more excited...unless we had twins. I've always thought that would be fun."

I tried to imagine not one, but two little babies growing inside me, two lives, two personalities. My brain spun at the notion, and I felt myself drifting away into sleep, held tight by Jeff, content that, at the very least, Jeff was ready for this. I wasn't entirely sure I was *ready*, but I was happy.

I was having Jeff's baby.

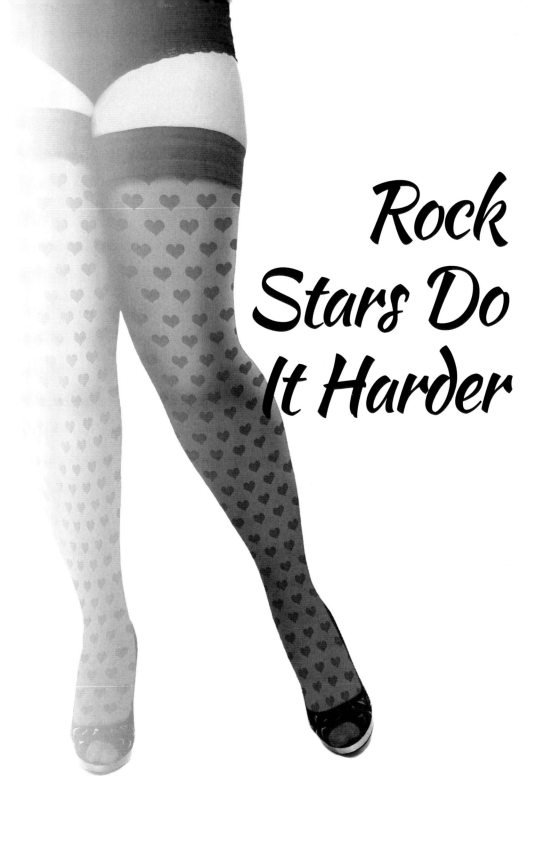

Rock
Stars Do
It Harder

Chapter 1

*T*he pain in Anna's eyes when she caught sight of him on the stage sent a bolt of agony through Chase Delany's heart. It was the ultimate rejection, even more than her words. She'd told him in no uncertain terms she didn't love him. Even that didn't hurt quite so much as seeing her soft, sweet, expressive gray eyes blaze with pain and surprise and anger at the mere sight of him.

Since she'd rejected him, Chase had thrown himself into the band, into tours and concerts. He wrote like a madman, pouring his pain and anger into songs that got progressively darker as the weeks passed. His bandmates noticed, but they didn't say anything. The darker music drew the fans, drew the crowds to swelling numbers, filled the stadiums and the bars and the casinos. Sure, they weren't headliners yet, but of all the opening acts, Six Foot Tall drew the most attention, garnered the loudest applause.

None of that mattered. Not to Chase.

The fans could scream their heads off, but it wouldn't fill the ache in Chase's heart, the hollow in his belly. Only *she* could fill him like that, and she'd chosen someone else. Even when fans sneaked backstage after shows and pressed their bodies against him, he couldn't find a single moment of contentment.

He'd let a girl take him all the way once—and only once—after Anna broke his heart. He'd rejected dozens of girls up until then, all skinny girls with small, hard breasts and waists he could span with his hands, ribs showing when they lifted their tops to tempt him with their pale, frail bodies. He'd rejected them all, politely but firmly.

Then a different kind of girl found him backstage, bribed security to give her a few minutes alone with Chase before a set. She was tall, with wide hips and heavy breasts, a luxurious fall of black hair, and bright green eyes. For the first time in weeks, Chase felt the stirrings of desire. He let her peel her shirt off, pendulous breasts swaying in front of his face, her areolas dark dimes against her pale skin. She'd pushed her skintight pants down to her feet and stepped out to stand before him naked and gloriously beautiful, a pale Diana. The cold air of the dressing room made her nipples stand on end, hard little beads.

Chase sat, waiting, heart thudding, his pose deceptively casual. She didn't say anything, just unbuckled his belt, tugged his pants down to his ankles, slipped her legs astride his, and impaled herself onto him, moved above him, her green eyes locked on his, full lips pressed thin, heavy breasts swaying. His body responded, but his mind stayed frozen and cold, his heart empty and black.

She isn't Anna. He pounded the thought through his mind, a harsh reminder, but to no avail. Black hair flashed into blonde locks, green eyes turned gray. Her name was poised on his lips, whispered in the cold air.

Her nostrils flared and her eyes narrowed, the black-haired beauty, but she smiled and said, "I can be your Anna, if that's what you want."

She moved faster above him, her eyes closed, and her breath came faster as she neared climax.

He came, and the release was brief and unfulfilling. She rose off him, plucked a few Kleenex from the box on the counter behind Chase. He watched with a kind of detached, apathetic disgust as she cleaned the white trickle from her thighs, swiped down the line of her lips, and then threw the tissue in the small metal trash can on the floor. She dressed, pulled her long black hair into a ponytail, and opened the door. Before she departed, she pulled a small white rectangle from her purse, a business card, and set it on the filing cabinet by the door.

"If you get over Anna and you want some real company, call me." Then she was gone.

Chase sat, his pants still around his thighs, cock limp and sticky against his leg. A fist knocked on the door, jerking Chase from his blank stare, and he tugged his pants on, buckled his belt, and called a hoarse, "Come in."

The security guard poked his head in. "You're on in five." He saw the card on the cabinet, and flicked a grin at Chase. "Nice, huh? That chick had some big ol' titties, right?"

"Yeah."

"Gonna bring her backstage again after?"

"No." Chase felt a flood of self-loathing wash through him. "In fact, don't let anyone else back here again."

The security guard lifted an eyebrow in surprise. "You sure? You don't want—"

"No, I don't."

"All right, man. If you say so."

After that Chase had taken to hiding in the green room, or in a crowd of other musicians. He'd started to heal, started to forget.

And then, a few weeks after the black-haired girl, he'd gone out onstage in Vegas, some music festival in a casino way off the Strip. The lights had gone up, the crowd had been wild, manic, infusing him with a crazed energy. The first number had killed. Then he'd paused, scanning the crowd, seeing only a sea of faces. Just as Chase was about to give the signal to kick in the next number, he'd seen a flash of blonde hair, an all-too-familiar face only a few feet away from the stage.

Anna.

One look, and his heart had crumbled all over again.

He'd written dozens of songs about her, but he'd only written one song *to* her, *for* her. It was, perhaps, his best song to date. The band had learned it, but they hadn't planned on performing it yet.

It was time, he decided.

Chase spun in place and waved for his band's attention. "We're doing 'I Found You.'"

"Now?" This was Gage, his bassist, and one of his oldest friends.

"Yeah, now. She's here. She needs to hear it."

Gage shrugged. "If you say so, man."

"Make it burn, boys," Chase said. He turned away and fixed his eyes on Anna.

Mic to his lips, he addressed her. "This next song is...special. It's brand new, so you guys are the first live audience to hear it played. I wrote it during a time of heartbreak and loss. Just listen—you'll see what I mean." Chase paused to tamp down the emotion rising within him. "I hadn't planned this, but the person...the woman I wrote this song about, she's in the audience today. Makes this performance especially personal. Anna, this is for you."

He watched her eyes darken with pain, and then the drumbeat kicked in and the music carried him away. He screamed himself raw, that song. But it didn't matter. She turned away, and he knew she'd made her final choice. Just as well. He was so hurt, so full of blind rage, he wouldn't have been able to speak to her.

He saw *him*, Jeff, standing behind her.

"Take care of her." Chase's raw, hoarse voice boomed into the silence of the stunned audience.

Jeff only nodded, and Chase was satisfied. Even through the boiling anger and searing pain, he wanted her to be happy, and it was clear Jeff made her happy.

The rest of the set flew by, and he collapsed in the green room, completely spent. He sipped water and settled in to wait for his bandmates to finish partying with the rest of the festival bands. He wasn't up for a crowd, not then.

The door opened, and he started to bitch out the security guard, but the face he saw poking through the gap stopped his heart. She hesitated, unsure.

"You?" Chase's voice cracked into a whisper.

"I know you probably don't want to see me, of all people, but—"

"No, it's fine. Come on in." He set his bottle down and tried to gather his scattered wits. "What—uh, what are you doing here?"

She shrugged. "I don't know." She held up a backstage pass. "I have this...Anna—sorry, *she* gave it to me. That looked like it was pretty rough, and I thought you might need someone to…I don't know. But here I am."

Her eyes held sorrow for him. That hurt, in an odd way. She cared about him? She saw his pain, clearly. "Here you are."

The silence stretched out, neither of them sure what to say, or do, or feel.

God, she's gorgeous. The thought struck him, unbidden.

For the first time in months, Anna was nowhere in his mind.

Jamie Dunleavy licked her lips and tried to slow her breathing. Chase was staring at her, his gaze inscrutable. He was sweaty, dark eyes narrowed, chest heaving, a bottle of water in one fist. His hand was so big it made the bottle of Ice Mountain look tiny.

She knew she shouldn't be there, with Chase, backstage. It was just asking for trouble. He wasn't with Anna anymore, but he was still off-limits. A best friend's ex was a big no-no, in her book. She'd fucked more guys than she'd care to count or admit, but she'd never, *ever* slept with the ex of anyone she cared about. She had *some* standards, after all.

So why am I here? No reasonable answer popped into her head.

He'd just looked so…angry and broken when Anna finally, truly, and literally turned her back on him. The look in his eyes, before he'd shut himself down, was one of soul-deep hurt. And Jamie was a sucker for troubled, hurting guys. She seemed pulled to them. It wasn't so much bad boys that she was drawn to as guys with serious issues. Endless hours of self-psychoanalysis and girl talk with Anna had given her enough insight to understand why she was drawn to the fixer-upper, dark, and dangerous types: She saw herself in them, and hoped they'd have at least a chance of understanding her, of getting why she was the way she was.

So far, no luck.

Lots of sex, some of it pretty damn spectacular, but that was about it. Lots of walks of shame, lots of guys who disappeared after a tumble or two.

Chase seemed to be the ultimate in tall, dark, and fucked-up. He was lounging in a chair, sweat pouring down his face and beading on his clean-shaven head, a pair of supple, faded black leather pants hugging his thick legs and showing off a bulge that had her throat going a little dry and her pulse pounding. He had a ripped, sleeveless Led Zeppelin T-shirt on, tight around his torso and showing his burly, toned arms. His wrists were adorned with thick leather metal-spiked bracelets, and tribal tattoos peeked out from beneath his shirt onto his shoulders and arms. His ears were pierced and gauged. His brown eyes were so dark they were almost black, narrowed and struggling for expressionless apathy.

Jamie saw through his efforts, though. He was hurting. She had no idea what she, of all people, could do for him, but she knew she couldn't just walk away and leave him to hurt alone.

"I don't know why I'm here, honestly," she said a second time. "Shit. I already said that. I just...I guess I wanted to see if you were okay."

Lame, lame, lame. Jamie kicked herself. Usually she was pretty good at saying exactly what she was thinking. To a fault, actually. She had tendency to take brutal honesty to a whole new level sometimes. But now, faced with Chase, her best friend's ex-lover, Jamie found herself tongue-tied, stammering, fumbling for complete sentences.

Chase swigged his water before responding. "Okay? I mean, I'm here. I'm alive. I'm..." He trailed off, rolling the water bottle over his forehead. "Fuck. No, I'm not. I'm not okay at all."

That was all the opening she needed. Jamie moved into the room and closed the door behind her. There was only the one chair, so she sat half on the counter, her back to the mirror and the too-bright light bulbs. She was within arm's reach of Chase, but not suffocatingly close. She tried to ignore how being this close to him had her feeling shaken up and out of sorts.

"Can I help?" she asked.

Chase laughed, humorless. "Help? What are you going to do? Get Anna back?"

Jamie flinched and stood up. "No, I can't do that. She's happy with Jeff. I just…I know how it feels. I—" She shook her head angrily. "You know what? Whatever."

She stomped toward the door, cursing herself mentally. She was stopped by strong, gentle fingers on her arm, spinning her around. Her lungs froze and her brain melted. Chase was suddenly inches away, his huge, hard body frighteningly close. She could feel the heat emanating from him, as well as the confusion and the hurt. And the attraction.

His eyes were on her, but she still couldn't make heads or tails of what he was thinking.

"I'm sorry, Jamie. That was a dick thing to say."

"Fucking right it was." *Damn it, there goes me and my mouth again.*

Why was he closer now? The glittery heart on her tank top, bulging with her breasts, brushed against his Led Zeppelin shirt. The contact, even that little bit, had lightning bolting through her. Her nipples weren't even hard, but she was still shivering when each of her breaths had her chest expanding and pushing her against him.

"Well, I said I'm sorry. It's just—I'm just—"

"No, now I'm the one being a dick," she said. "I shouldn't be here. I'm her best friend, and I'm probably just making things worse."

His hand was still on her arm, circling her bicep. He was so close now she had to tilt her head back to meet his eyes. His gaze was intense, and Jamie felt something in her stomach clenching at the way his stare washed over her, glancing from her face to her thick, curly hair and down to her cleavage. Her shirt wasn't low-cut, but it was tight enough that the outlines of her bra were visible.

And now, under his eyes, her nipples peaked and poked through her bra and thin cotton tank top to dimple the material.

She felt his body respond. *Oh, god. Oh, god. He's huge.* She felt her body quivering and straining to feel more, get closer. *Get your ass out, Jamie.*

She didn't listen to herself. He wasn't holding her arm so tightly that she couldn't have gotten away, so why was she stuck in place like she was about to kiss him?

No. No. *No.*

Yes…

She was falling forward…

His lips were salty with sweat, soft yet firm, scouring her mouth with something like desperation. His hand tightened on her arm, his other hand slipping to the small of her back and pulling her close. She moved into him instinctively, crushing herself against him before she knew what she was doing.

Then reality hit like a palm-strike from Jesus. *What the hell am I doing?*

Jamie threw herself backward out of his arms, away from his kiss. It hurt. It physically, mentally, and emotionally hurt to pull away so forcefully. He tasted, felt, and smelled like man-heaven. Hunk-nirvana. Sex-Valhalla. Were there other kinds of heaven she could compare that ten seconds to? Probably, but her brain was too fried to come up with them.

She'd kissed *him.* It hadn't been his fault. It was all her. She was a terrible, terrible best friend and an awful human being.

Jamie's fingertips touched her lips, as if to keep the memory of his kiss close. Her back was to the door, and her breath came in ragged gasps. "That…that shouldn't have happened. God. I'm so sorry." She ducked her head so her copper curls draped in front of her face. "I don't know what the fuck I was thinking. I'm sorry, Chase. I shouldn't have—" she cut herself off and groped for the doorknob.

Time to beat a hasty retreat before he could come up with a scathing response. Or worse, kiss her back. 'Cause that would be terrible. Wonderful, amazing, incredible…and totally wrong. If he kissed her, he'd be a cad. If she let him, it would push her past having just made an innocent mistake and into heinous-bitch territory.

He took a step, licking his lips, brows furrowed in confusion. "Jamie, wait. Just hang on a second. That was—"

"A mistake," she filled in for him. "Never going to happen again. It can't. I'm Anna's best friend, and you're her ex. Us…that kiss…it's not just 'hell, no' territory, it's like…full-on 'fuck no' country."

Chase's lips quirked. "You drop the F-bomb a lot, don't you?"

Jamie shrugged. "Yeah, I do. I know it turns a lot of guys off, but it's just how I am."

"I think it's hot."

Jamie backed up. "You're not allowed to think I'm hot."

"Why not?"

"Because. You just can't. It makes this that much harder."

"Makes what harder?" He took another step toward her.

She turned and spoke as she walked away. "This. The part where I do the right thing for once in my life. I'm gonna walk away, and we're both going to pretend nothing happened."

"But it did happen." He was chasing her, moving through the bustling hallways after her, shouldering aside techies and band members and stage crew. "Jamie, wait. Just hang on and let's talk about this."

She shook her head, curls bouncing. "No way. Not happening, Chase. Don't push me."

She tried to ignore him. She saw the exit just ahead, the red-lettered sign shining in the distance, a thin bright line of white spearing through the backstage gloom as someone stepped out. She scurried for the exit, not looking back, trying to ignore the part of her that was begging, *Just one more kiss, Jay. Just one more. It can't hurt anything.*

She made it. She hit the crash bar with her hip and stepped out into the oppressive, dry desert Las Vegas heat, squinting at the sudden brilliance of the day. She fumbled in her purse for her sunglasses and slipped them on, thankful for the emotion-blocking quality of the mirrored aviator shades.

But of course, he was right behind her. His hand was on her hip, spinning her around. How did he do that? She wasn't a small girl, and she worked out. She took kickboxing. Jamie knew she was buff. He shouldn't be able to manhandle her like she was some sprightly little thing.

"Jamie, just hang the fuck on for a second." His voice was a low growl. "Look, I'm not gonna pretend it didn't happen, but I know why you're bugging about this, and you're right. It's…complicated. But I don't think—"

Jamie smacked his hand away from her body, needing clarity, and god knew his hand on her wasn't helping. "Don't think what? Think it won't be a problem? Think we can just hook up and no one will be any wiser? She'll *know*, Chase. She's my best friend, and I can't lie to her. Trust me, I've tried. We're like…psychic with each other. She's lied to me, and I've known when she was lying. I know when she's hiding something, and vice versa. Not to mention, *it's wrong*. You don't fuck your friend's exes, Chase. You just don't."

"Who said anything about fucking, or hooking up? It was just a kiss."

Jamie snorted. "Sh-yeah. *Just* a kiss. Right. And I'm the Virgin Mary."

Chase smirked, the first real humor to enliven his face. "Then what would you consider it?"

"A gateway drug?"

Chase laughed, a belly laugh. "A gateway drug, huh?" He sobered and closed in on her; Jamie wanted to back away, but she was rooted to the spot, pinned by his intense gaze, his fierce presence. "Then I'd be interested in seeing what the hard stuff would be like."

Jamie forced herself away again. "No, Chase. That can't happen. How can you be thinking about that at a time like this?"

"You expect me to pine for Anna forever? I've had weeks to forget her, to move on. This was the clincher. Just…salt in the wound. I can't live my life in the shadow of her rejection."

"Bullshit." Jamie poked his broad chest with a finger. "You're not over her. I saw the look on your face."

Chase's face closed down. "I didn't say I was over her. I said I had to move on."

"Well, this isn't the way. Hooking up with me isn't the way."

Chase frowned. "You keep talking about hooking up. I never said or did anything to suggest that. You did."

Jamie clenched her teeth and turned away. "You're right. My bad. Have a nice life, Chase." She walked away again, and this time he didn't follow her.

Jamie found herself tensed and expecting to feel his hand on her; she was torn between hoping he would and fearing the consequences if he did.

Chapter 2

*C*hase watched Jamie leave, wondering why his heart was palpitating. It might have had something to do with the way her fine, round ass swayed, cupped by denim so tight it left little to the imagination. It also might have had something to do with the searing memory of her kiss on his lips.

Ten seconds of time, but he knew he was ruined for other women, other lips. He'd gone from limp to raging erection in a single breath, a single brush of her balm-slick, strawberry-tasting lips.

It also might have had something to do with her unequivocal rejection. She'd kissed him, then bolted as if stung. Chase understood her reservations, and damn it all if she wasn't absolutely correct, but that didn't make it any easier.

Neither did how soft she was, how perfectly she fit in his arms, how her curves had molded to his body like puzzle pieces snugging into place. She'd enjoyed the kiss as much as he had; she could deny it all day long, but Chase knew she'd felt the same things he had.

He wanted Jamie, hard.

But the way she'd walked off with her jaw set and her emerald eyes blazing with determination left little doubt that he'd ever see her again.

Which really, really, *really* sucked. Chase knew he'd walk through the Mojave desert stark naked if it meant getting just one more kiss from her. But she wouldn't let that happen.

Chase turned away with a whispered curse. She was right. Goddamn it, she was right. He had to forget about Jamie. He was still broken up over Anna.

Being faced with her so suddenly, apropos of nothing…that fucking hurt. She'd seemed so surprised, so conflicted. As if merely seeing him had pained her. Which just went to show that she wasn't as over him as she'd tried to make it seem.

One look at Anna's sweet, innocent face, blue eyes and blonde hair and lush curves...and Chase had been lost all over again. Wishing he could hold her, kiss her, hear the low, passionate moans she used to make for him as she came. She'd been so eager, so hungry, like no one had ever paid attention to her, like she just had no clue how sexy she was. It was a turn-on all by itself, her strangely erotic innocence. She'd changed the way he saw sex. He'd thought he was teaching her, and all along she was showing him how much more than mere hormones and pheromones and orgasms it could be. Sex had always been fun for him. When he first met her and invited her back to his place, he'd thought it would be an enjoyable night in the sack with a hot girl who had some killer curves. But then it had changed. No warning, no clue. Just...it was more. From the first kiss in the car, stolen as she drove away, Chase had seen her hang-ups and had wanted to fix them. She didn't see her own sexiness, and he'd made it his mission to show her what she was, what she had that men wanted.

In the end, she'd shown him that sex could have meaning. And goddamn if he didn't want that again.

But Anna was gone forever. She'd chosen Jeff over him. Chase had seen enough to know she really, truly loved Jeff. She was happy with him, and Chase wasn't going to begrudge her that. She deserved happiness.

He wished it could have been with him, but that wasn't meant to be, and he had to move on.

He just didn't know how. That random groupie who had seduced him...he could have pursued her. She might have distracted him for a while. But he hadn't.

Now Jamie had to go and show up, kiss him, rock his world, and ruin the little bit of progress he'd been making.

What now?

"Hey, Chase, there you are." Gage popped his head out of the door. "We need you inside, dude. Cleo from Murder Doll Asylum is looking for you. She wants you to do a couple songs with her."

Chase followed his bassist inside and through the backstage area. "Murder Doll Asylum?"

Gage shrugged. "Yeah, I know, right? Bizarre-as-hell name, but I listened to a couple of their songs on the way down, and they're fucking brutal, man. She's got a killer voice." He quirked an eyebrow at Chase, grinning. "And having met her, she's got a killer body to go with it. Could be fun, if you know what I mean."

Chase waved his hand. "I'll do the set, but that's it, man."

Gage made a disgusted face. "Dude, listen. You're all hung up on that chick. I know you liked her, but you've gotta get over her. You've been a mopey fucktard for weeks, man. Distract yourself. That one chick a few weeks ago, Shannon? The one with the black hair and the huge tits? You tapped that, right? She was asking us at the after-party why you weren't there. She wanted you, bro. Like, hard."

Chase could only shrug. "Yeah, I hit it. She was hot and all, and it was good, but...I just don't know. She didn't hold my interest. I don't know what else to say. I'm just not interested."

Gage shook his head again. "Well...I guess it's whatever you want, man. But we've been friends since ninth grade, man, and this ain't you. You're all...*depressed* and shit. We're on the way up, man! We're playing Madison Square Garden next week—how huge is that?"

"We're opening for the openers, Gage," Chase said. "But I know. Okay? I know. Just give me some time. I'll come around."

Gage slapped him on the back, playfully hard. "Just do me one favor?"

"If I can."

Gage grinned lecherously. "Don't count Cleo out before you've met her, bro. She's hot. Like...*hot*. And I'm pretty sure she's into you. I mean, fuckin' *every* girl on the *planet* is into you, but Cleo is fine as hell, and she can scream like a banshee, man. Their tracks are sick."

Chase forced a grin and a laugh so Gage would get off his case. "I'll try to keep my mind open."

"That's all I'm asking."

Murder Doll Asylum was an all-girl screamo band led by Cleo Calloway. They'd made a name for themselves as a band that could rock as hard on stage and play as hard off-stage as any of the all-male metal outfits. Six Foot Tall wasn't strictly metal, but they had enough hard numbers that they could fit in with billings that featured harder acts. This gig in Vegas was with a ton of metal bands of several sub-genres, headlined by acts like Hatebreed, Devil Driver, and Otep; it was the hardest grouping of bands they'd ever played with, and all the guys in Six Foot Tall were finding the process of adjusting from the tamer rock acts they usually played with to the darker, harder thrash, screamo, and death metal bands on this gig to be a strange but fun adventure.

Chase idly twisted the spiked bracelets on his wrists as they neared the stage. He could feel the music in his bones and his belly before he could really hear anything specific. Until you were close enough to hear the feed from the monitors, the music heard backstage was a wall of sound, thick and impenetrable, rumbling and grumbling in your body.

Now that he was in the side-stage curtains watching, he could hear the band's signature sound, a steady, growling bass line overlaid by high, squealing, technically stunning lead guitar work. Through it all, the drums pounded maniacally, topped by Cleo's unintelligible but emotive screaming, chanting vocals. Chase wasn't usually a huge fan of screamo bands, preferring a more melodic and artistic approach himself. He could appreciate the talent he was seeing, though. Cleo's face twisted and contorted with angst and rage, her thin, porcelain-pale features curtained by a thousand thin dark purple dreads as she bent over at the waist, mic held sideways to her lips, cupped by her other hand. He couldn't make out a damn word she was saying, but she sure did seem to feel it from the depths of her soul.

The number ended, and Cleo stepped off-stage as the lights darkened between numbers.

She grabbed a water bottle proffered by stagehand and stood next to Chase. "Hey. Wanna do a couple numbers together?"

Chase grinned at her. "Sure. I don't know any of your stuff, though."

She waved a hand dismissively. "We can do some covers. We're more than just screamo, you know."

"Cool. What do you want to cover?"

"You know 'Cowboys From Hell'?"

"Hell, yeah." Chase bobbed his head; the boys were all huge Pantera fans.

The bassist, a tall, willowy girl with blonde pigtails, tapped in a thrumming line, followed by the kick drum, and then the lights came on, bathing Cleo and Chase in twin spots. Cleo leaned in close to the lead guitarist, a short but svelte girl with black spiky hair and earrings rimming her ears from lobe to tip, muttering the song they were going to do. The guitarist nodded and strummed a few chords as the rest of the band cued in.

Then they were off, blazing through the beloved metal anthem, Cleo and Chase alternating verses and harmonizing on the chorus as perfectly as if they'd rehearsed it. They did "Sanitarium" by Metallica next, and then closed the set with "Killing in the Name of" by Rage Against the Machine. Chase was skeptical when Cleo suggested it, but Cleo assured him the band knew it backward and forward, and had covered it before. He found himself pleasantly shocked when the guitarist did indeed do justice to Tom Morello's guitar work.

Chase had paid close attention to Cleo while they performed, and she was as sexy as Gage had suggested. She was thin and pale, with small breasts and boyish hips, which was as far from Chase's taste as you could get, but she *was* beautiful, with wide hazel eyes and an expressive, kissable mouth.

Maybe she would provide enough distraction to help him forget; he had a lot of forgetting to do after all. Anna, Jamie…between the two, he wasn't sure he'd ever truly be able to forget, but he had to try.

It was midnight, and Chase was hammered, more than half-naked, and about to lose his third straight hand of strip poker. Of course, he wasn't necessarily playing to win, and neither were the girls from Murder Doll Asylum. Chase smirked as he thought, *Losing has never been so much fun.* And neither had winning. He was down to his leather pants, earplugs, and his socks, but then, the girls were faring about as well. He'd won twice as many hands as he'd lost, so Cleo was down to her bra and panties; Leah, the bassist, was topless in her Catholic schoolgirl–style miniskirt; and Kylie, the guitarist, was in a T-shirt and panties.

They'd been partying for hours, ever since their set ended earlier in the evening, with the drummer and rhythm guitar from MDA having gone with the other guys from Six Foot Tall to some after-party somewhere in Vegas.

Which left Chase to entertain three hot chicks on his own. He figured he could handle it.

He fanned his cards and examined them again, as if they might have changed. Ace of hearts, ace of diamonds, and three of hearts. A pair, but not enough. He was pretty sure Leah had a straight, and Cleo was holding something to beat that—a full house, maybe. He wasn't sure what Kylie was holding, but he was pretty damn sure it beat his hand.

Chase sucked in a breath and let it out slowly. Leah had just raised on his bet, which meant he was beaten three ways. "All right, ladies. I'm not gonna see that. I've got a pair of aces."

He laid his cards down and tried to keep his face neutral.

Leah whooped. "Hells, yeah! Straight, baby. Take 'em off, Delany."

Chase grinned and stood up, ran his hands over his abs teasingly. He watched as all three girls froze in anticipation. He decided to toy with them; he drew off one sock, and then the other.

"That wasn't the bet!" Cleo yelled. "Your pants, Chase. The bet was, if you lose, you take off those sexy leather pants."

Chase looked down at himself, as if surprised to see his customary leather pants. "The pants?" He glanced with overdone incredulity at the three girls. "You want me to take my pants off?"

"YES!" all three girls said in chorus, and then burst into a fit of giggles.

Which was funny in and of itself, since none of them were the giggling type. They were the type of girls who could hold their own in the most brutal of mosh pits, who could breed a sonic massacre onstage and then drink half their male counterparts under the table afterward. And they were giggling.

Chase laughed, swaying in place. Those last two shots of Patrón were starting to catch up to him. "Well, let it never be said that Chase mother-fucking Delany ever welched on a bet," he announced, a little too loudly.

He eyed each girl in turn, his gaze lingering on Leah's perky C-cup breasts, and then unbuttoned the top of his pants. He grinned when Cleo licked her lips, shifting in her chair. The zipper went down, and now they were loose around his hips, his semi-rigid cock bulging in his skin-tight CK boxer-briefs.

And then he paused. "I have an idea. How about the three of you play one last high-stakes hand." He poured a shot for each of them, handed out limes and the salt, and then, when everyone was ready, he lifted his shot glass in a toast. "Winner of the last hand helps me take off my pants."

Leah, Cleo, and Kylie exchanged looks, then grinned. Cleo scooped up the cards, shuffled, and dealt. Chase planted himself unsteadily into his chair, blinking at the double images he was starting to see. Time to slow down a bit; they were just starting to get down to the fun part of the night.

He watched the girls play, each one keeping her face straight and hard, giving nothing away. Watching them play, he started trying to figure out each girl's tell. Leah was worrying at her bottom lip with her teeth absently, fingering one of her cards with her thumb. Kylie was blinking a lot and uncrossing and recrossing her legs—either nervous, or she had to pee. Cleo was the hardest. She was perfectly still, no obvious sign of nerves or excitement. Then she glanced at Chase and licked her lips, pink tongue swiping with exaggerated slowness between her black lipstick–painted lips.

She's going to win, he realized. She wasn't nervous or excited, only confident, which meant she had a killer hand and she knew it. Chase found himself hardening at the thought of Cleo's hands stripping him of his pants. She *was* pretty sexy, in her own way. She had knowing eyes, busy hands, porcelain-doll features. Like a china doll turned goth-anime.

Chase shifted in his chair. This would definitely be a welcome distraction. He'd hoped the night would provide a few hours of forgetting, but he hadn't dared hope it would go *this* well.

He pushed away the doubts concerning what was about to go down. He owed no one anything. He could do what he wanted. If he wanted to spend the night in a *ménage à quatre* or whatever this would be called, then he had every right to. He was a goddamn rock star, for fuck's sake. Rock stars fucked three girls at once.

Cleo's whoop of triumph jerked him back to the present. Leah and Kylie were pouting while Cleo stood on the table, gyrating her hips and pointing at Chase. "Get over here, Delany. You're mine, now, bitch."

Chase stood up slowly, eyes on Cleo across the table from him, Leah and Kylie between them. He circled behind Leah. He paused with his lips at her ear and put his index finger on her bare knee near the hem of her skirt, then dragged it up her thigh, hiking her skirt higher as he went. He felt her breathing cease entirely as his finger moved up her hip to her naked side. She gasped when his finger traced the underside of her breast, and then whimpered when he flicked her rigid nipple.

"Don't worry, sweetheart," he whispered in Leah's ear, his eyes fixed on Cleo's. "I haven't forgotten about you."

He pinched her nipple, nipping her earlobe, letting his hot breath huff into her ear. She tipped her head sideways to offer him better access, and he took it, planting a hot kiss on her neck.

She deflated when he moved away, letting her breath out, her head lolling back on her shoulders. Kylie was next, and she was watching him out of the corner of her eye, palms flat on the table, drawing slow, deep breaths. He paused behind her as he had Leah, but instead of immediately touching her, he simply stood behind her, mouth against her ear, his hands planted to either side of hers. She was frozen, head turned slightly so she could see him. He waited. Chase could feel the anticipation rolling off her in palpable waves.

"I haven't forgotten about you, either," he whispered.

Kylie turned in place so her lips brushed his. Chase felt a bolt of lust hit him when her soft, moist lips touched his.

"What are you gonna do?" Kylie asked, breathless.

"I don't know. What do want me to do?"

She shrugged. "I'm awful hot in this shirt."

Chase grinned and touched her lip with his tongue, tasting the salt and the tequila and faint traces of lipstick. "Hmmm. I might be able to help you out with that."

Kylie sucked in her belly when Chase's fingers brushed the skin of her abs, lifting her tight red baby-doll T-shirt up over her head and off. Her spiky black hair was mussed by the shirt's removal, so Chase took the opportunity to run his hands over the spikes. She shivered when his palm grazed down her neck and across her shoulder, hesitating on the shoulder blade before plunging down her chest to her breasts, cupped by a plain black bra.

Chase dug his fingers into the cup and lifted one breast free, tweaking the rosy bud of her nipple. He lifted the strap and let it snap back. "Is this in the way, too?"

She nodded, unable to speak. Chase winked at Cleo, who watched the exchange with an amused lift of her eyebrow, arms crossed over her chest.

"You're next, Cleo," Chase said. "And you have a bet to keep."

Cleo just smirked. "Bring it, sexy pants."

Chase froze. "What did you call me?"

Cleo frowned. "Sexy pants. Why?"

Mr. Sexypants. Anna's voice echoed through his head, her nickname for him tugging on his heart.

He shook his head to clear it of the memory, and her voice. That was past. This was now, and he had three beautiful, willing women waiting for his attention.

"Something wrong, Delany?" Cleo asked.

"No, sorry. It's nothing." He turned back to Kylie, slipping the bra strap off her shoulder, then the other. "Now, where was I?"

Kylie reached behind her head to slide her hands over Chase's back, clawing with her nails. "I think you were helping me off with my bra."

"Oh, yeah," Chase said, "now I remember."

He deftly unhooked her bra with one hand, nibbling on her ear and cupping a breast as the bra fell away. He felt Leah's eyes on him, hungry. Cleo was watching, too, and he tried to decide if he was seeing hints of jealousy in her eyes or not. Cleo shook her head slightly, poured a shot of tequila and downed it sans salt or lime, then turned her attention back to Chase, who was prowling around the circumference of the table once more.

He stopped beside Cleo, who turned in her chair to face him. "My turn?" she asked.

"Your turn." Chase ran his thumbs around the inside of the waistband of his underwear, but didn't lower them. "You're the only one who's wearing a top," he pointed out.

Cleo laughed. "It's not exactly at a top," she said. "But I take your point. Want to fix that?"

Chase smiled, licking his lips, then lowered his mouth to her ear. "It would be my *extreme* pleasure."

He suited action to words, unclasping her bra and tossing it away from her body in a single motion. Cleo stared up at him, lifting her chin defiantly, as if refusing to feel embarrassed by her nudity. Chase let his gaze rove down her body, taking in her small breasts with their nickel-sized areolas and beaded nipples. He reached down and carved a narrowing circle around her nipple with his finger, feeling the skin tighten under the pad of his fingertip.

Cleo bit her lower lip, sliding her eyes closed slowly and then opening them again. "I don't think this was part of the bet."

"Nope."

"So what are you doing?"

Chase shrugged. "Three sets of beautiful bare breasts? How can I not touch them?"

Cleo didn't answer. She continued to stare up at Chase, then hooked her fingers through the belt loops of his pants and tugged them down. They were tight enough that his boxers shimmied down with them, revealing the broad tip of his cock, now fully erect.

Cleo grinned. "Well, that works." She tugged again, and Chase stepped out of his pants, naked now. "The bet was just the pants, but I'll take this, too."

Kylie and Leah glanced at each other, then burst into giggles again. They whispered to each other, then stood up and wove their way, a little unsteadily, around the table to Chase. Cleo poured four shots, and they each downed theirs. Chase looked at each woman in turn, all of them now clad in only panties—or, in Leah's case, a miniskirt.

Leah stood to one side of Chase, Kylie on the other, with Cleo still sitting facing him. No one moved for several long moments, and then Leah lifted her hand and slid it down Chase's chest to his belly. Kylie did the same on the other side, and now both girls' hands were on his belly, inches from his straining cock.

Chase, his eyes still locked on Cleo, who seemed to be battling some kind of discomfort or embarrassment, ran his hands up Kylie's and Leah's thighs. Both girls pressed closer to him, and then Kylie turned into him, pressed her lips to his arm and wrapped her nimble guitarist's fingers around his thick shaft. Chase slipped his palm under her panties to caress her ass, pushing the cotton boy-short panties down. Kylie wriggled her hips and shimmied out of them. Chase searched the hem of Leah's skirt until he found the zipper, and then, with one hand still kneading Kylie's firm, tight ass, he unzipped Leah's skirt and shoved it down, working his palm down one hip and then arcing across her flat belly to the other hip. Cleo sat motionless the entire time, her hazel eyes piercing into Chase's.

If he was going to be honest with himself, Chase knew he would rather have been alone with Cleo, and if he was any judge of her expression, Cleo was wishing for the same thing.

Instead, Kylie's delicate fingers were slowly stroking his cock near the tip, and then Leah took him in her hand as well, near the base, their pumping hands meeting in the middle.

Chase held himself absolutely still, except for his exploring hands, which were drifting up to curl around Kylie's and Leah's waists to cup their breasts and roll their nipples.

"I dare you to lick it, Cleo," Kylie said, her free hand grazing over Chase's ass.

Cleo hesitated, glancing from Chase's face to his cock.

"Yeah, Cleo. Come on," Leah urged. "Suck on his pretty cock."

"You first," Cleo said.

Leah shrugged. "I'd love to," she said, sinking to her knees.

Cleo's brows knitted as Leah put her lips around the broad crown just above Kylie's still-stroking fingers. Chase's breathing grew ragged, but he didn't move a muscle, even his hands frozen as Leah began to get into it now, sucking on the tip, licking around the groove, her fist pumping him near the base, her other hand gripping his ass.

Chase once again pushed away doubts, which were buried deep, and not enough to put a halt to this.. This felt good. Two hot women were all over him. This was awesome. Epic. He'd never been with more than one woman before, and this was shaping up to be even better than he'd dared imagine.

Except…Cleo.

She seemed as unsure as he felt, deep down. She wasn't touching him, her eyes locked on his.

Pour a shot, he mouthed to her. She nodded and poured shots. He need more liquid courage to really go through with this. He snaked his arm out from behind Kylie and took the shot, feeling his inhibitions burn away under the smooth burn of the Patrón.

Kylie knelt down on his other side now, and Leah moved away to make room for her. Kylie's lips wrapped around him, and she took him deep into her mouth. Leah had only worked his tip, never taking him deep. Kylie did the opposite, sliding him into her mouth as deep as she could before backing away slowly, only to deep-throat him again.

Chase closed his eyes and swallowed, his throat dry and his muscles burning from the effort to keep still, to hold back. "Girls, you have to stop now. I'm close."

Kylie laughed, her voice buzzing on his cock, and he flinched. She took him deep, and then moved away. Leah took her place again, working his tip with her tongue.

Chase frowned, realizing they had no intention of stopping. Cleo watched all this, her face struggling for impassivity. She abruptly stood up, and Chase shot his hand out to grab hers, stopping her from walking away. He slid his palm up her arm, stopped at her breast, then moved up again, slipping around the back of her neck beneath her purple dreads. He pulled her close, closer, and then his lips met hers. She gasped, stiffened, and tried to pull away, but Chase held her in place, darting his tongue between her lips. She melted slightly, and then eased into the kiss.

Chase pulled away after a moment, his forehead touching hers as he struggled to hold back. His hips were circling against his control, and now Leah backed away, too.

"You want it?" Leah asked Kylie.

Kylie didn't answer, wrapping her lips around him again and taking him deep. Her hand, along with Leah's, began to stroke him faster now, and Kylie's bobbing head matched the speed of her hand.

"I'm…I'm right there," Chase gasped. "I'm about to come…"

Cleo moaned into his mouth as he began to growl, and then she kissed him. Chase ran his hand over Cleo's ribs, then palmed her breast. She moaned again, then slipped her hand down between Kylie and Leah to cup his balls, pressing her middle finger against his taint. Chase let his head flop back, and his spine arched as he came with a loud roar. Kylie took him deep into her throat as he spurted a second time, and then her lips were replaced by Leah's, and she sucked his tip furiously, drawing a third spasm from him, hollowing her cheeks to glean every drop from him.

She drew him out of her mouth with a *pop*, and then Leah gave his tip one last lick.

Chase sagged, stumbling. Kylie and Leah stood up, pushing Chase toward the queen bed, and he crawled onto it. Cleo remained where she stood, hesitating. Chase held his hand out to her, meeting her gaze with his own.

A long moment passed before Cleo lifted her chin in a defiant gesture, then wriggled out of her panties and climbed onto the bed.

Chase planted sloppy kisses on her skin as she moved onto the bed with him. *She's going to be the first to come*, Chase decided.

Leah was already pressing herself in on his right side, Kylie on his left, their hands smoothing over his body, roaming his chest and stomach and thighs and cock. Cleo was perched awkwardly over his knees, her hands on Chase's shoulders to support her weight. Chase grasped her wrists in his hands and tugged her toward him, kissing her lips as she reached him, then pulled her higher yet, ignoring her confused expression. He planted his hands on her ass and lifted to settle her knees next to his head, her legs under his shoulders so her soft, damp, shaven core was hovering over his mouth.

Planting her palms on the wall, Cleo arched her back with a low, hesitant moan as Chase swiped his tongue along her crease. He adjusted her position slightly, then licked at her again, and still a third time before flicking at her clit with the tip of his tongue. Cleo gasped, a breathless sound that turned into a drawn-out moan as he circled her clit.

Chase was reminded of the girls to either side when their lips pressed moist kisses on his chest and stomach, their hands still exploring his body. Chase slid his palms on their bellies, and both Kylie and Leah sent up their moans of pleasure as he dipped his fingers between their thighs. Chase found his ability to multitask put to the test as he swirled his tongue around Cleo's clit while establishing a delving rhythm with his hands inside the other two girls' desire-wet clefts.

A chorus of moans filled the hotel room, Cleo's the loudest. Chase slowed his rhythm, finding his tongue and fingers working together. Each girl gasped in protest when he slowed his ministrations to nearly nothing, teasing their pussies with fingertips and tongue moving just enough to stimulate, but not enough to let them reach orgasm.

"Chase, god, please!" Cleo groaned.

Chase chuckled low in his throat. "Please what, Cleo?"

"Fuck you, Delany. Don't make me say it."

Kylie giggled on his left, her diminutive but nimble fingers stroking his limp but slowly solidifying cock. Leah was working his balls, massaging them gently in her hands, pressing a finger to his taint and rolling it in tiny circles as Kylie began to pump his now semi-rigid shaft. He felt Kylie leave the bed then come back, guiding his fingers back to her cleft. He didn't spare a glance, but he heard the crinkling of a condom wrapper, then felt the rubber stretch over him, rolled hand over hand down his length.

Chase sped up his rhythm, licking at Cleo's clit quickly, circling, flicking and sucking the small, hard, sensitive nub until she was writhing above him, gasping loud moans, arching and bowing her spine. She was at the edge, Chase realized.

He slowed his tongue, keeping his fingers moving inside Kylie and Leah, flicking his two long middle fingers over their G-spots.

"Say it, Cleo," Chase demanded, then speared his tongue at her clit.

Cleo tried to resist, groaning and lifting up, away from Chase, but then lowered herself back down to his mouth. "Goddamn it, Delany." She moaned again when he licked her pussy in slow, torturous circles. "I won't beg you."

"I'm not asking you to beg. Just say what you want."

Cleo growled. "You're a bastard." She whimpered when his tongue ran in narrowing circles around her nub, then shrieked when he flicked it again with his tongue. She was close now, only a few swipes of his tongue away from coming. "Goddammit, Delany. Fine. Please, *please* make me come."

Chase rewarded her with an increased tempo, licking her clit until she was undulating above him, caught up in the sensation and helpless to quiet her shrieks as she came apart.

Leah was right behind Cleo, moaning softly as she gyrated her hips on the bed, lifting her clenching pussy into his fingers as she came, her hands going still on his balls. Kylie was last, letting her voice rise up in a long scream when she came, slowing her fist on Chase's cock and curling into his side as she writhed in ecstasy.

Cleo was gasping, panting, sliding her core down Chase's chest to rest her breasts on his face. He took a nipple in his mouth, gently suckling until she wriggled on top of him, hypersensitive. She lifted up to meet his gaze, and for a split second, he saw something in her eyes, a moment of vulnerability swiftly erased.

Leah clambered over Chase's legs to slip between him and Kylie, turning away from him to face the other girl. Both girls giggled and then tangled their legs together, Leah half-straddling Kylie as they locked lips. Chase watched in fascination for a long moment as the two women scissored their legs together, palms scrubbing over breasts, groping and grabbing with a frenzy that shocked him.

Cleo laughed in Chase's ear. "Don't mind them. That's just what they do."

Chase ran his hands down Cleo's back to caress her ass, then grabbed her hips, pushing her downward until her cleft was brushing the tip of his cock. Cleo moaned, rolled her hips slightly, then lowered herself to impale him into her.

"Oh…my…god…" Cleo gasped, thumping her head onto his chest and swiveling her hips to help him find her sweet spot. "Right there, oh, god, yes, right there."

Chase thrust into her, trying to ignore the sounds of the other girls next to him, wet kissing, fingers moving inside pussies, giggles and moans. He was slightly embarrassed to be witnessing Kylie and Leah together, but in the end gave himself over to being turned on by it. Their soft, sinuous bodies writhed together, pale skin flashing in the lights of Vegas shining through the open curtains. Their laughter faded as they neared release, moans becoming frantic, feminine gasps of ecstasy rising in an erotic chorus.

Chase let himself grunt as he moved inside Cleo, raising his hips to meet hers, his large hands nearly spanning her tiny waist, lifting her negligible weight to crash her back down on top of him.

"I'm so close again, Chase," Cleo whispered in his ear, "but I need you on top."

Chase grinned up at her, then flipped her effortlessly, propping his weight on his elbows, his hips fitting between her parted thighs. "Like this?"

"Fuck yes," she moaned, wrapping her legs around his ass to pull him against her. "Harder, please."

Chase complied, driving into her slow and hard, drawing out and thrusting in. Cleo's hands clawed down his shoulders as she rolled her pussy against him, their bodies meeting in a slap of flesh, their mutual moans of pleasure counterpointed by Leah and Kylie next to them coming with tangled screams and shrieks.

Chase's low male growls braided with the three female gasps, and then all became a symphony of orgasm as they released together, Cleo curling around Chase and growling a high-pitched scream, Chase rasping low in his throat, Kylie's and Leah's moans echoing in harmony.

Then all was still and silent but for desperate panting for breath.

Chase moved his weight off Cleo, resting half on, half off the bed, one leg planted on the floor, the other across Cleo's legs. Kylie and Leah took up most of the bed, tangled together in a splay of limbs, their breathing soft and rhythmic, gentle snores.

Chase tried to relax and get comfortable, but there were simply too many bodies in the bed, so he slipped off the bed, tugged his boxers on, and made his way onto the balcony. The Vegas air was warm and dry, filled with the sound of cars rushing in perpetual traffic, voices filtering up from the sidewalk a dozen stories beneath him.

He was still a little drunk, he realized. The lights around him were blurring and twisting. He heard the sliding glass door open and then close. Cleo joined him, his T-shirt not quite covering her ass, showing she hadn't put on panties. Her bare skin flashed in the darkness, and he felt a stirring of desire for her, something strange and out of place that he didn't understand. He'd just had sex with her, but he felt awkward staring at her bare pussy peeking out from beneath the shirt. He looked away, and Cleo tugged the shirt lower.

"Couldn't find my panties," she said, sounding as awkward as he felt. "And I need a smoke." She smacked a new pack of Parliament Lights on her palm three times, then ripped the cellophane off, withdrew a cigarette, and lit it. She'd brought the nearly empty bottle of Patrón out with her, and she took a swig from it before handing it to Chase.

Cleo's pack of cigarettes sat on the railing with her clear orange Bic lighter, and Chase, feeling an odd compulsion, took a cigarette and lit it.

"I didn't think you smoked," Cleo said, blowing a plume of smoke out of the side of her mouth.

"I don't. Or at least, not anymore. Used to, back in high school."

"Why start now? It's a nasty-ass habit, but I love it too much to quit. At least not till I stop touring."

Chase shrugged, coughing as the acrid smoke hit his lungs for the first time in more than ten years. "Not sure. Had a craving, I guess."

Chase took the bottle from Cleo and drank from it, wincing at the burn. Cleo hit it after him, then set it down next to her foot, the shirt riding up to bare her small, tight ass. Once again, Chase looked away, unable to shake the strange embarrassment he felt at seeing her naked body, now that he was out of the passion of the moment.

They were standing next to each other, close, thighs brushing, arms touching. Cleo drew on her cigarette, snorted the smoke out of her nostrils, then turned her head to meet Chase's gaze.

On impulse, Chase closed the distance between them, his lips touching hers. Cleo froze in surprise, then eased a little, kissing him back. Their lips moved together, and it wasn't unpleasant, but it just felt…off.

Chase pulled away first, his brows furrowed in confusion. "Cleo, I—"

"That was weird," she said, cutting him off. "Not bad…just…not right."

Chase shook his head, then inhaled smoke, coughing once more. He glanced at the cigarette and tossed it away half-finished. "Not doing it for me," he muttered, then looked back at Cleo, who was examining the glowing orange tip of her cigarette.

"Cleo, listen—what happened, with us, in there…" Chase waved his hand at the glass door. "I'm not sure…I mean…"

Cleo laughed, puffing smoke from mouth and nose. "You don't have to explain, Delany. I get it. It happened. It was good, in the moment. You're...I won't deny, in one way that was the best sex I've ever had. But in another way, it was really, *really* fucking awkward. I've never gotten it on in a bed with other people." She drank from the bottle again, hissing as it went down. "That's more Kylie and Leah's scene. I've never shared a guy before."

"I've never done anything like that either," Chase admitted. "And like you said, in a way, it was great. Having all three of you go down on me...that was intense. But with you and me—"

"If we'd been alone, I think it might have been different," Cleo said, cutting in over him.

"Yeah."

"But as it is..." Cleo shrugged. "I don't think I could do anything with you again and not have the image of tonight in my head. Even now, all I can see is Kylie and Leah taking turns on you while you kiss me."

Chase ducked his head, a feeling of mutual understand washing between them. "Yeah, exactly."

Silence stretched out, and Cleo finished her smoke, tossed it away, and swigged from the bottle. Chase finished it, and they stood side by side, watching the three a.m. Vegas crowds hustle and bustle below them.

Finally, Chase broke the silence with the question burning unspoken between them. "So...you and I...is there something there?"

Cleo didn't answer right away. "I don't know, Delany. I don't know." She crossed her arms beneath her small, hard breasts, turning to face him. Her hazel eyes met his, and they searched each other silently. Eventually, Cleo shook her head. "No, I don't think there is. I think there could have been, but..."

Chase nodded. "Yeah, I know what you mean. I almost want to say, 'I'm sorry,' or that I'm kinda disappointed. You're a cool chick, and you're hot, and talented. I think there really could've been something."

Cleo shrugged, a little lift of one shoulder. "But that back there… it was fun, but it's not something I'll do again."

"Me either."

Cleo tilted her head, considering her next words. "Also, Chase? I'll say this totally honest. I don't think you're over that other girl. The one you sang the song to."

Chase looked away. "That's complicated."

"Meaning you don't want to talk about it."

Chase stared at the yellow headlights coming at them, the red taillights moving away; as a kid, he'd always thought of the stream of headlights as "bees" and the river of taillights as "wasps."

"I *am* over her. I mean, I know she's gone, that she doesn't want me. I'll admit that still hurts, but I'm past hoping it'll change. She's with Jeff, and she's happy. That's good enough for me. I'll move on. I'll be fine."

"I know it's none of my business," Cleo said, "but I don't think this is the way to go about getting over her." She waved at the hotel room again, meaning what had gone on earlier.

"No, you're probably right. But…I don't know. It's not something that makes sense out loud. I'm not trying to forget her, just…god, how do I say it? I need to get rid of the hold she has on my heart." Chase ran his finger back and forth on the railing, staring at the path of his finger rather than meeting Cleo's too-knowing gaze. "For a long time after she made it clear she didn't love me, I couldn't do anything. I couldn't make myself care about anyone. All I could do was play and write music. Which is all well and good, but…I can't let the pain rule me. I have to get over her."

"I thought you *were* over her."

"I said it's complicated."

"Meaning you have no fucking idea what you're feeling, because there's just too much going on."

Chase laughed. "Yeah, pretty much."

"My advice, for what it's worth? Give it time." Cleo rested her head against his shoulder, and they stayed like that for a long time. Eventually, Cleo pushed away. "Now get out of here."

"What about Kylie and Leah?"

"They'll be fine. This is what they do. They're…complicated. I'll tell 'em you said 'thanks for a good time.'"

After he got dressed and left the hotel, drunk and dizzy and confused, Chase wandered Vegas on foot, trying to sort out what he was feeling.

He'd told Cleo the truth about Anna; he was as over her as he would get, this soon. Seeing her had hurt, had dredged up a lot of emotions he'd worked to bury. But it had also reinforced the fact that she was gone.

But what he hadn't told Cleo was how Jamie had affected him. She was still there, in his head. Under his skin.

When he'd kissed Cleo on the balcony, the reason he'd pulled away was because all he could think of was Jamie. The pained, tortured look on her face when she'd torn herself away after their kiss. It was brief, but that one kiss had held more tantalizing pressure than Chase had ever felt. He'd been ripped apart by that kiss.

Cleo, Kylie, Leah…he'd had fun, but now, alone after the fact, all he could think of was Jamie. Where was she? What was she doing? Was she with someone else?

He imagined her at a bar, a bottle of beer in her hand, leaning into some half-drunk asshole with groping hands. The thought of some other guy's paws on Jamie's full, hypnotizing hips sent a pang of hurt through Chase. The idea of her going home with that guy, stripping for him, kissing him, caressing him, letting him touch her ivory skin… it made Chase crazy with irrational jealousy.

He tried to banish the images, but he couldn't. All he could see was Jamie's fiery curls and green gaze, and then he would see some faceless male clawing at her skin, the sweet flesh that should belong to Chase, but didn't.

He could feel her palm scraping over his scalp as she kissed him, her balm-slick lips sliding on his, teasing him, her full breasts pushing against him, nipples pebbling against her bra hard enough to feel through the cotton.

"Fuck," Chase growled aloud.

He swerved off the sidewalk and into a doorway, the bumping bass line from within the club promising a few hours of distraction, at least. He sat at the sticky, scratched bar, watching fake-breasted strippers undulate against silver poles. He stuck to beer, lost count, lost track, lost time. The strippers became the same person after a while, delirious images of Jamie, naked, dancing just for him.

Eventually, he felt Gage slump onto the stool next to him, pry the bottle from his fingers, and drag him out of the club. Gage never said a word, just propped up Chase's dead weight and dragged him into a cab, into their hotel, into bed.

Day came, and with it the oblivion of hangover pain, the haze of travel, setup, performance, and the familiar ritual of going from one show to the next, now drowned in a constant ocean of alcohol.

Women came and went, but none of them stirred his interest.

Jamie stayed in his thoughts, until eventually numbness set in.

Chapter 3

*J*amie was drunk. Like, really, *really* drunk. The kind of hammered where she couldn't remember where she was, how she'd gotten there, or what was going on. She was conscious, but unable to form coherent thoughts. She'd been this way for a while, she thought. She was starting to gain some control over herself, over her awareness.

Focus, Jamie, she told herself. *Wake up.*

She wasn't really asleep, but it felt that way. She needed to get her bearings. Something was happening, something was going on. Something not right. Deep breath, think hard, blink...blink.

Jamie breathed in, cleared her vision, squinting straight ahead. A blur of colors, a wash of inchoate images: the faint scent of booze on someone's breath close by, aftershave, male deodorant, male musk; soft breath on her face, the sound of male grunting above her, flesh against flesh, the wet sucking sounds of sex. She focused again, forcing coherency to the world: blank white above her, a ceiling with a trapezoidal area of brighter white from a window. Jamie squinted to her right, saw a window in triplicate, shadows beyond, an orange dot of a streetlamp, a gibbous moon.

The sounds of sex continued, and then Jamie became slowly aware of physical sensation. The sex was happening to her. Another sound filtered through the haze of alcohol: feminine moans of sex enjoyed. *Her* voice, moaning softly. *She* was having sex.

Jamie gathered herself together and focused once more, this time on the blurry pale skin and dark hair and pale blue eyes above her. No one she knew. Thick, shaggy brown hair the color of walnut shell, unkempt, uncut. A goatee, thick as an overgrown shrub, with a few days' worth of growth on his cheeks between the goatee and his long sideburns. Pale blue eyes watching her, slightly unfocused, dilated, reddened. A weak chin,; thin features; thin, dry, cracked lips. Jamie continued her perusal of the man she was having sex with, almost apathetically. She wasn't sure who he was or why she was having sex with him; he certainly wasn't attractive, not in the way she usually liked her men. He looked young, younger than she, more of a manling, a man-boy, which was also not her type. He was skinny, all hard angles and thin, wiry arms, hairy legs. Again, *so* not her type.

Jamie focused on the rest of her awareness. He *did* seem to know what he was doing, sexually. Decent rhythm, stroking evenly. He filled her well enough. Not huge, but not tiny. She could feel him inside her, so that was okay. He didn't weigh much, so she wasn't being crushed. That always sucked. He wasn't grunting like some kind of hog, which was nice, just softly groaning low in his throat, a constant sound.

Time to finish this and figure out what the fuck was going on. Jamie pushed at his shoulder. "Roll over."

"'Kay," he said, and complied.

She settled onto him, making sure to keep her weight evenly distributed. He was just a skinny little guy—no sense in breaking him. She would have to hold back a bit; besides, she was feeling queasy and dizzy, and not really in the mood for a wild frenzy.

Jamie adjusted the angle of her hips and set a slow rolling rhythm, supporting her weight with her hands next to his face. A little close for comfort, since she didn't know him and wasn't attracted to him, but she could feel a little orgasm coming along nicely, so there was no sense in stopping now. Maybe if she closed her eyes, it would help.

She arched her back and rolled her hips, and let herself gasp a little louder as the tip of his cock hit close to her G-spot. Not right on, but close. Close enough.

Then she felt a palm on her side, running up her ribs to cup her full, swaying breast. *Wait a second.* There were already two hands on her waist, holding her in place. The extra hand gripped her boob, too hard, groping and fumbling awkwardly.

What the fuck?

The hand roamed over her back and down her spine to explore her ass. Jamie turned her head, craning to see who else was in bed with her. She was too drunk to panic, and this seemed like consensual sex anyway. But...*two* guys? Hell, no. The hand slipped up her back and over her shoulder, then back under to grope her tit again. It was a pudgy, hairy hand, short fingers, greedy fingers. Strong, clumsy fingers.

She peered dizzily behind her and saw, yes, another man. This one was the polar opposite of the guy beneath her. Short, stocky, a bit of a belly around the middle, a mat of hair on his chest, small, beady eyes and wet, thick lips. Watery, bloodshot brown eyes, moon-face features. Way, *way* not her type. And he was on his knees behind her. Was he...? He wasn't. No. No....

Yes, he was.

The moon-faced second guy was on his knees behind her, gripping his short, thick, uncircumcised penis in his hand and stroking it along the crease of her ass.

Um, no.

She croaked, but couldn't get words to come out. She was close to coming, which wasn't helping matters, but having moon-face behind her ostensibly preparing to anally penetrate her was one hell of a turnoff.

She croaked again, trying to get the "fuck no, you aren't doing that" out past her lips, but it wasn't working.

Then Moon-face spoke. "Are you ready for Big Ben?" As he said this, he gestured with his penis, probing her ass-crack with the tip of his cock.

That got her powers of speech working. "'Big Ben'? Did you just refer to your penis as...'Big Ben'?"

The guy beneath her choked back a laugh. Jamie felt an orgasm quavering within her, absurdly, impossibly timed. She couldn't stop her body's rolling rhythm now. Couldn't.

Moon-face—whose name was probably Ben…she seemed to hazily remember meeting a Ben…and a Brad—hesitated, licked his lips, assessing whether she thought this was funny and/or hot.

"Yes?" he said, his tone of voice lost between a statement and a question.

Jamie, coming now, couldn't quite express her disbelief. "Are you—oh, god, oh, god—are you fucking serious? Big Ben? Does that make the rest of you—oh, god, yes—Little Ben?"

The guy beneath her laughed out loud now, and then groaned as he came. Jamie didn't feel the hot rush of seed when he spasmed, so he was wearing a condom, thank god.

Jamie felt something hot and hard probing her ass again.

"No, asshole." She threw herself clumsily off the guy beneath her, away from the probing nastiness of Big Ben/Little Ben. "And I also mean that literally. No asshole. Not for you. Not for anyone. Not ever."

Jamie may have been…experienced, sexually, but she drew the line at anal. Not gonna happen. Especially not like this. Not with him.

Ben shrugged, his face pouting comically. "Um…okay, then."

Jamie was overcome by a rush of dizziness, and lay back in the bed, palm over her eyes.

"So…can you at least help me out, here?" Ben asked. "You can't leave me hanging like this."

Jamie squinted at him, feeling floppy and disconnected from herself, severed from reality. She was beginning to come down a little, and she found herself not caring about anything, especially now that her virgin little asshole was safe from probing.

Ben was lying down next to her, not too close, thankfully. The bed they were all three in was big, king-sized, probably. Good thing, too. Jamie watched her hand reach out, wondering what it was doing.

Oh, that.

Her hand fisted around Ben's penis and began to pump. He grunted, porcine, thrusting his hips into her hand. Jamie felt her lip curling in something that would have been disgust if she'd been able to feel anything, but, thankfully, she was numb emotionally and mentally.

And that, she abruptly remembered, was the reason she'd gotten so hammered in the first place: to achieve numbness, to forget *him*.

Ben grunted one last time, hips thrust up, and then came onto her hand and his belly. Jamie's eyes were closed, sparing her having to watch. She cracked her eyes open and stared at her hand, barely suppressing a shudder of revulsion.

What... the fuck... am I doing?

Jamie slid down the bed and off the foot end, glancing around the room. The only article of her clothing she could find among the piles of towels and jeans and boxers and T-shirts was her panties. She scooped them up and donned them, grateful to not be totally nude anymore.

The guy whose name she hadn't remembered yet—but who she strongly felt might be Brad—got up and found her bra and T-shirt, handing them to her wordlessly before getting a pair of gym shorts from his dresser next to the window. Ben didn't move, just watched the proceedings disinterestedly. He stared openly, not even bothering to disguise his blatant ogling. Jamie tried to ignore his leering gaze as she hooked her bra beneath her breasts and then spanned it around her body to stuff her boobs in.

Eventually, she snapped. "Would you look somewhere else, please? Big Ben ain't gettin' nothin' else from me, I can promise you that."

The other guy, tugging his shirt over his head, glanced at Ben. "Dude. Enough already. Get the fuck out."

"I'm tired, now, man."

"I don't give a shit. Get the fuck out."

Ben frowned, shrugging. "Fine, man. Whatever." He stuffed his feet into a pair of shorts that hung past his knees, then tugged a Bob Marley shirt on. As he exited the room, he said, "Call me later, Brad. We'll blaze. I'm getting an 'O' from my hookup tomorrow."

Brad nodded. "Sure thing, dude."

Jamie watched all this in dawning comprehension. She pulled her shirt on, saw her Steve Madden sandals by the door, and slipped her feet into them, stumbling from one foot to the other. "You're a stoner?"

Brad shrugged. "I smoke down, yeah. Why?"

Jamie just shook her head. "I'm really hammered. I don't remember…well, shit. I don't remember a damn thing. I wasn't even sure what your name was until 'Big Ben' said it."

Brad's face pinched in confusion. "You don't remember anything?" He stuffed his feet into a pair of ADIDAS sports sandals. "We met at Duggan's. You sat down with us and started flirting. We did some shots of tequila, and then you suggested going back to my place for a threesome. I thought you were joking, but…you weren't. I couldn't believe my luck."

Jamie rubbed her forehead. "I suggested it? Shit. With you two?" She left the bedroom and found the kitchen, saw her purse sitting on the counter by the microwave.

"'With us two'? What's that supposed to mean?"

Jamie washed her hands in the kitchen sink, almost frantically. "Nothing. Don't worry about it. Did I drive here? Please tell me I didn't."

Brad shook his head. "I only had a beer and a shot, so I drove."

"Were you high?"

He shrugged, a tiny roll of his shoulders. "A little." He took a box of Cheez-Its from a cabinet and opened them, offered them to Jamie, who took some. "Does it matter? I wasn't drunk, and I wasn't, like, crazy-blazed. I was fine."

Jamie suppressed her desire to tell him driving high was just as stupid as driving drunk. He was her ride back to her car, so she held her tongue.

They munched on crackers, and then Brad pulled a pair of Dr. Peppers from the fridge.

After a while, Brad said, "Sorry about Ben. He's kind of a douche. He has this hookup for some seriously amazing bud, so I hang out with him. But…he's a douche."

Jamie studiously examined a cracker. "If he's a douche, why the hell did you agree to a three-way with him?"

Brad shook his head and shrugged. "I don't fucking know. You're the hottest girl who's ever paid attention to me, so I guess I just went with it for the chance to get with you. I may have been a bit more blazed than I thought, though. Now it seems like kind of a bad idea."

"You think? 'Are you ready for Big Ben'? Who the fuck names their cock that?"

Brad laughed. "Right? I can't believe he actually said that. Like, he was totally serious."

"No, he really was." Jamie laughed, but only to cover the shudder of disgust.

Brad was silent for a while. "I kind of feel like I should apologize. If you don't remember anything, you must have been pretty hammered when you sat down with us."

Jamie sighed. "Yeah. It's probably my own fault, though. I'm the kind of person who you can't tell how drunk they are. I could be obliterated, and you wouldn't know it. If you can see me looking impaired, like I'm stumbling or slurring or whatever, then I'm probably beyond schwasted and about to pass out."

Brad toyed with the tab of his soda can, not looking at Jamie. "So… you really don't remember anything?"

"No, honestly. I sort of came to in the middle of having sex with you. Everything before that is a blank."

Brad kept his eyes averted. "Oh. I guess I thought we sort of hit it off at Duggan's. I thought you and I…maybe we could—"

Jamie winced. "Brad, listen, I'm sorry. This whole thing is weird and uncomfortable for me. I don't know you. I don't remember meeting you, and that's just the hard, honest truth." She set her empty can by the sink. "I'd really like to just go home. Is there a bus stop nearby? Or…"

Brad shook his head. "A bus stop? Have you ever actually ridden a SMART bus? It's terrifying, and that's not even mentioning the crazy people." He set his can down next to Jamie's, staring at the two cans together as if they represented something that could have been but would never be. "I'll take you to your car. Come on."

The ride from Brad's apartment, which was in Hazel Park, back to Duggan's in Royal Oak was one long, awkward silence. Woodward Avenue was empty at three-thirty in the morning, a single SMART bus rumbling along the right-hand lane, spewing clouds of diesel exhaust. Duggan's was dark, Jamie's battered blue Buick LeSabre one of a few cars left in the lot.

As Jamie was sliding out of Brad's old red F-150, he touched her elbow to stop her. "Could I call you sometime?"

Jamie sighed, not turning around to look at him. "Brad, I'm sorry. I'm gonna be brutally honest here. I just want to go home and try to forget this ever happened. It's not really you, per se. You're a nice guy. Sex with you was nice. But I'm just...I'm fucked up, okay? This was a mistake, an awful drunken mistake. There's so much I'm trying to forget, and this is just one more thing." She shook her head, almost angrily. "I'm sorry, I don't know why I said all that."

Brad didn't answer for a long moment. "It was 'nice,' huh? That's the kiss of death for a guy. I get it, though."

"I'm sorry, Brad. Really. I wish I knew what else to say—"

"No, it's fine. It really is. I had a good time, except for—"

"Except for Big Ben," Jamie filled in. She turned and grinned at Brad as she stood up, leaning down to look into the open door. "A word of advice, from a woman to a man? Next time you try to score with a chick, leave the creepy douchebag out of it. Things might have gone differently if he hadn't have been there harshing my mellow, or whatever it is you stoners say."

Brad just laughed. "Yeah, I'm starting to see that." He put the truck in Drive. "Anyway, you're here. So...thanks. And Jamie? Good luck forgetting. But remember, sometimes you can't forget, and shouldn't. Sometimes you *need* to remember the bad shit, so when the good times come along, they'll mean that much more to you."

Jamie closed the door, and Brad drove away, back south down Woodward. She stood watching his taillights recede, hearing his last words echoing in her head.

Maybe forgetting Chase was impossible. Maybe she should just go on with her life and try to let go, rather than wishing for the impossible and hating life when it didn't happen.

Jamie drove home to her apartment in Clawson, barely seeing the road. With every mile, something hot and acidic rose in her gut, as much emotional as physical. By the time she was unlocking her front door, she was holding it back by force of will.

She slammed her door behind her and ran into the bathroom, dropping her purse on the floor as she fell to her knees and vomited into the toilet. She brought up everything she'd had to drink, everything she'd eaten, and then vomited more. When she felt done, she sank back sit on her thighs, her feet tucked beneath her, wiping her mouth with the back of her hand. Then her vindictive subconscious brought up an image of Ben, kneeling behind her, waving his chode-like penis at her, and then she had a sensory memory of Ben spooging onto her hand, and she vomited again, bringing up bile this time.

She slumped with her cheek against the toilet rim, holding back what felt suspiciously like tears.

She couldn't cry. She didn't cry. Not about guys. Not about doing the walk of shame. Not about waking up in strange apartments, or having sex with guys she didn't know. She did *not* cry.

She needed to talk to someone. Jamie dug her phone out of her purse and dialed Anna, knowing she'd answer even though it was four in the morning.

Anna answered on the third ring. "Jay? What's up? It's four a.m., hooker."

"I know, I'm sorry to call you at this hour, but…I fucked up, Anna. Really fucked up. Can you come over?"

"Shit. Are you hurt? Pregnant?"

"What? No. Not like that. Just…I need my best friend."

Anna paused before answering. "You broke your vow of celibacy, didn't you?" Jamie didn't answer, just sniffled as she struggled to hold back the tears, and that was enough for Anna. "Oh, shit. You're crying? I'll be there in a few minutes."

As she disconnected, Jamie heard Anna talking to Jeff in the background, telling him she didn't know when she'd be back. Jamie tossed the phone in her purse, stood up unsteadily, and brushed her teeth. She stripped, turned on the shower, and let it run hot, staring at herself in the steam-fogged mirror.

She stepped under the stream of scalding-hot water and scrubbed herself until her skin was red and raw, and then let the water soak her until the hot water ran out. Jamie was sniffling nonstop now, but refused to let the tears fall. She put on her favorite sleep T-shirt, an ancient thing with Eeyore on the front that used to be black but was now faded closer to gray.

Jamie climbed into bed, curled into a ball, and focused on not crying.

She'd been holding it back for so long. Not just tonight. The thing with Ben and Brad was the last straw, the tipping point. She'd been denying herself the emotions, pushing them down, bottling them up and ignoring them.

Now, whether she liked it or not, they were all coming up, coming out.

She heard the apartment door open and close, and then Anna appeared in her bedroom door, a box of donuts in one hand, the other holding a cup-tray with two Tim Horton's cups. Anna was sleep-mussed, long blonde hair tied up in a messy bun, wearing yoga pants, Uggs, and a several-sizes-too-big Dopey T-shirt every bit as old as Jamie's Eeyore one. She had makeup smeared under her eyes, and as she sat down on the bed, Jamie caught a whiff of sex from her.

"I brought you a hazelnut mocha, extra whipped cream. Plus, a dozen assorted donuts, with a few extra honey crullers." Anna set the donuts and coffee on the dresser, kicked off her boots, and sat cross-legged next to Jamie. "Talk, Jay. What happened?"

Jamie tried to sit up, but couldn't. She rolled to her back and met Anna's worried gaze. "I got drunk."

Anna frowned. "Well, that's not too unusual, though, right?"

"No, Anna. I mean, really, *really* drunk. Blacked-out drunk."

"Oh."

"And I woke up in a strange apartment."

Anna winced. "Shit."

"Yeah. Except it wasn't really waking up, exactly. It was more... coming to...in the middle of having sex. With a guy I don't remember meeting, whose name I didn't know until afterward."

Anna's eyes slid closed. "*Jamie.*"

"I know. Shut up, though. It gets worse."

"Worse? How the hell can it get worse?"

Jamie squeezed her eyes closed, near panic as the tears welled up. "There was another guy in the bed." Anna made a strangled noise, but Jamie spoke over it. "He...I was on top, and the guy I was having sex with had his hands on my hips, you know how they do, holding on right where your legs meet your hips? Well, then I felt this other hand start touching my boobs. And then I saw this guy behind me. God, Anna. You don't understand how drunk I was. It was hard to see anything. Like, past seeing double. I saw this guy, right? And you know what he was about to do? Yeah, you can guess, can't you?"

"You didn't, Jamie. Tell me you didn't let him."

"Hell, no. He had his short little chode-dick in his hand and he was...god, I'm gonna puke again...he was tickling my ass crack with it."

Anna put two fingers to her mouth and puffed out her cheeks, making a heaving noise.

Jamie laughed, a choked, humorless sound. "This is the best part, though. Or worst, depending on how you look at it. You know what this guy said to me? As he was about to anally penetrate me, he said, and I quote, 'Are you ready for Big Ben?'"

Anna blinked several times, processing. "Are you serious? He actually said that?"

"Yes, he did. And no, he wasn't joking. His name was Ben, and he named his dick Big Ben."

"That's…I don't even know what that is. Terrible. Funny, but terrible."

Jamie nodded. "Yeah. So I put a stop to the anal real fast. But I guess I lied when I said that was the worst part."

Anna covered her face with her hand. "There's *more*?"

Jamie closed her eyes and drew a deep, shuddering breath. "Let me just preface this with a reminder that I was still drunk, and I had no idea what was happening. I think I thought it was all a bad dream, or something. I still want to think it was. But…anyway. This Ben guy. He was sitting there, all pouty, with this pathetic hard-on. And he begged me to help him out."

"You didn't. Please, Baby Jesus, tell me you didn't go down on him."

"Well, no, I didn't do that. I gave him a hand job. I have this image in my head now. I mean, I didn't want to touch his dick. But part of me seemed to be…I don't know…acting by itself or something. I watched my hand reach out of its own volition and grab him. I closed my eyes at that point, but I can't get this memory out of my head of him coming on my hand. With the right guy, I don't mind that, you know? I mean, I'm not a money-shot kind of girl—that's nasty—but if I'm into the guy, I don't mind having his come on me. But this guy…I can't describe him 'cause I swear to god I'll puke again if I do. He was such a creeper. It wasn't how he looked, exactly, it was just…him. I was getting dressed, and this guy was just *staring* at me. Watching me get dressed. With what he'd said and was about to do to me…no lube, no prep, nothing? It was creepy." Jamie shivered dramatically, choking back bile and tears.

Anna slumped back against the headboard. "Jamie. Ohmigod, Jamie. How—and *why*—do you get yourself into these situations?"

"I don't know, Anna. I don't know. I wish I knew," Jamie heard herself say.

She knew it was a lie, though. She knew precisely why she'd gotten herself into that situation. She'd gone out drinking to drown out thoughts of *him*, of Chase. Then, at some point, she'd decided to try and erase her need for Chase with other guys.

She couldn't tell Anna any of this, though.

What she said was, "Anna, I'm tired of being a slut."

"You're not—"

"I *am*. We've been over this. I…am…a…slut. I know it, and I own it. I like sex. I *love* sex. I'm a twelve-step program away from being a nymphomaniac."

"So choose not to be."

"It's not that easy, Anna. I wish it was. I tried. I kept my vow from Vegas until now, no sex, not even my own fingers. Not even Mr. Pinky McVibrator. And you know how much I love my Mr. Pinky."

"Yes, Jay. I know you love him. I loved my Mr. Pinky, too."

"Then you found Jeff, and now you don't need Mr. Pinky, 'cause you have Mr. Long Hard and Attached to a Real Man Who Loves You."

"So what happened?"

"I don't know." Jamie hated the lie, hated that she could see the knowledge of Jamie's lie in Anna's eyes.

"Jay. I'm your best friend. Tell me."

"No."

"*Ja*mie."

"*An*na."

"Okay, fine." Anna stood up and paced away, grabbed her coffee, and sipped it. "There's something you're not telling me. If you need your secrets, then fine, whatever."

"It's not that I don't want to tell you. I just…can't. Not yet." Jamie managed to sit up as she said this.

The hurt in Anna's eyes was more than Jamie could take. One tear slid down her cheek, and then another, and then a third, and then she was bawling helplessly, curled up around a pillow, wracked with bone-shuddering sobs.

Anna knew there was nothing to say, so she sat grabbed the box of Kleenex from the back of the toilet and sat down next to Jamie with it, stroking the curly red hair out of her face as she wept.

When the storm of tears quieted, Anna drew Jamie's head into her lap and looked down at her best friend. "You know I love you, Jamie. You know I'll never judge you. You know there's nothing you could do to make me not be your best friend. I won't ask you again. Just know… I'm here, okay? If and when you're ready to spill, I'll be ready to listen."

"I know. And thanks."

Anna drew a deep breath, and Jamie knew the ass-kicking was about to ensue. "You know, too, that I can't let you get away with this bullshit without kicking your ass."

"I know."

"It's not about the vow of celibacy, Jay. That was just my attempt to help you see that you can enjoy life and enjoy being yourself without sex. Especially without *cheap* sex." Anna twirled the end of one of Jamie's curls between her index finger and thumb. "But in the end, you have to want to be different inside yourself."

"I know, Anna."

"No, I don't think you do." Anna met Jamie's eyes, her hazel eyes hard now. "Have some goddamn self-respect, Jamie. Quit putting out for chumps and douchebags. Wait for a real man, a good man. If that guy—*the* guy—comes along, and you have no standards, no self-respect, then he won't respect you. And a guy who doesn't respect you will walk all over you. You'll be little more than his sex slave. You have to want better for yourself."

Jamie couldn't help the renewal of tears Anna's brutally honest words engendered. "Easy for you to say."

Anna drew back, stung. "Really? You think so? You were there when I was with Bruce. You think I just magically figured all this out? Everything that happened with Chase…running off to New York to fuck him, and then running back to Jeff? God, Jamie. I hate myself for leaving Jeff like I did. I was too chicken to see what I had with a damn good man who loved me, so I ran off to be with someone else. Someone like Chase."

Jamie couldn't help defending him. "What's wrong with Chase?"

"Nothing. It's not about Chase. He's a good guy. He'll make someone very happy someday, if he ever learns to settle down. But he's a rock star, and you can't expect a rock star to be faithful. I can't live like that. He wouldn't have been able to give me the attention and love I needed. He's too focused on his career."

"You don't know that. Maybe he could have."

Anna looked at Jamie with suspicion in her eyes. "No, maybe you're right. But I've made my choice, and I don't regret it for a moment. Chase wasn't right for me. I didn't love him. I never did. Maybe I could have, but I'll never know that, will I? Why are you pushing this?"

Jamie wiped her eyes. "Sorry. I don't know. I just…I don't know. You have Jeff, and you're deliriously happy. I'm happy for you." She couldn't keep the jealousy out of her voice."

Anna sighed. "It'll happen for you, Jay. It will. Just…learn to be okay within yourself. For yourself. It'll happen. Probably when you least expect it."

Jamie felt exhaustion creeping over her. "I know. I will." She peered up at Anna through sleep-heavy eyes. "Just make me one promise."

"What?"

"Love me forever and be my BFF, no matter what?"

"You know it, hooker. No matter what."

Jamie pretended to fall asleep, listening to Anna let herself out. Real sleep soon washed over her, but not before the inevitable thoughts of Chase made their way through her mind and heart.

She couldn't tell Anna what she was feeling for Chase. Not yet. Maybe not ever. Anna had promised to be her BFF no matter what, but if Jamie and Chase were to be together, Anna would be reminded of everything that had happened between her and Chase every time she saw him. And considering how close Anna and Jamie were, that would be often.

Jamie sank into sleep, knowing Chase was an impossibility.

That didn't stop her heart from crying out for him, or her body from needing him.

Chapter 4

Jamie sighed as she placed the last stack of folded Cacique panties on the display table. She'd been folding and putting away the stock order for hours, after an insanely busy Saturday afternoon rush. She was exhausted, emotionally, mentally, and physically.

It had been a little more than two months since her drunken debauchery with Ben and Brad, and in the intervening weeks she'd kept almost strictly to herself. She worked a huge amount of hours at Lane Bryant as it was, and then she'd been promoted to assistant manager, and her hours had only increased.

The busyness had been good for her. She worked, went to the gym, and went home. She'd been studiously avoiding her drinking buddies, knowing if she went out with them, she'd fall right back into her old ways. Meaning, she'd end up doing the walk of shame again.

She'd gotten back on the celibacy wagon, which was good but sucked. She was busy, she was in shape, and she was learning to be content by herself.

But then, that was the problem: Jamie was lonely.

Anna was busier than ever with Jeff and their ever-expanding DJ business, so Jamie didn't even have her BFF to hang out with as much as she used to. That was fine, she told herself. Anna was happier than she'd ever been. Good for her.

Jamie was keeping her legs closed and staying off her back. That was a good thing.

Maybe when she met Mr. Right, sex with him would be, like, the best ever. The problem was, if she was keeping to herself all the time, how was she supposed to meet him?

The other problem, the real problem, was that Chase wouldn't leave her thoughts. She hadn't seen him in nearly three months, and all those weeks, all those days hadn't dulled her desire for him. He was still on her mind when she fell asleep, still in her heart when she sat in the bathtub with a bottle of wine and Mumford and Sons on Repeat.

Yeah, she still drank too much; she just did it alone. Which was even more pathetic, in her opinion.

Jamie glanced around the store one last time, making sure everything was in place for the opener tomorrow morning. She'd let the other two girls go home early once the rush died down, so she was locking up alone.

Just as well. No one to goad her into going out with them.

She shut off the lights, locked the doors, and made her way across the parking lot, nose buried in her phone as she checked Facebook. The status updates weren't helping, of course. It was Saturday night, just past midnight, and all her friends' statuses were the same. Everyone was out, and drunk, and having a great time.

"Lynn tagged you in a photograph…." But of course, the pic was a self-taken shot of Lynn and her boyfriend Aaron making out at The Post Bar, and the caption was, *Jamie u whore where the fuck are you, chica! You should b partying with us rt now!*

The Post Bar. Ugh. Posers and douchetards getting hammered and pretending to be cool.

That used to be me, Jamie realized. Suddenly, it didn't interest her as much. Yeah, she was turning into a lonely old hag, and she was probably only a few dozen cats away from being the crazy cat lady, but for some reason going to the bar to get blitzed and flirt with guys who'd bathed in cologne and popped their collars and shuffled around in their Puma shoes just didn't seem as appetizing as it used to be.

Jamie unlocked her Buick and opened the door, scrolling through her Facebook feed until she reached posts she'd already seen. She heard a vehicle approaching from behind her but didn't turn to look as she slid into her car, the leather cold on her thighs.

"Jamie!" a male voice called. "Get in!"

Jamie clapped her hand to her chest, having jumped clear off the seat in surprise. She glanced up to see Vince hanging out the window of his silver Excursion. Vince's girlfriend Nina waved from the passenger seat, and then the window behind Vince's rolled down to reveal the one face she couldn't say no to: Lane, her openly gay *other* best friend.

"Jamie, darling, we're going to Harpo's," Lane announced, throwing open the door, hopping out to drag Jamie toward the mammoth SUV. "We've got an extra ticket since my loser boyfriend got called in to work tonight. You're coming."

Jamie had to make a token effort to say no. "Lane, I can't. I'm exhausted. I worked a double today, *and* we had the inventory order come in. I just want to go home and collapse."

Lane stuck his tongue out at her, shoving her into the car, pushing on her ass to get her through the door. Lane was a twink, thin, absurdly beautiful with startling blue eyes and angelic features, manicured fingernails, and impeccable fashion sense. Jamie could have flattened him with ease if she wanted to, but she also knew Lane wouldn't take no for an answer. He would just pester and whine and harp on her until she agreed.

Besides, she'd been good for months. She could afford to unwind a little.

"Jamie, *chica*, you've been avoiding us for months. It's time to get out and have some fun." Lane reached across her body and buckled her in, then wrapped his arm around her shoulders and gave her a squeeze, kissing her cheek. "I can only let you be lame for so long, then it becomes my honor-bound duty to drag you out for a fun night of drinking with your gay husband."

Jamie laughed, Lane's irrepressible humor and infectious sense of fun getting to her and lightening her mood. "Fine, but you have to have my back."

Lane pretended to swoon as if mortally wounded. "Of *course* I have your back. How could you even doubt me?"

"I mean you have to keep me out of trouble. Drinking a bit, fine. Letting me do the walk of shame, not fine."

Lane lifted his index finger. "Ah. Now *that* I can do. When did you join the nunnery, if I may ask?"

"Don't be a dick, Lane. I'm not a nun. I'm just taking a break from my role as a hopeless slutbag."

"You're not hopeless," Lane said, smirking.

Jamie smacked his shoulder. "So you agree I'm a slutbag, then?"

Lane narrowed his eyes. "This sounds like a verbal trap, but I'll go ahead and spring it. Baby girl, you're probably the only person who's fucked more guys than me. And *that's* saying something."

Jamie sighed. "That's what I was afraid of. I mean, I knew it. But… maybe I don't want that to be me anymore."

Lane, ever on his toes, nodded, his expression serious and genuinely concerned. "Well, sweetie, all I can say is, if that's what you want, then you have to make it happen. Matty turned me around, that's for sure. I haven't so much as kissed another boy in the year and half I've been dating Matty. Which for me is a record. Usually I'm bored and sucking cock in the bathroom by week three."

Jamie laughed because it was funny, but also because it was true. Her expression sobered quickly, though. "Are you in love with Matt? Are you happy?"

Lane glanced past Jamie out the window, thinking before he answered. "Yes, I think I am. When my need to keep him happy and faithful to me outweighs my desire for all the shiny new boytoys, you know he has to mean something important. I don't want to let Matty down by being a ho, so I choose not to be a ho." He shrugged as if it was simple math.

Jamie nodded, but inwardly questioned how easy it really was. "Well, if works for you, it can work for me. I just need to find the guy to inspire me down the straight and narrow."

Lane laughed. "No, honey. The straight and narrow is a myth. I'm still kinky as hell. I just get everything I need from *him*. That's why it works."

They chatted for the rest of the ride down to Harpo's, and Jamie never even thought to question who they were going to see play. It didn't matter, after all. She wasn't going for the music.

When they entered the club, a band was finishing up their set with an instrumental hard rock number. Jamie and Lane got their drinks from the bar and then made their way to the railing overlooking the pit. Vince, Nina, and John and Kelly, who were friends of Nina's that Jamie didn't know, went down to the pit to get good spots for the next band, who it seemed they were there to see.

Jamie and Lane made small talk as the techies cleared the stage and reset it for the main act, and then the lights went down and the distinct sounds of the band warming up clattered over the crowd.

"Do you know who's about to play?" Jamie asked Lane.

Lane shrugged. "No, not really. I've heard Vince and Nina talking about this show for weeks, but they bought the tickets. I'm just along for the fun. I'm more of a Britney fan anyway, you know that. Hard rock is *so* not my thing."

The lights came up slowly, purple and red and blue washing in strobing pools over the stage. Then a spotlight lanced through the gloom to illuminate the lead singer.

Jamie's heart stopped.

"Hey, guys. It's great to be back in D-town. How's everybody doing?" The crowd went nuts, and when they settled down, he continued, "Awesome. Well, we're Six Foot Tall, as you might have guessed, and I'm Chase Delany. So tell me, are ya'll ready to rock?"

Jamie was frozen to the spot, one hand clutching her third vodka cranberry, the other gripping the railing in a fist so tight her knuckles were white. *No. No. Not now. I was just starting to be okay.*

That was a lie. She wasn't okay. She would never be okay as long as Chase Delany was alive and not hers.

She watched him rile the crowd all through the first number, getting them pumped and wild, moshing with violent abandon, psyching them into a frenzy. She couldn't take her eyes off him. She was close enough to see his features, but too far away to make out anything detailed. She needed to see him up close. She needed him to see her; she was afraid of what would happen if he did see her.

Jamie turned to Lane and sank her clawed hand into the muscle of his arm. "It's *him*."

Lane looked at her as if she'd sprouted horns. "Retract the claws, kitten, you're hurting my arm." Jamie forced her hand to her side, and Lane shook his arm, wincing. "Damn girl, you got some grip. Now what the hell are you talking about? You know him? I admit, he's one fine-ass piece of man-meat."

"It's Chase. *Chase*. Anna's Chase."

Lane's eyes widened. "Oh, shit." Lane looked from Jamie to Chase, who was standing at stage-edge, his eyes locked on Jamie, never missing a beat of his Kid Rock–style rap number. "Wait. You said 'him' like he meant something to you."

Jamie turned away, realizing she was dangerously close to admitting something no one could ever know. "No. Never mind."

Lane leaned back, examining Jamie as if seeing her for the first time. "Girl, you're lying through your teeth. It's me we're talking about here. If you can't tell your gay husband about it, who can you tell?"

"No one. Never. It's nothing. There's nothing to tell." She drained her rocks glass and shook it. "Whaddya know, I'm empty. How about another round?" She turned away to escape to the bar.

Lane grabbed her by the shoulders and span her around to face him. "I don't think so, sweetheart. You're not getting out of it that easy. Now, let me see if I have this straight. He's your BFF's ex. If I remember correctly, that was a messy situation, in which he ended up with a broken heart. Yes?" Jamie nodded. "And you're in love with him. I can see that much for myself. You don't even have to say it. The question is, does he know? Does he love you back?"

Jamie licked her lips and squeezed her eyes shut, refusing to let her emotions fly away from her. "It's impossible, Lane. *Impossible*. Completely and totally. There's no point in even discussing it."

"Nothing is impossible when it comes to love, kitten. Trust me on this. Matty is as far away from my type as a man can get, but it works. It may seem impossible, but you never know what can happen, right?"

Jamie shook her head, staring at the ceiling, refusing to even blink. When she had control over herself, she said, "No, Lane. He and Anna…they can't see each other. It would cause both of them too much pain. I just…I have to get over him."

Lane's voice was achingly tender. "Jamie, baby. You know I love you, so you know I'm saying this out of an attempt to help you. You're seriously about three seconds away from ugly crying over this guy right here in the middle of Harpo's. That's not something you can just get over."

"I have to," she whispered.

Lane shook his head. "No. Live your life for you. Anna's your BFF, she'll understand. She may not like it. It may be awkward, it may break every rule in the girlfriend handbook, but when love comes knocking, you answer."

"Lane—"

He cut her off with a palm over her mouth. "You listen to me, Jamie Grace Dunleavy. Go down there and *do* something. Just talk to him. Ancient Chinese proverb say, 'A journey of a thousand miles begins with a single step.' So take a step." He pushed her gently backwards, turned her toward the stairs leading to the pit and slapped her ass. "Go. And if things go FUBAR, you can blame me."

Jamie hesitated, then glanced at Chase, who was prowling across the stage like a caged lion, growling a metal number, his eyes never leaving her. She made her way through the jostling, moshing crowd until she was almost directly beneath him and stared up at him, her hands at her sides, perfectly still amidst the chaos of the pit. The song ended, and their signature ballad "Far From You" started, a haunting guitar refrain underlaid by a grumbling, chugging bass and almost jazz-like snare-drum taps. Chase sang the entire song crouched at the edge, his eyes locked on Jamie's.

She looked at him, unflinching, watching a bead of sweat run down his scalp to drip off his nose, then another skidding down his temple and drifting into a smear on his stubble-dark cheek. He was shirtless, a plain white T-shirt gripped in his fist, which he wiped across his brow every once in a while, and he wore a pair of leather pants and knee-high shit-kicker boots crisscrossed by straps and buckles and studded by short metal spikes. His thick, toned arms glistened with sweat, and his rippling abs moved as he breathed and sang, the sheen of sweat glinting, teasing, tantalizing.

Jamie wanted nothing so much as to jump up on stage, shove him to the floor, and rip his pants off, lick the sweat from his body and rub her hands across his slick skin. She wanted to feel his cock in her hands—she wanted to taste his come in her mouth and feel him fill her pussy as he thrust into her.

She wanted to let him tie her up and tease her for hours. She wanted to blindfold him and torture him with a thousand kisses over his flesh and on his stone-solid arousal until he begged and pleaded with her to let him come.

Jamie bit her lip, picturing these things. She felt her nipples harden, felt her core grow hot and damp. She found her fingers drifting down to the waistband of her skirt and slipping beneath it.

She wanted to touch herself, thinking of Chase naked for her, tied up and blindfolded, laid out to her mercy. She wanted to make herself come thinking about Chase's cock dripping with pre-come, smeared with her juices and her saliva, the thick purple veins standing out on the silky flesh.

Jamie gasped, realizing she was actually touching herself right there in the middle of the moshing crowd, with Chase watching her. She jerked her hand out of her skirt and wiped it on her blouse, then smelled her fingers out of some odd reflex. She stank of female arousal.

She glanced up at Chase, who seemed transfixed, his eyes wide, the cords in his neck standing out, his fist gripping the mic so tight she could see the straining tendons of his hand. He was still performing, still singing the final chorus of the ballad in his deep, rich voice. But as he stood up and turned away from the crowd, she could see a huge telltale bulge in his pants. His bassist nudged him and said something, laughing, and Chase shook his head irritably.

Chase didn't turn around for a few moments, waiting as the next number began, this one another driving metal song. Jamie stood watching him, keeping her thoughts away from dangerous territory.

Then, after an amount of time Jamie couldn't have measured, their set ended, and Chase left the stage with a backward glance at Jamie. A few seconds later, she felt a huge hand wrap around her arm. "Miss? Please come with me. Mr. Delany asked me to bring you backstage."

She complied, ignoring the jealous murmuring of the other girls around her who'd overheard. She followed the security guard, who was roughly the size and shape of a silverback gorilla, through the crowd to the backstage area. He led her to a door, knocked once, then opened it, ushering Jamie through. She stepped in, and the door closed softly behind her, latching with a *snick* of declarative finality.

Chase sat on a threadbare couch, one long arm slung casually across the back, one leg stretched out across the cushions, the other gripping his T-shirt in a tight fist.

Jamie stood with her back to the door, her breath coming in ragged, panting gasps. It took every ounce of willpower to keep from crossing the room and covering his magnificent body with hers, tangling her tongue against his, tasting the sweat and cold water on his mouth.

He rose up from the couch in a lithe, graceful movement, his expression roiling with emotion. Then he licked his lips, opened his mouth as if to speak, and Jamie was undone. The sight of his mouth, lips parted, teeth white...she *had* to taste him.

She lunged, crossing the three feet between them, crushing her breasts against his bare chest, wrapping her palms over the back of his head and neck. Her lips met his with desperate need.

He tasted as she'd imagined, as she remembered, of sweat from his lips, of ice-cold water from the bottle on the floor by the couch, and faintly of alcohol.

Jamie moaned as she kissed him, and that sound spurred him into life. His huge hand curled around her waist to rest on the small of her back, his other burying itself in her curls near her ear.

They kissed until their breath merged, until they were gasping, chests heaving. Jamie felt his erection at her belly, and her core surged hot and wet at the feel of him.

"I want you so fucking bad," she whispered into his lips.

"I'm right here," Chase growled. "And goddamn it, I've dreamt of you every night. Wet dreams of you naked, touching yourself like you did out in the crowd."

Jamie felt herself flush. "This is still impossible."

"I know. But…I don't care. I need you." He rumbled in his chest, a sound of frustration. "I don't care if that makes me weak for admitting. I *need* you, Jamie."

She sagged into him. "I need you, too. So what do we do?"

Chase shrugged. "Fuck if I know. I can't think for needing you, wanting you. All I can think of is kissing you again." His hand clawed into the muscle of her ass, sinking into the silk of her skirt, pulling her against him. "I want to take you on the couch, right now."

Jamie whimpered. "Don't you fucking dare say shit like that."

"Why not?"

"Because I want that so bad…so bad. I'm about to let you. I'm *this* close to ripping those stupid, sexy leather pants off and raping you on the goddamn floor." Jamie was trembling from head to toe, shaking with fear and need and lust and excitement.

Chase's hands were shaking, too, his breathing shuddering, his cock a hard rod between them. "Fuck, Jamie. We can't. We can't. If we do, there's no going back."

Jamie laughed mirthlessly. "There's already no going back."

"I know."

Jamie lifted her chin to gaze up at him, her palms caressing the stubble on his scalp at the back of his head. She knew she shouldn't be here. She knew this couldn't be, couldn't happen, but it already was happening.

She lifted up on her toes to kiss him, and something deep in her heart caught, tripped, and shattered. His lips were tender on hers, tasting her mouth, not demanding more but exploring, treasuring.

His palm slid down her ass to pull up the skirt, and she desperately, frantically wanted him to lift it, to touch her bare skin.

No. She couldn't do this to Anna.

Jamie snatched at the last vestige of self-control she had, a spider-silk tendril of hesitation. She stumbled away from him, backward, back against the door, clutching the doorknob in her fist.

She ignored the single tear slipping down her cheek. "*Goddammit.*"

Her heart was cracking, but she made herself turn the knob, thinking of Anna's face when she'd seen Chase in Vegas. It would be like that every single time they saw each other. That thought was impetus enough to twist the knob and slip out, her lips tingling, her body trembling, her skin on fire and her core throbbing with unsated need. She wiped the tear away with her knuckles and let herself feel the hurt.

Pain was better than need.

Chase watched Jamie slip away once more. She kept running from him, sneaking out of his grasp. She was right—he knew she was. He'd seen the thoughts pass across her face, seen the determination settle onto her features.

Anna's face crossed his mind, her eyes when she saw him onstage in Vegas. That moment…the surprised pain, it was reason enough to stay away. Anna and Jamie were closer than sisters, and Chase knew Anna still had feelings for him. They might have been buried deep and overshadowed by her love for Jeff, but if she saw Chase again, especially on a regular basis, those feelings would find their way to the surface. Which was a surefire way to break up a friendship.

He couldn't do that to Anna, or Jamie.

She was gone now. Really gone. He was back out on the road tomorrow; they had a show in Kalamazoo and then Grand Rapids, followed by Marquette and then Green Bay. He would stay far away from Detroit. Far away from Jamie.

He'd stay away if it killed him.

Chase slumped onto the couch, aching in his heart, aching in his body. He rubbed his hand across his scalp, trying to hold on to the feel of Jamie's hands on his head, on his face.

He nearly jumped up and followed her, then sat back down.

A second time he got up and paced to the door, then turned away. *No fucking way, dickhead. Don't do it.* But it was no use.

He needed her too badly.

He threw the door open and ran after her, needing to catch her, if only for one last kiss.

Rock
Stars Do
It Dirty

Chapter 1

Jamie heard Chase's feet behind her, heavy boots smacking the concrete. She ducked her head, doing her damnedest to pretend she didn't hear him. To pretend she didn't know what would happen if she turned around.

Jamie didn't turn around. She made it to Dale's car, clutching the leather strap of her purse in a white-knuckled grip. A part of her wanted to haul around and deck him. Another part wanted to turn around and kiss him, then take him somewhere, *anywhere*, and finish what they'd started.

She was tugging futilely at the locked car door when he caught up to her. His hand wrapped far too gently around her upper arm, near her armpit, his knuckles brushing her breast. She dragged a deep shuddering breath in, placed her palm on the window, refusing to turn around.

"What do you want, Chase?" Jamie hated how quivery and breathy and damned *needy* her voice sounded.

"You." His voice was raw, growling, as if the admission had been dragged out of his chest.

"Well, you can't have me."

"I know, but…" His grip tightened on Jamie's arm, and then he let go with a long, expelled breath. "That doesn't mean I'll ever stop wanting you."

She clenched her teeth and squeezed her eyes shut; the visceral pain in his voice tore at her heart.

"Chase…" Jamie could feel the intensity radiating off him, and she just *had* to turn in place to see his eyes. "God, you think I want—you think I don't—"

"Then why can't we make this work? Anna will be okay. She has Jeff. I'll be okay around her, if I have *you*."

Temptation raged through Jamie. "That's like…it's so wrong. I can't. I can't. It'd be ripping open wounds every time you two are in the same room."

She was standing against his chest, her hand curled up between them. She wasn't sure how that had happened, but it felt so right. And so wrong.

"It would get easier. Time heals all wounds, right? You heal the hurt inside me. You make it all go away."

Jamie blinked hard and bit her lip until it hurt. "*Stop*, Chase. *Please* stop. It would be a betrayal of Anna. My best friend. The one person I have in this world who's like family. I can't." The admission of her own feelings for Chase were on the tip of her tongue, and she choked them back. "I'm sorry. I'm *so* sorry."

She stepped away from him, and the hurt in his eyes deepened until Jamie thought she might be seeing the raw material of his very soul gleaming in the cracks of his heart, visible through his eyes. She felt a tear dragging down her cheek. Jamie knew this was the correct decision, but it still felt so wrong, so terrible. Chase was already hurt; she was only driving the dagger deeper.

She watched his eyes harden, watched as the shutters slammed down between them, between him and the world.

"Fine. I get it. You're right. She's your best friend. Your family. I'm just…some guy, right? I wish you all the best, Jamie." His voice was dead and cold, his words like stones. He turned and walked away.

"Chase, no, it's not like that. You're not just some guy, you're—"

He spun around so fast it startled her. "*Don't*, Jamie. Don't mitigate it. Okay? You can either heal me, or hurt me. Not both. That's not an ultimatum, it's just facts. I'm not going to try to make you choose between me or her."

"But that's exactly what you *are* doing."

"You're doing it, not me. I think it would work. I think it would be tough, but eventually, it would be okay."

"No, it wouldn't!" She slumped back against the door of the car, struggling for breath, for control. "Why do you have to make this so much harder on me?" Jamie slid along the side of the car, away from him; his nearness was intoxicating, suffocating. "What do you want to hear from me? Yes! I want you! Is that what you want to hear? But this *cannot happen*! I can't betray my best friend like that. Not even for you."

Chase backed away, his eyes dark, fathomless chasms. "Message received, Jay. Loud and clear. I won't bother you anymore." And then he turned away again.

He walked back into the building, shoulders tense, palm scrubbing frantically over his scalp. Jamie let him go, the hurt she could feel from him as powerful as the hurt inside herself.

He'd called her "Jay." No one but Anna ever called her that.

After Chase was gone, Jamie texted Lane, begging him to get her home. Lane appeared a few minutes later with Dale's keys and drove Jamie to her car. He didn't ask her any questions, didn't say a word the entire drive from Harpo's to Lane Bryant. He just drove, one hand on her knee. When he pulled up next to her car, he unbuckled his seatbelt and leaned over to hug her. She clung to his neck and choked back her tears, focusing on breathing until she had control over herself again.

"Thanks, Lane."

He nodded and kissed her cheek. "You know I love you, sweetie, and you know I'm here for you."

"I know." She pulled away and opened the car door, swung a leg out. "I'll call you later and we'll talk, okay?"

Lane smiled. "No worries, kitten. Just take care of yourself?"

She made it home without breaking down, somehow. She made it into her bed before unleashing a torrent of tears that didn't stop until she was simply too exhausted to weep anymore.

Anna showed up. "Jay?" she called from the kitchen. "Something told me you needed company."

Jamie didn't answer. She felt Anna's weight on the bed next to her, then fingers brushing curls away from her eyes.

"What happened, Jay?"

Jamie could only shake her head. "Just…life sucks."

Anna sighed, an irritated huff. "Jamie. Why aren't you talking to me? There's something big going on with you, and you're holding out on me. I'm starting to get mad."

"I can't tell you, Anna. It's complicated."

"Meaning you're afraid."

"Shitless."

Anna didn't answer right away. When she did, her voice sounded distant. "Okay, well, I can't make you talk to me. You know I love you. You know I'd never judge you."

Jamie sat up and faced Anna, working her feet beneath her into a cross-legged position. "Anna, please. Listen. It's not that…I don't know…it's not that I don't trust you or that I want to keep things back from you. You know I tell you everything—""Except the one thing that I've ever seen make you cry on a regular basis." She gestured at the bed they both sat on. "I've found you here, in your bed, bawling, more times over the last few months than in all the years I've known you. And we've been friends forever."

Jamie didn't know what to say. She fidgeted with a loose thread on her comforter. "Anna—god. I want to tell you. You're my best friend. You're the only one I've ever been able to tell everything to. But this is…it's fucked up, Anna."

"Are you in some kind of trouble?"

"No, it's nothing like that. It's just…"

"What? Just what?" Anna jerked the ponytail holder out of her hair, untangling her blonde locks with her fingers before smoothing it back and retying it. "I'm not gonna ask again, okay? If you won't tell me, fine. I get it."

Jamie flinched at the hardness in Anna's voice. "Why does this feel like a turning point between us? Like if I don't tell you, things won't be the same between us?"

Anna shrugged, a tiny lift of one shoulder. "I'm not trying to make demands or ultimatums or whatever. I just…I guess I sense this somehow has something to do with me, and I'm worried."

Jamie sighed, a frustrated expulsion of breath. "God. I need vodka."

"Me, too."

"No, I mean for real. If I'm going to do this, I'm going to need vodka." Jamie wiggled off the bed, wiping her face.

"Do what?"

"Tell you all of this."

Anna twisted to watch Jamie scrub the smeared makeup off her face at the *en suite* bathroom sink. "You're going to tell me?"

"I guess I have to. It does concern you. And…if I'm going to lose him over you, I might as well tell you, right?"

A pregnant pause, and then the question, in a low, tense voice: "Him?"

Jamie shook her head. "Vodka first." The two women went into the kitchen, and Jamie pulled a bottle of Grey Goose from her freezer. "I've been saving this for an emergency. I think this qualifies."

She poured two generous measures into a pair of juice glasses, then a hint of orange juice over them. She knocked hers back immediately and poured a second while Anna sipped hers more slowly.

"Jeez, Jay. Don't get drunk without me." Anna tried to laugh, but the worry in her eyes had Jamie swallowing the last of her second shot and pouring a third.

Jamie poured juice over the third measure and leaned back against the kitchen counter across from Anna. "Not drunk. Just tipsy enough to be able to get this out." She sipped, and then set the glass next to her. "Just remember when I'm telling you this, that nothing actually happened, okay?"

Anna frowned. "Okay…?"

"In Vegas, when you left the casino…the Six Foot Tall show. You gave me the backstage pass. I'm not sure what I intended to do, but…I ended up in Chase's dressing room. You should have seen him,

Anna—well, I guess I'm glad you didn't. He was so broken up. I just…I hated seeing him hurt. I mean, you could see how upset he was from the audience. I just wanted to make sure he was okay, you know?"

"What *happened*, Jay?"

"It was like…being hit by a bus. Something about him just struck me, deep inside. You know? It was more than his looks or charisma. I remember how you talked about him. Like he's got this magical presence. You just can't help yourself when he's around—he just takes over a room."

Anna's voice was quiet. Too quiet. "I remember."

"Well, this was more than that. It was…something totally different."

"Are you in love with Chase, Jamie?"

Jamie sucked down vodka, coughing before answering. "Maybe. I don't know. I haven't let myself think that far." She wiped her mouth with the back of her hand. "We kissed. In Vegas, backstage. I've never felt anything like it in all my life, Anna. I'm sorry. I can't even pretend to know how this is making you feel, but you wanted the truth."

"I'm not sure this is what I was expecting."

"Yeah, how could you, right?"

"How could I expect it? Or how could you do this to me?'"

Jamie shrugged, looking at Anna over the top of her glass. "Both?"

"I honestly don't know. Maybe I *am* thinking both. Keep going."

"Well, it was like that one kiss was more…I don't know…more intimate, or meaningful than *any*thing I've ever shared with another guy in my entire life. Like that one kiss was…a promise of everything he and I could have, and god…it was like an earthquake, it was so intense."

"Damn, Jay."

"Yeah. Damn. But then I remembered who it was I was kissing. I ran. I mean…of all the people in the world for me to finally feel a real connection with, it had to be *him*? Of course it did."

"So that was it?"

Jamie snorted. "Not hardly. I told him I couldn't do it, couldn't let anything happen between us. You're my best friend, and he's your ex. No way. Taboo, right?"

"Right." Anna's voice was oddly strained.

"So I managed to get away from him, which was like ripping out a chunk of my heart. We had your wedding and went home, and I worked my ass off, got the promotion. I tried to forget."

"And then you got drunk and had an accidental threesome with a pair of neanderthal potheads."

"Yeah. Fucking awful. Especially since it didn't help. It just made it worse. And not just because they weren't Chase, which was bad enough, but because even though we weren't together, I still felt like being with those two gumps was like cheating on Chase. Stupid, but it's how I felt, and it was rotten."

Anna rubbed her face. "God, Jay. No wonder you were so upset that night."

"Yeah." Jamie finished her vodka and poured a fourth, seeking oblivion, even though she knew it would never come. "I managed to bury myself in work enough to almost feel like I was moving on, and then Lane and the gang showed up after work tonight and dragged me out with them."

"Uh-oh."

"Yeah. They had an extra ticket to a show. They didn't tell me who was playing and I didn't ask, 'cause why should it matter, right?"

"Right. But let me guess. It was Chase."

"Bingo. So he brought me backstage this time, and we had another moment. It was all tortured and angsty and shit. We kissed again, and it was just as epic as the first time, only more so. I can't even put it into words. I never wanted to stop. I..." Jamie set the glass down and rubbed her face with her hands. "Anna, I swear, I never meant for this to happen. I don't know how it *did* happen. But I can't get him out of my head, no matter how hard I try."

433

Anna seemed to be at a loss for words. "Jay, I'm not even sure what to say, or what to think, or how I'm supposed to feel about this."

"Sshh-yeah. Tell me about it."

"I mean, in one sense, I want to be happy for you, but on the other side, you're my best friend and Chase *is* my ex. If I had to see him every time you and I got together, or something…it'd be impossible. It would hurt. I broke his heart, Jay. I did. He has every right to be pissed off at me. To never want to see me again. And I *hate* that I hurt him." Anna's eyes were downcast, as if the depths of her mixed drink contained some kind of answer to the situation.

There was a long silence then, during which both women sipped their drinks and tried to figure out what to say next.

Eventually, Anna broke the silence. "If he's what you want, Jamie, I'll deal with it. I love you enough to make it work."

Jamie groaned. "I already—shit. I already told him it could never work. I couldn't do that to you, Anna. I broke his heart again."

"For me?" Anna said, her words barely a murmur. "Because of me?"

"Not just—I mean, yeah, sort of. You're my best friend. You have such an intense history with him, and…" Jamie turned away and rummaged in the fridge, emerging with a bottle of cranberry juice. "I've had enough drama in my life. I don't need a relationship predicated on the kind of intense bullshit anything between Chase and me would come with."

"But, Jay…this is breaking your heart, too. I can see it."

Jamie shook her head. "It's done. Maybe in another life we could've…I don't know. It's moot now. He's gone."

Anna crossed the kitchen and wrapped her arms around Jamie. "Oh, god, honey. I'm so sorry. I wish I could—I don't know. I just wish it was different for you."

"Me, too." Jamie whispered the words so quietly they were barely audible.

Jamie sat alone in a bar an hour's drive from anywhere she knew. She'd been working sixty-hour weeks for nearly three months straight, working close-open shifts, doubles, extra inventory shifts, then working out at a twenty-four-hour gym, only going home when she was so exhausted she could barely make it through a shower before collapsing into bed.

Even still, she dreamed of him. She saw him on a stage, dark eyes boring into her, sweat running down his temple, down his chiseled cheek. She felt his scalp under her palms, woke up with her hands tingling from the vivid memory/dream of their stolen kisses. She woke up damp between her thighs, frustrated and alone and angry.

So, one day, she called in sick and drove away, pointing her car north on I-75 and just going. She blasted HIM and Hinder, Mumford and Sons and The Fray and everything on her favorite playlist until she was almost out of gas, and then she pulled off the interstate and found a bar.

And then she drank.

And drank some more.

She was in that pleasant place between buzzed and drunk, far enough gone to not care about what happened next, but sober enough to enjoy it. It was six in the evening on a Tuesday, so the bar—a just-off-the-freeway dive bar—was sparsely populated by a few isolated truckers and a table of drunk locals wearing John Deere hats and stained blue jeans. The only person of interest was a man who seemed to be none of the above, someone out of place, like Jamie. He was sitting at the end of the bar, a fitted baseball cap with a curved bill pulled low, sandy hair curling up from under the back edge. She couldn't see much else, but his jeans were dark and tight and clean, and his arms seemed thick and muscular, stretching the sleeves of his T-shirt.

Jamie pretended to watch the Lions-Falcons game, checking him out in brief sidelong glances. He never really looked her way, but she thought he might be doing the same as she was, watching her out of the corner of his eye.

Maybe I just need another distraction, she thought.

Then she mentally snorted, knowing it would be futile. She also knew she was going to go through with it anyway. She could tell from the way his finger traced patterns in the sweat on his beer bottle that he was preparing to make a move.

Yep, here it comes.

He stood up, strolled over to her, and sat down next to her. He lifted his beer bottle and tipped it toward her. "To passin' through, yeah?" He had a British accent, which did something fluttery to her stomach and made her toes curl in a way she hadn't felt in a long time.

Jamie clinked her glass of shiraz against his. "To passing through."

They both sipped, and then Jamie let herself give him a long once-over. He was hot, that was for damn sure. Gorgeous, piercing blue eyes in a classically beautiful face. His hands were strong-looking but manicured, large enough to make his Coors bottle seem small.

"So, where're you from, Blue?" he asked, his voice deep enough to pleasantly rumble in her ear.

She quirked an eyebrow at him. "Blue?"

He laughed. "It's an Aussie thing. People with red hair get called 'blue.' Haven't the foggiest why, though."

"You sound British."

"Well, I am. But my mum's from Perth, and I spend summers with her, so I've picked up a few mannerisms."

"You still spend summers with your mom?" Jamie said, amused but slightly worried.

He just laughed again, an infectious, unselfconscious sound that made her grin. "Not like you're thinking. I take a month every summer and go on holiday to visit her."

Jamie lifted an eyebrow at him. "You take a month-long vacation every year?"

He shrugged. "It's not uncommon, actually. For Europeans, at least. You Yanks are so obsessed with work you never take more than two weeks. A month is standard for most of Europe."

Jamie sighed wistfully. "A whole month off? God, I'd kill for that."

"Make it happen, then."

She shook her head. "I wish, but no. It's pretty much impossible." Jamie stuck her hand out to him. "I'm Jamie."

"Ian." His handshake was firm but gentle, his hand swallowing hers.

Jamie felt another flutter in her belly. Maybe this distraction would be more effective than she'd anticipated.

"So, Ian, where are you headed?"

He shrugged. "Actually, this is the time of year I'm usually in Australia, but Mum is traveling this year, so I came to America for my holiday."

Jamie laughed. "You came to Buttfuck, Michigan, on a vacation?"

"Is that the name of this place?" Ian asked, laughing. "I knew you Yanks were weird, but that really takes the cake. Kind of a strange name for a town, innit?"

Jamie found herself giggling. "I know you must get this a lot, but your accent is hot."

Ian swigged from his beer. Jamie got the sense he might be embarrassed.

"I might have gotten that before, yeah." He grinned at her, wiggling his eyebrows suggestively. "So...feel your panties dropping, then? 'Cause that's what one bloke told me, just this week past. He said, 'Your accent is a panty-dropper, man.'" He said the last part in a passable American accent, which Jamie found supremely odd-sounding.

Jamie shrugged nonchalantly. "Keep talking, and we'll see what happens."

"So your knickers *are* feeling a bit loose, then?"

"I'm not sure I'm wearing knickers."

Ian choked on his beer. "I didn't take you for that sort of girl, Jamie. Knickers is just another word for panties."

Jamie laughed. "Oh. Well, I am wearing panties, yes. But they *might* be feeling the slightest bit wiggly. Especially if you buy me another round."

Ian lifted his bottle at the bartender, then gestured at Jamie's glass, holding up one finger. "In that case, we should toast to sexy accents and dropping panties." He chuckled, making it seem like a joke.

Jamie clinked her glass against his bottle again, laughing with him. As she sipped, she wondered if he had any idea how close to the truth their toast was.

I'm back to my old tricks, I guess, she thought. *'Cause I'm about to take this boy back to his hotel and fuck him silly.*

She let him buy her a few more drinks, discovering over the course of two more hours that he was an IT consultant, and he was actually in Michigan on a mix of business and pleasure. He'd finished his contract in Detroit and had decided to venture northward with no real destination in mind. She also discovered that he was an only child, unmarried, and that he lived in London.

A couple more rounds revealed that he was staying in a motel just down the street from the bar.

"So, Jamie. What are your plans for the rest of the evening?" Ian asked.

"Don't really have any," she admitted.

She'd managed to avoid answering too many questions. Mainly, she didn't want to admit she was trashed in a bar hours from anywhere.

"Well, why don't you come back to my room with me?" Ian said. "Just…you know, till you sober up a bit?"

Jamie nodded, trying to calm her hammering heart; she wasn't sure why she was nervous, but she was. Being nervous was a good thing. "Sure. Sounds good."

"I hope you don't mind a bit of a walk, though," Ian said as he stood up, "seeing as I didn't drive from the hotel."

"No, that's fine. Probably do me some good."

"That it will, love. You seem a mite wobbly, if you don't mind me saying."

Jamie laughed as she stood up, swaying unsteadily. "Yeah, just a mite." She exaggerated her unsteadiness, using it as an excuse to wrap her hand around Ian's arm. "Mind if I hold on to you?"

Ian glanced down at her; standing up, he towered more than six inches over her. "Not a bit. Wouldn't want to go and have a spill, now, would we?"

Jamie just shook her head in response, concentrating on the feel of his thick arm, corded with muscle. It was a nice sensation. He smelled good, too, she realized, leaning into him. Faint cologne, not overpowering, a spicy, male scent, along with deodorant, and that other more indefinable scent of clean man.

Ian laugh rumbled through her. "Did you just sniff me?"

Jamie giggled in embarrassment. "Um. Maybe? Shut up. You smell good." She leaned in again and sniffed at his shirt. "A man who smells good is as much of a panty-dropper as a sexy accent."

"So…if I've got both…"

Jamie glanced up at him through her lowered eyelashes. "I plead the Fifth?"

Ian just snorted. "The Fifth Amendment is an American thing, love. I'm British, so it doesn't work on me."

"Oh, damn."

Ian didn't push it, and she let it go. She had to be a *little* hard to get, after all. *Right*, she thought. *'Cause this is hard to get.*

They were following the main road, walking across parking lots and stretches of yellowing grass, cars whizzing by to and from the freeway. A hotel sign about a quarter mile down announced their destination. They reached it after a few more minutes of walking in a surprisingly companionable silence.

Ian led her to a ground-floor room, unlocking the door and throwing it open with a flourish. "It's not much, but…well…that's it, really. It's a hotel room. Sorry I can't offer you better."

"We *are* in Buttfuck, Michigan. I can't really expect the Ritz, can I?" Jamie said.

She didn't spare the room much of glance; it was the same as any Best Western anywhere in the country. There was a pile of clothes on the bed, and Ian rushed over and scooped them into a Samsonite suitcase, which he closed and tossed into a corner.

"Sorry about that," he mumbled. "Wasn't expecting company."

"No problem," Jamie said.

An awkward silence ensued, in which Jamie wondered how long she should wait before attacking him with her face. Ian seemed, if Jamie was any judge, to be wondering the same thing.

"I'm not as drunk as you think," Jamie blurted. "I mean...I was kind of hamming it up. So I could hold on to you."

She heard the words coming out but couldn't seem to stop them. Embarrassment was shooting through her, centered in her belly as a knot of nerves. She hadn't been nervous around a guy in...a very long time. Since high school, probably. Even with Chase she hadn't been actually nervous; she'd been anxious, flooded with uncontrollable need and burning desire. She'd been mixed up around Chase, an emotional wreck, a physical mess. He turned her inside out and upside down and set everything about on fire.

Ian was different. He was...comforting. Familiar, somehow. And yet, she was nervous. She wanted him, but she didn't want it to be like all the guys she'd picked up at the bar. He was only in the U.S. for a month, she assumed, so it was a limited-time offer only. Maybe that was the source of her nerves. She wasn't really sure. She only she knew she didn't mind being nervous. It was a new feeling, something besides the ache in her heart and the coiled knot of need low in her belly.

Ian regarded her with something like amusement. "Yes, I'm aware. I wasn't going to say anything, since it seemed to be working in my favor."

Jamie shifted her weight from one foot to the other. "This is where I say 'I'm not usually this kind of girl,' except...I kind of am."

Ian lifted an eyebrow, the corner of his mouth quirking up in a smile. "Well, I guess we're evenly matched, then, because I'm in the same boat, more or less."

Jamie laughed. "Un-mix your metaphors, Shakespeare."

"I just mean I'm supposed to say something like, 'I don't normally bring girls home from the pub,' but I do, rather often, actually. I'll admit I'm relieved you said it first, though."

Jamie relaxed then. She sat on the edge of the bed, her purse still hanging from her shoulder, and glanced at Ian. "I'm in the middle of a big internal conflict, actually. Not about you, exactly, just…life. Myself. This tendency of mine to go home with guys from the bar. I promised myself I wouldn't do this anymore. But then there was this guy…and it was all Shakespearean forbidden love and whatever. So now that's over and I'm trying to go on with my life, but it's not that easy and you're here and I'm here, and—"

Ian crossed the space between them in a single stride, kneeling between her thighs and kissing her suddenly, silencing her. His hands were on her legs, and he tasted like beer and faintly of spearmint gum. "I get it, Jamie. I do. You don't have to explain."

Jamie wasn't sure what to say, for once. She *wanted* to explain. She wanted him to understand what he was getting into, but she wasn't sure what it was herself. It didn't feel like a one-time-only hookup, and nothing had even happened yet. They both clearly knew the score. They both knew how it was supposed to go: They'd fuck, and then Jamie would sneak out at some point in the early hours of the morning and walk back to her car. Only…she didn't want to.

She kissed Ian back, hesitantly, exploring the sensation of lips on lips, his hands daring up her thighs to curl around her hips inches above her ass. She felt butterflies in her stomach at his touch. She was looking forward to feeling him peel her shirt off, strip her of her jeans. It wasn't fire in her belly, but it was enough.

Ian might even be more than a distraction, she thought. She could run with that.

When he pulled away to slide up onto the bed next to her, Jamie kicked her shoes off and set her purse on the floor. She watched as Ian untied his shoes and tossed them near the table by the window.

"Ian?"

"Yeah?" He sat cross-legged and barefoot in the middle of the bed, combing his fingers through his shaggy blond hair.

"What if I said I didn't want to do the walk of shame tomorrow morning?"

He shrugged. "Then don't."

She picked at a loose thread on the comforter. "I mean...wake up here, tomorrow. I mean, we both know how this usually goes. This is your hotel room, so normally I'm the one who's supposed to sneak out at four a.m. But...I don't want to. I'm not sure what that would make this between us, but...yeah. What if I just want to do things differently?"

Ian nodded. "Ah. I...you know, normally that would make me rather uncomfortable. We've been honest with each other thus far, so I'll go ahead and continue the trend. I actually asked a girl to leave once. She was just...lingering. All bloody morning, she was there. Tea and break-fast, and checking her email and whatever, and I just wanted to tell her that wasn't how it worked. So I asked her if she would mind being on her way. I said I had business to take care of, only it was Sunday and I didn't. I felt like rubbish all the rest of the day. I kept seeing her disap-pointed face, like she thought we were going to *be* something and it was awkward. I hated that. I've never gone looking for a relationship, you know? I had one once. A serious one, too. Introduced her to Mum and Dad and went on holidays with her, all that rot. It was nice for bit, hav-ing someone to come home to, someone to watch the telly with." Ian's accent, fairly unpronounced until then, had grown stronger. "She was a beautiful girl, Nina was. Great in the sack. But...she was a slob around the flat. Couldn't make a decent cup of tea to save her life, either. And it was shite like that that did us in. The little things. No one cheated on anyone, we never really fought, and I really did enjoy having her around, but it was just...it wasn't *right*, you know?"

Jamie nodded, unsure where he was going with it. "Relationships are hard," she said, just to fill the silence. "I'm never sure how they're supposed to work. I always feel like it should be just sex, and he obviously thinks it's something more, but I never know *what* it's supposed to be, you know? Like, it's fun, and they're nice, and it's great not being alone at home all the time, but…"

"What's the point?" Ian finished for her.

"Exactly. If it's not just sex, and we're not getting married, what's the point?" Jamie pulled the thread free, popping seams until she had a few inches of clear thread like thin fishing line. "So…yeah. I guess I'll go, then. I really don't want to do the whole hook-up thing. I'm tired of it. I don't know what I do want, but I know I *don't* want that." She stood up, slipping a toe into her sneaker.

Ian looked up sharply, confusion on his face. "Go? No, that's not what I meant. I'm not sure why I said that. I shouldn't have told you all that. I'm sorry." He scooted across the bed and pulled her down by the hand so she was sitting on his lap. "Stay. Please? Stay here tonight. Let's both of us try something new. No expectations either way. You don't do the walk of shame, and I won't wake up alone, stuck somewhere between relieved and disappointed."

"So no expectations either way?"

"Right."

"I can do that." She let herself settle onto his lap, wrapping her arms around his neck. "I have to warn you, though, I'm pretty sure I'd make a shitty cup of tea."

"I drink coffee, too." Ian grinned, sliding his hands under the hem of her shirt to touch the skin on her back.

Jamie explored the muscles of his shoulders and back through his shirt. "Well, you're in luck then, 'cause I make a killer pot of coffee."

His lips touched her neck on the side an inch above her shoulder, then moved down to her throat, kissing the hollow at the base of her throat. Jamie let her head fall back, feeling an exhilarating rush of pleasure at the touch of his mouth on her flesh. She found the bottom edge of his shirt and lifted it up over his head, tossed it aside, then resumed her roaming of his torso with her palms. His skin was fair and smooth, his body toned and muscular, but not overly developed. He continued kissing her throat, then slid to the right, moving the neck of her shirt aside to touch his lips to her shoulder blade. With his other hand he touched her belly, dragging his fingers upward, lifting her shirt as he went. Jamie pulled back and raised her arms over her head, and Ian drew the fabric off, tossing it aside.

His gaze roved over her body, her full breasts held in by the red lace of her bra. "You're very beautiful, Jamie." He reached up and brushed one of the bra straps off her shoulder. "Very beautiful indeed."

Jamie glanced away. "Thanks."

His fingers slid the other strap off, and then he was unhooking the back with one hand, his eyes never leaving hers. Jamie held his gaze as her breasts fell free, and then her eyes slid shut involuntarily when his fingers grazed the underside of one breast. She clutched his forearm, and he cupped the heavy weight of one breast in his hand, then pinched the nipple between two fingers, rolling it. Jamie let herself gasp. She wriggled her bottom on his lap, feeling his erection thickening. Slipping sideways off him, Jamie lay back and pulled Ian down over her, tangling her fingers in his hair as he dipped in to kiss her lips. She felt her pulse quicken as their lips met. Butterflies again, more of them now, fluttering in her belly.

She slid her palms down his spine, curved around his waist and found the button of his jeans, popped it open and unzipped his fly. He was on his hands and knees over her, his palms by her face and his knees on either side of her hips. She pushed his pants down and he lifted up to let her get them off. She grasped his shaft in her hand, her pulse go from a rabbiting patter to a hammering thunder. He was well-endowed, thick, straight, pointing away from his belly. She slid her fist down his length, then paused at the base as he lowered his mouth to her breast, and she gasped when he sucked her nipple between his teeth. He reached between them and stripped her of her jeans quickly, then let his fingers roam along the outside of her hip, running in along the swell of her hipbone, across the dip where leg met groin, then down between her thighs.

Jamie let her legs fall apart, stroking his length as he slid a single finger along her crease. She reveled in the sensation of a man who knew what he was doing. He didn't just plunge in, but let the tip of his finger tease her, dragging up and down her pussy before probing in, ever so gently at first, then more and more, until his finger was inside her to the first knuckle, and then the second. She rubbed her thumb over the tip of his cock, drawing the pre-come out and smearing it over him with her fingers. Jamie let her hand move down to cup his balls, testing their weight, exploring them gently before resuming her slow and steady stroking of his cock.

He circled her clit with his middle finger, slowly, teasingly, then brushed the nub quickly, once, twice, and then she was arching her back and whispering a moan. He had her moments away from coming already, and they were just starting. This boded well. He slipped his fingers deeper into her, curling in to unerringly find her G-spot, then flicked his fingertips across it, pushing her closer to the edge, rubbing it, and now she was there, *right there*…Ian added his thumb, pressing it lightly against her clit, and that was all it took. Jamie gasped, shuddering, as the orgasm ripped through her. She pulsed her fist on his cock as she came, and then when the waves lessened, she pulled him toward her.

Ian pulled away. "Wait…wait. My trousers. I have a rubber in my wallet." He hung off the bed and dug his wallet out of his jeans while Jamie watched.

She was on the pill, obviously, but she didn't stop him. An aftershock rippled through her, and she pulled him to her as he sat up with the wrapper in his hand, moving toward her.

She took the condom from him, ripped it open, and slowly rolled the latex over his cock. He moved his hips into her grip, then settled himself over top of her again. He paused, his ocean-blue eyes pinning hers, and his mouth opened as if he was going to speak. She met his gaze evenly, waiting for him to say whatever was on the tip of his tongue. But he didn't. He just smiled at her, a half-curve of his lips, and then swiveled his hips to caress her nether lips with the tip of his cock. Once again, he didn't simply drive in but took his time, weight on one elbow, the other brushing her red curls away from her eyes and drifting down to cup her breast.

She ran her fingers through his coarse blond hair, then down his back, and cupped his firm ass, pulling at him, wanting him inside her.

He just shook his head. "Not just yet."

She didn't answer, held onto the hard globes of his ass and waited. His strong hand explored her body as he probed into her pussy with slow, soft rolls of his hips, teasing, teasing, and now he was inside her but only a few inches, and oh, god, he was right at her G-spot, gliding into her and away, sliding across that perfect place in a deliciously slow rhythm, driving her already orgasm-sensitive flesh wild. She clawed her fingers into the muscle of his ass, wanting to pull him in, pull him harder, but instead she merely held on and let him go at his own pace.

She felt his cock thickening inside her, felt his pulse beating hard against her chest, felt his muscles quivering and sweat sheen his pale skin as he moved inside her, slow, then a few quick strokes, then slow again until she was almost mad with frustration, wanting him to settle above her and drive in hard. But he didn't. She wrapped her legs around his hips and pulled at him, but he only laughed into her mouth, kissed her, and moved slower and more unpredictably than ever.

"Goddammit, Ian. Just—oh, god, that feels good. Just fuck me. Hard." Jamie whispered the words raggedly, her hips now fluttering against his with a life of their own, pushing in when he pulled away, pulling away when he began to drive in.

"You want me to fuck you hard?" Ian adjusted his position so he was directly over her now, his palms next to her ears and his hips between her thighs, his mouth next to her ear. "Is that what you want, Jamie?"

She clung to him, shuddering as the waves of her second orgasm began to tremble low in her belly. "Yes, Ian. Yes. Fuck me hard. I'm so close."

He planted a kiss on her neck and drove into her, deep, hard. Jamie whimpered, meeting his thrust with her own. "Like that?"

"Yes…yes…just like that. Again." Jamie arched her back, planting her heels to get herself closer, to get him deeper.

But he didn't drive in hard again. He fluttered at her entrance, shallow bursts near her G-spot, pushing against the ribbed flesh there until sensation overwhelmed her and she flopped back to the bed, whimpering helplessly, mad with need, close to orgasm but not there, while a new kind of detonation crashed through her, not quite orgasm, but like it. It was an emotional sensation, something entirely wrapped up in Ian, in this experience with him.

Ian shifted again, moved upward and began thrusting slow and deep, his body close to hers, and now she felt true release build up, pressure rising as his pubic bone slid along her clit, his shaft moving deep inside her.

It was then that Jamie recognized the emotion tangled up with the physical release: relief.

She had been worried she would never be able to truly enjoy being with a man if it wasn't—she stopped herself from even thinking the name—if it wasn't *him*. Even though she'd never actually been *with* him, she was worried no one else would be able to meet her needs, to spark her desire the way he did.

This, with Ian, was as close as she'd ever come to the intense welter of desires *he* ignited with Jamie. It wasn't the same, but it was close. And it was good.

She shook the thoughts free, feeling Ian begin to move with increasing desperation now, driving harder, if not faster. She was close, again. The pressure was a balloon inside her, pent-up need, layers of frustration building layer upon layer like a pearl in an oyster. The first orgasm had only added to the buildup, and now she was nearing a second, and felt a dizzying fear that this too would only add to the snowball effect.

It was just there, suddenly, that pulsating inferno of frustration, stress, pent-up need. It had been building up within her ever since she first saw Chase in the back room in Las Vegas, and now that she saw it for what it was, she couldn't see or feel anything else. It was like panic. She needed release, but she didn't think mere orgasm would do it; this was emotional in nature, internal, mental, psychological, not physical. The first orgasm Ian had given her had only put more on top of the pile. This second one was going to be intense, and Jamie found herself hoping desperately that it would give her the relief she needed. She felt doubt sneaking up on her, though.

The pressure mounted, and Ian's thrusts grew frenzied, his back arching and beaded with sweat. She clung to his shoulders and met him thrust for thrust, her legs around his hips, pleasantly filled by him, his tip striking her at just the right angle to give her the most pleasure. She heard herself moaning, felt the intensity building, felt the waves rolling through her. Jamie bit Ian's shoulder as she came, raked her nails down his back and cried out. The explosion of physical release made her writhe and cling even tighter to Ian, and then she was sent further into abandon when she felt him come moments after her, groaning and burying his face in her neck, grinding madly into her, and then they were still together.

Ian rolled off and lay next to her, breathing heavily. "Bloody hell, Jamie." He rolled his shoulders. "You took a layer of skin off, I think."

Jamie pushed him over so she could look at his back, wincing at the eight parallel gouges running down his back. "Damn. Yeah, I did. Sorry. Guess I got carried away."

Ian just chuckled and pulled her over to rest her head on his chest. "No worries, love. I wasn't complaining. I haven't had it off that well in an age."

"Me, either," Jamie said. "Assuming that last part means it was good for you."

Ian rumbled in sleepy laughter. "Precisely. It was more than good for me, darling."

Darling. Love. Jamie listened to his breathing as it slowed and evened out. Those were just casual words for him, she reminded herself. Not actual terms of endearment.

She was dizzy, drunk, fairly well-sated...and disappointed. Still burning with frustration. Need. The mountainous weight inside her was still there. She wasn't as sexually frustrated as she had been, but the root cause of her ache hadn't changed. She listened to Ian's sleeping breaths, felt his heart beating under her ear, watched his chest rise and fall, admired the contours of his body. He was damn sexy, and a good lover. A girl could do worse. He had a good job, a hot-as-hell accent, and he could make her come twice in a row, while they were both drunk. She should hold on to this one while she had him.

Maybe it would turn into love. Or at least...something like it. Something as close as she could come without—*no.* She wouldn't, *couldn't* go there. That wasn't a possibility. She'd made her choice.

Her instinct to flee kicked in. It was that time. Ian was asleep, her car was waiting, and by the time she made it to her car, she'd be sober enough to drive. Or she could just sleep in her car. Or even get a room in this same hotel.

As if sensing her inner dilemma, Ian's arm curled around her waist and held her tight against him. Jamie kicked the flight reflex down, choked it down, shoved it down. This was good. Ian was good. She reached down and tugged the flat sheet and the comforter up to her breasts, covering herself and Ian. This was nice. He was holding her. She'd be here with him when they woke up. They'd have breakfast together. She might even learn his last name.

This is good, Jamie told herself.

The problem was, she didn't quite believe herself. Not deep down. A voice in the shadowy corners of her soul, that place where one's darkest truths reside, was telling her this was still just another futile attempt to bury her heartache.

She felt the pressure in her belly, the burning need for release. She *wasn't* sated. Not by a long shot. Maybe she could wake Ian up in a few hours and go again, take the edge off. He'd be game, most likely. She knew, though, that for as long as she was with Ian, the edge would still be there. He simply wasn't capable of satisfying the blood- and soul-deep desires within her. He could—and would—try his best, and she'd let him. But it wouldn't be enough, and she knew it.

She fell asleep wondering how long she could keep this up.

Chapter 2

The music was fire in his veins. It was raw, primal fury pounding through his blood and his muscles and his brain. The shrieking guitars and chugging bass and pounding drums, the poetry flowing from his mouth in the growled and sung lyrics—these were the only things capable of drowning the hurt, capable of disguising the cracks in his heart.

Chase crouched on top of the speaker stacks, shirtless, sweating, screaming into the mic as thousands of fans watched, rapt. They could see the agony in his performance. He didn't try to hide it. Rather, he used it. He left his soul on the stage every single night, and the fans ate it up. Music journalists and bloggers were watching him carefully, offering write-ups praising his "raw, soulful, and deeply tortured performances," as one writer put it. Chase didn't care for any of that. Let them blog and tweet and and whatever else. Let them talk. The music was what drove him. He wrote on the tour bus, ignoring the wild parties, the joints and fifths his bandmates indulged in around him. Ignored the gaggles of topless girls. He wrote, worked out the melody, and gave it Gage and Linc to perfect.

The guys were increasingly distant. Or rather, they recognized his need for space and distanced themselves, left him alone. Didn't invite him to after-parties, didn't offer him the joints or the bottles. He hadn't had a drink in over a month by the time the tour schedule allowed them a few weeks off, and hadn't touched a woman since the experiment in Las Vegas with the girls from Murder Doll Asylum.

Back in Detroit, Chase didn't know what to do with himself. Without the rush of the performance, without the fans and the music, he was left loose and numb.

He'd long since used the money fronted him by the record label to pay off his house. He had a cousin drop by once a week to keep the place from looking abandoned, so when he finally walked into his house in the suburb of Sterling Heights, it was clean, the lawn mowed, the fridge empty of molding food and spoiled milk. He'd called his cousin, Amy, from Chicago and let her know he was coming home, and she'd stocked his kitchen with some food staples. In return, he'd mailed her money and a ream of tickets to the next Detroit show.

He stood in his living room, trying not to remember the last time he had been here. He had stood in this very spot, just to the left of the faded suede couch, while a certain blonde-haired, hazel-eyed DJ had stolen his heart, one stripped-off article of clothing at a time. Her bra and panties had been blue, lacy, and too fucking sexy for his own good. God, what a night that had been.

Chase shook himself. No sense in thoughts like that. It wasn't Anna on his mind or in his heart anymore, anyway. He hadn't really been truly in love with her, he had long since realized. He had been falling in love with her, but hadn't been there yet. She'd run off before that could happen.

Not that he was at all bitter about it.

Then Jamie had come along while he was at his most vulnerable and had wormed her way into the aching space in his heart. She was all curls and curves, red hair like fire-lit copper and fierce green eyes, soft lips that tasted of vodka and cranberry and lip balm. She'd given him the slightest taste of what it would have been like to be her lover, and then snatched it away from him.

Not that he was at all bitter about it.

He rummaged in the fridge, found a case of Harp lager, popped one open, and sipped from it while he made himself a sandwich. He was back in Detroit. Jamie didn't live too far away. Finding her would be a piece of cake.

No.

Chase scrubbed his face with his palm. That was over. She'd made her choice clear. She didn't want him. Although that wasn't true, exactly. She *did* want him, equally as much as he wanted her. She just refused to let herself have him. Sure, he understood her reasons; they were perfectly reasonable and correct reasons, after all. It's not like he *wanted* to see Anna all the time. It would have been difficult and awkward as hell.

But Jamie…she would have been worth it.

Would have been.

Chase finished his beer and swirled the suds on the bottom around, wondering what the hell he was supposed to do with himself now.

He picked up his phone and scrolled through his contacts until he found the one he was looking for: Eric Meridian. Eric owned a gym and kickboxing studio not far from Chase's house, and he had often gone there before the band really took off, sparring with Eric, pumping iron, or just pummeling the heavy bag until the stress was reduced to a manageable level.

Chase needed to vent. Badly. He sent a text to Eric asking if he had time to spar and waited for a reply.

Within minutes, Eric texted back: *I've always got time to spar bro. Drop by whenever you want.*

Chase grinned, changed into workout shorts and a tank top, packed a clean change of clothes, and drove to the gym. When he got there, Eric was taping his fists. Tall, wiry, nondescript of feature with short brown hair and brown eyes, Eric didn't seem to be the kind of person you should be afraid of, but he was. Eric was deadly proficient in several styles of martial arts, mainly Muai Thai, kickboxing, and Jiujitsu. He wasn't hugely muscled, didn't have any tattoos or piercings, and would pass on the street for an accountant or CPA, but Eric Meridian was, in reality, one of the hardest and toughest people Chase had ever met.

Chase taped his fists, stretched out, and then he and Eric stepped into the small roped-off ring. They began circling each other, fists raised, bodies twisted sideways to present the smallest possible target. Chase, full of angst and suppressed pain and anger, struck first. He didn't hold back, knowing Eric was perfectly capable of handling with ease anything Chase could throw at him. Chase lashed out with a right cross, which Eric blocked easily, then lifted his knee, leaping into Eric to provide impetus to the blow. Eric quick-stepped backward, grabbed Chase by the bicep, threw himself to the floor, and planted his heel in Chase's chest, kicking up and back to flip Chase over his head.

Landing with an *ooomph*, Chase was winded but scrambled to his feet, throwing up crossed arms to block the flurry of quick jabs Eric threw at him, designed more to distract and disorient than actually do damage. The real blow came suddenly as Eric danced backward then darted forward, left heel flashing out to catch Chase in the chest, winding him further and propelling him backward. It was enough to spur Chase into a fury. He launched himself forward, using Eric's own tactic of a flurry of jabs to distract, then plunging in with a knee, then a snap-kick to Eric's ribcage.

From there, the fight turned savage, in a friendly type of way. Eric seemed to sense Chase's underlying tension and began pushing Chase harder and harder, putting real force behind his blows and letting fewer and fewer of Chase's strikes through his defenses. After almost ten full minutes of all-out sparring, both men had bloody noses and bruised ribs. The core reason for Chase's distress hadn't changed, but at least he no longer felt like he was so on edge, so about to implode or explode, or just simply combust into a million pieces of sexual frustration and broken-hearted despair.

They sat on a bench side by side and swigged from water bottles.

"What's eating you, bro?" Eric asked.

Chase shrugged. Eric was a good friend and great source of stress relief, but he used the word "bro" in every sentence. It grated on Chase's nerves after a while, which was why he usually kept their conversations to a minimum. "Just life," he ended up saying.

"Life? I'd think life would be great. You're a fuckin' legit rock star, bro. Things should be off the chain."

Chase suppressed a sigh; Eric also spoke in an endless series of slang phrases and terms. "Yeah, well. Even rock stars have problems, man. I just need to blow off some steam. Thanks for letting me stop by."

"Hey, I getcha. No worries, bro. I've got a date in a couple hours so I'm gonna bust outta here, but you go ahead and do what you need. You know your way around." Eric bumped fists with Chase and then swaggered off to take a shower.

Chase finished his water, then refilled it and moved to the heavy bags suspended from the ceiling a few feet away from the ring. Chase rolled his shoulders, then slipped a soft right jab at the bag, an exploratory touch. A second, then a third, and then a pair of snap-kicks, followed by a roundhouse heel kick. With that, Chase was off in a frenetic rhythm of punching and kicking, letting out all of his anger and hurt, pummeling it all into the bag. He heard noises around him, people talking, the grunts and shuffles of a pair sparring in the ring, clinking and clanking of weight machines, but none of it penetrated through his awareness.

When he finally stopped to rest, his hands on his knees, dragging in quick, deep panting breaths, he realized someone was watching him from the heavy bag nearest him. She was tiny but full-figured, barely five feet tall but blessed with curvy hips and breasts even a sports bra couldn't hide. Her thick black hair was twisted into a braid dangling over one shoulder, and her eyes were a vivid green. Too green. Too reminiscent of—Chase cut that line of thinking off with brutal finality.

She had a quirky grin on her lips. "That poor bag must've really pissed you off, huh?" She had her fists taped, and sweat was beading on her face, neck and chest. She was breathing almost as hard as he was.

Chase found himself turned on for the first time in weeks. "Yeah. I caught it talking about my mom, so I had to beat the shit out of it."

"Remind me not to get on your bad side, then." She crossed over to him and stuck out her hand, which was dwarfed by his when they shook. "Tess."

"Chase." Chase smiled at her, a genuine smile. "It's a pleasure to meet you, Tess. Come here often?"

She lifted an eyebrow at him. "Really? You're using *that* line on me?"

Chase laughed, and felt the pall of numbness receding. "It's not a line, I swear. I don't come here often, so I'm honestly wondering if you do."

"Uh-huh. Sure. It's a pick-up line if I've ever heard one, but I'll take the bait." She rubbed her wrist across her forehead and shook her head to toss her braid away so it dangled down her back.

Chase found himself wanting to wrap that braid around his fist and use it to hold her in place while he drove himself into her from behind; faint shock rippled through him at the ferocity of the sudden desire. He felt a smile curl his lips, a feral, seductive smile. He felt satisfaction at the way Tess reacted, nostrils flaring, breasts swelling as she dragged in a deep, steadying breath. Her fingers tightened into the leather of the heavy bag, and her eyes narrowed. Chase took a few steps toward Tess until he loomed over her, staring down into her eyes. She didn't back up, but he could tell she wanted to. Instead, she seemed to swell in presence, meeting his gaze head-on, the corners of her mouth lifting in a smile as hungry and feral as Chase's.

Without warning, she shoved the bag at him, hard, knocking him back. While he reeled, stumbling for balance, she snapped a kick at his stomach, which he didn't quite block. He was knocked farther back, heaving in a breath. She didn't relent, however, and closed in with him, curling in a pair of swift uppercuts to his ribs. She wasn't trying to hurt him, he could tell, but she wasn't holding back, either. Her eyes gleamed with adrenalized excitement, and even as she crushed her knee into his chest, her eyes betrayed her desire.

Chase slapped away a straight right punch with his wrist, then darted his own blow at her ribs, hard enough to let her know he wasn't fooling around, but not enough to really hurt. He'd never sparred with a girl before, and it unnerved him. She was clearly skilled, more so than he was, Chase realized, but he still couldn't bring himself to open up the way he would with Eric. Chase might not have had much good to say about his upbringing, but at least his old man had drilled into him a bone-deep respect for women, a refusal to ever strike a woman under any circumstances.

Tess was inviting him to come at her, though. She was dancing around him, having lured him into the ring, bouncing from one foot to the other, fists up, braid-end swaying in a serpentine rhythm. She was a tiny ball of energy, quick and fierce and wild. Chase snapped a kick at her, worried it was too hard. If he connected wrong, he could easily send her flying, injured. He need not have worried, though. She dodged it with ease, knocking his heel upward with a forearm and lunging in underneath it to crash into him with her body. She might have been small, but that body-blow had a huge amount of force behind it, her fae frame slamming into him hard enough to topple him backward. He landed on his back, winded once more, gasping for breath like a fish out of water.

He felt a weight settle on him, blinked hard to clear his vision. Tess was above him, on top of him, green eyes glinting merrily, barely breathing hard. Her knee was in his groin, a subtle warning that nonetheless managed to be an erotic promise.

"Yeah, I come here a lot," she said, her face mere inches from his.

"I can tell," Chase gasped.

He wrapped his fingers around her wrists next to his head, holding but not restraining. Tess tensed, eyes narrowed, chin lifting in defiance, her knee shoving ever-so-slightly harder into his crotch. Chase moved his hands up Tess's arms slowly, non-threateningly, until he reached her shoulders. Tess was frozen now, eyes locked onto Chase's, waiting for his next move. Chase held her gaze as he slid his palms down her spine, hesitating at the small of her back for a millisecond before continuing down to cup her ass. Tess's eyes widened and her breath caught. Chase gripped the firm globes of her ass, kneading the flesh through the thin, skintight fabric of her knee-length yoga pants. Tess moved her hips—involuntarily, it seemed to Chase—so her ass worked deeper into his grip. Chase let his fingers spread apart, exploring the expanse of each cheek, then tracing the crease between them. Tess shivered above him, widening her knees and pushing her hips backward to open herself to him.

Chase felt his erection stiffening between their bodies, and Tess licked her lips and let her gaze flicker down to take in the bulge in his gym shorts. Without warning, Chase gripped Tess's hips and flipped them over so he was on top, one hand pressing her hips to the floor, the other capturing her wrists and pinning them above her head. Tess writhed beneath him, bucked and kicked, but Chase had his knees between her thighs, preventing her from gaining leverage against him.

Lowering his lips to her ear, Chase whispered, "How about this: I'll take you out to dinner, wherever you want, and then I'll bring you back to my house."

Tess bucked again, this time less to get free than to remind him she wasn't going to go down without a fight. Then she said, "Sure. But what are we going to do at your house?" Her voice was low and sultry, breathy against his cheek.

Chase nipped her earlobe with his teeth. "Hmm. We could play euchre?"

Tess laughed, a seductive, rippling sound. "You need four for that." She returned the bite, worrying at his ear with her teeth. "I don't share."

"Oh. Well. Hmmm." Chase shifted his position so his rigid shaft brushed against her cotton-covered mound. He could smell her arousal, a dizzying musk. "I have an idea. How about I bend you over my bed and fuck you from behind until you're screaming my name?

I'll wrap my fist around that sexy braid of yours and make you come a dozen times before I let you leave."

Tess's mouth opened in a breathless gasp of surprise. When she found her voice, it was shuddering and broken with desire. "Only a dozen?"

"Greedy? I can make it more, if you want. Maybe I'll tie you up and see how many times I can make you come before you pass out?"

Tess writhed her hips into his, and he nearly forgot they were in a public gym—empty, by the sounds of it, but still a public place. He had to tense every muscle in his body to keep from ripping her pants off and taking her there on the mat of the sparring ring.

"How about I give you three hours to make me come as many times as you can? If you can give me more than four orgasms in three hours, I'll do whatever you want, or let you do whatever you want to me, within the limits of safety and consensual agreement."

Chase laughed. "Is this a bet?"

"Yep. I don't think you can do it."

Chase narrowed his eyes. "Doubting me already? We just met, honey. You have no idea what I'm capable of."

"Oh, I'm not doubting *you*, I'm doubting *me*. I've never in my life orgasmed more than once in a row."

Chase laughed, but this time it was a rumble of pleasure containing a promise. "Then you've been with all the wrong men, sweetheart."

"Maybe I have," she said. "But I guess we'll see, won't we?"

"I guess we will."

They used the gym showers and dressed, then took Chase's rental car to dinner at P.F. Chang's in the Somerset Collection. They learned a bit about each other during their leisurely dinner. Tess was a flight attendant for Northwest Airlines, was currently single following what Chase gathered was a pretty bad breakup, although she glossed over it with a few curt phrases of dismissal. She was the youngest of three children, and the only girl, and her much-older brothers were both in law enforcement, so she'd learned young how to defend herself. For himself, Chase told her about his band's recent success and left out any mention of Jamie or Anna, saying only that he'd been single for quite a while. Tess's eyes narrowed when he said this.

"You know my brothers are both cops, right? I did mention that? You should realize they've taught me how to detect a liar, and how to cause intense physical pain to men who lie to me."

Chase didn't answer right away, dragging his last pea pod through the sauce on his place without looking at her. Finally, he met her eyes. "It's a lie of omission. Let's just say it was a complicated situation that I don't want to talk about. If it's something that needs to be told, eventually, then I'll tell you."

Tess nodded. "Eventually, hmm? I can live with that. As long as you're not secretly married or something." She finished her glass of red wine, then twisted the stem between her fingers. "Are you planning on there being an *eventually* between us?"

Chase shrugged. "I honestly hadn't thought that far. It's not impossible."

"Fair enough," Tess said.

"About our bet," Chase said.

"Yeah?"

"What do you get if I lose?"

Tess gave him an amused grin. "Hmmm. I'm glad you asked." She ran her tongue along her upper lip suggestively. "If you lose, you agree to be my bitch for three days. Sexually and otherwise. Everything. Do my dishes, vacuum my floor, wash my car...shirtless. Go down on me whenever I want without having the favor returned. Rub my feet."

Chase tilted his head to the side. "Damn. You drive a hard bargain. How about that's the bet both ways? I lose, I'm your bitch. If you lose, you're mine. Including the topless car washing."

Tess lifted her chin defiantly. "Deal." She extended her hand and they shook to seal the deal. "But you'd better bring your A-game, buddy, because I'm telling you, you've got your work cut out for you.

It's really difficult for me to reach climax, and I'm a mess afterward. Just sayin'. Be ready to be my bitch."

Chase leaned forward and kissed the corner of her mouth, a tease, a promise. He sat back without delivering on the kiss, leaving Tess with her lips parted in anticipation, her eyes half-closed, nearly panting.

"Pay the bill so we can go," Tess whispered. "I've got a bet to win."

"There's just one stipulation," Chase said, sliding cash into the black bill-folder. "You can't cheat. No pretending I didn't make you come."

Chase drove them to his house, and when he closed the door behind him, Tess stood in the middle of the living room, hands crossed over her stomach, grasping the hem of her shirt in preparation to strip it off.

"Not wasting any time, are you?" Chase said, crossing the space between them and capturing her wrists in his hands. "We're doing this my way, sweetheart. And my way involves stripping you myself. Slowly."

Tess released her shirt and stood, waiting. "Your way, huh? What if I don't want to do it your way?"

"Well, if you're having trouble coming, then maybe your way isn't working." Chase ran his hand between the bottom of her shirt and the top of her calf-length skirt, brushing her skin with the calloused pads of his fingers.

"Maybe you're just a cocky bastard," she said, gasping, the breathy catch in her voice stealing the vitriol from her words.

"Or maybe I just know I can make you come as many times as I want. Maybe I just I know I can play your sweet little body like a guitar."

Tess let her head loll back on her shoulders as he lifted the hem of her skirt up, dragging his fingers along the insides of her pressed-together thighs. "If I'm a musical instrument, I'm more of a mandolin: round at the base and strung tight."

"You're not self-conscious about your figure, are you?"

She shook her head. "Hell, no. I may be tiny, but I'll kick your ass. I've got wide hips and big tits, and I'm so short I'm nearly a little person. If you don't like it, that's your loss."

"I like it. I like it a lot." Chase brushed her silk-covered slit with his fingers, feeling her grow damp as he touched her. "In fact, I plan to spend the rest of the night showing you how much I like it."

"That works. I'd hate to have to break your arms."

"You wouldn't break my arms."

"Yes, I would. Especially if you don't quit teasing me and touch me already."

Chase was slowly working his middle finger under the elastic leg-band of her panties, tracing the outer edge of her labia. "All in good time. I'm not sure you're ready for me to touch you yet. You don't want it bad enough."

Tess clawed her fingers into his bicep, trying to tug his finger closer, deeper. "Yes, I do. I do. I want it."

"How bad?"

"Really bad."

Chase swiped his finger along her slit, feeling her slick, hot juices as they coated his fingers. "I don't believe you."

"I'm not gonna beg, Chase. You're the one who has to prove yourself to me, remember. If you lose, you'll spend three days licking my pussy and rubbing my feet."

His middle finger dipped deeper, curling into her tight channel and rubbing against the ridge of her G-spot. She shuddered; her knees buckled, and she stiffened her legs to catch herself. "Maybe I shouldn't tell you this, but that doesn't sound like a loss for me."

"You say that now..." she started, then trailed off as Chase hooked his fingers inside her panties and tugged them off with a single sharp motion, guiding her legs to step out of them one at a time.

Tess started unzipping her skirt, but Chase stopped her. "Not yet. You're going to have your first orgasm fully clothed."

"Except for my panties, you mean." Tess ran her hands over his shoulders as Chase knelt in front of her.

He slid his palms up the backs of her legs from ankle to buttocks, tickling and tracing the strong curves. Her skirt was still draped down around her calves, disguising the way his hands were slipping between her thighs from behind, spreading her stance until her feet were shoulder-width apart, granting Chase access to her desire-wet nether lips. He cupped her buttocks, then traced a finger down the crease of her ass.

"Is this off-limits?" he asked, letting his finger move in near her anus.

"For now? Yes." She pushed his hand away, moved it to her hip. "Ask me again later if you've managed to win our bet. I may change my answer."

"Fair enough."

Chase ran his hands down the front of her thighs and then back up, twisting his palm so it was facing up, cupping her mound. Tess's legs buckled again, and her weight bore down on his palm; she wiggled her hips so her clit rubbed against the heel of his palm, and she let out a soft moan.

"You're wet and tight, Tess. I think you might be ready," Chase said, dragging two fingers through her folds.

"About...oh, god...about damn time," she said.

Chase lifted her skirt up to her hips, steadying her with an arm around her ass. He curled his two middle fingers into her hot, wet pussy, flicking his fingertips across her G-spot. When she gasped, he sucked her clit into his mouth, turning her gasp into a moan. Her hands scraped over his stubble-dark scalp, her fingers turning into claws as he licked and flicked at her folds. Her breathing turned to panting, her knees began to dip and buckle with every swipe of his tongue, every feather-light brush of his fingers over her G-spot.

"I can't believe it...oh, god, oh, god, I'm close already." Tess's hands cupped the back of Chase's head in a familiar way that did something deep in his heart, something between pain and desire, its source nebulous and difficult to pinpoint.

He pushed the thoughts away and renewed the vigor of his tongue's assault on the sensitive, cream-wet nub of her clit. She clutched him tight, and his arm kept her upright when the first wave rolled over her. Chase felt it start low in her belly, heard her breathing grow frantic as her orgasm neared. As she closed in on climax, Chase slowed and then paused, drawing a curse from Tess.

"What? Why the hell are you stopping? I'm so close, you bastard!" She writhed into him, seeking release.

Chase let the fabric of her skirt droop around his face, obscuring him. He slipped his free hand up her belly and tugged the cup of her bra down to reveal her breast. Pinching it between two fingers, Chase began again with his tongue and fingers, rolling the tip of his tongue in circles around her taut clit, pressing his fingers against her G-spot and working in circles to match the motion of his tongue.

She was almost instantly on the cusp of climax, but Chase drew it out, increasing his pace until she was frantic once more, then slowing down, repeating this cycle until Tess was nearly mad with need for release.

"Goddamn it, Chase! You're making me crazy!" She clutched his face against her, shamelessly pushing him into her folds. "Fuck me, I'm *so* close."

"I know you're close, sweetness." Chase paused to answer, gently tweaking her nipple. "And believe me, I plan to thoroughly fuck you. And then some."

She tried to speak, but her words were subsumed beneath a strangled shriek of ecstasy as Chase pushed her closer and closer to climax with now-relentless fingers in her cream-drenched sex, his tongue whipping at her throbbing clit. He felt the pulse in her clit, felt the throb, felt the quavering in her belly and the clenching in her inner muscles.

Two fingers deep in her sex, Chase extended his pinky and pushed it against the tight bud of her anus, and as she came, he pressed just the tip of his littlest finger against the knot of muscles, not quite entering her. She screamed then, a full-voiced howl of release. Her body undulated as she came, her knees giving way even as she fought to stay upright. Chase continued to flick and suck and wiggle and pinch her every nerve ending until she was wrung limp. He caught her and carried her to his room, kicking open the door with his foot, settling her on the bed gently. Her body shook and shuddered with aftershocks, and her breathing was ragged.

Chase unzipped her skirt, slid a palm under her backside and lifted her, tugging the skirt off with a jerk. Then he peeled her shirt over her head, Tess cooperating with floppy limbs. He unhooked her bra and tossed it aside. She was naked for him then, and he was hard with desire. He felt the all-too-familiar pang of misplaced guilt rush through him as he pressed kisses to her breasts, the awful, unshakeable sensation that he was doing something wrong by being with someone *else* than Jamie.

Tess was oblivious to the thoughts racing through him, of course, and he was thankful for that. He nibbled on her nipple, worrying the taut bud with his teeth, eliciting a sexy little mewl from her. She was regaining her senses finally, and was clawing at his shirt, pushing it up over his head and exploring his torso with eager hands, then ripping at the button of his jeans and pushing them down.

Chase had left all his leather pants with the tour bus, so he was stuck with jeans, which he disliked and rarely wore. He let her strip him, let her look at him, let her take his turgid shaft in her small hands. She slid her palms along his length, rubbed her thumb over the broad mushroom head, caressed his cock with quick, soft, skilled hands. He knelt above her, letting her touch him until his felt himself begin to respond, begin to rise.

"No more touching. I'm yours to do with as you wish if I lose," Chase said, pushing her hands away and over her head, then tracing a line from neck down between her breasts to test her swollen folds with his index finger. "For now, however, you have three more orgasms to go."

Tess arched her back as he ever so gently began to move his finger inside her. "Shit...shit...that was so intense, I'm not sure I'd survive another one."

"Well, then, I hope you have life insurance, sugar, because that was just the beginning."

Tess moaned as he lapped his tongue around one nipple, working the other with the fingers of one hand and circling her clit with the fingers of his other hand. He was using the opposite hand in her sex as he had used before, and he could smell her musk on his fingers, along with another, darker scent from his pinky. She'd said her second entrance was off-limits, but she hadn't protested when he'd touched her there before, so he decided to push his luck a bit. The first orgasm had wrenched through her like a tidal wave, so if he drew this one out even longer, the second would be even more intense.

He worked her clit slowly with his fingers, getting her hips moving in gentle circles before slacking off, letting her subside a bit, then bringing her back up again, biting at her nipple, sucking on it, flicking and pinching the other. And then, abruptly, he moved down her body and lifted her legs over his shoulder, lifting her hips to bring her sweet wet folds to his mouth. She writhed in place, moaning nonstop now as he suckled her clit, slathering her own juices downward over the tight muscles of her anus. She groaned when his pinky touched her there, and then sucked in a ragged, whimpering breath when he penetrated up to the first knuckle. He didn't move his pinky, just left it there to let her adjust, slowing his pace and working her throbbing bud with soft, slow licks of his tongue. He was able to reach her nipples still, so Chase rolled one between finger and thumb in torturously slow pinches.

Tess was wiggling and arching and undulating as he drew out the process, working his pinky inward with careful, delicate pushes, timing them with thrusts of his tongue against the straining nerves of her clit. When he was inside her to the second knuckle, he began to work his finger in and out, once again synced with the rhythm of his tongue against her folds and his fingers on her breasts.

Tess began to buck into his finger, driving him deeper, her voice raised in a keening shriek. He felt her pussy muscles clench and quiver; her back arched and her heels dug into the bed. He pushed his finger and pulled it, licking furiously until his jaw ached and his tongue was on fire, pinching her nipple until he was sure the twinge of pain was adding to the pleasure.

She came with a cry, bowed upward in an arched bridge, only her heels, head, and neck touching the bed. Wave after wave crushed through her, shaking her, ripping shuddering sobs from her as she lowered her body to the bed. Chase relented then, and kissed his way up her flat, taut belly, kissed each breast, then her neck, then her mouth, tasting the salt of sweat and tears on her mouth and cheeks. Tess clung to his neck, shaking uncontrollably.

He kissed her neck and shoulder as he fished a condom from the bedside table drawer, ripped it open with his teeth and rolled it over his straining cock. Tess was oblivious to this, gasping for breath.

"Ready for number three, sweetness?" Chase said.

"What? Oh, god. Oh, god…I can't—I'm not ready. I'm not ready." Tess was barely able to whisper, the words mumbled drunkenly. "It's too much."

"You asked for it, babe." Chase probed her entrance with the tip of his cock, working himself slowly inside. "Too much? Want me to stop?"

Tess's fingers scrabbled at his back as he filled her, stretched. She was tight, so tight, almost too tight. He went as slow as was humanly possible, working himself in an inch, then pausing to let her adjust before pushing gradually farther in. He watched her face work through a myriad of emotions, surprise, delight, even fear.

He paused again before he was fully inside her. "Seriously, Tess. I don't want to hurt you. You're so fucking tight. Should I stop?"

She shook her head, the snake-tip tail of her braid jiggling near one of her breasts. "No…god, no. Please don't stop. Just…like you are. Slow."

"Slow," Chase agreed, thrusting incrementally.

He'd been straining with need to release for what felt like forever, turned on by the noises Tess made as she came, the sight of her tan skin and rounded curves, but still he held back, squeezing his eyes shut in concentration as he felt himself drive in to the hilt, almost too big to fit inside her tiny channel. He had to be careful with her, he knew, even after she'd adjusted to him, even after climax had her loose and pliant.

He moved into her in sinuous thrusts, barely moving still, but enough for her to feel it, enough for him to feel it. Tess began to whimper again, mewling noises in the back of her throat, moving her hips with his now, meeting him careful thrust for thrust. Her fingers tightened on his shoulders and her legs circled his waist, holding him deep inside her.

Chase decided to give her the illusion of control for a while; he flipped her so he was on the bottom, and she readily adjusted to ride him, knees wide to straddle his hips, palms flat on his broad chest. Her braid dangled over her shoulder to tickle his throat. He grabbed the braid and tugged gently until she was sitting upright, and then he held her in place with his hands on her hips. His middle fingers were mere inches apart on her belly, and he began to lift her, guiding her motions. She arched her spine inward, tipping her head back and moving on her own, now, finding her rhythm on top of him.

Chase was barely thrusting, letting her do the work while he held himself back. He had to give her a break, let her recover before he brought her to climax again. She wasn't ready yet. He let her move on top of him, surging up and down now, impaling herself on him, driving herself deeper than he'd imagined she'd be able to take him. She collapsed forward after a few minutes, writhing with increasingly desperate movements.

Now.

He lifted her off him, bodily removing her, ignoring her frantic moans of protest. He put his lips to her ear and whispered, "You didn't think I'd forgotten my promise back in the gym, did you?"

She shook her head. "No...what? What promise?"

He slid off the bed and drew her after him, flipping her onto her stomach and pulling her toward him by her ankles. "I'm going to bend you over this bed and fuck you from behind."

"Oh, my god, Chase. I can't take that. I could barely handle your finger." Real fear was evident in her voice.

He settled her on the bed's edge so her feet didn't quite touch the floor, so she was at his mercy. He carved his palms over her arched spine and to her ass, tiny and taut. He gently caressed each cheek, then teased her anus with a finger. Tess whimpered, pushing into his questing finger even as he could feel her shivering with a mixture of fear and anticipation. Chase spat saliva onto his hand and smeared it onto the knot of muscles and worked his ring finger around the circle of muscles, while with his other hand he gripped his shaft at the base and probed her pussy with the tip. He hadn't inserted his finger into her yet, and he gently, carefully pushed in as he thrust into her wet, ready folds with his cock.

"Oh, god," Tess whispered, relief in her voice.

Chase leaned over her. "I would never do that. I would never hurt you," he murmured. "The tip of my pinky finger is one thing. *That* is something else entirely."

He was telling her the truth, in that he would never push a woman past what she wanted and what she was capable of doing with enjoyment, but he didn't mention how much he *wanted* to take her like that. He was riding a knife-edge of control, his ring finger now in her to the first knuckle, his shaft moving into her sex in small, shivering thrusts. He wanted to plunge hard and fast, but he held back, riding gently into her pussy, her fine, firm ass quivering gently with each thrust.

He was learning her noises. She began to mewl again, a kitten-like noise high the back of her throat, a sound that he now knew signaled her impending orgasm.

Chase allowed himself one concession to the fury pounding through him: He wrapped her braid twice around his fist and gently but firmly tugged until her back was arched and her head lifted off the bed. She planted her fists on the bed and undulated her body into him. She was still unable to reach the floor, and Chase began to plunge up into her, lifting her up with each driving plunge, still holding back, still restraining himself from crushing into her with the kind of intensity he desired.

Tess took all of him, though, and gave back with everything she had, losing herself in the delirium of sexual abandon. She lifted herself up with her torso muscles and back, then let herself crash down onto him, spreading her thighs farther apart and wiggling to get his finger deeper into her asshole. Chase gave her what she wanted, more of his finger, pushing in until his other fingers were splayed against the muscular flesh of her ass, until his finger was impaled inside her as far as it would go, and he began to thrust his cock into her harder and harder, never fully penetrating, knowing he might hurt her if he did so. He held on to her braid and let himself drive into her, and now, finally, she began to lose the rhythm in the frenetic frenzy of orgasm.

Chase felt her muscles clamp down, squeezing his finger as she came. He finally let himself loose then, coming with her, driving as deep as he dared in slow but powerful thrusts. Tess was wild, thrashing beneath him, shrieking and writhing and sobbing. Chase came hard, desperate from having held back for so long, from having gone so long without sex.

After nearly a minute of body-wracking climax, Tess went still, but for her ragged breathing. Chase withdrew from her, lifted her to the middle of the bed and drew the blankets over her. He went into his *en suite* bathroom and discarded the condom before washing his hands twice. When he approached the bed again, Tess was snoring.

He smiled to himself, then slipped on a pair of gym shorts and got himself a beer from the fridge. He hiked himself up onto the kitchen counter and drank his beer, head slumped back against the counter, lost in thought. After a trackless amount of time, he finished his beer, and then a second, and then a third, his mind and heart a muddle of half-formed desires and fears and worries.

Foremost in his mind was the knowledge that he was far, far from sated. He'd ravaged Tess and left her passed out in his bed. She really was a fiery, spirited little thing, but he'd simply wrung every last drop from her. He didn't think she'd be complaining come morning, but he knew for as much fun as he'd have with her, eventually it would end.

He, however, was still burning with need, adrenaline, desire, and pent-up frustration.

Tess simply couldn't give him what he needed. It was through no fault of hers, though, and that was the part that left him sad. Throughout their dinner conversation, he'd come to like and respect her, and the fact that she could kick his ass in the ring turned him on something fierce. He wished they were more compatible in bed.

He drained his fourth beer and then slipped into bed next to Tess. She moved against him, instinctively spooning with him.

She half-turned to face him, opening one eye. "You lose the bet, Chase."

"What? No way. I'm not done yet."

Tess laughed. "I hate to say this, but *I* am. I can't take any more. I really can't. I'll be sore as hell in the morning as it is. I cannot physically handle another orgasm. The bet was four in three hours, and that's not happening. Therefore, you lose."

Chase laughed. "Fine. I concede."

"You would. Bitch."

He laughed again, and Tess smiled sleepily at him, then turned back over and was soon asleep once more.

Chase fell asleep thinking of green eyes. Only, these green eyes were framed by red curls as fiery as the woman beneath them.

Chapter 3

A fall wind blew hard down the corridor of Michigan Avenue in Chicago. The sidewalks were full of pedestrians burdened with shopping bags and the streets jammed with taxis and buses and private cars. The sky overhead between the towers was gray and heavy. Flecks of something cold and wet—possibly snow, or rain, or a mix of the two—spattered against Jamie's face as she bustled from the door of the high-rise condo building. She had her phone in her hand, an iMessage in the gray bubble: *Meet me at the corner, babe. Dinner reservations in twenty.* Her response, in blue: *K. B right there.*

She flipped the collar of black pea coat up and hunched her shoulders, hustling through the post-Thanksgiving shopping crowd to meet Ian. His mother had relocated to Chicago, and Ian had ended up moving to Chicago with her. He didn't live *with* his mother, but nearby. Laura Collins, his mother, was a short, sweet woman with iron-gray hair and steely blue eyes. She adored Jamie, but had hinted in more than one conversation that she didn't think Jamie was entirely happy.

Which was true, of course. She'd put everything she had into making things with Ian work. She commuted to Chicago every Thursday after her last shift and spent Friday and Saturday with Ian and his mother, then made the four-hour drive back for work Sunday afternoon. Ian met her in Detroit a few times a month as well, and overall, things worked. They worked.

But...Jamie was restless. She spent most of the four-hour trip twice a week trying not to think about how much longer she could pretend she was okay.

Ian knew. She saw the knowledge in his eyes at times, in the way she'd catch him gazing sadly at her, expectantly. Waiting.

Ian had something planned for today. He'd made reservations, which was unlike him. Usually they did burgers and beers at a local pub, or ate in. This was *an event*. He had something to say to her, and she knew it. It was probably a preemptive strike. His way of sparing her feelings, in an odd manner.

She found Ian waiting at the street corner, watching her approach. The sad look was in eyes again, distant and semi-hollow.

"Hello, love," he said, with false cheer.

She kissed him, a brief touch of the lips. They pulled away at the same time. "Hey, yourself."

"Hungry?" Ian took her hand, and they walked through the crowd together.

"Famished. Traffic into the city was hellish."

"Sorry to hear it, darling. I worry about you making the drive so often in that dodgy old auto of yours. I'm always afraid it's going to go tits up on you halfway here."

Jamie chuckled at his turn of phrase. "Yeah, it's definitely a possibility, I guess. But it's fine for now. Besides, if it does go tits up, I'll just call you, and you'll rescue me." Out of habit, she nudged closer and smirked at him. "And then as a reward, *I'll* go tits up for you."

Ian laughed. "Oh, god, I *really* don't think that phrase means what you think it means."

Jamie shoved him with her hip. "Oh, shut up. I know exactly what it means, I was just using it in another context."

"And *I* know *that*. I was just teasing you."

They had a long, leisurely dinner, filled with the idle conversation of a couple familiar and comfortable with each other. It was laced with tension, though. Jamie felt it, and she saw it in Ian's eyes.

Finally, she leaned back in her chair with a sigh. "Out with it, Ian."

He shifted uncomfortably. "I—I'm not sure where to start."

"Just start with the truth." She flagged the waiter and held up her wine glass.

Ian sipped from his own wine and then set it aside. "You aren't happy. With me, I mean."

Jamie pinched the bridge of her nose. "No, it's not that. Not really. It's…complicated."

"Un-complicate it."

"God. That's a lot easier to say than to do. As cliché as this is, and as much as I hate how it's going to sound…it's not you, it's me."

"That's fucking bollocks, Jamie."

"I know, I know. But it's *true*." The server arrived to pour Jamie another measure of cabernet, and she sipped it greedily. "There's just—"

"Someone else?"

"Yes. No. Sort of. There isn't anyone else in the sense you're thinking. I haven't been seeing anyone else. I promise. But my heart is…I just can't—" Jamie cut herself off with a huff. "Shit. I'm making a mess of this."

"Sorry, darling, but you kind of are making a bit of a muddle of it. Just spit it out. You're in love with someone else. I get it."

"It's not that simple, though. It's just one of those things that won't go away, you know? No matter how hard I try, I just can't seem to let go."

Ian scratched his jaw and then fiddled with the cloth napkin on the table. "I do remember that conversation we had. In my hotel room in Buttfuck, Michigan. You said some rot about forbidden love. You said you were over him."

"It wasn't rot, Ian."

"It's just a word, Jamie. I know it wasn't. I just meant I remember you mentioning this other guy. And you're still not over him enough to be happy with me."

"It's not like I don't want to be over him, Ian. I do. I really, *really* do want to be over him. But I just…can't seem to do it."

"And I can't do this with you if you're not." Ian tossed back the rest of his wine and watched Jamie's reaction.

She only nodded. "I know. And I'm sorry. I'm sorry to have wasted so much of your time." She stood up, leaving her half-full wine glass, and turned to walk away.

"Jamie, wait. You didn't waste—shit." He cut himself off when he realized Jamie wasn't listening.

She was already out the door and into the flurries of hard, stinging snow. She wasn't crying. Not again. Her eyes were stinging from the wind, was all. There was no reason to be upset. She knew it was coming. She would have done it herself soon. She wasn't being fair to Ian, or to herself.

It still didn't explain why the hole in her heart ached so badly.

Chase flopped over onto his back, and Tess let out a long, contented sigh.

"Chase, baby. I don't know how you do that to me every time," Tess said.

Forcing a smile onto his face, Chase turned over and kissed her. "I'm just that good," he said.

Tess pinched his thigh. "And you're just that arrogant."

"It's not arrogance, it's confidence."

"Same thing, babe." Tess scooted out of bed and gathered her clothes, tossed them in her suitcase, then dug out a clean pair of panties and a bra. Her uniform was already pressed and hanging on the rack near the hotel door.

Chase watched her diminutive form as she moved around the room, gathering the rest of her things and packing them away, then hopped in the shower. He was every bit as attracted to her as the day he'd met her three months ago, but his ability to pretend she satisfied him was waning. He hated the pretense. Hated feeling like shit when he had to paste on a smile and act exhausted after a vigorous session in bed with her, when the truth was he was always holding back and was usually just getting started when she was finished, left partially sated and entirely frustrated.

He had an inkling she knew, but he hadn't had the courage to broach the subject. She had a flight to Boston in a few hours, so he doubted the discussion would happen right then. He had a gig himself in a while, headlining at the Mayne Stage here in Chicago.

He liked Tess, a lot. He had a good time with her.

But…it just wasn't enough.

Tess emerged from the shower to find Chase standing naked at the eleventh-floor window, staring out at the swirling snow. She stood next to him in silence for a while, then looked up at him.

"This isn't working, Chase."

He glanced down at her. Serious green eyes gazed back up at him, calm and collected. "No, I guess not." He turned back to the view of downtown Chicago. "I'm sorry."

"Why are you sorry?"

"I don't know. It's…I'm just sorry this didn't work. You're an amazing girl, and I wish—"

"I can't keep up with you. I know I can't. But I think that's only a part of the problem. There's something else. That thing you said you'd tell me 'eventually.'" Tess leaned her head against his arm. "This is eventually, but you still don't have to tell me. It's someone else. I see the way you look at me sometimes. Maybe I look like her, or something. I don't know. But that's what it is."

"Yeah, sort of. But it's—"

"Complicated," Tess said in sync with him.

"Yeah," Chase said. "It's really complicated."

Tess turned away from him, dropped the towel, and stepped into her panties, then hooked her bra around her middle and slipped it on. "I don't need to know the details. But I'll tell you this: A lot of the time, when someone says something is complicated, what they really mean is they're afraid of the truth. They're afraid of what will happen, afraid of the consequences." She turned back to Chase. "Good things often come with tough consequences. It just makes us appreciate the good that much more."

"You're right," Chase said. "But it's not me you have to convince. It's her."

Tess shrugged. "*I* don't have to convince anyone. *You* do. And if it's meant to be, it'll happen." She put on her flight attendant uniform, zipped her bags, and then set her rolling suitcase on end, handle extended. "I care about you, Chase. You're a good man and an incredible lover. I really am sorry this didn't work out, too."

Chase thunked his head against the cold glass, then moved toward Tess. "I haven't been fair to you, Tess. And that's what I'm sorry for."

She smiled at him, a little sadly. "I knew this was coming a long time ago. I knew it was coming when you said you didn't want to talk about it back in Eric's gym. I was just being selfish. I wanted a piece of you for myself."

"Well, you got a piece. A big piece." He grinned lecherously, but his heart wasn't in it, and neither was hers. "Seriously, though. This goodbye sucks."

Tess nodded. "Yes, it does. All goodbyes do."

He leaned toward her and kissed her, careful not to smudge her makeup or wrinkle her uniform. When he let her go, Tess took a deep breath and let it out.

"Goodbye, Chase."

"'Bye, Tess." He watched her leave, wondering what he was supposed to do with himself now.

He took a long shower and dressed, packed his one duffel bag, and left the hotel. The snow was bitterly cold against his shower-hot skin, and the wind was even worse, snatching his breath away. He walked aimlessly, trying to empty his heart, snuff out the turmoil inside himself. He shrugged deeper into his thick coat, eyes downcast, attention wandering. His bag was slung over one shoulder, and his hands were dug into his pockets. He thought he might be capable of just walking,

walking, walking until the snow buried him or the cold froze him, or the hole in his chest ate him from the inside out.

Then he rounded a corner, and something soft yet firm slammed into him, knocking him backward. He slipped on a patch of ice, tangled up with whoever he'd run into, and tumbled to the sidewalk, slamming his head into the concrete. He saw stars, squeezing his eyes shut against the pain. Then something familiar spiked through the fog and the thunder in his skull to his awareness. It was subtle at first, a combination of scents, lotion and perfume and shampoo, woman-scent…and then a series of sensations, the way her body fit against his, a tickle of hair on his face, and the heat of an intense gaze.

Chase cracked his eyelids open to see the burning jade orbs that had haunted his dreams for months staring down at him.

"Y-you?" Her voice broke.

Chase tried to catch his breath and speak, but the wind scoured past his nose and mouth, taking it, and the pain in his head and the ache in his heart all conspired to keep him gasping. Most of all, it was her beauty that left him breathless.

Her hands were on his chest, resting lightly. Her lips were inches from his, red and full. Her breasts were crushed against him, and…he was instantly erect, hard as a rock and near to bursting in the space of a single heartbeat. And all Jamie was doing was looking at him.

Then he truly looked at her. Her eyes were red, and unshed tears were pooling, threatening to spill out. "Jamie? Are you okay?"

She could only shake her head. She tried to get off him, to stand up, but she couldn't. Chase let his head touch back down to the cold concrete, snow drifting around his eyes, and gazed up at her.

"Yeah, me either," he said.

Jamie laughed, a choked sound. "Help me up. I can't…"

Chase stood up gingerly, helping Jamie to her feet. He didn't let go when they were upright. He drew her instinctively into his arms, and she went willingly, seemingly unconsciously. "What's wrong, Jay?"

"Everything. You. Me. Just…everything."

Chase laughed again, knowing what she meant, somehow. "I wish I didn't understand that, but I do. All too well."

"Why are you here? Why do you always show up at the worst times?"

"I wish I knew." He felt truth boiling on his lips. "But then...I do know. I keep showing up because we're meant to be."

"It can't be."

"But it is."

Jamie sobbed into his chest, as if a dam had burst open, then cut herself off just as quickly. "Why? Why, Chase?"

"Why what?"

Jamie pulled back to meet his green piercing brown. "Why did you have to make me fall in love with you? I wasn't supposed to fall in love with you."

Chase felt something hot and wet burn down his cheek. "I don't know, Jay. But I've been wondering the same thing. Why, oh, why did I have to fall in love with the one girl I can't have?"

Jamie's eyes slid closed, fluttered, then opened. When her eyes met his again, he saw a new kind of determination in them. As if she'd made a decision. The hot wetness stung his eyes, almost as if he was crying, but that wasn't possible. He hadn't cried since he was in elementary school, if not before. Certainly not over a girl.

Then he felt moist, soft, wet lips touch his cheek where the saltiness stung his skin, heat on his cold flesh. Again and again her lips touched his face, cheek, chin, forehead, throat, neck, then...a pause... bated breath...and her lips touched his. Chase's eyes were closed tight, blocking away the world, and he almost flinched, so intense and visceral was the sensation of her lips on his. Like hot wine, like a drug.

He had no chance of resisting.

He kissed her back, softly at first. So softly. Then her lips pulled away, and he heard her drag in a shuddering breath. He opened his eyes and saw her, tear-tracks on her cheeks, wiping them with trembling fingers. Chase mimicked her gesture, kissing away the salt of her tears, trailing kisses across her face, over her lips, tasting hesitantly, then taking hungrily. She met him with equally sudden ferocity, and they were lost together then.

Chase pulled away first. "If you walk away again, if you tell me no again, I'll be broken in a way that can never be fixed," he said.

Jamie shuddered, and then collapsed into his chest. "Me, too." Her words were muffled by his coat, but he heard them.

"Is this happening? Us?" he asked.

She nodded. "It has to. It can't not." Jamie looked up at Chase and let him see into her heart through her eyes. "I'm terrified."

Chase licked his kiss-swollen lips. "Me, too."

"Where do we go? What do we do?" Jamie asked.

"Well, first I have a show to play. Then I'm going to find a hotel, and I'm going to kiss you and make love to you until you beg me to stop."

Jamie shuddered into him, but this was a different, more feral and salacious, kind of shudder. "I'll never want you to stop." She arched into him, wind-blown red curls tangling around them both, and he felt fire blaze through his body, instant heat, instant need. "Never."

"Then I never will," he answered.

Chase kissed Jamie again, and this time it was slow and languorous and full of promise. Their eyes met again as they pulled apart, and the heat flying between them was hot enough to melt the snow as it drifted between their bodies.

The promise in her eyes had him ready to explode, and he knew when they finally came together, it would stop his world.

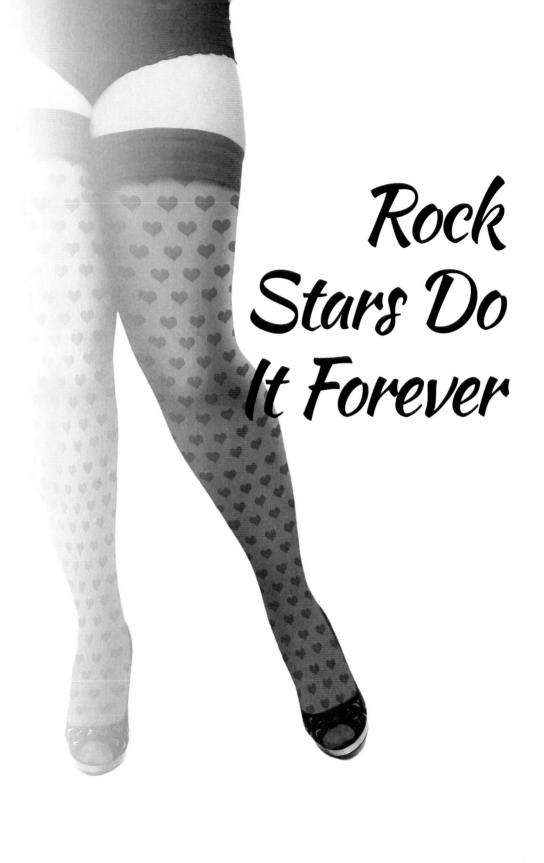

Rock Stars Do It Forever

Chapter 1

Snow swirled, small stinging flecks drifting and windblown and never accumulating, touching Jamie's nose and cheeks like frozen fingers as she rested her face against the scratchy wool of Chase's coat. Her heart thudded crazily in her breast, adrenalized with the knowledge that she was indulging in something forbidden, something that surely would come with a high cost. She was giving in to something that felt inevitable, as unavoidable as the movement of stars across the sky, as unstoppable as gravity or time or each breath drawn into shuddering lungs.

Chase's arms were wrapped around her, strong and thick and comforting, holding her close to his warmth and spicy male scent, blocking out the world. The cold around them only added to the sense of isolation, the feeling that they two were the only ones in the world. Jamie had spent so long denying her feelings for Chase, reminding herself why she couldn't be with him, why it was wrong, why it couldn't happen. Now, here she was in his arms, and nothing had ever felt so right. Standing chest to chest, breathing in his scent and his strength... nothing had ever felt so much like home.

For Jamie, whose life had been one ratty, barely-able-to-afford-it apartment after another from the age of sixteen, home was a nebulous concept, a thing to be desired but never had. Home was the latest one-year lease, non-refundable deposit, one-room apartment with a galley kitchen and blank white walls. Home was wherever she had a bed and bottle of vodka.

Now, home suddenly had become this man, wherever he was. She'd spent weeks and months traipsing from suburban Detroit to Chicago, back and forth every weekend, until she was more familiar with the inside of her battered blue Buick LeSabre than the inside of her battered Clawson apartment.

Home. Jamie breathed in again, deeply. Wool of Chase's thick navy peacoat, his cologne—some spicy, citrusy smell that seemed at once exotic and deeply masculine—tangled up with body wash and the smell of fall morphing into winter, the smell of fresh snow and cold, crisp air. She tightened her grip on Chase's shoulders, her arms curling up from underneath his armpits, clinging to his shoulder blades for dear life, as if he might be ripped away.

"You don't need to crush me, Jay," his voice rumbled, amused. "I'm not going anywhere."

"Yes you are." She fought the overwhelming rush of emotions threatening to choke off her words. "You're always going away."

Chase laughed, another rolling rumble. "Hate to break it to you, babes, but you're the one who kept running from *me*."

Jamie sniffed—from the cold, of course. "I had to."

"So…what changed?"

Jamie shrugged, a small movement almost lost against Chase's bulk. "Nothing. I just can't fight it anymore."

"Fight what?" Something in his voice had Jamie thinking Chase knew the answer but wanted to hear her say it out loud.

She pushed back a little and tucked her hands in between them, gazing up into his dark eyes. "You know."

"Yeah, but I just want to hear you say it again."

Jamie let her forehead rest against his chest. "Fine," she said, wrapping her arms around his neck, "if you must hear it again. I love you, Chase Delany."

His eyes burned, lit from within, fiery brown locked on her wavering green. "You love me."

"Yep."

His hands rested on her waist, skated up her sides, to her shoulders, then cupped her face, powerful calloused paws cradling her cheeks with tender gentility. "I might like you a little bit, too."

Jamie frowned. "*Like* me? A *little* bit? I'm not so sure this'll work if that's all you got for me." She pushed up on her toes and bit Chase's lower lip between her teeth.

Chase turned the bite into a kiss, and unlike the others, this kiss was not the product of desperation. He took her mouth and her lips with hungry determination, devouring her breath with his, driving his tongue into her mouth and exploring with possessive need. His thumbs brushed over her cheekbones and his lips crushed hers, his tongue tasted hers, and his body was hard and solid against hers. Jamie melted into the kiss, feeling the edges of her soul bleeding into his, the joining of their mouths only the beginning, only the visible tip of the mountain.

"Does that help?" Chase asked.

"Nope. I need to hear it. I need the words." She pressed a kiss to the hard line of his jaw. "I need you to *show* me."

"I can do that," Chase murmured. "I've loved you since the second you walked into my dressing room in Las Vegas."

"Now we're getting somewhere," Jamie said. "About showing me...?"

Chase laughed. "Well, I have a show. Have to be on stage warming up in an hour. Come with me."

"Like you could pry me away from you, at this point," Jamie said.

"Hungry?"

Jamie shook her head. "No, I just ate."

Chase cocked his head. "Something tells me I won't like the answer if I ask who you ate with."

Jamie's eyes narrowed. "No, you wouldn't."

"Is that why you were crying when you ran into me?" Chase said.

"I wasn't crying when I ran into you. I was trying *not* to cry. Then I smacked into you and that's what started me crying."

Chase pulled her into a walk and tangled his fingers in hers. "Who was he?"

"Why do you want to know?" Jamie glanced up at him. "Does it matter?"

"Yes. If he made you cry, then I need to kick his ass."

Jamie snorted a laugh. "If you're gonna kick the ass of the person who's made me cry the most in my life, then you'd have to kick your own ass."

"There's something confusing about that statement, but I'm not sure what it is." Chase shook his head. "But for real? You've cried about me?"Jamie ducked her head, watching the snow drifting in circling swirls between her feet. "Chase, I've never cried so much in my whole life as I have since I met you. It's not…it's not really your fault, directly. It's just the situation. I'm not a crying type, honestly. I don't go bawling into a pint of Ben and Jerry's every time something shitty happens. But something about this whole situation between us just fucks me up in the head."

Chase nodded. "I know what you mean." He squeezed her hand. "Tell me about him, though. This situation is fucked up enough without any secrets."

"It's not a secret. But fine, if you must know. His name was Ian. He was from London. I met him…" she trailed off, laughing. "Actually, I met him when I was trying to run away from how I felt about you. I ended up somewhere north of Flint in a shitty dive bar off the freeway. He was the only one there who wasn't a trucker or a gap-toothed yokel."

"Good reason to like a guy, I suppose."

"I liked him because he made me feel something. I'd been trying to just *not* feel for a long time. He wasn't you, but he was nice. Kinda sexy. Had a hot accent." Jamie sucked in a long breath. "Ian was… wonderful. Treated me great. Eventually moved here to Chicago to be with me. He claimed it was because his mother moved here, but I think she moved here to be closer to him. I don't know. I've been coming to Chicago to be with him every weekend for months now."

"He made you come to *him* every weekend?" Chase sounded incensed.

"I did it voluntarily. He came to Detroit too, but I liked driving down to Chicago, because driving was…a relief. I could shut down and just drive."

"Am I missing something? You said he was wonderful, but it sounds almost like you were trying to get away from what he made you feel."

"Damn your insightfulness." Jamie dug her other hand into her coat pocket. "I didn't love him. I couldn't, and I didn't try to convince myself I did. I just wanted to not be alone. I couldn't have you, but I thought maybe if I tried hard enough, I could be happy with *some*one. If it could have been anyone, it would have been Ian."

"But?"

"He knew I wasn't happy. I met him for dinner a few blocks away, maybe two hours ago. He just wanted to know what was going on, why I wasn't happy. I tried to explain…well, no I didn't. I knew he wouldn't get it. How do you explain this thing between us?"

Chase expelled a breath heavy with sympathetic understand. "You don't. Fuck, I didn't even *try* to explain it to Tess. She broke up with me just before you ran into me."

"Tess?"

"My version of Ian. My attempt to be okay without you."

Jamie glanced up at him. "Didn't work any better than mine, did it?"

Chase huffed a sarcastic laugh. "Not hardly. Clearly. Staying away from you…it's like…trying to defy gravity."

"Gonna sing me some *Wicked*?" Jamie teased.

Chase quirked an eyebrow at her, then did a surprising rendition of the iconic song in question. Jamie found herself stunned. Chase's voice, what little she'd heard of it, was lower, growly, more of a rock song and she hadn't thought him capable of hitting some of the notes in that song. He did, though, and amazingly well.

"You just can't help it, can you?" Jamie asked, laughing.

"Being incredible."

He shrugged, grinning. "Not really, no. I was just joking with you, though, singing the song. It was shitty too. That song is written as a duet, and it's *way* out of my range."

"I didn't notice anything off."

Chase waved a hand dismissively. "Most wouldn't. I did it fair justice, but a real Broadway singer would have cringed."

"I don't know. I thought you sounded amazing. You shouldn't doubt yourself

He just shrugged. "I'm not doubting myself. I'm in a rock band. I have no designs or aspirations on Broadway. I have enough of a musical ear to be able to sing pretty much anything I hear, but my voice just isn't that kind of voice." He glanced at her. "You know I majored in musical theater in college?"

Jamie stopped walking, staring at him. "Are you shitting me?"

Chase rubbed the back of his neck. "No. Why is that so surprising? I've always loved music, and yes, I've always loved being the center of attention."

"I guess I shouldn't be shocked," Jamie said, walking with Chase again. "I guess you just seem so much like a natural born rockstar that I can't picture you prancing around singing 'Maria'."

Chase laughed. "Actually, I did that show my sophomore year of college. I was a kick-ass Tony, I'll have you know."

"I'm not about to debate that," Jamie said, trying to picture Chase with slicked-back hair and tight black jeans. It wasn't a difficult image to summon, oddly.

Chase stopped into a pizzeria and got a couple to-go slices, ate them as they made their way to the venue where Six Foot Tall was playing. Jamie sat at the bar and nursed a glass of wine while she watched the band set up and warm up. She watched Chase test his microphone. Doubts crept in.

What the hell am I doing? She shouldn't be here. Shouldn't be considering what she was considering. A couple kisses, a declaration of love…those were all good and well, but nothing had changed. Being with Chase would still be fraught with problems.

She should just get up and leave. Not tempt either of them anymore.

Jamie stared down into rippling red depths of her wine, arguing with herself. If she walked away again, she wasn't sure she would ever recover. She'd turn into a cat lady. Or a dog lady, since she hated cats. Or maybe a fish lady. One of those really, *really* crazy people with fishtanks on every wall. Chase would be okay, right? He'd get over it. Just like she would.

Right.

Part of her kept wondering why she was fighting this so hard. Hadn't Anna said she'd find a way to deal with it if Jamie and Chase got together?

"Not thinking of bolting on me, are you?" Chase's deep voice rumbled in her ear.

Jamie started, not having heard him approach. "What? No! Yes. Maybe. No." She took a swallow of her wine to cover her nerves.

Chase dragged a fingernail across her hand clutching the wine-glass, then to her wrist, then up her forearm. Jamie shivered and swiveled her gaze from the ruby liquid to his intense mocha gaze. The heat in his eyes had the doubts melting like an ice cube under a summer sun, had desire pulsing from a flicker into an inferno. The only point of contact between them was his finger trailing a line of fire from her elbow up her shirtsleeve to her shoulder, but that was enough to push a balloon of pressure into her womb, to send heat cresting between her thighs.

If he touched her any more intimately, Jamie would combust on the spot. He brushed his finger back down her arm, slicing down the skin mere millimeters from her breast. She ached for his touch, suddenly. If he would just nudge the outside of her breast, even through her shirt and her bra, she might find some satisfaction. Some release. The pressure, the mountain of frustration piled up within her was heavier than ever, pushing at the walls of her sanity. She *needed* Chase. It wasn't a matter of desire. Not anymore.

She *had* to feel him. Hold him. Touch him. Taste him. His face was an inch away from hers, his spicy male scent filling her nostrils, his breath on her neck, his finger now teasing her, tracing the curve of her breast. His freshly-shaven scalp gleamed dully in the dim lights, and Jamie couldn't resist scraping her palm over the smooth skin, drawing his lips closer to hers, drawing his mouth against hers, from sucking his tongue into her mouth and running her tongue over his teeth and tasting the faint tang of toothpaste layered under the pizza and the more recent beer he'd been sipping as he set up.

His body closed the space between them, his hips between her legs, his mouth returning her kiss with equal fervor, his hand kneading the denim clinging to her thigh, his fingers tickling the underside of her breast. He was her world, the distant thump of the drums being tested fading, the hum of a guitar and the rumble of a bass drowned beneath the rush of blood in her ears, the pound of need in her mind, the crush of desire like sunfire in her veins.

"I want you…" she gasped, the words torn from her lips as the kiss broke.

"I need you…" he answered, murmuring the words in a ragged rhythm, his lips moving against hers.

Her legs wrapped around his waist, her arms around his neck, and they kissed once more, or perhaps it was the same kiss continued, broken and resumed. *That was it*, Jamie decided: they'd only kissed once over the blocks of months they'd been denying their love for each other. It was only one kiss, interrupted.

Howls and wolf-whistles finally had them splitting apart.

"If we don't stop now, we'll never stop," Chase said, his voice a husky whisper.

"But I don't want to stop," Jamie said.

"I don't either," Chase said, "but the things I want to do to you are best done in private."

"What are you doing to my privates?"

"A lot of things," Chase promised, "but none of them here."

"At least give me a hint?"

Chase kissed her again, slowly, driving his tongue into her mouth, dipping in and retreating, laving her lips and tongue. "I'll do that to you…" he whispered, "over…and over…and over."

"Oh god…please?" Jamie's voice was a pleading whimper. She sounded desperate, and she didn't care, because she *was* desperate. "What else are you gonna do to me?"

"Hmmm." Chase rumbled. He scratched her jeans on her thigh, high up, dangerously close to the V where she wanted his touch, his fingers moving in a mocking rhythm. "I might do this to you…and if you're good, I might even kiss you and touch like that at the *same time*. I might even let you come."

Jamie laughed against his mouth, her smile mirroring his. She reached between them to cup his bulge through the leather of his pants, felt a thrill of satisfaction as she realized he was huge and hard inside his pants, aching for her as she ached for him. She traced the hard lines of his cock with her thumb and forefinger, stroking him through the leather. "And I might just do this to you," she whispered back to him. "I might just let you come, too. *If* you're good. I might just put my mouth on you and let come down my throat. You want that? Hmmm?"

"Oh god." Chase's voice was thick with barely-restrained desire. "God…do I want that. So bad. *So* bad."

"Well then…you'd better be good. And you'd better finish this show so you can take me home." Jamie felt a pang of emptiness shoot through her as Chase backed away, watching her for several backward steps before turning away and swaggering to the stage. The ache between her thighs was an all-devouring pressure now, a pounding, pulsing, fiery burn.

It was going to be a long show.

Chapter 2

*C*hase knew he'd never been more on fire as that night on stage. The knowledge that Jamie was waiting for him at the bar infused him with a manic energy, a contagious drive that had the band playing better than they ever had. The crowd felt it too, and turned the concert into a wild party, several mosh pits starting in various areas. Chase worked them up into a fury, adjusting the intended playlist to include numbers the crowd could participate in, goading them into singing back to him. He bounded across the stage, feeling the music in his veins like liquid fire. Every once in a while he would glance to where Jamie watched from her seat at the bar, and he would feel a new rush of energy burst through him at the sight of her.

By the time the show was over, the crowd was insane, and began chanting for an encore until the band had to go back out and play another mini-set. Chase was impatient by this time. As much as he loved the rush of performing, he was ready to be done, ready to scoop Jamie up and find the nearest hotel room. He crossed back and forth at the edge of the stage, eyes now locked on Jamie in the distance, finishing their last encore number.

Off-stage, Chase had a quick celebratory shot with the guys, who knew his moods well enough to know he wasn't in the mood for a party. They'd grown used to him taking off on his own while they partied.

Gage followed him away from the group, cornering him against a doorway. "Something happened." Gage knew him better than anyone, and knew there was a reason for his renewed energy.

Chase shrugged into his coat and moved to push past him. "Yeah, something happened. I'll catch up to you guys."

Gage narrowed his eyes, blocking Chase's exit. "You've doing better recently. Since you've been with Tess. The guys need you on point, man. I don't know what's going on with you, but something's changed."

"Tess broke up with me."

Gage rocked his head back on his shoulders, eyes closing, scrubbing his palms down his face. "Shit."

"It's okay though. It had to happen. I knew it, she knew it. It's better this way."

"You don't seem real broken up about it." Suspicion crossed Gage's face, his pale blue eyes searching Chase's.

"It's complicated. We're in Milwaukee next, right?"

"Yeah, why?"

Chase shrugged, going for nonchalance. "Go without me. I'll meet you there. I've got some shit to take care of."

Gage's lips quirked. "Does the shit you're taking care of happen to have curly red hair?"

"Might."

Gage shook his head slowly and blew out a long breath. "Just be on stage in Milwaukee on Wednesday, man," he said. "That's all I ask."

"I will. You know I will."

Gage clapped Chase on the shoulder and turned away, then stopped and gave Chase a long, level look. "Also, because you're my best friend...be careful, okay? When everything happened with Anna, man, you were a hot fucking mess. Having you on an even keel makes everything better for all of us."

Chase nodded and gave Gage a man-hug, their right hands clasping as if arm-wrestling, then bumping chests and right shoulders. "I know. That was kind of a shitty time for me. Thanks for putting up with my bullshit. This thing I've got going on now...it could be good. Really good."

"And if it doesn't go the way you're hoping?"

Chase didn't answer immediately. "It will. It has to."

Gage gave Chase a hard shove toward the exit. "Go. And good luck."

I don't need luck, Chase thought. *I just need her.*

He found her on the same stool where he'd left her, finishing a side of cheese fries, dipping the last one in ranch. She had a nearly empty glass of red wine in front of her, and she tossed the last bit back as Chase approached.

"That was a seriously great show," she said, standing up and putting on her coat, then slipping her palms around to the backs of his shoulders. "You kicked ass."

The familiar affection in the way she touched him sent a thrill of excitement through Chase, the kind of upwelling of emotion that had his throat closing and his heart pumping harder. He fit his hands to the swell of her hips, holding her tight against him.

"Thanks," he said. "I was pumped. I felt good. Knowing you were watching…it just gave me this jolt of energy."

Jamie pressed even closer to him, crushing her breasts against his chest and gazing up into his eyes. "So now what do we do?" She curled her fingers into the muscle of his shoulders, nails raking through the thin cotton of his T-shirt, sending chills of arousal shivering down his spine and into his balls.

"Now…we have three days to ourselves. My next show isn't until Wednesday."

Her lips touched his jaw between ear and chin, then his throat; Chase had to focus on catching his breath each time a kiss planted fire on his skin. "And what could we possibly do for those three days?" Her voice was low and sultry and thick with overt suggestion.

Chase let his fingers crawl down to caress the upper curve of her ass, scratching the denim. "Hmmm. I might be able to think of a few things."

"Less thinking, more doing." Jamie bit him, a sharp nip of the skin on his neck near his shoulder. "I can't take the waiting anymore. I need you. Right now."

Chase rumbled a husky laugh in reply, turning away and taking her hand in his. He pulled her into a swift walk, leading her out of the club and into the cold Chicago night. The air was still and thin, cold as the upper atmosphere, dark as space. A yellow cab drifted by, its light off, tires buzzing against the road. A few isolated flecks of snow skirled through the street, blown from some secret place. The sky above was clear and cloudless, blackest black between skyscraping towers. A sliver of gibbous moon glinted low in the sky, and Jamie's hand was warm in Chase's.

He took a deep breath of the frozen air, glanced at Jamie. "There's a hotel just around the corner. We can go there."

"The closer the better."

Chase pulled her into a walk in the direction of the hotel. "Eager much?"

Jamie shoved him playfully. "Yeah. You're not? Maybe I misjudged the situation, then."

Chase pulled her into him and grabbed a handful of her ass and kneaded it roughly. "I'm about two seconds away from bending you over that car and taking you right here," Chase growled, "so don't tempt me."

Jamie gazed up at him with serious eyes. "You don't hear me protesting, do you?"

Chase just shook his head and pulled her back into a walk. They reached the hotel soon and Chase stood at the concierge desk arranging for a room. The lobby was deserted except for the concierge. As he worked with the young woman behind the desk, Chase felt Jamie's fingers slide down over his stomach and down to his groin. She found the shape of his cock behind his zipper and traced its length with her fingers. Chase gave her a look in warning, but she only smiled innocently at him. The concierge named the total for the room and Chase dug his wallet out of his coat pocket, working to keep his expression neutral and his hips still. Jamie's stroking of his shaft through the leather increased in tempo as he waited for his card to be run and then signed the slip. He was growing harder with every stroke, burgeoning, thickening. He felt pre-come gather at the tip, soaking the cotton of his boxer-briefs. He sucked in a deep breath and let it out slowly, turning away and pushing Jamie in front of him to hide his arousal. They stood back-to-front at a bank of elevators, waiting for a car to arrive. As they stood, Jamie pressed herself back against him, subtly writhing her hips to rub her ass against his cock.

Chase hissed between his teeth, finding it ever harder to contain his arousal. He was nearing the point of having to physically hold himself back. He'd been so turned on for so long that he was near to bursting. He'd been turned on and ready to go since the moment Jamie slammed into him on the street, since she kissed him, since her body pressed against his. His arousal had only kind of gone away during the show, and every time he'd glanced at Jamie from the stage he'd felt a bolt of desire.

He was so hard, so ready…and she was making it impossible to hold back, reaching behind herself to cup the back of his head, turning her face sideways to plant desperate kisses on his cheek and lips, writhing against his cock shamelessly. There was no one in the lobby at all, the concierge having vanished, but Chase still felt exposed.

"Goddamn, Jamie. You have me right on the edge," he said, whispering in her ear. "I'm close already. You'd better back up and give me a chance to get myself under control or I'm gonna come in my pants right here."

The elevator doors opened right then and they stepped into the car, pushing the button for the seventh floor. The doors swooshed closed and as soon as the car began moving, Jamie turned to face Chase.

"Maybe I don't want you to have control…" she said, fumbling with the button of his pants. "Maybe I want you to come, right here, right now."

"That could be messy."

His pants were open, now, and she was pushing his zipper down, freeing his rigid shaft and taking it into both hands. Chase couldn't breathe, suddenly, could only hold himself absolutely still, every muscle tensed and locked, focused on holding back. Her hands were hot on his skin, soft and tender and greedy, working him steadily, her body pressed against his, backing him into a corner.

He felt himself rising, then, against his control. Her eyes were on him, searching him. He had to close his eyes, then, squeezing them shut and gritting his teeth, sucking in a breath and holding it, ducking his head and straining with every fiber of his being.

She didn't relent, kept up her slow, intimate ministrations, both fists on his length gliding up and back down, rubbing his crown in her palm now as she pumped his base, then moving her fists on him hand over hand.

He gasped raggedly, then ground out the warning: "I can't…I can't hold it back. Goddamnit…*fuck*." He clawed his fingers with crushing force into the denim and muscle of her ass, squeezing so hard she gasped. "I'm gonna come, Jamie. Right now."

She sank quickly to her knees and took him in her mouth, one hand stroking his cock at the base, the other cupping his balls, middle finger pressing against his taint and massing the muscle there. She sucked hard, taking him deep. Chase came with a soft grunt, fisting his hands in her soft curls, holding her but not pushing at her. She drew him out of her mouth to lick his tip, then sucked him deep again as his muscles clenched once more, releasing a second stream into her mouth. She was grinding her fist on his base in a furious rhythm, drawing his orgasm to a wild frenzy, her finger pressing against his taint and spurring him to a third spasm, her mouth bobbing on him, taking him deep and then backing away.

As he shot the last of his seed into her mouth, the elevator came to an unexpected stop on the fifth floor, the bell dinging and the doors sliding open. Jamie jumped to her feet at the *ding* of the bell, tugging his pants up. She pressed Chase into the corner, wrapping her arms around him and burying her face against his cheek shielding his still-throbbing cock from the view of the elderly couple that got onto the elevator with them.

Chase heard her giggling, then heard her swallow, and giggle again, her shoulders shaking. Her hands were cupping the back of his head, stroking his stubble, her breath huffing on his ear.

"You came *a lot*," she whispered, her voice so quiet as to be barely audible.

"I can't believe you did that," he said, his voice equally low.

The couple in front of them were whispering to each other as well, muttering and casting disapproving, disgusted glances at Chase and Jamie.

"I told you I needed you," Jamie whispered. "And I still do. That was...just a taste."

Chase chuckled helplessly at her turn of phrase. "Well, you did get quite a taste."

"You taste so good," Jamie said. "And your cock...it's perfect."

"Think we could get away with me tasting *you* on the elevator?"

Jamie laughed. "Maybe if I was wearing a skirt."

"You mean I have to wait?"

"Only a few more seconds."

The elevator dinged again, letting them off on their floor. As they exited, Chase still pressed against Jamie's front, they heard the man on the elevator mumble, "Damn kids. Smells like sex in here."

They broke into laughter as the doors closed. Their room was only a few feet away from the elevators, and as Chase reached past Jamie to slide the keycard into the slot, Jamie tilted her head back to whisper in Chase's ear.

"I need you inside me." She reached back and stroked a finger against his soft shaft, causing him to twitch and harden. "Hurry up and get the door open."

Chase was fumbling, inserting the key and pulling it out either too fast or too slow so the light wouldn't switch from red to green. Finally, after a few muttered curses, he got it open and they stumbled into the darkened room. The door snicked closed and Chase flipped on a light.

He stopped, pants unzipped and unbuttoned, his cock thickening in anticipation as he watched Jamie turn in place to face him, a hungry look in her eyes. She licked her lips, breasts heaving as she sucked in several deep, steadying breaths. She bit her lower lip, then crossed her arms and peeled her shirt off, revealing her full, ivory breasts pushed up in a violently purple front clasp bra.

Chase felt his cock twitch and grow harder, and Jamie's eyes flicked down to it, a grin spreading across her face.

"I didn't really get to see it before," she said. "It's so pretty."

Chase glanced down at himself, then back to her. "If you say so." He took a step towards her, then another, stretching out a hand to caress her waist. "You're so fucking gorgeous, Jamie. You take my breath away. I get hard just looking at you. You're incredible. You're perfect."

Jamie shook her head, ducking her face to glance at the carpeting. "No. But I'm glad you think so."

"You are. You're perfect. Not just perfect to me, but actually perfect." He stepped closer yet, and his naked cock pressed hot against her warm, silk-soft belly.

"Perfect? I'm not, I'm—"

Chase shut her up with a kiss, a deep, endless, claiming of her mouth. She melted into him, digging her fingers against his back and pushing his T-shirt up, breaking apart to rip the cotton away and toss it aside before reclaiming his mouth with hers. Her hunger for him made Chase dizzy, wild with disbelief, breathless with anticipation.

She explored his body with her hands, roaming from his bare shoulders to his chest, his back to his stomach, scrubbing her palms over his bald scalp in a now-familiar gesture of affection that had Chase's heart seizing.

Jamie pushed his pants down, sinking to her knees and brushing his torso with hot kisses as he did so, then caressing his leg with her hand and lifting his foot from the leather, peeling it off one leg at a time, kissing each thigh as it was bared. Chase tried to lift her to her feet, uncomfortable with the kind of attention she was paying to him, overwhelmed by the sheer potency of the emotions she was displaying. She cupped his balls in both hands, pressing kisses to his belly, his thigh, the crease of his leg beside his sack, then touched her lips to his shaft. He gasped, and she turned her face sideways to take his length in her mouth, sliding her wet lips across his skin, tongue tasting his flesh. She wasn't giving him oral sex, he realized. She was kissing him, arousing him, showing desire for him. As if he needed further arousal.

He pulled away from her forcefully, feeling himself rising yet again. *Not this time*, he thought. *This time is about her.*

He pulled her to her feet, captured both of her wrists in one of his hands. "My turn," he said.

She let her hands go limp, stood straight, lifting her chin and gazing at him, cool and collected. "Touch me, please," she said.

Jamie's heart was pounding in her chest. She had the taste of Chase in her mouth, the musk of his seed from the elevator, the salt of his skin. She couldn't put words to what she was feeling in that moment. Desire, need…these weren't strong enough. She hadn't meant to go down on him in the elevator. She'd just been unable to resist touching him in the street, in front of the concierge, and then when they were alone in the elevator, she'd simply had to feel his skin in her hands, feel his huge cock fill her fists. And then she'd realized how close he was. She then simply *had* to feel him come, had to taste him. His cock felt so perfect in her hands, filling both hands and spilling over the top of her uppermost fist. She knew there might be cameras watching, knew someone could get on the elevator with them at any moment, but she didn't care. If he'd stripped her naked and banged her up against the elevator wall, she wouldn't have cared. Nothing mattered in the moment but Chase, but his skin and his heat and his body and his heart, his emotions so potent and completely bared on his face, in his eyes.

She'd tasted him, taken him in her mouth, swallowed him, caressed him and brought him to completion, felt his seed fill her mouth, hot and salty and thick, felt his tip touch the back of her throat, felt his balls seize and clench, and she'd taken more, wanting all of him.

And now she stood in front of him, vulnerable, letting her love show in her eyes, nearly naked and shivering with need. Except...what she felt was so far past a paltry word like "need." Every atom in her body was vibrating with desire for him, with the blood-hot need to feel his hands on her bare skin, his lips on her body, his thickness filling her.

She stood stone-still, shirtless, breath coming in slow, deep gasps, waiting. His eyes were dark and hooded, his chest rising and falling with his desperate breathing. He was naked, gloriously nude, bared for her perusal. She openly stared at him, taking in his thick arms scribed with tattoos, his hands curling into fists and releasing at his sides, his narrow waist and hard, round ass, his proudly jutting cock, huge and thick and dark, purple-veined and heavy. His thighs were thick and hard too, quadriceps cut and defined. His bald scalp was beaded with dots of sweat, and one drop trailed down his cheek. Why was he sweating? It was cold in the hotel room and he was naked.

She forced herself into stillness, wanting to rush over to him, press her body against his and beg him to put his hands on her, his cock inside her, his mouth on her. She'd already asked him to touch her, and now she would wait for him to do so in his way, in his time.

Her hands trembled. She'd tasted him, touched him, given away her feelings. She'd given herself over to him, knowing there was never any going back now. That kiss on the street had done her in. She was his, now, for better or worse.

Jamie swallowed hard past the lump in her throat. He wasn't moving, wasn't doing anything but staring at her, his gaze suddenly inscrutable. His hands tightened into fists at his sides and his jaw clenched, his eyes narrowing.

Suddenly, fear shot through her. Maybe...*god no*. Maybe since she'd gotten him off, he was done with her. Maybe all he'd wanted was a cheap thrill, and the rest of it had been a game. Maybe he was about to walk away. He was tensed, hard, almost shut down.

"Chase?" She couldn't help his name from escaping. "I..." one of her hands reached for him, then dropped to her side again. "Was this not what you—"

He crossed the space between them with one bound, lips crushing against hers, his hands curling around her waist and pulling her body flush with his. His cock was a hard rod between them, thick and hot against her bare belly.

"I love you so much it hurts," he whispered.

Jamie's soul clenched. "What?"

"You heard me. I...you're so beautiful. So perfect. You're really here? With me? You're not going to leave again?" His face twisted and his voice was low and hard. "I need you. Now. Always."

Jamie caressed his spine, then clutched the cool muscle of his ass. "I'm not going anywhere," she said. "I'm here. I'm waiting for you to make love to me. Please, Chase. Is that what you're waiting for? Me to beg you? Please, Chase. *Please* make love to me."

Chase's eyes blazed. "I should be the one begging you. I *am* begging you. Let me love you."

In answer, she reached up and unclasped the bra, pulled it off her shoulders and dropped it to the floor next to her with a flourish. She reached for the button of her pants, but Chase stopped her.

"Let me," he said, and sank to his knees in front of her.

She caressed his scalp as he pressed a line of fiery kisses down her stomach, then gasped as he *thankgodfinally* freed the button of her jeans, unzipped them, worked them down her hips. She wriggled her ass as he shimmied them down to her feet, then stepped out of them. When she wiggled her hips, Chase's nostrils flared and his mouth seemed to latch almost involuntarily onto her hipbone, his teeth nipping her skin, as if the sway of her hips drove him wild. She did it again, but this time to a rhythm, swaying side to side in his grip in a belly-dancing bounce. Chase growled, eyes sliding closed as if he couldn't contain his desire. His fingers scraped down her spine, stiff-ened into talons, raking off her panties—a purple thong matching her bra. She was naked, then.

Kneeling in front of her, Chase merely gazed at her once again for several long moments, eyes raking over her full breasts to her wide, curvy hips, to her thick thighs. He reached up, traced his hand down her side, caressing the edge of her breast, then down farther to her hip. Her breath caught as his hands swept around her hips to clutch her ass, exploring the firm flesh, kneading, digging, caressing. His finger swept down the crease, and she instinctively widened her stance to allow him better access. She didn't care where he touched her, she just wanted, *needed*, his touch. Anywhere. Everywhere. She trusted him to touch her anywhere, everywhere. He didn't push in, but simply explored her body with his hand, caressed the weight of each cheek of her buttocks.

She began to breathe a little, then, as he kissed her belly, sucking in long, shuddering breaths. He reached up to cup her breast, merely holding its weight at first, then exploring it more thoroughly as he had her ass. She let her head tip back as he rubbed his thumb over her nipple, felt it harden under his touch. Having been settled back on his haunches, Chase now rose up to his knees and kissed the underside of one breast, then the other. Jamie felt her lungs seize again when he took a nipple in his mouth, sucking it between his lips, past his teeth. She moaned gently, and then louder when he worried the nipple in his teeth, gasped when he pinched the other nipple in his fingers. His free hand carved down her ass, down the back of her leg, then back up her thigh, along the inside now.

Jamie let her legs widen a bit more, and his fingers found the damp heat of her entrance. He didn't enter her channel yet, but, as he had her breasts and ass, he merely explored at first, tracing the line of her labia, one side and then other, tickling, probing, touching. He was moving his mouth from one breast to the other now, his one hand clutching her ass, fingers of the other hand daring into the wet heat of her desire.

She smelled the musk of her arousal, potent and pungent, and then, to her mortification, she heard him sniff her, smelling her.

"God, Chase, don't do that!" She said, feeling her cheeks flush. "I smell—"

"You smell incredible," he said, cutting her off. "You smell so good. So good, I just want to…taste you, eat you."

"God…Chase…" this time it wasn't a protestation, but an affirmation.

He had accompanied his words with a swipe of two fingers into her pussy, and her legs buckled, her capacity for speech stolen along with her breath. Jamie rested her hands on the top of his head, rubbing her thumbs in tiny circles, letting her eyes shutter closed. He curled his fingers to explore her inner walls, stroking her insides, exploring her there as thoroughly as he had everywhere else, not seeking yet to bring her to orgasm, but merely learning her body.

Jamie loved his exploration. She would be content to let him explore forever, even if she never came. This touching, this tender, hungry searching of her body sated her in way she'd never felt, filled the ache in her soul. Already the mountain of frustration was gone, replaced now by wellspring of contentment, and they'd only begun.

He suckled her nipple into his mouth and drew his face away from her body, stretching her nipple to its fullest, almost painful extension, and then he released it with a wet smack. She felt his gaze on her, opened her eyes to see his wide and full of vulnerability. His hand was resting on her ass, holding her, the other was delving in her woman-hood, dipping and curling and swiping; now, his eyes locked on hers, he traced his middle finger up the wet crease of her pussy and began to circle her clit. He didn't make direct contact, yet, but merely let his finger drift almost lazily around it. Jamie held her breath, legs buck-ling to get her core closer to his touch, then, after an endless moment, he brushed the sensitive nub, seemingly by accident. Jamie expelled the breath on a short, sharp moan.

His touch was like fire, like magic. Nothing had ever felt so good. He seemed to know exactly how to touch her, how to give her the most pleasure. She kept her eyes on his, forced her heart open, letting her every thought, every emotion show in her eyes. She'd been holding herself in for so long, containing her feelings, pushing everything down, and now here he was, the man she'd dreamed about, wanted, needed for so long, here in front of her, kneeling before her and worshipping her body with his hands and his mouth.

The hand on her butt trailed down her leg, curled around her ankle and gently guided her stance wider. She complied willingly, spreading her feet apart until she felt air cold on her bare, bald pussy. Then she held her breath once more as Chase slowly lowered down on his haunches, his gaze never leaving hers. She stroked his head, fingers playing across the ripples and ridges of his scalp, down behind his ears, tracing the hard, masculine line of his strong jaw, thumbs skittering lovingly over his cheekbones before resting once more on the back of his head. His gaze pulled away, then, and turned to her core.

"God, Jamie. So sexy. So hot. So perfect." He kissed her belly, cutting a line of kisses across it, making clear he liked it, loved it, found it as sexy as the rest of her, and for once she believed him, knew he believed it and felt sexy for him, because of him; his mouth touched lower now, just above her pubis. "Your pussy is so beautiful, Jamie. Just like the rest of you. Hold on to me now. I'm going to kiss you here. I'm gonna make you come *so* hard."

She clutched the back of his head and shamelessly, wantonly pulled his mouth onto her pussy. "Yes!" She cried out, the word a gasp of intense pleasure.

His tongue teased her clit, lapped up the crease from bottom to top and then again, licking her. His fingers had never left her, had been slowly working toward her G-spot and were massaging it gently. When he thrust his tongue against her clit, he began to work her G-spot harder. She arched her back and let her knees buckle once more, lowering herself to his mouth. He began a rhythm, now, tongue circling her clit, moving his fingers against the sensitive ribbed flesh high inside her walls, free hand caressing and clutching her breast, cupping it, thumbing the nipple, pinching it.

She held on to him, held him against her, bobbing her body up and down into his tongue, into his fingers. She was close, already, despite his promise to make it slow.

Then he pulled away, and she heard a whimper of frustration rip from her lips. "Chase! Don't stop, I was close—"

"I said it was going to be slow." He stood up, leaving his fingers inside her, moving them from her G-spot to her clit, circling and stimulating, but not enough to let her come. "You need to lay down, love. I wouldn't want you to fall."

"You seem pretty confident you're gonna make me come that hard, huh?" She tried to make her voice steady and flippant, but it still came out breathy and small.

"It's not confidence, babes. It's knowledge. I *know* how hard I'm gonna make you come."

"Oh yeah? How do you know?"

He pushed her back toward the bed until her knees hit, then pushed her again so she was bending awkwardly backward, her feet still planted on the floor. He crushed his body against hers, his cock against her belly, hot and hard. She wanted it. She hooked her feet around his waist and jerked him toward her, reaching between them to grab his shaft.

He laughed and let her touch him, their wrists crossed and bumping as he mercilessly and skillfully caressed her stiffened clit with his fingers, her hand pumping cock greedily. He kissed her lips, and she tasted her own juices on his lips, his tongue, as she knew he tasted himself in her mouth. He crawled up onto the bed, forcing her to let go of him or risk hurting him, so she scooted backward until she felt pillow beneath her head. He stopped, and then began to slip back down her body, taking his cock out of her reach. She wanted to touch him more, hold him, caress him, kiss him. She wanted him in her mouth again, in her pussy, against her belly and between her breasts, all over her. She wanted him everywhere—

Then his teeth brushed her clit, his lips forming a seal against her labia, sucking her nub into his mouth. She let her legs fall apart and went limp into his touch, gasping a whimper when he slipped his fingers deeper once more, pressing circles onto her G-spot, and she knew she was rising again, nearing orgasm again.

So, of course, he slowed down. She wanted to cry out in frustration, and opened her mouth to do so, but her growl turned into a moan as his free hand drifted between her legs, beneath his other hand and sought out her most secret place. She clenched up, legs squeezing, buttocks tensing.

"Chase...no...not yet."

He grunted, still swiping his fingers inside her. "No? Not ready for that yet?"

She shook her head, unable to get a word out past her trembling, shaking lips. She was on the verge of orgasm still, held there by his fingers inside her, by his tongue inside her. She wasn't able to fall over the edge, though, clenched up and tensed up and and quivering at the feel of his long middle finger waiting at the crease of her ass, mere centimeters from the tight knot of her anus.

He left his finger there, and she tried to forget its presence, but couldn't, and that kept her just this side of orgasm.

"I want to come, Chase, please!"

"Then come."

"I can't—I can't. You...your finger. It's too close to my asshole. I'm...I can't. Not that. Not yet."

He moved his hand away, drifting upward with deliberate slowness to cup her left breast, the larger one, the one he seemed to favor. She arched into his touch, gasping, scratching lightly down his scalp with her fingernails. He shuddered and moaned when she did that, and the vibrations of his voice on her clit sent her spiraling over the edge, writhing uncontrollably beneath him, pushing her core into his mouth, shameless, needing more, more, and he gave her more, tonguing her relentlessly, milking her orgasm, sliding his fingers within her, pinching her nipple almost-but-not-quite too hard, just this side of painful.

She rode the waves of climax, clinging to Chase's head, pushing him between her thighs until she couldn't take any further stimulation, and then she pulled him upward. He let himself be dragged up to lay next to her, stroking her skin with his palms, roaming over her belly and arms and thighs, but giving her sensitive, swollen tissues a brief respite from his attentions.

Jamie held him to her chest, then pulled him to her mouth for a kiss, tasting herself on him even more strongly. The kiss sparked her need all over again, and she twisted on the bed so she was facing him, partly on top of him, tracing the contours of his chest with her fingers. She slowly drifted her touch downward, following the hard lines of his ribs, then the ridges of his abdomen, then the sexy V-cut leading to his achingly hard cock.

He gasped into the kiss when she took him in her hand, moaned low in his throat when she caressed his length.

"I want you inside me," she whispered, her lips moving against his.

He took her hips in his hands and lifted her all the way on top of him, then paused to grunt a single word, "protection—"

"I have some in my purse." Jamie looked away, then back to Chase, their eyes meeting in an acknowledgement of the awkwardness brought on by the tacit understanding of what that meant. "I know that's—I'm sorry if—"

Chase slid out from beneath her and grabbed her purse from the floor, handing it to her. "I know. You don't need to be sorry. You're here with me now. That's all that matters, right?"

"Right," Jamie agreed.

She dug in the purse and produced an unopened box of condoms, set them on the table beside the bed. They both stared at the box. Jamie pushed away the niggling worm of doubt deep inside her, the part of her that wanted to bring up the reasons why there might be other things that mattered besides being there in the hotel room with Chase. She wanted so badly for that to be all that mattered, but there *were* other things.

"Chase, I—"

He flopped backward, rubbing his face with his palm. "There *are* other things that matter. That's what you're going to say, isn't it? I know, Jay. I know."

"No one has ever called me Jay except…except—"

"Except Anna. You can say her name, you know. I'm not gonna flip out or get weird. She's my ex-girlfriend, not my ex-wife. And honestly, I'm not sure 'girlfriend' is even the right word for what we had. We never discussed the nature of it, never put our relationship into a box. But whatever. That's completely beside the point." Chase sat up again and took Jamie's hands in his. "The point is, you don't have to tiptoe around the subject of Anna with me. I'm here. You're here. There are issues, yes, and I'm not saying I don't care about them, because I do. But…I don't want to care about them right *now*. I just want to be with you right now."

Jamie shifted on the bed, torn between awkwardness and worry and desire. "I want to be with you too. I just…I'm worried we're…I don't know. Never mind. It's nothing."

Chase hissed in exasperation. "Oh, come on Jamie! Don't give me that 'it's nothing' bullshit. Say what you think. Say what you feel."

Jamie tugged the blankets down and tucked the flat sheet over her chest. "I'm worried we rushed into this."

"Rushed—Jamie…how can you think that? How long have we been denying what we feel for each other?"

"Not that. This," Jamie said, gesturing to their naked bodies, to the bed. "Both of us were with other people, like *today*."

Chase growled in frustration, rubbing his palm over his head, a gesture Jamie was learning meant extreme distress and helplessness. "Fuck. Fuck, you're right." He settled the sheet over his lap, hiding his softening erection. "I wish I could deny it, but I can't. I can't say it didn't mean anything to me, because it did."

"What did?"

Chase hesitated. "Being with Tess."

"Oh." Her voice was small. "I'm sorry, Chase. I wish...I wish this conversation could have waited until after we'd been able to—"

"No, it's probably better this way. I don't know what we're supposed to do, though. You know? I mean, yeah, I was with someone else earlier today. So were you. I don't like the thought of you with another man anymore than you like the thought of me with another woman. But it's the facts, and you can't change facts." He took one of her hands in his, rubbing the pad of his thumb across one of her fingernails. "So are we supposed to wait a specific period of time? A day? A week? A month? How long is appropriate? We've already talked about why we were with other people and what it meant to us and all that. I don't see any reason to go back over all that."

"I don't want to wait either, Chase, but—"

"How long is long enough? What's the right reset period, or whatever? I'm not being flippant. I'm not just trying to gloss over the problem so we can get it on. I'm asking honestly."

The sincerity and confusion and anguish in his eyes had Jamie scooting closer to him. Chase moved so he was leaning back against the bed, partially sitting and partially reclining, then pulled Jamie over to him so she was resting her head on his chest, the sheet covering both of them. Jamie took a few deep breaths, taking in his scent, the feel of his muscle under her cheek, his broad male bulk a comforting presence as much as it was a sensual turn on. Her hand settled on his diaphragm, between chest and belly, and he tangled his fingers with hers.

Silence stretched out as Jamie tried to come up with an answer, but all she could think of in the moment was how perfect and comforting and warm it was being held by Chase. His arm around her shoulders, tucking her close against him, his fingers tangled with hers, the rise and fall of his breathing, the faint thump of his heartbeat….

He felt like home.

"I don't know what the answer is, Chase. But I've just spent so long ignoring the truth about so many things, I can't—I can't do it anymore."

"What truths have you ignored?"

She snorted. "God. Everything. For most of my adult life I've ignored how lonely I was. How miserable and fucking pathetic my life was. I ignored how shitty I felt about myself, how trashy I knew I was."

"You aren't—"

"*Don't*, Chase." She cut him off sharply, almost snapping. "I *was*. I fucked anything with a cock from the time I was sixteen, okay? Sure I had fairly legitimate reasons. But that doesn't change it. And I got good at pretending it didn't bother me, to the point that I almost believed it. But I can't pretend anymore. This doesn't even really have anything to do with you. When I met you in Vegas, Anna had dared me to go celibate for two months. The dare was no physical male contact. No kissing, nothing. I couldn't even go a day. I kissed you. Then I went home and did okay for awhile, but then I got drunk and…well, bad things happened that I don't want to go into with you just yet."

"Jamie—"

"Shut up and let me answer the question."

"'Kay."

"I pretended a lot of things. I pretended I wasn't in love with you. I pretended I was okay without you, that this between us wasn't the most powerful thing I'd ever felt. And now…I can't pretend. I just want the truth out there, good or bad."

"So what is the truth, for you?"

"I want you. Even still, in the middle of this whole heavy conversation, I can't stop wanting you. I'm partially wishing I could let myself just stop talking and get you hard and take you. Ride you. Suck you off again. Let you do whatever you want to me. But…I can't push away the truth that this thing between us is still impossible."

"It's not impossible. It's just complicated."

Jamie laughed. "It's impossible, baby. It is. We were both broken up with less than twelve hours ago. I have no clothes but the ones on the floor over there. Everything else is back in Ian's condo, including my car. I may be with you, now and in the future, but I still have to deal with Ian. I kind of ran out on him. What if he changes his mind and tries to tell me he wants to get back together, give it another shot? I wouldn't do it, whether I was with you or not because my thing with Ian was nothing but a distraction from how I really felt. I knew that from the beginning, but that was another one of those truths I pretended not to care about."

"I like it when you call me baby." Chase rubbed her knuckle with a thumb. "I know what you mean, though. My thing with Tess isn't as complicated to untangle, but it's still there. She has a few things at my place back in Detroit, but that's easy enough to take care of. My cousin can send them to Tess. The emotional thing is harder. I know…I know it's hard. I know it's tangled up and fucked up and complicated. But it's not impossible. We just…we have to be honest and take things one step at a time."

Jamie sighed. "Yeah. But none of this answers the original question. What do we do now? Is it wrong for us to be together like this so soon?"

"Wrong?" Chase shook his head. "Being with you can never be wrong, if you ask me. *Not* being with you would be wrong. Maybe we just stay like this tonight, just…sleep. Hold each other. Cuddle and shit."

Jamie giggled. "You're funny."

"What?" Chase sounded confused. "How am I funny?"

She shook her head, giggling into his chest again, helplessly lost in laughter. "Just, the way you said that." She made her voice gruff and growly, at the bottom of her register, chin tucked against her breastbone. "'Cuddle and shit.' Like it would make you less manly to just suggest we cuddle. It was just funny to me for some reason."

"Guys aren't supposed to want to cuddle. It's not a manly word."

Jamie laughed even harder at that. "Call it something else if you want, but you *like* this. Holding me. Not having sex or foreplay or anything. Just…being together."

Chase turned his face to her hair, breathed deeply, clutching her against him. "Yes, Jay. I like it. I love it. Call it cuddling if you want. I'm secure in my manhood. Just don't tell the guys I wanted to cuddle. Especially *before* sex."

Jamie huffed, not laughing anymore. She turned her face up to meet his gaze. "I won't tell anyone. Your secret is safe with me."

His eyes bored into hers and she felt warmth running from her cheeks down to her chest, filling her stomach with tingling anticipation. Their fingers were still twined together on Chase's torso, his arm around her shoulders, but suddenly Jamie was much more aware of his body, of his desire, of her own need. She felt mercurial, being a raging tempest of desire one moment, then an emotional mess the next, and then back to wanting his body again, all within a matter of twenty minutes.

"I'm sorry I'm so back and forth on you," she said.

Chase smiled at her, the kind of smirk that said he thought she was being ridiculous. "We're both back and forth. That conversation wasn't just you. I was thinking the same thing. You were just more willing to say it out loud than I was."

"I still don't know exactly what we should do."

"*Should* do, or want to do?" Chase asked. "They're very different things in this case, I think."

"And that's where my confusion comes from." Jamie untangled her fingers from his and let her hand roam over his chest, her eyes fixed on his chiseled, beautiful face.

Chase put his finger to her chin and tipped her mouth to his for a soft, chaste kiss. "My desire for you isn't going anywhere. *I'm* not going anywhere. We don't have to do anything right now. We can just *cuddle*." He grinned as he said it, tangling his fingers in her hair, cupping the side of her face.

Jamie twisted in his arms slightly so she was pressed against him. "Maybe we could just kiss a little bit. Make out like we're teenagers."

Chase smiled at her again, an indulgent, knowing smile. "Yeah. That sounds good. Just kiss."

He pulled her face closer to his, their lips brushing but not meeting. Jamie moved to close in for the kiss, but he darted back out of reach, then brushed her lips with his again, his hand in her hair, eyes open and searching her face. She tried to kiss him a second time, and he evaded it again, this time touching her upper lip with his mouth, then her cheek. Jamie caught on to the game, grazing his lips with hers, waiting, waiting, then when he moved to kiss her chin, she intercepted him, crushing her mouth to his and claiming it, curling her hand around his head and holding him in place, stealing the kiss.

Chase sighed through his nose, softening into the kiss. Jamie smirked and pulled away, turning his game back on him. She touched her lips to the corner of his mouth, dipped her tongue against his lips, then darted away to hover near his mouth once more. He laughed and slid the arm that had been wrapped around her shoulders lower down, curling around her waist. Jamie unconsciously arched into his hold, turning more fully onto her stomach atop him, her weight more than half on his chest, the sheet tangled between them, a thin barrier between their skin.

Jamie shifted, pushing the sheet away so they were skin to skin, her left arm underneath her to support her weight. The fingers of her right hand skated over his bald scalp, down to cup his cheek as she moved in for a kiss, no games now in this one, only full passion, unrestrained. She slid her leg over his, toes digging into the mattress between his feet, shoving herself forward so she was directly above him, hips to hips, face to face.

The kiss opened up, heat breathing between them, igniting each of their desires. Jamie felt his need in his kiss, felt it in the way his mouth moved hungrily on hers, in the way his tongue speared into her mouth to taste her tongue, trace her lips and her teeth. Jamie's heart began to thunder in her chest once more, the same lightning excitement at his touch thrilling through her body. His hand on her waist thrilled her, excited her. The prospect of his palm drifting down to clutch her ass excited her. His cock hardening between their bodies excited her. She needed this. She wanted it. She couldn't go another minute without it.

The issues remained, but when he kissed her like this, so raw, so full of vulnerable hunger…nothing else mattered. She could give in to this now, or later. The hunger wouldn't change. It would only increase. She'd been starved for this her whole life.

Jamie felt the truth in that thought and accepted it. She had been waiting for Chase all her life. She may not have known it, but the way he kissed her, held her, spoke to her…he was the thing that had always been missing, the element she had been searching for in all those other men, those other boys. Those *guys*. Chase was a *man*. He wasn't just a guy. Jamie wasn't sure what defined the difference, but she knew it was there, saw it and felt it. Chase was so much *more* than those other guys in her past had ever been.

He saw her, saw into her heart and her soul and her mind and knew her, completely. He may not have known the details of her life, but he knew *her*.

All this, in the space of a kiss.

Jamie pulled away and saw the fire in Chase's eyes, felt it the way his hands curled on her stomach. He was waiting for her to tell him what she wanted. She couldn't speak, finding her words buried under a wave of need, a wildfire of hunger. She could only kiss him again, dipping down to touch her lips to his with aching, deliberate gentility, putting all of her heart into the contact of mouths. She felt her hair fall down around their faces, red curls framing their faces, curtaining them off from everything else.

She felt Chase's hands rest on her waist, both of them now, holding her sides, fingers splayed to touch her ribs. He hesitantly, almost gingerly smoothed his palms down to hold her ass, cupping and caressing. She arched her back, gasping into the kiss, loving that single intimate gesture with all of her soul and body in that moment. Chase captured her gasped breath with his mouth, touching her tongue with his, inviting her passion to higher peaks.

Jamie responded by shifting her weight to fully straddle him, her thighs on either side of his waist, forearms on the pillow next to his face. She felt the broad soft tip of his cock touch her inner thigh, and was filled in that single instant of touch with an inferno of want, flooding her belly with clenches of desire, her slit with slicking juices. She was wet immediately, and she let her thighs split farther apart, spreading her nether lips wider. Without breaking the kiss, Jamie slid down his body until the crown of his cock was nudging her entrance. Chase groaned and swiveled his hips into hers, mouth stretching open, breaking the kiss. He let out a long, deep, rumbling moan when she rolled her hips up to work his tip inside her.

He didn't move to thrust in, though. She felt him stretch out his arm, grab the box from beside them, shred it open and fumble a string of condoms out, rip one free. Jamie moaned into his mouth, then kissed his jaw, his chin, his shoulder, his throat. She couldn't help herself. She writhed her hips, wanting so desperately to drive him deeper into her, but knowing she had to wait.

He moved his hips down and rolled the latex over himself. Jamie rose up on her elbows, moving so he was poised at her slit once more.

She met his dark, hooded gaze. "Please? Now?" Her plea was breathy and desperate and she didn't care.

"Yes, god yes, now." He took her by the hips, hands holding her tight and pushing her down.

Jamie buried her face in the hollow of his neck, exhaled, and impaled him inside her. "Oh...my...*god*." Jamie heard the words escape from her as a sob of raw ecstasy.

She couldn't take him in all the way. Not yet. She wanted to savor every second, every inch. She only slid him in to the groove beneath his crown, then stopped, panting. He stretched her, filled her. She bit his neck, arms wrapped beneath his head in an embrace, knees drawn up to spread herself wide.

"God…god*damn*, Jay. You feel so—so perfect. So incredible." Chase's voice was just as ragged as she felt, shredded by the potency of fulfillment after so long a denial.

At the sound of the nickname, Jamie clung him even tighter, then drew in a deep breath. She paused, breath held at the apex, torso stretched taut, hips drawn up…then exhaled once more and sank down onto him, slowly sliding his huge, incredible, soft yet iron-hard cock into her all the way, stretching her body down his until he was buried in her softness to the root, until they were joined fully.

"*Jamie…*" her name emerged from his lips in a shuddering gasp, his head lifting from the pillow in a gesture of helpless intensity.

Then he thrust, once, slowly, and Jamie came. Without warning, without a breath to prepare, just a sudden tidal wave of clenching, ripping, juddering orgasm. Jamie sobbed into his shoulder and rode it out, rolling her hips on him.

"Yes, Jay, yes. Come for me." Chase whispered the words into her ear, breathed them so softly she might have imagined them.

But Jamie heard his words, and now she couldn't help but come even harder, lifting and lowering herself onto him in rhythmless abandon, sucking in deep, sobbing breaths and letting them out as high cries of climactic delight.

Chase fluttered his hips, rolling in and out in small thrusts, grunting as her inner muscles clamped down on his cock. Jamie felt herself clenching, every muscle contracting, especially her inner walls squeezing him mercilessly.

When Jamie went limp as the waves subsided, Chase rolled them over so he was on top. Jamie splayed her hands on his back, rubbed them up his neck to cup the back of his head, pulling his mouth down to her breast. He suckled her nipple and thrust into her, slowly and sinuously, one hand supporting his weight, the other fondling her breast.

"God, Chase. More." She arched her spine, shoving her breasts into his touch, lifting her hips to meet his in a steady rhythm. Jamie clawed her fingernails down his back lightly, then clutched his ass and pulled him against her. "I need more, Chase. More. Harder."

Chase lifted his mouth from her nipple and smiled at her, then deliberately slowed his thrust until he was sliding oh so slowly. He puled nearly all the way out, so only the very tip of his cock remained inside her. He paused, then, meeting her eyes, making her wait. She wanted him to crash into her, hard and fast; she also wanted him to go as slow as he could, to draw out this union as long as he could. She decided she didn't care how he made love to her, as long as she had him there with here.

"You want it harder?" Chase asked.

"Mmm-hmmm." Jamie caressed his ass gently, stroking his flanks and the hard muscle of cheeks. "I like it hard. But...slow and soft is good too. Just make love to me. Please...please."

Chase dipped down to kiss her, still holding himself barely inside her. He pulled away from the kiss to meet her eyes. Jamie searched his face, memorizing his features, absorbing greedily the look of wonder and tenderness and love. Then, she felt him move into her. He glided in with deliberate slowness, barely moving at all, and Jamie felt his entire body shivering with the effort to move so slowly. Jamie's mouth stretched wide in a silent scream as he filled her past, and her fingers dug into the flesh of his ass in urgent claws, pulling at him with fierce power.

"*Chase...*" his name was a plea, a whispered epithet.

He repeated the action, pulling out almost all the way, pausing at her entrance, then sliding in as slowly as he could. Jamie scrabbled at his back with her hands, digging at the bed with her heels. Chase drew a hand back and curled his elbow around the crook of her knee, planting his hand near her hip so her leg was drawn up, then he did the same with the other hand, and now Jamie was stretched open and her hips lifted up and her body bare for his pleasure.

"God!" she shrieked. "Yes!"

Jamie reached up behind her head to grasp the headboard, lifting up to meet his first stroke. He delivered the initial thrust slowly, as he had all the rest, worshipful and prolonged. Jamie waited, quivering, as he drew himself out, then when he began to glide back in slowly, she lifted herself off the bed to meet him, hard.

Chase slumped over her, forehead touching her belly, breath huffing on her navel, his entire body trembling with restrained need.

"I need it, Chase," Jamie whimpered. "I need you. I *need* you. Please. Don't hold back anymore. Give me all of you. Hard."

Chase growled at her words, a primal sound of capitulation. He drew out, shudderingly slow, and then, with an infinitesimal pause, he slammed himself home with nearly savage force. Jamie loosed a scream of rapturous bliss, dragging her nails down his back so hard she knew she'd drawn blood. Chase growled, thrusting again, hard and slow, pulling out and crashing in against her in a rhythm now, and she could only return her hands to cling to the headboard and cry out in euphoric delight as he slammed into her, harder and harder now, faster and faster, feeling her body shaking and trembling with the coiled tension of impending orgasm.

Jamie met him thrust for thrust, using the headboard for leverage to get herself off the bed, crushing her folds against him desperately, wanting more even as he gave her more. She was unable to control the sounds emerging from her throat, tiny mewls, shrieks, screams, ragged sobs. Chase grunted and growled with each thrust, moaning with every furious pump of his hips.

Chase released Jamie's legs and she wrapped them around his waist, clung to his neck with her arms and pressed her lips to his ear.

"I love this, Chase," she whispered. "I love you. Yes…oh god, yes."

They were moving together frantically, desperately.

"Jamie. Oh, Jay. I need you... Don't stop," Chase said, his voice guttural and thick.

"Come with me, Chase," Jamie said, feeling the waves begin to roll over her body. "Oh god, I'm gonna come right now, so hard, so hard."

Chase lost the rhythm, grinding into her with stuttering, shattering force, groaning every time his body slammed into hers. "Say it again, baby."

Jamie knew exactly what he wanted her to say. "Come with me." She clung to him, her hands on the nape of his neck and the back of his head, holding his face against her throat. "Come with me, Chase. Now. Oh. Oh...oh god, oh fuck!"

Jamie felt lightning strike inside her, a detonation so intense Jamie couldn't stand it, couldn't take it. She felt herself coming apart at the seams, shattering, splitting apart, full past bursting with all of Chase, with the infinite potency of his love, of his body inside her, of his arms around her, and all she could do was sob and cling and come, and come again and again while Chase undulated into her, making an incoherent sound in his throat that was part sob, part feral growl, and all man. He pushed and pushed and pushed, his mouth quivering between her breasts as he thrust frantically, arrhythmically. Jamie felt wave after wave of climax wash over her, each one more earth-shattering than the last, until she knew she was experiencing something far beyond mere physical orgasm.

Then she felt Chase unleash, felt his body tense and clench, then felt him judder and thrust hard, twice, and go still, laying on top of her, his lips pressing delirious kisses to her throat, chest, shoulders, cheek, and then her lips.

Jamie kissed him back, devouring his mouth, his breath, taking his love into her through the contact. Tears slipped out, trickled down her cheek and onto the pillow. She wasn't sure why she was crying, except perhaps for the sheer overwhelming amount of emotion running through her, from the intensity of her climax.

"Jay? Are you crying?" Chase carefully pulled out and rolled over with her, effortlessly shifting her to cradle her in his arms.

She nodded. "It's not sad tears though. Promise." She breathed deeply, shuddering involuntarily as an aftershock rippled through her. "I'm just...overwhelmed. In a good way."

"That was crazy intense, wasn't it?" Chase said.

Jamie moaned in satisfaction, wriggling against him. "Intense is an understatement. Like saying the ocean is a little wet." She felt him softening against her leg. "You'd better take care of that and come back to me. I need cuddles. And shit."

Chase laughed. "Mock if you will. Real men cuddle."

Jamie agreed, but was too entirely sated to say anything, and too fully enjoying the sight Chase's tight naked ass as he went to the bathroom to clean up. She also enjoyed the view as he returned, and enjoyed even more the feel of his arms curling around her as he drew her into a tangled embrace. She nestled into him, hearing his heart beat beneath her ear, his fingers toying idly with a curl, his breathing slow and steady, his body hard and strong but soft in all the right ways. Jamie closed her eyes and sighed deeply.

She was drowning in a sea of contentment, and nothing had ever been sweeter.

"Okay, baby?" Chase murmured.

"Never, ever been better."

"Good. Me neither."

Jamie felt herself drowsing. She wanted to stay awake, to savor the moment, the feeling of being held and loved, but sleep was stealing over her, an unstoppable force. She shook herself awake and turned her face up to look at Chase.

He rumbled in laughter. "Relax, Jay. Just...relax. We're together now. Let me hold you."

Jamie felt like a child fighting sleep. She sighed again and let sleep sweep her away.

Chapter 3

Chase was dreaming. It was a good dream, a pleasant dream. It was more than that, it was a fantasy, a wet dream. It wasn't real, he didn't think, because that would be simply too much to bear, too much wonder to contain. *She* was the dream, the one woman of whom he'd dreamed so often lately. The dream had been a long one, hours of ecstasy, it felt like. He'd dreamed of running into her after a show, and discovering she loved him after all, wanted to be with him despite the impossibility of such a thing. They'd gone to his show, and then to a hotel, and they'd made love. In that dream, she had taken Chase to a place he'd never thought possible, beyond sex, beyond climax, beyond anything that had ever been. He hadn't just come harder than ever before in his life; he'd felt her soul merge with his.

They'd fallen asleep together, in the dream.

And now, dreaming, he felt her lips on his body. Pressing fiery kisses down his chest, across his nipple, light lip-touches on his ribs, his side, his hip. Oh god, what a dream. She was kissing his thigh, and her hands were carving hot lines of sensual contact over his arms and inner thighs and now…oh shit, now she was *touching* him. Holding his aroused flesh in her fists. Stroking him slowly. Running her tongue up the side of his cock, licking his length as if he was a popsicle, taking him in her mouth and sucking hard.

"Oh god," he heard himself say. In the dream.

It was all a dream. He would wake up alone in the hotel room, hard and aching and ready to burst with no way to release except his own hand.

She fisted him, then feathered her fingers over his shaft in achingly soft caresses, sucked his tip hard, and then moved her lips gently on his crown, so soft, so wet, so delicate and loving and…

"Jamie. Oh god, Jamie, that feels so good." He heard the words, and the sound of his voice, in the dream, was ragged, thick and stuttering.

It felt so real, though. So real. Too real. But it wasn't, was it?

He didn't want to wake up.

"I love the way you taste," she said, then took him in her mouth again, deep now.

"It feels so good," Chase heard himself say. "Don't stop. Please don't stop until the dream's over."

He felt her pause. "Do you think you're dreaming, baby?"

Baby. The endearment tore at his heart, made it swell and fill.

"I'm dreaming. It's a dream. You're a dream. I don't want to wake up and still be alone." He shouldn't tell her that, even in a dream.

It sounded almost like she sobbed, then choking it off. "God, Chase. I'm so sorry you woke up alone so often." She caressed his cock with both hands, fist over fist, fingers trailing up his length, cupping the sensitive swollen flesh of his balls in tender hands, kissing him, deep-throating him, licking him, swirling her tongue around his tip. "What if this isn't a dream? What if you opened your eyes and it was real?"

Chase squeezed his eyes closed tighter, in the dream. "It's a dream. If it was real, I would die from happiness. I love you so much, and I don't want to wake up and not be with you." He knew he shouldn't tell her this. Not even in a dream.

She sobbed again, a sound of joy, he thought. Her voice sounded so real. Her hands on him, her mouth on him, her breath on his skin, it all felt so real. He felt a leg slide across his hip, then her weight settle on his hips. He felt her moist, hot entrance touching the tip of his cock, and he gasped in need. He wanted to touch her, take her hips in his hands and hold her, slide into her, feel her heavy breasts in his hands. He didn't dare.

He worried if he touched her the dream would pop like a soap bubble.

He felt her lips caress his chest, her hands rest on his pectoral muscles, and then she kissed his throat, and Chase couldn't help arching his back and tipping his head back to let her kiss him there again. He heard himself groan, a long sound of pleasure when her lips touched his adam's apple, and then his jaw, and then the corner of his mouth, and her breath was so hot on his lips, her mouth so wet and her tongue so demanding on his.

"Wake up, Chase." Her voice was a breathy whisper in his ear, and then she kissed him again, slow tongue in his mouth driving him wild with desire and heat and wetness and softness. "It's not a dream. I'm here. I'm real. I need you. Wake up and make love to me. Touch me."

Chase heard his voice raise in a moan of need, a raw, low, vulnerable sound of desperation. He wanted to believe the words of the dream-vision. He felt his hands unfisting from the sheet, which he'd been clutching with desperate strength, and drift up to touch the dream-her. She felt real, too. Soft as silk, skin like velvet, like heat and love and softness and sex made flesh. Her thighs under his hands were thick and strong, yet still as soft as down. He was touching her, and the dream continued. He dared to touch more. Her hips, wide and round and intoxicating, curves like deepest fantasy in his hands, under his needy fingers. Her sides, her belly, her padded ribs, her spine and her long, sensual back. He breathed deep, almost panting with the fullness of his love for her, the drunken ecstasy of merely touching her. She was sitting on him, palms resting low on his belly, near his diaphragm, her thighs split wide across his hips, poised above his rigid, throbbing cock. Poised and waiting.

He wasn't ready to be inside her yet, even in this dream so like wonderful reality, like fantasy made truth, this dream he'd dreamed so many times and always woken to the emptiness of a dark hotel room. He slid his dream-palms up her ribs to cup her breasts, and yes, they were every bit as large and heavy and silky-soft as he'd always imagined.

"Open your eyes, love," her voice came, like music.

"No, no. Not yet. I don't want to wake up yet." He ran his thumb across her nipple and felt it bead into a hard, stiff nub. "I want to make love to you before I wake. I need you, even if you're a dream."

She writhed on top of him, rubbing her wet slit over his tip, and he could've come just from that. "I'm not a dream. This is real, Chase. It's real. I'm real." She leaned down and kissed him, full and furious and passionate and hungry. "Remember? We're in Chicago. I watched your show. We made love. And now I want you again. Wake up."

Chase moaned, running his palms between her breasts, up her collarbone and up farther, cupping her face, her neck. He buried his fingers in her curls.

So real. Too real.

He felt her palms on his chest, her hips writhing in undulating, sinuous circles, working the tip of his cock inside her soft folds, just the first inch slipping in and out. He smelled her, faint shampoo, perfume, sex.

The scent of sex was what woke him. He'd never smelled anything in a dream.

He cracked one eye open, hesitantly, then the other. Her weight above him didn't vanish with the return of sight. Her sweet beauty greeted him like dawn after a long night. Red sleep-tangled curls, tickled his face and his shoulders as she leaned over him, smiling down at him.

"There you are, baby." She crushed her lips to his, then lifted up to gaze down at him. "You wouldn't wake up."

He had his hands fisted gently in her curls, so he tugged her down for another kiss, devoured her mouth greedily. "I didn't want to. I thought it had all been a dream."

"But it wasn't," Jamie said. "It was real. I had the same thought when I first woke up, so I had to touch you, make sure you were real. Once I started, I couldn't stop. I want you so bad it hurts."

"Thank god it wasn't a dream. I would've died, I think."

527

She lifted her hips, wide green eyes locked on his. "Me too."

"But it's real. Right?"

"Right." She hovered there, just the tip of him inside her pussy. "But I think you'd better tell me you love me again. Just in case."

He released her hair, trailing his fingertips down her breastbone, over each nipple, down to the soft field of her belly, then slipped a single finger into her, brushing her clit. She gasped, arching her back as she writhed on top of him, driving him deeper.

"I love you, Jamie. I love you." He whispered the words, his voice low and fierce.

Jamie shivered, trembled, and then gasped his name as she sank down onto him, impaling him to the hilt, their hips colliding. Chase groaned in ecstatic relief as he felt himself filling her, and Jamie's voice rose to match his, and then they both began to move in perfect sync, moaning together, lips touching but not kissing, simply stretched wide in silent screams, breath shuddering in and groaning out.

Their motion together was slow, glacial, coursing in like a tide, drifting out like an exhale. Jamie's palms pressed onto his chest, her breasts swaying in the rhythm of her body's thrusting, her hips rolling, drawing him deeper. She took control of their pace, and Chase let her. She leaned forward, lifting up, hesitating at the apex, then sinking down, repeating this motion, drawing out every impalement, crying out as he dove deeper with every thrust.

Chase cupped one of her swaying breasts in his hand, scratching his fingers along her spine and clutching her ass as she undulated on top of him. He whispered her name as he moved, over and over, "Jamie...Jamie...Jamie..."

He felt himself rising, felt his climax nearing. He held it back, clenching every muscle, gritting his teeth as Jamie moved, gliding him in and out, her wet heat slicking his throbbing cock. She was so wet, so tight, and Chase struggled with every breath now to hold back.

"God, Jay. I'm so close. I can't hold it back much longer." Chase grabbed her hips to slow her motion, but Jamie resisted his hold and moved harder, faster. "Jamie…come with me."

"Don't hold back," Jamie whispered, and collapsed forward to lay chest to chest with Chase, burying her lips against his, moving only her hips now.

Chase felt his throat burn as he growled, hips juddering up against hers. He couldn't hold back. She was milking him, working her hips on his in a relentless rhythm, and all he could do was let go.

"Jamie…" he gasped her name as he felt himself about to release. "Now, Jamie. I can't stop…Please don't stop."

He grabbed her hip with one hand and drove her down onto him, arching upward as he climaxed, scratching the fingers of his other hand down her spine. He felt her inner walls clamp down around him and she screamed, coming with him. He felt liquid heat burst out of him, filling her, and then she crushed herself down hard onto him, riding a wave of climax and he shot again, thrusting hard enough to lift his entire lower half off the bed.

Jamie collapsed, limp, onto him, shuddering and quaking with wave after wave of orgasm, and Chase couldn't stop, couldn't slow his manic plunging into her. She gasped breathlessly into his ear, making desperate sounds as Chase finally slowed.

They lay silent together, panting, shuddering. At long last, Jamie rolled off of him, carefully drawing his softening member out of her.

"I have to pee *so* bad," she said, slipping off the bed.

Chase watched her naked body as she walked, feeling desire roll through him, even as he was still trembling with the aftershocks of climax. She was *so* beautiful. He felt his breath catch as she came back to him, breasts swaying slightly in a pendulum rhythm, hips gyrating from side to side as she walked. Chase rolled to a sitting position and shifted his legs off the bed. Jamie stopped just out of reach, copper curls wild around her shoulders, pale skin like flawless ivory, eyes like luminous chips of jade.

"God, Jay. You're so lovely, you take my breath away. Literally. I had to remind myself to breathe just now, watching you, naked and sexy and just-fucked."

Jamie's face twisted with emotion, clearly overwhelmed by his words. "You're too sweet, Chase."

"It's nothing but the truth, sweetness."

Jamie moved closer, one step at a time, until she was standing between Chase's knees. He reached up to hold her hips, and she rested her hands on his shoulders. "You like when I look just-fucked, do you?"

Chase laughed. "Yes, I do. I fully intend to keep you looking just-fucked as long as I can. I might feed you once or twice. I might even take you out to dinner, if you please me."

Jamie's eyes narrowed dangerously. "Oh, if I please you, hmm? And how do I go about pleasing you, *master*?"

Chase grumbled low in his throat, a ruminating sound. "Hmmm. You've done well so far. But I'm still feeling a bit...peckish."

Jamie huffed a confused laugh. "Peckish? What the fuck does that mean?"

"I means I'm hungry. I need to eat."

"Oh, I see." Jamie's expression told him she wasn't following yet.

He pressed his palms together, flattening his hands, and slipped them between her thighs, pushing them apart. "Yes. And at the moment there's only one thing I want."

Jamie let him part her thighs, thrusting her chest out as he pressed his lips to her belly, then trailed kisses lower and lower. "And...oh god...and what would that be?"

Chase lay back on the bed, leaving his feet planted on the floor, and pulled her toward his face, causing her to climb up onto the bed on her hands and knees. He cupped his hands between her thighs to cup her ass from beneath, pulling her forward, then guided her torso upright so she was kneeling above his mouth, core directly over his lips.

"What would that be?" Chase murmured. "Can't you guess?"

"No." Jamie shifted, seeking balance. "This is dangerous, Chase. I've got no way to balance myself like this."

"I'll hold you." He extended a hand up and Jamie took it in both of her hands, clutching tight and sucking in a sharp breath as he flicked his tongue over her slit. "*This* is what I want. Your pussy."

"Chase...we just..." Jamie trailed off, mewling in her throat as he laved his tongue inside her.

"Don't care," Chase said. "Besides, I'm only going to kiss you *here*."

He suited action to words, pressing his stiffened tongue to her clit. Jamie whimpered and rocked forward, and Chase straightened his arm, holding her upright. Her legs buckled and she forced herself back upright, then had to lean into Chase's arm as he began to circle her clit with his tongue, setting a fast, relentless pace. Chase's arm trembled as she leaned all her weight against his arm, lifting up and rocking her core back and forth into his tongue.

His index and middle fingers dipped into her folds and sought out her G-spot, and Jamie threw her head back and shrieked as he found it, massaging gently in rhythm with his mouth. Then, without warning, Chase's middle finger extended outward, tracing the line away from her pussy, backward.

"Oh god, Chase...no..."

"Please? Trust me?" Chase broke away from her juice-wet slit long enough to murmur the words.

He tasted himself in her faintly, but she'd cleaned herself before coming back to bed, so it wasn't too strong. He didn't care anyway. He had a mission, now. He wanted to feel her come apart above him. He was going to make her next orgasm shatter her.

He pressed the tip of his ring finger to the hard knot of muscle, but didn't push in. He continued to circle her clit with his tongue, occasionally flicking the taut bead, drawing a sharp intake of breath from her. She didn't demur when he moved his ring finger in small circles, ever so gently depressing into her tight channel. She growled as he worked his finger into her, carefully and slowly. He continued

531

his assault on her clit, working his other two fingers against her ridged inner flesh, holding her upright with a burning arm.

She slid her legs apart and rolled her hips, still growling low in her throat at the invasion of his ring finger. He was nearly in to the first knuckle, and that was far enough. He began to move the finger in and out in tiny gyrations, working to keep the rhythm of all three fingers in tandem.

Jamie straightened her body, lifting up and giving Chase's trembling arm a respite. He felt the first quivers of climax begin, tremors in her belly against his forehead. She was chanting now, "oh, oh, oh, oh," and he felt her muscles clench. She went limp again, falling forward against his supporting arm, letting go with her hands and placing his palm against her breastbone, supporting her weight there.

She was rolling her hips against him helplessly, working his finger deeper into her tight, forbidden entrance. Jamie curled over his hand, and he had to use every ounce of strength to hold her upright. She was close, now, so close.

He sucked her clit into his mouth past his teeth and pressed his fingers against her G-spot, digging his third finger deeper; Jamie came with a keening cry, and Chase milked her climax until she began shuddering.

"No more, no more, let me down, please…" She sobbed, gyrating her hips helplessly, her entire body shaking as she continued to climax.

Chase gently withdrew his finger and slid out from beneath her. She collapsed onto her hands and knees, gasping, heaving. Chase knelt behind her, stroking her back with both hands, rubbing in gentle circles, then down to her buttocks, cupping and kneading. Jamie moaned.

"Oh my god, Chase. Fucking hell." She twisted to look at him over her shoulder. "Give me a minute. I'm not sure I can take another one just yet."

Chase laughed. "Oh yes you can." He moved closer into her so his erection was nestled upright between the globes of her ass. "And you will. Right…now."

He bowed his spine outward, grabbed his shaft and guided it to her entrance. Jamie sucked in a breath and shifted her hips, lowering her spine and lifting her ass to meet him. He nudged her labia with the tip of his cock, rocking his hips to nudge in, one hand on her hipbone. Jamie moaned, buried her face against the backs of her hands on the rumpled comforter, arching for him to split herself wider, granting him access.

He slid in deeper, slowly, slowly, gliding silkily into her folds, groaning in his chest as he penetrated her. When he was impaled to the hilt, he paused. "God, oh god, Jamie. You feel so fucking good."

Jamie could only moan in response, rolling her hips in invitation for him to thrust.

"Oh god." Then a realization washed over him. "Shit, Jamie!"

She heard the change in the tone of his voice, twisted her head to look at him over her shoulder. "What? What's wrong?"

"We haven't been using protection this morning."

Jamie huffed, something like a sigh or a laugh, Chase wasn't sure which. "It's fine, baby. I'm on birth control and I was just tested last month."

Chase hesitated still. "You're sure?"

Jamie lifted up on her hands and pushed back into him, ducking her head between her arms, doing a half-pushup, then pulled forward and crushed backed into him. "God, yes. I'm sure. I'm sure…"

Chase let her reassurance push away all the worries and lingering doubts, the feel of her firm, soft ass meeting his thighs and her tight pussy clenching around him driving him wild. He shifted his knees farther apart, leaned over her back to plant kisses on her spine, then her lower back, then her ass.

"God, Chase…I need you deep." Jamie was panting, rolling her hips into him, waiting for him, encouraging him.

Chase took her hips in his hands and pulled her back as he thrust forward, a first, slow, gentle surge. Jamie cried out softly, bowing her spine down to raise her hips, sinking back on her haunches to meet him. Chase pulled back slowly, until he was nearly falling out, then, unable to hold back any longer, drove himself home, slow but hard. Jamie cried out again, and then Chase's control was lost.

"Jamie…I can't hold back. I can't go slow." He drew back and then slammed himself in, the slap of flesh against flesh cutting through their mutual panting.

"Don't—don't be gentle," Jamie gasped, rocking back and forth to meet his ever-more-urgent thrusts. "Fuck me hard…yes! Fuck me hard, just like that!"

Her words made Chase even crazier, fingers digging into her hips so hard she sucked in a breath. He forced himself to let go before he bruised her pale flesh. Harder and harder now, no semblance of control or sweetness or gentility. His back was straight, his hands scrabbling at her thighs and hips, resting on her back as he slammed into her again and again, her cries of pleasure, her breathless gasps of "yes yes yes, fuck yes…" sending him even further over the edge. She was meeting him stroke for stroke, her hands planted forward, her knees wide, her hips high, moving back into his nearly savage thrusts and encouraging him to give her more, more, more.

He was close, then, and she felt it in his loss of rhythm. She snatched a pillow and shoved it under her stomach, bending down so her breasts and face were on the bed and her ass lifted as high as she could get it, welcoming the loud slap of his thighs into her ass. His balls were striking her folds with every stroke, his cock slamming deep, his body convulsing as he prepared to come.

"*Fuck*, Jamie, I'm gonna come so hard.."

Jamie's voice rent the air with a feral snarl. "Come for me, Chase. Fuck me hard!"

Chase felt her clenching around his shaft, and knew she was close too. He fumbled at the crease of her ass with his hand, finding the rosebud knot of muscle with the same ring finger as earlier, discovering it to be more pliant than the first time. He spat on his fingers and smeared it on her entrance, sliding his finger.

"Oh my fucking god, Chase!" Jamie could barely speak through the moans emitting from her throat, and she nearly collapsed as he worked his finger in to the second knuckle, then pulled it back.

He felt her quivering, choking on her breath and her screams. He was holding back, slowing himself down to long hard thrusts as he carefully inserted his middle finger. Jamie screamed out loud, then, writhing against him and biting the bed spread.

"What are you doing to me? *Ohmyfuckinggod* that's good!" Jamie spread her thighs as wide as they would go, leaning back into his hand so her ass was stretched wide for him.

Chase let himself begin thrusting harder again, moving his fingers back and forth, not really in and out but merely insinuating the idea of motion. Jamie instinctively and unconsciously began to feather her hips into the movement of his fingers, timed with his thrusts.

"It...doesn't hurt...does it?" Chase asked between panted breaths.

"NO! No...it's fucking incredible." Jamie was lost in primal lust, then, growling and groaning, shoving back against him, driving his fingers deeper.

Chase let his two fingers begin to actually move, then, when he felt the muscles of her pussy begin to clench and clamp around his cock, her groans turning to full-voice screams. He had no idea how he'd lasted this long, since he was already dripping pre-come when first thrusted into her. They were moving in perfect sync, then, his fingers deep inside her now, moving in with every slap of flesh meeting flesh.

"I'm coming, Jamie...come with me, love, *now*."

"Holy fuck, Chase! Fuck me harder...I'm so close..."

Chase gave it to her, pulling back and driving in so hard his pubic bone was bouncing off the flesh of her ass, harder than he'd ever fucked in his life. He gripped her hipbone with his free hand and jerked her back into him, even though she was already willingly ramming herself into him with every stroke.

And then they came, their voices shouting in unison, her voice shrieking, piercing, his a lion-like roar of ecstatic fury.

He unleashed his seed into her in a thick, hard rush, feeling it shoot deep, and then he was totally lost in her, frantically and arrhythmically driving into her, milking his orgasm along with hers. Jamie's inner muscles clamped down around his cock and his fingers so hard when she came his thrusts were slowed by the coiled tensity of her flesh, and he let himself go slack, moving languidly as his last throbbing spurts of come leaked into her.

He collapsed forward onto her ass, sweat sticking between them, slick and salty and stinging his eyes and mouth, his sweat mingling with hers. Chase extricated himself from her tight openings and rolled to the side with her, spooning her.

Jamie twisted her neck to kiss his lips, her mouth quivering with the intensity of her still-shuddering aftershocks. "Chase...Chase, baby. That was fucking intense..."

Chase laughed. "No, that was intense fucking." He kissed her throat, behind her ear, lifted her hair with his clean hand and kissed her nape beneath her hairline, then her shoulders. "You think that was intense? Just wait till I fuck you in the ass, baby. You'll come so hard you'll think you're being ripped in half."

Jamie shivered against him. She twisted in his arms and put her lips against his ear. "You want to fuck me in the ass?" She clutched his ass and jerked him against her body. "You want me to let you do that? I just might let you, if it's anything like that last orgasm. I think I want it. I want your big hard cock in my tight little asshole. I want to feel you come deep in my ass."

Chase's eyes closed at the sound of her whispery breath in his ear, at her dirty words. "Good. 'Cause I'm going to." He reached up between them and tweaked her nipple, drawing a sharp gasp from her.

"But..." she traced her finger up his spine then back down, lower, lower, until she was teasing the crease of his ass. "But you'll have to let me do something back to you."

Chase felt his ass clench tight in response. "Oh? What's that?" He went for nonchalant, but didn't quite make it.

Jamie laughed, a throat, sultry, amused sound that had his cock twitching with renewed desire. "Mmmm...not telling. It'll be a surprise. You'll like it, though. I promise."

Chase felt nerves shoot through him at her words. "Um. You're not putting anything back there."

"Nothing you haven't put in me. How 'bout that?"

Chase wriggled uncomfortably. "I don't know."

Jamie laughed again. "That's my terms, *sweetness.* You want to fuck me in the ass? You have to trust me back, then." She tilted away from him to take his flaccid cock in her hands. "You have to know I'd never do anything I didn't think you'd like. That's how this works, right? I trust you, you trust me?"

"I trust you, but—"

"There's no 'but' when it comes to trusting someone. I let you put your fingers in my ass. I've never let anyone do that. I was an ass-virgin. I trusted you." Jamie traced his length with her fingers.

"I didn't know that was your first time."

"It doesn't matter. It was awesome." Jamie kissed the round part of his shoulder. "Beyond awesome. Every time I come with you, it's better than the last. If that pattern keeps up, I might actually die from orgasm overload."

Chase rumbled a laugh. "I don't think that's possible."

"Well, if it is, you're determined to find out." Jamie closed her fist around him, feeling him begin to respond, pushing him onto his back and sitting up cross-legged next to him, facing his prone body.

"God, Jamie. You have me ready to go again. You make me feel like a teenager. Horny, insatiable, unstoppable."

"You *are* insatiable." Jamie began to stroke her fist up and down, achingly slow.

"So are you."

"Then we're a good match."

Chase met her eyes. "The best match. I've…I never knew I could feel this way about someone."

"What way?" Jamie's eyes told him she knew, but wanted to hear him say it; he wanted to say it out loud.

"Like I can just let go."

Jamie's face scrunched up in confusion. "What's that mean?"

He rolled one shoulder in a shrug. "Just that I've always held back a little. With everyone I've ever been with, *everyone*—" the emphasis made it clear who he meant, without having to say more, "I've held back. Emotionally, physically. I move fast, Jamie. I fall hard and I fall fast. I mean, we've been dancing around this thing between us and avoiding it for months, but despite that, this is the most time we've actually spent together. But already I know, I *know* I'm in love with you. And I love that that doesn't scare you off."

Jamie laughed, a disbelieving scoff. "Scare me off? Chase, I don't think you understand how bad I have it for you. If you didn't return how *I* felt, *that's* what would scare me off." She continued to move her fist on his shaft as they talked, almost as an afterthought.

Chase just nodded, then said, "But it's also physical. I've always felt like if I just really let go, did everything I wanted…how I wanted, as hard and as intense as I wanted, it would hurt the person I was with, or scare them." His breath was coming in long gasps now as Jamie's fist on his cock began to pick up pace.

"Baby, listen. I know we've only spent this last, what, twelve hours together, but I feel like we've been together forever. Like, I know you. I know your soul. I know your heart. I know your body. I want all you have to give. All of it. Don't ever hold back." Jamie glanced down at his turgid cock, smiling hungrily as a pearly drop of pre-come glistened on his tip.

Chase couldn't get any words past his closing throat, past his gasping breath. She was stroking him with both hands, fist over fist. He began to move his hips into her hands, throwing his head back. Jamie slowed, then, until one hand was nearly at his base, sliding molasses-slow, before she slicked the other over his tip, and she continued this erotically slow manipulation until Chase was thrusting up with his entire spine and nearly begging for her go faster. He didn't, though, because as teasing as her pace was, it felt like pure heaven, drawing his desire into a furious boil.

Jamie adjusted tactics, then. She began to pump him with one hand, just as slow as before, working her fist up his length, rubbing her thumb around the smeared pre-come and then gliding back down. With her other hand Jamie cupped his sack, merely holding at first, then massaging gently. The hand stroking his shaft clamped down around his crown and squeezed, and Chase gasped at the feeling. Still cupping his tightened sack, Jamie extended her middle finger to his taint, still squeezing his tip in a quick pattern of clenches. Chase shifted on the bed, not thrusting up but wriggling and writhing under her touch. She pressed her finger in circles around his taint until he began to moan, then slid her finger back further, into the tight-clamped juncture of his ass.

"Relax for me, baby," she whispered, and plunged her hand down his length, squeezing his shaft in the tight sphincter of her fist.

Chase forced himself to relax, spreading his thighs apart, trusting her. Jamie loosened her hold on his cock, sliding her hand up and down loosely now, so loose she was barely touching him. Her finger worked its way in, towards his anus. He felt a bolt of fear, quickly squashed. She was touching him there, finally, just a fingertip on the knot of muscle, the way he'd initially touched her. Jamie applied a hint of pressure as her fist began to pick up pace on his length, and Chase knew it wouldn't be long before he came. The boiling need to release was reaching an unbearable intensity, and her gently-probing finger was only adding the desperate inferno of pressure within him, hot and hard and ready to explode, despite how many times he'd already come with her that morning.

He felt her finger push harder, and he couldn't help his reaction. He pushed his torso downward, an involuntary motion, his legs falling apart as his heels pulled up higher. A welter of emotions tumbled through him, a slight twinge of embarrassment at his position, knees drawn up and back arched, with Jamie's finger beginning to probe deeper as his climax rose. The embarrassment grew as he began to roll his hips, feeling the tip of her finger now inside him, an alien, foreign pressure sending spasms through his entire body.

"Don't fight it, Chase," Jamie murmured. "Give in to it."

Chase forced himself to relax again, and his knees fell apart and his body began to move as her finger dipped in and pulled back, the same kind of faux-motion he'd used on her. And god…it *did* feel good. Strange and intensely powerful, pressure building inside him like a steam boiler gone wrong, about to detonate.

Jamie was stroking him at a middling pace, a steady rhythm. She leaned over as her hand reached his crown, forming a cup with the top of her fist, and spat into it, slicking her saliva over his shaft with a slow downward stroke. Chase gasped raggedly, then groaned in rapturous need when she began to work him more quickly, harder and faster, her finger not going any deeper but moving in and out more fully. Chase was wild, desperate, undone.

"Jamie, I'm…gonna—gonna come…" he could barely form the words.

She leaned over again and continued pumping him at the base, wrapping her lips around the very tip of him and stroking her fist up to her mouth and back down. He felt her tongue on his tip, then she began to suck, hollowing her cheeks. Her hand moved in a blur on his cock, her finger working inside him, her mouth sucking with vacuum force.

And then he came, a feeling his entire body emptying up and out, as if his very insides were being torn up and shooting out into Jamie's suctioning mouth. He couldn't make a sound, even the breath in his lungs emptying through his spasming shaft, all sounds, all breath, all sensation throbbing in his cock as he came, and came, and came, and

Jamie drew it all out of him stroking him relentlessly, his body bowing upward and her finger moving in and out and his brain scrambling.

He didn't think he could come any harder, but she didn't let up, milking him with her mouth and her hands until he was gasping for air and scrabbling at the sheets with his heels, and still he came, orgasming so hard his body ached.

Finally, she let his cock go with a wet *pop*, withdrawing her finger from him, slowing her fist on his shaft until she was merely holding him as he panted.

"Fuck, Jamie. Just...*fuck*."

She just smiled at him and lay down to nestle against his chest. After a long, comfortable silence, Jamie spoke up. "We should get cleaned up. We're all...dirty."

"I'm not sure I can move yet," Chase murmured.

"Don't, then. I'll go first." Jamie slid off the bed and went into the bathroom.

Chase watched her as she went, beyond sated, wrenched thoroughly dry, yet still finding a throbbing core of desire inside himself for all of Jamie. He watched her wash her hands, turn on the shower and brush her teeth with the complimentary toothbrush and toothpaste. He watched her rinse her mouth and spit, and felt an ache in his chest at the beautiful normalcy of watching her doing such mundane things.

He watched with a welter of emotions, all of them centered around and springing out from love, as Jamie stuck her hand into the stream of steaming water, adjust the temperature slightly, and then step in, sliding the curtain closed.

Her phone rang, a sudden, jarring, shrill interruption cutting through the silence of his the thoughts and the sounds of Jamie showering. He contemplated answering it, but decided against it. He thought about finding it and seeing who showed up on the caller ID, but decided against it. The phone went silent, and then rang again a few seconds later. Silence, and then a third ring. The bleeping tone of a voicemail received.

Jamie emerged from the bathroom, wreathed in steam, wrapped in a thick white towel, her red hair wet and tangled and dangling down her back. "Did I hear my phone going off?"

"Yeah," Chase said. "It rang like three times. You have a voicemail, I think."

She crouched and dug it out of her purse, swiped her finger across the screen to unlock it, and tapped the screen, bringing up the missed calls screen. She tapped it a few more times, and then a voice came out of the speakers, male, British, and smooth.

"Jamie, love. I know we had a tiff, and I said some things I mightn't've meant. You know it goes. I just...I'm sorry. I hope you'll come home, come to my flat, I mean." Jamie paled, falling backward onto her butt on the floor, scrambling to silence it.

"Shit," she said.

Chase sat up and pinched the bridge of his. "That complicates things."

Jamie looked up sharply. "No! No it doesn't. There's no complications. I walked out. I left him because I didn't love him, didn't want to be with him. I left him *before* I met you."

"But he clearly wants you back."

Jamie stood up and crossed the room to sit next to Chase on the bed, phone clutched forgotten in her hand. "But I don't want him. I never really did. That was the entire problem. I was trying to convince myself another man could take your place. I couldn't keep up the pretense, Chase. I just couldn't. And now that I've been with you—made love to you—I could never ever spend a single second with anyone else." She pivoted to sit cross-legged on the bed, and Chase's eyes were drawn to the shadowy vision of her folds between the gap of the towel. She took his face in her hands and forced his eyes to hers. "Eyes up here, Tiger. You need to understand what I'm saying to you. You've ruined me for all other men. You did that the first time you kissed me."

He felt a hesitancy it her words. "But?"

"No buts. I just have to get my things from his condo. Make sure he knows I'm really done."

"Want me to go with you?"

Jamie considered. "I don't know. That could get awkward. But I really don't want to go alone either."

"How about I go with you, but wait in the lobby?"

"That would work," Jamie said. She pushed Chase toward the bathroom. "Now go clean up. You're crusty."

Chase showered and dressed and they left the hotel. Chase felt as if something in the world had shifted, as if everyone should know how completely his life had changed since the last time he was outside. When he and Jamie had entered the hotel, he had been bursting with need, every fiber of his being aflame with frustration and love and lust. Now, leaving the hotel not even a day later, he felt like he was almost a different person. One night with Jamie and she'd stolen his soul, hidden it within herself. She had shown him what he'd been missing his entire life, and now he couldn't fathom being without it…couldn't fathom being without her.

They caught a cab and Jamie gave the driver the address. A few minutes later they pulled up in front of an upscale high-rise condo building right on Lake Michigan. Chase went into the lobby with her, holding her hand. He stopped with her at the bank of elevators.

"I'll come up with you," Chase said.

Jamie shook her head. "It's fine. It's not like I'm scared of him or anything. He's a good person, and…I don't know. I just feel like if I leave your side, even for ten seconds, this whole thing will pop like a bubble. Like you and I finally being together is a dream that I could wake up from any second."

Chase laughed in relief and put his forehead to hers, one arm around her waist, the other tangled with hers at their sides. "God, I'm glad I'm not the only one feeling that way."

The elevators dinged and the doors whooshed open. A disbelieving huff of male laughter sounded from within the elevator directly in front of them.

"Fucking bollocks, Jamie. Didn't imagine you'd move on quite *that* fast." The British voice from Jamie's cell phone.

Jamie jumped in Chase's arms, gasping in surprise. "Ian…I—um…"

Chase felt her pulse leap into a frenzy. He stepped away from Jamie, still holding her hand.

"I don't guess there's much to say, then, is there?" The man, tall and good-looking with sandy hair and blue eyes, flicked his gaze from Jamie to Chase, his eyes alternating between angry and hurt and confused. "I'll just go."

"Ian, wait. I'm sorry for this, but—well…I don't know. I told you it was complicated."

"Complicated?" Ian laughed, a sarcastic sound. "Complicated is having feelings for another bloke when you're with me. Complicated I can deal with. Having a tumble with him in the lobby of my flat building is a bit different, I'd say."

"I wasn't—" Jamie started. "Listen, I just need my stuff, okay?"

"You've been fucking him all along, haven't you?" Ian said, fists clenched at his sides.

"What? No! Ian, don't make this into something it's not—"

"You stormed off yesterday and I thought you'd just need some time to cool off. I thought…I thought you'd come back and we'd discuss it a bit, figure things out. I—you—" Ian turned away, paced a few steps, and then turned back. "You ran straight to him, didn't you? Straight from his bed to mine."

Chase couldn't keep himself from intervening. "Now hold on just a minute, pal. You don't have to like the situation, but you've got no call to insult her."

"Sod off. I'm not talking to you, Yank." Ian dismissed Chase with a flick of his fingers. "I'm talking to Jamie, so you can just shut your fucking mouth."

"Fuck you. You're being a dick."

"Chase, don't." Jamie pushed at Chase's chest. "Just let me talk to him."

"Like I said," Ian punctuated his next words with a finger poking hard into Chase's shoulder. "Sod…off."

Chase knocked Ian's hand away and stepped in front of Jamie, putting his back to her so he was inches away from Ian. "Don't touch me."

Chase heard Jamie moan in frustration when Ian's fist flashed up and into Chase's stomach, knocking the wind from him. He saw red, lunging.

Chapter 4

Jamie groaned in irritation. *Fucking stupid posturing males.*

She saw Ian's fist moving in slow motion, slam into Chase's stomach, then watched a transformation overtake Chase. He grunted, sucking in a breath, then straightened. His face was a rictus of rage.

She had to stop this before it got really ugly. She stepped in front of Chase and shoved him back as hard as she could, taking his face in her hands. His eyes dragged from Ian to her.

"Don't, Chase." She spoke so low only he could hear it. "*Do not* do this."

"Motherfucker sucker punched me," Chase snarled.

"I know," Jamie said. "I know. But please just let it go. It's not worth fighting over. I hurt him, okay? He has a right to be angry, he's just being a child about it. Taking it out on you instead of me. Just walk away, okay? There's a pub a couple doors down. Go have a drink while I get my stuff. Please?"

Chase's chest heaved and she saw the rage warring with his desire to please her. "Fine. Only for you." He span on his heel and stormed off, fists clenched.

"Pansy," Ian's voice said from behind her, goading.

Jamie whirled, seeing Chase's shoulders tense and his strides slow. "Shut the fuck up, Ian! You're being a shithead. I just diffused the situation *you* created." She shoved him onto an elevator as it opened to let off a businessman. "Get *on*, Ian. Don't piss me off."

She stepped onto the elevator behind Ian and stood against the far wall, away from him. The ride up to Ian's condo was long and awkward and tense. Jamie followed him down the hallway and to his door, waiting while he opened it up, then stood in the foyer. Ian set his keys on a thin table by the wall, sighing deeply. His shoulders slumped and he turned in place, scrubbing his face with one hand.

"I'm sorry, Jamie. I shouldn't have done that. I was just…I'm right pissed and I've got every reason to be, I'd think."

Jamie flopped back against the closed door. "I know. And I'm sorry. I know you're hurt, and you do have a right to be. I haven't been fair to you."

Ian ran his hands through his hair, tilting his head and peering at Jamie as if exhausted. "Did I mean *anything* to you?"

"Of course you did, Ian. It was just…I don't know. It's hard to explain."

"You've said that before. I don't care to hear it again. Try to explain."

Jamie let her head thunk against the door. "You *did* mean something to me. I had a good time with you. You…you're wonderful. In any other situation I think we really could have had a good chance at something long term together."

"But?"

"But you never really had a chance with me, through no fault of your own. I've just…I've been in love with Chase for a long, long time. Since before I met you. I was running from my feelings for him when I met you. I told you all this yesterday."

"Feels like a thousand years ago."

Jamie blew a long breath out. "You have no idea." She looked up at Ian, who was leaning against the wall with one shoulder. "Look, I don't really know what to say to you that I haven't already said. I'm sorry I hurt you. I'm sorry you saw me with him like that. It's not like you think. I never even talked to him on the phone until yesterday. I literally ran into him in the street and I just…I couldn't deny how I feel for him any longer."

"And how you feel about me no longer applies, is that it?"

Jamie couldn't answer, since it was true.

"I see," Ian said. "Well then, there's only one thing left for me to do."

Something odd in his voice had Jamie glancing up to see Ian inches away and closing, hand scooping around the back of her head, his lips crashing against hers. Jamie froze in shock, felt herself melting just slightly—Ian *was* a damn good kisser, after all—and then she felt the rush of outrage and anger blast through her.

She pulled back, shoved him as hard as she could, and then slapped him. "*Seriously*, Ian? You kiss me? All that, and you *kiss* me?" She scrubbed her mouth with her palm, as if to wipe away the fact that she'd nearly let herself enjoy the kiss.

Ian shrugged. "I had to see. There is nothing left, is there? Was there ever anything?" Jamie opened her mouth to answer but Ian cut her off. "That was rhetorical. Wait here. I'll get your things."

Jamie dug the heels of her palms into her eye sockets hard enough that sparks flashed in the blackness of closed eyes. She heard his tread, lowered her hands to see Ian holding out two small duffel bags, the kind given out as freebies at the tech conferences Ian frequented.

"Pretty sure this is everything. If there's anything else I discover I'll ship it to you."

"Thanks." A long silence expanded between them until Jamie broke it. "You're a good man, Ian, and I'm sorry for...using you, I guess. Wasting your time."

Ian sighed, and rubbed his jaw with his wrist. "You didn't waste my time, Jamie. You just broke my heart." He ran his hands through his hair and Jamie had to look away from the raw splinters of emotion in his blue eyes. "I was falling in love with you. I'd thought about proposing."

Jamie let out a sound that was half-sob and half-laugh. "You were going to—? Ugh. I wish there was something else I could say besides 'I'm sorry.'"

Ian shook his head. "There really isn't anything, is there? Goodbye, Jamie."

She turned and opened the door, pausing to pick up her bags and glance at Ian. "I really am sorry. You deserved better treatment."

Ian didn't answer besides a shrug. Jamie left, and the elevators closed on her vision of Ian standing in his doorway, one hand in his pocket, the other rubbing the back of his neck, his eyes betraying pain even from a distance.

She found her car in the garage, tossed her things in the back-seat, pulled it out into traffic, found a parking spot on the street near the pub where she'd told Chase to go. She sat in her car trying to collect herself. It had been harder than she'd thought it would be to say goodbye to Ian. To see him hurting. To know she'd been the one hurt him.

The passenger door opening startled Jamie into alertness, but she knew it was him even before she opened her eyes. She smelled him first, bodywash, cologne, faintly of beer, that male scent and the unique essence of Chase, comfort and desire turned olfactory.

"I'm sorry I made it a scene, babe," Chase said as he settled into the seat next to her.

She glanced at him in amused disbelief. "It was going to be a scene regardless. An ex and a current is always messy, no matter what. You were defending me, and that's…so sweet. And really, the fact you were able to walk away from the fight? I love you so much for that. Any guy can beat someone's ass for his girl. It takes a real man, a strong man to walk away from a confrontation for his girl."

Chase reached out and took her hand. "Neither of us needed that." He examined her face. "It was pretty rough, huh?"

"That obvious?"

Chase laughed. "You look emotionally wrecked. Gorgeous and glorious as always, but you look like that took it out of you."

"He kissed me after I told him I'd been in love with you since before I met him. And then he told me he had been falling in love with me and that he was thinking about proposing."

"Shit."

"Yeah. It hurt."

"I'm sorry you had to go through that," Chase said.

"It's over now." Jamie noticed Chase had his bag on his lap. "You checked out?"

Chase shrugged. "Yeah. I figured we've spent enough time in Chicago."

"Sounds good to me. I have to be back in Detroit for work on Monday, but that's it. I'm free till then."

They headed away from Chicago, going vaguely west and north toward Wisconsin. They stopped at Holiday Inn off the freeway about halfway to Milwaukee, checked in, and had dinner. Jamie felt antsy for most of the time, wanting nothing more than to erase the bad taste in her mouth left by the scene with Ian. She wanted to feel more of Chase, experience more of many mercurial sides. She'd only scratched the surface of him, she thought. He seemed just as tense, just as full of coiled intensity. His head was freshly shaven, his jaw and chin clean and the hard lines of his handsome face accentuated by the low lights of the diner. His arms stretched the sleeve of a charcoal henley shirt, the sleeves pushed up to his elbows.

She wanted those arms around her, those hands holding her.

They went back to the hotel, and the door had barely closed behind him when Chase's voice washed over her. "Strip."

She turned in place to face him, her heart thudding. "Excuse me?" He was leaning back against the door, one leg crossed over the other, arms akimbo.

A faint smile traced his lips. His eyes twinkled. "I said, strip. Take your clothes off."

Her chin lifted. "Oh yeah? Just like that?" She *wanted* to strip, but she also wanted to see where he'd take it if she refused.

He took a step forward, his gait loose and powerful, his eyes predatory. "Yeah. Just like that."

"And if I don't?"

"You will." He smirked again. "Well…you'll be naked in about thirty seconds either way."

Jamie sucked in a deep breath and let it out, then crossed her arms beneath her chest. "No."

Chase lifted an eyebrow and stepped toward her again, arms uncoiling. Jamie took an involuntary step backward at the intensity in his gaze. An excited smile played over her lips, and her heart crashed in her chest.

He lunged, catching her in his arms, squeezing them to her sides. She gazed up at him evenly.

"Now what are you gonna do to me? Spank me?" Jamie asked.

"Tempting," Chase said. "But no."

He returned her even gaze, and then, before she could blink he had spun her in his arms so her back was to his front, both of her hands pinned in one of his, firmly but gently. Jamie struggled to free her hands, but she couldn't. She went still, waiting for his next move. His breathing was hot and loud in her ear, his chest hard at her back. With his free hand, he traced her cheek, following the line of his grazing fingers with his lips. Jamie tilted her head to the side as he lined kisses down her neck. Chase moved them forward so her torso was pressed to the wall, pinning her there with his hips, his erection against her jeans-clad ass. Jamie was wearing an old Counting Crows concert T-shirt, thin and tight; Chase released her hands, gripped the collar of her shirt and ripped it open down the back and brushed it off her.

"I liked that shirt!" Jamie protested.

Chase just chuckled. He grabbed her hands again before Jamie could think about finding a way to get free, and besides, she didn't really want to. She was interested in where he was going with this. But, for form's sake, she had to put up a fight. So—in the name of the game—she writhed her ass against his erection, a distraction, and then when he sucked in a breath and loosened his grip on her wrists, Jamie shoved him away and broke free. Chase laughed and caught her around the waist with one arm, jerking her back to his chest.

"I don't think so, sweetness. You could've done a little striptease for me, and I'd already be inside you, making you come for me." Jamie couldn't quite stifle a whimper. "But no, you had to play tough girl, hard-to-get. So…we do this the fun way."

"Fun for who?"

Chase dragged a finger down her chest, between her cleavage, and then traced the rim of the bra cup. "Fun for me. It'll be fun for you… eventually. But you might get a bit…desperate before I'm done with you."

He tugged the cup down and a breast popped free; he did the same to the other side, and then began toying with the nipples, one and then the other, pinching and rolling, flicking and cupping each breast with the taut bud caught between his middle and index fingers. Jamie's breath caught and she couldn't stop herself from arching her back into his touch. He slid his hand down her belly, dipped his fingers beneath the denim to cup her mound over the silk of her panties. Jamie froze as he stroked the damp line of her entrance with one finger, making the silk even wetter. She found herself panting and on the verge of begging him to put his finger inside her. She didn't beg, and he didn't touch her skin to skin. He seemed content to stroke her through the silk, digging in slightly to put pressure on her clit. Her hips writhed on their own, despite her attempts to stop it.

"Chase…" she heard herself whisper, and then clicked her teeth together on the rest of the plea.

"Yes, love?"

She only panted in reply, resting her head back on his shoulder.

Chase released her hands, withdrew his fingers from her jeans and placed her palms flat on the wall, pulling her hips back until she was forced to take several steps backward. She was now standing as if she'd been arrested, feet shoulder-width apart, palms flat on wall.

"Stay like this," Chase ordered, his voice gentle in her ear.

"Or?"

Chase's finger trailed up from her hip to her side, and then up to her armpit. Jamie tensed, realizing what the punishment would be if she moved. He ever so gently traced her underarm, and she choked back a giggle, flinching away.

"No, no! Please don't tickle me," she said, putting her hands back on the wall. "I hate being tickled."

Chase rumbled in amusement. "Good to know."

Jamie cursed herself for having given him leverage. She lost her train of thought when his fingers came back around her belly, both hands dipping beneath both denim and silk to cup her flesh, one hand remaining on the dip of her hip. His middle finger dove down to press against her clit, and Jamie hung her head, gritting her teeth against a whimper. He circled her once, twice, and she couldn't stop a single gasp from escaping.

"I want to hear you," Chase said.

So, of course, Jamie decided to make a game of her own out of how silent she could stay. He made wide, slow circles around her throbbing nub, and she had to clench her jaw to keep from panting. He increased his assault, circling faster and faster, and just as she was about to lose her own game, he stopped. That was almost her undoing. She wanted to beg him to keep going, but bit her lip to keep quiet.

He unbuttoned her pants, then slowly unzipped her fly. She tensed, waiting for the pants to be pushed down, but he didn't do that. Instead, he skated his palms up her sides, cupped her breasts in both hands, tenderly kneading the soft flesh. He abruptly unsnapped her bra, but left the straps on her arms. Jamie wriggled her shoulders, hating the feel of the loose straps, but Chase stilled her with a single press of his palms to her shoulders.

Her breasts were hanging free, unsupported now, but the bra was still partly on. It was driving her nuts, but she forgot that soon enough as his hands came back up to cup her breasts, now stimulating her nipples until she was shifting in place, holding back moans. And then his touch was gone again, sliding down to her hips, pushing the pants down to her knees and leaving them. She lifted her leg to pull the pants off, but Chase made a negative sound in his chest.

"Leave it," he said.

Jamie blew out a sigh of exasperation that nearly turned into a moan of appreciation as he began to massage her buttocks through her panties. It wasn't an erotic touch, oddly, the way he kneaded the muscles there, but it still turned her on even as it relaxed her. Of course, she couldn't get much more turned on, she didn't think. Then he slid his palms under the silk to caress her bare skin, and she realized how wrong she was; she could get *a lot* more turned on. He traced the crease between her ass cheeks with one finger, and she found herself wanting to spread herself wide to allow him entrance. She didn't though, and he didn't press in. She was almost disappointed.

He pressed his erection against her backside, leaning in with his mouth to her ear. "Soon, sweetness." He writhed his shaft into the crack, the zipper and button scraping against the silk. "Soon I'm going to be deep inside you…here."

"Soon, like now?"

Chase made a noncommittal sound. "Maybe, maybe not. You want me to?"

"Maybe." Jamie tried to sound blasé, but couldn't quite manage it.

If she was being honest with herself, she *did* want it. A lot, actually. His two fingers had been intense enough, but if he managed to fit his entire huge cock into her? It would be…mind-blowing, she was sure. As long as it didn't hurt, and she knew for a fact he wouldn't do it if was going to hurt.

"You lie," Chase murmured in her ear. "You want it. You're a dirty girl. You want my cock in your ass."

Jamie hung her head and bit her lip to keep from responding. Chase abruptly shoved her panties down to her knees with her pants, and then carved a line up the outside of her thigh to rest at the apex of her hip.

Chase murmured in her ear. "Which way should I go? This way?" He slid his finger towards her core. "Or this way?" He ran his fingernail back toward her ass.

Jamie wanted him in both places, so she didn't answer. Not that she would've answered anyway. He took her lack of answer as freedom to both. One hand curled forward to cup her mound, now pulsating with heat and dripping wet. His other hand clutched one ass cheek, and then the other before digging his fingers in between her thighs and ass. Jamie wanted to widen her thighs so he could touch her more freely, but her pants around her knees wouldn't let her, and neither would her own determination.

He moved both hands simultaneously, slipping one long finger into her pussy and the fingers of the other hand deeper between her thighs from behind. Jamie allowed herself a long breath in and then out as he circled her clit. Then, abruptly, both hands were gone and so was his presence behind her. She started to twist to try and locate him, but his voice at her left ear stopped her.

"Mmm-mmm. No moving," he admonished.

Jamie clenched her jaw around her sarcastic comeback, and waited. He took one of her hands in his, slid her bra strap off, then repeated it with the other side. He stepped away to hang the bra off the bathroom door knob. Jamie watched him, then snapped her attention back to the wall when he returned to his place behind her. He knelt down behind her, kissing her spine on the way, then each buttock, then underneath each one. He wrapped his hands around the front of the her thighs, stroked upward until his fingers brushed the line of her entrance. Jamie's breathing became more labored as slid his hands down and then back up her legs, stopping again just at the apex of her thighs.

"Step out of the pants," Chase instructed.

Jamie obeyed, stepping on the cuff one pant leg and tugging her foot out, then did the same on the other side. She was naked now, trembling with anticipation. She waited, and waited, but Chase did nothing, just knelt behind her with his hands on her thighs and his mouth pressed in a stilled kiss to the rounded outside of her ass.

Then he was gone. "Don't move," he ordered. "And don't look. Close your eyes."

Jamie closed her eyes, listening to a zipper of a bag *zzzzhrip*-ing open, then the sounds of clothing being rummaged through. She smelled him, felt his presence. Cloth touched her eyes, tied behind her head. She opened her eyes, but all was dark. He tugged her hands away from the wall and guided her to a different position, standing her in place and leaving her, then spinning her a few times so she was disoriented but not dizzy.

"What are you doing, Chase? What's going on?"

He didn't answer. She heard a soft footfall to one side, and then the other, she smelled him as he passed by her, then the scent was gone with the breeze of his passage. A finger trailed across her belly in one direction, a palm slid over her ass in the other. Lips pressed to hers briefly, gone as soon as she began to respond to the kiss. Fingers carved over her hips and into the wet folds of her core, stroking slowly and languorously, then were gone before she could begin to respond. His lips touched hers, tilted slightly sideways, and this time stayed until she opened her mouth, his tongue sliding in and tangling with hers, tracing her lips.

He was gone again, and then Jamie heard a zipper, cloth rustling and falling to the floor, and then she caught his scent and felt his presence in front of her.

"I'm right in front of you," he said. "Touch me."

She reached out, found hot flesh. She explored the area and found it to be his elbow. She followed his arm to his shoulder, his neck, devoured his bare torso with both hands then, over the toned bulk of his muscles, the cut and rippling perfection of his abs, down to his hips. He was naked, thank god. She felt the cool, hard, tautness of his ass, cupped it, clutched it, then around to grip his erection. She stroked him a few times, then he pulled away.

"Come back," Jamie said, "I want to touch you more."

He ghosted back into her outstretched hands, and she caressed his body all over, pressed her face to his chest, kissing across it, touching his shoulder with her lips and running her tongue over the small bead of his nipple, tracing the grooves of his abdomen with her mouth, falling to her knees and laving the hollow of hip, finding the V-cut and worshipping it with her fingers and her tongue. She paused, turning her face up to him, as if to look at him through the blindfold. She could almost see him in her mind: absurdly, gloriously gorgeous face turned down to look at her, his brown eyes wide and dark and glinting with unrestrained desire, his broad, hard muscles rippling as he held himself still for her touch, tribal tattoos across his biceps and forearms. She kissed his thigh, then skated her palms over his taut ass, pulling him closer, closer, until she felt the heat and iron and silk of his cock against her lips. She kissed him, smiling at the gasping intake of his breath, then took him into her mouth and slowly lowered her head, taking him deeper and deeper, relaxing her throat and going deeper yet.

"Fuck, Jay, what are you doing?" His voice was thick and quavering. "Don't gag yourself! Jesus…"

He lost capacity for speech then as she backed away, sucking on his tip and then downed his cock once more, deeper than before, until she felt his close-trimmed curls against her face. She backed away slightly, then bobbed her head until he hissed and pulled himself away.

She smiled up at him, licking her lips. Judging by the fraught silence stretching between them, Jamie knew she'd made her point. She stayed on her knees, waiting, hands on her thighs, face turned up to where she knew he was. She could feel his intense gaze on her.

Then she felt his hands on her arms gently lifting her up to her feet. His mouth touched hers, his tongue spearing through her lips in a demanding kiss. She melted instantly, moving to let him curl her into his embrace, but instead of his arms around her, she was swept up off her feet.

"Ohimigod, Chase! Put me down, you lunatic! You'll break your back!"

Chase just laughed and walked with her in his rock-solid arms—no hint of trembling or straining—and set her slowly onto the bed.

He kissed her breastbone, then suckled her nipple until she gasped and moaned, switching to the other breast and doing the same, scraping the sensitive peak with his teeth until she whimpered. He moved down her body, kissing as he went, and when his mouth reached her mound, Jamie eagerly slid her legs apart, cupping his bald scalp and shamelessly pulling his mouth to her hot, wet sex. Chase chuckled at her eagerness, and the vibrations of his laughter had her lifting her hips to press herself into him. He teased her with his tongue, light butterfly-gentle flicks against her clit followed by slow, fat licks of her entire opening, then a darting tongue-tip into her channel. Then his fingers curled into her to stroke her G-spot and his mouth worked her throbbing nub until she was bucking underneath him, moaning a nonstop sound of need as she drew closer to climax. She held onto his head for dear life, holding him tight against her.

"Oh god, Chase! I'm gonna come right now!"

And then he was gone.

"Where are you going? Come back here!" She writhed on her back, reaching for him, growling in frustration. "You can't do that!"

She heard him moving around, and then her hand was enclosed by his hand, something cool and soft wrapped around her wrist. Her arm was drawn back and over her head, a pause and the sound of rustling, and then she felt his presence move around the bed to the other side. She reached for him, only find her right hand stop abruptly, as if…

"Did you just tie me to the bed?"

"Maybe."

Her left hand was held in his unbreakably gently grip, tied to the bed, and then he was gone once more.

"Chase Delany. You *cannot* tie me up and blindfold me and then just leave me here on the edge of orgasm. You'd damn well better come back here and finish what you started." She heard the tinge of desperation in her voice, but couldn't quite manage to erase it.

"Oh, don't you worry, my love. I'll finish you off. When I'm ready." Chase's voice came from across the room.

"What are you doing way over there?"

"I'm looking at you. You're tied up and naked and at my mercy. I'm deciding what to do to you. You're so fucking sexy like that, all spread out for me...I could come right now, just looking at you."

Jamie spread her legs apart and writhed on the bed, an invitation. "You better not come. I want it. I want you. Give it to me."

Chase's voice was closer, now. "You want it? You want my come?"

"God yes. All of it."

Closer yet. "Where?"

"Anywhere. Everywhere." His fingers grasped her ankle and she sucked in a sharp breath; his palm ran up her thigh and Jamie wantonly spread her legs apart for his touch. "There. Inside me."

His weight settled on the bed, and then she felt him climbing up her body to kneel over her. "What if I want it somewhere else?"

Jamie lifted her body, wanting his skin against hers, wanting pressure on her aching clit. "Anywhere. Just...finish it. I want you."

She felt something hot and soft and broad nudging her sex. Jamie moaned, arching her back to get him deeper. He matched her thrust to move away, and then replaced his tip at her entrance. "Be still. Don't move. Don't make a sound."

Jamie froze, clamping her lips together. He moved his cock in circles, rubbing her clit with his crown. Jamie's body wanted to writhe in circles with him, but she forced herself into stillness. He moved himself faster and faster, and then pulled away, leaving Jamie gasping, head craned back in desperation. She wanted to plead with him.

"Stop moving."

"I can't help it."

"Try. The more you move, the more you make those sexy little sounds, the longer it will take. I can't take those moans. I'm so close to coming, Jamie. If you keep making those noises, I'm done."

Jamie felt him nudge her throbbing clit, and she had to flex every muscle in her body to keep still, biting her tongue to keep quiet. He circled her hot, hard nub again, and she felt the pressure of impending climax building up. Without warning Chase drove himself inside her, a fast, hard thrust, fully impaling his thick shaft inside her. Jamie shrieked in surprise and pleasure, and he pulled himself out.

"I'm sorry, I'm sorry," Jamie gasped. "I'll be quiet. Give it back, please."

He slowly entered her again, and Jamie wrapped her fists around the cords binding her—neckties, it felt like—and held them for leverage to keep still as he slid his pulsing shaft into her drenched slit. She bit her lip until she tasted blood, but she kept quiet, and he buried himself to the hilt, his hips bumping hers. He held there, and she heard his breathing, fast, ragged, as if he was barely staving off his own orgasm. Jamie flexed her vaginal muscles as hard as she could around him, clenching and releasing in a pulsating rhythm.

"Fuck, Jay. Fuck, that's incredible." His breath huffed hot on her throat. "Do it again."

Jamie clenched him tight again, flexing hard as long as she could, and then releasing with a gasp of exertion. Chase kissed her throat, then moved down to her breast and kissed the mounded flesh with soft, wet lips. Jamie struggled to contain her groan as he sucked her nipple into his mouth and flicked it with his tongue.

She nearly screamed when he drew back and slammed in, then twice, a third time, and with each hard thrust Jamie fell closer to orgasm. He plunged deep a fourth time and then withdrew completely, and this time Jamie did mewl in irate frustration.

Chase's body slid down hers and his mouth pressed to her sex. Jamie stifled a whimper as he licked and lapped and laved her aching clit in arrhythmic flicks, driving her mad with need for pressure, need for rhythm.

She was desperate now, so close to climax but held away from the edge by his endless teasing. She was drawing close now, and she struggled to hold absolutely still and remain completely silent, hoping if she could keep him from knowing how close she was he might send her over the edge. He settled into a rhythm, finally, licking directly against her throbbing nub. She called on every shred of will she possessed, but as she neared climax, her traitorous body bucked beneath his skilled mouth, and the delicious wet pressure of his mouth was gone.

"*Dammit!*" She couldn't stop the cry of crazed need from escaping, either.

He laughed, a predatory rasp in his throat, sinuously gliding up the length of her body, the slick tip of his cock dragging up her leg to nudge against her entrance.

"Are you ready for me?" Chase asked, his voice an almost inaudible whisper in her ear.

"Yes!" She let all of her desperation into her voice, let herself abjectly plead with him. "Chase, *please*, please...no more. No more. Just...be with me. Come with me. Come inside me. Shit, come *on* me, if you want. Come on my tits, or my face or anywhere. Just let me go, let me touch you."

Chase's tongue flicked her earlobe, and then his mouth kissed her ear, her jaw just behind it. Jamie panted, thrusting her pussy against the tip nudging her slit. He kept away until she went still, and then nibbled her neck, sucked her shoulder near her armpit hard enough that she'd have a mark later. She tugged on the ties binding her, wanting to feel his back move, feel his ass rippling, wanting to draw him in. She thrashed her head, trying to dislodge the blindfold. She curled her legs around his hips and jerked, but it was like trying to move a statue.

His breath returned to her ear. "I'd never degrade you that way, my love." His whispering voice was sweet and tender. "Never. Now, tell me where you want me to come."

She twisted her face to bite his earlobe. "Inside me. In my pussy. Now. *Please.* No more teasing. No more games."

He nudged in, a tiny movement that had only the very tip inside her, but it was enough to make her whimper.

"Like that?" he said, his voice a low rasp.

She could feel him trembling, holding back, straining for control.

561

"Yes…god yes. Just like that. More. More." She fought for still-ness. "I'm begging you, please, more."

Chase fluttered his hips, a series of slow, shallow movements that had Jamie flailing in paroxysms of delight, moaning. He kept up the tiny thrusts, barely moving in before he was pulling back. Jamie wasn't about to complain since it was better than nothing, but she wanted, *needed* more. He'd brought her so close so many times now, had her rising up and up and closer and closer until she was nearly mad with raging pressure, pent-up climax. And these butterfly thrusts weren't going to get the job done.

"Chase…stop teasing me." Her voice was a broken whisper.

He laughed again, the same low gravelly rumble of leonine amuse-ment. "Teasing? This isn't going to do it for you?" He thrusted even more shallowly, if possible, the tip barely moving between her labia.

"You bastard. You know it's not." Jamie jerked on the ties, but only succeeded in tightening them around her wrists.

Chase froze. "A bastard, am I?" He pulled out, barely stifling a hiss that told Jamie he was teasing himself as much as her.

He lowered his mouth to her breast, cupping it with his hand and flicking the nipple with his teeth. His other hand snaked between their bodies, a single finger racing around her clit. Jamie groaned and writhed in frustration, in pleasure, in confusion. What he was doing felt amazing, felt incredible, but she needed *him*. He didn't stop when she bucked beneath him to the tempo of his lick-ing tongue and flicking fingers. He didn't stop when she began to arch off the bed, and he didn't stop when she began to let full-voiced cries escape.

"Oh god, oh god, oh *god*," Jamie cried, finally cresting over the verge of climax.

At the very moment the wave broke over her, Chase plunged into her, hammering deep in a single thrust. She screamed in delirious ecstasy, curling her legs around his ass and clutching him with all the considerable strength in her legs. Wave after wave crashed through her, the pressure releasing in an inundating barrage powerful enough to leave her heaving sobbed breaths.

Chase didn't relent as she came, however. He drew back and pounded in, unleashing another scream from Jamie, and then he did it again, and she couldn't scream, could only gasp for breath. He began a driving rhythm and Jamie tried to keep up, tried to thrust back into him, but the blasting waves of climax weren't letting up, were only intensifying with every thrust of his cock. She had her fists wrapped around the ties tightly enough that she was sure her circulation was suffering.

"Untie me," Jamie pleaded between ragged sobs.

Chase never slowed his plunging thrusts, reaching up with one hand and deftly untying her right wrist, then shifting his weight to the other hand and releasing her left. As soon as each hand was free, Jamie clawed at his back, pawing at his sweat-slick skin, gripping his bulging biceps and pistoning hips and tensing buttocks. She smeared the sweat on his scalp, dragging his face down to hers in sloppy, desperate kisses, missing his mouth a few times and not caring. She wanted his skin, his sweat, his body. She clung to him, driving her hips into his madly now as she began to match his furious rhythm. She was panting wildly, each breath a loud moan.

Her climax had never retreated completely, and she was shuddering with aftershocks every few moments. Then, as he began to pump faster, Jamie felt the aftershocks morph and burgeon, turning into yet another orgasm. She clung to Chase's neck, her legs locked around his back, holding on to him as she rode out the orgasm, struggling for breath as the waves grew stronger, ripping through her like a tsunami.

The climax receded slightly, but didn't dissipate completely. Chase shifted positions slightly, slowing his pace but still driving deep. He brought his knees beneath him, slid his palms beneath Jamie's ass, gripping her hips and lifting. She moved down the bed toward him and arched her back, lifting her hips to meet him, reaching back to grip the headboard with both hands. Chase held her hips up, plunging hard and deep. Jamie's voice rose in a sound that wasn't quite a scream, a high-pitched keen of rapture as his cock filled her deeper than she'd thought anyone could be. He drove in deep this way a few times, and then, against all sense, thrust shallowly, pivoting his body so the broad head of his cock struck her G-spot dead-on.

Less than thirty seconds later, Jamie came again, and this time she couldn't bear it, couldn't stand it, couldn't even ride it out. All she could do was release a guttural scream and rake her fingers over his shoulders.

Tears of raw overwhelmed emotion tracked down her cheeks and she didn't bother to wipe them away.

Chase's movements grew rough and clumsy, and Jamie recognized the signs of his impending release. She planted her heels on the bed and met him thrust for frantic thrust. She moaned his name in his ear when he finally released her hips and collapsed forward onto her, grinding raggedly and arrhythmically, growling and groaning with every thrust.

"Chase, baby…oh god…come for me." Jamie held the nape of his neck and the back of his head, her body wrapped around his. He came with a counterintuitively soft sigh, slamming his pulsating cock into her with almost brutal force. "Yes, yes! Hard, I love it like that, so hard."

Chase couldn't speak as he came. Jamie felt his hot seed hit her inner walls, and his thrusting became deep-driving insanity, frenzied and wild. His pelvis crushed her clit, and she felt another impossible orgasm wash over her, impossible, absurd, and spastically potent. She bit his shoulder, dug her fingers into his back and pounded her core against him, their hipbones crashing like colliding tectonic plates, slow and unstoppably forceful thrusts.

All the while, liquid heat filled Jamie, wash after wash spurting from Chase into her cleft, and she took it all, clamping down on his throbbing cock with every ounce of power she had within her.

"Jamie…oh god, *fuck*, I love you so goddamn much." Chase's voice was gravelly and ragged in her ear, his thrusts finally slowing, abating. "I love you…so much. You—god…you shatter me so wonderfully, Jamie."

He rolled with her so she was cradled against his chest. She was a dribbling mess, but she didn't care. Nothing mattered but closeness, the warmth of his huge hard body radiating like a furnace against her sensitive skin, his manhood softening and throbbing against her thigh, his palms skating softly over her shoulder, his fingers tangling in her sweaty curls…

Jamie fell asleep more contented than she how to understand. She felt full in her heart, in her soul, in her mind, beyond exhausted, wrung limp and sated to surfeit.

"Promise me this will never end," she whispered, her voice muzzy and heavy.

Chase threaded his fingers through hers. "I promise you this will never end. You and me…this is just the beginning."

"Please?" It was a mumbled reply, meant to be thankful sigh of relief, coming out as something else.

Chase just tightened his grip on her, kissed her eyebrow, and she heard his breathing even out as sleep stole over her.

Chapter 5

*J*amie fumbled for her ringing cell phone. By the time she found it on her bedside table, it had stopped ringing. Figured. She struggled to a sitting position in her bed, wishing she could've stayed asleep for a bit longer. She'd driven from Chase's show in Milwaukee straight to Detroit where she worked a nine-hour shift before finally going home. All this had been on barely four hours of sleep. She'd woken up at oh-dark-thirty to pee and had ended up pinned beneath Chase's hard body, his sleepy eyes tender and lustful. She couldn't—and didn't—say no to him, so she'd never gone back to sleep.

Now, Tuesday morning—Jamie glanced at her phone and swore—ok, fine, Tuesday afternoon…and she was still feeling groggy and in need of sleep. She'd crashed hard when she got home, but it had been a broken and not-entirely-restful sleep. She'd kept partially waking and finding herself alone in bed.

Two nights with Chase and I already miss him in my bed, Jamie thought. *I've got it bad.*

The voicemail notification beeped, and Jamie played the message. "Hey, hooker, it's me," Anna's voice said. "Haven't seen you in forever, and I miss your face. Call me. Or better yet, lunch at BD's at one? K, good. See you there."

Jamie leapt out of bed, swearing. It was twelve-twenty. Knowing Anna, she'd show up at Mongolian Bar-B-Q at one and expect Jamie to be there. Showering and dressing in record time, Jamie skipped makeup except for the basic blush, mascara and lip gloss, and bolted out the door. As she expected, Anna was waiting with a diet Coke when Jamie showed up ten minutes late.

"There you are," Anna said, getting up to hug Jamie. "Wondered if you'd gotten my message."

"Yeah, sorry I'm late," Jamie said. "I had a bit of lie in."

Anna laughed even as her face wrinkled in confused frown. "A bit of a lie in? Starting to talk like Ian, are we?" Anna shook her head, chuckling. "Shall we carry on to the table and have a spot of lunch?" She said this with a terrible faux-British accent.

Jamie frowned. "Did I say that?"

"Yeah, you kind of did."

Jamie tilted her head back and groaned volubly. "I can't believe I actually said that. That was one of Ian's favorite phrases."

Anna cast a quizzical look at Jamie as they scooped uncooked chicken and vegetables into their bowls. "Was?"

Jamie bit her lip. She wasn't quite ready for that part of the conversation, but Anna knew her too well for Jamie to be able to dissemble for long. "Yeah, well…you know what I mean."

Anna scooped teriyaki sauce into a ramekin and set the dishes on the counter for the grill guy. "Maybe I don't." She dug her cell phone out of her pocket and tapped a message, then sent it and turned back to Jamie. "You're being purposefully vague and I don't like it. Spill, sister."

Jamie watched the grillers show off with their grill-sword things, trying to come up with a suitable response that would still buy her time. In the end she just sighed. "How about I ignore all interrogative queries until after I've eaten."

Anna frowned, shrugging. "Okay, guess I can handle that. But I get the feeling I'm not gonna like this very much, am I?"

Jamie couldn't answer that. She accepted her food with a smile for the sweaty but good-looking young guy behind the grill, tossing a couple dollar bills in the tip jar and banging the gong. Anna was true to her word, letting her eat in peace. When they'd both finished, Anna toyed with her chopsticks and leveled a serious look at Jamie.

"Ok. We've eaten. Now...*spill*." Anna stabbed Jamie's hand with the chopstick playfully. "Ian didn't knock you up, did he?"

Jamie sighed, half-laughing. "No." She took a deep breath. "Ian and I broke up about an hour after I got to Chicago, actually."

Anna's brow wrinkled. "Really? I thought things were going well. I was half-expecting you tell me you were moving to Chicago."

Jamie shook her head. "It was never going, well, Anna."

"What do you mean?"

"Ian...the whole thing with him. It was never going to work, and I knew it from the get-go."

"I don't understand. You seemed to like him. You were always talking about him whenever we hung out."

Jamie rolled her eyes. "Yeah, well...I was trying to convince myself everything was fine."

"So you broke up with Ian on Friday...it's Tuesday, and I know you work every Monday...so what happened Saturday and Sunday?"

"Actually, technically, he broke up with me, but I was gonna do it soon anyway."

Anna waved her hand dismissively. "Irrelevant. Where were you the rest of the weekend? What are you not telling me?"

"Um." Jamie tied a knot in the empty paper wrapper from her drinking straw, not looking at Anna. "Nothing?"

"Fuck you, hooker. Give me the truth."

"You can't handle the truth."

"Okay, *fine*, Tom Cruise." Anna scooted her chair back and prepared to stand up. "I'm going to the bathroom. If you can't talk to me, I get it. Or really, I don't, but I'm not gonna try to drag the truth out of you. You've either avoided the truth or outright lied to me every time we've talked for like months now. I'm getting sick of it." Anna left, her messy blond braid hanging down her back, swaying as she walked.

Jamie put her face in her hands, groaning in despair. "This is gonna suck," she muttered to herself.

Anna came back and sat down, crossing her arms over her chest. "Last chance, Jay. Or we're fighting for real."

Jamie took a deep breath, shredding the straw wrapper between shaking fingers. "I ran into Chase after I left the restaurant where Ian broke up with me."

"Shit." Anna's eyes slid closed slowly. "I knew it. I *knew* it. You fucked him, didn't you?"

Jamie looked up sharply. "It wasn't just *fucking*, Anna."

"Whatever, Jamie. You slept with him. You had sex with him."

"It's not...it was more than that." She could barely manage a whisper. "I can't even explain to you how much has changed for me. It feels like...I don't know how to put it into words. It's hard to believe it was just a single weekend. Two days. Two days, but everything is different. *I'm* different. He changed me, Anna."

Anna drew a long breath and let it out slowly. "Yeah. He has a way of doing that, doesn't he?" She reached out and took Jamie's trembling hands in hers. "I'll bite my tongue as long as I can, but you have to talk to me."

Jamie nodded, pushing back the huge weight of emotion bearing down on her chest. "I'm in love with him, Anna. I have been since Vegas. I tried so hard, *so goddamn hard* to deny it. To pretend it wasn't true. I did. I swear to you, I didn't want this to happen, but it did. We both tore ourselves apart for months trying to act like this wasn't inevitable. Ian...he was just an attempt to be okay without Chase, and it never had a fucking chance in hell of working."

"And Chase? How does he feel?"

"He did basically the same thing. Hooked up with some girl from around here named Tess. He was in Chicago for a show and she dumped him, pretty much at the same time as Ian dumped me. We were both hurting innocent people with this, Anna. Tess, Ian? Neither of them had any part of Chase or I. But now that Chase and I...happened...you're hurt. I don't know what to do."

"He loves you, huh?" Anna's voice was small and tight.

"Yeah."

Anna didn't answer for a long, long time. "Shit. I—shit. I don't know how to deal with this. It's not like he's my boyfriend and you went behind my back with him. I'm married to Jeff and I wouldn't change that for the world, but...it's *Chase*. You know how hard that whole thing was for me."

Jamie half-shrugged, sniffling back a tear. "Yeah...I know. But... you don't know what I went through trying to act like I don't need Chase."

"No I don't, because you weren't talking—"

"How could I talk to you about it? About him? You still care about him. I know you love Jeff with all your heart, but you can't sit there and tell me there's no part of you that doesn't wonder what could have been if you hadn't ran away from him in New York. What was the right choice in this, Anna? I tried the right thing. I tried to walk away from him. I *did* walk away from him. So many times, I did, and it nearly broke me every time. That kiss in Vegas. It was one of those moments that define you, that change who you are, what you want in life..."

Anna sighed. "I know the feeling all too well."

"Every time I saw him just made it worse. It's not just an attraction. I don't know what to say. It's...*need*. I was completely exhausted last night, but I still couldn't sleep right because he wasn't there, and I'd only spent two days with him. It's like...I don't know...like he's inside me."

Anna stood up abruptly and walked out of the restaurant, wiping at her face. Jamie slumped forward, resting her head on her arms on the tabletop for a minute, then followed Anna out to her car. She slid into the passenger seat and rested her head on the seatback. Next to her, Anna had her forehead pressed to the steering wheel. Her shoulders shook.

After a while, Anna sat up and scrubbed her face. "I...I love Jeff. I don't want anyone else. He's...he's perfect for me. But goddamnit, Jay.

You're right. I do sometimes, in very pit of my heart, wonder sometimes. I ran before he had a chance to explain, and later I realized he probably hadn't done anything wrong. But by then it didn't matter, because I was in love with Jeff already."

"I know."

"But…how can I ever look at Chase without that little niggling worm of doubt popping up? How can I look at him and not see us— him and I? You're my best friend, Jay. I want to be able to ask you about things with your boyfriend. We're supposed to have dirty little secrets about our men together. I want to ask you…I mean, I know what Chase likes, and I'm guessing I can imagine how the weekend went, and—" Anna shuddered and ducked her head, "but then I think of him and *you* in bed together and I get sick. It's not jealousy, exactly. I don't know *what* it is, but it hurts, Jay. It hurts."

Jamie leaned across the console between them and hugged Anna. "I don't know either. That's how I feel when I think about you and Chase together. I mean, like…he's *mine*. I don't know what I'm gonna do while he's on tour. I'm already going insane and it's been less than twenty-four hours since I saw him. And sometimes you come up, and it's awkward. And I…I don't know, Anna. This is what's been tearing me apart about the whole situation. I love him so much. I've never been happier in my entire life than when I'm with him. Nothing else matters except being in his arms. But I have to live life and so does he, and then everything comes crashing back down around me and…" Jamie rested her forehead against Anna's shoulder. "Reality sucks."

Anna laughed through a sob. "Yeah, it does." She leaned her ear against Jamie's head. "Don't take this the wrong way, Jay, but—fuck you for falling in love with my ex." After a silent moment, Anna shoved Jamie away playfully. "It was pretty amazing, though, right?"

Jamie dragged in a deep breath and let it out with a shriek and whole-body freak out. "Anna, it was so far beyond incredible! I didn't know it could be like that. I didn't know…" she took a deep breath and tried again. "He took me places I didn't know the human body could go." She said this last part quietly, lending intensity to the statement.

Anna sighed, almost wistfully. "You two are perfect for each other." She picked at her thumbnail, keeping her gaze cast down. "I never said this to anyone, or even admitted it to myself out loud before now, but I kind of felt like he wanted things I didn't know how to give him. He was just so crazy and intense and...it was exciting and fun, but it was overwhelming sometimes. I think that's the largest reason I ran. Emotionally, yeah, there were things there I couldn't figure out how to face, but I think unconsciously I was a little overwhelmed by the things he wanted to do with me, *to* me."

Jamie rubbed her palms on her thighs. "Yeah, see, for me, that's exactly what I need. I've been so...closed off, numb...and just *bored* with sex, with men in general. Chase makes me feel alive. Like I've just been dreaming until now and Chase is reality."

Anna giggled, a little hysterically. "This is a strange-ass conversation." She twisted the engagement ring and wedding band around her finger. "Jeff is exactly what I need. Being with him, making love to him is...it makes me feel cherished. He takes his time, he's so slow and sweet and thorough, and he can get a little freaky sometimes, but mainly, it's just...so completely what my soul and my heart and my body needs." Jamie wasn't sure what to say to that, so she kept silent until Anna blew out harsh breath and turned to Jamie. "I'm trying really hard to be cool about this. But...I'm upset. I'm confused. I'm hurt. I'm kinda angry, actually. I mean, I know this wasn't something you intentionally chose, so it may not be *fair* for me to be pissed off, but it's hard to ignore how I feel just because it's not 'fair.'" Anna used air quotes when she said the last word.

"I'm sorry, Anna. You have every right to be pissed at me. I get it. And yeah, I didn't ask for this, but...I can't—I don't know what to do. Just don't make me choose between you and him, please? I couldn't— couldn't do that. I love you, you're my best and oldest friend. But Chase? He's...I feel like he's my future."

"I'm not gonna make you choose, Jay. I wouldn't do that. But I need time. I need to talk to Jeff about this. Just…give me time." Anna stuck her key in the ignition but didn't turn it. "I'm not gonna lie, Jay. The more I think about this, the harder it feels like it's gonna be, the first time we all get together."

"It's gonna be—"

"Impossible." Both women said the word simultaneously, and then laughed together.

The gaiety quickly faded and Jay pushed the passenger door open. She got out and paused, bending down to look at Anna, her hands on the roof of the car. "I don't know what else to say besides I'm sorry, and thank you." Jamie felt like she'd said some version of that last phrase a thousand times in the last few days.

"Thank you?" Anna asked, her face screwing up with the tension of someone trying not to cry.

"For trying to understand. For being my friend anyway, despite this. I can't shake the feeling that I've betrayed you, somehow. Unintentionally maybe, but still." Jamie felt her voice break.

Anna squeezed her gray eyes closed around stubborn tears. "BFF's, no matter what." She reached out her fist, and Jamie bumped it with hers. "Now go the hell away before you make me ugly cry."

Jamie sniffed and laughed, then turned away without another word and drove home. On the way, she realized that, despite the number of times she'd apologized to Anna, her friend had never said it was okay.

Probably because it wasn't.

Anna may not have been actively in love with Chase, but old, dormant, and mostly-forgotten feelings still had the potential to cause heartache.

Sitting at home catching up on her DVR'd episodes of *Teen Mom 2*, Jamie found herself wishing she could quit her job and just follow Chase on his tour. Or fly out to wherever he was for each show and be with him that way. Or…anything other than sit at home missing him, jealous of the fans who got so much of his time and attention.

She Googled his tour dates, switched shifts around with the other assistant manager at work, and bought a plane ticket to St. Louis, where Six Foot Tall was performing next. The ticket nearly cleaned out her savings, but she'd just paid rent and all of her other bills were up to date. Everything else could wait.

Chapter 6

*C*hase finished his last encore number and stepped off the stage, the screaming of thousands of fans bolstering him despite his exhaustion. The band's tour schedule was brutal. The last several weeks had been a whirlwind of non-stop shows, back to back, sometimes with a few days in between. Demand for Six Foot Tall was growing exponentially, and there was talk of the band headlining a show in Detroit sometime soon. Jamie had met him for almost every show, Chase paying for her airfare and hotel stays. Their relationship had deepened over the last two months, but it was still very much like a long-distance relationship. They spent more time talking on the phone or texting than they did in person, and they rarely had more than one night together in a row. Chase needed a break. He needed a few consecutive days spent not on stage, not warming up or writing new material or traveling. He needed private down time with Jamie, without the specter of the next show looming, cutting short their time together. Jamie understood, of course, and never complained. She came to every show she could, and was traveling almost as much as he was, flying all over the country to meet him. Chase's credit card was racking up serious frequent flier miles.

That night's show was one of the rare and blessed dates that was followed by three days in a row off. He'd already booked a suite for the two nights he had with Jamie. They were in Phoenix, Arizona, and the next show was some tiny club somewhere in New Mexico, an unplugged acoustic set. He accepted a towel from the stagehand and wiped his face and head with it, searching the backstage area for Jamie's wild red curls. There she was, facing into a darkened corner, her phone pressed to her ear, finger plugging the other. He sidled up behind her, wrapped his arms around her waist and kissed her neck while she finished her phone call.

She hung up and stuck the phone in her purse, then turned in his arms and met his lips with hers. "Hey, baby. Great show!"

Chase smiled into her lips. "Thanks. Who was that you were talking to?"

She shrugged. "Work call. The M.O.D. messed up the inventory order and I had help her unfuck it."

"Gotcha. So, ready for three days and two nights alone with me?"

"God, am I ever," Jamie said. "Are we staying here in Phoenix?"

"Yep. I have a suite booked. I'll meet the guys at the next show in New Mexico."

"And you're in L.A. after that?"

Chase nodded and pulled her into a walk out of the building where the limo rented by the label was waiting. "That's gonna be a huge show. Biggest yet, I think. If that one goes well, our agent says we might get a headliner billing at the Palace."

Jamie lit up, gripping his arm in excitement. "Really? That would be so huge! Headlining in your hometown? I bet it would sell out."

Chase laughed. "Yeah, probably not, but nice try. We're a long way from selling out the Palace, baby."

Jamie shoved him playfully. "You so would. I've heard people talking about you guys. You're getting a lot of radio play on the WRIF and 89X."

Chase glanced at her. "Really? Jim told us we've been getting more air time, but I guess it didn't quite register what that meant." He handed her into the limo and slid in next to her. "It's kind of weird. For as much as I'm all over the country, I still feel isolated from reality in a way. We're playing in front of sold-out crowds, but they're there to see the other bands as much as us, if not more so. We play and we keep going. We're getting paid a shit-load of money, but it's not really *real* most of the time, you know? Someone tells you, 'you're getting a lot of radio play,' and you're all like, 'oh, that's great,' or whatever, but it doesn't *mean* anything most of the time. It's not like I'm in those cities hearing our songs on the radio, you know? Right now, it feels like the whole word is broken up into the bus, the stage, and you, and nothing else even exists except in theory."

Jamie turned on the limo seat and draped her legs over his, curling her arms around his neck. "You're building a brand, baby. A name. Recognition. It'll all pay off. It already *is* paying off. People are starting to know who you are, on a household level." She nuzzled her face into his throat. "And now none of that matters."

"No?" Chase asked, tangling his fingers in her hair.

"Nope. For the next few days, you're mine. You're not a rockstar as of this moment. You're just my Chase."

He sighed into her hair. "Your Chase. Perfect."

The limo dropped them off at the hotel, where they ordered room service and drank two bottles of expensive white wine. They sat side by side on the bed, finishing the last of the second bottle.

"How long can you keep this up, Jay?" Chase asked, apropos of nothing.

Jamie tilted her head to rest it against his shoulder, swirling the wine at the bottom of her glass. "I don't know. Like you said, my life feels compartmentalized into work, airports, your shows, and hotels. I love traveling, honestly, but…it *is* getting exhausting. I'd give anything to spend a week on a beach with you." She tossed back the last of her wine and set the glass aside before turning to straddle Chase. "I'll do this as long as necessary. As long as this is your life, your career, this is how I'll see you."

"Do you even see your friends anymore?"

Jamie shrugged. "I have lunch with Anna when I'm back in Detroit. I went out with Lane and his partner Matty the other day. The rest of the people who I called my friends? They weren't really friends. They were drinking buddies. I only drink with you, now. They don't call me or try to catch up. The only people who keep up with my coming and going anymore are Lane and Anna, so they're really all that matter."

"Funny how that happens, huh? When you're gone all the time, the fake friends have a way of getting culled out." Chase slipped his hands beneath her shirt to run his palms on the hot skin of her back. "It works for me, though. The guys are my friends. The roadies and the driver, the security guys, they're friends too. Jim, our agent. You. That's about it."

"Who else do you need, really?"

Chase kissed the base of her throat. "Besides you and the band? No one. Who else is there?"

Jamie reached down and peeled her shirt off, her curls bouncing down to hang around her shoulders. She'd let it grow recently, and it was now almost to mid-back. Chase loved her hair, loved to hold on to it, run his fingers through it, grip it in his fist as he made love to her.

He'd been planning this night for a while. He'd hinted at what he wanted to do with her, and she'd not demurred. He skimmed his hands over her shoulders, across the lace of her bra, feeling the hard beads of her nipples, then reached behind her to unhook her bra. He felt his cock twitch and harden as her heavy breasts fell free. He took them in his hands, cupping them, kneading the silky flesh, grazing his thumb across her nipples. He flicked a nipple with his tongue, a featherlight touch, and Jamie gasped sharply, arching her back.

She shifted her weight backwards and unsnapped his pants, unzipped them and gripped the waistband of his pants and boxer-briefs, tugging them down. Chase lifted his hips and she slid them down to his knees, where he toed them off and kicked them aside. She peeled his shirt over his head, and then shimmied down his body, her soft breasts brushing his skin. All thoughts left his mind as she took his erection in her mouth. She worked her jeans and panties off while she licked and kissed his cock, and then they were both naked together. He let her work his cock for a second, and then drew her up so her face was level with his.

"I have plans for you," he told her.

"Oh yeah?" Her voice was low and sultry, and her eyes hooded.

She rolled over and lay on her back, posing for him. Her palms skittered over her breasts before moving down to cup her sex, teasing and inviting. "What kind of plans?"

Chase hopped off the bed and dug in a pocket of his suitcase, producing a bottle of lubricant and couple of condoms. "Plans that involve this."

Jamie's eyes widened and her nostrils flared, her tongue running over her bottom lip. "Oh. Oh god. Okay." She sat up, then moved to her hands and knees.

Chase laughed, crawling across the bed toward her. "Eager, are we?" He curled his hand around her hips and drew her to him, so his cock slipped, upright, between the firm, soft cheeks of her ass.

She writhed into him.

"Yes…" she breathed. "So eager. You've been teasing me about this for so long."

Chase sucked in a hard breath, pulling his hips away to caress her ass with his palms, sinking back on his haunches behind her. "It's not teasing. It's…getting you ready for it."

"I'm ready." Jamie watched him over her shoulder, biting her lip

"Not just yet," Chase said. He skated his hand over her spine, then around her ribs to cup a breast, working his other hand between her legs to trace her damp heat with one finger. "First, I need this. I need to taste you. Feel you come. I'm so hard for you, I couldn't last long enough to get deep enough, slow enough in your tight little asshole."

He fingered her clit, feeling her juices begin to flow. He circled the sensitive nub, tweaking a nipple as he did so, and within minutes Jamie was quivering and rocking back into his hand, near to orgasm. Before she came, she reached behind herself and found his cock, guided him into her silky wet folds. He was throbbing already, and had to hold back after only a few slow strokes. She began to thrust back into him, and the feel of her ass pushing against him brought him to a boiling point all too quickly. He slowed, then, clenching his teeth and forcing himself down. He reached for the lubricant, squirted some onto his fingers and slathered it against Jamie's tight anus, massaging at first with one finger. She moaned in ecstatic relief as he nudged his finger in to the first knuckle, then began to whimper when he worked a second finger in, liberally working her entrance with lube.

"Fuck me, Chase. I want it. Fuck me in the ass."

"Not yet, baby," Chase gasped. "Come for me first."

He began to stroke into her pussy, sliding his fingers in and out of her ass, gently, in sync with his thrusts. She began to buck hard against him, and Chase had to focus all his strength in holding back his own orgasm as she let go, whimpering softly into the blanket as she climaxed.

He pulled of out her folds, then, and reached for the condom. Jamie took it from him, ripped it open and handed the roll to him. He slid the latex over his cock, gritting his teeth, and then smeared himself with lube.

Jamie craned her neck to watch him. "Now, Chase? Please?"

Chase pulled his fingers out of her slowly, and then settled the tip of his cock against her asshole. "God, yes. Now, my love." He hesitated, though.

Jamie rolled her hips, inviting him. "What is it?"

Chase held her hip in one hand, meeting her gaze. "This is both of our first time for this."

Jamie quirked an eyebrow. "Really? I didn't realize it was yours too."

"It is. This is something we're doing together."

Jamie swiveled her hips into groin. "I'm ready, love." She bit her lip, her hair hanging down to one side, bouncing lightly as she moved. "I need you inside me, baby. I want you in my ass."

Chase searched her eyes for hesitation, trepidation. All he saw was love and desire.

Jamie watched Chase grip his shaft by the base and gently probe her anus. She forced herself to relax, even though her belly was fluttering with nerves. She wanted this with him. Especially now that she knew it was his first time doing this, too. Lust burned through her, dark and dirty. His fingers inside her back there was always intense, every time. She never came as hard as when he was knuckle-deep in her ass, and she loved the feeling. Now, he was finally about to put his cock inside her, after weeks of promising.

She admitted, deep down, to being a little afraid. He was huge, and that entrance was small.

She felt a hint of pressure, and tried not to tense. His breathing was ragged, as was hers. A bit more pressure, and then the now-familiar feeling of tightness and penetration and stabbing thrill, shooting pleasure. This was more, though, so much more. She twisted her head back to look at Chase. He had his head thrown back, his spine straight, his thick, beautiful cock held in one hand, his other on her hip, steadying her. His eyes were closed tight, sweat streaking his scalp and forehead. His muscles were straining, and she knew he was holding back. He nudged in a little further, and Jamie felt a gasp escape at the pulsing invasion. She was stretched wide, so wide. It hurt, just a little, but the pain was laced with lovely thrill, delicious desire and hot need.

Jamie reached forward and jerked the pillows toward her, stuffed them beneath her belly, propping herself on one elbow. With her other hand, she touched herself, a gentle circling of her clit at first. She moaned, and Chase slid in another inch, prompting the moan into a loud groan. He growled, tensing, freezing. She felt herself adjusting, loosening. Her fingers pulled pleasure from her core and sent it out in hot waves, turning the stretching into filthy need.

"More, Chase." She barely recognized the animal growl of her own voice.

He gave her more, slowly. She moved her fingers faster, now, in the confident speed of a woman touching herself, the way only a woman can pleasure herself. Chase let go of his shaft and gripped both hips, then bent slightly over her and tweaked a nipple, once, and it was enough to bring Jamie nearly to the edge. Chase thrust again, and she felt him to be all the way in, then. He held still for a moment, gathering himself and giving her time to finish adjusting.

Then he drew back with aching slowness, and Jamie felt a lightning bolt shoot through her, like an orgasm multiplied by a thousand. She shrieked, then bit the comforter, stifling her building scream. Her mouth went wide, but no sound came out.

Chase reached the apex of his pull-out, hesitated, then began the slow plunge in. A squeak scraped out of her throat, and Chase took that as encouragement to let the thrust in morph into an immediate withdrawal.

Jamie needed him to move faster. Each slide was an agony of ecstasy, and if only he would give her more, faster, she knew it would get better. Her mind was so scrambled by need, she couldn't get words out of her mouth. She tried to speak, she really did, but all that emerged was a whimper. He plunged in, faster now. He pulled out, paused, and Jamie felt the cold touch of lubricant, and then he stroked in again, incrementally harder. Jamie keened, a high-pitched sound from the back of her throat, and pushed back into him as he thrusted in.

"Oh god, Jamie. Oh god, you're so tight. So...so fucking tight." Chase growled.

His fingers dug into her hips and began to tug her back into his thrusts. Jamie let herself moan, then felt a scream building again. The pressure inside her was a mountain, heavy and overwhelming, huge and sun-hot, fire in her belly, lava in her core. She shook all over, and now she was moving with him.

Jamie shoved the pillows away, stretched her arms in front of her and let go, gave in to need. She rocked into his plunging shaft, a scream bubbling up. His hand slid up her spine, his touch achingly gentle in counterpoint to his rampaging thrusts. Brushing over her shoulders, he tangled his fingers in her thick copper curls, caressing and massaging at first, then he gripped a fistful and tugged her backward, holding close to her scalp and jerking in time with his thrusts, his other hand still clenching the flesh of her hip. Chase was growling now, wordless and primal, and Jamie matched his feral sounds, gasping and grunting as he slammed into her ass.

"Chase..." his name grated past her lips, dragging more words with it. "Fuck me hard, Chase. Fuck my ass so hard..."

"Jamie, *fuck*, Jay. I love you." He pulled her back by the hips, hard, giving her a slamming thrust, flesh slapping against flesh, and a scream ripped from Jamie's trembling lips.

The sound of her scream set Chase free, unleashed him. He drove in without restraint now, and Jamie rocked forward as he pulled back, slammed her ass into his body on the in-thrust, crying out as the tensing, shaking, quivering muscles of her buttocks crashed into him.

The pressure was an inferno, now, volcanic heat, titanic and unstoppable. She felt the crest rising within her and let her front half go limp on the bed, half-supported one arm, reaching down with the other to touch herself once more.

Now, the touch of her fingers on her throbbing clit was nearly too much, an overwhelming erotic shock to her shattering system. She was splitting apart, bursting at the seams. Screams were ripping from her throat in staccato ululations, peaking as he plunged deep, hard and fast, quieting as he drew back. He was roaring non-stop now, a leonine rumble as he began to pump with manic speed and crushing force, and as hard as he was fucking her, Jamie needed more, craved more, lifting up with her core and thighs and slamming down to meet his thrusts.

Lust bled into love, need and desire bled into starvation-like hunger for the way he filled her and stretched her with every thrust, felt tears squeezing from her eyes, salt drops of overwhelmed ecstasy, pressure of her impending climax leaking from her tear ducts.

"Jay...I'm gonna come..." Chase's voice was rough and thick.

She couldn't summon coherency. "Yes...yes!" That was all the sense she could make as she rocked into his thrusts, her fingers a blur on her clit, teeth clamped on her lip so hard she tasted blood.

Chase lost his rhythm, thrusts stuttering and frantic. He drew back, paused, and then slammed home hard enough that Jamie was bumped forward off-balance, then jerked back by his hands at her hips. She let him control her body, acquiescing willingly to his primality, his dominating power exactly what she wanted. He made a sound in his throat, and she felt his cock pulse. She came in that instant, screaming louder than she'd ever sounded, not caring who heard. The pressure was a tsunami roaring through her, magma rushing through her core, wave after wave clenching her muscles around his cock.

He pulled back and then rammed into her again, throwing her forward, a sustained growl coming from his chest. She was pulled back again and felt another wave of orgasm rolling over her as he blasted into her ass a third time, and this one had them both screaming, his voice louder than hers, even.

She felt him thrust once more, softer now, and then a last, soft fluttering push, and then he was still. Jamie couldn't support her weight, not with arms or legs. She was still impaled by him, held up by his hands. She sobbed ragged breaths, whimpering.

"Holy...fuck," Chase gasped.

"Love you...so much," Jamie managed.

She cried out when he began to draw out. He was achingly tender as he withdrew, and she wanted to cry out again when he left the bed and stumbled to the bathroom to toss out the condom and wash his hands. She murmured in pleasure when his heat and weight settled behind her, spooning her. She turned in his arms, and he cradled her close, holding tight for long minutes. Her lips turned up, touched his, and then she let tears of...everything...fall as she lost herself in his kiss.

His hands roamed her back, her hip, her ass, her thigh. She bit his lip when he pulled back, sighing as his fingers tangled in her sweaty curls.

"Did I hurt you?" Chase mumbled.

Jamie took his face in her hands, fixed her eyes on his hesitant brown gaze. "*No*, love. No." She kissed him with all the affection and tenderness she had. "You were perfect. So incredible. I can't even describe what I just experienced. It wasn't just an orgasm, it was…a super-gasm."

"Good. I kinda lost control." He sighed in relief. "I was worried I'd hurt you."

Jamie reached down and curled her fingers around his softened cock, knowing his refractory period was almost over already. "I love that you lost control. *Love* it." She bit his chin, then kissed his shoulder, squeezing his cock in soft pulses, feeling him harden. "This time, though, I want it slow and gentle and soft. I want to ride you slowly. I'm gonna ride you until you come apart beneath me."

Chase rumbled in laughter, leaving his fingers threaded in her hair, letting her touch him. "Damn, girl. You're insatiable."

"Complaining?" Jamie asked, caressing him into full erection.

"God..hell no. I love that about you. I love that you initiate as much as I do." Chase tilted so he was on his back, drawing Jamie on top of him. She straddled him, low on his thighs, leaning down over him so her breasts hung down to brush his chest. She kissed him, slowly at first, then losing herself in his mouth, the wonder of his hands on her skin. She sighed into the kiss as he thumbed her nipples into taut beads. She gasped when he shifted his hips so his pelvis applied pressure to her clit, which drove her nearly over the edge from the very start.

Jamie arched her body away from his, fisting his rigid cock slowly and gently, then lifted up on her knees and pulled his shaft back towards herself. He stilled, her breasts cupped in his palms, waiting. Jamie knelt above him with his crown poised at her nether lips. Her mouth was slightly open, her breath coming in shallow puffs, her gaze locked on Chase's. One hand propped her weight up on his chest, the other gripped his shaft at the base. His hands tensed, then relaxed, began roaming her body, sliding over her spine, clutching her hips briefly, grazing her face and tracing the line of her throat. She waited, waited, the very tip of him nestled between her labia. When his fingers dared down between their bodies to circle and carve and caress her clit, Jamie sank down on his thick length, abrupt and swift, without warning or preparation, moaning on an exhale as he filled her channel. She settled both hands on his shoulders, holding herself still at full impalement, drawing deep breaths, meeting his gaze with unrelenting vulnerability.

She was lost to this man. She'd been telling the truth when she promised him she'd meet him at every show she could for as long as it took. Nothing mattered but him. She shifted her hips back and forth, settling him deeper, feeling so full of him, physically and emotionally, and wishing she could be even more filled by him, wishing she could drown in him, hold all of him within her body, let his essence merge with hers.

Chase groaned, fluttering his hips in restrained thrusts, wanting to plunge up into her, but holding back, relinquishing control to her. Jamie sat back, balancing on her shins, stretching his cock away from his body. He moaned, wincing as she pulled him as far away as he could go. He spread his palms on her thighs, fingers digging into the firm muscle and soft flesh. Jamie rose up with her thigh muscles, pulling him nearly out but not relaxing the stretching of his cock. She sank down and rose up once more, then began a slow rolling rhythm with her hips, rocking her core back and forth over his slick, solid shaft. He moaned continuously as she rode him, clutching her thighs and rocking into her.

Jamie kept the pace slow and soft, balancing above him, her eyes locked on his, her hands resting on his on her thighs. Chase traced up her torso with one hand, cupped her full breast and tweaked the nipple, causing her to gasp in pleasure. His other hand delved down between her thighs to where their bodies joined, one long finger lazily caressing her clit. Jamie began to pulse above him faster as he fingered her closer to climax, and she felt his stretched, strained cock begin to throb, saw the tension in the lines of his face and the veins in his neck. A crushing pressure ballooned into life within her, centered on her core, and it only built with every stroke of his fingers, every throbbing plunge of his thick shaft inside her soft, sex-slick slit. She was breathless already, and when she came, it was with a gasping, keening cry, arching backward. She clutched her breasts, one hand resting over Chase's, encouraging his caressing grasp. She rolled and rocked on his body, but still she didn't relax forward.

"Jamie…I can't—can't come like this. I'm—pulled back too far," Chase said, panting.

She smiled wickedly, pinching her own nipple and sliding up and down his cock slowly, torturing him, feeling his need for release. "I know, baby," she whispered, bending forward while keeping her hips tilted back. "You're not going to come until I'm ready to let you."

Chase arched and humped up, seeking relief, but Jamie followed his movements, keeping him stretched far enough to prevent him from coming. He groaned and grunted, arching into Jamie's still-slow rhythm. His eyes squeezed shut and sweat streamed down his forehead, his breath coming in harsh pants, his fingers fisting in the sheets at his sides. All was forgotten but for his need for release. Jamie watched him carefully, measuring his desperation.

As she sinuously impaled herself on his shaft, she felt yet another climax burgeoning inside her, and she pressed two fingers to her aching, hypersensitive nub, skyrocketing the pressure into sudden supernova heat. Her other hand went to her breast, rolling her nipple between her fingers, hard, just this side of painful, and she began to slide on his cock with increasing speed. Urgency filled her, frenzy overtook her. This climax would be intense, she knew. The pressure was unbearable, fire in her belly, lava in her veins. She held it back, slowing her pace on Chase's body, letting the heat and pressure build yet more.

"Jay…please…*fuck*, I'm dying. I'm gonna explode." Chase's eyes were feral slits in his face, his voice a rasping growl like a rockslide.

"You wanna come, baby?" Jamie whispered the words, pleased with how sultry she sounded, even to herself. "You wanna come inside my pussy?"

"Fuck yes. I need it. Let me go, please. *Please.*"

Jamie tilted her hips even farther back until Chase cursed out loud, then she relaxed the tension slightly, ever so gently. "Beg me," she whispered, each word a breathy moan.

Chase laughed. "I *am* begging you. Please let me come. I need it. I need you."

"You have me," she said.

"Promise?" His eyes were wide now, brown pools of fire locked on her.

"Yes, Chase. I promise." Jamie tilted and slid up his cock so the thick shaft pulling wet against her clit, shot lightning through her core; then, feeling the climax crest inside her, she paused at the apex, his crown between her lips. "I love you. Forever."

"Forever." He tensed, still, frozen, waiting. "I love you."

"Come with me." Jamie fell forward on the last word slicing her core down around his cock in frantic rhythm.

"Oh fuck, oh fuck, oh…*fuck!*" Chase thrashed into her wildly, and she felt his seed spread through her in a flood of wet heat.

She bit his shoulder, meeting him thrust for frenzied thrust, her body flush against his, only their hips moving as they climaxed together. Chase's arms were steel bands around her back, one hand fisted in her hair at her neck, the other curled around her waist, holding her tight against him as he crashed into her core, spurting deep with every thrust, filling her, filling her. She wept against him, overcome by physical sensation and emotional floodtide, love for Chase pounding through her in place of blood, need for all of him firing in place of synapses. She sobbed, heaving in the rhythm of their frantic, pounding pace. She felt her body clench around him, felt her womb contract and her muscles clamp and her core clench.

She felt her her heart expand, and she knew if she hadn't been already, she was irrevocably *his.*

After a timeless eternity of mutual climax, they went still, Jamie collapsed on top of him, still impaled by him, filled by him. His breath huffed in her hair, his fingers toying with tangled curls, tracing her skin, the lines of her hips.

Neither spoke as sleep stole over them. Jamie eventually shifted so he slipped out of her folds, and she slid off him and curled into his arms, more contented than she'd ever been. It seemed every night she spent with him saw her more full of his presence, more contented with life, with love.

She wondered muzzily how she could find any further happiness, how she could be anymore wonderfully full of Chase.

Chapter 7

*C*hase tried to calm his nerves, tried to force himself into relaxing. It didn't work. He was uneasy, unexplainably anxious. Well, his anxiety was partially explainable: Six Foot Tall was headlining at the Palace of Auburn Hills that night. It was their first headliner venue, and it was their hometown. It was also nearly sold out. The guys were amped, and so was Chase, but the other source of his nerves were less pleasant.

Jamie had been off lately. Just…distracted, almost distant. Snappish, at times. He'd asked her if anything was bothering her on a number of occasions, but she always denied it.

Matters weren't helped by the fact that she'd had the other assistant manager at her work quit, leaving her to cover most of the shifts on her own. She'd only been able to get away to see him twice in the last two months, and most of the time he tried calling her she could only talk for a second, or was so tired she fell asleep while talking. He'd been busy too, of course. They'd done an interview in *Revolver*, played on Conan O'Brien's show, as well as their usual aggressive tour schedule.

But none of that mattered to Chase, if something was wrong with Jamie.

He sat backstage at the Palace, watching the seats fill up, plucking strings on his guitar. He'd played the guitar most of his life, in a hobby sort of way. He was a singer more than anything, but if he got a few minutes of downtime before shows or on the bus between venues he would pull out his old acoustic six-string and play. He wrote most of Six Foot Tall's songs that way, although he'd never played the guitar on stage for the fans. Kyle, the guitarist, was talented enough for six people, so there was never any reason for Chase to play on stage.

This time around, he was working on a song, but not one for the band. He'd written the lyrics over the last couple weeks, tweaking them here and there until they were perfect. Now he was putting them to music, and he was almost done putting the finishing touches to the melody. He wasn't sure when he would sing the song, since it was a special piece he'd written for Jamie, and their relationship seemed strained as of late.

He glanced back down at the black-and-white composition book he wrote his lyrics in, made a note changing a chord. He soon lost himself in the song, and didn't emerge again until he heard someone approaching from behind him. He closed the notebook just as he felt Jamie's arms slip around his neck, and her lips touched his jaw. He reached up over his head and pulled her down for an upside down kiss. Jamie moved around his body without breaking the kiss, sitting on his legs facing him, and the kiss deepened.

His body responded immediately, thickening against the button fly of his leather pants. Jamie clearly felt his response, shifting on his lap to rub her core against him. He moaned into the kiss, and wished they were alone.

"God, I missed you," Jamie whispered against his lips.

He sighed in relief. "I've missed you too," he said. "So much. I really love this kind of hello."

Jamie smiled, her lips tightening and curving against his. "Want to go somewhere more private for an even better hello?"

"The bus is empty," he said. "The guys are out to dinner."

"Let's go." Jamie stood up and pulled him up by his hands.

He shrugged his coat on and led her to the tour bus, into his room, locking the door behind them. When he turned around from locking the door, Jamie already had her coat, shirt and pants off and was clawing at his zipper. He let her strip him naked, and then he unhooked her bra and slid down her panties while she stroked his cock with her fist. Before he could stop her, Jamie had dropped to her knees and took his cock between her soft, perfect lips, running her skilled tongue around his tip, caressing his base with her hand and his balls with the other. He let her take him deep a few times, and then when he felt himself rising too fast, he reached down and lifted her up by the arms.

"Enough," he growled. "I need to be inside you. Now."

"Then take me," she breathed.

He kissed her, reaching down between their bodies to stroke her silky, wet folds with his fingers. She was juicy and dripping and incredible, ready for him. He pushed her backward onto the bed, positioned her at the edge of the bed with her legs over his shoulders as he knelt between her thick, powerful, perfect thighs. He felt his cock twitch as she gasped when he lapped at her sex, then nearly came when she whimpered again. He licked and flicked her into a frenzy, curling his fingers inside her channel in a "come here" gesture, and she obeyed, coming immediately, arching up off the bed and keening as she fell apart under his mouth. At the crest of her climax, Chase rolled Jamie onto her stomach and plunged into her, fisting his hand in her wild, lovely red curls, loose like he loved her hair. She moaned and rocked back into him, humping her back and pushing hard against him.

"Fuck, Jamie. You feel so good."

"Oh god, Chase. Fuck me hard. I need it. I need you." She settled onto the bed, rising up on her tiptoes and falling down as he thrust up. "Come inside me. Right now. Don't wait."

Chase couldn't help but obey her command, pumping hard, once, twice, a third time, then found his release buried deep inside her, watching sweat bead on her spine. She crawled away from him, up onto bed and rolled to her back. He stood panting, slumped forward, breathless and still shuddering with the aftershocks. Jamie spread her thighs apart and held her hands out for him. He slid up her body, his still-hard cock pushing easily back into her wet folds. He kissed her lips, one hand planted on the bed next to her face, the other cupping her cheek.

He slipped his tongue between her teeth, sighed in his throat when her feet hooked around his waist. He needed her again, and soon. His hand found her breast, cupped and hefted its weight. He thumbed her nipple, then pinched it.

"Ow, not so hard," Jamie said. "My nipples are sensitive."

He gentled his touch, but found himself wondering at her complaint. She'd never said anything like that before. Usually she liked it when he pinched her nipples, and he was always careful not to cross the line into real pain. He knew he hadn't pinched her too hard. He went back to kneading and caressing her breast as he kissed her, beginning a subtle shifting of his hips, testing his hardness. She tensed her vaginal muscles around him, and he felt himself hardening. Her breasts seemed slightly heavier, he thought. He looked at her, took in her beautiful face and lush body.

They definitely seemed bigger. Not that he minded. He caressed her body, stroking her face and sides and belly, and then, his palm pressing over her stomach, he found himself wondering if her belly seemed firmer, harder beneath the padding of silky flesh. He returned his attention to her breasts, and this time Jamie pulled away from his kiss.

"What?" She asked. "Is something wrong with my boobs?"

He shook his head. "No. They just seem a little bigger than normal. I like it."

Jamie froze, her vivid green eyes searching him. "Are they? I've been really busy lately, so I haven't been working out as much. I might have gained a little weight."

"That wasn't what I—you're beautiful, baby. Perfect. I love your body, love your big breasts and perfect hips and amazing ass."

She smiled, but it seemed forced. "Thanks, babe." She shifted her hips and curled her arms around his neck. "Make love to me."

He pushed aside his thoughts and stroked into her. "I love you, Jamie."

She pressed her lips against his shoulder and her body shook, almost as if she was crying. She spoke with her face in his neck, meeting his soft and steady thrusts. "I love you, Chase. So much." She pulled away and her eyes were wet. "You love me forever? No matter what?"

He frowned, slowing, but she ran her hands down to his ass and pulled him against her, encouraging his pace faster. "Of course. No matter what. Always." He felt himself rising to climax, and Jamie's harsh breath and frantic hips told him she was close too. "What's wrong?"

She shook her head. "Nothing. Nothing." She clawed her hands into his ass and jerked at him, as if she needed him closer. "Just make love to me. Don't stop...please...never stop."

He pressed himself hard against her, his base crushing her clit, rolling deep into her. "Never...I'll never stop. I promise. God, Jamie... come with me."

"Yes! God, Chase." She whimpered, buried her face against his neck once more and held him tighter than she'd ever done before.

He burst into her, filling her with his seed, thrusting hard several times, feeling her walls clench around him, her legs tense against his thighs, her fingers digging into his ass. She was sobbing, and he knew something was wrong.

He took several deep breaths, then pulled out. "Jamie, baby, what is it? And don't say 'nothing.'" She shook her head. "Honey, talk to me."

"I'm fine, Chase."

He pulled her over, cradled her against him. "Bullshit, Jay. Something's up."

She sighed deeply. "I don't want to talk about it right now."

"Are you okay?" He put his fingers to her chin and tilted her face up so he could search her jade eyes. "Are *we* okay?"

Her eyes wavered wetly, jumping from side to side as she gazed at him. "Yes, oh god yes. It's nothing like that. I'm not about to break up with you or anything like that."

He sighed in relief. "Thank god." He glanced back down at her. "Don't put it off till after the show, if that's your plan."

She took his face in her hands and kissed him deeply. "That's not it. I promise you, I vow on my soul that's not it."

"But there's something you're not telling me." It wasn't a question.

She ducked her face, then. "Yes, baby. But just trust me, okay? We'll talk after you perform. Please don't worry, okay? It's fine. We're fine. I'm fine. We're all alright."

"You know that's just gonna drive me crazy, now, right?" He pulled her against his chest to hide his frustration. "I'm gonna be wondering what's going on."

"Just try to forget it for now, okay? If it was something urgent, you know I'd tell you."

He sighed. "Okay. Fine. But we're going out alone after and we're talking."

"Absolutely."

They were silent then, Jamie ruminating on whatever was on her mind, and Chase going in circles in his head trying to figure out what it could be.

He dozed with her in his arms, and a thought floated through the back of his head, an idea.

No, he thought. *That's not it. It can't be.* He held her close, breathing in the familiar scent of her shampoo and her body lotion and the musk of sex. *But if it was?*

He tried to honestly consider the possibility running through him.

If it was that, I'd be happy. Among other things.

An unknowable amount of time later, he heard a knock on the door. "Chase, dude," came Gage's voice from the other side. "We gotta be onstage to warm up."

"Coming," he rumbled.

Jamie stirred in his arms. "Gotta go already?" she asked sleepily.

"Yeah. You stay here for awhile."

She pursed her lips for a kiss, and he gave her one, slow and deep and passionate. "Okay, baby. I'll see you up there. Love you." Jamie pushed his shoulder to get him moving.

Chase forced himself out of bed and got dressed, knowing if he didn't, he'd get lost in her, lost in the kiss, lost in a third round of lovemaking. He slipped out the door with his boots, which he didn't remember taking off in the first place, and glanced back at her. She was dozing with one hand draped over her stomach.

He paused, watching her sleep, wondering.

Jamie woke up alone in the bed on the tour bus. She stretched lazily, listening to the thump of distant bass and drums of the opening acts. She crawled out of bed and stepped into her panties, then hooked her bra under her breasts, spun it around and slipped the straps on, tucking her breasts into the cups. She put her pants on, but left them unzipped and unbuttoned. There was a mirror on the back of the door, and she examined herself in it, turning sideways to look at herself in profile.

She wondered if he'd noticed the changes in her. Probably. He was observant like that. She ran her hands over her belly—still flat, thank god—then hefted her breasts. He'd obviously noticed her breasts, but he might've bought her story about gaining weight. Which, she had, just not for the reasons she'd given him. She'd been working out more assiduously than ever, taking up yoga with a vengeance.

She wasn't ready to tell him yet. She knew how important this performance was to him, and she wanted him to put his whole attention on the show. If she told him, he'd be too upset to focus. It was why she hadn't said anything yet. He was consumed with interviews and TV appearances, show after show. Obviously she couldn't tell him via text, and she hadn't been a hundred percent sure when she'd seen him the last couple times.

She was sure now, of course. Doctor-verified sure. Nerves and fear fluttered in her belly at the thought.

She wished she knew for sure how he'd react when she told him. God. Would he be happy? Afraid? Mad? The last possibility was the one she feared most. That wasn't like him, but…she couldn't be sure.

The band was just starting to reach their true potential. This was the worst possible timing for this news.

For her too. She'd been shouldering a huge burden at work, taking the place of two people. The GM had hinted that she was being considered for a regional position, which would make Jamie the only real choice for the next GM. Now was not the right time for this.

Except…you couldn't really pick the timing in these sorts of situations, could you?

Jamie finished getting dressed, fighting off panic.

She'd been pretending she was okay, trying to put on a brave face for Chase until the time was right to tell him, but she knew he'd noticed a change in her. Of course, he thought it meant something was wrong with her, or that she was going to dump him. She needed him more than ever, but—if she was going to admit the deep, dark truth—she was terrified he'd leave her to figure this out on her own.

If the pattern her life had taken thus far kept up, that's what would happen. The man she loved would abandon her at the time she needed him most. She didn't think he would. Her gut told her he'd be what she needed, he'd stick around for this. But…the fear remained.

This was the one eventuality she'd always been afraid of. It was why she was always so careful about protection and about taking her pill every day. She didn't need this, didn't want it. Not yet. Maybe not ever.

But now here it was, her worst fear realized.

She slipped her coat on and stepped out into the late December cold, shivering deeper into the wool jacket. A Palace security guard met her halfway across the parking lot.

"Mr. Delany sent me to escort you backstage, miss Dunleavy." His voice was a throaty croak. The guard was short, stocky, with a bald white scalp and kind dark eyes that hinted at capable confidence.

"Thank you." She extended her hand and shook his. "Jamie."

He squeezed gently but firmly. "Gary."

His smile transformed his face. He wasn't an attractive man, but he had that spark of charisma that drew her, made her like him. She followed him through the Palace underground to the entrance to the backstage area. The last opening act was still performing, a lively local rock band. She found Chase sitting in a dark, lonely corner, plucking at guitar.

She stood beside him and rested her hand on his shoulder. "I didn't know you played the guitar. How the hell did I not know this?"

He shrugged. "I don't play much. Usually only when I'm writing a song, which I only do on the bus, lately."

"What are you playing?" she asked.

He shrugged again, shook himself and reached out to close a notebook on a stool in front of him. "Nothing. Just a song."

The notes he'd been playing had been haunting and somehow familiar, even though she knew she'd never heard it before.

An awkward silence sat between them. He was obviously brooding on the news she hadn't told him.

"Chase, look, I'm not trying to keep anything from you—" she began.

He cut her off. "Then just tell me. Whatever it is, I'd be better of knowing. This not knowing is killing me."

"But this show, it's so important. I don't want anything to get in the way."

He set the guitar down and grabbed her ams. "Nothing about you, nothing about *us* could ever be in the way."

She nearly caved, nearly told him, nearly blurted out the two heavy words. But she didn't. Afterwards. That was the best time. Once he got on stage everything else would vanish for him. It always did.

When he realized she wasn't telling, he sighed. "Fine. Afterwards, then."

He stood up, clearly irritated. The opening band had finished and the crew was resetting the stage for the main act. Chase's gaze burned into her, digging at her secret. She wanted to tell him.

She rushed into his arms and felt a soft rush of comfort in his embrace. "I love you, Chase. Just hold on to that until we can talk after you're done, okay? I love you, and everything's okay."

Except it's not. She fought back the flood of words bubbling on her tongue.

"Let's go, Chase. We're on!" Gage appeared, smacking Chase on the back.

"Coming." Chase turned and pasted on a grin for Gage, mimicking his best friend's exuberance.

Jamie saw through it, though. He was worried.

She met his eyes when he turned back to her. His dark eyes locked on hers and she saw a heady, dizzying depth in them. *He knows*, she realized. Her mouth opened, but nothing came.

"Just tell me," Chase whispered. "Say it."

She couldn't. The kickdrum pounded onstage, the guitar twanged and whined as Kyle tuned it in.

"Chase! Fucking come on! Hometown headliners, motherfucker!" Gage appeared once more and this time physically grabbed Chase by the arms and pulled him away from Jamie. Gage met Jamie's eyes and smiled apologetically. "Sorry, Jamie. I'll give him back after the show!"

"I love you!" she called after Chase. "Kick ass!"

He smiled, and then he turned toward the stage and she saw the transformation happen. He shook his head, rolled his shoulders, hung his head back on his neck and drew a deep breath, shaking his hands. Then he stood straight, arms loose at his sides, leonine and powerful and graceful. He strode onto the stage, accepting a wireless mic from a techie on the way.

Jamie found her place just off stage, where she could see everything but remain invisible. The lights were down, thousands of people filling the seats and the boxes and the pit near the stage. The crowd was screaming, shrieking with anticipation. Jamie felt nerves flutter through her at the thought of being out in front of that many people. *No thanks.*

A single spotlight clicked on, bathing Chase. He was wearing his signature tight, faded, black leather pants, heavy black combat boots, a white button-down dress shirt with the sleeves ripped off, thick black leather wristbands glinting with silver spikes. His head was freshly shaven, glistening in the spotlight. His gorgeous face was limned in the light, and she could see him composing himself, pushing everything away. He just stood for a moment, bathing in the applause. From her vantage point, she saw him flick a finger at the drummer, a subtle gesture, and the drums kicked into life, a pulsing heartbeat rhythm. The crowd went even crazier. He raised his head, looking out over the sea of people, and the volume of the audience raised even more. They were in a frenzy, and Chase was eating it up, pulling into himself like oxygen.

He spread his arms wide, and Jamie was deafened.

Then Kyle plucked a single string, sending a long, high, wavering note over the crowd, which Gage underwove with a throbbing bass note. Kyle watched Chase, drawing out the single note. Chase slowly brought the mic to his lips, and Kyle held his pick poised over the bridge of his black and red electric guitar. Chase drew a deep breath, held it, mic to his lips, and then on some signal Jamie missed, Kyle brought the pick down to produce a wild rush of noise, a huge, deafening power chord. At the same time, Chase belted a wordless note, half-sung, half-screamed.

And then it was on. The song took off, a popular radio single that everyone knew. Jamie sang along, trying to relax into the show.

Song after song, and Chase was on fire. He was turning his anxiety into heat, energy, and Jamie knew this was their best performance yet.

Finally, one of their artistic numbers came up, a long instrumental song written by Gage and Kyle. Chase stepped offstage and found Jamie.

"You're amazing," she told him, kissing him.

"It felt good. We were on." He was wired, almost vibrating with energy.

"*You* were on." She rested her hands on his back, meeting his gaze.

The song soared, providing a dramatic counterpoint to the tense silence between them.

"Tell me," Chase said.

"Not yet," she whispered.

The song ended and the crowd filled the silence with roaring applause. The band left the stage and downed bottles of water, then met for shots. Gage beckoned to Chase, who backed away from Jamie. Gage handed him a shot glass, and the guys all clinked glasses and downed their shots. Chase turned back to Jamie.

"Please," he said. "Tell me. Say it."

The crowd was insane, wild.

Gage appeared. "We gotta go back on."

"One second," Chase said without looking at his friend.

"We don't have a second. They're gonna fuckin' riot, man." Gage looked frustrated, sounded irritated.

"Go," Jamie said.

"No. Tell me."

Jamie squeezed her eyes shut. "Go, Chase. A few more songs. Then we can talk."

Chase took her arms in his hands, ignoring the screaming fans. "I'm not going on until you tell me. Say it."

She was hyperventilating, fear boiling through her. She couldn't resist the pleading note in his voice. A tear slipped down her cheek.

She forced her eyes to his. "I'm pregnant."

He blinked, rocked back on his heels, his fingers loosening on her arms, blinked again, sucked in a deep, ragged breath. Then he blinked fast, as if holding back tears of his own. "I knew it," he said, more to himself. He pulled her against his chest. "You're positive?"

"I saw a doctor. No question. I'm eight weeks."

"Phoenix," Chase said.

"Yeah. Phoenix."

Gage grabbed Chase's shoulders. "I know something heavy just went down, and I'm sorry to interrupt it, but we *have* to go back on. They're seriously about to fucking riot. *Now*, Chase."

Chase struggled for composure, clearly fighting emotion. "Jamie, god...I—"

"This is why I wanted to wait. I'm sorry, Chase, I'm sorry—"

"Sorry? Fuck no. Don't be sorry. I love you. I gotta go, but...shit. Fuck." He kissed her roughly, desperately. "I love you. I love you."

Then he was gone.

Chapter 8

*C*hase ran through the last part of the show on autopilot. He felt a distant sense of amazement that he was able to function at all. He was numb. He was terrified. He was shocked. He was thrilled and excited.

He was happy.

He didn't know what he was, too overwhelmed by too many emotions to sort them all.

It all translated into a raging performance of their signature hit, ironically the number he'd written for Anna and performed in Vegas. He'd performed it so many times by this point that all emotional meaning had been leached out of the lyrics. Thank god for that.

The last notes hung in the air, settled over the wild audience like a blanket. The band bowed as Chase introduced them all, then they began to file offstage. As he passed out of view of the crowd, Chase felt a bolt of inspiration hit him. He knew what he wanted to do. It was crazy, but it was inevitable, once the idea hit him.

He grabbed his guitar and a little black box he'd been carrying around for almost two weeks. The house lights had started to come up, but then the tech saw Chase onstage with a guitar and lowered them, hit him with a spotlight. The crowd froze, returning their seats. Offstage, confused whispers echoed.

He turned, beckoned a stage tech and whispered a few requests. The tech scurried away and returned with a guitar amp cord, a mic stand, and two stools.

Chase adjusted the stand, plugged in the guitar, and then turned to the crowd. "This is unplanned, me being out here alone. I hope you'll bear with me for a few minutes." He lifted the guitar in a gesture. "A little known fact about me is that I play the guitar. I don't play on stage because, shit, you've all heard Kyle. The guy can shred better than anyone I know, so why would I bother? But…this is a special occasion."

The crowd howled and clapped, then fell silent when Chase lifted his hand. "As you may be aware, this was our first show playing as the headlining band, which, of course, is fucking huge. Right? And we're all from the D, so it's extra special. You guys are awesome. I know I speak for the rest of the band when I say there's nothing like playing at home. And to be here? In the Palace? It's a dream come true. So yeah, special occasion." The crowd went nuts again, and Chase had to quiet them. "But that's not why I'm out here alone with my guitar. You guys are about to hear a song no one has ever heard before. Not even the other guys in the band. Will you let me play you my song?"

They screamed, and several yells of "yes!" rose above the din.

"Awesome," Chase said, readjusting the mic, fidgeting with the tightening knob, then strummed a chord. "This song is for Jamie. In fact, I think you guys need to meet Jamie. She's the love of my life, and she should be sitting here with me when I sing this. Jamie, come on out."

Gage appeared, pushing a stunned, terrified Jamie. She sat on the stool next to Chase, her green eyes wide.

Chase took her hand, whispered in her ear. "Just sit there and be beautiful, okay? You don't have to do anything but look at me and listen, okay? Just listen. This is what I was playing earlier."

Jamie nodded, sucking in deep, shuddering breaths.

Chase turned on the stool and moved the mic so he was half-facing the crowd and half-facing Jamie. Into the mic he said, "I've been working on this song for a while now, and waiting for the right opportunity to sing it to Jamie. Initially the plan was for it to be at a picnic or some shit, somewhere romantic where it was just us. But…" he glanced at Jamie and offered her a bright smile, "but Jamie gave me some…news just a little bit ago, and that changes everything. Everything. So, here it is.

"It's called 'A six-word spell.'"

Chase cleared his throat, then picked a simple but haunting melody on the guitar. He met Jamie's eyes and began singing in a high, clear voice, at the upper end of his register.

"A skein of kisses
Trails from my heart to yours,
Tangling our souls one with the other
In an endless web of heat and desire.
I hold you tight and whisper as we kiss,
You clutch me close with desperate fingers
As we drowse in the afterglow,
Drowning delightfully in satiety."

He paused in his singing and repeated the opening notes as an instrumental chorus, eyes locked on Jamie, his gaze unwavering and fierce. He saw the emotion in her eyes, the wonder and hope and stunned confusion. She glanced out at the crowd, then back at him. He smiled at her, then returned his lips to the mic and resumed singing.

"The days and moments and weeks that went before this night
Are but a dream, lost and burnt by the fire between us.
And now all that remains is love,
Our fingers twined as we sleep,
Our hearts beating as one.
Apart from you, I bleed.
Without you I mourn.
How can I bind you to me?
How can I seal closed the spaces between us?
With a six-word spell, a vow spoken:
'With this ring, I thee wed.'
Marry me, my love.
Be my forever."

Chase repeated the chorus notes again, playing through his own emotion, fighting a thickness in his throat, stinging in his eyes. Jamie's face was streaked by a flood of tears. Chase let the guitar go silent, set it down on the stage and slipped off his stool, grabbing the mic from the stand. He had the little black box in his hand, and he sank to his knees in front of Jamie. She put her hands over her mouth, shoulders shaking.

"Jamie, I know this is totally crazy. This is probably not a really typical way to do this, but…it's the only way I know. And…I love you. Too much to let another day go by. That song was my proposal." He opened the box to reveal a one-carat, princess cut diamond ring, simple but beautiful. "Will you marry me?"

The crowd lost it, and Jamie's whispered "Yes," was lost in the screams and applause. Chase heard it, though, read it on her lips and on her face. He stood up scooped her against his chest, holding the mic away so it didn't *thump* noisily. He kissed her, to the delight of the audience. He heard a question shouted by someone near the stage and lifted the mic to his lips.

"Oh, I didn't tell you what the news is, did I?" He glanced at Jamie, lifting his eyebrow in a silent question. She shrugged and nodded, laughing. "Well, the news is, Jamie is pregnant. We're going to be parents together. Now, just so there aren't any questions from you guys *or* from her, I was writing this song with the intention of proposing well before Jamie told me she was pregnant."

Jamie laughed, almost hysterically. She took Chase's hand, gazing at the ring on her finger, then glanced out at the crowd, which hadn't stopped screaming since the moment Chase asked the question. She leaned close to his ear and whispered, "Get me off this stage, Chase. I need you alone."

He grinned at her, then looked back out at the crowd. He took her hand in his, turned them to face the crowd and raised their joined hands. "I love you, Detroit. Thanks for putting up with my sappy proposal song. I hoped you liked it." They screamed their approval. "Now, if you'll excuse us, we have some celebrating to do."

The screaming went on and on, well after Chase and Jamie had left the stage and the house lights had risen.

The moment they were offstage, Jamie shoved Chase with all her strength against the wall, slamming him into it so hard his breath left him in a huff. He was stunned by her sudden fierceness, looked into her eyes. The intensity he saw in her jade-green orbs left him breathless.

She kissed him hard, kissed the hell out him. Kissed him so fiercely he couldn't breathe, couldn't do anything but kiss her back.

"Did you mean it?" Her voice was a harsh, ragged whispered plea.

"Did I—? *Yes,* Jamie. I love you. I love *us.* I want to marry you."

"But not just because I'm pregnant with your child?"

"God no. No. That just made me want to marry you even sooner. Now. Tomorrow. Next week. I don't know when. But…You're mine. And I want you to be mine forever."

"I am yours forever. I just…I was so scared." She ducked her head. "I'm *still* scared."

Chase laughed, a nervous chuckle. "Me too. You're pregnant. We're having a baby. I don't know shit about fatherhood. This is…so unexpected."

"I know, I know it's bad timing, and I'm sorry but—"

"Don't apologize. Never apologize. This is perfect. Just like you." He pinned her with an intense stare. "You weren't afraid I wouldn't… that I'd run, or something, were you? That I'd leave you to raise our child alone?"

Jamie shook her head. "No, I know you better than that. But it was still scared of it. I couldn't help it." She laughed and cried at the same time. "This is just the worst possible timing. Your band is bigger than ever and still growing, especially with how this show went, and I'm about to be promoted to GM at work, and…I'm not ready. I don't…I don't know how to be a wife, or a mother. I never thought I'd get married. Really *really* never thought I'd be a mother. I don't know *how.* I'm not even sure I want to, but I'm going to be, like it or not."

"Unexpected, yes. Unwanted? No. I'm not ready either. But we can do this together. Okay?" He took her cheeks in his palms, drew her close to him and kissed her, gently and carefully. "I'm happy you're pregnant. Scared shitless, but ready to take this on, with you."

Jamie thunked her head against his chest and went limp. "Thank god. I didn't know what you'd say. I didn't know—god. I've been so scared for so long."

Chase led her into a walk, took her to the bus and into his room. They needed privacy. Chase felt his own emotions spiraling out of control, needed time alone with her to process. To hold her.

To make love to her.

He pulled her down onto the bed with him and held her close. She nestled in his arms, then turned her bright gaze on him, her eyes burning.

"I need you," she whispered. "Take me."

Jamie's heart was pounding a million miles an hour. As if they hadn't made love a hundred, hundred times by now, as if she didn't know every inch of his body. As if she hadn't felt him settle above her just like this a thousand delicious times. She watched him peel off his clothes, lifted up to let him strip her, watched rapt as he stood raking her body with his gaze. She couldn't take her eyes off his erection, pink skin ridged and purple-veined, broad head dark with rushing blood. He simply stood, breathing, each breath causing his cock to bob, beckoning her touch.

She resisted the call, waiting for him. She wanted his touch, wanted to follow his lead. Before Chase she'd always been the one setting the pace, initiating and leading, hoping the flavor of the night could keep up with her. They never could, they could only try to last long enough to make it worth her time.

Chase? Oh god. He led her, he set the pace and took away the need for her to make decisions in the bedroom. She could trust him, wait for him, follow him. She could lay on her back and just breathe, knowing without a doubt Chase would take her to heaven and back.

She held her breath as he knelt on the bed and crawled over her. She forced her anticipation-tense body to relax as he prowled on all fours between her thighs, his eyes dark and predatory, his thick, heavy muscles rippling. She lifted her chin, arched her back up into his touch, sucking in a breath as his palms skated across her belly.

The look on his face told her what he was thinking. She stilled his hand on her womb, her palm on his, breathing deep and watching his eyes shine. The gleam of love turned to the glint of lust, and Jamie led his hand down her belly, over her pubis, guided his fingers into an inward curl, her eyes going hooded as he took the cue, took her away from now and into ecstasy. He captured both of her hands in his and raised them over her head, lifting her breasts to his lowering mouth. His hand left her wrists, and she forced herself to remain as he'd placed her. His hand traced a line down her cheek, his mouth sucked her nipple into an elongated ribbon of shooting heat, his fingers curled against her core and sent lightning thrilling through her womb. He pinched her nipple in his fingers, and now he set a complicated rhythm of suckling, curling, and pinching, a fiery trinity of sensation blazing like a comet through her body.

She fell willingly over the edge, bucking against his touch, biting her lip to remain silent. Chase didn't take mercy on her, kept her writhing with his mouth on her taut nipple, and as she crested the wave of her climax, he sliced into her, sent her juddering over the edge once again. He pulsed into her, deep and slow, lips worrying her nipple, fingers rolling the other, his hips pistoning with gentle force.

He knew what she needed, and he gave it to her. He raised his head and settled his torso against hers, cradled her head beneath his strong arms, held her in a hot embrace and moved with her, breathing her name in her ear, a prayer to their mutual pleasure. He met her eyes, locked gazes with her as they slid and slipped and tangled together, her arms scraping over his broad shoulders and lean waist, her feet catching at the tensing and releasing muscles of his ass, her lips stuttering on his neck and his stubble-rough jaw, her breath coming in hard gasps as he took her to new heights of need.

There were no words, no cries or screams or moans, only synchronous breaths in the silent room, only the sweat slick sliding of trembling limbs and eyes locked in an unwavering meeting of souls.

They came in unison, each gasping the other's name, the only spoken words.

There was no talk after that, either. Only fingers tangled and resting on her belly, both of their eyes staring at her womb. Jamie's thoughts were running in circles, incredulity at the life growing inside her, fear of screwing up, fear of not being enough, joy at Chase's crazy, romantic proposal, at his unflinching devotion to her. His bone-deep knowledge of exactly what she needed and his ability to make her feel loved and cherished and protected in a way uniquely Chase's.

She heard his breathing change and turned her eyes to his face, relaxed and handsome in repose. Her thoughts wandered back to before the concert. He'd been the rockstar, taking her with fierce, forceful, erotic power, then took the stage with the same dominant charisma, working the already-pumped crowd into a frenzy. He'd bled out on the stage, left pieces of his soul in the audience's ears. Then, when she'd spilled the news to him, he'd turned an arena into a coffee shop, transforming instantly from rockstar into singer-songwriter, using a simple, beautiful song to move every heart in attendance.

She held her hand up so the light caught the diamond and sparkled brilliantly. She felt an overwhelming rush of joy and fear bolt through her at the significance of the ring.

She let sleep steal over her, knowing Chase would wake up soon and want to go out with her.

Her last thought before succumbing to unconsciousness was, *what am I going to tell Anna?*

Chapter 9

*J*amie clenched her hand into a fist in a vain attempt to still the trembling. *I can do this*, she told herself. No, she couldn't. But she had to. She was distantly aware of the bright beauty of downtown Rochester, every building bathed in multicolored strings of lights. The streets were busy, bustling with bundled shoppers, breaths puffing white in the cold December air. Christmas was a few days past, and Jamie had spent it with Chase. They'd both been introduced to each other's families, which was fine. Chase's mother was kind, small, dark-haired, with the same intense brown eyes as Chase. His father was absent from his life, a story Chase had shared late one night in a hotel in Indiana. His father had left with another woman when Chase was thirteen, and that had shaped his young mind and heart. It had also nearly destroyed, Kelly, his mother.

Chase had bought his mother a condo and a car, sent a huge check to her every month. He called her once a week.

Jamie's family was a bit more awkward of an experience. Her father and mother were still together, somehow, but she didn't see them very often. She had a strained, almost non-existent relationship with them, which was putting it nicely. Her parents had always made it clear they considered her a disappointment, when they bothered with her at all. Her mother had, during the last holiday get-together argument, called her a whore. Of course, her mother was the one strung out on prescription painkillers at the time, and her father stank of cheap perfume—the kind prostitutes wore.

Jamie had left, and hadn't seen her parents since.

Chase knew all this, and had been still willing to go with her for a Christmas Eve dinner. The shock on their faces when she'd introduced

Chase Delany—whom even they had heard of—as her fiancé and the father of her unborn baby, had been worth the awkwardness.

Chase's mom, however, had taken the news with joy, hugging Jamie like a daughter and asking a thousand questions about pregnancy to which Jamie didn't know the answers.

Now, Jamie was about to meet with Anna.

Jamie pulled into a parking spot and made her way into Gus O'Connor's. Anna was sitting at a high-top, sipping diet Coke from a straw. *That's odd*, Jamie thought, *Anna's not drinking wine*. They'd agreed to meet at Gus's, which had long been a favorite hang-out of theirs. They always split a bottle Kendall Chardonnay.

Jamie hugged Anna and sat down across from her. Anna seemed even happier than usual, glowing, almost. The server appeared and Jamie ordered a diet Coke and a burger, and as the server left to put in their order, Jamie noticed a puzzled expression cross Anna's face. Much like the one that had probably crossed her own, Jamie reflected.

"So, I have some big news," Anna said, grinning from ear to ear.

Jamie knew instantly what Anna was about to say. "I have some news too, but you go first."

Anna's features flickered in consternation, then shifted back to joy. "Okay, so you can't tell anyone yet, since only Jeff knows, but…I'm pregnant!"

Jamie smiled and squealed with Anna, asked the right questions about due dates and whether she thought it would be a boy or girl. She was happy for Anna, she really was, but in light of what Jamie had to say to Anna, her excitement was largely a show for Anna's benefit.

Finally, after they'd both eaten, Anna pushed her plate aside with a sigh. "Okay, hooker. Spill it. You said you have news too."

Jamie twisted her paper napkin between her fingers, struggling for calm. "Well, um. It's kind of a two-fold thing." Jamie had been trying to keep her left hand out of sight for most of the meal, and now she set her palm on the scuffed wood tabletop in front of Anna. "Chase proposed."

Anna blinked, then her eyes widened. "Ohmigod!" She seemed more stunned than happy. "He did? Ohmigod. Jamie, that's...that's wonderful! That ring is gorgeous!"

Jamie grinned, a real smile this time. "Yeah, it is. Wonderful, I mean. And the ring *is* beautiful."

Anna's eyes narrowed, her gaze zeroing in on the diet Coke Jamie was sipping on at that moment. "Oh...shit. You didn't order Coke just because I did, did you?" She leaned forward, both hands on the table, her eyes blazing. "You're *pregnant!*"

Jamie ducked her head. "Yeah. Nine weeks."

Anna sank back in her chair, clearly trying to process the news. "So he proposed when he found out he'd knocked you up, huh?"

Jamie physically flinched. "No!" She scrubbed her face with her palms. "Well yes, but it wasn't like that. He was going to propose anyway. He...it was—I'm happy, Anna. Be happy for me, can't you?"

"I'm just shocked, Jay. I don't know what to think. It was hard enough when I heard you'd slept with him. Now this? It's just a lot." She averted her gaze to the table. "If you're happy, then I'm happy for you."

"I am happy. I'm scared, I'll admit. I wasn't expecting this. Husbands and babies? Never thought they'd be in my future, but yet... now I can't imagine anything else. It just seems okay, with Chase. It's scary, but I know it'll be okay."

Anna nodded. "I know what you mean. I'm married to Jeff and everything, but I'm still scared. I don't know how to be a mom. I'm still learning how to be a wife."

Jamie tilted her head. "How is being a wife different from being a girlfriend?"

Anna laughed. "It's totally different. If you're dating someone, you know, in the back of your head, you can always just break up if things go wrong. You know, even if you're afraid of the process of breaking up, that you'll be able to move on. But once you're married, it's permanent. It's legal. Getting a divorce is messy and difficult and expensive, if nothing else. And...there's an element aside from all that. I'm his wife. I want to make him happy. I want to be everything he needs. It's not gender role thing, or a *Leave it to Beaver* thing. I'm not June Cleaver by any stretch of the imagination. But I still want to be the best wife I can be for Jeff. Maybe that makes me old school, or traditional, or oppressed by some women's standards. But it's what I want."

Jamie didn't answer for a long time. When she did, her voice was hesitant. "See, I don't even know where to start with all that. You know, for all the sleeping around I did before Chase, I've never lived with a boyfriend. I've never had a boyfriend long enough for that to be a consideration. Living with you was different. We were roommates, and we barely saw each other at home. I don't know the first thing about being married. Am I supposed to do his laundry and cook his meals? He's a rockstar. I don't know how being married to him is supposed to work. I don't know how to be a mother. I'm terrified of how bad giving birth is going fucking hurt. I'm—I'm happy, but I'm scared."

"Don't take this the wrong way, but I'm just worried all this with Chase and you is happening too fast. He's a man on the move. He was just on Conan O'Brien, for fuck's sake. Headlining concerts, *sold-out* concerts at that. How is he supposed to be a father? A husband? I'm not gonna lie, I'm worried, Jay."

"You think I'm not?" Jamie snapped.

"But this is what you want?"

Jamie sighed, holding back tears. "Yes. I love him. But regardless of what I want, I'm pregnant with his child, Anna. And he's not gonna just run off, you know that as well as I do. He wrote this song for me, and it was how he was going to propose. He had the ring and everything, for like two weeks. And then I found out I was pregnant but didn't tell him right away, because he was touring and it just never seemed like the right time, and I was scared of how he was going to react and—and then the show at Palace happened. He was so amazing, Anna. You should have seen him. But he knew something was up with me, and I didn't want to tell him until after the show, not wanting to distract him or whatever."

"But that didn't work," Anna said.

"No, that didn't work. He looked so torn up by whatever it was he was thinking I was gonna tell him. I think he kinda suspected. So I told him, right near the end of the show. Right in the middle of the fucking concert."

"Like, he was onstage when you told him?"

"No, dumbass," Jamie laughed. "He was offstage during an instrumental number the rest of the band was doing. He pulled me aside and begged me to tell him what was wrong. So I did. Then Gage dragged him back on to finish the concert, which he did. I don't know how, but he did."

"He's a consummate performer, if nothing else. The man knows what he's doing onstage, I'll give him that."

"So then the show ended and the lights were going up and everything. I mean, people were getting up to leave, and Chase just swaggers out on stage with a guitar."

"He plays the guitar? I didn't know that."

"Yeah, neither did I, oddly. I mean, he's a singer, and he writes all their songs, so I guess it shouldn't be too much of a surprise, but it was. So he gets a mic and a stool and plugs in the guitar and goes into this whole bit about how he doesn't usually do this kind of thing but it's a special occasion."

"Oh, shit. I think I know where this is going."

"Yeah, it's going there. So then he calls me out onstage with him. In front of a sold-out Palace crowd. *Me*. And then he sings this incredible song, which ended with him proposing, *in the song*. The song *was* the proposal. And then he showed me this ring and I said yes and we kissed on stage in front of thousands of people…god, Anna. It was the craziest thing that's ever happened to me. And he'd been planning on proposing that way all along, just not in front of a huge crowd, I guess. But then he found out I was pregnant and just couldn't wait."

Anna shook her head. "That would have mortified me, but...it works for you, I think."

"I was shitting myself, Anna. It was sweet and romantic and incredible, but...terrifying. I'm not even a performer like you."

They sat in silence for several long minutes, each thinking.

Then Anna spoke. "So we're going to have babies together, Jay. You realize that? I'm a little over nine weeks myself."

"That's crazy, Anna. You and me, both with men, both about to have babies. At the same time."

Anna threaded her fingers through Jamie's. "BFF's, Jay. This thing with you and Chase is tough, but...You're clearly happy with him, so all I can do is be happy for you. We'll be fine. It'll be fine, right? Our men will learn to be friends, and Chase and I will get over the awkwardness, right?"

"There's only one thing to do, at this point, you know that right?" Jamie took a deep breath. "We have to go on a double date."

Anna's eyes widened. "You do remember that Jeff punched Chase, right?"

Jamie winced. "It might be a little awkward, yes."

Both women giggled nervously at the prospect.

Chase tried to ignore the butterflies in his stomach as he and Jamie followed the hostess back to the booth in Andiamo's where Anna and Jeff were waiting. He held Jamie's hand loosely, forcing himself not to clench her hand as tight as he could.

"Hey, it's gonna be fine," Jamie said.

"Yeah. I know."

"Just breathe and be yourself, okay?"

"It's been more than a year since I saw her last, and a lot has changed since then," Chase said. "In my head, I know it's fine. But I just can't help being nervous."

Jamie just squeezed his hand. Anna and Jeff both stood up as Chase and Jamie approached. Chase eyed Jeff warily, resisting the urge to rub his jaw where Jeff had decked him. Jeff seemed relaxed, but the tension in the corners of his eyes betrayed his nerves. Anna had always worn her heart on her sleeve, so Chase could easily see that she was every bit as nervous as he was.

Chase shook Jeff's hand, then turned to Anna. "Hi," he said.

His hands hung loose at his sides. He wasn't sure if he should hug her or not, and Anna seemed just as confused. He settled for leaning in from far away and giving her the kind of hug he'd give to a great aunt he didn't see but once every few years: careful, hesitant, and awkward.

"Hi," Anna said, stepping away.

Her jaw was tight, Chase saw. She was taking slow, careful breaths, hands at her sides, rubbing her dress as if to dry sweaty palms.

"You look great," Chase said. "Jamie told me you and Jeff are expecting, so…congratulations."

"Thanks. Yeah, we're pretty happy." She glanced at Jeff, seemed to draw strength from his presence. "I hear double congratulations are in order for you and Jamie. Engaged *and* pregnant."

"Yeah, thanks…"

Jeff pinched the bridge of his nose, groaning. "You two are so awkward right now, it's making *me* nervous." He put his hand on the small of Anna's back. "As much as I hate to suggest this, the only way for any of us to enjoy dinner is if you and pretty boy here go and talk this out. Get the awkward shit out of the way."

Chase rolled his eyes at the nickname, then nodded. "You're probably right, cowboy." He and Anna went to the bar, found seats side by side. "Mind if I have a drink?" He asked.

"No, go ahead. I could use one, but I'm saving my one half-glass of wine allowance for after dinner."

Chase ordered a whisky on the rocks, and they sat in silence while the bartender poured it. Chase took a sip, then turned sideways on the barstool and faced Anna. "You really do look great, Anna. You're glowing."

She laughed. "Everyone says that about pregnant women, and I have to admit, I don't see what the hell people are talking about. Jamie looks happy, but glowing?"

Chase shrugged. "It's kind of a stupid phrase, isn't it? I mean, clearly you're not actually glowing, 'cause that'd be weird."

"Yeah, probably not too great for the baby, either."

They laughed together, and the tension seemed to ease. Then Anna drew a deep breath, and Chase knew the serious part of the talk was about to happen.

"I don't know if I believe that everything happens for a reason, but I want to preface this by saying, I'm glad things happened the way they did. I wouldn't change anything—"

"I wouldn't either—"

"Let me finish," Anna cut in. "What I need to say is that I'm sorry for not giving you a chance to explain, back in New York. It seems like a million years ago, like it happened to someone else. But the fact remains, I wasn't fair you."

Chase let out a breath he hadn't known he was holding, a breath he felt like he'd been holding since that day in New York. "Thank you, Anna. You can't know how much that means to me." He found her gray eyes wit his, shocked by how familiar, yet how foreign her eyes were to him, after all this time. "I didn't do anything with them, you know. Not that it changes anything, but...you should know. Those girls were coming on to me. I was pushing them away."

"I know that now. But then, all I saw was the thing I was most afraid of, happening. I heard you say something about not wanting me to find out, and—"

"What I was going to say was, 'I don't want Anna to see this and think I'm cheating on her.'" He sipped his whisky. "I was really mad for a long time, Anna. I felt so *wronged*, you know?"

"Like I said, I'm sorry. I didn't give you a chance to explain, then or later. But...I don't think it would have worked with us, even if there wasn't Jeff in the picture."

Chase nodded. "Yeah, you're probably right."

Anna paused for a long moment, then said, "Chase…do you still have feelings for me? Truly?"

He set the tumbler down and stared into the amber depths. "Now? No. Is there some tiny part of me that wonders what might have been? Sure. A tiny part. But the rest of me knows that if you left like you did, then we weren't meant to be. If you had wanted it to work, then you would have given me a chance to explain." He met Anna's eyes. "Do you, for me?"

"Like you said, there's a tiny part of me that wonders, but it's so insignificant in comparison to the way I love Jeff, and the way I already love this little life inside me, that it doesn't even matter."

Chase nodded his agreement, feeling the same way. He let himself really look at Anna. He could admit to himself that he was still attracted to Anna on some physical level, since she was a beautiful woman and was glowing with the shine of pregnancy, but it was the kind of attraction a guy would feel for a movie star, distant and idle. He'd been worried that if he saw Anna all he would be able to think of was the time they'd spent together. He was worried he'd have images of her in his head, the way they'd been together.

That wasn't there, though. All he saw was Anna, his fiancée's best friend. Those images had long ago been scoured away by the force of Jamie in his mind, in his soul, in his heart, in his body. If he closed his eyes and thought of sex, all he could see was Jamie, green eyes bright and copper curls wild as she came apart beneath him. There had never been anyone else but her.

"So we can be friends?" Anna asked.

"Friends," Chase answered, shaking her hand.

There was no spark when their hands touched, no electricity between them. He finished his whisky and they went back to the table, finding Jamie and Jeff deep in discussion about some movie or another.

The rest of the dinner was comfortable. There were still some awkward silences, but it was clear the bulk of the brooding tension everyone had been worried about had dissipated.

When they all parted, Chase gave Anna a hug, a real hug this time. "I'm happy for you," he said to her. "All I ever wanted was for you to be happy, and to see your own worth. Now you do, and I'm—I'm happy for you."

Anna stepped away from him, toward Jeff, but she kept her eyes on Chase, a tear shining in one eye. "You did, Chase. You helped me see my own worth, and that was a priceless gift. So…thank you."

She turned away before he could respond, and he was glad.

Jamie twined her fingers in his, gazing up at him as he watched Anna and Jeff drive away.

Chapter 10

Jamie tried unsuccessfully not to fidget while Kelly Delany adjusted the pins holding her veil in place. She couldn't help shifting in the chair, however. She was jittery with nerves and excitement. More excitement than anything else.

"Hold *still*, Jamie," Kelly hissed. "I've almost got it, if you would just sit still for five seconds."

"I'm sorry, Kelly. I'm just excited."

"Of course you are. But unless you want to marry my son with your veil half on, you'll sit still."

Jamie drew a deep breath and let it out slowly, closing her eyes and picturing Chase in his tuxedo. She tried *not* to picture herself helping him out of it; she wasn't quite successful in this either, and she felt her belly flutter and her core grow warm at the images running through her head. She must have shifted unconsciously, because Kelly hissed as a pin came loose. Finally the veil was in place and Kelly was standing back, admiring her handiwork. Jamie finally allowed herself to stand up, turn in place and look at herself in the mirror.

She wore a strapless, high-waist dress, the material gathered beneath her breasts and draping over her curves. Her belly was still obvious beneath the dress, but it still managed to conceal the slight bump while flattering her figure. Her hair was mostly down, the curls brushed to a shine and teased and sprayed into a luxurious fall of springy copper ringlets, just the curls around her face drawn back behind her head. She fought a rush of tears at her own reflection, at the realization that she was about to walk down the aisle and marry Chase.

She breathed deeply, pushed the welter of emotions down and turned back to Kelly. "Thank you so much, Kelly. I don't know what I would have done without you."

Anna returned from the bathroom at that moment, and immediately held a crumpled Kleenex to her eyes. "Jay, you look—" she sniffed back tears. "You look incredible. So beautiful. You're gonna take his breath away."

"I hope so."

"I know so. Hooker, you sexy." Anna frowned. "I probably should stop calling you, that, huh? Now that you're being made an honest woman."

Jamie glared at her best friend. "If you stop calling me 'hooker,' we'll be fighting. How am I supposed to know you're my best friend if we don't call each other names?"

Anna laughed and pulled Jamie into a hug. "Seriously. You look stunning. I can't believe you're about to get married."

"Me neither. Now let go before you mess up my veil. Kelly might kill you if you mess it up," Jamie said, backing away.

"Fine, ho."

"Shut up, bitch."

Anna smoothed her dress over her belly. "Two pregnant women hugging. That's awkward."

"You're awkward."

Kelly stepped between them, fluttering her hands. "Enough, you two. We have a wedding to get on with."

Jamie took a deep breath, sobering. "Lead the way, Mom-to-be."

Kelly and Anna walked ahead of Jamie, leading her to the double doors leading into the chapel. Jeff was waiting by the doors, rugged and handsome in his tuxedo. Jamie took his proffered arm, let out another deep breath, then nodded. Kelly and Anna pushed open the doors, preceding Jamie down the aisle.

In the months between Christmas and the wedding date, things between Jamie and her parents had grown worse, a combination of jealousy over Jamie's happiness, hypocritical disapproval of her being pregnant and unmarried, and just plain cantankerousness. Eventually, Jamie had made the decision to have Jeff give her away at the wedding, and left her parents out of it. The moment she made the decision, she'd felt a weight fall away from her, and the well of happiness inside her had only grown deeper. Her parents had never been much to her besides a source of trouble and hurt, so the decision to stop trying completely had been a relief.

Now, she walked down the aisle at a stately pace, the wedding march played by live string quartet. The chapel pews were about half-filled, mostly with Chase's friends and family. Jamie's aunt and uncle on her mom's side had shown up by invitation, and a few of her other friends, most notably Lane and his partner Matty. There was no bride and groom's side, although Chase's band and their girlfriends took up a large portion of the chapel on the right side.

Her eyes found Chase's. He looked stunned, his eyes wide, jaw slack, gaze wavering in shocked adoration. Jamie felt a hot bolt of desire for him. That need, it was always there, simmering just beneath the surface. No matter how much time she spent with him, her hunger for his sculpted body and skilled hands and hot mouth never lessened.

If anything, she wanted him more than ever with every passing day.

His eyes raked over her a second time, and this time she saw the tender lover give way to the fierce fires of lust. She took his hands when she reached him, barely hearing the words passing around her. She barely heard as the minister spoke the words, although she reacted in the correct places, her attention was focused on Chase, on his chiseled features, high cheekbones and strong jaw, blazing brown eyes and simple black plugs in his gauged ears, plain black leather bands circling his wrists beneath the sleeves of his tuxedo. His head was freshly shaved, gleaming in the light. His arms stretched the material of the suit, custom cut to fit his powerful physique like a glove.

The service passed quickly, to Jamie. They exchanged the standard vows, which Jamie made it through dry-eyed.

Then, after the minister pronounced them man and wife and they'd kissed, Chase turned to Jamie with a grin. "I proposed to you with a song, so it only makes sense that I marry you with one," he said.

A guitar was brought to him from somewhere, and he slipped the strap over his head, strummed the strings with the pick, adjusted the tuning a bit, and then took a deep breath, letting it out slowly. He strummed again, then set about picking the tune of song he'd proposed to her with. A Youtube video of his proposal song had surfaced and gone viral, so many people in the pews had probably heard it already, but Chase had a way of capturing attention and keeping it, no matter what he did.

He sang the song through, his eyes never leaving Jamie's. Then he got to the ending lines, which Jamie realized he'd altered slightly to suit the occasion. Now, he sang,

"How did I bind you to me?
How did I seal closed the spaces between us?
With a six-word spell, a vow spoken:
"With this ring, I thee wed."
You married me, my love.
You are my forever."

Now Jamie's emotions, contained up to this point, burst free. She flung herself at Chase as the last notes hung in the air, and he slung the guitar by its strap around his back to wrap her in his arms. He pressed his lips to hers and devoured her mouth, then pulled away, whispering, "I love you, Jamie Delany."

She grinned at the sound of her name joined with his, but she was still crying too hard to speak the words back. She just pressed her cheek to his and let him guide her out of the chapel. He stood with her on the steps in the bright spring sunshine, his arms strong around her. Now, alone with him, albeit briefly, she was able to speak.

"I love you so much, Chase. So much." She rested her chin on his chest and gazed at him, letting her eyes take on a lustful, playful burn. "You look so hot in that tux, by the way."

Chase rumbled in laughter. "You, in that dress…I'm not sure how I'm gonna make it through the reception without pinning you against a wall and fucking your brains out."

Jamie smiled lasciviously, reaching between their bodies to stroke his zipper, feeling him come to life under her touch. "So don't."

"Seriously?" He quirked an eyebrow at her.

"Would I joke about such a thing?"

He kissed her again, but it was broken up by the doors opening. They pulled apart and greeted the people streaming out of the chapel, thanking them for coming and exchanging other pleasantries. Eventually the last of the attendees were gone and she and Chase, along with Anna, Jeff, and Kelly, and Gage, the rest of the bridal party, took the requisite pictures.

The reception was long, loud, and fun. She ate, danced and mingled for hours, always mindful of her promise to Chase. Finally, she found a moment to slip away to the bathroom. She paused in the doorway, catching Chase's eye. He grinned at her and nodded. She watched him casually break off a conversation with Gage's girlfriend's brother and make his way toward her. She scurried ahead of him, waiting until she reached the end of the hallway. He caught sight of her, and she ran ahead. She heard his rough chuckle of amusement as she bustled ahead of him in as fast a run as she could manage with her dress. She came to another corner, waited until he was in sight of her, then ran ahead. Finally she came to a darkened but unlocked office at the farthest end of the reception hall, far away from the crowd and the staff. She made sure he saw her enter, then leaned back against a wall, breast heaving, laughter on her lips.

Chase burst into the office, caught sight of her, his eyes glinting with predatory amusement. He was barely panting, despite having jogged after her across the building. He closed the door behind himself, the *snick* of the latch closing deafening in the silent room. He simply stood there for a moment, hands loose at his sides, head tilted slightly as he devoured her figure with his gaze. She felt his eyes like heat on her every curve, felt his lust for her, his raw, potent desire as a palpable force.

She didn't move a muscle, simply stood with her back pressed to the wall, chest heaving, breasts straining against the white chiffon of her dress, her breath coming in deep gasps—from anticipation and desire now rather than exertion.

Chase swallowed the short distance between them in two long strides, pressing his hips against hers, his forehead bumping hers, palms flattened against the wall to either side of her face. She brushed her hands up his torso, resting them on his shoulders.

"You're beautiful, Jamie. Breathtaking. A goddamn vision."

Jamie smiled. "Thanks." She slid her mouth across his, then bit his lower lip. "So. Gonna fuck my brains out now?"

"Yeah, sure am."

She breathed a sigh. "Oh, good."

He chuckled, then lowered one hand to her waist, across her belly, then up to her breast. Her breath caught as she forgot to resume breathing. His fingers tugged the cup of the dress down and her breast up, baring one dark pink nipple. He lowered his mouth to it and flicked it with his tongue. Jamie's breath returned with a gasp.

His hand curled into the fabric of her dress at her hip, bunching the material, gathering it, revealing her legs an inch at a time. He pulled the dress up past her hips, and then his breath stopped with a long groan.

"*Fuck*, Jamie. You haven't been wearing any panties this whole time? Jesus. *Jesus*, Jay. It's a good thing I didn't know until now or we wouldn't have made it through the wedding."

She laughed, reaching between his arms to unbutton his tuxedo pants, then slid the zipper down. Jamie bit her lip as she dragged his boxers down to his knees, freeing the erect weight of his cock.

She circled her fingers around him, sliding down his length and back up. Chase sucked in a breath, closing his eyes briefly. When he opened them, they were on fire with need. He slid his palm around the back of one her thighs, lifting it up to his waist, then he moved his hand to her other thigh and Jamie's eyes widened, realizing what he intended.

"God, are you crazy? You can't lift me up—"

She was cut off by him doing exactly that. Jamie clenched her legs around his waist and braced her back against the door, wrapping her arms around his neck. She was split immediately in two by his impatiently thrusting cock. Jamie lifted her face to the ceiling and whimpered in her throat, filled and stretched and impaled and completed by his manhood in her sex.

Chase buried his face in her breasts and crashed up into her, heedless of her weight, his palms cupping her ass beneath the draped dress. She'd been filled by Chase before, had felt him drive deep in a thousand different positions, but never had he been this deep. The base of his cock pushed perfectly against her clit as he drove into her with short, hard, piston thrusts. Her fingers curled around his nape, her palm flattened over the bald dome of his scalp, and she found herself lifting up and sinking down to meet him, her mouth pressed to the front of his head, muffling her cries.

Chase grunted and growled into the soft flesh of her breasts. Jamie lifted up and sank down with an exponentially-increasing urgency, and the chorus of sighs and gasps coming from them both filled the tiny office. Jamie felt the delicious heat and pressure coiling in her belly, the weight and lightning of impending climax, and she knew by the constant growling coming from Chase—from her husband—that he was close too.

"Now, baby," Jamie whispered. "Come with me."

"God, yes," Chase answered, and she felt the liquid heat of his essence fill her at the same moment that her entire being exploded from within, wave after wave billowing through her. She cried out into

Chase's shoulder, biting the rough fabric of his suit coat, and he in turn muffled his bellow of release in her cleavage.

Chase held her aloft for another moment, then extracted himself from her folds and let her slide down to her feet. He held her dress up around her hips with one hand and reached to snatch a handful of Kleenex from the nearby desk with the other. He cleaned her carefully and thoroughly before letting her dress down.

She smoothed out the wrinkles, although by this point in the night it didn't really matter, watching as Chase made himself presentable once more.

He grinned at her. "How are your brains, Mrs. Delany?"

"Very thoroughly fucked out, Mr. Delany, thank you." She adjusted his tie for him, and he rubbed her upper lip with his thumb.

"You'll have to fix your makeup," he said. "You're a bit…smudged."

Jamie nodded, glancing down to make sure she was presentable. She looked up, feeling Chase's gaze on her. "What?"

His eyes were blazing, his fingers flexing into the fabric of her dress at her hips. "I just…I guess it just struck me that we're actually, factually married, now. You're mine. Really mine, forever." His voice was thick with emotion, and Jamie felt herself melting at the unusual sight of tears in his eyes. "I don't know how I got so lucky, Jay. You're… so much more than I could ever have dreamed for myself. I don't know what I'd do without you. Thank you for marrying me, Jay. I just…I hope to be the husband you deserve."

Jamie threw herself against him. He was open with his emotions, with her at least, but she'd never seen him bare himself this way, raw and completely vulnerable. She wanted to say something back, something equally as dramatic and poetic, but words escaped her.

"You already are, Chase. You wrote it in your song. 'You are my forever.'"

He pulled her into a kiss more potent than anything they'd ever shared before, a scorching, melting, soul-merging kiss that left them both breathless and bated.

"We'd better stop now, or our guests will start wondering what happened to us," Jamie whispered.

Chase's hands skated around her waist to cup her ass. "They're all drunk already anyway, most likely," he said, his voice rough with renewed desire. "Let them wait."

"Fuck 'em?" Jamie asked, laughing into his mouth.

"No," Chase said, turning her to the desk and bending her over it, lifting her dress. "I'm gonna fuck you."

"Oh, good." Jamie lifted her hips, giving him access as he freed his erection and rubbed its length against the seam of her ass. "I was hoping you would say that."

Chase slid into her, and she moaned, writhing back against him.

"God, Jay. You feel so good," Chase growled. "So fucking tight."

"I love feeling you inside me," Jamie breathed. "Don't stop."

"Never."

"I want you like this forever. Deep inside me."

Chase's palms caressed her hips, and then pulled her into him. "Forever."

They breathed together, moved together, then their rhythm stuttered, and they came together, gasping in unison, panting.

When he slipped out of her, Jamie straightened and turned in his arms. "Forever? You promise?"

"Yes, my love, I promise. Forever."

THE END

Big Girls
Do It
Pregnant

Chapter 1: Anna

Jeff groaned in frustration, scrubbing his face with one hand. "Again, Anna? We've barely gone a hundred miles."

I sighed. "I'm sorry, Jeff. It's not like I can help it, you know."

He glanced at the GPS unit attached to the windshield beneath the rearview mirror. "Can't you hold it a bit longer? The city isn't that far away."

I shook my head. "I've *been* holding it. I had to go an hour ago, I just didn't say anything. Now I *have* to go, and no, I can't make it all the way downtown."

Jeff blew air out between his lips. "Never gonna make it to New York at this rate," he muttered under his breath as he began merging across traffic towards the interstate exit. "Stop to pee every hour, need a snack every half hour. Jesus."

I laughed. "Quit complaining, Jeff. I wanted to fly, but no, you didn't think it was safe."

"The doctor said no flying the last trimester. You're five months. I don't want to take any chances."

I slipped my hand under his. "And I get that. I appreciate your concern for me and our baby. But if you want to take a road trip with a pregnant woman, you have to know the risks. It's not like you haven't been living with me peeing and eating all the time for the last twenty weeks."

He huffed again as he pulled into a McDonalds parking lot. "I know, I know. I just didn't even want to go to New York in the first place. And now it's taking double the amount of time it should because you've suddenly got the bladder of a fucking chipmunk."

I snorted. "And you're an expert on chipmunk bladders, now? What if chipmunks can hold it forever?" I shoved open my door and heaved myself up and out. I wasn't a beached whale yet, but movement was getting more difficult every day. "And I know you didn't want to go, Jeff. But it's Jamie's baby shower. I can't miss it."

I closed the door on his grumbling about parties for babies who aren't even born yet, laughing at him still. Jamie was having her baby shower in New York City a lot sooner than normal because Chase's tour was hitting Madison Square Garden and he wouldn't be home again until she was about to pop.

I peed and got back in the Yukon, settling in for the last leg of our trip. Jeff grumbled a lot, but was always sweet and understanding. He'd dealt with my craziness for weeks now, and his complaints were always in good humor. If I asked him to get me a snack at two in the morning, he would. Fortunately, I hadn't had a lot of odd cravings so far. Mainly, I was hooked on Triscuits and cheese and sparkling lime water. Like, a box of crackers and a block of cheese a day, that kind of hooked. Jeff was buying the lime water by the case from Whole Foods. I also couldn't stand the smell or taste of chicken, tuna, or nail polish. I hadn't painted my nails since about the eleventh week, which was driving me nuts, as I'd been getting weekly or biweekly mani-pedis for years. I even tried pinching my nose and having Jeff paint my nails, but the smell lingered in the air and made me nauseous anyway. And I was already nauseous all the time, so that sucked. When Jeff made himself a tuna sandwich, I nearly barfed and started yelling at him so bad he actually took the tuna and threw it out the back door so I'd stop shrieking at him. Of course, I couldn't go outside until he'd cleaned that up, which sucked since I liked to sit on the porch and read.

The other truly awful part of being pregnant, so far, was that I had zero sex-drive. Just none. No motivation whatsoever. It wasn't that I found Jeff suddenly unattractive or anything, I was just nauseous all the time, and if I wasn't nauseous, I was tired or cranky, or some other combination of ridiculous hormonal imbalances. Which, of course, translated into a cranky, testosterone-ridden Jeff. He refused to take care of things himself, for some odd reason. He couldn't or wouldn't explain his aversion to it except that he believed, since he was married to me, that he wouldn't do that, even if it meant going weeks without sex. I kept telling him I wouldn't mind, since I just couldn't get in the mood even for a handjob, let alone a BJ.

I tried to go down on him, once, actually. It was about fifteen weeks in, and I was feeling okay that day. Jeff had been especially sweet, bringing me tulips and chocolate when he got back from work. I wanted to reward him for being so nice, especially after he rubbed my feet for twenty minutes. So after we'd gotten in bed, I ran my fingers along his bare stomach, pushed off his boxers and fondled him into erection.

His lips curved into a lazy smile as I glided my fingers around him, and then he sighed when I slid on my side down his body until my face was level with his shaft. I had him going, pumping him steadily until his hips began to move in time with my strokes. *So far, so good*, I thought. No nausea, no roiling in my stomach. Finally, as he was nearing climax, I took him in my mouth, shallowly at first, just the tip past my lips, sucking gently, cupping his balls and stroking his base still. He was groaning and sighing my name, and I felt good giving my man what he needed.

He tugged gently on my hair twice, crying out, "Oh god, Anna, yes...don't stop please...I'm coming now—god, thank you, thank you—" and then his voice trailed off into a wordless cry of release as he shot weeks-worth of pent-up come into my throat.

When he came, he came *hard*. Like a firehose, straight down my esophagus. Usually, that was fine. I don't think that's any girl's favorite thing ever, despite what I've heard some chicks claim. I mean, how could it be anyone's favorite thing? Even when you're ready for it, it's surprising. Jeff always tasted good to me, never bitter or too musky, and I really, truly didn't mind going down on him. I usually enjoyed the feeling of making him lose control, giving him such pleasure. I may not have found the actual experience erotic for myself, as in, I didn't get off on giving him head, but it was something I enjoyed doing for him.

I was suitably shocked, then, when I went from pleased with myself and loving Jeff's frantic gasping and groaning and almost pathetically desperate whispered thanks as he came in my mouth, to sudden and violent nausea.

It was like being shot by a vomit-cannon. The thick, salty, musky seed hit my throat and the back of my tongue, and instantly I felt my gorge rising. I wasn't gagging as if he'd pushed himself too deep; it was an immediate sickness.

I literally leapt off him, his cock leaving my mouth with an audible *pop*, and scrambled off the bed, barely making it into the bathroom before I heaved violently into the toilet.

Jeff—god bless the amazing man—was right there beside me, holding my hair back. He was panting, naked, still half-erect, and confused, but he was still thinking of me.

Even as I puked again, I felt a rush of love for him.

"I'm sorry," I gasped, glancing up at him between heaves. "It wasn't you, baby, I promise, I just...oh god—" and then I lost it once more, heaving until my now-empty stomach turned it into futile retching.

He held my hair with one hand, snatched a washcloth off the towel rack with the other and wet it down under the sink. Which wouldn't mean much to most people unless you knew that I tended to get sweaty after vomiting. Jeff had knelt beside me often enough at that point in the pregnancy to know this about me. He helped me sit back on my ass on the cold tile floor of the bathroom and wiped my face with the washcloth, brushing stray tendrils of my blond hair out of the way. I was gasping for air, clutching my still-tumbling stomach, groaning and praying that the nausea would pass.

When I finally thought it was passing, I struggled to my feet, clutching to Jeff for dear life. He helped me back to bed, slipped on his underwear and cradled me against his broad chest.

"I'm sorry, Anna. I should have known that would make you sick. I shouldn't have let—"

I cut him off. "I wanted to, Jeff. I really did. It just hit me really suddenly. I was fine all the way up until you came, and then I was just sick, like instantly. I don't know if I can do that again, though."

He sighed. "No kidding."

I couldn't help a little laugh at the wistful tone in his voice. "I really am sorry, Jeff. I know I've not really been in the mood lately. Hopefully the morning sickness phase will pass at some point."

He smoothed my hair away, and when he spoke his voice was heavy with sleep. "It's fine, baby. I'll live."

"Yeah, but you'll be cranky-horny all the time until I give it to you again," I said, sleepy now myself.

I barely registered his lazy grunt in response as I fell asleep.

After that, I hadn't even tried. I'd joined him the shower once, a week before we left for New York, and got him off with my hand, but when he tried to return the favor, I found myself unable to find a release. Eventually he gave up, both of us frustrated.

Now, with my feet sticking out the open car window to rest on the side-view mirror, I realized I hadn't been nauseous yet that day, or the day before. I hadn't puked in almost a week, actually. I glanced at Jeff, who had his chin propped on one hand and the other wrist draped over the steering wheel. As I watched, he absently took his hand off the wheel, reached down and adjusted himself inside his gym shorts.

Watching that, the brief movement of his hand tugging himself into a more comfortable position, or whatever it is guys do when they adjust their junk like that, I felt a twinge of something that could have been desire. It also may have been heartburn from having eaten McDonalds for the last five out of eight meals, but I was pretty sure it was desire.

I didn't say anything, I just tilted my seat father back, rested my head on an angle so I could watch Jeff without being obvious about it.

See, this whole no sex for the last three months thing was shitty for me too. I *wanted* to want him. I'd gotten used to having Jeff whenever I wanted him, daily, or nearly daily. Some days we'd both be busy or tired, but we'd never, since first getting together, gone more than a week without some kind of sexual liason, whether it was actual inter-course, oral sex, or just groping hands and kissing. So this whole *I want to want you but can't* business was getting old for me too. I watched him drive and tentatively imagined myself reaching over the console and touching him, perhaps just exploring the muscle and skin and dusting of hair on his belly at first. That went well. The picture fit, as it should. I pushed the idea, thought of running a single finger under the loose elastic of his shorts, feeling the scratchy pubic hair under my finger. That was a good image. No problems, yet. No nausea, no disinterest, no apathetic exhaustion.

A little further, mentally, then. I imagined—or maybe it was remembered—the feel of the soft, springy, warm tip of his cock against my hand, swelling in my fist as I lightly squeezed him. I pic-tured my hand loosely curled around his thickness, feeling the ridges and ripples and veins throbbing with life and desire and heat and seed. Mmmmm, yes. I liked that picture. This was good. I even felt my nipples harden a little as I pictured my fist sliding up and down his length. They peaked even more when I explored the memory of his body above mine, stroking deep.

I had to clamp my thighs together at that image. I thought I might have caught a whiff of my own sudden musk of desire, there and then gone, snatched away by the wind through the open window. We were approaching the outer edge of the city, suburbs becoming denser and highrises higher.

"How long till we're at the hotel?" I asked. I may have surrepti-tiously tugged the neck of my sleeveless camisole down to reveal a larger expanse of cleavage.

Jeff glanced sidelong at me, then did a double take at my breasts before looking away again. "Gotta pee again already?"

I laughed and crossed my arms under my breasts, which, by this point, were nearly spilling out, my nipples hard and visible against the fabric of my shirt. "No, surprisingly. Just...antsy."

He glanced again, and his gaze lingered longer on my mostly-exposed breasts. "Antsy, huh? Are you cold? Should I close the window?"

I gave him a confused look. "No, I'm fine. Why would you think I'm cold?"

He licked his lips, his gaze flickering to my breasts and then back to the road. He shifted in his seat and adjusted himself again, then gestured with a finger at my nipples. "You just look like you could cut glass, there."

I waited till he glanced back at me, then tugged the shirt down to reveal one breast with a hardened, erect nipple, which I tweaked with two fingers. "They are hard, aren't they?"

Jeff groaned and leaned forward in his seat, clutching the steering wheel with both hands. "God, Anna. Put that shit away. You're teasing me, here, babe."

He leaned back again and tugged the waistband of his shorts away from his body. When he let the fabric lay against his skin once more, I saw the telltale bulge.

"Who says I'm teasing?" I asked, pulling the other side down so both breasts were bare now.

It was past midnight at this point, and the city around was still bustling, cars passing on either side of us, street lights shedding orange glow, stoplights cycling, horns honking, steam billowing from manhole covers.

Jeff's eyes narrowed. "Anna, it's been three fucking months. Don't start something you can't finish." He glanced to either side of us, see-ing cars pull parallel to us. "And put your tits away, babe. Those are mine, not for public consumption."

I laughed and tucked myself back into my bra, but left the shirt tugged down to give him a good view. "No one's consuming anything, but fine, if that's how you want it. And that's my point, Jeff: I'm start-ing something I *want* to finish. So get us to the hotel already."

I pulled my feet back in the car, shut the window, and leaned toward Jeff, twisting in my seat to partially face him. I settled my hand on his thigh, and he covered my hand with his, following my touch as I let my hand drift up his thigh and under the hem of his shorts.

"I'm driving as fast I can." He glanced at me as I snaked my hand into the leg of his boxers to touch bare skin, finding his shaft. "Where are you going with this, Anna?"

I shifted in my seat for better leverage. "I don't know. I just want to touch you." I gave him a long, slow stroke, and smiled as he sighed, sliding down in his seat.

"God, Anna. You're making it hard to drive." He let his head flop back against the headrest.

"Want me to stop?" I clamped my fist around the tip of him, then rubbed the top of the head, smearing the sticky pre-come around him.

"Hell no. But I also don't want to have to change in the car before checking in. And there's no way I'm letting you go down on me in the car in the middle of New York City."

I slowed my stroking of him, but didn't let go. The more I touched him like this, the more I wanted him. It felt like my libido was coming back all at once, and with a vengeance. Suddenly, I found myself almost not caring if anyone saw. I was about to climb over the console and straddle him while he drove. Of course, my baby bump might get in the way, and he wouldn't be able to drive. I just held on to him, gripped him, touched him. He took corners too fast, stopped too abruptly. I grinned at his impatience, because I felt it too. My heart pounded in my chest as I imagined his arms around me, his body hard against mine. It had been forever, for-fucking-*ever*. An actual eternity, it seemed. Suddenly, it felt like a lifetime had passed since I last felt him sweat into my skin, felt his breath on my neck hot and fast as he panted my name.

I slid my thighs together and tried to get closer to him, but the stu-pid console and my baby bump were in the way and all I could do was touch him, feel him thick in my hands and hope the hotel was close. Jeff glanced at the GPS in the dashboard, made a few turns, and then slowed to enter a parking garage.

"Fucking finally," he muttered, stopping and rolling his window down to take the ticket.

I had to withdraw my hand, then, as he searched for a parking space. He found one, jammed the truck into park, and nearly jumped out to grab our bags from the trunk. I was slower to get out, but not by much. I smirked at Jeff as he set my suitcase down to adjust himself, his bulge clearly defined in his shorts.

"See what you do to me?" He asked, grinning.

I let my smirk fade into a sultry smile. "That's the whole idea, isn't it?" I sidled up to him, pressed my body against his and leaned up on my tiptoes to kiss him.

His lips met mine, tasting of Coke and faintly of Doritos. He moaned softly into my mouth as I slid my tongue between his lips, then louder as I slipped my hand between us to rub him through his shorts. My belly was a hard lump between us, not in the way, yet, but I realized within a few weeks, it would be. I wasn't sure how I felt about that.

A car passed by us, circling downward to a parking spot, honking as they slowed to watch us make out. Jeff pulled away, chuckling, and pushed me toward the elevator. When we were on and the door were closed, Jeff dropped the handles to our rolling suitcases and pinned me in the corner, taking my wrists in his hands and pinioning them above my head. I tilted my head back and bared my throat to the hot, wet kisses he planted there, moving down to the hollow at the base of my throat, and farther, to the valley of my breasts.

I gasped, sighing his name, needing more than breath to feel his hands on me, his mouth on me. I felt his hardness against my thigh as he kissed my cleavage, and I reached down to grasp it in my fingers. More, I needed more. I dug my hand under his shorts to clutch him bare in my hands, relishing the hot hardness of him. I was frantic, suddenly, trying to push his shorts down and my loose cotton skirt up.

And then he pulled away, leaving me limp and gasping and stunned in the corner of the elevator.

"I'm not going to fuck you in the corner of a dirty elevator, Anna," he growled, scrubbing his hand over his close-cropped scalp. "You have no idea how bad I want you right now, babe, but not like this."

I wanted to cry. A tear of absurd rejection slipped down my face. I brushed it away, irritated with myself. I was being stupid and I knew it. Jeff was right, so right, but the sudden inrushing of my sex drive was erasing my reason.

"Anna, I—"

I shook my head, cutting him off. "No, Jeff. You're right and I know it. I'm having one of those stupid hormonal reactions I can't exactly help." I laughed at myself through a sniffle, then tipped forward into Jeff's embrace. "Just take me to the hotel and fuck me until I can't walk."

Jeff's fingers tightened in my shoulders. "That I can do."

The elevator doors opened then, letting on a man, his wife, and three children, all chattering loudly in Arabic. Jeff and I traded glances, laughing. If Jeff hadn't stopped things when he did, this family would have gotten an eyeful.

Fifteen minutes later, we were checked in to our hotel and riding another elevator up to our floor. Jeff still had all of our luggage in his hands, refusing to let me carry more that my purse. My stomach was doing flip-flops as he slid the card into the reader and pushed the door open, flipping on lights and setting our suitcases against the wall.

I hadn't gotten three steps into the room when Jeff stopped, turned in place, and wrapped a large, strong hand around my elbow, drawing me inexorably against his chest. I dropped my purse on the floor at my feet and placed my palms on his pecs, staring up into his hot brown gaze. My heart was hammering in my chest, as if this was my first time.

Except, I knew what was coming and I needed it as much as my next breath.

He didn't do anything for the space of several heartbeats, only clutched my elbow, his thumb drawing a slow circle on my skin. I stood waiting, breathing, anticipating.

Then, he lifted his hand and brushed my cheekbone with the back of his index finger, trailed the pad of his finger down my neck, across my collarbone and down between my breasts. I sucked in a deep breath, swelling my breasts, and held it. He slipped the digit under the elastic of my camisole, pulling it down to bare one breast. I was already holding my breath, so when he touched his lips to the slope of my breast, I expelled it a long sigh, tipping my head back in ecstasy. He kissed down the breast to the nipple, paused to look at me, then took my nipple in his mouth and suckled it. *Oh sweet Jesus, thank you.* Electricity shot down my body to strike at my core, sending trembles through my thighs and dampness slicking my folds.

Jeff's hand left my elbow and slid up my arm, over my shoulder and down my back, stopping to cup my ass, drawing my hips against his. His mouth left my flesh, and he murmured, "I need you naked."

"Fuck yes," I whispered.

He pulled my camisole over my head and my heavier-than-ever breasts fell free, bouncing and swaying. I watched in pleasure as his eyes fixed on them, revealing his desire.

Is there anything better in the world than knowing your man thinks you're beautiful? Not to me, there isn't.

He pushed my skirt off, leaving me in my panties. He liked me like that, naked except for panties. Even now, with the burgeoning roundness of my belly, he liked to kneel in front of me and take in my body, as if he was drinking in my beauty to slake an unquenchable thirst. Then he knelt forward to sit on his calves, wrapping his hands around my ankles, sliding his palms up my legs, up the back of my thighs, caressing the ever-expanding globes of my ass. He buried his face against my hip, just above the waist of my panties, kissed my skin, dug his fingers into the leg-opening to stroke my wet folds. I gasped when his middle finger slid inside me, ever-so-slightly. I gasped again when he abruptly jerked my panties off and nudged my legs open. I spread my stance and steadied myself with my hands on his shoulders.

He swiped my folds with his tongue, clutching me close with his hands on my ass. Then, outrageously, he stopped.

"What—why are you stopping?" I demanded. "God, you can't stop now!"

He stared up at me, his brow wrinkled in confusion. "Didn't I hear somewhere that pregnant women shouldn't receive oral sex?"

I growled in my throat. "That's an old wive's tale," I said, putting my hand on the back of his head. "Just don't do a hot kitty and we'll be fine. Now…give me orgasms." I pressed his face between my thighs and whimpered as he complied, spearing my clit with his tongue, slipping a single finger into my channel and curling it to brush me just so.

Then he stopped again. "Hot kitty?" He curled his finger again, and my legs almost gave out.

"Blowing—blowing hot air into me." I locked my knees as he stroked inside me.

"Oh." He kissed my folds, then lapped at my opening, inciting a blissful moan from me. "That's too bad. I know you like that," he murmured, the vibrations of his voice making me shiver.

"Yeah, but just don't stop what you're doing and I don't think I'll miss it."

He started a circular rhythm with his tongue around my swollen clit, which made my knees buckle in time with his tongue. I felt the sweet burning pressure well up within me, rising and rising with each swipe of his tongue, each curling caress of his finger. And then he added a second finger, pressing against the inner ridge and sucked my stiffened nub into his mouth. He reached up to pinch a thick nipple between two fingers, and with that added stimulation, I exploded, falling forward against him and crying out, holding on to his shoulders for balance as my body convulsed and spasmed, heat billowing through me, lightning bursting behind my shut eyes.

He moved me backward and I felt the edge of the bed against my knees. I let myself collapse backward, gasping, feet planted on the floor. Jeff slid his body between my thighs, and I reached up, eyes still closed as aftershocks washed through me, to tug his shorts down. He peeled his T-shirt off as I took his erection in my fist and slid my hand down around his rigid, silk-soft cock. I drew him toward me, needing him, needing more of him, all of him.

"Give it to me, Jeff," I panted. "Please."

"Goddamn, Anna. You're so beautiful when you come." He leaned over me and I felt the broad tip of his erection nudge my opening.

I pulled him closer, guided him into me. I whined in the back of my throat, a sound of pure relief, utter bliss. Jeff groaned low in his throat as he slid deep. He straightened, tucking one hand under my right knee and lifting my leg around his waist. One foot still on the floor, one around his waist, I was at the perfect height for him stand and drive into me, his sliding shaft striking every nerve ending inside me, gliding deep, so deep, so gently and wonderfully deep.

"Oh fuck, Anna. You don't even know how much I needed this, how much I missed this."

"I think I do."

He pulled back, almost out, then slid home again, groaning when our bodies were flush against each other. "You feel so good, Anna. God*damn* you feel so good." He was trembling, holding back.

I fisted my hands in the blanket and lifted my hips to meet him. "More, Jeff. Harder. Please."

"I don't want to—"

I pulled at him hard with my leg, jerking him deep. "I need it, Jeff. I'm not going to break. Please, just fuck me harder."

Jeff slid out and back in, a thoughtful, hesitating thrust, then another. Then he gave me an exploratory harder thrust, and I cried out his name. That seemed to encourage him, and he pushed into me again, harder this time.

"Yes, like that," I panted. "God that's good. More."

He rumbled in his chest. "So good." He set a fast rhythm, then, and each stroke sent me further in ecstasy, each thrust had me whimpering and moaning.

And then I exploded second time, almost out of the blue. It washed over me like a tidal wave, rolling and rollicking and detonating and forcing a scream out of me. Jeff's hand went to my hips and pulled me hard against him. I wrapped my other leg around him and now all that held me aloft was his arms under my ass and his shaft inside me, ramming deep in a pulsating series of short thrusts. I felt him tense, felt his buttocks clench under my legs and knew his climax was imminent.

I clenched him with my inner muscles, clamping down as hard as I could. He groaned loudly and I felt him release, liquid heat billowing through me, filling me. I cried out with him, not so much from my own orgasm, which was still rocking through me, but from the sheer joy of feeling Jeff come inside me, seeing the bliss on his rugged, handsome face.

I felt a second spasm rock his body, then a third smaller one and then he was letting my legs down and pulling out of me. We crawled backward on the bed and I curled into his side, his heart thumping under my ear, lulling me into a state of sated bliss.

As I was about to drift off to sleep, I heard him murmur, "Gonna be Caleb."

I snorted sleepily. This was an ongoing debate with us. I was sure it was a girl, but he was convinced it was a girl. So we had this argument, and it always came up just like that, as one of us was falling asleep, or on the way out the door. We each tried to get the last word in, me as he was leaving to DJ a shift, he as I was about to drift off to sleep.

I let him get the last word in, knowing I'd get him back later. Of course, the main reason I let him get away with it was that I was too sleepy to summon speech, too limp from his loving to even grunt an "unh-uh."

We still hadn't decided if we were going to find out the gender at the next ultrasound, and that was the source of a less playful debate.

He wanted it to be a surprise, and I wanted to get the nursery ready with gender-appropriate decorations. Of course, Jeff was all like, "Just paint it green," but that was cheating to me.

My last thought was of my own inability to decide whether I wanted it to be a girl or boy more. I wavered from day to day. I would think of big, burly Jeff holding a little baby girl with blond curls and Jeff's brown eyes, a big pink bow in her hair, and I'd have a mini-emotional meltdown, and then I'd picture him with a little boy who'd be the spitting image of Daddy and I'd have a different kind of breakdown, and I just couldn't decide.

I fell asleep with images of baby boys and baby girls dancing in my head. In the end, it didn't matter, because girl or boy, they'd be *ours*, and that was the only important thing.

Chapter 2: Jamie

I slid my palms flat over my belly, turning sideways to look at myself in profile. My red curls were longer than they'd ever been, hanging loose nearly to my waist. They were actually kind of out of control, at this point. I'd been thinking about cutting my hair for weeks now, but hadn't done it. Chase would freak, for one thing. He loved my hair long. He liked to bury his fingers in it when he came inside me. If I cut it off, he'd absolutely shit his shorts.

I giggled as I pictured his reaction if I showed up at his show tonight with my hair chopped off. What if I actually, factually shaved my head? We'd be matchers. It could be funny. Chase would probably have a heart attack. Maybe shaving my head wasn't a great plan. I took a long sheaf of springy red curls in my hand, narrowing my eyes at myself. My belly was getting ridiculous. I wasn't even twenty weeks along and I was already getting mammoth. Stupid Anna was barely showing at all, the bitch. Here I was, big as houses when she could get away with most of her normal clothes. I was shopping in the maternity section already.

I sighed, smooth my hand over my belly again, then returned to examining my hair. I held the bulk of it up at my nape, trying to picture myself with my hair at chin length. Just holding my hair up out of the way was a relief on my neck, and that was what decided me.

Time to cut my hair, for the first time in my adult life. The last true hair cut I'd had, not counting the odd inch or two trimmed off now and again, was before I'd moved out on my own at seventeen. I let my hair go and felt it bounce free at the small of my back, then reached for my cell phone on the bathroom counter. I got my stylist friend Lindsey to pencil me in last minute, called a cab, and then spent the next few minutes trying to figure out how I'd explain my sudden decision to Chase.

I'd have to seduce him, of course. As long I left my hair long enough for him to have something to tangle his fingers in, we should be fine, I thought.

There I went, again, with the 'we'. I'd been referring myself in the plural, lately. Myself and the baby, I guess. We. *We're gonna take a shower. We're gonna get some breakfast. We'll be fine. We're feeling nauseous.* It wasn't something I did intentionally, it just happened. It cracked Chase up to no end, which only irritated me further. I always corrected myself when I caught myself doing it, but it kept slipping out.

After putting on the sexiest bra and panties I could fit in, I put on my favorite outfit, the only thing I felt sexy in, a floor-length, high-waisted dress, scooped low in front and back to show off my ginormous preggo boobs, tucking in just right to give me some curves around my hips and ass without hugging my belly. It was ivory in color, soft against my skin, loose and comfortable yet still let me feel attractive.

I wore it more frequently than I should, mainly because I'd never been able to find another dress like it.

The cab honked outside and I snagged my purse and phone on the way out the door. Chase had paid a fortune for our house, but it was perfect, a brownstone walk-up in a hip but fairly quiet section of Manhattan. We had the entire first floor, and he'd let me furnish to my heart's desire. I loved our home. I'd love it even more when his tour was over and he could stay home with me every day. His label was giving the band a couple months off, since Chase and I were having our baby and Gage, the bassist, claimed to need personal time. No one knew what his deal was, but Chase had made the hiatus happen since he'd noticed Gage was had been acting off lately, in a funk. I'd get Chase all to myself for six whole months before they went into the studio to start recording their first full-length album. They'd put out a couple EPs up that point, each recorded in whirlwind, marathon sessions between tour dates, but they hadn't put out anything full-length yet.

Six Foot Tall had gone viral, in a way. Someone had recorded his performance and proposal to me and uploaded it to YouTube, and it had gotten well over a million hits, which spurred the sales of their music and sold out the rest of the shows on the tour. They'd played on Leno and Late Late Night with Jimmy Fallon, and had been on the cover of *Rolling Stone* and *Revolver*.

All of which, of course, translated into me not having seen my husband—even after more than year, I still got giddy thinking that—in more than three months. We FaceTimed and Skyped, of course, but it wasn't the same. Skype sex wasn't anywhere near as satisfying as having Chase in my bed. Not by several orders of magnitude.

I pushed the thoughts from my mind as I sat down in Lindsey's chair and told her what I wanted, more or less. Which was, namely, shorter. Not so short Chase's couldn't grab into my hair, but shorter. Lindsey made quick work of my hair, keeping up a constant chatter in her thick New York accent, black bob nodding and ducking as she snipped and fluffed and snipped until she was satisfied. I had made her turn me around so I couldn't see myself. When Lindsey finally stepped away and tucked her scissors in her apron, I felt nerves shoot through me.

What was I thinking? Cutting my hair? Shit! Chase was going to kill me. He'd hate it. I'd hate it.

"You seriously look amazing, Jamie," Lindsey chirped, teasing my curls with her fingers before turning me around. She must have sensed my nerves. "Honest, Jamie. He'll love it, I promise. You've got to, like, trust me."

I had my hands over my eyes, refusing to look still. "What was I thinking, Linz? I don't know why I just did this, I really don't."

Lindsey laughed and took my wrists in her dainty little fingers. "You're pregnant. You know how many pregnant women I get in here who have had a sudden urge to cut their hair? It happens all the time.

I'm not sure why, really, but it's a fact. It's kind of my specialty, actually. The other girls always send me the preggos, because I can usually tell when they really want to cut their hair and when they think they do but really just want it to look different. Sometimes that's all it is. Part of the nesting phase, I've heard, where you go through and like change everything for the baby."

I laughed. "Maybe that's it. But I don't think I'm nesting just yet. I just…wigged out, like, I all of a sudden *hated* my hair and wanted it gone, off my neck. But now? Oh god, I'm scared to look. I haven't had it noticeably shortened in, god, like fifteen years."

Lindsey pried my hands away from my face. "Look at yourself, Jay. You're beautiful."

I sighed and opened my eyes, heart in my throat. I gasped. I looked totally different. Like, completely altered.

I interrupted my own thoughts to tell myself to stop talking like Lindsey, who, at 22, had a tendency to still say 'like' in every sentence.

I turned my head from side to side, marveling at how much lighter I felt. I shook my head, laughing as my hair bounced around, now hanging just above my shoulders. She'd cut away a good bit near the front so I had springs of curls as bangs that drifted across my cheekbones. It was a perfect cut for me, I realized, emphasizing my heart-shaped face and accentuating my eyes. It sharpened my jawline, somehow, and brought out the curve of my throat.

Plus, there was still a good bit of hair left, so Chase could do his thing.

I pulled Lindsey into a hug, and felt my eyes prick. I cried at the drop of a hat, these days. A Hallmark commercial had me bawling just the day before, and it was driving me nuts.

Lindsey pulled free and unsnapped the apron from around my neck. "So you like it?"

I nodded happily, sniffing back the traitorous tears. "I *love* it. I really do."

"And you think Chase will like it?" She grabbed a nearby broom and started sweeping up the mess of hair on the floor.

I took a deep breath. "I hope so. I think so. He'll be surprised, but once he gets over the shock, I think he'll be happy. I'll find out in a few hours, I guess."

Lindsey's gaze sharpened. "They're in town? The whole band?"

I nodded, wondering what her angle was. "Yeah, they're playing the Garden."

Lindsey crouched to brush the hair into a dustpan. "Is it sold out?"

I laughed at the hopeful tone in her voice. "Who do you have a crush on?"

Lindsey blushed, her fair skin going pink across her cheeks and on her nose. "Gage."

I nodded. "You and half the country, the half that isn't in love with my husband."

"I met him by accident the last time they played New York. He was being dragged around by some girl, a groupie, I think. She dragged him in here and got him to pay for a cut and color. I felt bad for him. She was, like, heinously obnoxious, and he was realizing it, I think. She was hot, in bimbo sort of way. He was really nice to her, though, despite the fact that she was, like, clearly a gold-digging fame whore. He was really classy about it."

I nodded, having gotten to know Gage pretty well by that point. "That's Gage for you. He's got some rough edges, but he has a great heart, if you can get him to show you his real personality. He's got this whole hardass rocker persona that he puts on, but it's not really him."

Lindsey nodded. "I kinda got that same impression." She blushed again. "I like both sides of him."

I laughed. "The front and the back, you mean?"

Lindsey turned red. "That's not what I meant!"

I elbowed her playfully. "Sure it's not. You know you were checking out his ass."

She rolled her eyes, then leaned in to whisper to me. "Actually, he *was* wearing these tight, ripped jeans that hugged him, like, *all* over. I couldn't stop staring at him." She dropped her voice to almost inaudible. "He sat so I had this crazy crotch-shot of him, and I swear, I nearly cut a chunk out of his bimbo friend's ear because I was staring at his bulge the whole time."

I laughed so hard I snorted. "Would've served her right. But, while he's not my husband, Gage *is* pretty hot."

"Yeah, he is," she muttered, her tone wistful.

I waited for her to ask, but after a few moments, it became clear she wasn't going to. "You want to come with me?"

She looked up, hope gleaming in her eyes. "Oh god, really? You have an extra ticket?"

I laughed. "I'm married to the lead singer, honey. I don't need tickets. I've got a box wherever he's playing, he made sure of it."

"That's the coolest thing ever." She clapped her hands. "I get off in an hour, and now that's gonna be the longest hour of my life!"

I stood up slowly and walked with her to the register. "You know where I live, right? Drop by when you're done and we'll go early to see the guys."

As I left, Lindsey hugged me and thanked me about fifty times, and refused to let me pay her for the cut. I laughed as I hailed a cab, watching her pull out her phone and text furiously. I don't think I'd ever seen anyone so excited in all my life. Maybe she could pull Gage out of whatever funk he was lost in.

I ate a quick dinner at a bistro near Lindsey's salon and then went to my standing weekly mani-pedi appointment. About a week after we got back from our honeymoon, Chase had insisted I make the appointment and set it for every week. He claimed I'd been beans-and-ricing it for too long and it was time to let him take care of me. Apparently, now that money was rolling in for the band, that meant all sorts of lavish treatment I'd never imagined would be a part of my life, such as standing manicure appointments, shopping trips to Fifth Avenue, and even a car and driver if I wanted it. I'd drawn the line at being chauffeured. Chase was quickly becoming a rock star and a household name, and that meant lots of money, but I'd lived a relatively simple life, taking care of myself and using the occasional indulgence as a treat for meeting my respon-sibilities. I couldn't take the swing in the complete opposite direction, not all at once, at least. A new purse whenever I wanted it? Awesome. Louboutin pumps and Chanel pajamas? Hell yes. Pretending like I'm some swanky celebrity, with an entourage and a driver and bodyguards everywhere I go? Hell no. I may be married to a rock star, but I'm still Jamie Dunleavy—Jamie Delany, now—and I'm no poser.

Lindsey was *click-click*ing up the sidewalk toward my house as I was stepping out of the cab. I had to stifle a smile and a giggle, as she'd kind of overdone it in her excitement. She was wearing a miniskirt that only barely covered her tiny little ass, and tight-fitting, low-cut sleeveless shirt that very blatantly accentuated her decent-sized tatas—and by accentuated, I mean pushed up to overflowing. She was also wearing a pair of four-inch spike heels which were ridiculously impractical for a rock concert.

"Wow, Linz," I said, eyeing her outfit skeptically, "You're really… going all out, huh?"

She grinned. "Yep."

"Well, there's no way Gage could possibly resist you in that outfit," I said.

She ducked her head. "That's the point, isn't it?"

I poured Lindsey a glass of wine and wished I could have some myself. Yeah, the doctor had said half a glass every once in a while was fine, but I knew myself, and I knew there was no point to drinking half a glass of wine. Half a glass of wine was like being brought to the edge of orgasm and then abandoned.

I regretted my analogy as soon as it passed through my head: I hadn't seen Chase in three months. Which meant I hadn't had an orgasm in three months. I'd tried, of course. We'd Skyped and tried getting a little nasty that way, but it just fell flat for both of us. My own fingers were useless, now that I'd become addicted to Chase's. Even my vibrator hadn't gotten me anywhere. And now I was mere hours from getting what I so desperately needed, namely, an exhausting marathon session of fucking Chase's brains out, followed by some epic cuddling.

I shivered in anticipation even as I thought about it. I felt my nipples tighten and my panties dampen just picturing Chase above me, naked, sweaty, and mine.

"Come on, Linz," I said, "I can't wait anymore. I need Chase."

Lindsey laughed and tossed back the last two swallows of wine. "I'm ready."

A cab was letting out my neighbor as we stepped out of the brownstone, and we climbed in, exchanging hugs with Mrs. Lettis as we passed. Mrs. Lettis was a hugger. She hugged everyone and anyone. When Chase and I had first come to look at the brownstone, she'd shown up to chatter about the previous tenants and Chase and I hadn't been able to get away without at least three hugs each from the sweet, elderly, buxom woman.

Linz giggled as the cab pulled away from the curb. "She's…nice."

"She really is. I once watched her hug a drug dealer. Seriously. I walked her to the store once, and a this guy was in the freezer section buying ice cream. He stank of weed and paid for his ice cream from a roll of hundreds so thick he needed an industrial sized rubber band." I scrolled through my Facebook newsfeed on my phone as I spoke. "Well, this guy had all this cash, but the cashier didn't have enough correct change to give him back, since the dealer only had hundred dollar bills. This was at like eight in the morning. So Mrs. Lettis, being the kind of woman she is, paid for the guy's ice cream. Now you have to understand, this guy was *scary*. Tattoos all up and down his arms and on his throat, pierced lip, ears, and nose, arms bigger around than your waist, 'thug life' tattooed across his knuckles. Mrs. Lettis paid for his ice cream without batting an eyelash at him. He was stunned, like, speechless. He tried to thank her and pay her back, and she just clucked at him, and leaned in to give him a hug. He just stood there, frozen, like 'what the fuck do I do?' God, Linz, it was *so* funny.

She patted his face and said, 'everyone needs ice cream, dear.' The cashier, who'd been pissing himself, couldn't believe it."

Linz giggled. "She sounds awesome."

"You have no clue. I'm pretty sure that dealer visits her every week, like staking out his turf so no messes with her. It's cute."

The cab dropped us off at the gate where I showed the security my backstage pass and were waved through. Linz stuck close to me as we wove our way through the bustle of techies, roadies, band members, and all the other assorted people necessary to make a concert happen. It was huge show, with Six Foot Tall being only one of the headlining bands, along with Theory of a Dead Man, Drowning Pool, and System Of A Down. There were also almost half a dozen opening bands, a mix of local talent and up-and-coming acts. Needless to say, finding my husband in the chaos proved to be nearly impossible. The backstage area was huge and crowded, everyone scurrying and chattering into walkie talkies, checking lists on tablets as they walked. We found Gage first, sitting on a black box that once held sound equipment of some kind, restringing his bass. He glanced up as we approached, and his face lit up, hazel eyes bright. He ran a hand through his long, loose, pale blond hair, his massive bicep flexing with the motion. Gage was huge, standing at least six-four and weighing a good two-fifty in solid muscle. He was an MMA fighter before he joined the band with Chase, and it showed in the rugged, scarred features of his face, which, despite the roughness were still handsome in a Dolph Lundgren sort of way.

" 'Sup, Jay." He stood up and gave me a one-armed hug, resting his bass on the toe of his Timberland boot. "Who's your tasty-looking friend?" His eyes took on an avid, hungry gleam.

I heard Lindsey suck in a surprised gasp at Gage's words, but she recovered quickly. "I'm Lindsey," she breathed, sticking her hand out.

Gage took her hand in his, but instead of shaking it, he used it to pull her closer. "I'm Gage."

Lindsey stood with barely an inch separating her from Gage, each breath she took swelling her breasts to touch Gage's chest. "I know," she said. "I cut your girlfriend's hair the last time you guys were here."

Gage frowned, struggling to remember. Then his face cleared and he guffawed in laughter. "She was *not* my girlfriend. I didn't even bang her. She was too fucking obnoxious. She was a fucking slut, and coming from me, that's saying something."

Lindsey snorted. "She only wanted to be near you 'cause you're famous."

Gage nodded, then his gaze sharpened. "And you? Why do want to be near me?"

"Because I think I could like you."

Good answer, Linz, I thought. I passed behind Lindsey and fixed Gage with a hard stare, telling him without words that if he hurt my friend, I'd have his balls. He smirked and nodded subtly, letting me know he heard my unspoken message.

I heard the tell-tale *rat-a-tat-tat* of Johnny Hawk, the drummer, tapping his sticks against a counter, and the click of a pick hitting the strings of an un-amped guitar. I found the door, peeked my head in and said my hellos to Johnny and Kyle and asked if they knew where Chase was.

"He's by the stage, I think," Kyle said, tweaking the tuning of his guitar without looking up at me. When he had the tuning right, he looked up at me with a bright smile, which morphed into a surprised expression. "Damn, Jay. You got *really* pregnant."

I gave him the finger and a nasty glare. "Smooth, Kyle. Real smooth. What you meant to say is, 'damn, Jay, you're huge.'"

Johnny, the youngest of the band at barely twenty-three, made an *oh shit* face, which made me laugh. Kyle held up a hand in a gesture of surrender. "No! That's not—I just meant…" He sighed in exasperation. "Damn, you pregnant chicks are touchy. You look good, Jay. You really do."

I grinned at him. "I'm just giving you shit, Kyle. But don't say that to any other pregnant lady. You'll get your block knocked off."

I left the room then and went toward the stage in search of Chase. I heard his voice before I saw him, and he sounded irritated.

"This isn't the time or place, Jenna. And I'm not the guy. I'm married. You know that."

A whiny female voice, breathy with overt seduction, responded. "Oh, come on, Chase. It doesn't have to be like that. You know you want to. You've been such a good boy all tour, don't you think you deserve a little treat?"

I felt rage boil through me. Who was this bitch trying to seduce my husband? I tried to take a few calming breaths, but it wasn't working. My Irish temper was up and hotter than was safe. I felt my hands clench into fists, and before I knew it, I was rounding the corner to the dead-end emergency exit hallway.

What I saw had me even angrier. The groupie, Jenna, was on her knees and crawling toward Chase, who was backing away from her, toward me. She had his belt in her hands, and had clearly fallen to her knees to try and go down on him, but had only managed to snag his belt off him before he got away.

The little bitch saw me at that moment and paled, scrambling to her feet and dropping the belt. Chase span in place, eyes flying wide.

"Jamie!" He took a step toward me and I held out my hand to stop him. He halted, sucking in a harsh breath. "I didn't do anything, Jay! I swear!"

"I saw everything, baby." I cut my eyes at him, let them soften so he'd know I wasn't mad at him. I then fixed my glare on the groupie. "You. What the *fuck* do you think you're doing?"

"I—I—I'm sorry, Jamie, I mean, Mrs. Delany. I just, I wanted—" she shook her head, bleached hair flying.

Mrs. Delany, I thought. *I like the sound of that.*

"You wanted a piece of Chase," I said, my voice deceptively calm. "I can understand that. He's a hot piece of man. But the problem, here, is that he's *my* husband."

She took a step backward, away from me, as I stalked closer. "I know, I'm sorry—"

I was within striking distance now, but I wanted to make my point first. "That's right, you are sorry. You're a sorry piece of shit whore." I was caught up in the rage, now. I knew should stop, but I couldn't. "He's my *husband*, you cunt. Stay the *fuck* away from him."

She was trembling, now, but anger and panic were replacing fear. "Listen, bitch, I said I'm sorry, now move—" She didn't get the chance to finish her statement.

My fist cracked against her nose, breaking it in a spray of blood. My hand immediately went numb, and then began radiating pain as my knuckles absorbed the force of the blow. The groupie dropped to the ground, screaming. I heard a muffled laugh behind me and turned in place, shaking my hand, to see the whole band watching. They were all laughing, shoulders quivering in mirth, fists covering their mouths as they cackled.

"That was fucking *epic*!" Johnny yelled, doubled over, hooting.

I grinned as the other guys clustered around me, patting me on the back and chattering all at once. The laughter abated as a black T-shirted security guy pushed between us, lifted Jenna by the arms to her feet and shoved her, just this side of too-rough, toward the exit. As they rounded the corner, she leveled an evil glare at me, the entire lower half of her face a wash of blood, her huge fake tits coated in red.

Chase stepped in front of me, took my hand in his and rubbed my knuckles with a gentle thumb. "You okay?"

I nodded, stepping closer to him so our bodies were flush, my belly and breasts crushed against him. "I can't believe her. Does she do shit like that often?"

Chase tilted his head back and groaned. "Unfortunately, yeah. She's the sister of one of the roadies and she's always around. I'm pretty sure ninety percent of the guys on the tour have fucked her at least once. They kind of pass her around. It's gross."

I spared a glance at the other guys from the band. "None of you have fucked her, have you?"

Gage and Kyle both made disgusted grimaces and shook their heads. Johnny, however, looked embarrassed.

"Johnny!" I yelled. "Tell me you didn't. That's fucking nasty! She's gotta have more diseases than a cockroach!"

He shrugged. "I didn't sleep with her, I just—she...she gave me BJ, once." He turned eight shades of red, tugging on the end of his long, braided black goatee.

Gage shoved him, hard enough that Johnny slammed into the wall opposite. "Stay away from that bitch, Johnny. She's a ho. She's poisonous, man. She'll fuck anything with a cock, and she'll do anything to get what she wants."

"Well she's *not* getting my man," I growled, and the guys all laughed. "You think it's funny now, but it won't be so funny when I go to jail for assault and battery."

Chase took my face in his hands and his mocha-brown eyes delved into mine. "You have nothing to worry about, baby. There's only you."

I kissed his hard, stubble-rough jaw. "I know. I trust you. It's other women I don't trust."

Chase turned his face down so his mouth met my next kiss. "That was hot, Jay. Seriously. I like you when you're possessive."

I let the heat of my desire blaze in my eyes as I looked up at him. "You're *mine*, Chase."

I heard Gage clear his throat. "Let's go, guys. I think it's about to get hot in hurrr." He slurred the last word as a play on the hip-hop/pop song from a few years ago.

Chase chuckled against my mouth, then cupped my ass with his hands to pull me tighter against his body. "It's gettin' hot in hurr, so take off all your clothes," he murmured, slipping his hands over the bare skin of my back where the back of the dress dipped down.

"Find me room with a lock and I will," I said, dragging my finger nails down the back of his faded, tattered black *Return of the Jedi* T-shirt.

His fingers clawed into the soft flesh and firm muscle of my backside, then released me. "Wait a second…goddamn Jay, what happened to your hair?" He ran his fingers through it, fluffing it, tangling his hands into the shortened curls.

"Took you long enough to notice," I said. "Do you like it?"

Chase stepped back and scrutinized me. "It's different."

My heart palpitated crazily. "That doesn't sound good."

"No! I just, I have to get used to it. You cut a *lot* off, baby. It's a shock. I didn't notice before because of the excitement, but now that I'm really looking at you…I like it. I do."

I narrowed my eyes at him. "Liar. You hate it." I turned away, feeling my heart clench. It was just hair, I knew, and it would grow back, but…the thought of Chase not being attracted to me had me sick to my stomach.

I stormed past him, but I didn't get three feet before his arm wrapped around my waist and pulled me back against him. My breath caught at the familiar feel of his body against mine, the power in his hands as they smoothed down my hips, the heat of his breath on my neck, now bare and open to his mouth. His palm skated over my belly, briefly tender and loving, and then skimmed up to cup my breast, his thumb nudging the edge down to bare more skin, then yet more, digging down until one nipple was peeking out. I felt my thighs clench as desire rocketed through me. His erection was a hard, thick rod against the top of my buttocks and the small of my back.

He ground his hips against me, pressing his shaft into me. "Feel that?" His voice was low rumble in my ear. "Does that feel like I hate it? You just surprised me is all, baby. I love it. Now I can kiss your shoulders, just…like…this…" He suited action to words, planting hot kisses along my shoulder blade and up my neck between each word.

I shivered under his mouth, pressed my thighs together, needing pressure; one of Chase's hand—not the one thumbing light circles over the tip of my nipple—slid down my side to my hip, bunching in the cotton where my hip dipped in to my thigh, and brushed the V where I so desperately needed his touch. In that moment, I didn't care where we were, who could round the corner and see.

Chase walked forward with me, never breaking contact or pausing in his kissing of my skin, now behind my ear, beneath it, over my jaw-line and to my chin. He found a doorknob, twisted it, pushed it open. We startled a group of men in the act of snorting lines of cocaine, three roadies by the look of them, and one guy who looked like a rocker, with spiked dyed red hair and spike-studded leather bracelets on his wrists.

"Out," Chase growled.

The rocker drew a short straw along the last line, blinked hard as he sniffed. The guys stood lazily, one of them brushing his fore-arm over the low table they'd been snorting from. The rocker was the last one out the door, and he threw a lecherous glance over his shoulder. "Fuck her good, mate," he said, his voice thick with a British accent.

"She's my wife, asshole," Chase said, shooting a hard glare at the man. The British rocker just smirked as he sauntered off, not bother-ing to reply, pulling a guitar pick from his back pocket.

Chase pushed the door closed and twisted the lock, then turned to me. "Sorry about them."

I shrugged. "It's a concert, they're rock stars. What do you expect?"

Chase pulled a face. "I just hate that shit. Coke, I mean. When Gage and I started the band, we made a pact that we'd never do drugs, and that no one who played with us would either. We actu-ally fired our first drummer for that same thing, not long before I met Anna. We caught him doing lines off a stripper's tits in the back room of a nightclub, when he was supposed to be with us, practicing."

"I knew people who did it regularly. I never liked it. I tried it once, but I hated it. Plus I watched too many friends fuck up their lives using it."

Chase nodded. "A buddy of mine OD'd. Right in front of me. I watched him go, and I couldn't stop it."

His eyes darkened and narrowed with memory. I closed the distance between us, pushing my breasts up against him and running my fingers up under his shirt.

"Hey," I said, tilting my face up for a kiss, "enough of that. Where were we?"

Chase shook his head to clear it, and when his eyes descended to mine, they were hot with lust once more. "God I missed you. Do you have any idea? If I didn't love performing so much, I'd quit because I just can't stand being away from you so much."

"I'd never let you quit," I said. "It's what you do, part of who you are. I miss you too, more than *you* know, but it just makes these reunions that much better."

He grinned at me, and the sight of his smile still had the power to take my breath away. Then he kissed me, and my breath was truly snatched, sucked away by the desperation of his mouth moving on mine. I melted into him, slid my palms up under his shirt and clawed my nails down his spine, feeling tingles begin in my core. Chase curled his fingers into the fabric of my dress at my hips, gathering the material into his hands to slowly bare my legs. The anticipation of his hands on my flesh caused me to shiver all over, to lean up on my toes to deepen the kiss. I put every shred of my desire, my need, my three months worth of pent-up sexual frustration into the kiss. At some point I pushed his shirt off so I could roam my hands over his rock hard, sculpted torso, and then I was fumbling with his belt and zipper and button, pushing his boxers away as well.

And then—god, yes—he was naked for me, right there in the office or whatever this room was. Hard for me. So hard, so huge. Thick and pink and veined and ridged and rippled and begging for my touch. I trailed my fingers slowly down his stomach, nibbling on his lower lip. Chase sucked his belly in, still slowly gathering my dress up at my hips. I loved this teasing, this give and take. Chase blew out a sigh of ultimate pleasure and relief as I finally wrapped my hand around his cock, and when he did, I smiled at him, my lips curving against the line of his jaw.

"God, Jay. God, I love your hand on me."

"You like that?" I teased. "You want more?"

He bucked his hips into my plunging fist. "Yes, *fuck* yes."

"Then touch me." I straddled his knee, clenching my thighs around his leg and rubbing myself against him.

Chase waited a beat, then peeled my dress off over my head and tossed it aside. He pushed me back a few inches and took in my body, and his eyes went heavy-lidded with appreciation. "God, Jay. You're… you are honestly the sexiest goddamn woman in the world. You're heaven, my love. Absolute perfection."

Again with the prickling eyes. I reached up behind me to unclasp my bra, letting it fall away so Chase could gaze at me. He closed the gap slowly, cupping my bare breasts in his big, hard, callused hands, gently massaging them. He knew by now that they were sensitive, so he was extra gentle. Of course, I'd gotten three months more pregnant since he'd seen me last, and they were even more sensitive. Just the ever so slight brush of his palms over my nipples had me wet and shivering, gasping. And then he bent and pulled me to him, lowering his mouth over my breast and suckling a rigid nipple between his lips. I cried out against his shoulder, and then full-on bit him when he slipped his fingers between my thighs, cupping me over my panties.

I had his erection in my fist again, sliding my fingers around him, rubbing the tip with my thumb, squeezing low on the base the way he liked it, pulsing my fist around him in short squeezes as I slicked his pre-come over him. His thumb hooked over my panties and jerked them down, and I stepped out, widening my stance, and then whimpered into his bicep when he slipped two thick fingers into my wet, arousal-pungent folds.

"I need you, baby," I said. "Now. Take me now."

Chase laughed, almost mockingly. His fingers curled inside me, eliciting a muffled shriek, and then his thumb pressed over my ultra-sensitive clit and I was undone. I latched my teeth onto the round of his shoulder and let myself scream as I came apart.

"Goddamn, Jay. You came fast." Chase didn't relent when I came, but curled his fingers inside me again, and I had no choice but to ride his hand, rubbing against him and whimpering, crying out. My orgasm hadn't slowed, hadn't abated, and when he slid to his knees in front of me, I let my head fall back and steadied myself on his broad shoulders, knowing I was about to be ripped in two by his talented tongue.

His tongue stroked up my crease, and I shivered, shook, trembled, aftershocks hitting me with sledgehammer force even as another orgasm built up within me. The tip of his tongue touched my clit, lightly, and then circled it. I moaned long and low, the sound rising in pitch until I was keening in my throat, dipping with my knees at each curling lap of his tongue in me. I rode his face, arched my back and fucked his tongue with my folds, greedily gorging myself on the high. I cried out his name as the third orgasm punched through me, leaving me breathless and limp.

Chase chose that moment, the instant of utter satiety and complete bonelessness, to move behind me and spin me in place. He lifted my foot and placed it on the low coffee table, which was pushed up against the wall. I bent forward, planting my palms on the wall and braced myself, waiting.

He took his time. He slid up against me, dragging the tip of his cock along my thigh, nudging my folds. I gasped at the presence of him there, held my breath, tensed and waiting, needing it. He pushed against me, and I whined when he moved away.

"I need you inside me, Chase." I could barely gasp the words.

He mouthed my neck in the hollow between shoulder and throat, cupping my breasts with both hands. He put his foot next to mine, nestled his tip in my folds. I arched my back, silently begging him. I heard him suck in a breath, and then he was sliding up, sliding in, and I sobbed in relief, in desperate ecstasy. I heard him moan, felt the vibrations of his voice on my skin. I held my breath and waited, every muscle tensed, my heart hammering absurdly in my chest.

And then he was inside me, sweet and deep and slowly pushing deeper. I let out my tension in a gasp, sinking down to meet him. He lifted up on his toes to drive himself deeper, swiveling his hips in a circle as he reached full impalement. I draped myself against the wall, head down, watching his hands cup and caress my breasts. His right hand slithered down my belly and between my thighs, and then his fingers curled in to slide against my clit, and I screamed into my forearm, biting it until pain laced the pleasure. I grabbed Chase's thigh and pulled him, urging him harder, faster, but he resisted. He lowered himself down from his tiptoes and onto flat feet, then pulled his hips away until he was nearly out of me and I was whimpering with the loss of him within me. He held there, circling my clit with his fingers, then began pulsating his hips so his tip slipped shallowly in and out between my swollen labia.

"Oh fuck, baby" I moaned, "stop teasing me. Give me all of you."

He clutched my breast in one hand, pressed his fingers against my nerve endings with the other, hesitated for a beat like that, then thrust hard into me. Once, twice, three times, hard and arrhythmic, and then he was gasping against my neck and pumping his cock into me, fast and hard and so perfect.

"Like that?" He asked, rolling my nipple in his fingers.

"Yes, yes...like this. Don't stop." I clutched his thigh in my hand and pulled him closer, arched my back and lowered my hips into his frantic thrusting.

I came a fourth time, a nuclear detonation within me, my inner muscles clamping down around his thick, slick, sliding shaft, my breath stopped and gasping in stutters, heart palpitating, fire and heat and lightning shuddering through every fiber of my body.

I knew, in that moment, what Chase needed. I knew he was close, and I knew how he liked to come. I pushed away from the wall, lifted up to pull him out of me, ignoring his curse of protest. He followed me to the floor as I settled on my knees and forearms, presenting my ass to him. I was quivering all over, aftershocks crashing in my muscles and my core, but I held the pose, watching him over my shoulder. He grinned, licked his lips dramatically, and settled on his knees behind me. He grabbed himself at the base, feathered his fingers into my slick folds, and guided himself in, sliding deep.

"Oh fuck, Jamie. God you're perfect. So tight." He grabbed my leg at the quadricep and lifted so my thigh was resting on his outstretched knee, and I nearly collapsed at how deep he went, how he struck every sensitive place inside me from the angle of his penetration. "I've dreamt of being inside you like this every night for three months."

"Me too," I gasped.

I didn't think I would, or could, come again, but when he started shifting his hips to drive into me deep and slow, I felt it rising again. Impossible. I almost feared how hard I would climax if he took me over the edge a fifth time. Five times in thirty minutes? I'd be a puddly mess.

But I did. As Chase began to groan and grunt with each staccato thrust, I felt it rip through me. "Chase, baby...come with me. Right now."

He thrust hard into me and I felt him unleash within me, filling me, and his voice filled the room with a long, low growl. I didn't scream, didn't cry out or whimper, I was left too breathless by the potency of my climax. I could only clench my fists and open my mouth wide in a silent scream, rocked forward by his crashing hips. And then he was limp behind me, his cheek resting on my back and his cock softening within me.

"Holy shit, baby," I said, collapsing onto my belly on the floor. "That was…incredible."

Chase flopped to his back next to me. "Yeah it was." He twisted onto his side to smirk at me. "That was just the beginning, babe. You have no idea what I'm going to do to you tonight, after the show. You won't be able to walk tomorrow."

I rolled to my back and pulled him over me. "I already won't be able to. You just ruined me. I'm done."

Chase lowered his lips to mine, kissing me with a sweetness that belied the ferocity of our lovemaking from just moments ago. "I wasn't too rough, was I?"

I held him by the nape and met his gaze. "No, baby. You were perfect. Exactly what I needed, just like you always are. You won't hurt me, or the baby." I squirmed beneath him. "You did make me all drippy, though. I think you came an entire gallon."

He laughed. "I had a lot built up."

I scrutinized his face. "You didn't take care of yourself at all?"

He shrugged, rolling off me. "Once, about two weeks after I left. It sucked. It's just not the same, not satisfying at all. I'd rather have blue balls and wait until I can be with you." He extended his hand to me and lifted me to my feet.

I put on my bra and slipped the dress over my head, stuffing my panties into my purse.

"Not gonna put those back on?" Chase asked as he dressed.

I shook my head. "No, not until I can go to the bathroom and clean up. I don't think you understand how much you came, Chase. Even after I clean up, I'll be dripping for days."

He tied his boot and stood up, pulling me against him. "Sorry. I didn't think to bring a condom."

I shrugged and scrubbed my palm over his shaved head. "It's fine. I like feeling you bare inside me. I'll just be…squishy for a while." I rubbed his head again, then looked into his eyes. "You should grow your hair back. I'm tired of bald Chase."

He smirked at me. "Fine, if you want me to."

At that moment someone knocked on the door. "Sorry guys, but we gotta be on in ten," Gage said.

"Coming right now," Chase said.

I snickered. "You already did," I said.

"Whoa, TMI guys," Gage said, laughing.

Chase kissed me, long and slow, and then we exited the room. Gage gave us a knowing smirk as I ran my fingers through my hair, which very likely looked as thoroughly just-fucked as I was in all actuality. I walked with Gage and Chase, chatting about the other bands on the tour.

They escorted me to the hallway, and I glanced at Gage. "Where's Lindsey?" I asked.

"In the box already."

"You better be nice to her, Gage Gallagher," I warned. "She's a sweet girl, not one of your groupie sluts. Don't hurt her."

Gage met my gaze, his eyes serious. "I know, Jay. I won't, I promise. I'm taking her on a for-real date after the show."

I gave him a surprised look, as I'd never known Gage to take a girl on a date before. He was in many ways a stereotypical rock star, especially when it came to women.

Before we parted ways, I pulled Chase aside. "Will you be here for the ultrasound on Thursday?" I tried to sound casual, and didn't entirely succeed.

I would never tell him how much I wanted him there. If he couldn't make it, it wouldn't be his fault, and I knew it. I'd been putting off asking him until I saw him in person, and I wanted to keep putting it off, because I knew what the answer would likely be. I held my breath as he considered.

"I honestly don't know, babe," Chase said, grimacing. "I really want to be there. All I can promise you at this moment is that I will do everything in my power to be there."

I swallowed, hard. "That's all I'm asking. Do your best."

Chase's eyes found mine, and they were piercing. "What aren't you saying?"

I shook my head and brushed a wayward red curl out of my mouth. "Nothing, honey. It's just…I'm really hoping you'll be there." I put my hand over his mouth before he could speak. "I know you can't promise me. And if you can't, that's how it is. I knew there'd be the risk of this kind of thing when I married you. Just try, okay? Now go kill 'em." I leaned in, kissed him, and then turned him around by his shoulders and pushed him away, smacking his ass as he went.

I made my way to the private box and slid into my seat next to Lindsey, who was, as usual, busily tapping away at her phone.

She looked up when I appeared, and grinned at me. "Well well well," she said, "don't you look pleased with yourself."

I rolled my eyes at her. "More like pleased with my husband," I said, covering up my inner turmoil over the upcoming ultrasound appointment. "So I hear Gage is taking you out later."

Lindsey blushed. "Yeah, I wasn't expecting that. I mean, he's Gage Gallagher. He's got a reputation already, and they've only been a big deal for like a year." She picked at a thread on the hem of her mini-skirt. "I'm kinda nervous."

I patted her knee. "You should be, hon. Gage is a force of nature. The fact that he's taking you on an actual date? That's huge, Linz. He likes you."

She narrowed her eyes at me. "Did you say something to him?"

I shrugged and accepted a diet Coke from the server. "I might have told him I'd cut off his balls if he hurt you. No big deal. Not like he could possibly mistake you for one, but I just didn't want him to treat you like one of his little groupie hookers. You're a classy chick, and he needs to treat you like one." I turned a serious look at her. "If he doesn't treat you right, ditch his ass. Just 'cause he's a rock star doesn't mean he can treat you like shit."

Lindsey frowned at me. "I appreciate your intentions, Jay. But I think I know what I'm getting myself into."

I laughed. "You don't know Gage, if that's what you think."

Lindsey turned to the stage as the lights went down, and I caught a thoughtful expression on her face before the stadium went dark. I wasn't about to tell Lindsey some of the things I knew about Gage, none of them bad, per se. He was an intense person, and not someone to lightly enter into any kind of a relationship with, rock star status aside. I wondered if Lindsey really had any clue what she was in for.

Those thoughts were erased as a four spotlights bathed each band member, Chase in front, right at the edge of the stage, Gage and Kyle to either side and Johnny in the middle on his elaborate drum set. The crowd went wild for several moments, screaming and clapping, then gradually faded into silence as the band merely stood in place— or sat, in Johnny's case—waiting. When the silence was complete, Johnny hit the kick drum in a slow rhythm, *bang...bang...bang...*building anticipation, getting blood boiling. The beat gave nothing away as to which song they'd start off with, and the crowd became restless and the kick drum rhythm continued, drawing out the tension. Chase extended his hand out the side, low, and then slowly raised it. For every few inches Chase raised his arm, Johnny increased the tempo of his kick drum, until Chase's hand was vertical over his head and Johnny was kicking the pedal faster than I'd thought possible. They held this for a heartbeat, and then Chase dropped his hand in downward slice. The gesture cut Gage and Kyle loose, and they both cut into a blistering power riff, the stage lights bursting into a flashing pattern. Chase bobbed his head in time to the music, then slowly brought the mic to his mouth and began the intro hook to one of their hardest numbers, a piece Chase told me was a tribute to Slipknot, Gage's favorite band.

I watched them perform, watched my husband work the crowd into a frenzy, bringing them in on the crowd-favorite numbers, jumping out into the front rows of the mosh pit at one point, which had my heart in my throat until the security men had him safely onstage once more.

I wasn't really into the show, though. Not all the way. My mind was on the ultrasound, and if I really had what it took to be the wife of a rock star when it came time to have the baby. If I went into labor early, would he be able to get there in time? Would he be around for the baby's first smile, first word, first step? Every once in a while I'd catch a pensive look on Chase's face, and I knew he had the same concerns.

It was the day of the ultrasound, and I'd been fighting tears all day. Chase had called me the day before to tell me he had an interview today and wouldn't be at the appointment. I knew it was silly. I knew it was just an ultrasound. At least, that was what I told myself to keep myself calm. He'd be here if he could.

Right? It was hard not to question everything, with the way my emotions were running rampant.

I sat in the waiting room, reading through old text conversations between Chase and I, just to feel any kind of a connection with him. My heart was in my throat, my eyes burning.

A nurse in maroon scrubs called my name, and I followed her down a short hallway, where she weighed me, and then ushered me into a dimly lit room. I slid onto the elevated chair, my phone clutched in my fist, waiting for the technician.

My phone buzzed in my hand and I slid the green icon across the lock screen to open the thread.

You have wifi access right now?

I went through the requisite steps to access the guest wifi for the doctor's office, and then texted him back. *Yep. Why?*

The three dots in a gray bubble appeared, and his response came through a few seconds later. *I put the interview on hold until after your appointment. FaceTime me.*

I put my hand over my mouth and held back a sob. He'd found a way to be here anyway. I sucked in a deep breath to calm myself, hating how emotional I was all the time. I'd never been the kind of girl to cry at every little thing, so this was especially frustrating, since I couldn't stop it. The technician came in and sat down in her chair, greeting me. She was a thin, younger woman with black hair cut in a short bob, and she had the coldest hands I'd ever felt.

The nurse tapped at the keyboard, slid my shirt up, lined the waistband of my yoga pants with a white towel before slathering the frigid blue goo on my belly.

"Is it okay if I have my husband on the phone with me for this?" I asked her. "He couldn't be here for the appointment, but he wants to involved."

"Sure," the technician responded without looking away from her screen.

I tapped the *FaceTime* button on my phone and after a few rings, Chase's face appeared on the screen of my iPhone. I smiled at him and we talked about the upcoming interview for *Spin*. When the nurse began sliding the wand across my stomach, Chase asked me to show him what was going on. I turned the phone around and showed him to the nurse, who flashed him a distracted and slightly irritated smile, which turned to awe when she realized who he was. I showed him the ultrasound equipment, and then focused on the screen showing the baby.

The nurse hit a key and the room was filled with the distorted *thumpthump—thumpthump* of the heartbeat, and Chase gave a choked laugh at the sound.

"Is that the heartbeat?" he asked.

"Yes," the nurse replied. "And it's a good one. Right in the middle of the best range. I'm gonna see if I can get a good shot at the gender now."

I swiveled the phone so I could see Chase, and felt love for him ripple through me at the emotions I saw written on his features.

"Where are you?" I asked him.

"I'm in the hotel room in Columbus," he replied. "The guys are all down in the conference room waiting for the interview to start."

"Oh, here, look!" The nurse pointed at the screen, holding the wand low on my belly at an angle.

I turned the phone so Chase could see the monitor clearly. There was a blob of white against grainy black, moving and shimmering as the baby wiggled inside me. I couldn't make anything out at first, but then I realized what I was seeing.

"It's a girl, Chase, you see it?" My throat was thick as I spoke, and I mentally cursed the damned emotions.

"I see, baby. I see. It's a girl. Our daughter." He was equally as emotional, so I didn't feel as embarrassed by my own.

I turned the phone back to me, seeing a single tear streak down Chase's face. "God *damn* it, Jay. I wish I was there with you. We're having a daughter. A baby girl." He wiped his face and forced a laugh out. "It didn't seem really real until now, you know? Seeing it there on the screen made it…god. Fuck, I'm really going to be a father." He scrubbed his palm over his scalp, which was now darkened by growing hair.

"I know what you mean," I said. "I knew it was real because I'm the one with the baby growing inside me, but this makes it all the more real."

"Do you guys have a name picked out?" the nurse asked.

"We've discussed a few," I said. "He likes Beth and I like Samantha, after my grandmother. We haven't decided yet."

"Actually," Chase cut in, "I've been thinking, and I want to go with Samantha. Sam."

I looked at him in surprise, seeing the satisfaction cross his face. "Are you sure?"

"Yeah, I'm sure." He smiled at me, and I wished I could run my fingers down his cheek. "Samantha Delany. It's got a great ring to it, don't you think?"

I could only nod until I had control of myself. So damn emotional. Ugh. I sucked in a deep breath and smiled at him. "Yeah, it does. Sam Delany." I laughed. "I knew you'd see things my way."

"Don't I usually?" He asked.

The nurse smiled at our conversation as she continued to tap keys and shift the wand. "The rest of the appointment is just taking measurements and stuff. I heard Dad mention an interview, so if you have to go, you won't be missing anything dramatic."

I blew a kiss at the phone. "Call me after the interview," I said.

"I will," Chase said. "I've been told I have a couple days between shows after Columbus, so I'm going to fly back. We'll do the nursery all in pink or whatever you want then, okay?"

I said goodbye, and we hung up. As the appointment wound down, I found myself alternating between a confusing welter of emotions. I was ecstatic at the thought of having a daughter, and I was so grateful to Chase for making the effort to be as involved as possible in the ultrasound; on the other hand, I was still terrified.

I stopped in the hallway as the thought hit me. I'd been skirting it for awhile, but now it was out there. I was terrified. I'd never had to take care of anyone but myself. Even now that I was married to Chase, I was still basically independent most of the time. I'd held babies on a handful of occasions, when friends had them, but that was it. I had never interacted with a baby for longer than ten or fifteen minutes.

And Chase would be gone for much of it.

Could I do this?

I managed to make it home before the emotions overtook me. I sobbed in the bathroom for nearly an hour, only pulling myself out of it when my phone rang. I stared at the screen with the picture of Chase, trying to suck down the tears and rub away the redness. He'd still know I'd been crying, but there was nothing for it.

I sniffed, wiped my face, and slid the answer key across the screen. "Hi, baby."

"What's wrong, Jamie?" His voice was soft with concern.

"Nothing. Just hormones." I knew he wouldn't buy it, but I didn't want him to worry.

"Oh come on, Jay. Don't feed me horseshit. What's up?"

I sighed. "Just…it's hard, sometimes."

"What is?"

"Having you gone." My voice was tiny, hesitant. "I know I signed up for it when I married you, and I love what you do, I'm so proud of you but—it's just hard sometimes is all."

I heard Chase sigh, a deep, soulful sound. "I know, Jay. It's hard for me too, you know that, right? I hate being away from you. I hate that I wasn't there with you in the office today. I hate that I'll probably miss other big stuff while I'm gone." His voice strengthened. "I can make you this promise, though: I will be there with you when Samantha is born. I don't care if I have to walk off stage in the middle of a show, I'll be there. You have my word."

I nodded, even though he couldn't see me. "Okay. Thank you." I heard people in the background calling his name. "You should go. I love you. Call again when you can."

"I will. Love you. Bye." And he was gone.

I put my hand over my belly, picturing a girl with curly black hair and brown eyes. "We can do this, can't we, Samantha?"

As if she'd heard me, I felt a flutter in my belly, and then a sharp poke. My hand clapped over my mouth and I sobbed in a hiccuping laugh as I realized I'd just felt my first kick.

I was really, actually, factually having a baby. A real live human being was going to come out of my hoo-ha.

Oh shit.

Chapter 3: Anna

I watched Chase and Jeff standing awkwardly side by side, Miller Lites in hand, their faces locked in matching rictuses of agony. Jamie's mother-in-law shrieked particularly loud when Jamie unwrapped the third set of cute little onesies with cute little sayings like "Mommy's little monster" on them. Chase rubbed his forehead with the rim of his beer bottle at his mother's high-pitched squeals of excitement.

"Chase! Look!" Kelly Delany said, rushing over to her son. "This one says 'Daddy's Girl' on it! Isn't it just adorable!"

Chase stifled a sigh. "Yes, mom, it's adorable. It's as adorable as the last fifty-seven I've seen. They're all adorable."

Kelly shot her son a scathing glare. "Well don't sound so enthusiastic. I wouldn't want you to get over excited or anything. It's not like you're about to be a father or anything."

Chase spoke into his beer bottle. "I'm excited to have a baby, Mom. What I'm not excited about is sitting around watching a bunch of women squawk about diapers and trade breast feeding secrets."

Kelly huffed. "Then why are you here?"

Chase rolled the side of the bottle across his forehead. "I don't *know*, Mom. *Some*one told me I had to be here." He shot a dirty look at Jamie. "I've always sort of thought baby showers were a women-only thing. Guess I was wrong."

Jamie sighed. "Fine, leave then. I just thought you would want to share in this experience." She gave him the dirty look right back. "Guess I was wrong."

"Fuck me," Chase muttered. "Don't turn this into something it's not. I'm excited for the *baby*, Jay. I could care less about diapers and bizarre little shirts that snap together under her ass. I don't know."

677

Jay glared at him, then relented. "Fine. You're such a guy, Chase."

"Well no shit," he muttered. "Was it the cock that gave it away, or the balls?"

I nearly snorted diet Coke out of nose at that.

"It was the fact that you're a jackass, I'm pretty sure. Or the giant asshole where your face is supposed to be."

I did snort soda out my nose at that. "Jay, I'm sorry, but I don't think any guy on earth likes baby showers," I said.

Jay glared at me. "You're *not* helping, Anna."

"Actually, I like baby showers, and I have a cock," Lane—Jamie's GBFF (gay best friend forever)—said, raising his hand.

"Yeah," I said, "But you don't count. You're basically a girl."

Lane shrugged. "Yeah. But I'm still male. I'm on both sides with this one."

I glanced at Jeff. "You want to leave too?"

He examined me carefully, then looked around the room and back to me. "You really have to ask?"

I sighed. "Ugh. Men." I looked at Jamie. "I think we have to let them leave for awhile."

Jay waved her hand without looking up from her phone. "Fine. I already said fine."

Chase groaned. "But we all know what 'fine' means."

She clicked the button on the top of her phone to put it to sleep, and then gave Chase a sickly sweet smile. "Yeah, but we wouldn't our men to be bored, would we? Go get drunk or something. Just go."

Chase set his bottle down and grabbed Jeff by the shoulder, dragging him away and pushing him toward the door. "Let's go now, before they change their minds. God knows we don't want to get stuck playing fucking baby bingo or some shit."

I laughed at that, then fell silent when Jamie glared at me. Jeff mouthed *I love you* as Chase dragged him out the door. Jamie stared at the door, then turned back to the stack of wrapped gifts. "We're not playing baby bingo, are we Jamie?" I asked, suddenly suspicious.

She huffed, looking offended. "No!" She lifted a box from the floor beside her. "Would I make you play something as dumb as that? We're playing 'pin the sperm on the egg.'"

I choked on my Coke a third time, spewing it out of my mouth and nose, coughing and laughing. "We're playing *what?*" Kelly patted me on the back and handed me a paper towel. I patted my yoga pants dry and wiped my face. "Are you serious?"

Jamie stood up slowly and made her way to a wall, where she taped a filmy piece of plastic-y material to the wall. It was yellow with a cartoon diagram of the female reproductive organs in purple. Along one edge of the uterus was a pink dot with a bizarre smiley face on it. Jamie showed us little black squiggly bits with bulbous heads, fixed with a pin near the head, obviously meant to represent sperm.

I groaned. "You're serious." I took one of the sperms from Jamie and examined it, shaking my head. "Where did you find this, Jay? And we're not seriously going to play this, are we?"

Jamie snatched the sperm from my hand and set it neatly in a pile with the others on her coffee table. "I found it online. It looks like fun. There was actual baby Bingo, but that's dumb."

"This isn't dumb?" I demanded.

She glared at me. "No, it's cute and funny." At my skeptical expression, she gave me a hurt look. "What the fuck do I know about baby showers, Anna? I've only even held a baby a handful of times in my life. I've never been to a baby shower before. I'm not the kind of girl you invite to baby showers. Bachelorette parties, yes. Baby showers, no. I'm trying, okay? I don't know how to do this. I don't know how to be—" she sobbed suddenly.

I levered myself out of the chair and wrapped her in a hug. "It's fine, Jay. It's great. We'll have lots of fun pinning little spermies to happy eggs."

"It's not about the fucking game, Anna!" Jamie pulled away from me to shoot me an evil look. "I don't know shit about babies or how to be a mother. And Chase is gone, and I don't know how to do this!"

I sighed, not wanting to admit my own very similar feelings. Kelly came up on Jamie's other side, joined by Lindsey, two of her friends, and several other girls I didn't know but thought were somehow connected to Chase's band.

"I'm scared, Anna." Jamie whispered it into my ear so the other women wouldn't hear.

Kelly turned Jamie's face with a palm. "You're allowed to be scared, Jamie. Every woman is scared for her first baby. I think you're scared for every baby, no matter how many you have. Babies are scary. No one here thinks any less of you for being afraid."

"What if something goes wrong and Chase isn't here?" Jamie said. "What if I go into labor early? What if we have this baby and I'm shitty mom? What if I fuck her up? I don't want to fuck up my daughter, but I will. I fuck everything up."

I laughed, crying with her now. "No you don't, Jay. You'll be a great mother. You're not going to fuck up your daughter. You won't, I promise you."

Jamie sniffled, then looked at me. "Are you scared, Anna?"

I laughed again. "Jay, I wake up in the middle of the night having panic attacks. Every night for the last month I've woken up at two in the morning barely able to breathe, panicking. You guys can't tell Jeff because he'll just worry and I need him to be the one who's not worrying. I'm terrified, Jay." I knew I shouldn't say the next part, but I did anyway. "I wish I had my best friend. I know you live in New York now, but…I sometimes wish you didn't. I know you're happy here with Chase and everything, and it's selfish of me, but I just wish sometimes that we could have our babies together."

Jamie lost it again. "I'm not happy, Anna! That's the worst part! Chase is on tour. He's gone more than he's here. I talk to him several times a day, and I'm so thankful for that. He's making a huge effort to keep in contact with me and I realize that, and I appreciate it. He FaceTimed me instead of doing an interview with a magazine just so he could sort of be there when we found out Samantha's gender. It was so sweet. But...I'm still alone when I go to bed and when I wake up. When he's here, I'm deliriously happy. But...he's only here until Wednesday, and then he's gone again right up until I'm full term."

Kelly subtly shooed the other girls away so it was just her, Jamie and me. "I might have an idea, Jay. I'm not sure it will work, but...you could always stay with me. The last trimester is always the hardest, and you really shouldn't be alone. I can help you, and then when you go into labor, Chase can just fly in to Detroit instead of New York. I know you and I don't know each other all that great, but I'd love to have the opportunity to fix that." She picked at her cuticles with a fingernail while she spoke, as if afraid of rejection.

Jamie's eyes lit up with relief. "Really? That would be so cool! I just...I don't want to do this alone. And that way Anna and I could have our babies together."

I pulled Jamie and Kelly into a hug. "I think it's perfect."

Jamie sniffled. "Thanks, Kelly. You're the best."

Kelly just smiled and hugged us together.

We played Pin the Sperm on the Egg, which was actually really fun. It degenerated into a frenzy of sex jokes and all around bawdy silliness, and by the time the shower was over Jamie seemed to be in better spirits. The boys came back about an hour after the party was over, and they were surprisingly sober. I never thought I'd see the day, but they seemed comfortable with each other.

It was still awkward for me, sometimes, seeing both Jeff and Chase together, but as time passed and the memories faded, so did the awkwardness. Jeff and Chase were laughing at a joke as they clomped through the foyer of the Jamie and Chase's beyond fabulous Manhattan brownstone. Jamie and I exchanged a pleased glance at the way our men seemed to have bonded while they were gone. I gave Jamie an *I told you so* smirk and she just rolled her eyes in acknowledgement.

When the party mess was cleaned up, Jeff, Chase, Kelly, Jamie and I all sat down in the living room.

"So, Chase." Kelly sat on the arm of the couch next to her son. "I was talking to Jamie while you and Jeff were gone. I was thinking it may be a good idea for her come stay with me in Birmingham for her last trimester. She really needs someone to help her while you're gone."

Chase looked from his wife to his mother, and then stood up with a sigh. He crossed the room to look out the window onto the busy street beyond. "Meaning she'd have the baby in Detroit, rather than here."

"I know it's not what we originally planned," Jamie said, moving to stand next to Chase. "But…I think it would be good for me."

Chase didn't answer for a long time. "It's that hard for you here by yourself, huh?" He ran his palm back and forth over his head, a gesture I knew meant he was upset.

"Yeah, it really is." She moved to stand in front of him, wrapping her arms around his waist and staring up at him. "I like your mom a lot. It would be nice to get to know her, for one thing. And for another, I'm barely twenty weeks along and it's already getting harder for me to move around. When I'm thirty-four weeks and can't get up without a fricking crane, being here alone while you're touring would be…god, it'd be impossible."

Chase nodded. "I get it." He let out a long breath. "So you're moving back to Detroit. Okay then."

Jamie frowned up at him. "No, Chase. I'm not *moving* anywhere. I'm staying with Kelly temporarily, until I have the baby. By then your tour will be over and we'll come back home together." She put her hand to the back of Chase's head, tilting his face down to hers. "This is home. Here, with you. I know this tour is important, and I'd never ever ask you to stop, or change it, or cut it short. I just—I need help, baby."

The hard, tense set of Chase's shoulders relaxed. "You're right. You're right. It is a good idea. I just—I wish I could be here. I wish it wasn't necessary. That's all." He lowered his face to hers for a kiss.

When their lips met, I looked away and found Jeff watching me. He tilted his head toward the door, indicating that it was time to go. Kelly had already snuck out the front door, and when I turned to say goodbye to Jamie I realized why: she and Chase were lip-locked in a kiss that had all the signs of not stopping, regardless of who was or wasn't in the room. I felt myself blush when Chase's hands slid up the backs of Jamie's thighs to pull her against him.

"On that note, I think it's time to go," I said.

Jamie lifted up on her toes and peeked at me over Chase's shoulder. "Bye, Anna. Bye, Jeff. Call me tomorrow."

"Sure thing. I think we're leaving after lunch so we can do breakfast together."

Jamie just waved at me with one hand, already lost in Chase's mouth. I turned away before awkwardness descended any more thickly on me. When we were in a cab headed toward our hotel, Jeff twisted on the seat to look at me. "You alright?"

I shrugged. "Yeah, why wouldn't I be?" Jeff just frowned, but I knew what he was getting at. He wouldn't be able to say it out loud, but I knew. I decided to put him out of his misery. "I'm fine, Jeff. I'm happy for Jamie and Chase. Did you have fun with him?"

Jeff nodded. "Yeah, once I got past that it was fucking pretty boy Chase I was hanging with, yeah." That was as close as Jeff would come to acknowledging the elephant in the room that was my previous relationship with Chase. "He's cool. We drank some scotch at the sports bar down the street and watched the UConn-Nebraska game. I'm not really into the whole March Madness thing, but I'll watch a game here and there. Chase is the same way."

"I have no idea what March Madness is," I said.

"College basketball playoffs, basically." He glanced at me to gauge the effect of his next words. "Chase is pretty mixed up about the whole being gone while Jamie's pregnant business. He admitted that he's thought about cutting the tour short to be with her full-time."

"He really can't do that," I said. "This tour is a make it or break it thing. They're getting big, but this tour can really cement them as one of the biggest up-and-coming bands in the business. If they cut the tour short, it could ruin all the progress they've made. They're not so big that they can do whatever they want, not yet at least."

Jeff nodded. "He said the same thing, basically. I think Jamie going back to the D until the baby's out is a good plan."

"I think so too. And I'm really excited that she'll be around for awhile. It would be so cool if we could have our babies at the same time." I smirked at Jeff. "You know what else is a really good idea? Finding out the gender on Monday."

Jeff let his head fall back onto the seat with a sigh. "Here we go again."

I just laughed.

Jeff squeezed my hand gently as the ultrasound technician prepped me, lining my belly with white towels and splooging a glop of frigid blue goo onto my stomach. The lights were dim, a computer monitor on the wall opposite the chair showing a black screen with indecipherable words and abbreviations on either side. My name, Anna Cartwright, was written across the top of the screen. I was still getting used to writing "Cartwright" as my last name, but I felt a thrill every time I did.

"So," the technician said, rubbing the tip of the wand into the goo on my belly. "You're not finding out the gender?"

"That's what *he* says," I jerked my thumb at Jeff. "I want to know, but he doesn't. Maybe you can tell me and he can cover his ears or something."

"That's cheating," Jeff said with a grin.

"Well, we could do it that way," the technician said. "I wouldn't recommend it though. You should know or not know together, as a couple. I will say, though, that you'd be surprised by how many couples have this same argument in here. It's not uncommon."

"I just want to be able to decorate the nursery." I watched the screen shifting as she slid the wand around my belly.

"Okay," the nurse said. "Look here, you can see the head and a little arm, see it?"

Jeff and I looked at each other, then the screen. I clenched Jeff's hand as we saw our baby for the first time. My heart stuttered, leapt, and then began hammering as the reality of our baby hit me.

"Can you tell what it is?" Jeff asked.

"I'm looking," the nurse said. "I want to get a fix on the heartbeat first, though. Here, listen."

She tapped a key on the keyboard, and then another, and the sound of the heartbeat filled the room. I covered my mouth with my free hand, hearing a real live heart beating inside me. I looked at Jeff, who was as transfixed as I was.

There was something odd about the heartbeat, an odd overlapping in the rhythm. It made my stomach drop. "Is that how a heartbeat is supposed to sound?" I asked. "I'm looking into that, just wait a second," the nurse said. "I think—" but she cut herself off as she wiggled the wand around, sliding it from one spot to another, the sound of the heartbeat distorting.

"What is it? Is everything okay?" Jeff demanded.

"She's fine, it's just...wait...now listen." She swiveled the wand a fraction and the distortion of the heartbeat cleared, and then she swiveled it in the opposite direction, making the sound fade, distort, and then clear up again. "Hear that?" She turned in her seat to grin at me.

I felt an inkling of realization strike me. "Is that...*two* heartbeats?"

"Two? Like twins?" Jeff asked.

I turned to look at him, seeing surprise on his face as I'm sure it was on mine. The nurse repeated the effect of producing two distinct heartbeats, then tapped a few more keys and searched my belly some more. I watched the view on the monitor shift and adjust, and then, as she brought the wand around to my side, I saw it, saw *them*, two distinct forms. Four arms, four legs. Two heads. Two heartbeats.

Two babies. *Holy shit.*

The nurse searched and tapped some more, and then pointed at the screen once more. "Congratulations, Mr. and Mrs. Cartwright. You're having twins!"

Jeff and I traded stunned glances. Jeff's mouth flapped open and closed as he tried to speak. "Twins? How—how—*twins?*"

The nurse just laughed as she continued to adjust the wand for different views. "That's a very common reaction, actually. Are there any twins on either side of your families?"

I nodded my head, almost absently. "Yeah, yeah, we both have twins in our family."

"Well, there you go. It's a genetic thing, although there are rare cases of twins in families with no history of it." She printed out some pictures of the babies—*babies, plural…oh god*—and put them in an envelope, then proceeded to swivel the wand and tap on the keyboard, sometimes making parts of the screen turn technicolor. "So, do you still want it to be a surprise, now that you know you're having twins?"

Jeff and I exchanged glances.

I touched his cheek so he looked at me. "Jeff? You're the one who wanted it to be a surprise in the first place."

He shook his head slowly. "I think…I think we've got enough of a surprise now."

"So you want to know?" The nurse adjusted the wand to focus on one of the babies. "Well…it looks like this one is…ooh, this is a great potty shot. It's a girl. See?" She moved the wand, searching for the best view once more, talking to herself. "Okay. Baby number two…where are you? There you are. That's your head, and there's your legs, come on baby, give a good look. Ah, gotcha. Baby number two is…a boy! They're fraternal twins, a boy and a girl."

I sucked in a deep breath to calm myself. "God, twins." I looked at Jeff, who seemed to be still struggling with shock. "You called it, remember?"

He shook his head, then met my eyes. "I called it? Oh yeah. Way back, just after I proposed." He laughed. "I did, didn't I?"

"We're having twins, Jeff." I said it out loud, again.

"Oh god. Oh god. Twins." He gave me an odd smile. "So, miss interior decorator. How are we doing the nursery now that we're having a boy *and* a girl?"

I just shook my head. "I have no idea. I like green?"

Jeff laughed. "What I said in the first place? Nice, Anna." He turned to the nurse. "So aside from the fact that there's two babies in there, does everything else look good?"

She nodded. "Yes, everything looks great. All the measurements are right on target for twins. The high-risk doctor will want to talk to you, though."

Jeff's face paled. "The high-risk doctor? Why? I thought you said things were good?"

She patted his hand. "Any time a woman carries twins, she's considered high-risk. Giving birth is complicated enough with one baby, so when you have two, we just have to be extra careful so the mother and the children are all safe and healthy. It's just a precaution, Mr. Cartwright. No need to worry."

When we were back home, I kicked off my shoes and lowered myself to the couch. Jeff sat next to me and lifted my feet onto his lap, rubbing my instep with his thumbs. Several minutes passed in silences, until I felt myself drowsing.

As I was about to drift off, I felt Jeff's hand cover my belly. I felt his face touch my stomach, and opened my eyes sleepily. His eyes were locked on mine, molten brown love, tender hands caressing my belly. "Caleb and Niall," he whispered. "Caleb *and* Niall."

I smiled at him, brushing his hair across his forehead. "Caleb and Niall. A son and a daughter. Are you ready for this?"

He laughed. "No. Not even close. But it's happening. It's real." He leaned toward me, taking my lips with his. "And I'm glad."

"You are? You're glad?" I spoke into his lips as they covered mine, tasted mine.

"Mmm-hmmm. Of course." His fingers touched my cheek, then traced down the curve of my neck. "A little nervous, I admit. But glad. I'm excited to be a daddy."

"I'm excited to be a mommy." I twisted and lay back on the couch, pulling Jeff over me. "I'm also excited for you to get me naked and plunder me on the couch."

Jeff pushed my shirt up over my head, and I unclasped my bra while he tugged my pants off. A few more moments passed and I was naked and wrapping my knees over his shoulders and burying my fingers in his hair while his tongue dipped into me, slowly at first, in circles and gliding upward strokes. I let him tongue me into a frenzy, but when I was on the cusp of orgasm, I pulled him away, pulled him up to me. He'd shed his shirt and unbuttoned his jeans at some point. I slid my fingers under the band of his boxers and freed his heavy erection, pushing his jeans away and guiding him to me. He nudged my knee aside so my foot planted flat on the floor, the other stretched out along the back of the couch. Kneeling above me, Jeff put one foot next to mine on the floor and nestled his tip into my folds, one hand on the armrest of the couch just past my head, the other caressing my face and my breasts and my belly, then dipping down to cup my mound. I lifted my hips and he slid in, both of us sighing as he filled me. His fingers slipped between the joining of our bodies and circled my clit, driving gasps from me.

He was only barely moving, but something about the angle and the placement of our bodies on the couch gave him incredible leverage, letting each stroke drive deep and slick along all the best nerve endings. I needed more. God, more. I pushed up off the floor with one foot, bracing the other on the opposite end of the couch, lifting my hips to crash against his in a pleasingly punishing rhythm. Jeff seemed surprised by my sudden desperation. I wasn't sure where it was coming from, but as he slid into me, driving deeper with each thrust, I found myself needing more, more, even though I'd had him just the night before. Each stroke of his shaft into me drove me crazier, wilder, incited my need.

"God, Jeff. I love you so much. Don't stop, please." I clutched his ass with desperate fingers, pulling him into me, thrust up to meet him stroke for stroke until we were thrashing on the couch together, frantic, moaning into mouths and against shoulders, riding the cusp of climax together. Then his fingers found my clit and his mouth found my nipple and I passed over the edge, screaming his name. I clamped down with inner muscles and arched my entire body off the couch, crushing my soft folds into his hardness and pulsating in shallow thrusts, whimpering and gasping as he hit me deep inside. I felt his stomach tense, heard his breath catch and felt his rhythm falter.

"Give it to me, Jeff. Give it all to me, right now." I wrapped my arms around his neck and pulled him down against me, relishing his weight on me, the feel of hips hard against mine, his shaft piercing deep and his balls slapping against me, his fingers in my hair and on my nipple.

"You want it, baby?" He kissed me, quick and sloppy, pumping into me madly now.

"God yes, Jeff. Let me feel you fill me up. Come for me, love. Come hard." I dragged my fingers down his back and felt him shudder, felt him tense. I kissed his temple, his cheek, his shoulder, his chin, whispered his name into his mouth and wrapped my legs around his hips as he came, and I kissed his quivering mouth as he gasped my name with his release.

After the shocks had faded, I curled into the back of the couch, holding Jeff close as we both shuddered. "I think that was the best couch sex we've ever had," I said.

He made a growl of agreement in his chest. "Yeah. Although, once we have the twins, our days of rocking couch sex are numbered."

I laughed. "I think once we have the twins, our days of sex of any kind are numbered."

He lifted up to look at me in mock horror. "Don't *say* that!"

I quirked an eyebrow at him. "You know we can't have sex for six weeks after I give birth, right?"

He put his face into my shoulder and pretended to sob. "More weeks without sex? I'll die. I'll die dead of blue balls."

"No you won't," I said, cradling his head with my hands. "I'll take care of you, don't worry."

"Promise?" He looked comically serious. I think he may have been serious.

I laughed and kissed him. "Yes, baby. I promise. No blue balls for you."

I found myself wondering about my own need for orgasms, though. I know you weren't supposed to put anything in your vagina for six weeks after birth, but I could I let Jeff twiddle my button? Or would I be so stretched out that he wouldn't be able to find it? I kept these worries to myself. Jeff seemed horrified enough as it was.

Twins. Holy shit.

Chapter 4: Jamie

I rubbed my shoulder beneath the bra strap, trying to alleviate the twinge in the muscle. Kelly frowned at me, watching me massage my shoulder.

"Something wrong with your shoulder?" she asked, stuffing the last of my maternity clothes into a suitcase.

I shrugged, rolling my shoulder. "No, I'm fine. My shoulder's just been achy recently. No big deal." I zipped my toiletries case closed and tossed it into the suitcase next to my hair straightener and blow dryer. "That should be it. Let's go."

Kelly didn't move, just stared at me thoughtfully. "Have you had any other odd feelings? Achy back, nausea as if morning sickness was coming back? Anything like that?"

I zipped the suitcase closed, set it on the floor and pulled the handle up with a *click*. "I've been a little nauseous, yeah, but I think it's just heartburn."

Kelly shook her head, chin-length black hair bouncing. "Don't ignore that stuff. We're going to the doctor as soon as we get to Detroit. How long have you been having those symptoms?" Kelly was a nurse, I had found out, and was taking her role as my caretaker very seriously.

"Symptoms? Why are you calling them symptoms? It's just normal pregnancy stuff, right?" I buttoned up my sweater, stuffed my phone and charger in my purse, and gave my beautiful home one last look-over.

It was clean, tidied, and dark. Mrs. Lettis was coming over once a week to check on things for us, which she would have done for free I'm pretty sure, but Chase insisted on paying her. I locked the front door behind me and let Kelly take the suitcase and stuff it into the trunk of the waiting cab.

"Because they very well could be symptoms," Kelly said.

I slid into the seat, puffing embarrassingly from the exertion necessary to just sit down in a car. I was twenty-three weeks now, and officially the size and shape of a beluga. I wasn't sure I'd be able to get out of bed by the time I was full-term, if I kept getting bigger. Stupid Anna, even with her twins, still wasn't as big as me. I didn't get it.

"Symptoms of what?"

"Preeclampsia." Something in her tone of voice had me worried.

"I've heard that word, but I don't know what it is," I said.

Kelly patted my knee. "It's complicated. I'm not going to worry you until we know for sure. Just be sure to tell me if you have any more things like that. Even if you're positive it's just usual pregnancy discomfort, tell me. Okay?"

I was worried now, but no sense in telling her that. I just shrugged. "Okay."

We chatted aimlessly the rest of the cab ride to the train station. Once we were in our seats, Kelly pulled out a paperback and was soon lost to the world. I dug my iPad out of my purse and opened the browser. I typed "preeclampsia" into the Google search bar and brought up the first hit, a .org website dedicated solely to preeclampsia. The more I read, the more frightened I became. By the time I'd read everything on the website, I was in full-blown panic attack mode.

"Kelly." I closed the cover to my iPad and met Kelly's eyes over the top of her book, a bodice-ripper by the looks of it. "You think I have preeclampsia?"

Kelly sighed and set the book face down on her thigh. Her kind brown eyes, so much like Chase's, searched mine, were soft with worry. "You Googled it, didn't you?" I nodded. "Jamie, it's going to be okay. I don't know that you do. I just don't want to ignore the possibility."

"But I'm experiencing everything listed on the website. Everything. And it said there's no cure but to induce labor or to abort. I'm not—I can't—I mean—"

Kelly leaned forward and took my hands in hers. "You're freaking yourself out needlessly. You're fine. Samantha is fine. Okay? We'll go see Dr. Rayburn first thing, I promise."

I took several deep breaths and tried to push away my panic, my tears, my sense of impending doom—which, by the way, was also one of the possible symptoms. For something which and no cure except to have the baby, and I wasn't even close to full-term yet.

I managed to calm myself down enough that I didn't hyperventilate, but it was close. I marinated in my own worry for most of the excruciatingly long train ride from New York to Detroit. When Chase called, he picked up on my worry within minutes, but I wasn't ready to saddle him with the possibilities yet, especially since, as Kelly said, I wasn't even sure I had preeclampsia. It was hard not to tell Chase, though. He was, beneath everything else, my best friend. I told him everything. So to keep this from him, even if it was just a worry at that point, was painful. I wanted him to comfort me, tell me it was fine, I was just being silly. But if I told him, he'd worry. And when he worried, he would be off his game and this tour *had* to go well.

By the time we pulled into Detroit some fifteen hours later, I was delirious from exhaustion and I'd run through every possibility in my head a dozen times, from emergency C-section as soon as I saw the doctor to being hospitalized for the next twelve weeks to being told I was an idiot for worrying so much over nothing. Kelly had slept most of the way, and I'd read the book she'd brought, as well as another one I had on my iPad. I'd watched half of the first season of *Downton Abbey*. I was bored, scared, tired, cramped, worried, and panicked. And horny. How could I be horny at a time like this? I had no answer for myself, and no relief in sight until I saw Chase again in a couple weeks.

Kelly woke up as we pulled into the station, took one look at me and groaned. "You've been working yourself into a fit the entire time, haven't you?"

I just shrugged and tugged my sweater higher up my shoulders. I knew if I answered her out loud, I'd snap, and she didn't deserve that. We made our way to Kelly's car in the long-term parking lot, shoved my suitcase in the backseat of her Lincoln MKZ. Chase had wanted to buy her something fancier, but she'd refused to let him, he claimed. So he'd gotten her the Lincoln and had it stuffed with every available option. He'd laughed when he related how she'd chewed his ear off after the car was delivered. I don't know what she was complaining about; it was a nice car that I wouldn't mind driving, if it had been practical to even own a car in New York City.

I fell asleep in the car and didn't wake up until Kelly gently shook my shoulder an hour later, sitting in her driveway. It was past two in the morning and I followed Kelly sleepily as she unlocked her front door and showed my my room. I didn't even look around me at Kelly's house. I fell face-first into the bed, felt Kelly slip my shoes off, tug the blankets free from beneath me and drape them over me. I couldn't even summon the strength to murmur a thanks to her. And yet, even in the grip of utter exhaustion, I dreamed of being chained to a hospital bed for the next three months.

I woke up in a sweat, near tears, and rubbed my wrists where I'd felt the shackles in my dream. As I fell asleep, I felt the dream coming back, felt the panic, the bone-deep fear.

The next morning—or, well, it was past noon by the time I woke up—Kelly forced a healthy breakfast down my throat and shooed me into her car. My OB/GYN in New York had referred me to a colleague of hers in Detroit, and had insisted I go in for an appointment when I arrived. Now that Kelly had so kindly instilled in me the fear of pre-eclampsia, I was all too willing to get poked and prodded again, if it meant putting my mind at ease.

Two hours and half a dozen tests later, I sat in the passenger seat of Kelly's car, sobbing hysterically into the phone while Chase begged me to calm down and tell him what the problem was. Eventually, Kelly took the phone from me and explained preeclampsia and all its attendant issues and worries to him. By the time she'd educated Chase on my problem, I had calmed down enough to carry on an intelligible conversation.

Kelly handed the phone back to me and I pressed it to my ear, sniffling but calm. "Hi baby," I said. "So. How's the tour?" I asked, with overly-fake enthusiasm.

"Fuck the tour," Chase growled. "I'm coming back."

"No, baby," I said. "Not yet. You're almost done at this point. Just finish the tour. You can't quit now, Chase, and you know it. Doctor Rayburn said we just have to watch my blood pressure for now. Worst case scenario, they'll induce me at thirty-two weeks. I'll call you every day and tell how I'm doing, okay?"

Chase growled again. "No, it's not okay. I should be there with you. I should be the one taking care of you."

"You will be. You have to finish the tour, Chase. You *have* to. The label will be pissed if you quit."

"I'm gonna worry more than ever now."

I sighed. "I know. I didn't want to tell you, but…I'm scared. I know it's going to be okay, but I'm scared."

"Goddamn it, Jay." I heard the anguish in his voice. "I should *be* there."

"You're where you have to be for now. If something comes up, I'll be the first one to call you, okay? I promise."

"But if something comes up, I'll be hours away. What if—what if I don't get there in time?"

Kelly took the phone from me. "Listen, son. I'm here with her. This is why she came to Detroit. I'm a nurse. I know what to look for. I'll monitor her blood pressure and make sure she rests. I'll take care of her. You need to focus on doing your job. Keep your fans happy."

"Okay Mom," I heard him say. "Just…take care of her, okay?"

"I will Chase. It'll be fine."

I took the phone back, told Chase I loved him and hung up. Kelly tried making conversation on the way back to her house, but I ignored her. I didn't mean to be rude, but I just couldn't summon the will to care. Eventually, she relented with a sigh and turned on the radio to a pop station. Even Rihanna couldn't get me out of my funk, it seemed.

Bed rest sucked. I wouldn't let Kelly take time off work until absolutely necessary, especially since Beaumont Hospital, where she worked, was barely a ten minute drive from her house. Which meant, of course, that I was home alone and relegated to complete bed rest. Like, don't get up to pee unless you absolutely have to. I've always been an active person. I wasn't a gym rat by any stretch of the imagination, but I liked to do stuff. I worked hard, I played hard, and I kept busy. I've never been the type to sit around and watch TV all day, and now, suddenly, that and read was all I had to do. For the first couple days, I watched every movie Kelly owned, which was quite a few. She had everything from *The Breakfast Club* to *Walk the Line*, even a few action/adventure movies featuring hot shirtless men. After I'd gone through her movie collection, I started in on daytime television programming.

Fuck daytime programming.

I watched all her movies again, and then went through all the movies available on her premium cable package's On Demand section, even the ones I'd never heard of and didn't really like. I even watched *3000 Miles to Graceland* twice.

At which point, a single week had passed.

Fuck bedrest.

Fuck preeclampsia.

When Kelly came back from work at the end of the second week, I begged her to help me find something to pass the time. She stifled her laughter and brought out her knitting kit.

I just stared at her.

"You expect me to knit? Do you know me at *all*?" I held the needles in each hand like knives, pretending to stab her. "What am I going to knit? Socks? Sweaters?"

Kelly laughed and fended me off with a clipboard. "Figuring that out will be part of what passes the time." She gestured at the TV. "You know I've got Netflix on there, right?"

I frowned at her. "What?"

"The TV. When I went to finally buy a new TV after having the same one since nineteen-ninety, the salesman talked me into getting this fancy one here. It's a smart TV, apparently. You can surf the web on it, which I'm not entirely sure what the point of that is, but you can." She picked up the remote and hit a button, bringing up a menu bar across the bottom of the screen. "I had to have the Best Buy Geek Squad come out and set all this up for me, but now that I have it and know how to work it, it's awesome. Netflix has pretty much everything, including entire seasons of shows—"

I rolled my eyes and snatched the remote from her. "I know what it is, Kelly. Why the hell didn't you tell me about this two weeks ago? I was about to start watching all your movies through for the third time. Jesus."

Kelly flushed with embarrassment. "Sorry, I just…I forgot. I guess I just thought you'd be able to figure it out on your own or something. Technology is my worst enemy." She sat on the couch next to me and untied her white Keds. "When the hospital started the transition to tablet computers, I seriously almost lost my job because I couldn't figure them out. When Chase insisted I have smart phone, I had to take it in to the Verizon store and have them show me how to use the damn thing. I couldn't even figure out how to answer a stupid phone call. I kept hanging up on Chase and then redialing him."

I laughed with her as I flipped through the Netflix options. Thank sweet baby Jesus for Netflix. I might actually come out of this whole bed rest thing with most of my sanity intact.

I wondered if bed rest meant I couldn't have sex with Chase. That would be bad, very, very bad. The doctor hadn't said specifically no sex, but she'd said I can't do anything to raise my blood pressure. Chase definitely had a tendency to raise my blood pressure, you might say.

The next day while Kelly was working, I sat down with the second season of *The Walking Dead* queued up and the reusable Whole Foods bag full of colored string. Okay, *fine*, they were skeins of yarn, I suppose. I chose yellow, orange, green, and red yarn, pulled up a "how to knit" video on YouTube, and got started.

It took three days of clicking needles and unthreading my knots before I got the hang of it and was able to start trying to make something for real. I'd finished *The Walking Dead* and was going through *Spartacus.* The first thing I knitted was an unrecognizable, misshapen thing that vaguely resembled something a Rasta might wear over his dreads, if knitted by a blind and drunk old woman. I had meant it to be…well, I didn't really have any idea what it was supposed to be. A hat maybe. Or a pillowcase. It could function as either, really.

By the time I was done with the pillowcase/hat, I had watched through a couple seasons of *Sex and The City.* I'd already seen the entire the series—and all the movies—but it was a comfort food kind of thing. I could quote my favorite lines from the first season to the last, and to re-watch it—for the third or fourth time, possibly—was like hanging out with old friends. I could partially tune it out and try to focus on actually knitting—or crocheting or whatever—something useful.

I managed a scarf, first. It was about four feet long and six inches wide and had holes big enough you could fit your fist through them, but it was recognizably a scarf.

#Winning.

Kelly laughed her ass off at my scarf, and then showed me how to tighten my knots or whatever the hell they're called. Stitches? Loops?

They're knots, fancy knots. So I made another scarf, this one longer and wider and with fewer gaping holes. It was pink and purple, so I gave it to Kelly, who actually wore it, bless her heart. I think she did it to be nice to me, since it was warm out and the scarf was the ugliest thing I'd ever seen. The edges curled and refused to lay flat, the ends were crooked, and the whole thing was just fucking ugly. But Kelly wore thing to and from work for a solid week before I told her she didn't have to actually wear it. She looked relieved.

Now that I had more of a hang of it, I decided to make a pair of socks for Chase. Which was stupid, because they'd be more like something Santa Claus would wear over his boots or something, but still. I knit the damn things and give them to him and he'd be grateful, damn it.

I managed one "sock" while I watched the best of John Cusack's eighties movies. By which I mean *Say Anything*, *Sixteen Candles*, and *Stand by Me*. I also tossed *High Fidelity* in there even though it's not technically an Eighties movie, but it's awesome and has Jack Black in it.

Chase walked in at the end of *HiFi*, and I shrieked happily. I also might've peed a little.

No one told me about that, and I wish they had. I mean, I've heard all sorts of stand-up skits by women who have kids, but I thought it was a joke. Like, haha, you pee by accident. So funny.

NO. Not funny. You really do pee by accident. I laughed too hard once watching *Liar, Liar*, and I peed so bad I had to change my panties. For real. I was so embarrassed I started a load of laundry, even though I was alone in the house and not supposed to lift baskets of clothes. So yeah. Pee. I thought about wearing a pad all the time.

Chase knelt beside me as I struggled to a sitting position on the couch. "I had a couple days between shows and decided to fly back and see you." He put a palm on my belly and the other on my cheek, kissing me slowly and deeply. My toes curled.

I pulled away, all too soon. "Don't get me worked up," I whispered. "I can't have sex."

Chase frowned. "What?"

"Yeah. Apparently orgasms raise your blood pressure or something, and that's a no-no." I slid my fingers through his hair, which was now long enough to be spiked in two inch-tall gel-stiff prickles.

"That sucks, baby." He moved to sit next to me. "Here I was hoping to make you scream for me."

I moaned and thumped my forehead onto his shoulder. "I'm so mad. I miss you so much. I'm horny, and after I have the baby it'll be another six weeks before you can put anything into me."

Chase gripped my T-shirt in his fists, growling. "God. We're both gonna fucking die before we can make love again."

I grinned, putting my palms flat on his chest and pushing him backward until he was laying against the arm of the couch. "Just because I can't come," I said, unbuttoning his tight blue jeans, "doesn't mean you can't."

Chase sucked in a breath and caught my wrists. "But, what about you?"

Ignoring his question, I freed my hands from his grip and unzipped him. "Commando?" I tugged his jeans down under his taut buttocks.

He groaned and watched me fist his erection with slow strokes. "I was planning on ravaging you into exhaustion. I thought it may take some of the stress away."

"It would have," I said, loving the blissful expression on his face as I worked his shaft with both hands, "and you're so sweet for thinking of me."

Chase lifted his head to quirk an eyebrow at me. "You're mocking me, aren't you?"

"You're a sad, strange, little man," I said.

Chase laughed and let his head thump back again as I wrapped my palm around his thick mushroom head and twisted gently with a slight pumping motion, rolling my palm over his head and then twisting again. I thumbed the clear pearl of pre-come around his tip until he was slick under my hand, and then resumed the twisting, pumping motion, increasing in tempo until he was arching his back off the couch. I curled my other hand around his base and pumped him swiftly. The motions of each hand were hard to keep separate, but I made a challenge of it, twist and roll and pump. Chase groaned deep in his chest and I felt him tense. I stopped all motion, just holding his cock in my fist and letting him back away from the edge.

Chase slammed his head against the arm of the couch. "Damn it, Jay. God, I was right there."

I slid off the couch to kneel on a pillow on the hardwood floor next to him. I leaned over him and ran my tongue up his throbbing length, then took him into my mouth and sucked once, twice, three times, just enough to get him moving, and then spitting him out and kissing back down his length. He tangled his fingers in my hair, holding the wayward strands away from my mouth, brushing my cheeks and my forehead, cupping my face, each touch tender. I planted kisses all the way down his shaft, then opened my mouth to take his sack between my lips, careful to cover my teeth. He hissed and cursed under his breath as I massaged his tender skin with my lips and tongue, holding his rigid cock in both hands.

When I thought he'd backed far enough away from the edge of climax, I resumed moving my hands up and down his length, tugging upward and sliding down to plunge my fingers against his base. He lifted his hips to meet each downward thrust of my hands, and now I lowered my mouth to him, taking his tip between my lips at each thrust.

The upward crush of hips grew desperate and his breathing ragged. "God, Jay. So fucking good. Feels…so good."

"Fuck my mouth, Chase." I whispered the words and then took him deep into my mouth.

He sucked in a raspy breath and let himself go, thrusting hard into me. I gripped his length with one hand, wrapping my lips around his tip and sucking hard as he thrust. When he pumped toward my throat, I sucked hard, when he pulled away, I released the suction; when he thrust, I pumped his length. I cupped his balls in my other hand and massaged them, letting my middle finger extend back toward his taint and rubbing gently.

He buried both hands in my hair and held tight, not pushing me down, just holding, fisting his fingers in my curls. "God...*damn*. Oh god, I'm close. So close. Don't tease me, baby. Let me come, please." I slowed my rhythm on him, just to tease him. "No, fuck no..." He wanted to pull me onto him, but didn't.

I laughed with my mouth still latched around his soft salty skin, and the buzz of my voice drove him wild. I let him thrust deep, relaxed my throat and took him deeper, clenching him with my fist and lips and my throat muscles, working him into a frenzy. His hips lifted off the couch and he fluttered his cock in shallow, desperate thrusts. I didn't relent, then, but worked him faster, fingering his taint and fisting his base with a blurring hand, my grip loose so I was barely brushing his skin.

I felt him tense in my hands, heard him groan, curse, and gasp. He fell down onto the couch, then thrusted again, and this time he did pull me against him, just a little, just enough to let me know he was about to explode. I hummed in my throat as I swallowed his tip as deep as I could, fisting him furiously.

"Oh god..." Chase's fingers tightened in my hair. "I'm coming..."

He detonated with groan. I felt his balls tense and then hot liquid splashed down my throat. I backed away and took him deep again, setting a bobbing rhythm as he came again, and then again, spurting hard each time, groaning and cursing nonstop.

The payoff for him was almost as much of one for me. I loved watching him lose control, completely sated, eyes rolled back in blissed-out ecstasy. I continued to suck and stroke him as he softened, milking every last drop of pleasure from him.

Eventually I released him and sat next to him on the couch.

"Fuck, Jay," he said, pulling his jeans back on. "I think that may have been the best blow job you've ever given me."

I pushed his hands away and fastened his pants for him, enjoying the fact that he was panting, out of breath and sweating. "Good," I said. "That's the goal. Each BJ should be the best one yet."

"I think you succeed, if that's your goal." He leaned in and kissed me, as he always did after I went down on him. "So, how can I make you feel good?"

"You just did," I told him, sliding into the nook of his shoulder.

He snorted. "No, sweetheart. That was you making *me* feel good. You're getting things backward."

I laughed. "I get pleasure from that. Not sexual pleasure, like it doesn't give me an O, but I enjoy your reactions, making you feel good. We've talked about this."

"I know," he said, stroking my arm with his thumb. "But I still don't entirely believe you when you say you like it."

"Do you like going down on me?" I asked him.

"Yeah, for the same reasons you said. I like giving you pleasure, making you feel good."

"Well, there you go."

"So can I do that to you, then?" He asked.

I shook my head. "Sadly, no. There's nothing I'd love more than have you munch my rug until I can't breathe, believe me. But at this point, it's not penetration that's the problem. It's my blood pressure. It's why I'm not supposed to exert myself. I have to stay off my feet so the effort of walking doesn't become too much. In which case, I'm pretty sure your expert skills in cunnilingus would make my blood pressure spike through the fucking roof."

Chase laughed. "Expert cunnilingus skills, huh?"

I nodded, patting his chest. "Yep. Masterful. You're an artisan of pussy-licking. A connoisseur of oral orgasm administration."

Chase laughed so hard my head bounced on his chest. "Good to know you enjoy it." He met my eyes. "I feel bad that you gave me that, and I can't do anything for you back."

"Well it's not like I'm keeping score, you know. I did it because I wanted to. You came to visit me, and I can't tell you how much that means to me. I know you're insane with this tour, so I know how much it took to take the time away." I smirked at him. "But if you're that worried, you can just keep a tally of how many orgasms I give you, and when I'm cleared for sex, you can pay me back."

Chase nodded seriously. "Okay, then. A tally system it is." He dug his phone out of his hip pocket, swiped it open, and tapped the yellow *notepad* app.

I laughed as he wrote "Orgasm Tally Card" on the top line. He spaced down a line, and wrote the numeral *1* on the next. "I was actually joking, Chase. It's not a who's-come-the-most competition, babe."

"It is now." He pushed his phone back into his pocket. "So, how have you been passing the time, my love?"

I laughed again, this time more in deprecation. "Poorly. I'm bored out of my fucking skull, Chase. I'm restless. Antsy. I've never spent this much time being lazy in my life."

"It's not laziness, Jay." Chase squeezed me against his side. "It's doctor-ordered bed rest. You're the least lazy woman I know."

"Nice try, babe, but that's not how it feels to me." I sighed. "All I do is sit on my ass, watching Netflix and knitting."

Chase guffawed. "Knitting? You? Since when do you *knit*?"

I frowned at him. "Why couldn't I knit? Maybe you just didn't know I did."

He rolled his eyes. "You don't knit, Jay. You just don't. No more than I do."

I glared at him, more offended than I had a right to be, since my reaction when Kelly first suggested it wasn't too far from Chase's. "I do too knit. Now, at least." I reached over the side of the couch and set my knitting bag on his lap.

A stunned expression on his face, he rummaged in the bag, pulling out my pillow/case hat, the holey scarf of shitty knitting, and my latest project, one sock out of the pair for Chase. "Damn, Jay, you *have* been knitting." He held up the pillowcase/hat, clearing his throat in an effort to not laugh. "Um…honey? What is this?"

I snatched it from him. "Shut up, you. It's a hat. Or a pillowcase. It can be both, if it wants to."

Chase took it back and set it on his head. His entire face was obscured by the multicolored yarn. "A hat?"

I snatched it off his head. "For a Rasta. To cover his dreads."

Chase laughed harder. "Do you even know any Rastas? And he'd have to have like, the biggest, longest, thickest dreads ever for this thing to fit."

I smashed it onto his head and pulled it down over his face. "Shut up. It was the first thing I tried making. I've only been doing this for, like, a week." I grabbed a square throw pillow and stuffed it into the hat; it fit, barely, and the corners poked through the holes, stretching it to ridiculous proportions. "It's harder than you might think."

"I'm not making fun of you, baby. I promise. It's just…it's funny." Chase pulled out the scarf next and wrapped it around his neck, posing and batting his eyelashes. "Does it go with my outfit?"

"Now you're just being a dick." I took the bag from him and dug in it until I found the one sock I'd finished. "I did make you something, but you probably don't want it now, since I'm such a crappy knitter."

Chase laughed and kissed the nape of my neck, knowing how that melted me. "I do want it, baby. I'm just teasing. I'm sorry."

I handed him the sock. "It's a sock. I've only finished one."

Chase's face twisted in his effort to not laugh. "Um. It's a sock?" He coughed, trying gamely to keep a straight face. "A sock for me?"

He unlaced his boot and tugged it off, then held the sock up to his foot. I had to hold back a snicker myself as I saw the thing I'd made against his foot. The sock was a cylindrical tube, and it was clear he wouldn't be able to get even part of his foot into it. It was too narrow across the opening, and wouldn't even cover his heel, even if he could get it on.

I bit my lip as Chase nonetheless tried to lever his foot into the "sock". He managed his big toe and the one next to it.

Then genius struck.

"It's not a sock for your foot, honey." I kept a straight face, miraculously.

"It's not?" He peered at me in confusion.

"Nope."

"Then what—" He broke off as I glanced to his crotch, a smirk on my lips. "No. No way."

"Yep. It's a cock sock." I choked on my laughter.

"You're full of shit," Chase said, "you did *not* make me a cock-sock."

"I did too. Look at it. It's just big enough to fit on that third leg of yours." I reached for his pants. "Try it on. Come on baby, model that cock-sock for me."

Chase buried his face in his hands. "No. Uh-uh. No way."

"Yes! You have to! I want to see how it fits." I fought his hands away and managed to unzip him, freeing his cock.

Chase sighed theatrically and stood up, his pants open and hanging loose. He snatched the sock from me with a glare and slid it onto his cock, but it didn't quite fit yet. "It's too big, honey."

"It'll fit when you're hard," I said, taking his yarn-clad cock in my hands and caressing him into erection. When he was fully hard, the sock fit perfectly. "See?"

Chase waggled his hips so his shaft waved side to side, the green, orange and white sock tight around his turgid cock. "The latest in men's fashion…the cock-sock!" He strutted from one side of the living room, hands on his hips, mimicking a catwalk sway until his pants fell around his ankles.

I laughed so hard I stopped breathing, gasping and snorting. "Stop, stop, oh god!"

"It's quite comfortable," he remarked, waving his cock in my face. "I think it'll be great for keeping my cock warm when I get morning wood."

"What the *fuck* is going on?" Kelly's voice screeched from the kitchen doorway. "Oh my god. I'm scarred for life. Chase Michael Delany, put some goddamned pants on before I have to rip out my eyeballs!"

I had just calmed down, but Kelly's surprise appearance into our little fashion show and Chase's mortified reaction sent me into paroxysms of laughter once more. I watched Chase tug his pants on and button them hurriedly, the cock-sock still on.

"Don't you work until four, Mom?" Chase said, tugging the sock out of his pants.

Kelly made a grimace of disgust. "Oh my god. I'm going to have nightmares for the rest of my life." She turned away from us both, scrubbing her face with her hands. "There was a scheduling mess-up, so I got sent home early. Jesus, seriously, what were you two doing? Jamie can't have sex, Chase, surely you know that."

"Yes, Mom, I know that." He lifted the sock. "Jamie knitted a sock for me, but it didn't fit my foot—"

"La-la-la! Not listening!" Kelly yelled, covering her ears. "Forget I asked. I don't want to know. I really, *really* don't want to know."

"I'm sorry you saw that, Mom."

"I'll just have that image burned into my brain forever, no big deal." She pinched the bridge of her nose while Chase and I exchanged glances and tried not to laugh. "It's good you're here, though, Chase. Jamie has a doctor's appointment tomorrow morning. You can come."

He nodded. "My flight out isn't until the day after tomorrow, so that'll work."

I woke up the next day with a headache so bad I didn't want to get out of bed. The sunlight streaming in through the window was too bright, piercing my closed eyes and making my head throb even worse. I heard the door squeak open and smelled coffee and toast.

"I brought you breakfast, baby," Chase said, settling onto the bed next to me.

"My head hurts so bad, Chase. Can you close the blinds for me?" My voice sounded tiny, hesitant and weak. I hurt too bad to care.

"Yeah, sure," he said, getting up to slide the blinds closed. "You want some tylenol?"

"Please. Regular extra-strength tylenol."

He came back, and I heard Kelly's light tread behind his. "Your head hurts, Jamie?"

"Yeah. Really, really bad. A migraine, I think. I get them sometimes. I haven't had one in a long time, though."

Kelly didn't answer right away, which worried me. "Why don't you let Chase help you get dressed? We should head to Dr. Rayburn's office."

I peered from beneath the blanket at the clock, which read eight-fifteen in the morning. "I thought the appointment was at eleven?"

"It is," Kelly said, "but the headache isn't a good sign. I'd rather get you checked out earlier."

I was almost twenty-eight weeks at that point, and looked like someone had stuffed a beach ball under my skin. I let Chase help me dress, which was awkward and embarrassing, and then rode in the back seat of Kelly's car to the doctor's office. Tests, pee in a cup (so incredibly fun *that* is), more tests…oh and Mrs. Delany, can you please collect your urine every time you pee for the next twenty-four hours?

Um, I pee every six seconds. I'll need a fucking vat to put all the pee in at that rate. But, it's for the baby's wellness and my own, so in a cup I pee…every six seconds. It's every bit as exciting as it sounds, and infinitely more messy than you can possibly believe.

Chase pushed his flight back till the afternoon and went back in to see Dr. Rayburn with me in the morning. Marcia Rayburn was a short, svelte, older woman with steel gray hair, quick witted and no-nonsense.

"I think I'm going to admit you to the hospital, Jamie. Your protein levels are really high. That, combined with the headaches and the back and shoulder pain? I'm going to need to observe you for a few days. If your levels don't go down, we might need to look at an induction earlier than I'd originally planned." Dr. Rayburn offered me a reassuring smile that seemed at odds with her foreboding words.

"For a few days?" I said, my voice catching at the end. "Like how many days?"

"Three or four? It depends on how things go." Dr. Rayburn clicked her pen in and out.

"Worst case scenario," Chase asked. "How early would you need to deliver the baby?"

Dr. Rayburn didn't answer right away. "I can't say with any degree of accuracy. It all depends. Jamie has reported some changes in her vision, which along with the headache today, could mean she's at risk for eclampsia, or seizures, or at the least severe preeclampsia. If her symptoms worsen to any significant degree, we would need to deliver immediately. Obviously we want her to go closer to full term, or at least thirty-two or thirty-four weeks. Thirty-six would be best, but I don't really see that happening, honestly."

"If you have to deliver this soon, what would happen?" Chase's voice was heavy with worry.

"Well it would be a premature birth, obviously. At twenty-eight or twenty-nine weeks the baby would require an extended stay in the NICU as her lungs would likely not be totally viable yet. There are a lot of factors, and honestly I don't want to worry you with them needlessly until we're sure it's going to come to that, and it very well may not." Dr. Rayburn tucked the pen into the pocket of her lab coat and stood up. "I'd like you pick up a home blood pressure cuff and monitor your blood pressure as well. If you notice any increase at all, and I mean at *all*, call the emergency line for my office and have them page me. If the increase is significant, go straight to the hospital. Same thing for the other symptoms. If your headache worsens, if your vision changes at all, or if the back or shoulder pain worsens, go to the hospital. Don't dismiss it or try to tough it out. Okay?"

I nodded and tried to swallow my panic. "Sure, whatever you say."

She patted my knee. "It's going to be okay, Jamie. I promise. We'll take care of you and the baby. Don't stress yourself out with games of what-if, okay? That's important. You need to rest and relax and be calm."

I laughed, somewhat mirthlessly. "I'll try, Doc, but this is stressful. I'm worried. The what-ifs are running rampant already and I'm not even alone yet."

Dr. Rayburn just nodded and opened the door, pausing to look over her shoulder. "Mr. Delany, I understand your band requires constant travel, but I must stress how vital to her wellbeing—and that of your baby—your presence is. Call her, text her, Skype her, visit her as often as possible. You simply cannot know how much your mere presence will help her. I implore you to make every effort to see her as much as possible."

Chase nodded, his expression unreadable, which meant, to me, that he was seriously stressed. "I understand, Doctor. Thank you."

We left the office in silence, and drove home in silence, the radio off for once. We pulled into Kelly's driveway and Chase turned off the car, but didn't move to get out.

"I love my job," he said, staring out the window. "I love being in a band. I love making music. I love the crowds, I love the attention. The guys…they're my brothers, you know? There's nothing else I'd rather spend my life doing. But this? God, it's impossible. It's fucking…fucking impossible. I need to be here with you. I *need* to. I can't sleep at night worrying about you. I lay in the bunk on the bus and stare at the ceiling, wondering if you're okay, if Samantha's okay. I play the set, I sing my goddamn heart out every night, but I'm not there, on stage. I'm on autopilot, the rest of me is here. With you."

I squeezed my eyes shut, knowing me breaking down is not what he needed right then. "You're doing what you have to do, babe. I know that. It's hard without you, I'm not gonna lie about that. It's fucking hard and I miss you. But don't think for one second that I regret anything, that I hold it against you or resent you, or your job."

Chase finally looked at me. His eyes were a study in complexity, at once tender and hurting and loving and molten and determined. "Thank you, Jamie. That's...you don't know how bad I needed to hear that." He took my hand in his and simply held it, threading his fingers through mine. "I'm not sure I can stay away. I'm going crazy. I'm burning out. I haven't—haven't really talked to anyone about this, and I hate that I'm adding to your stress, but I have to vent. I'm starting to hate the tour. I'm cranky. I'm snapping. I'm—I'm drinking alone in my room after shows, just to dull the edge of my worry. I just have this pit of fear in my stomach that something's going to happen while I'm on the fucking tour and I won't be able to get there in—in time."

I had never seen Chase so distraught. He scrubbed his hand through his hair again and again until it was wild. His hand squeezed around the steering wheel so hard I heard the material squeaking under his grip. I touched his shoulder, hesitantly at first, then, when he flinched before leaning toward me, I leaned across the console to pull him into a hug. I put my lips to the shell of his ear, nuzzling him.

"You only have a few more shows, honey. Call me every night, okay? Fall asleep on the phone with me. Don't drink, please? Don't go there. Call me. Even if we don't talk, just be with me on the phone. I know it's hard, and I—I won't lie and say I don't wish you were able to just cut the tour short, but that has to be the absolute last resort. But it won't come to that. I'll get to thirty-two weeks, at least. You have to finish the tour. I know it, and you know it. The guys are counting on you."

Chase nodded, his face buried in my shoulder. "I know. I just hate it." He pulled away and rubbed the heels of his hands into his eye sockets. "Thank god for Mom, huh? I'd be out of a job for sure if you were stuck alone in New York for all this."

I laughed. "No shit."

Chase glanced at his phone then slammed his hand into the steering wheel. "Fuck. I have to go. My flight out is in less than three hours." Chase leaned in and kissed me, slowly and thoroughly. It was a farewell kiss, and I was crying by the end of it. "If you cry, I won't be able to leave."

I sniffled and wiped my eyes, summoned the dregs of my courage and shoved the selfish sadness down, ran my hand through his soft black hair and kissed his cheekbone. "Go. I love you. Call me." I got out of Chase's rental car and backed away. "Go be a rock star, baby."

He smiled sadly. "I'd rather be here being a husband and daddy."

"Soon. Go." I waved at him, one hand on my belly.

What I hadn't told him was that I had the same sense of foreboding, a feeling that my three or four days in the hospital would turn in to an emergency C-section and Chase would miss it, and I'd be alone in the OR, trying not to cry.

I rubbed my belly. "Stay in there for me, Sam. Okay?" I felt a flutter and then a foot or elbow pushed against my hand, eliciting a laugh. "Be a good girl for me and stay in there until Daddy can be with us. Please?"

Chapter 5: Anna

*O*ur OB, Dr. Michaela Irving, paused for a terrifyingly long moment before delivering the news. "You're measuring a little over three weeks behind where you should be, Anna. Both twins are small, worrisomely so." She glanced at the papers in the file folder, more to gather her thoughts, I guessed, than for any actual information.

I struggled with accepting her news. "What? I'm eating healthier than ever before in my entire life. I'm—I'm doing everything I can, I swear! I don't—I don't get it."

Dr. Irving held up her hands to stop me. "Anna, it's got nothing to do with what you're doing or what you're eating. You're doing everything right. Sometimes these things just happen, especially with twins. I know I've explained the risks associated with having twins, well, this is one more that exists. You're thirty-one weeks tomorrow, and I'd like you to make it to thirty-four, if possible. We'll have to have you in to measure your progress at least once a week, but if I don't see sufficient progress I'm going to schedule an induction. A lot of my colleagues will only do a C-section for twins, but I'd like you to try to deliver naturally if you can."

"I'd like to deliver naturally too," I said. "But whatever you think is safest for the babies."

Dr. Irving stood. "Just stay positive and keep doing what you're doing. See Tasha on the way out and schedule an ultrasound for next week, 'kay?"

I just nodded and squeezed Jeff's hand. He'd been silent for the entire ultrasound and Dr. Irving's prognosis. "I'm scared, Jeff."

He didn't respond immediately. "It'll be okay. Just—we'll just take it one day at a time, one ultrasound at a time."

The next week, Jeff had a gig DJing a blow-out Bat Mitzvah in Bloomfield Hills that was paying too much money to ignore, so I went to the ultrasound alone. I had progressed some, but Dr. Irving still seemed more worried than she was saying. She had me come in three days later, rather than the next week, which had me in a panic. At my thirty-third week ultrasound, Dr. Irving again remained silent for several minutes.

"You're still measuring far enough behind that I'm worried the babies aren't getting what they need. It's always a balancing act with twins, especially in situations like this. Obviously the farther along you're able to go, the better it is for the babies, but with twins, it always gets more complicated. With your measurements and the rate of progression I'm seeing, my feeling is that it would be best to induce you next week."

I twisted the strap of my purse between my fingers. "Are they... will they both be viable?"

"I believe so," she replied. "I'm the most worried about the boy, since he's measuring smaller than his sister. Their lungs both look good, though, so I'm very optimistic."

I hated that phrase. *Very optimistic.* Like she was discussing the weather for an upcoming ball game or something, rather than the lives of my babies. I didn't express this, though. I just nodded and squeezed Jeff's hand so hard he frowned at me. He was, as he'd been through most of the appointments, silent, watchful, a solid presence beside me, calming me as much as possible.

On the way home, I turned to Jeff. "Can we swing by Kelly's house? I want to see Jamie." He just nodded, staring straight ahead. "Talk to me, Jeff. I can feel you stewing over there."

He frowned at me. "I'm not stewing."

"You've barely spoke three words to me all week," I said.

"What do you want me to say?" He jabbed the radio off with an impatient stab of his thumb.

"I don't know. Anything. I mean, I know you're a man of few words, but this is ridiculous."

That got a chuckle from him, but he quickly sobered. "I'm worried, Anna. Is that what you want to hear? I'm scared for you, and for our babies. You're gonna deliver six weeks early? Isn't that, like, a fucking lot? And she's having you do a vaginal birth when just about every other doctor in the field recommends a C-section for twin births? What if she's wrong? What if something goes wrong?" He swung around a corner too fast, and hit the gas until we were going so fast I clutched the handle with white-knuckles. "What if—what if…god, there's so much going through my mind I don't know where to even start, so I just—don't. I keep it in, because you're worried too, you're scared too and you need me to be the strong one, the calm one."

"Slow down, Jeff, you're scaring me." He took his foot off the accelerator and we slowed down enough that I could relax. "Like I said, you're stewing. We're both scared, Jeff. We've never done this before. Yeah, I need you to be my rock like you always are, but I also need you to talk to me. You do me no good if you're lost in your own head. You may as well not even be here if you're gonna do that."

"I don't know how to deal with all this, Anna. It's so much. There's so many elements to this, so many factors, so many ways it could go wrong and I'd—I'd lose you. Lose the babies. I can't—"

I took his hand and kissed his palm. "That's not going to happen, honey. Nothing's going to go wrong. Dr. Irving knows what she's doing. I trust her. No one is going to lose anyone."

He smiled at me, but it didn't entirely reach his eyes. "Just—I love you. And I'm worried. That's all."

"It's going to be fine, baby."

"Why are you the one comforting me, here?" He laughed, tangling our fingers together and bringing my knuckle to his lips. "It's going to be fine."

"It's going to be fine," I agreed. He pulled into Kelly Delany's driveway and I stopped him before he shut the truck off. "Why don't you go out and have a drink or something. Relax. Have some alone time."

He seemed baffled by the idea. "A drink? At two o'clock in the afternoon on a Tuesday?"

"Or whatever. I'm not saying go get hammered. Just go and relax and let me have some time with Jay."

He nodded. "There's a shooting range not far from here. Maybe I'll got shoot some rounds."

I kissed him and made my way to the front door, where Jamie was already waiting, waving at Jeff as he backed out.

"Hey hooker," I said, hugging her, our bellies bumping as we awkwardly tried to maneuver in for a proper embrace. "You look great!"

Jamie snorted. "Shut up, you lying sack of shit. I look like fucking Shamu at this point. Except Shamu can jump through a hoop, and I can barely get my ass off the damn couch to take a piss."

Anna laughed. "Well, I'm finally catching up to you in the whale department. We're about the same size, now."

She stood beside me and we compared bellies. "Except you're almost two weeks farther along than I am. And you have twins."

My smile faded a bit. "Yeah, well, that's why my doctor wants to induce me next week."

Jamie frowned and took my hand in hers. "Really? Mine too."

"I thought she said things were looking better?"

Jamie shrugged. "Yeah, well, not anymore. After being basically chained to a hospital bed for three days, my protein count and blood pressure had leveled off a bit, but now they're back up and worse than ever. She's not sure I'll make it to next week. I'm supposed to go in tomorrow to get checked."

"Sorry I couldn't come see you while you were in the hospital, hon. We had that gig in Jackson and then I had an ultrasound that just took forever and I was so tired by the end—"

Jamie clapped her hand over my mouth. "It's fine, Anna. You already explained. It really wasn't that bad. I had wifi and my iPad and my knitting. I just hate hospitals. You have to stay in bed and wait and wait and wait for absolutely nothing. And then they tell you, 'oh we'll check on you in a couple hours,' but really they mean like, some time the next week they *might* remember to come back."

I laughed. "Yeah, not looking forward to that."

"So we'll be having our babies together, huh?" Jamie handed me a caffeine-free diet Coke—*gross*—and we sat on the couch together.

We both burst out laughing when we approached the process of sitting down the same way: bracing one hand on the arm of the couch, leaning forward into a sitting position as we lowered ourselves to the cushions, easing down until our leg muscles couldn't support our weight any longer and then falling the rest of the way.

"I guess we will," I said, hand on my belly to feel a little foot kick-kicking away so hard it took my breath away. "Jeez, kid, take it easy," I said, looking down at my stomach.

Jamie laid her hand where mine was and I moved her palm over slightly so she could feel the kicking. "Damn, that kid can kick!"

"I know!" I winced as the other baby started in on the other side of my belly.

"Do you know which one that is?" Jamie asked.

"I think Caleb is on the left, Niall on the right."

"So that's Niall kicking you over here, then," she had her palm on the right side of my belly, where Niall was trying to punt her way out, it felt like.

"Pretty sure that's where they were last ultrasound."

Jamie laid her head back on the couch and looked at me sideways. "Are you ready, Anna?"

I mirrored her pose. "Hell no. I'm not ready for *one* baby, much less two. I never thought I'd be a mom, you know? Even after I started dating Jeff, I didn't really think it'd happen. Not that I didn't want it to, I just…I don't know. I never really let on to Jeff, but I was, and still am, scared I won't be a good mom."

Jamie sighed, and it sounded like relief. "God, thank you. I thought that was just me. Sometimes, despite feeling her kick and like, *knowing* there's a baby in there, I don't really feel like this is real. Am I really about to have an actual human being squirt out of my hoo-ha? For actual-factual real? A little human being that's going to be completely dependent on me? What if I fuck up?"

I laughed. "I think there won't be a lot of actual squirting, Jay. I think it's going to be more screaming and trying to shit, from what I've seen on *A Baby Story*.""You watch that too? I hate it, but I can't stop watching. I keep thinking it'll help me be ready for actually giving birth, but then all it does is freak me out even worse."

I took a sip from the flat, watery-tasting caffeine free Diet Coke and tried not to grimace at it, in vain. "We're not gonna be shitty moms, are we, Jay?"

Jamie sighed, staring out the window at a robin hopping across the lawn. "I fucking hope not. I mean, there's no real manual for this shit, you know? All the self-help books and TV shows and *What to Expect When You're Expecting*...all that won't make a difference when it comes time to actually have the baby, to actually be a mother. Doesn't stop me from reading it all and watching it all, hoping it'll help or something. But I know, deep down, once the baby comes...everything is going to change. And all you can do is hope you're able to figure it out as it all happens."

I groaned. "Damn Jay, that's pessimistic as all hell."

"Well, do you have a better way of looking at it? 'Cause I'd love to hear it."

I watched carbonation bubble up and stick to the sides of the glass rather than meet Jay's eyes. "Not really, I guess. I think I'm more hoping that, like, I'll just know what to do when the time comes, you know? I mean, is anyone ever really prepared to be a parent? No, but also yes. I mean, it's part of the human cycle, you know? It's programmed into us, into our genes or DNA or whatever, to reproduce and to take care of our offspring. Not everyone is the same, and some people are more suited to parenthood than others. I mean, look at my parents. They were shitty parents. But I'm determined to love my kids and take care of them the way I wish my parents had me."

Jamie nodded. "Exactly my feelings. I may not get any 'Mom of the Year' awards, but at least I'll be better than *my* folks were."

Anna watched as the corner's of Jamie's eyes tightened, as if from pain. "Are you alright?"

"Yeah, just a headache."

"*Jamie.* Didn't your doctor tell you not to just ignore a headache? Especially at this stage?"

"God, Anna. Yes, yes, you're right. But—"

"But nothing." I levered myself to my feet. "Are you packed?"

"Packed?" She gave me a panicked look. "Packed for what?"

I called Jeff, ignoring Jamie's squawks of protest. "Hey baby. You can come get us now."

"Us? Referring to yourself in the plural, now, are we?"

I snorted. "No, that's Jamie that does that. But Jamie's got another headache and I'm making her go in to the hospital."

"Oh," he said, and I heard the sounds of pistols in the background fading as he left the range. "I'll be there in ten."

Jamie sat on the couch, glaring at me as I slid the phone into my purse again. "Anna, seriously—"

"No, you seriously. Quit fighting me on this. You know you have to." I grabbed both of her hands and pulled her upright, then smacked her ass as she shuffled toward her bedroom. "Now go get your hospital bag and let's go."

"Fine. Hooker."

"Stubborn-ass ho."

The fact that she didn't put up more of a fight told me what I needed to know. The increasing tension around her eyes, and the way she clenched her jaw as she slid into the back seat gave me enough of a clue that I knew I was doing the right thing.

When we were nearly to the hospital, I turned around to look at her. "Should you call Chase?"

She shook her head. "Not yet. Not until I hear what the doctors have to say."

After a couple hours' wait, and a battery of tests later, she was officially admitted to William Beaumont Hospital's Labor and Delivery unit. She called Chase.

Samantha Delany was on her way.

Bridge

*C*hase was uneasy. He was backstage waiting for Six Foot Tall to go on. Device, David Draiman's new band, was on, finishing their last set, and they were killing. It was Draiman, though, so of course they killed. Disturbed was a huge influence on Chase's harder music, so the opportunity to play with David Draiman last minute in Chicago was a dream come true. He was geeked, nervous, a bit star-struck, and on top of it all, the down-deep fear that something was wrong was growing.

He was edgy, bouncing on his toes, cracking his knuckles over and over again, checking his silenced phone in the back pocket of his signature leather pants. He knew he needed to get his shit together, but he just couldn't shake the jitters, the sinking feeling in the pit of his stomach. He'd nearly called Jamie at least six times, but never had.

Now, he didn't have time. Device had already done a three-song encore and Six Foot Tall was set to go on within minutes of Device leaving the stage, which had been curtained off toward the back so the next band's equipment could be set up.

"Thank you Chicago! Good night!" David waved one last time to the screaming crowd, hometown for him, and left the stage, handing the mic to a stagehand and accepting a hand towel and bottle of water, and was gone before Chase could open his mouth. Device had origi-nally been slated to play a small acoustic set in a club as a soft launch for their newest tour, but the gig had been cancelled at the last minute. Then the local band that was supposed to open for Six Foot Tall had cancelled, citing an OD'd lead singer, and Device had agreed to fill the slot. Of course, David Draiman was a huge draw, so they'd taken up nearly half of Six Foot Tall's original time. Chase didn't really care, and the fans loved it. They'd just have to go over time, which shouldn't be a problem.

The stage was cleared and reset, and Chase prepared to go on. He took a deep breath, let it out, shook his hand, then trotted out onstage. The crowd went wild as the spotlight hit him. Johnny Hawk hit the kick drum a few times, and Gage thumped his bass, setting up a rumbling line as the band got settled in.

Blue stage lights bathed him, then turned purple. He felt the nerves leave him as Kyle fingered the opening chords to their latest hit, "Shadow Thrall". Performing was the only time he felt any kind of peace, lately. When the chorus came with the shrieking guitar solo underlaid by the scudding bassline, Chase was crouching at the edge of the stage, howling the lyrics: "The shadows hold me in their thrall, I cannot deny their call, I'm falling, falling, and I cannot stop this fall..."

Even then, though, the fear remained. It ate at him, dug under his skin and made his heart thump crazily, made his stomach roil and constrict. The next song fit his mood. It was their hardest metal piece to date, and it written entirely by Gage. The lyrics were dark, darker and harder than anything Chase had ever penned, but his fear gave him the edge needed to sell them.

The lights dropped to black and Gage took front and center stage, bathed in a single red stage light. He held his black bass guitar vertically against his body, his long, fine blond hair loose around his face, obscuring his features. The crowd was silent except for a few isolated whistles and shrieks, and Gage milked it, thumping the lowest string with his thumb in a reverberating tone that washed across the audience. When the tension was thick enough to cut, he began to slowly ramp up the speed of his hammering thumb, until the waves of basso reverberation were crashing back on themselves, reaching a crescendo. When the peak hit and he couldn't tap any faster, his back arched and the bass resting on his chest, he slammed forward and let loose with a thundering series of chords, headbanging to the punishing rhythm. As the rhythm reached crescendo, Johnny began pelting the snare drums in a stuttering march pattern. When their rhythms snyched, Kyle wove a repeating series of riffs through the wall of sound created by Johnny and Gage.

Then it was Chase's turn. He had slunk into the shadows near the side of the stage to accept a guitar and had returned to stand between Kyle and Gage, waiting until the song hit a second crescendo and paused in single beat of silence. When sound returned, Chase added a driving backbone rhythm pattern. By now, all four members of the band were bathed in lights and the song was in full force, the crowd jumping and moshing with wild abandon.

Chase gradually moved toward the mic stand as the song progressed toward the first verse and began growling the lyrics to "Ablation":

"Down this dirty hole
You and me we crawl
Through this recurring nightmare
Of me against you
Rage against recrimination
Blame against damnation
Domination of my past
Versus ablation of my heart
Your nails on my spine
Was once erotic
Your eyes on mine
Was once Hypnotic
But this nightmare
The way it flares
Ignites into hatred
Slices through the skin
Of your demonic beauty
Revealing the evil within
This recurring nightmare
Of me against you

Rage against recrimination
Blame against damnation
Your lies ablate my hope
Your betrayal perpetrates my hate
You were once erotic
Hypnotic
Now you're just demonic
Chthonic
A chronic cyclonic storm
Wrecking all my dreams."

Chase's voice was raw by the end of the song, by the time he'd screamed the chorus through three more times. He knew he'd sold it. He'd given in to every fear and nagging worry and put it all into the song, let it feed the lyrics with all his inner darkness. He stood in the pool of white spotlight, sweat dribbling down the shell of his ear and into the gauged hole of his piercing, heart hammering, stomach clenching, adrenaline pumping. The instruments around him all fell silent and he forced himself to breathe through it, ignore the fear that was quickly turning into unreasoning terror.

Then his phone buzzed. He ignored it until the lights doused between songs, then spun around and dug it out of his pocket, shielding the glow with his body.

The name across the screen made his heart stutter and stop. *Jay.*

What was he supposed to do? She knew he was performing tonight. She wouldn't call him unless it was an emergency, but Johnny was already clicking his sticks to count in the next song, and the lights were up.

He shoved the phone back in his pocket and forced himself through the next song. He felt his phone buzz again, and almost lost his place in the lyrics. When the song ended, he edged up to Gage and Kyle and told them to do a solo or something, an instrumental piece to buy him time.

Chase left the stage and stood under the light of an emergency exit sign with his phone clutched in his trembling fist.

"Hey guys, I'm Gage. We're, uh, we're gonna do an instrumental song for you guys. It doesn't really have a name, it's just a jam we put together. Hope you like it." He heard Gage's bass kick in a fast rhythm, then the other guys came in.

You wouldn't know they were making it all up as they went along. They'd never done an all-instrumental number before, hadn't practiced it or written it or jammed out to even have an idea. But it was buying him time, and that's all that mattered.

He pulled up the text message. *Hey Babe. I know you're onstage, sorry. It's time. The headache came back and I've been admitted to L and D. They're gonna start a pitocin drip around midnight to induce labor. I need you here.*

Midnight. Fuck. That was in three hours. He was in Chicago, four hours away. There were no flights out till morning. He didn't have a car. The band was only three songs in to an eleven song set.

He swore again under his breath and typed a response, a promise he didn't know how to fulfill: *I'll be there. I promise.*

Gage came out to get him. "Come on dude, you're on. 'Long Night Gone' is up next."

He met Gage's gaze. "They're inducing her in three hours, Gage. I gotta be there."

"What's that mean?"

"It means they're forcing her to go into labor early. It means she's having the baby, like now."

"Fuck." Gage flipped his hair back from his face with an angry motion. "Fuck. What are you gonna do?"

Chase shook his head. "I don't know. I don't fucking know, man."

"Problem?" Darrel McKay, said. Darrel was the lead singer for Blood Oath, a local Chicago metal band that had been the pre-opener.

"I'm about to have a baby, and I'm here. She's in Detroit. We're not even halfway through our show." Chase rubbed his hand over his head, again and again. "I don't know what to do."

"I can fill in. I don't know your material, but we can do some covers." Darrel ran his fingers through his shoulder-length black hair, flipping it back.

"That works for me." Gage said. "Let's do it. You make the announcement, Chase, and then get going."

Chase shook hands and bumped fists with his band-mates and then took the stage, sitting on the very edge with his feet hanging off. He lifted the mic to his lips, shaded his eyes against the glare of the stage lights and the spot bathing him. "So, hey Chicago. How's it going? Having a good time?" The crowd cheered and applauded until Chase lifted a hand to silence them. "Some of you may know I got married a little while back, and my wife is expecting a baby."

There was more applause, a few boos from the disappointed female members of the audience, and some shouts of congratulations.

"So, the reason I'm sitting here like this talking to you rather than singing the next song is that I just got a text from Jamie, my wife, and she just went into labor." He paused and scratched his head. "Well actually, she's getting induced, if you want to get technical, but that's beside the point. The point is, I have to go witness the birth of my daughter. This is—and you have to believe me—this is the *only* reason I would ever leave in the middle of a concert. I hate doing this, I really do. You guys are the reason I'm here, the reason the boys and I are able to live our dream like we have been."

He stood up, waved to the other guys, and took center stage. "So, you guys paid good money to hear us play, and just because he's a badass, David has graciously offered to kind of fill in for me. So, is anyone here a fan of Blood Oath?" The crowd screamed wildly for the local talent, and it was several long moments before anyone could be heard over the noise. "I take it that means you'll let us change things on you? The guys from Six Foot Tall are gonna play, and Darrel is gonna sing, and I personally think Darrel is fucking badass. They'll rock your shit, I guarantee you. They might even take a couple requests."

Darrel lifted the mic to his lips. "Hey, you're about to have a kid, man. It's least I could do to help a brother out." He pushed Chase toward the side of the stage. "Now go, get the fuck out of here and be with your wife."

"If you follow me on Twitter or Facebook, check for updates. Thank you, Chicago!" Chase waved to the crowd and left the stage as the band kicked in the opening notes to "Down With the Sickness" in tribute to David Draiman, who was watching from backstage.

Less than half an hour later, he was in a car borrowed from a roadie and flying as fast as he could safely drive toward Detroit. The fear in his belly had faded a bit, but hadn't gone away completely.

Something told him the insanity had just started.

Wait for me, Samantha, he thought. *Wait for me.*

Chapter 6: Jamie

A long, growling groan ripped from my throat, a sound of frustration, pain, and panic. The OB on duty, Dr. Clayton, had ordered
a pitocin drip to start labor, but the anesthesiologist hadn't shown up
yet, despite the passage of more than two hours, so I was feeling the
full force of every contraction, and they were increasing in intensity
with every half-hour.

Chase still wasn't here, and all I'd heard from him was a single text
an hour before: *OTW, driving now, be there soon.*

Anna and Jeff had gone home, at my insistence; I knew it would
be several hours before anything happened, and they had Anna's complicated pregnancy to deal with. I was, once again, alone and in pain.
I breathed in through my nose as a contraction gripped my core and
squeezed. It felt like a menstrual cramp amplified by a million. I whimpered, trying to breathe through it, counting in my head, *One-one
thousand…two-one thousand…three-one thousand…four-one thousand…*
and then it passed, leaving me slumped back against the thin pillow,
sweating and panting.

"Where the fuck is the drugs man?" I growled, to the empty room
at large.

A nurse breezed in at that moment and checked the charts and
beeping monitors, adjusted the fitting of the circular monitor pick-up
strapped to my belly. "He's coming, hon. Another patient had a complication with her epidural."

"A complication?" I heard her voice squeak at the end, panicking at
the idea of a complication happening to her.

"Nothing for you to worry about, dear." The nurse was a young
brunette with wide brown eyes and an easy smile. "Just a slightly-off

placement is all. You'll be just fine. Dr. Harris is an excellent doctor. You have nothing to worry about, I promise."

"God, don't scare me like that. I'm freaked out enough as it is." I sucked on the straw in my miniature can of Vernor's.

"Do you have anyone here with you, Mrs. Delany?" the Nurse asked.

"Yeah, my friends just left, and my husband is on the way."

"Where's he coming from?"

I felt my womb tensing in preparation for another contraction. "Chicago, he actually left in the middle of a show."

The nurse scanned the print-out coming from the monitor, assessing the frequency and intensity of the contractions. "Oh? What does he do?"

I laughed. "You must be the only nurse in the whole L and D who doesn't know." I gritted my teeth and breathed through the contraction, then exhaled in relief when it passed. "My husband is Chase Delany from Six Foot Tall."

I could tell the nurse tried to contain her excitement, but she wasn't entirely successful. "Oh my god! I love them! I saw them at Harpos before they blew up!"

"Well, you'll meet him as soon as he gets his ass here." I took another sip from my soda and then crunched an ice chip, wishing desperately for something other than ice and soda.

"Did he really leave in the middle of a concert to be with you?" The nurse asked, clearly awed.

"That's what I hear. I haven't actually talked to him yet, but I know he's supposed to be playing right now and instead he's driving to get here."

"Well, things seem to be progressing pretty quickly, especially since this is your first baby. It'll still be several hours more before the baby gets here, if everything happens like it should." She turned to leave, pausing at the door. "Dr. Clayton should be here to check how far you've progressed in a little while, and Dr. Henry should be along with the epidural any minute."

"Awesome," I muttered, thinking about how large Dr. Clayton's hands had been when he'd first checked me upon admittance to the L and D ward. Large, hard, and cold.

Not a good combination when your profession was shoving your hands up the hoo-ha of unsuspecting women. There should be a requirement that all OBs have small, warm hands. Careful hands. I also thought the idea of a male OB was kind of contrary. What the hell does a man know about girly bits? He doesn't have them. Clinical knowledge only got you so far, after all.

What it amounted to was I wishing Dr. Rayburn to get her ass to the hospital for the actual birth. She'd been paged when I had first arrived at Beaumont, but there hadn't been any word as yet. Dr. Rayburn's hands were perfect, small, gentle, sure, and not frigid. She also possessed the ability to make me feel like it would all be okay with a few calm words. There was just something about her demeanor that set I at ease.

Dr. Clayton? Not so much. He was over six feet tall, middle aged, built like a grizzly bear, and not given to talking unless necessary. He wasn't surly or taciturn, just gruff and quiet. He really was a nice enough guy, and if he'd been any other kind of doctor, I would have been reassured by his quiet competence. As an OB/GYN, though, he put me on edge.

Speaking of whom…Dr. Clayton strolled in at that moment, reading something on a tablet. He slid the pad in his lab coat pocket and went to the monitoring station, glancing through the contraction chart and checking the pick-ups for the monitor. Still without speaking, he snapped a pair of rubber gloves on, kicked the door shut and plopped onto the rolling stool, scooting into position between my knees. He pushed the sheet up to my hips, and without so much as a preparatory how-do-you-do, slid his hand between my legs.

I winced and tried to contain my curses as he wiggled his huge finger around inside me, then sighed in relief when he withdrew his hand and stripped the gloves off. A quick hand-wash, and the doctor resumed his seat on the stool, repositioning the sheet to cover me.

"Well, Mrs. Delany, you're progressing pretty quickly, actually. You're about sixty percent effaced and dilated to almost five. You have a ways to go yet, but at this rate it shouldn't be too much longer." He scratched the salt-and-pepper stubble on his jaw and stood up. "Just sit tight for now. I'm going to leave the pitocin where it is for now, since you seem to be progressing nicely. I'll check you again in a few hours. I saw Dr. Harris just a minute ago, so that epidural is on its way."

And he was gone, just like that. I wondered why he thought it necessary to to tell me to sit tight. Like I was going anywhere? I sighed and gripped the railing as another contraction ripped through me. This one lasted longer, clenched her tighter, and left me breathless with relief when it finally passed.

In the background, Tom announced the next dancers on *Dancing With The Stars*, and I tried not to cry. I knew Chase was on his way, but that didn't help me feel any less alone in that moment.

"Come on, Chase, hurry up, baby." I hissed through my teeth as the next contraction hit me like a ton of bricks, barely five minutes after the last one.

It was another hour before the anesthesiologist showed up. Dr. Harris was an older American-Asian man with thick black hair barely contained by some kind of scrubs-hat. He helped me to a sitting position on the edge of the bed and wiped my back with iodine from the kit he'd unpackaged on the moveable table. I tried to keep my breathing even and pushed away my desperate wish for Chase's hands to hold as the needle—which looked about eight feet long—pierced through my skin and slid, cold and alien, into my spine. Sharp lances of pain shot through me with each motion of the doctor's careful hands, with each sliding inch of the needle. I held as still as I could and tried not to breathe as he inserted the line and taped it to my back with medical tape.

I couldn't stop a whimper from escaping as a contraction clutched me in a vise-like grip. Sweat beaded on my forehead and dripped down my cheek, tangling with my hair and causing strands to stick to my skin. My eyes squeezed shut, I started when I felt Dr. Harris' hands touch my shoulders as he urged me back to a laying position.

"I got it in first try," he said, touching buttons on a box attached to the IV hook of my bed. "There, the drip has started. You should feel relief almost immediately."

I whimpered again, this time in relief. Numbness spread through my lower half, cutting away the spearing pain of an on-rushing contraction. I still felt pressure, but not pain. It was odd, actually. The contractions clenched me still, and I felt the vise-grip pressure around my womb, but it was pressure absent pain.

"Thank you sweet baby Jesus." I closed my eyes and relaxed into the uncomfortable bed.

I heard the doctor chuckle as he cleaned up. Exhaustion stole over me and I felt sleep tug me under. The contractions gripped me every few minutes, but I was able to doze off into a restless sleep. When I woke up, Chase was sitting with his elbows on the edge of the bed, worry etched on his gorgeous features.

"You're here," I mumbled, reaching for his hand.

"I'm here, finally." He scooted the chair closer, reaching out to brush a tendril of hair away from my eyes. "There was a huge accident on seventy-five, so I was stuck for a fucking hour and a half. I almost got arrested for trying to go on the shoulder around the pile-up."

I laughed. "You did not, did you?"

Chase grinned. "Yeah I did. For real. The cop only let me go when I told him who I was and why I needed to get here."

"You missed the giant needle," I said, scooting slowly and awkwardly up to a reclined sitting position. "It was seriously like a fucking sword."

"What giant needle?"

"The epidural," I said, holding my hands about two feet apart. "It was seriously like this big."

"Honey, it couldn't have been *that* big," Chase laughed.

I huffed. "It was too. Six inches, at least."

"Did it hurt?"

I stared at him. "I have a six-inch needle sticking out of my spine, Chase. What do you think?"

"The needle is still in?" Chase asked.

"I don't know. I don't think so, but it's not like I could see what he was doing. Yes, it hurt, but it makes the contractions bearable."

"What are the contractions like?" Chase threaded his fingers through hers and shifted in the visitor's chair.

I widened my eyes as I felt the squeeze of a contraction. I glanced at the monitor read-out and saw that the contractions had ramped up significantly while I dozed. They were frequent and powerful now, the chart looking like a mountain range of peaks and valleys.

"Before the epidural they were, no lie, the most painful thing I've ever felt. I don't even know how to describe it to you. There's nothing like it, especially that a man would experience. It's like menstrual cramps, but times a million, but you don't know what that feels like." I adjusted the blanket to better cover my toes. "The best I can put it is like a giant fist squeezing your stomach. Now that I've got the epidural in, it's more like how you feel something happening when you're getting dental work done under local anesthetic. You can feel the tugging and the pressure, and it's kind of uncomfortable, but it doesn't exactly hurt, you know?"

Chase nodded. "I guess I get that." He ran a hand over his head, the already-messy black spikes getting even messier. "So what's happening? I mean, where are we, or whatever?"

I shrugged. "Just waiting, I guess."

"Waiting for what?"

"For my body to be ready to have the baby?" I reached for my cup of ice, discovering it to be empty. "Can you get me more ice? There's a little room down the hall, a pantry kind of thing. You can get something from the fridge if you want, or coffee."

"All you want it is ice?"

I rolled my eyes. "Don't get me started. If you have anything in your stomach, the epidural makes you nauseous, so you're not allowed to eat anything. It's awful. I'm so hungry, but all I can have is liquids and ice chips."

Chase stood up and leaned over me, pressing his lips to mine. "I'll be back, then."

He left, and I watched through the open door as the nurses all stared after him, whispering behind their hands. One of them glanced at me and blushed, then came in.

"That's your husband?" she asked.

I grinned. "Yeah. I know, I'm a lucky girl."

The nurse, a tiny blond thing in the maroon scrubs of an intern, giggled. "What's it like being married to a rock star?"

I shrugged. "Its got its ups and downs. I mean, he's Chase Delany, and he's even more awesome than you can probably imagine, so there's that. But he's also gone a lot, so it's hard not being jealous of the fans that are getting more of his time and attention than me. In the seven or eight months I've been pregnant, I've seen him in person exactly three times, four including today."

"God, that sucks! I'd go crazy." She glanced over her shoulder at the nurses station to make sure she wasn't needed. "Does it bother you when girls like me get all giggly around him?"

I shrugged again. "No, not really. I mean, he's hot, you can't deny it. I get it. I just happened to be lucky enough that he fell in love with me. What drives me nuts is the groupies that follow his band around on tour and try to seduce him even knowing he's got a wife."

The nurse's eyes boggled out. "They do that? For real? I mean, yeah, he's hot, and it's fun to imagine—I mean, um—yeah. He's hot, but I'd never *do* anything."

I laughed. "You're funny. The sad thing is, there are girls who'd do anything for a hot guy. It's kind of ridiculous. I mean, there are so many men out there, why do you have to be deprived of morals that you'd seduce a married man?" I looked up at the little blond nurse. "What's your name, by the way?"

"Andrea." She bit her lip and blushed scarlet when Chase came back in, carrying a styrofoam cup of coffee, another mini-can of Vernor's and a cup of ice.

He smiled at Andrea as he handed me the ice. "I'm not sure I remember the last time I had coffee this burnt," he said, chuckling.

I glanced at Andrea, who was slowly edging away toward the door. "Andrea, this is my husband, Chase. Baby, this Andrea, one of our nurses."

Andrea shook his hand, her eyes wide. "Hi, Mr. Delany. I can make some new coffee for you, if you want. I'm not really a nurse yet. I'm an intern, so I'm really just here to observe and to help, but I'll do whatever you need, so if something comes up, just—" She cut herself off as if realizing she was rambling. "Anyway. I'll just—I'll go. Nice to meet you, both of you." She scurried out of the room and vanished before Chase could get a word in edgewise.

He laughed, giving me a puzzled look. "Well…that was odd. She didn't even give me time to see if she wanted an autograph."

I shook my head, shoulders shaking in silent laughter. "She was starstruck, baby. We were just talking about you, too, so she was probably kind of embarrassed."

Chase frowned, then shrugged. "Oh. She ran off like she was afraid of me or something."

"You *are* intimidatingly sexy, babe." I said, crunching on a piece of ice. I glanced at the group of nurses behind the desk, the number of whom seemed to have grown. "Maybe you should go out there and take some pictures with them or something."

Chase pinched the bridge of his nose. "I'm not here to take pictures with the nurses, Jay. You're about to have a baby. I'm here for you. For us."

"I know that. But they'll just keep clustering there and staring at us. Maybe if you take a few pictures and sign a few autographs, they'll be more likely to leave us alone." I sipped the soda and then tugged Chase closer by his hand. "Plus, it's hot watching you be all celebrity."

Chase winced as he swallowed a mouthful of coffee, which to my nose did smell incredibly burnt. "Yeah, I guess."

He set his coffee down and moved to stand in the doorway, waving over one of the nurses. He said something to her, too low for me to catch, then smiled at her, the brilliant, brain-melting smile that I realized was his professional smile, one that didn't quite reach his eyes. I watched the shift in him, the straightening of his posture, the eyes darting everywhere as the room filled with women of varying ages in scrubs of all colors. I watched in amusement as he worked the room with ease, spending a few minutes with each person, completely attuned and focused on the person he was talking to. He took individual pictures, then a couple with the group as a whole. He signed cell phone cases, scrub sleeves, receipts, a $20 bill, the inside of a romance novel cover, and the back of an e-reader.

His smile never faltered, and even in the midst of it all, he glanced at me frequently, a question in his eyes. I knew he'd clear the room out in an instant, if I asked him to.

Eventually, the nurses left Chase slumped down into a chair. "God, that's exhausting," he said.

"Is it?" I said, genuinely interested. "It seems like it would be fun."

"It is fun, but it's tiring. Each person wants to feel special, wants your attention on them, but you can't ignore everyone else. So you have to be focused on whoever you're talking to, but still be aware of the people waiting. I've had people show up to more than one show and wait in line to meet me several times, and they always hope I'll remember them from show to show. And it's like, I try, but I meet hundreds of people at the post-show signings, and I just can't remember them all." Chase waved his hand, dismissing it. He leaned closer to me and touched my belly beneath the monitor lead. "How are you doing?"

I shrugged. "I want to have this baby. I've been here for like six hours already."

"How much longer do you think it'll take?" Chase asked.

"I have no idea," I said. "It could be hours still. I remember my mom saying she was in labor for like two days with me."

"God, I hope it doesn't take that long," Chase said.

"Me too, believe me." I shifted in the bed, watching the monitor as another contraction clenched my uterus. "Even with the epidural, this is uncomfortable at best."

Three hours passed, with Chase slugging cup after cup of burnt coffee.

Five hours after Chase's arrival, Dr. Clayton appeared, checked my progress, and then washed his hands. "Good news and bad news. Good news is, you're almost completely effaced. Ninety percent or so, I'd say. Bad news is, you're only dilated to seven, so you haven't moved very much there. I'm going to turn up the pitocin a touch and see if that breaks things loose. If that doesn't help you along, I might think about breaking your water, but I don't necessarily want to do that just yet." He touched a button on the IV box and then turned to leave.

I nodded. "Okay." When he was gone, I addressed Chase. "All that just means I'm not ready yet, so we wait some more."

"Yay, more waiting!" Chase said with fake enthusiasm, laughing at the end to make it a joke. He sobered and asked, "Why wouldn't he want to break your water yet?"

I thought. "It makes you progress even faster, which can make you have the baby pretty much immediately. But there's only a short window of time to have the baby after breaking the water. If it takes to long, you have to have a C-section."

Seven in the morning brought a new on-call OB, a delicate Lebanese woman wearing a hijab. She said I had dilated to a nine and that my primary OB, Dr. Rayburn, was supposed to be at the hospital in an hour or two to decide whether to break my water or not. Chase had dark circles under his eyes, and I'd heard his stomach growling.

"Chase, you should go get something to eat. Nothing's going to happen until Dr. Rayburn gets here."

He shook his head. "I'm fine, baby. I'm not leaving."

I narrowed my eyes at him. "Go, Chase. Get some food. There's a cafeteria in the hospital. Just get a sandwich or something. You need to eat. Just because I can't doesn't mean you can't."

"Are you sure?"

I flapped her hands at him, since I couldn't actually get up to push him out the door. "The sound of your stomach growling is making me crazy. Go eat."

He hadn't been gone five minutes when I felt something wet spreading beneath my butt and up my back. I sat up and pushed the sheet away, touching the bed between my legs.

"Of course my water would break now." I touched the call button and then reached for my phone to text Chase to come back immediately. The message sent and the 'delivered' notice popped up.

A chime from the chair where Chase had been sitting brought another curse from me. He'd forgotten his phone.

A nurse came in, and that sparked a flurry of activity. The on-call showed up, put on one glove and checked me.

"Oh yes, it is time, Mrs. Delany. I can touch her head with my finger." The on-call's pager went off at that moment, and she stripped off the glove as she checked it. "Dr. Rayburn is here to deliver you. Just in time, it would seem."

"My husband is in the cafeteria and doesn't have his phone with him," I said. "Can someone find him for me?"

One of the nurses left at a run, and that was when I realized this wasn't just happening *soon*, it was happening *now*. The other nurses were moving around the room with quick efficiency, one shutting off the epidural and pitocin drips, transforming the room in readiness for the delivery.

Dr. Rayburn showed up, gloved, masked, and aproned, smiling calmly at me. "Ready, Jamie? You're about to be a mommy!"

I was dizzy and weak and couldn't breathe, but I listened.

Nothing.

Nothing.

"Why isn't she crying?" I heard my own voice from far away. "Dr. Rayburn? Why isn't Samantha crying?"

There was no answer, and I knew fear like no other.

"Samantha? Chase? What's going on?" Tears, in my eyes and clogging my voice.

I looked up at Chase, saw terror on his features. He was watching Dr. Rayburn, clutching my hand so hard it was going numb.

"Got it..thank god," Dr. Rayburn's voice, pitched low, more to myself than out loud but falling into a space of silence.

I couldn't see anything but Chase, and I saw relief flood his eyes. I heard a *smack*, and then the most welcome sound I'd ever heard.

The indignant squalling of a newborn.

I breathed, really breathed, for the first time in what felt like days. As I sucked in cool air into her hot lungs, I felt a presence at my side and opened my eyes to see Dr. Rayburn cradling a blue paper wrapped bundle.

I struggled upright, took the crinkling paper and tiny weight into my arms. A little pale pink fist waved in the air and the cries filled my ears, washed over me. Little dark eyes met mine and the cries stopped for a moment.

Mother gazed at daughter, and for a moment, the universe stopped.

Something within me shook, shuddered, broke open, and I was filled an inrushing flood of overwhelming love. I heard myself sob, took the tiny fist between two fingers and brushed my daughter's face, her cheek, her scalp, touched her so-soft skin still crusted with blood and effluvia.

"Hi, Samantha." I kissed her nose and tried not to drip tears on her. "Samantha May Delany."

Chase's grandmother was Samantha's middle namesake, since Samantha was my grandmother's name.

Chase's face filled my vision, and I turned my face up to his, saw his eyes wet and tears streaming down his face, his eyes glazed with a welter of emotion. "You did it, Jay. You did it." His voice was barely audible.

I sobbed again and gestured to him with the bundle of baby. "Go see your daddy."

Chase leaned down and gingerly settled his daughter into the crook of his arm, the baby seeming even smaller against his huge frame and burly, tattooed arms.

"We did it," I whispered.

Chase just shook his head without taking his eyes off Samantha. "No, baby. *You* did it. God, you're amazing." He glanced at me, love and adoration in his eyes. "I love you so much, Jay."

I couldn't respond, too exhausted and amazed and overwhelmed to speak.

A nurse came and took Samantha from him, talking about tests. Chase came over to me and held my hands as the afterbirth was delivered, put his head next to mine and breathed with me as Dr. Rayburn did something painful to my bottom half.

After a few minutes, she stood up and stripped her delivery gear off. "You did amazing, Jamie." She washed her hands and stood next to me opposite Chase. "Four pounds six ounces, eighteen inches. You want to go take some pictures, Daddy?"

I watched in bleary-eyed wonder as Chase took pictures with his phone, and I laughed when the nurse pressed Samantha's ink-black foot to his forearm, leaving a footprint on his skin. He took pictures of her after she was wrapped in a blue and white blanket, snuggled in my arms.

After the baby had been taken to be measured and tested, Dr. Rayburn came back. "Well, overall she looks pretty good, all things considered. She is a few weeks premature, so I'm worried about her breathing. She's not quite as pink as I'd like, and she seems to be taking some pretty shallow breaths. She might need some assistance for awhile, so just be aware she might have to stay here for awhile, until her oxygen levels even out and she gains a little weight." She patted my leg. "You look great, though, Jamie. You tore a little, so I had to give you about seven or eight stitches, but nothing excessive. For now you need to eat and get some rest."

And then we were alone once more. Chase sat on the edge of the bed and traced my face with a forefinger, and I in turn touched the miniature footprint on his forearm.

"I'm gonna get that tattooed on, right there," Chase said, touching the dried ink.

It would make an awesome tattoo. Maybe I'd get one to match.

A nurse brought a tray of food, which I devoured faster than I should have, probably. Exhaustion was washing over me, then, tugging me under, drowning me. I'd been fighting it, knowing I needed to eat and wanting to see Samantha again before I slept, but it futile. Chase stroked my hair and my back with a tender hand, his fingers eventually moving to thread into mine, and I let myself go, feeling complete and safe under his watchful gaze.

I fell asleep, and the last thought before descending into the drowsing depths of sleep was, *I'm a mommy.*

Chapter 7: Anna

I heard my phone ringing. It was distant, hazy. I struggled up through the fog of sleep, reaching for it even as I felt Jeff stir next to me, nudging me with his foot and mumbling, "Phone's ringing."

I snagged it off the nightstand and brought it to my ear. I'd forgotten it was plugged in, though, so the cord jerked it out of my hands to fall, still ringing, between the nightstand and the bed. I cursed floridly, reaching for it, unable to quite grasp it. Still swearing, I finally managed to grab it with my thumb and forefinger, swiping the 'answer' tab immediately.

"Hello?" I sounded out of breath and frustrated. The clock on the nightstand read eight-oh-six in the morning.

"Uh, hi, Anna. It's Chase." He sounded exhausted and exhilarated.

"Hi Chase. How's Jamie?" I felt Jeff sit up next to me.

"She had the baby about an hour ago."

"An hour ago?" I shrieked. "She was supposed to call me first so I could be there! God, we're so fighting!"

Chase laughed. "I'll tell her you said that. Things happened really suddenly, though. We were in a holding pattern for a long time, just waiting. Then her water broke and she had the baby within like, fifteen minutes."

"Gotcha. We'll be there in a few minutes. Congrats, Chase! You're daddy! How does it feel?"

"It's amazing. It was, no lie, the most incredible experience of my entire life." I heard him sigh, holding the phone away from his mouth. "She's actually sleeping right now, but they're going to move us to a recovery room soon. Well, soon in hospital terms."

"So like, four hours?" I said.

"Exactly. Have some breakfast before you come up. There's no rush. We'll be here."

"Ok. What room are you in?" I asked.

"I'll text you the room number when we get moved."

"Okay." I paused. "Chase? I'm happy for you. You'll be a great daddy."

"Thanks, Anna." He hung up, and I flopped back on the bed.

"She had the baby an hour ago," I said.

"Well, lets get our asses up and showered, have some breakfast, and go see them." Jeff suited action to words, moving into the bathroom and starting the shower.

Instead of getting in himself, though, he returned to the bed and dragged me out, pushing me to the bathroom, stripping me of my nightshirt and panties in the process. I had been laughing up until he pushed my panties off and knelt in front of me on the bathroom tile, a hungry look on his face. I leaned back against the sink, staring down at Jeff's blazing brown eyes. He ran his hands up from my ankles to my knees, up the backs of my thighs, carving hot trails around between them in a teasing brush along my folds.

My breath caught and I closed my eyes in anticipation. I felt his fingers close around my ankle and lift. I cooperated, setting my foot on the closed lid of the toilet, holding the edge of the sink with both hands for balance. His fingers slid up the inside of my thigh, sliced through my folds and swiped through the slick heat deep inside me. I gasped and felt my knees weaken, then buckle when his tongue slid against my clit and began slow circles around it. I let go of the sink with one hand to run my fingers through his soft, brown, close-cropped hair, pulling him against me as the fire began to boil in my core. Two fingers slipped inside me and curled against my G-spot, buckling my knees again and sending lances of lightning through me.

I felt myself riding the edge, teetering on the brink of climax. Instead of letting him bring me over the edge, I tugged him up, tilting his face away from my core. "I need you. I want you inside me. I want us to come together."

He stood up slowly, and I felt the tip of his cock nudge against me. I wrapped my leg around his hip and he held it there, lifting up on his toes to enter me. As he slid into me, he leaned in to kiss me, his tongue spearing into my mouth. My belly was in the way, though, so he had to lean back to thrust into me. I still had one hand gripping the sink for balance, and I put my other hand on his shoulder, pulling myself up and sliding down to meet his thrust. He leaned away from me, stretching his cock as far as it would comfortably go, and we both watched as he drew out and slid back in, setting a slow rhythm. I watched my folds stretch around him, watched his thick length driving in and sliding out, finding something erotic in the play of skin against skin, against the wet glistening of his cock and the way we fit together so perfectly.

Jeff's free hand slipped between our bodies to touch the hypersensitive nub of my clit, barely touching it, brushing it with a feather-light touch that had me jerking and arching my back, needing more, wanting all he could give me.

The only sound was our bodies meeting, wet sliding, slick sucking, mouths kissing and breath gasping, fingers scratching and scraping. Then the heat billowed through me and stirred me hotter and Jeff's strokes grew frantic and his fingers on my clit circled rough and pushed against me and made me wild and touched me so perfectly. He lifted up on his toes and jerked me closer by the leg, fingers clutching my thigh and pulling me behind the knee, and each thrust of his cock had me gasping, sent my body to trembling and spasming and gasping. My head lolled back on my shoulders and I felt my breasts bouncing with each thrust, and I knew he was still holding himself back, still forcing himself into a measure of gentility and I loved him all the more for it.

I careened over the edge into climax without warning, digging my fingers into his bicep and whispering his name in a breathless prayer. I felt him release in that moment, at the exact instant of my orgasm.

I knew he'd been keeping it back, holding, waiting until I came. God, the man always, *always* knew how to give me exactly what I needed.

Is it bad that one of the things I loved most about my relationship with Jeff was our sex life? I mean, don't get me wrong, that's the only thing, and it's not the thing I love the most about Jeff as a man, but our sexual relationship never failed to leave me breathless. Even when it was plain old vanilla missionary in the dark on a Sunday night, it was perfect. He was perfect. Slow and sweet when I needed him tender, rough and ready fucking when I needed him powerful and erotic.

And this? Standing up in the bathroom, thirty-four weeks pregnant? God, so amazing.

If you'd told me yesterday that I'd be fucking Jeff like this, I'd have laughed at you. I'd have told you there was no way I could manage standing sex at this stage of my pregnancy. Yet here I am, coming so hard I can barely breathe, clutching Jeff for dear life as my entire body convulses, my leg slipping from his grip and driving him deeper inside me, his cock still spasming and thrusting, our mouths crashing together in a rough and raw kiss of desperate love, furious expression of need.

We breathed together for long minutes as we regained our bearings.

And then contractions struck. The first one hit me like a ton of bricks, my womb clamping down with enough force to leave me doubled over, gasping for breath.

"Anna? Shit, Anna?"

I pulled myself upright, clinging to Jeff with both hands as another contraction hit me hard on heels of the first. "It should pass," I gasped. "Sex can cause contractions, but it rarely induces labor. Just…just give me a minute."

I felt Jeff's worried gaze on me, and but I ignored it, resting my cheek on his chest and breathing through the pain. Finally the contraction left me and I was able to straighten and stand on my own.

"See?" I said, "It's gone."

"Maybe we shouldn't—" Jeff started.

"Oh hell no," I interrupted. "Unless the doctor tells us we can't, you're not taking away my orgasms. Especially since I'll be without them for six weeks after the birth. I read on some internet mommy's chat-board that these contractions are actually good somehow. They soften the cervix or something."

Jeff frowned. "It looked painful."

I shrugged. "It was. It's worth it to me, though." I pushed him toward the shower, which was still running. "Now get in, before we don't have any hot water left."

I was getting worried. I hadn't said anything to Jeff, but the contractions hadn't actually stopped completely. I'd read that they could last on and off all day after sex, but that they should be irregular. Mine were spaced about ten minutes apart like clockwork, and they had been all throughout the shower, breakfast, and the drive to the hospital. I managed to keep my reactions down to a wince every now and again. Jeff noticed, I think, but didn't say anything.

Jamie was awake by the time we got to the hospital around ten-thirty. She was eating and talking with Chase we entered the room, looking alert, although both she and Chase wore rather subdued expressions. I hugged Jamie, sitting on the edge of her bed.

"Hey, hooker. How are you feeling?"

"Like I just shit a bowling ball," she joked. "Actually, I feel okay. Tender, tired, and happy."

I examined her closely, and the tension lines around her mouth and eyes didn't escape me. "What aren't you telling me?"

She shrugged. "Samantha is a preemie, Anna. There's complications. She's having trouble breathing on her own. She's at risk for RSV. I haven't even seen or held her since she came out, except for literally a minute when I first had her." Jamie sniffed, and I could tell she was barely holding herself together, which made sense of the angst I could feel radiating off of Chase from across the room.

"Why don't you give us a minute, guys," I said.

"I'm not gonna—" Chase began.

"I'm fine, Chase. Just go. Give me a minute with Anna." The guys both left, reluctantly, and Jamie threw her arms around me. "I'm scared for her, Anna. I mean, she's not in critical condition or anything, but I'm just…I just hate this."

"She'll be okay, Jay. You know she will. She'll be out of here and home with you and Chase before you know it." I held her tight. "I'm proud of you, Mama."

Jamie sniffled again and then pushed me away playfully. "What about you? When are you getting induced?"

"Supposed to be next week." I touched my belly as another contraction rippled through me, right on time, ten minutes from the last one.

Jamie didn't miss my reaction. "But it might be sooner, huh?"

I grimaced as the contraction blistered through me. When it passed, I shrugged, shaking my head. "I don't know. Jeff and I had sex this morning, and it started these contractions. They're supposedly normal, and they're supposed to go away eventually."

"But?"

"They haven't gone away. They're coming every ten minutes, and they're freaking *strong*."

"Have you told Jeff?" Jamie asked.

"Not yet. I don't want to worry him unless I have to. I keep hoping they'll go away. I've been moving around, walking, all that." I stood up and walked the few steps across the room and back.

"I think you probably should ask someone about it. What if you're in labor? I mean, you don't want the babies to just fall out, you know?"

I snorted, sitting down on the bed next to Jamie again, giving her shoulder a playful shove. "You're such an idiot, Jay."

"Yeah, but you love me." She rubbed my belly. "You really should get checked out though."

Jeff, Chase, and a nurse pushing a mobile bassinet entered the room. The nurse brought the cart with the clear plastic cradle to a stop at the foot of the bed and lifted up a tiny bundle wrapped in the blue and white hospital swaddling blanket. She settled the baby into Jamie's arms and stepped away.

"She's been doing a lot better for the last few hours," the nurse said. "Her O-two levels have been pretty stable on her own, so Dr. Mansour thought you might like to spend some time with her."

The transformation that came over Jamie was immediate, and shocking. She cradled her daughter against her chest, a blissful smile on her lips, her eyes wide and shining and happier than I'd ever seen her. "Oh my god, hi," Jamie said, her voice pitched high in that tone of voice we instinctively use with babies. "Hi there, beautiful. Look at you, oh, you're awake. And you look just like Daddy, such dark hair and beautiful brown eyes."

Chase circled to the other side of the bed and stared down at his wife and daughter. Surreptitiously, I watched Chase as he gazed at his family. I may not have been in love with him, but I still cared for him, and to see him so happy made me happy.

I turned to look at Jeff, who was watching the whole thing with an expression of rapt interest. *This is going to be us soon*, his expression said.

At that moment, of course, another contraction hit me, harder than ever and less than ten minutes since the previous one. I couldn't stop a hiss from escaping, my hand covering my belly, the other braced on the bed. Before, they'd only lasted maybe twenty or thirty seconds total, but this one had me in its grip for nearly a minute.

"Anna? I thought they'd stopped?" Jeff, from beside me, hand on my back, voice a complex mix of concerned and irritated.

I blew out a long breath between pursed lips as the contraction finally passed. "Well, they didn't," I said, irritable from the pain. "I thought they would. They're getting stronger and closer together."

Jeff growled. "Damn it, Anna. You should have told me *hours* ago."

"I didn't want to worry you if it was nothing."

Jeff tugged me to my feet. "Well now I'm worried and irritated at the same time, which is just super awesome." He pulled me out into the hall, pressed me back against the wall beside the door and cupped my face in his hands, forcing my gaze to his. "Anna. You're *supposed to* worry me with this shit. It's my job. Letting me love you means letting me worry about every little thing."

"Jeff, I—" I tried to look away but he wouldn't let me, so I brought my eyes back to his. "I'm sorry. I should have told you."

"Damn right." He touched my lips with his, a caress more than a kiss. "Now, let's go find a doctor for you and see if you're in labor."

I was in labor.

Eighty percent effaced and dilated to a seven.

My doctor was pissed.

Then came the bad news: Caleb was in a breech position, and if he didn't turn, they'd have to do a C-section.

Bridge

Jeff paced the hallway, trying to get his breathing under control. The helplessness was a fiery rage in his blood, a dark and angry force shuddering in his blood, his brain. His hands shook, his heart hammered, stuttered, machine-gun pattered.

She was in pain, contractions ripping through her in relentless waves, pain turning her lovely features into a rictus of agony. Sweat dampened her hair, fine strands sticking to her forehead, lines etched into her brow, mouth set, full lips pressed flat. Fingers clutching the bed rail so hard her knuckles turned white.

And Jeff could do nothing. Nothing.

They were only giving her another hour before they did an emergency C-section. Before they cut her open and pulled the babies out. He knew it was normal, but the idea of C-section still freaked him the hell out.

Jeff found himself at the end of the hallway, fists clenched, head pressed against the cold wall. He felt a hand on his shoulder and turned around.

"Hey man. You all right?" It was Chase, of all people.

"Do I look okay?" Jeff knew he was being a dick, but he couldn't help it.

He'd learned to get along with Chase to an extent, but he'd never be best friends with him.

Chase withdrew his hand and stood a few feet away from Jeff, spinning his cell phone between a thumb and forefinger. "I know you and I aren't, like, best buddies or whatever, Jeff, but…look, I know it's hard, okay? It sucks, not being able to do anything." He shoved his phone in his pocket and moved to stand in front of Jeff. "It's going to be okay. Anna's tough. You and I both know that."

"She's in pain, and there's nothing I can do. It fucking sucks. I need to do something, help her, I don't know. Not just stand there and hope for the best."

"I know. How do you think I felt when I found out Jamie was getting induced and I was in fucking Chicago? What if something had happened and I wasn't there? But you gotta know they know what they're doing. They'll take care of her. She'll be fine. Just be there with her. Be there for her." Chase clapped Jeff on the shoulder. "Like I said, I know we're not necessarily friends, Jeff, but I do still care about Anna, in that I want to see her happy and healthy. You make her happy, and I can see you're a good man. If you need a friend, you've got one." Chase turned away, then, leaving Jeff stunned.

He stood watching as Chase slowly walked away, only finding his voice after several heartbeats. "Chase?" he called out, and the other man stopped, turned around. "Thanks. And congratulations. Samantha is beautiful.

Back in the room with Anna, Jeff found her in the same basic position, clutching the railings, sweating, grimacing through the pain. He sat beside her, soul wrung dry, hands trembling with raw emotion. When the contraction subsided, all he could do was whisper love to her, hold her limp hand, and wait some more.

Each time a contraction ripped through her, she tried to tough it out in silence, but couldn't, and long, groaning, soul-searing screams of pain were drawn from deep within her. Each scream, each moan, each gasp shredded Jeff. Then she went limp when the contraction passed and her eyes turned to him, fixed on him with such complete adoration that he wanted to weep.

An hour passed, taffy-stretched slow in some moments, and rocketship fast in others.

A technician moved an ultrasound wand over Anna's belly, and even Jeff could see the truth: Caleb was still breech.

Chapter 8: Anna

I didn't want to scream anymore. I wanted to be that tough kind of woman who endures the pain of childbirth in silence; my throat ached, scraped raw, because I wasn't that kind of woman. I sucked in long breaths, eyes closed and knees drawn up, fingers clutching the bed railing so hard I didn't think I could let go on my own.

I felt Jeff next to me, and I knew he felt helpless. I wanted to tell him it was okay, it would be worth it all when we held our little babies. Words wouldn't come out though, stolen as another wave of excruciation sliced through me.

I heard voices, felt something wet and cold on my belly, then a hard probing and sliding across my skin; an ultrasound. I tried to pry my eyes open to see the screen, but my sight was blurred and wavery.

"He's still breech," a voice said. "We'll have to do an emergency C-section."

I wanted to cry, but I also knew it would mean an end to the pain.

I saw ceiling tiles overhead, moving. Long breaths in and out, wrenching pain, more voices, fluorescent lights, doors opening, Jeff telling me to breathe *it's okay baby, just breathe for me, in and out, breathe in and one, two three* more pain, things happening to my body, motion, blue papery fabric wrapped over me. Things happened around me, and then the massive clenching pressure of contractions stopped and I could breathe. The absence of pain was so blessed, so incredible that I was woozy, dizzy, disoriented with relief. I felt Jeff's hand in mine. I forced my eyes open, relieved all over again that the pain had stopped, and I knew I should know why, but didn't.

"Hi." It was all I could manage.

"Hi, baby. We're in the OR." Jeff's voice was tender and quiet.

"I can't feel my toes." I tried to wiggle them; nothing. "What happened to my toes?"

"Anesthetic, Anna." Jeff's fingers squeezed mine. His strength and warmth was reassuring.

"So I still have my toes?" It seemed important, but I wasn't sure why. I felt foggy and delirious.

"Yes, honey. You still have your toes." Jeff was laughing, and I saw his face above me, smiling at me.

I sucked in deep breaths, blew them out, and gradually clarity returned. "They're doing the C-section?"

Jeff nodded. "There you are. Back with me, now?" He brushed strands of sweat-damp hair away from my face. "Yeah. Caleb is still breech and they can't wait any longer."

A wall of blue blocked my sight of my body from the waist down, but Jeff was by my head, dressed in scrubs with worry etched in his rugged features. I felt pressure on my belly, tugging. Voices issuing calm instructions floated to me from the other side of the partition. I was glad I couldn't see what was going on. Out of the corner of my eye I saw a nurse turn away from my body, and her gloved hands were coated in blood. I had to look away, focused on Jeff's jawline, hard and strong and rough with days worth of beard. It kind of suited him, actually.

"I don't think I tell you enough how handsome you are, Jeff." I was filled with fear and excitement and panic and worry, and it seemed like an important thing to tell him.

He looked down at me, carving a caressing line down my cheekbone with his thumb. "You're amazing, Anna. I love you so much. You're doing great. They've almost got the first baby out."

I felt a strange pulling sensation, and then I heard a sound that forever be imprinted on my soul: the shuddering breath and stuttering cry of a wailing infant. Jeff's face contorted as he watched over the top of the curtain, and I could read the play of emotions across his face: awe, amazement, wonder, love, shock.

"It's Niall, honey. They have Niall. God, she's beautiful, she's perfect. Just like you." His voice caught and he blinked hard several times.

A few heartbeats passed and then a female voice spoke up. "Dad? You want to cut the rest of the cord?"

I turned my head to the side. A warmer sat a few feet away, this side of the curtain and away from the sterile surgical area. Niall lay on the warmer, mostly cleaned up and kicking and wailing, waving tiny fists. A nurse had a length of purplish-red umbilical cord clamped off and held it out to Jeff, while another handed him a pair of odd-looking scissors. Jeff turned to look back at me, and I smiled my encouragement at him, barely recognizing the activity still happening to the rest of me. He slid the scissors between the clamps and cut the cord, and then Niall was wrapped in a blanket and handed to Jeff.

Just as I'll never forget the first time I heard Niall's crying voice, I'll never forget that image: Jeff, huge arms flexing in the sleeves of his scrubs shirt as he reached for his daughter, a tiny, wailing bundle of swaddling blanket and waving fists fitting snug into the crook of his arms. His face, so handsome, turning soft and tender and awestruck. The feather-light kiss of his lips to her forehead, the barely-contained emotions warring on his features. His eyes smiling at me, looking at me with such love that my heart couldn't contain it all.

The strange tugging sensation came again, and then I heard Caleb's voice cry his displeasure.

Jeff was next to me again, and this time he couldn't hold it back. A tear slipped down his cheek and he bent over me, kissed my forehead, then my lips. "Anna, god, Anna. Caleb is here. Caleb is out. He's so amazing." He looked down at me, his deep brown eyes soft with emotion, wet with tears. "I love you so much. You did it. God, Anna. I'm so proud of you."

The cord-cutting ritual happened again, and then Caleb was hurried away, all too soon. I barely got a glimpse of him, and then he was gone.

"Will I get to hold them soon?" It was all I could think of. I reached for Jeff, now cradled in Jeff's arms, only to discover that my arms were strapped to the table.

A young male face, acne-scarred, hair contained in the stupid-looking sterile hat, a mask around his mouth, appeared from behind the curtain. "You'll get to hold them soon, Mrs. Cartwright. You have to get stitched up first, okay? As soon as you're able, we'll bring your babies to you."

"Can I at least kiss Caleb?" I had to touch one of my babies, at the very least. I had to know it was all real, that this was happening, that it wasn't a dream, that my babies were healthy.

The nurse nodded his approval and Jeff brought Caleb over to me, crouched down and put Caleb's forehead to my lips. When my lips touched his skin, when I saw his thick thatch of dark wet hair, I lost it. Tears streamed down my face, and I couldn't wipe them away.

Another nurse took Caleb from Jeff and set him in the warmer, recording his weight, stretched him out and marked his height at head and foot on the paper liner with a pen, then Caleb was gone and Jeff was next to me, wiping my face with gentle fingers.

The next few hours passed with startling swiftness. I was wheeled out of the OR, unstrapped—to my great relief—and brought to a recovery room. I was shaking uncontrollably, my hands trembling so badly Jeff had to hold the straw in a can of soda to my lips, because when I tried to pick up the can on my own, I shook it so bad it sloshed over my hand. I ached, so badly. The anesthetic was wearing off and my entire lower half was a knotted mass of pins and needles, as if my legs had fallen asleep. The pins and needles got so bad that I wanted to scream. It felt like a thousand bees were buzzing under my skin, crawling and stinging. I rubbed my thighs almost frantically, trying to erase the sensation, but it didn't work. Eventually, Jeff took one of my legs and settled it across his lap and began massaging the muscles, starting at my thigh and working his way down to my calf and then my foot, moving to the other leg and repeating the process.

It was the best massage I'd ever gotten.

An older, silver-haired woman in the colorful pattern-printed scrubs of NICU nurse entered the recovery room, followed by two other women in plain dark blue scrubs.

"Ready to meet your babies?" The NICU nurse asked.

"God yes. How are they doing?" I tried to stand up, but didn't even manage to rock forward to a fully sitting position.

"Why don't you let us help you into a wheelchair and we'll take to them, so you can find out for yourself?" The nurse, whose name tag announced her name as Sheila, helped me get my feet under me.

I was helped into a wheelchair, and they pushed me down endless corridors and around corners and through open doorways to the NICU ward. It was a wide room with rows of incubators and warmers, smelling of baby and milk and hospital. Machines buzzed quietly and efficiently, a baby fussed hungrily in one of the warmers, and in one corner, a nurse cradled a baby in her arms, teasing the baby's lips with a bottle of formula.

Jeff walked beside me as I was wheeled to a stop between side-by-side incubators. I looked from one baby to the other, drinking in their features, seeing my nose, Jeff's eyes, a mix-up of both of us. I couldn't tell them apart. I didn't know which was which. Shouldn't I be able tell? Guilt hit me. These were my babies, and I didn't know which was which? Did that mean I was a bad mommy? I had to hold back tears.

"Which one is which?" I asked, my voice quavering.

Sheila smiled at me, understanding pouring from her in nearly-visible waves. "It's perfectly normal to not be able to tell them apart yet, hon." She reached in to one of the incubators and carefully lifted the swaddled bundle out, settling it in my arms.

It? Had I just thought of my baby as an it? Another shudder ran through me.

"This is your daughter," Sheila said, fussing with the little cotton cap on Niall's head, tugging it further down around her ears.

Niall was awake and quiet, brown eyes wide, searching, roving, and then…she fixed her eyes on me, focusing. A hot rush of emotion hit me, a Niagra flood of love and overwhelming protective need and awe and wonder. I'd made this warm thing in my arms, this little human, this tiny person. She was mine. Mine and Jeff's. I looked up at him, smiled at him, felt his love wash over me.

Sheila smiled at us, patted me on the back. "Dad, you can hold Caleb if you want, then you can trade. They're doing very well, both of them. They have mild jaundice, but that's normal for any baby, premature twins especially. They're breathing fairly well, although they'll need some help now again. We'll have to see how they eat, though."

"How big are they?" I asked.

"Niall is three pounds nine ounces, seventeen point three inches," Sheila answered. "Caleb is three pounds four ounces and sixteen point eight inches. They've both taken a bottle, but Caleb had a bit of trouble latching on. His sister didn't have any trouble, though. She latched on right away and sucked the bottle down like a champ."

I looked at Caleb, nestled in Jeff's powerful arms. "Let's switch," I said. "I want to hold him now."

Jeff slipped his hand under Niall in my arms, lifted her free and for a moment had both of his babies in his arms. His smile in that moment was one of absolute joy. I saw his phone denting the breast pocket of his scrubs, so I reached up and grabbed it out of the pocket, pulled up camera and took several pictures of my husband holding both of his children. He settled them both in my arms and I felt the same look of contentment wash over me. I saw Jeff snapping pictures out of the corner of my eye, but I had eyes only for my babies. Niall, on the left, drowsing now, eyes closing, hands lax against her chin, Caleb on the right, fussing noisily, mouth working open and closed, hands waving and little fingers flexing.

Such tiny fingers. Everything about them was just…so small. So fragile. So perfect.

Jeff took Niall from me and then Sheila brought me a bottle. I held it to Caleb's lips, and he nuzzled it with his mouth, but didn't take it. He cried louder, his mews of hunger turning to wails of anger. A drop of formula touched his tongue and he wailed even harder, but refused to take the nipple of the bottle. Sheila showed me how to encourage him to take it, teasing his upper lip with the dripping tip. After several tries, he latched on and began sucking, his cries silencing.

"Will I be able to breastfeed them?" I asked.

Sheila stood back, watching him drink. "Yes, of course. For now we need to be able to monitor how much they're eating, though, so we'll have to continue to bottle-feed them. They both have to be at least four pounds eight ounces and able to drink an entire bottle at every feeding before they go home. We might have you try to breast-feed them next time they're hungry, just to see how they latch on."

"How long will they be here, do you think?" Jeff asked.

Sheila shrugged. "It depends, really. A few days at least, maybe a week or two."

It wouldn't end up working out quite that easily, though. I didn't know that then, of course.

Chapter 9: Jamie

*A*week and half had passed since I'd had Samantha. She'd done well enough after birth that they'd sent her home, but now, as I held her in my arms, I worried. Her legs were mottled various shades of red and pink, splotches of color and paleness alternating like the patches of a jaguar. She seemed to be struggling to breathe, sucking in hard for each breath, lifting her chin to gasp for air. Her shirt was hiked up around her armpits, and I watched as her stomach dipped in with each breath, distending with each exhale, her diaphragm showing at the inhale.

Something was wrong.

Chase was out on the back porch of Kelly's house, where we were staying until we got the okay to drive home to New York. The sliding glass door was open and I could hear the start-and-stop guitar of Chase writing a song. I looked back down at Samantha, her sleeping face looking distressed.

Kelly sat down on the couch next to me. "How are we doing, Mama?"

I looked at her, and I knew my worry was stamped on my face. "She looks like she's having trouble breathing."

Kelly took Samantha from me, resting the baby face-up on her legs. She pressed her thumb into Samantha's skin, watching as the thumbprint remained for several seconds before disappearing. She pushed up Samantha's shirt a bit more and watched her chest retract and expand with each breath, tilting her upside-down watch to time the space between breaths.

Kelly turned to me with concern in her eyes. "I think you need to take her to the ER, Jamie. I don't have an at-home pulse oximeter to measure it, but I'm pretty sure Samantha's levels are low. It could be RSV."

That was a word I'd heard tossed about before they let us bring her home. I wasn't sure what it was exactly, but I knew it had something to do with her breathing. "Will she be okay?"

Kelly wouldn't quite meet my eyes. "You need to take her to the hospital to get checked out, sweetie."

I picked up Samantha and held her to my chest. "Get Chase, tell him what's going on. I'll get Sam in her car seat."

Within minutes, we were making the short trip back to Beaumont. Chase dropped Sam, Kelly and I off at the emergency entrance and went to park the car. We were hustled to a triage room almost immediately, probably thanks to the fact that the nurses all knew Kelly. Chase joined us shortly thereafter, and then after more than thirty minutes, a young Indian man in a lab coat—looking too young to me to possibly be a doctor—checked over Samantha, almost cursorily.

"It is RSV, there is no doubt. She is not yet coughing or wheezing that I have seen, so it does not seem to be bronchiolitis as yet, but that is my worry. Her pulse-ox is seventy-four, which is very worrisomely low. It should be one hundred, or very close to it." He traced a fingernail along her diaphragm, which was visible at every inhale. "You can see here that she is having to work to take in breaths. I am going to admit her and have her taken up to the pediatric ward."

I struggled to keep my tears of panic at bay. "What can you do to help her?"

He gave me a serious, compassionate look. "Unfortunately, at her young age, there is nothing we can give her beyond saline and a little very diluted oxygen. She is too newly born to be given steroids or anything like that." His faint accent lilted at every other syllable. "We will monitor her, and we will do everything that we are able to keep your daughter healthy."

After an hour's wait, a nurse showed up to take us to the pediatric ward several floors up. My heart pounded, and I had to focus on deep breathing to keep from breaking down. Chase's hand in mine was a lifeline, warm and solid and comforting. It was all that kept me sane.

The room was tiny, barely ten feet wide and fifteen long, split in half by a thin curtain. Against either wall was a huge crib that could be converted into an incubator. A well-built male nurse in his thirties with sandy blond hair cropped short and a day's worth of stubble on his fair skin greeted us warmly. He introduced himself as Brian, and said he'd be our nurse until shift change in four hours. He spent several minutes with Samantha, checking her over himself, familiarizing himself with her chart, taking her temperature, listening to her breathing with a stethoscope, changing her from her own clothes to a hospital onesie that allowed him to attach monitor leads to her wrist and and a pulse-oximeter to her big toe.

That was what broke me: the sight of my baby, not even two weeks old, with a miniature cannula inserted into her nose and trailing over her shoulder, red and green wires with monitor leads taped to her wrist, an oximeter pinching her big toe, glowing red. I collapsed backward into a plasticky leather recliner, buried my face in my hands and sobbed. Chase didn't try to comfort me beyond a heavy hand on my shoulder.

"I know it's scary to see her like this," Brian said, "but she's going to be okay. We're going to take great care of her, and you'll be home as soon as possible."

I nodded, barely hearing him. It didn't seem like it was going to be okay. Samantha lay in the crib, swaddled in a blanket with the lead wires trailing out near her shoulder, eyes narrowed but open. Her little mouth was partially open, and she was visibly struggling to draw in breath. I could only watch her, eyes burning with unshed tears, and try to breathe for her. I sucked in a breath as she did, let out mine with her, as if I could lend her my oxygen, as if I could heal her with sheer force of will.

Hours passed, streaming by like water, then stopping to creep by in a sludge-slow crawl. I sat in the chair watching Samantha try to breathe, ignoring Chase's attempts to call me. At some point, Kelly left. Each labored breath in caused my heart to ache.

I was completely helpless.

I didn't notice him leave, but at some point, Chase shoved a styrofoam cup of khaki-colored coffee in my hands, too hot, burnt, too sweet, but exactly what I needed. The only sounds were Samantha's breathing, now laced with an occasional wheeze, and the incessant coughing of the baby on the other side of the curtain. When Sam coughed for the first time, I cried again.

There were no windows and no clocks, no way to measure the passage of time. It could have been midnight, it could have been noon. We'd left for the hospital about four in the afternoon, I thought, but wasn't sure. Chase was antsy, bouncing his knees, sitting in another chair drawn up near mine, continually running his hands through his hair. Then he began humming, mumbling, standing up and pacing the few steps down the length of the room and back, clearly caught up in something in his head. He left the room and I heard him ask the nurses at the station for a pen and pencil, and then he returned and resumed his seat on the edge of the chair, scribbling on the pad of paper furiously.

I didn't disturb him, knowing he'd share it when he was ready.

Abruptly, he stopped pacing, facing me. "I'm supposed to be onstage in Lancaster, Pennsylvania right now," he said.

I wasn't sure what his point was, so I just stared at him, not trusting myself to not completely lose my shit at him.

"I had this song for Samantha just pop in to my head. I need to get it out."

I just nodded, glanced at Samantha while chewing on my nail.

He took a breath, then started singing *a capella*. The melody was a lullaby, lilting and sweet and kind of haunting and quiet.

"I can't breathe for you,
My darling,
I can't hold you close enough.
There's nothing I can do,

I doesn't matter if I'm strong or if I'm tough.
Because there's no way for me to imbue
Any of my strength into you.
I can only watch and pray,
I can only stand and stay
In this room close by your side,
Praying to a God I've long denied.
You're so tiny in that bed,
My darling,
You're so pale, and, god, so still.
And I can only watch and pray,
I can only stand and stay,
Wishing your body wasn't ill.
I can't breathe for you,
My darling,
There's just nothing I can do.
But I'm here, just the same,
Praying over you, I'm watching over you.
I can't ever hold you close enough,
My darling,
I can't ever be strong enough.
But I'll always, always try,
I'll comfort you when you cry.
I kiss away your tears,
I'll quiet all your fears.
I can't breathe for you,
My darling,
I can only watch and pray,
I can only stand stay
In this room, close to you."

By the end of the song, there was a crowd around the door, nurses, doctors, parents, orderlies. Chase's voice had never sounded so sweet or so soulful. He'd poured his heart into that song as fully as if he'd been on stage in front of thousands of people. When people realized the song was over, they seemed unsure what to do. Clapping seemed inappropriate to them in this setting, I think, but they knew a performance when they saw it. In the end, they scattered one by one, and Chase and I were left alone with our sick, sleeping daughter.

Chase swayed on his feet, stumbled, fell backward and landed in the chair, scrubbing his face with his hands almost violently. When his shoulders began to shake, I realized he'd finally cracked the façade of his composure. I left my chair and knelt on the floor between his knees, still sore from childbirth but uncaring of my own discomfort in that moment. I pulled his face against my breast and held him, just held him. He only allowed himself a few moments of shuddering, silent tears before he breathed a harsh, gusting sigh and sat back, wiping his face.

"I don't know what came over me," he said, "I'm sorry—"

"Don't you dare apologize," I said, cutting in over him. "Our baby girl is sick and there's nothing we can do but wait. You're allowed to be upset."

He nodded, rubbed his face again, breathing deeply. He pulled me onto his lap and I curled up into him, resting my head against his chest, listening to his heartbeat, watching the gentle rise and fall of Samantha's labored breathing.

At some point I dozed off, and was woken by a wet hacking cough coming from Samantha. Chase was asleep as well, head lolled back uncomfortably on the chair. I slid off his lap and stood over Samantha, taking her hand in mine. She curled her tiny fingers around my index finger and held on tight, cracking her eyes open to peer at me. Her face scrunched up and she coughed again, a wet, wracking cough that tore my heart to shreds.

A nurse came in, a different one now, a pretty woman in her thirties with blond-streaked brown hair pulled into a bun. She introduced herself as Laurie and gently but firmly insinuated herself between me and Samantha, placing her stethoscope over Samantha's chest and listening as she coughed.

"I know this cough sound really horrible," she said, turning to me, "but she doesn't have any crackles going on, and her pulse-ox is holding steady right around eighty. She's not ready to go home yet, but I don't think she's getting any worse. We'll keep the oxygen on for now, and if you notice a lot of drainage clogging her nose, you can clean it out." She showed us how to do that, squirting some saline into her nose and suctioning it out with a green bulb syringe.

Samantha absolutely hated this process, kicking and screaming flailing, but she seemed to breathe easier after it was done.

More hours passed. My birth-sore body protested the long hours in the same position in the chair, watching the monitors, watching her pulse-ox fluctuate from seventy-two to eighty-four, but never any higher. Chase eventually left, returning with a couple pre-made sandwiches, bags of chips and bottles of soda from the cafeteria.

More coffee, more waiting. Watch her pulse-ox obsessively, willing it to rise. Dozing off fitfully, only to be woken by coughing, by the nurse checking in, by Chase shifting, by my own thoughts.

Mundane things like TV, music, Facebook, Twitter, Instagram… they all fall away when you're in a hospital room, watching your child suffer. All that matters is the bizarre fast-yet-slow passage of time, the monitors, the read-outs and the child. The only status that counts is that of your baby.

She breathes, she coughs, she sleeps, she needs a bottle. She shits and you have to change her without making a mess of the monitor leads. You feed her another bottle, holding her against your chest and feeling guilty for each clean, easy breath you take. You do everything so carefully, so thoroughly, in case that one thing you do just right might just possibly make the difference and get her well sooner. You try to sleep, and can't. Your eyes burn, heavy and hot from exhaustion, but there's no comfort, and even if there was, you wouldn't take it, because to be comfortable while your child lays ill is some kind of betrayal. The hospital room, the whiteboard with its layers of not-quite erased dry erase writings, the machines and monitors against the wall, the bevy of wires, the TV on mute, tuned to a local channel and playing soap operas and *People's Court* and *Judge Alex* and now-ancient and partially-familiar reruns of *Cheers*. The crib, your baby, finally seeming to be asleep, truly resting, for once not coughing or wheezing and giving you a glimmer of hope, despite the pulse-ox readout of eighty-eight, when you know it has to be at least ninety-five before they'll send her home.

Eventually, a kind of panicked claustrophobia sets in. It's a claustrophobia of time, hour after hour in the tiny room, maybe venturing to the bathroom, choking down food and coffee, listlessly watching crap TV without really caring. You grow desperate for something to change, for healing to occur while you're looking the other way, for the endless monotony to shift. And then you feel guilty for feeling bored when just there she's still gasping, her chest still retracting, because if she's not retracting, she might be getting better.

Eventually Chase made me walk down to the cafeteria, just to get away for a minute. I hated him for making me leave, because I was positive something would happen while I was gone. Interacting with people was an oddity, suddenly. I wasn't sure how long we'd been in the hospital. My phone had long since died, and the only marker of time I had was staff shift changes and news broadcasts and which rerun was playing on the TV attached to the wall by a long swivel arm.

In the cafeteria, I ordered two cheeseburgers and watched the cook as he flipped and pressed them. The cook was an enormous black man, easily six foot six and over three hundred pounds, a chef's hat slouched sideways on his head. He moved with a slow, graceful economy, sure and efficient behind the counter. He wore loose clear plastic food service gloves, black-and-white checkered pants, a white coat-like shirt with two rows of buttons, over which was a spattered apron; his sleeves were spotless, despite the myriad of stains on his apron. He gave me hesitant smile as he slid the burgers on to buns and put them into sty-rofoam containers.

"What day is it?" I asked him.

His gaze shifted, and I saw understanding in his eyes. "Thursday. 'Bout seven in the evenin'." His voice was impossibly deep, gravelly, raspy.

"Holy shit," I breathed. "I've been here for two and a half days."

He nodded. "Time turns into somethin' odd in them rooms. Makes you forget just about everythin' but them that's sick." He turned away, pulled the basket of fries out of the deep fryer and shook them, dumped them into a pan and sprinkled fries on them before scooping some into the to-go containers and handing them to me. "What'chu here for?"

"My daughter has RSV."

He nodded. "That shit is awful. My youngest had that. Only three months old."

"Mine isn't even two weeks old." I popped a scorching hot fry into my mouth.

He grimaced. "Goddamn. Sorry to hear it." He scratched his cheek with a huge finger. "She'll be okay though. They come through it all right. Kids are resilient, you know? They bounce back. She'll be fine. I got four kids, and all but one of 'em got that RSV. They all fine, now."

"Thanks," I said. "It's hard to see, sometimes."

"I know it does. It's hard just sittin' there. Can't do nothin'. That's the hardest thing."

I took a deep breath, nodding. "That really is it, isn't it? Being helpless is awful."

"I know that's true." He slapped the top of the counter with his paw and then waved at me. "Your girl'll be fine and so will you."

I nodded. "Thanks."

I sat down and ate one of the burgers, dipping fries into ketchup squirted out of packets. I was halfway done when someone slid into the chair next to me. It was Anna, in yoga pants and a loose sweater.

"Anna?" I twisted in my seat to give my best friend a hug. "Why are you here?"

She looked like how I felt: faded, exhausted, sore. "Caleb is still in the NICU." She snatched a fry from me. "You?"

"Samantha has RSV."

"Ugh." She snatched another fry, then rubbed one eye with the heel of her palm. "I haven't even her and she's sick."

"Is Niall home, then?" I asked.

She nodded. "Yeah. She's fine. Jeff is home with her. I…I haven't seen him in a week, except in passing. One of us is home, one of us is here."

"This is the first time I've left the room in three days." I'd finished my burger and was picking at the fries, but found I wasn't hungry any longer. I pushed them to Anna, who picked at them as well. "Can you believe this is us? Married, with babies?"

Anna laughed, shaking her head. "No, I really can't. I really can't. I feel like a totally different person than I was three years ago. Even one year ago. You know? Like, was that really you and me going to the bar every night? Getting drunk, hitting on guys?"

I snorted. "*I* hit on guys. *You* always chickened out and made me go up to them alone." I bumped her with my shoulder. "You just sat there watching, sipping your pinot grigiot and acting aloof."

"Aloof? Me?" She gave me an incredulous look. "That wasn't me being aloof, that was me being too scared to get off the stool."

"I kinda wish I'd been more scared than I was. That may have saved me from being as much of a skank as I was."

"Yeah, maybe." She said it with straight face, then broke down into snickers of laughter.

I pretended to glare at her. "Very funny, bitch."

"Hey," she said, laughing, raising her hands in a gesture of defense, "I always tell you you're not a skank, and you just argue with me. So this time I agree with you, and you get mad? Pick a feature, hooker."

I laughed with her, and it felt good. "Hey, I'm a girl. I'm allowed." I stood up, and Anna stood up with me. "You should come up and see Samantha."

She nodded. "I'd love to."

Chase was holding Samantha in his arms, feeding her a bottle when we got to the room. As they always did when he saw Anna, Chase's eyes flickered with scabbed-over pain. It didn't bother me anymore, not much, at least. There would always be pain there, I realized. When your husband has a history with your best friend, there would always be an element of buried pain and unavoidable awkwardness. He smiled at us, his face lighting up as his eyes met mine. *That* was what made the awkwardness worth it: His eyes always lit up when he saw me, a smile always spread on his face when I entered a room.

Anna slathered hand sanitizer on her hands from a dispenser on the wall, then crossed the room to crouch near Chase, touching Samantha's cheek with the back of her index finger. "God, she's adorable. She looks so much like both of you!" Samantha sucked down the last of the bottle, and Chase handed her to Anna, who looked from Samantha to me, and then from Samantha to Chase. "She's got your eyes, Chase, but Jay's nose."

"Thank god for that," Chase said. "She'd have been doomed if she got my nose."

Anna laughed, and touched the baby nose in question, speaking in the high-pitched voice people use when talking to babies. "Well hi there, Samantha. I'm your Auntie Anna. You have to get better so your mommy and daddy can take you home. Just like your cousin Caleb. He's got to get better too, so you can play together. That's right. You'll have so much fun together, yes you will."

Chase laughed. "Why do people do that? Talk like that?"

I slapped his shoulder. "Studies have shown that babies register high-pitches better, they respond to them better. We do it naturally because we somehow just know it works."

Chase gave me a strange look. "Where'd you learn that?"

"I was stuck with nothing to do but read books and watch TV for *weeks*. I learned all sorts of shit."

Anna handed Samantha back to Chase. "I'd better go. You'd better bring her over as soon as possible, okay?"

"We will," I said. "Now go be with Caleb."

When she was gone, life in the hospital room resumed their pattern. After an unknowable amount of hours, a doctor swept into the room, an older man with delicate hands and wire-framed glasses and steel-gray hair. After a surprisingly thorough examination, he settled Samantha back in the crib and turned to us.

"She's doing very well," he said. "She's on the mend, I'd say. Another day, maybe two, and she should be ready to go home. Her breathing seems clear, her retractions are nearly gone, and she's not producing a lot of mucus. I wish I could let you take her now, but I'd rather keep her for another twenty-four or forty-eight hours, just to be safe. Sometimes they reach this point and then have a relapse. I'd hate to have you go home only to have to turn around bring her back."

We both nodded, understanding the logic, but not liking it.

"She'll be okay, though?" I asked, my voice embarrassingly tremulous.

The doctor nodded, exuding reassurance. "Oh yes. She'll be just fine. You'll have to watch her breathing for a while, of course, especially as we get closer to winter. You'll be watching for the retractions along here," he explained, tracing a finger along her diaphragm. "If you see that, this working to breathe, that's when you should bring her in. Hopefully, of course, you won't need to, but that's what you should be on the look out for, just in case."

He left then, and Chase and I looked at each other in relief. We finally had a goal in sight, an end in view. I settled myself on Chase's lap once again, and he wrapped his arms around me. His breath tickled my ear and my hair; I'd never been so aware of something so simple as breathing. Even relaxed, sitting here on my husband's lap, I was listening to every breath Samantha took, attuned to every sound.

I fell asleep on Chase, and I dreamed a mundane and wonderful dream of rocking Samantha in the darkness of her nursery in our Manhattan brownstone.

Chapter 10: Anna

After two and a half weeks in the NICU, Dr. Sherman finally let me take Caleb home. Jeff was at our house with Niall, who, he said, was eating and shitting faster than he could keep up with. He sounded slightly hysterical when he said that. I tried not to laugh. I dressed Caleb in a green and white onesie that had a picture of frog on the front, and the words "hop to it". I buckled him into his car seat, covered him with a blanket despite the eighty degree July weather, and left William Beaumont Hospital after nearly a month straight. I'd spent most of my time at the hospital, unable to stay away from Caleb for more than a few hours. I knew Jeff was overwhelmed at being alone with a newborn, and I certainly missed him, but I couldn't stomach the thought of something happening to Caleb while I wasn't there.

I clicked Caleb into the seat base, then leaned in to kiss his forehead. His eyes were open, and he tracked me as I closed in on him, batted at me with his little fists. I laughed at him, letting him grip my finger for a moment. I don't think I've ever driven as carefully as that ride from Beaumont to my home. I watched every intersection with paranoia as I passed through, braked early and accelerated slowly. Normally a twenty minute ride at the most, it took me over half an hour to get home. When I did, I found Jeff asleep on the couch, Niall on his chest covered in a pink blanket with a burp cloth under her face. Jeff's hands were wrapped around her, his long fingers spanning her body and cradling her in place. A bottle sat on the floor, and the TV was tuned to ESPN.

Caleb was sleeping soundly in his carrier, so I left him there. I gingerly lifted Niall from Jeff's chest and pressed her tiny sweet sleeping face to my breast, breathing in the clean scent of her hair mingling with the faint essence of Jeff. She didn't stir, so I just held her for a few moments, eyes closed, inhaling her presence. My eyes watered, teared up, and I had to quietly sniff them away.

When I opened my eyes, Jeff was awake, watching me with love shining in his eyes. I smiled at him over the top of Niall's head. I set Niall down in her crib in our room, covered her with a blanket and stood over her, watching to see if she stirred. When I was content that she wasn't going to wake up, I went back into the living room and lay down to slide into Jeff's waiting embrace on the couch. He curled his arms around me and pillowed my head on the crook of his arm. Neither of us spoke for long minutes, content to bask in the glow of being home together.

"I'm finally home," I whispered.

"You're finally home." Jeff murmured in my ear, then nuzzled the hollow of my neck with kisses until I giggled.

His lips trailed kisses around to the base of my throat and upward, planting a blaze of heat deep inside me. My doctor had told me I *should* wait six to eight weeks before resuming sexual activity, but followed that up by saying that as long as I'd stopped bleeding it should be fine, but he should be gentle. I hadn't told Jeff this, though.

He slid kisses further along my throat to my jaw, then across to my lips, and then we were lost in each other. Of all the kisses I'd ever shared with Jeff, I think that one, laying on our couch with our new-born babies nearby, was the sweetest, most desperate. I'd barely seen Jeff in the previous two and half weeks of Caleb's stay in the NICU, and kisses had been the last thing on our mind in the days leading up to and immediately after giving birth. I kissed him like I'd lost him and then found him again. I kissed him as if I'd been starved of his breath, as if I was drowning and he was my air. I delved into the kiss, lost myself in it. I caressed his face, ran my fingers through his messy hair, rubbed my palms on his jaw and relished the feel of his stubble under my skin. I breathed a sigh of joyful relief at the wondrous feel of his hands arcing down my spine, at the power of his arms as they cradled me close, at the heady intoxication of his tongue against mine.

He pulled away, leaving us both breathless. "I'm gonna get carried away," he whispered.

"What if that's what I wanted?"

He gave me a puzzled look. "I thought we couldn't for like two more months?"

I grinned at him. "I had a C-section. Different rules." I slid against him, insinuating my body into his, pressing my curves into his hardness.

"Oh?" He let his hands wander down my sides to grip my hips and pull me harder against him. "What are the rules, then?""As long as I stop bleeding, it's fine. You just have to be gentle." I pushed my hands up under his T-shirt to roam his firm stomach and the hard slabs of muscle on his chest. "I stopped bleeding three days ago."

Jeff stared at me, as if assessing my words. "You're sure? I couldn't stand it if I hurt you."

"Just…go slow and gentle, okay?" I angled my body away to push his gym shorts down, freeing his still-swelling erection.

I took his shaft in my hands and caressed him into diamond hardness, and I didn't stop there. I slid my fist around him, toying with him, enjoying the slide of silk around steel, the familiar beauty of his manhood and the way it fit perfectly in my hands. I felt heat welling up inside me, burgeoning into roiling pressure as Jeff's hands found bare skin, pushed away my yoga pants—carefully avoiding my belly and the healing stitches. He delved downward, achingly slow, delicate and tender. The slowness was delicious, building the need inside me to an inferno. He didn't stroke and circle my folds with his customary sureness. No, this time, he explored me with an almost virginal hesitancy, and I delighted in each exploratory touch, each slow swipe.

He knew me too well, though. He still knew how to read my reactions, gauging each gasp and each sigh.

As he worked me gradually into a feverish pitch of need, I did the same to him, caressing his length with my fingers, stroking him with both fists, rubbing his turgid tip with my thumb, tracing the swollen veins and rimming the hollow groove beneath his head with an index finger. Touching him, relearning him, loving him with my hands.

"We have to put one on," I whispered.

He didn't answer, he just reached out to the coffee table a few feet away, slid open the narrow drawer and withdrew a string of condoms, ripping one free with dextrous fingers. We'd kept some there forever, from when we were merely enjoying each other and not "not trying" to get pregnant. We didn't use them often, but we kept them on hand. Now, I was glad we had.

He rolled it on and we shifted on the couch, Jeff's spine against the back of the couch, me facing him. I spread my leg over both of his and held my breath as he guided himself into me. He stopped when I gasped in surprise at the way he stretched me, holding still until I opened my eyes and resumed breathing. He waited, watching me. I let myself adjust to him, my hands clutching his shoulder and the nape of his neck, my forehead against his. Our eyes locked and I slowly swiveled my hips to slide him into me, my gaze never wavering from his. It was almost like being a virgin again, tightly stretched, a slightly unpleasant pinch that quickly faded into the familiar ecstasy of his thickness filling me. When he was fully immersed in me, I held tight, not moving, just absorbing his heat and hardness.

Then, with glacial slowness, we began moving, our bodies writhing together in synchronous perfection. He always knew exactly what I needed, and was always able to give it to me perfectly. He kissed my neck, my throat, my lips, my shoulder, sliding slowly into me, withdrawing in an achingly tender caress, and then slipping back in again. I could only hold him and gasp, breathe with him, move with him.

When I came, it wasn't an explosion; I slid slowly and inexorably into climax, like an inrushing tide slipping gradually up the beach, wetting the sand further inch by inch. I clung to Jeff like a shipwreck survivor clutching a spar, holding on to him and gasping breathlessly, ignoring the twinge and ache of stitches pulling, moving my hips with his, hissing as the crest washed over me, whimpering his name as I was left limp and sated. I held tight still as he came with a soft gasp, his entire body shivering with the effort to keep still and slow rather than plunging into me as I knew he wanted to. He stroked deep, gently, stilled there and bit my shoulder, pulled away and gasped my name.

And then Caleb began crying. We both laughed, my head falling forward onto Jeff's shoulder. At first, Caleb just whimpered a bit, a thin mew of just-woke-up displeasure. Then, in the time it took me to disentangle myself from Jeff and re-dress, he had launched into a full-fledged arm-flailing wail of anger.

I unbuckled him from his carseat and lifted him out, cradling him against me, only to realize in a rather messy way he was crying: he'd blown out his diaper, smearing my hands, arm, and shirt. Jeff laughed, but took Caleb from me and changed him while I cleaned myself off.

In the process, Niall woke up and added to the cacophony with her own quavering infant cries. Having stripped my shirt off and tossed it into the laundry room, I was left in only my bra as I brought Niall out of her crib, discovering with a certain amount of hilarity that she had blown out too. So, I put her on the changing table vacated only moments ago and changed her as Jeff shook a bottle of Enfamil and screwed a nipple onto it.

When Niall was changed and dressed again, I plopped down onto the couch next to Jeff, who watched in fascination as I freed one of my breasts from the confines of the bra and tickled Niall's lips with my nipple. She mewed and nuzzled, worked her mouth, cried in frustration, and then latched on with a vengeance, eliciting a gasp of surprise from me. I felt a tug inside my breast as my milk started.

"That's amazing," Jeff said, watching Niall feed.

"Yeah it is," I agreed, then glanced at him with a smirk. "You know it means my breasts will be basically off limits for awhile, though, right?"

He frowned. "Yeah, that's crossed my mind. I'm not super thrilled with it, but it is what it is." He paused to set the bottle down and move

Caleb to his shoulder, patting his back gently. "As long as I get them back at some point, I'll be fine."

"You'll get them back, don't worry," I said, teasing him. "I might let you play with them sometimes, you'll just have to be careful, 'cause they're super sensitive."

Jeff opened his mouth to reply, but Caleb chose that moment to belch so hard he lurched forward on Jeff's shoulder, sending us both into laughter. Jeff cradled Caleb on his back, supporting his neck with one hand. Caleb's eyes rolled around in his head, searching his surroundings, looking shocked by the massive burp that came of him.

We passed the day peacefully enough, feeding, changing, burping, and holding the babies, finding a pattern together. It was overwhelming at times, especially when both babies decided to get hungry at the same time, or when they both went apeshit in their diapers together. I also knew the time was coming when Jeff would have to work and I'd be here with them alone, but that in the future. I held on to the present, clung to the joy of watching the love of my life hold his son, or bounce his daughter in his arms.

I'd thought I was content before, with Jeff. That feeling of being full of love was blown away by the sheer power of my love for my babies. When I finally lay down, that first night in my own bed with my husband next to me and my babies in their cribs a few feet away, I felt a peace and happiness wash over me that defied description or quantification. There was simply no holding it in, no way to express it. I was completely flooded by happiness, so overwhelmed by it that I had to turn my face into Jeff's shoulder and cry.

He held me, seeming to understand, or maybe he just knew that sometimes women need to cry and there's just no explaining it. It was tears of joy and happiness, yes, but then, once they were loose and flooding down my face, I found myself also crying from the fear and stress and worry of Caleb's stay in the NICU, being so unsure when he'd get to go home. I'd held it all in while I was there, unable to let it out. Now that Caleb was home, I could cut loose and let myself be weak, let myself feel everything.

Jeff just held me. His arms closed me in, clutched me against him and cradled me, comforted me, soothed me. The storm of tears rocked through me, and Jeff's lips whispered love to me as I wept.

After an unmeasurable time, the flood stopped and I drifted to sleep, nestled in the nook of Jeff's arm, spent from crying, still filled with a happiness I couldn't even begin to describe.

The happiness persisted, even when Caleb woke up two hours later, waking up his sister in the process.

Laying in bed with Caleb suckling at my breast and Jeff feeding Niall a bottle on the other side of me, I thought back to that day so long ago when I'd stumbled out of a Ram's Horn, fleeing uncertain feelings I didn't know how to process for a man I'd just met. My journey had been a convoluted one, that was for sure. I couldn't help wondering where I'd be if I'd decided not to go to Ram's Horn that day, or if I'd ignored the letter with the plane ticket to New York. Or if I'd stayed in New York and dealt with my fears rather than running from them. Every choice I'd made had led me here, to this moment.

Did I regret anything?

No.

I regretted hurting both Jeff and Chase, in different ways, but that pain had also led us all to this point in time. Chase and Jamie had their own happiness, and I had mine.

Jamie had texted me earlier in evening that the doctor had finally given her the okay to take Samantha home. She'd promised to come over some time in the next week so we could hold each other's babies and catch up some more before she and Chase drove back to New York.

My thoughts fell into a jumble of disordered ideas and slow musings, and then Caleb was done and burped and asleep once more and I cradled my son to my chest, listening to his breathing, to Jeff's and to Niall's, feeling my heart swell with an all-encompassing love for my family.

My family.

Once upon a time, I'd given up on ever having a family, on ever having a man love me the way Jeff did.

Which just goes to show you, Life is a strange place, a mirror-maze of twists and turns, an incomprehensible adventure in which heartbreak that leads to love, in which mistakes lead to perfection, in which tears dry away and reveal beauty beneath.

Such is my experience, anyway.

THE END.

Continue reading for an excerpt from the spinoff series

Big Love Abroad

Featuring Ian from Rock Stars Do It Dirty

I clutched the armrests of my seat, staring fixedly out the window to the wet tarmac below. I had my headphones on, Björk playing loud enough to drown out everything else. My breathing was erratic, and I was sweating; we hadn't even finished boarding yet and I was in the middle of a full-blown panic attack. My black hair was frizzing out from the side of my face and sticking to my forehead, sweat pulling it out of its normally tight ponytail. I hated flying. *Hated.* I'd been on a flight several years back that had gone through such violent turbulence more than half of the passengers had been vomiting by the time we'd made an emergency landing to get out of the storm. I'd never forgotten the helpless horror and nauseating drops in altitude, the way the gusts of wind had tossed us to and fro like a toy.

I didn't have much choice but to take this flight, though. I'd been accepted to the University of Oxford, where I was going to study English Literature. I'd recently received my BA in Lit from University of Michigan, and now I had a once in a lifetime opportunity to study Jane Austen and the Brontë sisters in the country of their birth. My thesis focused primarily on *Jane Eyre* and *Pride and Prejudice*, and was concerned with how those two works influenced the birth of the romance genre. I had the whole thing mapped out, and had already exchanged emails with a few professors from Oxford over the summer, planning the first steps in solidifying my thesis. I was beyond excited to be moving to England, but first I had to survive the flight.

I felt someone move into the seat next to me. I smelled him first, citrus overtones of some faint cologne, a touch of male sweat, not unpleasantly, and a whiff of copper, like blood, oddly. I turned my head and pulled my Beats by Dre headphones off to hang around my neck.

My heart stopped and my mouth went dry.

Well, hello Mr. Chunk o' Hunk…

He wasn't sitting yet, but was facing me as he shoved his carry-on into the overhead compartment. His faded *The Kooks* T-shirt was riding high enough to reveal delectable washboard abs with just a hint of happy trail hair leading down to the Promised Land. I let my gaze slide upward to take in his toned arms flexing as they worked his bag into the compartment, and then his face…oh lordy-lord, he was beautiful. Clean, classically beautiful lines, a strong jaw but not too square or caveman-ish, striking cheekbones and piercing, vivid blue eyes that were somewhere between cornflower and periwinkle and completely hypnotizing as they flicked down to me.

I was caught staring and flushed red, turning away to stare out the window. We were taxiing now, and he slid into the seat, a pair of iPhone earbuds trailing down his chest, one stuck into his left ear. He pulled the other bud out and tapped his phone, silencing the faint, tinny music thumping from the dangling earbud. I glanced at him from the corner of my eye, and was mortified to realize he was smirking at me.

Smirking. *SMIRKING*.

Bastard.

I twisted in my seat to face him, my Latin temper flaring at the smug expression on his face. Of course, my temper might have been fueled by my fear and the panic attack I was currently fighting off.

"I don't bite, you know," Mr. Smirky said, with a damnably sexy British accent lacing his words.

"I do."

His smirk widened into a grin. "Well, I might need to get to know you a bit before we start biting each other. You know, exchange names at least." He stuck his hand out. "Ian Stirling."

I shook his hand, noting with an uncomfortable amount of plea-sure that his hand was huge and hard and strong, and his nails were well-manicured. Dirty, chewed-up fingernails is a sign of mental lax-ity, to me. An unfair judgement, I suppose, but I just cannot abide a man who cuts his nails to the quick, all squared off and hacked to pieces, or greasy and dirty. I like clean hands. Not dainty, effeminate hands, I like my men as manly as the next girl. Just…manly but *clean.*

As I shook his hand, I noticed the source of the coppery scent I'd noticed when he first arrived: his thumb was bleeding a gash along the cuticle. "You're bleeding," I pointed out, releasing his hand.

He frowned at me, then glanced at his thumb. "Oh, shite. I hadn't noticed. Not sure how that happened." He stuck his thumb in his mouth and sucked the blood off.

I freaked. "That's so gross! Do you know how unsanitary your mouth is? Here, give me your thumb." I grabbed his hand, reaching down into my purse at my feet. I always kept a small first aid kit in my purse. My friends at U of M made fun of me for it, but I liked being prepared for all eventualities.

I'm a type A person, dominant, prepared, and bossy; or, as my best friend Alexa says, an anal retentive bitch.

I pulled out my first aid kit, dabbed a dot of Neosporin on the cut, unwrapped a bandaid and fixed it to his thumb. "There. All better."

He was smirking again. "Thanks." He said it with a wry tone to his voice, staring at the bandaid as if he'd never seen one before.

"What?" I asked.

He shook his head. "Nothing."

I crossed my arms under my breasts, which only served to push them up and nearly out of my top. I'm a well-endowed sort of girl, sporting the kind 36DDD breasts that can only fit in Lane Bryant and Cacique bras. Well, I'm sure there are other stores that sell bras I *could* fit in, but I like nice things, and the way I'm built, there's really only three stores worth shopping at: Torrid, Cacique, and Lane Bryant. The rest of me is fairly well-endowed as well, and for the most part, I own it and I rock it. I'm not afraid to show off what I've got, and I've got a lot to show off. The only time I feel insecure is when guys come around, especially guys like the one sitting next to me. He's the kind of hot that can snag any woman he wants. He could be on the cover of GQ. He could stand next to Ryan Gosling and not feel ugly. Sandy blond hair with hints of red brushed across his forehead, intentionally messy, a bit long in the back, curling in an adorable way. I wanted to tangle my fingers in the slight curls at the back of his neck.

"Not nothing. I heard the tone in your voice." I quirked an eyebrow at him to let him know I was serious. I don't always do the eyebrow lift, but when I do, men obey me. Take that, Dos Equis hot old guy.

He chuckled and waggled his bandaid-wrapped thumb. "I've just not had a bandaid on since I was boy. It feels a bit odd, is all."

I shrugged. "You were bleeding. There's nothing unmanly about putting on a bandaid."

"It's a Hello Kitty bandaid." He delivered the *coup de grâce* deadpan, with an admirably straight face.

I managed to hold my serious expression for a few more minutes. "So?"

"It's pink." Still deadpan, not even a hint of a smile.

"So?"

"So, I know real men wear pink, but this might be overdoing a tad, don't you think?" He finally grinned at me, and we laughed. "And besides, bandaids in general aren't very manly. Like umbrellas and hand lotion."

"So real men let themselves bleed everywhere, get needlessly wet, and have chapped hands?"

He nodded. "Right."

I laughed. "That's stupid."

He shrugged. "It's what we're taught as men. You're supposed to just deal with whatever happens and be tough." He glanced at the bandaid again. "But thanks anyway, I do appreciate the gesture, though. You never told me your name, you know."

"Nina Herrera."

He smiled at me, and if I hadn't been sitting down, my panties might have fallen off. "It's a pleasure to meet you, Nina Herrera. So. London?"

I nodded. "I'm attending Oxford in the fall."

"Ah. I had a few mates attended there. Beautiful place." He unplugged the earbuds from the phone and tucked them in the breast pocket of his lavender button-down dress shirt and shrugged out of his dove-gray suit coat. "What are you going to study at jolly old Oxford, then?" He said the last part with an exaggerated Jeeves-the-butler accent.

"Literature. Jane Austen and the Brontë sisters, specifically."

Ian pulled a face. "Ugh. Not my cup of tea, personally. I could never get past the boredom of all the who-said-what rot. Nothing ever really *happened*, you know? Give me Milton or Lord Rochester any day, if I've got to read boring old English nonsense."

I clutched my chest as if wounded. "Rot? That's the best part! It's all subtle. Every word had so many layers of meaning, everything every person said held importance. The conversations are where *every-thing happens.*"

He shrugged. "Well, to each his or her own, I guess."

I clutched the armrests again as we began the slow roll down the runway, my chest tightening with pressure as the jet picked up speed. I bit my lip so hard I tasted blood, but it was better than crumbling into hysterics, which was the other option, as the roar of the engines picked up the sense of weightlessness sent my stomach roiling.

"Afraid of flying?" I heard Ian ask.

"Yes. Very," I said, the words clipped out.

"Clearly." He said it with a chuckle. "If you wanted to hold my hand, all you had to do was ask."

I glanced sharply at him. "What?"

He gestured to my right hand, which, instead of the armrest, was gripping his hand. My nails were digging into his flesh, dimpling the skin where each fingernail touched the back of his hand. I forced my hand open and let go, but then Ian reached out and took my hand in his, this time threading our fingers together.

"I'm not fond of flying either," he said.

I stared at our joined hands, mine small against his, my tan fingers nestled against his fair-skinned ones. He didn't let go, just squeezed my hand gently, and then jutted his chin at my head phones.

"What are you listening to?" He asked.

We were airborne now, but we were still rising steeply and beginning a bank, so my terror ratcheted up even higher as my view out the window angled away from the ground to show nothing but overcast gray sky."Björk," I answered, my voice barely audible.

"I love Björk," Ian said. "What's your favorite song?"

"'Pagan Poetry'," I answered. "But I have to watch the video if I'm going to listen to that song."

"God, that video is brilliant," Ian said, watching me intently, despite his casual conversational tone. "You would look sexy in that dress she's wearing."

I turned to glare at him. "You'd like that, wouldn't you? Seeing me in that dress." I snorted. "I'd flopping be all over the place. It wouldn't be good. I need some serious support for these puppies."

"I would like that, yes." His gaze traveled down to blatantly peruse the "puppies" in question, namely, my breasts.

"Eyes up here, tiger." I pointed at my face, but I said it with a grin, letting him know I wasn't offended by his perusal.

Truth be told, I was all a-twitter inside. He'd *perused* me. Ogled me. He was holding my hand and talking to me, maybe even flirting with me. And he'd checked out my rack. Given, most men did, since it was on display even if I dressed demurely—which I didn't very often—but the way he'd looked me over had almost seemed…like he liked the rest of me, not just my boobs. Usually, a man's gaze took in my breasts, flicked over the rest of me, dismissed me, and then moved on.

Not Ian. He *saw* me; he saw *me*.

And he was still holding my hand, even after the jet leveled out and my nerves receded. This could spell something beautiful, or something heartbreaking, I realized. Maybe both.

Don't miss the rest of

Big Love Abroad

coming soon